Love is the most powerful magic of all.

Ava Matheson has traveled the world, running from the voices in her mind and a family who rejected her. A chance meeting in Istanbul brings a mysterious warrior into her life and plunges Ava into a magical world of fallen angels, ancient brotherhoods, and prophecies that will lead her to the destiny she was always meant to find.

"A towering work of romantic fantasy that will captivate the reader's mind and delight their heart."

— CAT BOWEN, ROMPER.COM

This special edition paperback contains the first three books in the Irin Chronicles series *The Scribe*, *The Singer*, and *The Secret*. It also includes a bonus novella, *On a Clear Winter Night*.

PRAISE FOR ELIZABETH HUNTER

This series, which features warring descendants of Fallen and Forgiven angels, has been complex and emotionally charged to the max. ★★★★★

— RT MAGAZINE

THE SECRET is a magical love story, a story of offering & assenting redemption through grace.

— CROSS MY HEART BOOK REVIEWS

Irin Chronicles had captivating, vivid world-building as a background to the unique story of scribes, angels & Grigori.

— NOCTURNAL BOOK REVIEWS

THE IRIN CHRONICLES
THE SCRIBE-THE SINGER-THE SECRET

ELIZABETH HUNTER

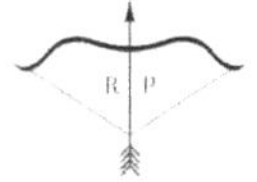

THE SCRIBE

IRIN CHRONICLES BOOK ONE

To the Telerant-Faith clan

For making me feel so very much at home,
even thousands of miles away.

PROLOGUE

Tel Aviv, Israel

"You're going to think I'm crazy."

"Are you?"

"No. Though I suppose most crazy people think they're sane. So it doesn't matter what I say."

There was a pause as the doctor studied the young woman. The listless mouth and relaxed demeanor were belied by the fierce expression in her gold eyes. Barely suppressed anger and… resignation. An odd combination for one so young.

"Why do you assume I will think you're mentally unstable? You're a professional woman. Obviously intelligent based on our previous conversation. University educated. Successful in a highly competitive field—"

"They all think I'm crazy, Doctor Asner." She shifted in her seat, letting her gaze drift out the window to the tree-lined street as a mother with two laughing children passed. A flicker of sadness in her eyes, then nothing again. "It's okay. I'm used to it."

"You hear voices?"

"No question mark on the end."

He blinked and looked up from his pad of paper. "Excuse me?"

The look she gave him was almost amused. The woman's dark curls fell over her shoulder as she angled herself toward him and crossed her arms. "No question mark. I hear voices. Your intonation held a slight lift at the end of that statement, indicating you questioned what you were saying. There is no question. I hear voices. I told you before. I've heard them for as long as I can remember. You can believe me, or you can think I'm insane. But it's not a question."

"You've studied linguistics."

"Linguistics. Phonetics. Ancient languages. Modern languages. I have a very generous stepfather who likes it when I'm not home. Getting several degrees seemed like a good way to pass the time."

"But you became a photojournalist."

"I'm a travel photographer. You don't have to make it sound more important than it is."

He shrugged. "Your work has appeared in major magazines. You make your living with what you do. Are you embarrassed by your work?"

"Not at all."

"Then why qualify?"

"I don't believe in putting on false fronts. Dishonesty irritates me. I am not a photojournalist. Remember the generous stepfather? He also gives me a very generous allowance in order to keep me out of his hair and out of the country. I can afford to travel lots of places that make for pretty pictures. Magazines like to buy them. I'm not saving the world or exposing the horrors of war. What I do is fun, not meaningful."

"Would you like to do something more meaningful?"

A rueful laugh was her first reaction. "God, no."

"Why not? The... voices?"

"There's that unspoken question again. Yes, the voices."

"Is that why you've never had a serious relationship?"

"So my mom called you before the session, huh?"

Asner smiled. "She's concerned about you. That much was evident. Are you and your mother close?"

"I suppose so." The young woman shrugged. "She's the reason I'm not locked up, so I can't really complain about her."

Her eyes drifted to the window again.

"Miss Matheson?"

"Ava."

"Excuse me?"

Ava blinked and turned her eyes back to the doctor. "Call me Ava. Matheson is my stepfather's name."

"But he raised you? Your stepfather and your mother raised you, didn't they?"

"Yes."

"And you only recently met your biological father."

Her eyes narrowed. "Is that why Mom and Carl insisted on this appointment? Because of my father?"

"He's a new presence in your life."

"Not really. I've been a fan for years."

He gave her blank look.

Ava sighed. "Yes, he's a new presence."

"He's a musician?"

"Please don't pretend you don't know who my father is. It's irritating. I knew him as an old friend of my mother's—that's it. When I found out he was my actual father, it wasn't a big deal. I've known since I was little that Carl adopted me."

"But you had no idea the man was your real father."

"No."

"Did he know you were his?"

"Yes, but he agreed to let my mom raise me. He's not the most… together person. He knows that."

Asner paused thoughtfully. "Do you think your voices have anything to do with your father? A shared… creativity, perhaps?"

She curled her lip. "My father—as messed up as he is—is a brilliant composer. He hears music in his head and writes it down and makes lots of money. I hear garbled voices I don't understand. Not really the same thing. You don't get locked up for being a brilliant composer."

"Do you fear being institutionalized?"

The fierce expression returned. "Why would I? As you said, I'm a successful photojournalist. Plus, thanks to my surprise dad, I'm rich enough to be eccentric instead of crazy."

He couldn't stop his own smile. "Tell me more about your voices. What do they say?"

She shifted again, and her eyes drifted back to the window. "I don't know."

"What do you mean?"

"I mean exactly what I said."

"So you *don't* hear language. You don't hear other people's thoughts?"

"I don't know what I hear." Her eyes swung back and narrowed on him. "But I know you believe me more than the others. I wonder why that is."

"I'm an open-minded individual."

"Maybe."

"Tell me more. How do you know I believe you? Can you hear me?"

"Yes."

"What am I thinking?"

"I can't tell you that. That's not the way it works."

"Do you sense my feelings?"

"It's all in the tone of your voice. The voice I hear, anyway."

"And what voice is that?"

"The one everyone has."

"Everyone?"

She took a deep breath and he saw the hints of resignation again. "Every country and every age. Different voices speaking the same language. That's what I hear."

He leaned forward. "Every voice sounds the same?"

"Of course not. Everyone has a different voice. They just all speak the same language."

"Everywhere in the world?"

"Everywhere I've traveled so far. So… a lot of it."

"What language is it?"

"I don't know."

"What are they saying?"

Frustration flashed. "I don't know."

"So how do you—"

"It's a language, doctor. There are rises and falls in the rhythm. There are common words and phrases I hear again and again. I hear the same things from the minds of people all over the world. I just don't know what they're saying."

He had to pause to contain his reaction. It didn't matter.

She cocked her head. "That's exciting to you."

He smiled. "It's very interesting, Ava."

"Interesting is one word for it."

He heard the irritation in her voice. "Though I'm sure it is frustrating, as well. I imagine it can be quite distracting."

The corner of her mouth turned up. "It's enough to drive you crazy."

Asner laughed a little, and Ava relaxed a bit. "How do you sleep?"

"Probably the same way you do. A bed is usually involved, but I'm pretty comfortable on trains, too. Planes are harder. Buses, practically impossible."

"What a clever and humorous deflection of my question." He stretched his legs in front of him, almost spanning the small office. "When you sleep, do you dream?"

"Vividly. Always have."

"And these voices… do you hear them in your dreams?"

She frowned, and Asner wondered if he was the first mental health professional to ask that question. Ava Matheson had seen more than her share.

"No. No, I don't hear them in my dreams."

He smiled. "That must be a relief."

"Yes, it is."

"Is that part of the reason you prefer to work alone? No voices?"

"Yes."

"And happy, relaxed places. Vacation spots instead of conflict areas."

"It's all falling into place, isn't it, Doc?"

"Have you tried medications?"

"All sorts of them." She reached out and grabbed the arms of the chair she sat in. "Most of them make me sleepy. Kill my appetite. That's about it."

He nodded, jotting down more notes as she examined him. "Do the voices… are they always the same volume? Are some louder than others?"

"Everyone is different. Some people are clearer than others. Yours right now is very quiet, but… urgent. You want to get this information as quickly as possible, but you're trying to remain calm."

He stopped and looked up at her. "That's very disconcerting, Ava."

She gave him an innocent smile. "Imagine what it must be like for me. What do you want, Doctor? You want something."

He paused, trying to decide how to answer. "I'd like to refer you to a colleague. He's someone I think might be able to help you."

"Why?"

"I remember him speaking once about a patient with similar symptoms. Do you mind traveling to see him?"

She waved at the distant ocean. "I was in Cyprus when my mom called and told me to go to a doctor in Israel for my yearly 'what's-the-matter-with-Ava' appointment. What do you think?"

"Excellent."

"I might not go, though." She shrugged. "Carl and Mom get pushy about once a year, but mostly, they leave me alone. Especially now that I have Jasper's money."

"Jasper is your father?"

"Yeah." A hint of a smile crept across her face. "I guess you could call him that."

"I don't want to take up too much of your time. I know we've gone over the hour—no charge, of course—but…" Asner scribbled down a name and telephone number from memory. "I do hope you'll see my colleague. He's in Istanbul. Have you been before?"

Ava's eyebrows furrowed together. "No, but I've been told it's beautiful, even though it's crowded."

"And you don't like crowds because of the voices?"

"That and the lack of deodorant on hot days. I might check it out." She shrugged. "Like I said, no guarantees. If I happen to be in Istanbul, I'll look him up."

He smiled politely and rose to his feet as she stood to gather her things: a large messenger bag, a battered camera case, a light scarf thrown around her neck to keep the dust of the city away. She grabbed the paper from Doctor Asner's hand and had started toward the door before he spoke.

"May I ask…?"

The young woman turned, tucking a curl behind her ear before she put her sunglasses on. "You can ask whatever you want. If I don't want to answer, I won't."

He frowned. "Your name—Ava—means 'voice' in Persian. Did you know that?"

The sunglasses hid her eyes. "Yes."

"Who gave you your name?"

She paused. "My father did. It was the one thing he asked for. To name me Ava."

"Do you know why?"

"No."

"And you never asked?"

She shrugged. "Does it matter? It's a nice name. Maybe he just liked the actress, you know?"

"Names are important."

She smiled a little. "Good-bye, Doctor Asner. Fun chatting with you. I probably won't see you around."

MIKHAIL ASNER WATCHED HER THROUGH THE WINDOW AS SHE WOUND through the narrow streets of Neve Tzedek and wandered north toward the city center. The slight woman with curly black hair melded into the city landscape effortlessly, a seasoned traveler accustomed to blending with her surroundings. He watched for a few more minutes, then picked up the phone, dialing a number from memory.

"You haven't called me in some time," said the voice on the other end.

"I found someone of interest."

"Did you give her my number?"

"Yes."

"Her name?"

"Ava Matheson. American."

A notable pause followed Asner's declaration.

The voice asked, "Will she come?"

"I honestly don't know."

"Did you tell her I could help her?"

"Of course."

"Then she'll come."

CHAPTER
ONE

Istanbul, Turkey

Malachi spotted the Grigori foot soldier at the edge of the bazaar. The man walked slowly through the spice market, stopping occasionally to examine wares he wouldn't buy, scanning the crowd for…

Her.

Dark curling hair shielded her face, but her figure was slight and quick. The human woman radiated energy, even as she strolled through the cacophony of sounds, sights, and smells that careened through the market in the heart of Old Istanbul. Vendors yelled out their wares as tourists sampled the variety of spices, dried fruits, and nuts the market held, and deft boys dodged the traffic, delivering trays of dark tea.

The woman seemed to exist in her own space, blending into the colorful mosaic of the bazaar, though she spoke to no one.

Malachi's gaze drifted away from her, back to the Grigori soldier. In his mind's eye, he approached the man quietly, stalking him to a deserted corner before he grabbed him silently and stabbed a sharp blade into the base of his skull, killing the murderous creature and releasing its soul to face judgment. Then he melted into the crowd, another passing traveler at the crossroads of the world.

You're reckless. Looking for trouble instead of using your head.

The voice of his last watcher mocked him, so Malachi did none of those things that morning. Instead, he fought back the instinctual rage and watched the man carefully.

The Grigori was hunting.

Casually adjusting the silver knives he wore under his shirt, Malachi tossed a few lire toward a vendor, then grabbed a small bag of roasted almonds, just another nameless tourist in the market that morning. Though he was one of the taller men in the crowd, hundreds of years had taught Malachi the art of blending into his surroundings. He followed the Grigori as the creature followed the woman. Hunting him, hunting her. The soldier kept his distance but never let the woman stray too far ahead. There was no sense of urgency as was usually seen when a Grigori was tracking his prey. The man almost looked relaxed if one didn't notice the dark eyes that never left the figure as she wound her way toward the courtyard that separated the bazaar from the mosque.

The man was nondescript, as the best soldiers were. Local, if he had to guess, though he'd never seen him before. But Malachi had returned to the country of his birth after hundreds of years away. It was possible one of his brothers was familiar with the soldier who was tracking the woman with such restraint.

Who was she?

Her face still obscured by her thick hair, she could have been Turkish or foreign, local or tourist. Her clothes were unremarkable, a loose pair of linen pants and a long-sleeved T-shirt. Modest, but not religious. The only feature that struck him as notable was the messenger bag she carried. It was expensive. Worn. A man's bag. Once belonging to a father? A brother? It was a decidedly masculine accessory for the delicate female.

She stopped at the exit of the L-shaped building, turning back to take a picture with a small black camera, just another tourist taking in the sights. As her face lifted to the sun, he saw her features. European... with a distinct hint of something else. A common enough look in a city like Istanbul. The breeze lifted her curling hair as she raised the device and held it away from her body as she framed the entrance to the building. The Grigori stopped near a small mountain of hazelnuts and tried to ignore the eager vendor who shouted at him about a sale.

The woman paused, and with his shoulder turned away, the

Grigori missed the quick glance she gave him as well as the slight shift in angle as the woman captured his image with her camera. Malachi had to smile. The clever female had spotted the tail, and she'd captured her pursuer before he could duck away. But she didn't give Malachi notice before she turned and sped out into the sunlight just as the call to prayer began to echo through the heavy summer air.

Who was she?

The Grigori finally shook off the hazelnut vendor and turned, picking up his pursuit. Malachi continued to follow at a distance, watching him, watching her. The woman ignored the müezzin who called the faithful, stepping lightly along the crowded streets as she made her way back toward the train station. She turned right near Gülhane Park and followed the tram line up the hill, walking a few blocks before she stopped near the lobby of one of the larger hotels.

Then she stepped into the glass-fronted building and out of sight. The Grigori stopped a block away, watching for a few moments before he pulled out a mobile phone, called a number, and spoke animatedly to whoever was on the other end. After a quick conversation, the man took one last look at the hotel, then walked away, back toward the train station.

But Malachi waited. The Grigori didn't know he had been spotted, but Malachi had seen the quick recognition on the woman's face. She hadn't recognized the man, but she'd known she was being watched. Perhaps, like him, she could sense it. She was more perceptive than the average human; Malachi would have to be careful. He sat down at an outdoor café to wait, ordering a tea and continuing to munch on the roasted almonds as he scanned the streets from behind black-shaded glasses and pretended to read a newspaper someone had left on the table.

A full forty-five minutes later, the woman emerged. She lingered at the entrance for a few minutes, holding a map in front of her as she scanned the streets from behind her glasses. Satisfied her follower had left, she started back up the hill.

She crossed the street, heading toward the hippodrome. The hairs on Malachi's neck rose as he walked. The walls whispered, centuries of secrets held in the cobbled brick and marble of Byzantium. As he strolled, ancient graffiti flickered black and grey in the corner of his eye. He saw the woman pause and take a picture of an old graveyard before she kept moving. As Malachi passed, he saw a lazy cat stretching in the sun.

Who was she? And why had she attracted the attention of the Grigori that morning? More, why had the soldier not hunted her in the common way? Grigori didn't show restraint when seducing a target. Their wicked charm was relentless. If the woman survived the encounter, she was discarded. To follow a woman so discreetly indicated some other, more enigmatic, motivation.

She walked the length of the hippodrome, past the obvious tourist traps, then turned right near a small café. Climbing up a side street, she dodged a car coming out of a parking lot as she put her map away. It looked as if she was walking into a dead-end street before she took a sudden left and disappeared. Malachi followed cautiously, hoping to not appear too conspicuous as he approached a building tented for renovation. He stopped to read a sign detailing the improvements to the structure, which housed a museum. Then he watched from the corner of his eye as the woman approached what looked like an old Ottoman house but was probably one of the many boutique hotels that had sprung up in the last few years. A discreet doorman stepped outside, opened the door, and spotted him. Without a pause, Malachi walked away.

He turned back to the hippodrome, pausing to take note of the glowing red lanterns in front of the Chinese restaurant near her hotel before he began the trek back to Galata. The woman, whoever she was, was staying at the small hotel. He'd find her again if he wanted to. As for the Grigori's odd behavior…

He'd have to ask Damien if he'd seen anything like it before. His watcher had centuries more experience than Malachi. He might be prone to recklessness, but he knew how to use the resources he was given.

Stuffing the almonds back in his pocket, Malachi's thoughts turned to decidedly more practical matters. With the heat of the day rising and too many salted almonds in his belly, he needed a drink. Throwing one last glance toward the wood-fronted house, he started back toward home.

• • •   • • •

He slammed the door shut on the small refrigerator.

"Doesn't anyone buy beer besides me?" he yelled to the empty kitchen. "If you don't buy it, you shouldn't drink it!"

From upstairs, a faint voice came. "You spent too much time in Hamburg. You're back in Istanbul, Mal; we drink raki." It was Maxim, no doubt lying in bed, waiting for the city to cool before he emerged.

"Or tea," another voice added in the same thick Russian accent. If Maxim was upstairs, so was his cousin, Leo. "Gallons of tea."

"Oceans of it."

"If only the Bosphorus flowed with vodka."

"We should get the brothers in Odessa working on that…"

Damien walked into the kitchen, glancing upward as the cousins continued to rib each other. "Drink water. You're not used to the heat yet."

Malachi grimaced. "I'll be fine. I was born here."

The watcher pulled a bottle of water from a cupboard and threw it toward him, the tattoos on his bare arms rippling as he threw the plastic bottle. "But you haven't lived here for hundreds of years. The city has grown, and that makes it hotter."

"Anthropogenic heat," said Rhys, walking into the kitchen from the library and holding his hand out to Damien for another bottle of water. The pale man had been sweating nonstop for three days—not surprising considering the air conditioner had broken around that time. His dark brown hair was plastered to his forehead, and his normally pale skin was flushed. "Human activity produces heat. More humans. More heat. Not to mention climate change. Bloody humans and their automobiles will kill us all."

Damien and Malachi exchanged amused glances. The cranky British scholar was constantly nostalgic for preindustrial times.

"Heat can't kill us, Rhys!" Leo called from above.

"But your whining is doing a fairly good job of torture," Maxim added. "Is whining a violation of the Geneva Convention?"

"Does the Geneva Convention apply to us?"

"Ask Rhys. He knows everything."

The scholar's face only grew redder. "Maybe if I wasn't the only one working—"

"Stop." One quiet word from Damien was all it took. The three men fell silent, even the ones on the second floor, who could hear their watcher's voice from a distance.

Damien was of average height and weight. His face could make humans stop and stare, or he could blend into a crowd, based solely on his demeanor. The only remarkable thing about him was the intricate tattoos he had inked all over his arms. Malachi knew the work covered most of the man's legs as well, though he kept them carefully covered. Malachi glanced down at his own markings. Four hundred years of scribing himself still hadn't left him half as covered as Damien. Who knew how old the man was?

Damien continued in a low voice, "Leo, did you call the man to repair the air conditioner?"

A thundering set of footsteps came down the stairs and the hall. The man they belonged to stopped in the door, filling it with his massive frame. "They said they will come tomorrow. Beginning of the summer means lots of work. They're busy." Sweat dotted a pale forehead topped by a thatch of sandy-blond hair. Maxim followed Leo, a mirror of his cousin. The two were inseparable, cousins being as rare as siblings in their race. Their mothers had been twin sisters, and the men looked like twins themselves. Even their tattoos were almost identical, though their personalities couldn't have been more opposite.

"So no air-conditioning until tomorrow?" Rhys asked.

Damien shrugged. "Sleep on the roof. There are beds up there and the breeze will be better when the sun goes down."

For some reason, Malachi's thoughts flicked to the woman slipping into the wooden house near Aya Sofia. The house had a plain street view, a classic Ottoman; it was probably cool and shaded in the interior. There might have been a courtyard. And air-conditioning.

"I should have kept following the woman," he muttered.

Damien's ears caught it. "What woman? Why were you following her? You know you're not allowed to—"

"Do I look like a foolish boy?" He glared at the man. "There was a woman at the spice market. She'd caught the attention of a Grigori soldier. I was watching him, and he was watching her."

All amusement fled the group. Each man knew the danger of a Grigori attack.

Maxim asked, "Did you kill him before he got to her?"

Rhys offered a bloodthirsty smile, forgetting his misery in the contemplation of Grigori death. "Set his soul free to be judged, brother? I wish I could have helped."

"I didn't. I'm being cautious, remember?" He aimed a pointed look at Damien. "Besides, his behavior was… odd. I wanted to ask you about it."

Damien narrowed his eyes. "Odd how?"

"He was hunting her, but he wasn't. He never approached her. Never tried to charm her. He was actually trying to remain unnoticed."

Leo shook his head. "No, that's not how they work. They seduce. They—"

"We all know what the Grigori do, Leo." Damien was staring at Malachi. "What happened?"

"He followed her back to a hotel, and…"

Maxim said, "And what?"

"Nothing. He just watched her, called someone on the phone, then left."

Damien was silent. The others were silent. It was, just as Malachi had suspected, unusual behavior for the Grigori of Istanbul. He had hoped Damien would have some clue, but the man's face registered nothing. Not shock, not recognition. Nothing.

The watcher finally said, "So you know where this woman is staying?"

He smiled. "I do, but the Grigori doesn't."

"I thought you said—"

"She spotted him at the market. Took his picture when he was looking away. She went into the lobby of one of the hotels near the palace, waited for forty minutes until he'd left, then went to her real hotel. The Grigori never saw where she's actually staying."

Damien nodded, seemingly impressed with the resourcefulness of the human. "Clever."

Leo nodded and grinned. "I like the clever ones. Was she pretty, too?"

Maxim elbowed his cousin. "That's not important." Then he turned to Malachi and narrowed his eyes. "But was she?"

"She was… interesting." She had been pretty, Malachi realized. He'd been concentrating so hard on the chase that he hadn't really noticed until he remembered her fine features, the slope of her eyes. "Yes, she was pretty." Not that it mattered to him, but the cousins were still young enough to find human women attractive. They had never known true beauty like the older men had.

"I want you to go back to her hotel tomorrow," Damien said. "Find out more. And you're sure she wasn't…?" There was a slight, hopeful rise in his voice.

"I don't think so," Malachi said quietly. "She would have heard me if she was. And the Grigori wouldn't have shown any restraint."

"Of course." Damien looked away. All the men found things to look at, other than each other. "Go back tomorrow," Damien said. "Find out more. We need to know why she's attracted their attention this way. This is different."

Malachi took a deep breath, alternately concerned and excited about the chase. It might be his most interesting day in the Old City yet.

THE WOMAN TOOK A LOT OF PICTURES. AND FROM THE LOOK OF HER equipment, she was a professional. She took picture after picture of the Sultanahmet's mosques and streets. The alleys and corner gardens. Odd angles a tourist wouldn't think of. Glimpses of old women selling lace and children selling toys. She even lay down on the dirty sidewalk at times. She ate corn and chestnuts from the carts in front of Aya Sofia and watched the tourists feed the pigeons. She captured it all, from the grand to the gritty.

No one was with her, and the Grigori hadn't found her again. Malachi watched her for hours the next morning as she made her way through the old city. Every now and then, she would duck into a quiet alley or deserted shop, hold her head in her hands, and rub her temples.

Was she dehydrated? She'd been sipping water all morning but looked to be suffering from a terrible headache. Still, she didn't return to her hotel. Her face, now that he was looking at it, was a picture of well-concealed tension. Crowds seemed to make her particularly nervous, and she avoided the swarms of tourists that came off the cruise ships at regular intervals.

Was she afraid of them? Was that why she took shelter in the quieter corners when she could? Malachi didn't think so. She looked, more than anything, exhausted, though every now and then a child or group of children would pass and her face would light up. She liked children. So did Malachi. The thought made him smile.

Despite her exhaustion, she continued taking pictures all morning, checking her phone every now and then. He would guess she was a regular traveler. The way she navigated the city, the way she talked to people, there was something about her manner that told him she was very comfortable with new places. If she was a professional photographer, it would make sense. What didn't make sense was why the Grigori soldier had been following the human woman yesterday, but not hunting her.

She worked her way through the Sultanahmet and toward the Galata Bridge, closer to the neighborhood where he and his brothers made their home. She picked up the tail just before the tram stop.

There were two this time, still watching. Still hanging back far enough that Malachi could keep them in sight while watching the woman. She paused near the train station, then turned back and turned left to an emptier side street. What was she doing? Was she headed for the park? The police station? No, she turned right again. She was headed back up the hill. Malachi tried to get closer, only to see her turn to look over her shoulder at the two Grigori following her.

She'd spotted them.

He could tell she was trying to lose the tail, ducking into crowds when she could and darting across the street, coming far too close to cars for his liking. She walked quickly, but the soldiers were good. Just before the street opened up, she made a quick left into an alley and Malachi's heart leapt.

Bad move, woman. Why were humans so stupid at times?

He sped up. They wouldn't attack her in the open during the day, but Grigori would have no qualms about disappearing with her. If they caught up to her, she was history. No government in the world would find a trace. The soldiers turned left and followed her into the alley.

Malachi started running, no longer worried about attracting attention. He had to get to her. Had to keep them from—

"And that is why you don't fuck with someone with pepper spray, asshole! What? Did you think because I'm a tourist I wouldn't be able to protect myself?" She kicked one in the kidneys, standing over both men and holding a small can. Malachi turned his head away as the breeze drifted toward him. Both Grigori soldiers were on the ground, writhing and clutching their faces, holding preternaturally sensitive eyes and noses that were, no doubt, in agony from the pungent concoction she'd sprayed from the can.

Malachi was gaping. How had she caught them by surprise? Their race could move almost silently. No human should have been able to fend off—

"And you!" The woman was pointing at him now, aiming the can in his direction. He brought his right thumb to his left wrist and began tracing, silently rousing the spells that would protect his senses should she choose to attack. He felt it, the warm glow of magic spreading up his arm, suffusing his body with power, activating the tapestry of magic that protected him. In seconds, Malachi would be covered with an armor even the fiercest warrior could not penetrate. "Why the hell have you been following me?" she demanded.

"I haven't been following you."

"Don't lie to me."

"I saw these men follow you into the alley." He lifted his hands, no longer worried about the pepper spray. He could feel the ancient power swirling over his skin. "I'm just trying to help."

"I said don't lie to me!" Her energy was high, her adrenaline staining the air as she walked toward him. Malachi backed away, drawing her out of the alley and into the safer street. "You were following me yesterday. You've been following me all morning. Why?"

How had she known?

"I haven't been following you," he lied. "Do you need some help? Is there someone I can call for you?" She was attracting enough attention just by her raised voice. He didn't want to attract the police. That was the last thing either of them needed. "Put the pepper spray down. I'm not going to hurt you."

"I might. If you tell me why you were following me all morning."

"For the last time, I have not been—"

Her temper burst. "I heard you, you lying asshole! Do I look stupid? Why were you following me?"

The ground beneath him shifted. The spells on his arms pulsed.

I heard you.

Malachi blinked as his vision scattered, and then he focused on the fearless woman in front of him.

"What did you say?"

CHAPTER

TWO

I heard you.

Time stopped as the words left her mouth of their own volition, launching into the air between Ava and the stranger who stood at the mouth of the alley. A thousand whispers surrounded her, and the voices of the city washed over her mind. The words flew, cutting through the cacophony that followed her. Three words that never should have left her mouth.

The man halted immediately, eyes widening as they reached him.

"What did you say?"

He knew.

"Nothing. Leave me alone." Forget her questions, she had to leave. Ava stepped over the prone bodies of the strange men who were still writhing on the ground. Instinct told her the man whose voice she'd heard following her since the day before was far more dangerous than the thugs who'd caught up with her near the bridge. She'd been lulled by it; something about the tone and pitch of this man's inner voice was more resonant than most. She'd allowed the voice to follow her, soothed by its tone. It had been the one pure sound in the redolent, clashing air of Istanbul.

"What did you mean, 'I heard you?'" he called.

He was following her out of the alley, abandoning the wounded men to their own moans and the growing crowd of concerned citizens and tourists. Ava slipped through them, never gladder to have perfected the art of weaving through crowds with as little contact as possible.

The stranger's whispers followed her, alive with excitement. Curiosity. Hope? She walked faster, trying to leave his voice and the memories it brought behind.

He wasn't completely unique. Ava had come across the strange resonance before in India. Another time back in Los Angeles. Once, outside a lonely house in Ireland. The resonance of his inner voice was different, though no more understandable, than the rest. Most of her waking hours were filled with the whispers of anyone and everyone she passed, but Ava had no clue what they were saying. It was as if she stood in a crowded room where everyone was whispering. Crowds blended into an off-key hum she'd battled to control for as long as she could remember.

What do your whispers mean, Mommy?

What whispers?

Everyone has whispers.

The strange looks, then the voices others could hear, too.

Crazy.

Troubled.

Dangerous?

Ava's eyes caught the corner of a leg sticking out of a blanket. A homeless man sat up from a bench near the entrance of the park, eyes wild and body swaying. Their gazes locked for a moment and Ava fought back the pang of sympathy and kept moving. If not for her mother, she might have been him.

She crossed the road at the entrance to the park, headed back to the hippodrome and the relative safety of the heavily touristed areas. Her camera banged against her hip as she walked. Normally, it would be out. She wouldn't pass up a chance to capture the smiling couple or the woman rolling out bread in a window. She would have captured the small dog watching the young woman tying a carpet in a store window. The two boys ducking behind a display in a shop. Snatches of life in the city. Family and friends going about their lives.

It was a bittersweet triumph, to capture moments she would never have.

The stranger's voice still followed, the lone bright thread running through the tapestry of the Sultanahmet. It was as if a single voice whispered to her, not off-key, but in a melodious timbre that stroked her mind. It wrapped around her as it had the day before. She had known it followed her, but she felt no instinct to run. The voice called to her, tempting her to turn and follow it. Urging her to abandon caution and seek it out.

The tone of the stranger's voice revealed his mood, though the meaning was still a mystery. Disbelief, frustration, and hope, all wrapped together. Ava ignored the urge to turn, stubbornly focusing on navigating the streets, dodging traffic, and avoiding the frightening swarms of tourists trailing mechanically behind the cruise ship guides.

Despite the crowds, she couldn't stop the thrill and awe as she passed Aya Sofia and the Blue Mosque. She loved it here, which had been a surprise. Ava hadn't loved a city in a long time. But this city was seductive. Layer upon layer of history. East meeting West. Modern colliding with ancient. Istanbul had been a revelation of the senses.

The stranger's voice was still following her when Ava turned the corner near her hotel, almost jogging up and down the completely unnecessary hill the house sat on. If you didn't look closely, it might have been no more than a very gracious residence in the heart of the city. In reality, it was an exclusive hotel that catered to travelers looking for luxury, safety, and privacy. Made of wood in the Ottoman style, it was almost plain from the front. But as she approached, a guard opened a door, letting her into the cool interior of the refuge, searching behind her when he saw the hint of panic still evident on Ava's features.

"Ms. Matheson?" he asked in lilting English. "Is there a problem?"

She shook her head. "I'm fine, thanks. I thought… It was just my imagination, I'm sure. Is the roof garden open?"

The guard's eye widened. "Right now? It is open, but the day is very hot, miss. Perhaps when the sun goes down—"

"It's fine." She shot him a tense smile. "I just need some privacy."

"Of course." He nodded and lifted a hand toward the elevators, but Ava didn't want to chance that someone might join her. Voices always grew more agitated in confined spaces, and the elevators in the hotel were small. She walked toward the stairs instead. Her phone was already out and she was dialing her mother's number when she pushed the door to the terrace open. Sunlight flooded over her, baking the tile that covered the roof. Ava took shelter under one of the generous shade covers that marked a quiet corner. As she suspected, the terrace was deserted. Keeping away from any windows or open doors, she let the phone ring across the world in Los Angeles.

"Hello?" Lena Matheson answered in a groggy voice. "Ava, what's wrong?"

It was just past midnight in L.A.

"Did you and Carl hire someone local?"

"What?" She heard Carl's voice in the background, a quiet growl that her mother shushed. "What are you talking about?"

"Did you hire someone, Mother?"

There was a quiet huff. "Well, really, Ava, what did you expect? You asked Carl to have pepper spray delivered to your hotel. He—"

"That's precautionary, Mom! I do that anywhere I've never been before when I'm traveling alone." A tight, nervous part of her stomach relaxed. It wasn't a stranger after all. Despite the unusual voice, the man following her was just another guard hired by her overprotective mother and stepfather. Nothing she couldn't handle.

"Just go about your business and ignore him. He has a job to do, and you know Carl won't fire him."

No, but he might hire more if he got wind of the incident in the alley today. "This is Istanbul. It's very safe as long as you're smart. I'd probably be in more danger traveling in New Jersey. You really don't need to—"

"Have you forgotten Cassie Traver? She was in Paris and she was kidnapped. Let's not take any chances, Ava. You know how he worries."

You mean how his accountant worries. The only reason her stepfather had started up with the guards again was because of the enormous amount of money the Travers had been forced to pay to Cassie's kidnappers. Ava had no illusions of paternal concern.

"Just tell him to keep his distance. I know you won't fire him, but I don't want to see him anywhere near me."

"Do you want to talk to Carl?"

"What do you think?"

There was a heavy pause on the line. "Okay. Are you… having fun?"

She heard Carl growl again. Her mother covered the phone with her hand.

"It's late, Mom." Ava swallowed the lump in her throat. "I'll call you back another time."

"No, it's fine. I'll just—"

"I gotta go. There's someone I need to meet with. For work."

"Call me back tomorrow?"

"I don't know—"

"Later, then. Just call me later."

"Sure." Ava collapsed in one of the luxurious chairs under the shade and ran her fingers along the frond of a potted palm. "I'll call you later."

"I love you."

"Love you, too. Bye." Ava hung up before Lena could say anything more, then stared over the rooftops of Istanbul, far above the crowds.

Silence. At last, silence.

* * * * * *

AVA STARTED EARLY THE NEXT DAY. SHE'D BEEN TO TOPKAPI PALACE before but had woken when the first prayer calls floated over the city and couldn't get back to sleep. She lay in bed for a few hours, loading and editing work on her laptop, then decided to beat the crowds and some of the heat. She headed toward the opulent palace in the center of the old city, walked past the first gate, and started working.

Photography had been her escape for years. There was something about the intense visual focus that helped Ava block out the voices around her. She could get lost behind the lens. An observer instead of an outsider. She snapped pictures of the stunning architecture, trying to capture it from unique angles in the morning light. But more and more, she found herself drawn to the people who began crowding the various courtyards.

Whispers of excitement.

Routine hums.

The clear, pure thoughts of the youngest children, uncluttered by the static of their parents and guardians.

And each and every one completely unintelligible to her. She recognized common words and phrases. She could probably quote things from memory, though she had no idea what she would be saying. People's inner voices didn't work the way their spoken voices did. They thought in slips and starts. Their minds drifted from one emotion to another, often so quickly it made her ill.

"Excuse me," she said, working her way through a tour group and toward an empty corner where she could watch the growing crowds.

Workers. Tourists. Families on holiday and the odd wanderer like herself. Ava turned her camera on them, capturing their fleeting expressions and sudden smiles. People were nice... from a distance. She'd avoided cities for years, preferring the peace of wilderness destinations and hidden enclaves where the voices of the locals weren't quite so overwhelming. She was still in shock that she'd agreed to come to Istanbul. Couldn't explain why, exactly, but she'd felt drawn to it. Maybe it was the promise of help. She couldn't allow herself to believe this doctor—Doctor J. Sadik—could actually help her. But perhaps she *could* allow herself to be curious.

She wandered the edges of the palace, looking out over stunning views of the sea and snapping pictures for hours. Every now and then, she'd catch a glimpse of him at the edge of her frame.

Hello, stranger. Ava snapped another picture of him, pushing a button on her camera to examine him more closely.

At least they'd hired an attractive one this time.

He looked Turkish. Taller than average. Most professional bodyguards were far from the romantic notions portrayed in movies or books, even farther from the giant thugs who followed musicians around. The best were men and women who could blend into any crowd. They were overlooked until they became necessary, and they rarely garnered an admiring stare.

But this man was... not handsome. Compelling. Something about him made her eyes want to linger. Lean muscle covered his frame, and despite the heat, he was clothed from head to toe, though his suit appeared to be made of linen and not some hotter material. His collar lay open, exposing the edge of an intricate tattoo. That was unusual. His hair was dark and straight, falling onto his forehead and almost into his eyes. He could use a haircut, which meant he was probably not married. She glanced at the three college-age girls who checked him out as he pretended to read a book at the café. He didn't even give them a glance. Focused. He blended into the crowd admirably for someone as physically imposing as he was, but there was still something about him that drew Ava's camera over and over again.

Or maybe it was just his voice.

She'd caught it almost as soon as she'd left the hotel. Thankfully, the bodyguard was keeping his distance. Carl must have clarified his instructions. The man followed, but not too closely. Occasionally, Ava would turn and deliberately snap his picture, letting him know she'd seen him. He looked away every time she did, a slightly irritated expression crossing his face.

She caught him at the edge of another frame just as he was pulling out a mobile phone. Probably calling Carl to complain about her.

"Won't do any good," she sang under her breath.

Her stepfather had tried for years to understand how Ava could pick up on any security he assigned to her. He knew she could hear them—her mother had never hidden her secret from Carl—he just chose not to believe. He wasn't a bad guy, really. Carl adored her mother, and he was honest to a fault. The fact that he'd been saddled with a stepdaughter who was slightly crazy was just the cost of capturing Lena Russell's heart. Ava couldn't fault his indifference as she'd never made an effort with him, either.

The stranger was still talking, so Ava grabbed a coffee and perched on a bench, lifting her camera to capture a boy who was laughing at something his mother had said. They teased and giggled with each other as Ava clicked. A common moment between mother and child set in the grandeur of the old Ottoman court. It was exactly the kind of photograph she loved.

A young man brushed a little too close, causing her to tense, to grip her cup as her coffee spilled hot over her fingers. Her bodyguard started toward the man, but Ava gave a small shake of her head.

Not a threat. The unspoken message seemed to reach him, because he stopped, looking between the retreating man and Ava.

She closed her eyes and breathed deeply, trying to rid the angry sound of the young man from her mind.

Sharp, piercing tones. His thoughts were shot through with a deep thread of pain. Most people's inner voices were like tiny orchestras in the moments before a concert. An odd cacophony of emotion and tone only occasionally smoothing out into a discernible voice. The young man who had just passed her was angry, but also in pain. It was all there in his voice.

Ava took a few more deep breaths and looked up to find her bodyguard staring at her. His voice, in contrast, was the smooth, clear note the moment before the orchestra played. Perfectly in tune. She didn't know quite what to make of it.

Time to say hello.

If she wanted him to cooperate and leave her be without reporting every flinch to her mother and Carl, she'd have to play nice. Tossing her coffee in a nearby trash can, she stood and walked over. He didn't run. Didn't look away. He stared at her from behind shaded lenses as she tucked her camera in her bag and held out her hand.

"Hi, I'm Ava. I imagine you know that already."

The bodyguard just blinked at her, staring at her hand as if it might bite. Finally, she dropped it. She had surprised him. His silent voice whispered in circles so rapid she felt as if she was in the middle of a minor storm. But he didn't speak to her, not out loud.

"I know I heard you speak English the other day. It might not be your first language, but I'm sorry, I don't speak any Turki—"

"English is fine."

His spoken voice was deeper than his silent one, but it held the same odd resonance that had drawn her since she first heard it. Ava tried not to lean closer, even though the urge was there.

"Okay." She nodded. "I just wanted to introduce myself."

"Hello."

What about his one-word greeting did Ava find amusing? She didn't know why she smiled, but she did. "That back there? With the guy... I get headaches—it's a medical thing that's not a big deal—so don't panic if you see me looking like I might pass out. I've never passed out in my life. And I have no idea why Carl hired you, but since I can't get him to fire you, we might as well be friendly."

He just shifted in his seat, clearly uncomfortable with the conversation.

"I know you're going to be following me, so please don't feel like you have to hide. If you could just keep your distance and stay as unobtrusive as possible, that'd be great. I've had guards before, but I'm pretty independent. I'm honestly not sure why Carl felt like he had to do this, but since there never seems to be any reasoning with him, let's just go with it, okay?"

The big man was still blinking at her silently. Ava tried not to sigh. His eyes had seemed intelligent enough, but maybe they hadn't hired the guy for his intellect.

"What I'm trying to say is... The incident you saw in the alley doesn't need to be reported to my stepfather. I took care of it, and we really don't need more people at this little party, do we?"

Complete and utter silence. It was almost inhuman. She caught him taking a breath when the collar of his shirt moved, revealing more of the tattoo work around his collar. They were letters, she thought, but nothing like she'd ever seen before. Other than that one breath, he could have been one of the statues on display.

"Do you have a name?" she asked.

He frowned. "You want my name?"

"Well, it would feel rude to refer to you as 'the big, silent guy' in my internal monologue, so yeah, a name would be nice." He was still silent. Ava frowned. "Is that not part of your job or—?"

"Malachi."

She smiled. "Malachi?"

"My name is Malachi."

"Nice name."

"I like yours."

She shrugged off the internal pleasure. "It's… easy to spell. Anyway, I have an appointment this afternoon, so I'll be heading back to my hotel now. I'll be trying to take a nap for approximately forty-five minutes, but will realize it's too hot, so I'll then take a shower and read a book. Maybe dump my pictures on the computer. All of this will be happening *in* my hotel, which has very good security, but please feel free to lurk around the entrance so you can shadow me to my appointment later."

Malachi stared at her, still silent. Finally, he put down the book and crossed his arms over his chest, leaning back in his chair and looking at her as if he was trying to solve a puzzle.

"Nothing to add? Any questions? I'm not sure how much Mom and Carl told you. I'm just here in the city for a while. Taking pictures… for my job. With a magazine."

More silence.

Ava shook her head and stood. "Fine. Whatever. I'll see you around, Malachi."

She turned to go, but he said her name in that low voice and she turned back.

"Ava."

"Yes?"

He stood and walked toward her. He didn't hold out his hand, didn't touch her in any way, but she still felt surrounded. Her breath caught as his inner voice took on an urgent tone.

"I will protect you."

She could feel her face heat. There was something intimate about the words, despite knowing he was only doing his job.

"I know. And I want you to know that I appreciate—"

"If there is any threat to you, I will protect you." He took another step closer, and Ava tried not to shrink back. "I promise."

She felt short of breath. Not from panic, but... "Wow, you take your job pretty seriously, huh?"

The first hint of humor crossed his face, and she saw the corner of his mouth inch up. "I do."

"Okay." She stepped back, no longer able to sustain his presence. There was something magnetic about the man, and she didn't want to know more. "I'm going back now. Don't forget, appointment later."

"After not-napping."

She forced a smile. "Exactly. See? You're an expert at my schedule already."

He said nothing more, but his quiet amusement followed Ava all the way back to her room.

• • •   • • •

HE PICKED HER UP AGAIN ON THE CORNER NEAR THE HOTEL BUT STAYED a polite distance back and didn't try to approach. She walked to the tram station and hopped on board, Malachi shadowing her. Then she stood, swaying with the movement of the car as the tram followed the tracks, down the hill and across the bridge to the New City. Instead of marble and brick, she was met with concrete and glass when she got off. Soaring buildings that would have been at home in any metropolitan area of Europe or Asia.

Malachi came a little closer as she walked toward the modern building that housed the doctor's office. Ava noticed several names and office signs that seemed to indicate it was an office building for different medical or mental health professionals. She took the elevator up to the third floor, ignoring her shadow, who seemed thankfully content to linger in the lobby.

"Ms. Matheson?" A receptionist greeted her in the small waiting room.

"Ava, please."

"Dr. Sadik will be just a few moments."

"Of course."

A few minutes later, a nurse peered into the waiting room and smiled before escorting her back to an utterly common office. There was a desk in one corner and a grouping of comfortable chairs in another. A chaise as well.

Ava had to smile. Apparently, Dr. Sadik was a traditionalist. She hadn't seen a chaise in a psychologist's office since she'd been a kid.

Green plants filled a small corner solarium, lending a verdant energy to the room, and Ava settled into a chair to wait.

She knew very little about Dr. J. Sadik other than the recommendation of the psychiatrist in Tel Aviv. Still, the shrink in Israel was supposed to be one of the best in his field, so Ava was willing to give his recommendation a chance. There wasn't much online about him, but maybe that was common for Turkish doctors. She had enough experience with mental health professionals to spot a quack from a mile away. So far, everything about the office and the staff seemed exactly like what she would expect.

"Ava?" She heard her name from the back of the room. Odd, she hadn't sensed the man before he entered. She must have been more distracted than she realized.

A thin man wearing glasses approached, holding out his hand for Ava to shake. He looked like he was in his early forties, younger than she was expecting. A pair of green eyes peeked out from behind simple gold rims. His English was slightly accented; Ava would guess Dr. Sadik had studied in England.

"You must be Dr. Sadik." She smiled, trying to be polite. She could be polite. He was probably a perfectly nice man, even though he wouldn't be able to help her. He took her hand in his and grasped it warmly.

As soon as he did, an unprecedented sense of peace filled her. It was as if the tension fled the room. Ava felt… clear. Unburdened. She cocked her head and smiled at him.

"What on earth…"

"I hear you have had trouble with voices, Ava. I'd like to help. From what little Dr. Asner has shared, I think I have had other patients with the same affliction."

"You have?" Nothing about this made sense, but not a single alarm bell was going off in her mind.

"I believe so. I hope my treatments might help you as they've helped others. My other patients have learned how to manage their condition, allowing them to live more serene lives. I believe I could do the same for you, if you'd be willing to meet with me. I'd very much like to help you."

The peace stole up her arm and through her shoulders, loosening them as Dr. Sadik still grasped her hand.

"That sounds…"

"Yes?"

"Wonderful. It sounds wonderful. But I'm not going to lie—"

"You have doubts." He cast an understanding smile toward her. "Of course you do. You're an intelligent woman. But let us sit." He motioned toward the chairs. "And talk more. Ask me whatever you like, Ms.—"

"Ava," she interrupted. "Just call me Ava."

"Very well, Ava." Dr. Sadik smiled and settled into his own chair. "What would you like to know?"

CHAPTER

THREE

A cruise on the Bosphorus was hardly how Malachi would have chosen to spend a ninety-degree day, but that didn't matter. He was still following Ava, which meant he did what she did. And currently, that meant sitting through an uneventful narration of the history of Istanbul while on the water. Ava perched on the port side of the cruise ship, snapping pictures. She was evenly split between amusement and boredom if he had to guess from her expression. He'd become reluctantly familiar with the human woman in the days he'd been guarding her.

There, the privately bemused smile.

There, the bored lift of her right eyebrow.

There, the slight pinch of her mouth when someone passed too close.

Malachi might have had his suspicions, but he questioned whether they were mere figments of his own hopeful imagination. He hadn't spotted a Grigori in days—not surprising since the two who had approached her in the alley had seen Malachi, as well. No Grigori would willingly take on a trained Irin scribe alone, or even with a partner. But could Ava be what he suspected without attracting their attention? None of it added up.

Malachi heard his phone ring.

"*Allo?*"

"It's Damien. Anything new?"

"You're missing out. It's a beautiful, hot day on the water. Lots of tourists. Sadly, no beer."

His watcher ignored him. "No one is following her?"

"Other than me? No."

There was a pause.

"If there has been no other threat to her—"

"They saw me." He stood and moved to a more secluded part of the deck near the back, where the wind would carry his voice out over the water. He still kept an eye on Ava. "I imagine they're being cautious. And since she thinks I'm some personal bodyguard her family hired to protect her, I don't even have to hide. She sees me and says nothing. It's the perfect cover to find out more about her."

"Malachi, Rhys and I have been looking into her family history. There is no evidence—"

"That she's Irina? I told you what she said."

"She said, 'I heard you.' One statement that could mean any number of things, and then she ran away. If she was Irina, even if she didn't know it, she'd be drawn to you. It's part of who we are. And how could she be unaware?"

"If she was born after the Rending—"

"She was born Ava Russell, to Lena Russell, a single mother, in 1985. Born in Los Angeles, raised in Santa Monica. The scribe house there has no record of her or her mother. There is no father listed. What Irin would leave a child without giving her a name, Malachi? What Irina would raise her child outside the safety of a retreat?"

He had nothing to say. Damien was right. The number of Irin children born after the Rending could be counted on a few hands. They were never unguarded, particularly the young Irina. They were hidden away and treasured by their mothers, most of whom were in hiding. His people hadn't been whole for two hundred years.

"I still think there is something different about her." His voice was irritatingly hoarse. "How else would you explain the Grigori watching her like that?"

It was Damien who paused then.

"Jaron is..." His voice was halting. "Not as some others are. Since he has moved West, his people have not been as aggressive."

A derisive snort was the only answer Malachi gave him.

Damien said, "It's in their nature to be predators, yes. But there haven't been as many deaths in Istanbul as you'd expect in the past twenty years. And yes, preying on women in the middle of the day like that is unusual. It's possible that whoever was following her has been taken care of. He's very controlling. That's why this area has experienced the relative calm that it has."

"You're acting as if there is some kind of truce between you and him."

"There isn't. There can't be; you know that. His nature has not changed, nor has ours. But he keeps a lower profile than what you were used to in Germany. Jaron is not Volund. He doesn't like attention, and his Grigori are more subtle in their pursuits."

Their pursuits. Malachi sneered. What a polite name for the Grigori practice of aggressively seducing and bedding human women, often leaving them half-dead or impregnated with children that could kill them simply by being born. Malachi had been tracking and killing Grigori soldiers for over four hundred years. It was his burning purpose in life. He had yet to see any soldier exhibit restraint.

"Nevertheless, I am going to stay with her."

"And when she leaves? Rhys said she's scheduled to leave Istanbul in another two weeks."

"Then we'll see what happens in two weeks."

"You're not following her out of the city, Malachi. I won't allow it."

Malachi bristled instinctively at the command. "Damien—"

"I am your superior," his watcher reminded him coldly. "I will not allow it. Leave the human woman to whatever fate the Creator has for her."

Malachi struggled to put into words the compulsion he felt. Ava Matheson needed to be protected. He knew she couldn't be one of his kind, but there was still something…

"I sense something in her, Damien. Something different. I feel—"

"You feel hope, my friend." The watcher's voice softened slightly. "Something most of us haven't felt for a very long time. But this hope… it's your own desire. Nothing more. You're not thinking clearly. She's not Irina. She can't be."

"I know that."

"Do you?"

Did he? His eyes returned to her. Ava was sitting next to a group of children, her eyes easy, her expression relaxed. Everything Damien had said about Ava made sense. There was no logical way she could be one of their kind. None. But something about her—her reactions, her energy—screamed that she was more than human. She was other. Different. Even the way she held herself away from the crowd while trying to blend in was familiar.

"I'll follow her while she's in the city. After that…"

"You'll return to your duties, Malachi. You have a job to do. Leo and Maxim are already covering your shifts."

A smile touched the corner of his mouth. "But I thought Jaron's Grigori were the civilized ones."

"A civilized Grigori is still a threat and an abomination. Some things will never change, including our mission."

Malachi was tired of Damien's constant discipline. Tired of the endless nights of stalking and waiting and violence. Perhaps someday he would join the more peaceful of their brethren in a rural scribe house like Rhys was always talking of doing. He would cloak his armor and spend his days copying sacred texts and his nights watching the stars, perhaps even some day counter the spells that prolonged his life so he could fade into the heavens as so many Irin had after their mates were torn from them.

Malachi had no mate. Only a handful of scribes did. And it was because of the cursed Grigori that he and all his kind were fated to spend their long lives alone.

He was kidding himself. He'd never retire from a warrior's life. Malachi would fight them as long as he lived.

"You have a job to do, Malachi." Damien was still talking. "And that job is not following a human woman who happens to catch your eye."

"Yes, Watcher."

"Keep me informed of your movements. I want to know where you are."

"Have Rhys enable the tracker on my phone. He can do that now, you know. You can watch me move on the map, if you want."

Damien paused. "He can do that?"

Malachi chuckled. "Welcome to the twenty-first century, old friend."

* * *   * * *

THE TOUR BOAT HAD REACHED THE END OF THE GOLDEN HORN AND had turned back toward the Galata Bridge when Ava approached him. He'd been playing a game on his phone, some mind-numbing activity Leo was addicted to that involved shooting birds at pigs. It was oddly satisfying; the pigs exploded in a puff not unlike the Grigori when you put a knife in the right place. He glanced up when he saw her move, then watched silently as she approached the bench in the corner where he had positioned himself. Her camera bag bumped against her thigh as she walked, an unwieldy cargo he'd never seen her without.

She paused in front of him, then sank onto the wooden bench opposite as Malachi hid his phone.

"I'm incredibly bored."

He shrugged. "So why did you take the tour?"

"You're supposed to take a tour of Istanbul from the sea. Didn't you know that?"

He smiled. "Do you always do what you're supposed to?"

"Hardly ever, but this is work."

"What do you do?" He already knew. Rhys had given him a full profile on her the day after he'd discovered her name.

"I take pictures for travel magazines."

Ava Matheson was considered one of the top travel photojournalists in her field, distinguishing herself by her willingness to go to the most remote location and capture it for the hungry print and online world. In fact, the more remote the location, the more attractive the job seemed to be for her. She'd climbed mountains in Peru and Nepal, traversed the Gobi Desert, and boated the Orinoco. The burgeoning ecotourism industry loved her. Ava specialized in finding the luxurious in the most remote places in the world. She seemed to avoid cities unless there was a specific assignment calling her to one. Malachi had no idea what she was doing in Istanbul, as Rhys could find no record of a commission from any of her usual clients.

"Which magazine do you work for?"

"Lots of them." Her gaze drifted off for a moment until it snapped back to his face. "I don't want to talk about work. Isn't that boring? I bet you hate to talk about bodyguard gigs. You probably have some great stories you can't tell anyone though, huh?"

You have no idea. He lifted an eyebrow. "So what do you want to talk about?"

He hoped she wasn't thinking about coming on to him. That was destined to end badly, then she'd call her parents—or whoever she thought had hired him—and start asking inconvenient questions.

"Are you Turkish? You don't have the same accent as most of the people I've met."

He could actually be honest about that one. "I am, but I've traveled a lot. Lived in a lot of other places. I imagine that's influenced the accent. You?"

"All-American girl."

"They write songs about your kind, you know."

She laughed. "*My* kind? That's a good one. I can pretty much promise they don't write songs about *my* kind. Not good ones, anyway. Have you been to the States?"

"I lived in Chicago for a time, but that was years ago."

Ava leaned forward, resting her chin in the palm of her hand as the breeze pulled dark hair into her eyes. "And what did you do in Chicago?"

I helped kill the upper echelon of Grigori soldiers belonging to a fallen angel who preys on the women of the Upper Midwest. And his pack of dogs. He was pissed about the dogs.

"The same thing I do here."

"Exciting."

"It has its moments."

"Did you ever guard Oprah?"

"I don't think so." He frowned. "Not directly."

"So, Malachi..." She shifted again, leaning back and lifting her face to the sun. It poured over her, warming her pale skin and lighting the red in her hair. She tilted her head back, closing her eyes behind her sunglasses. "Are you an independent contractor, or do you work for one of Carl's usual companies?"

She was subtly digging for information, but he couldn't figure out why. He decided to play along for now. It would be less suspicious.

"I'm somewhat independent, but I work with a larger company. The headquarters is in Vienna. I imagine Mr. Matheson was referred from there."

"Probably. He's doing a lot of work in Eastern Europe lately. Low production costs."

Her stepfather was a film producer, but Ava seemed unimpressed. In fact, everything about her spoke of boredom. Jaded expression. Cynical quirk to her mouth. Malachi sensed something else, though.

Lonely. The woman was desperately lonely.

"Do you like to travel alone?"

She seemed surprised that he'd asked a question. Her head tilted forward and she looked at him. "What?"

"Am I not allowed to ask you questions?"

"It's unusual."

"Call me unusual, then."

She smiled then, a genuine smile untouched by cynicism. "Yeah, I like it. I'm not the most social person in the world."

"I've noticed."

"Wow. That bad, huh?"

He shrugged. "You just seem to like your own space. I don't see you chatting with many strangers like a lot of the tourists do."

"My own space?" Her smile hinted at some inside joke. "You could call it that. I don't travel much in cities. They're very…"

He waited, but she seemed to expect him to interrupt. He didn't.

Finally, she said, "They're crowded. Noisy. Too many smells and sounds and sights all crashing together. I don't like them, usually."

"Not even Constantinople?"

"You mean Istanbul?"

He grinned. "Are we going there?"

"We better not." She laughed again. "I'll have that song stuck in my head for days. But to answer your question, despite the noise and the people and the heat—"

"The heat is something else, isn't it?"

"No worse than L.A. most summers. Despite all that…" Her eyes drifted toward the water. "I like it here. There's something about it, isn't there? It's…" Her eyes sought his. "Seductive."

Malachi could feel the tattoos covering his chest pulse. *No… Not going there, either.*

He straightened and cleared his throat. "It's a fascinating place. Very complicated history."

"I can tell." Her golden-brown eyes seemed to mock him. "Just by looking at it."

Silence fell between them as she held his stare. The wind picked up, teasing the fine hair at the back of his neck. He saw her glance down at the tattoo work along his collar, but she said nothing. Asked nothing.

"Why are you here?" he asked. "Really?"

"Headaches." The mask fell over her face. She had answered without thinking. He was betting she didn't do that often.

"Headaches?"

"The condition I mentioned the other day." She waved a careless hand. "There's a doctor here who specializes in it. The appointment last week, remember? I was referred to him. And you don't need to report that to Carl or my mom."

"I don't report on your activities to anyone unless I think there is some aspect of your safety in jeopardy. I'm not a stalker; I'm a guard."

"Good."

"Is he helping?"

"The doctor?"

"Yes."

Her head bobbed back and forth, considering the question. "Maybe. I try not to get my hopes up, you know? I've lived with the headaches my whole life."

Malachi knew all about not getting his hopes up. So why was he having a hard time believing Damien?

"And there is no cure for them?"

"Not that anyone has found. It's not a tumor or anything. They're a bit of a mystery."

As are you, woman. It wasn't headaches. At least, that wasn't all of it. He didn't know exactly what was going on with the interesting American woman, but he was determined to find out.

Malachi said, "It's better to be cautious, even with doctors. If there is any background information you'd like on this doctor, let me know. I know many people in Istanbul. Maybe some of my friends or associates have gone to him."

From her expression, she didn't like that idea. "I'll keep it in mind. I'm fine for right now."

"I just wanted to offer."

"Noted." She forced a smile. "But not necessary. I'm fine."

You are anything but fine.

The tour boat was pulling into the dock, and passengers rose to their feet. Ava joined them without a word, leaving Malachi behind to watch her walk down the gangway. Wordlessly, he stood, then followed her at a comfortable distance as she grabbed a fish sandwich from one of the floating restaurants and walked back toward her hotel, lonely and silent in the afternoon crowd.

Malachi strode into the house and straight to the library, not even stopping to rib Maxim about the bottle of beer the younger man was drinking in the kitchen. He'd left Ava exhausted. He was fairly sure she was done for the day, but the tiny tracker he'd slipped in her bag would alert him if she left the perimeter he'd set up around the grounds of the hotel. And if she was done for the day, then he had some questions for Rhys.

"Sadik," he said when he spied the shorter scribe sitting at his computer. "He's the doctor she's seeing. I saw it on the directory at the building we visited. J. Sadik. I need to know everything about him."

Rhys turned and frowned. "Had a great day, thanks. The air conditioner is fixed, and the activity logs have been updated and sent to Vienna. And I covered your patrol last night. How was the dinner cruise? Was there a show?"

"No dinner. No show. It was hot but informative." He paused and tried to slow his brain. "Thank you for covering my shift."

"Well, since you're on babysitting duty for the mysterious human, we're all *more* than happy to pitch in." Not even Rhys's polite accent could hide the sarcasm. Malachi knew the others thought he was following a rabbit trail, but he didn't care.

"Dr. J. Sa—"

"Sadik." Rhys turned back to the computer. "I heard you the first time. I'm just trying to force you into social niceties you seem to have forgotten living among the barbarians." Rhys's fingers began typing rapidly. The three-hundred-year- old scribe had taken to modern information technology like a duck to water. Not all Irin did. Damien still considered anything more advanced than a telegraph suspicious.

"Thank you, Rhys."

"Don't mention it. Really. What kind of doctor?"

"I don't know. She says she has headaches."

"Headaches?" he muttered. "That could by physical, psychological... You have no idea what kind of headaches?"

"She wasn't exactly forthcoming. She said he was a specialist she was referred to."

Rhys gave him a quiet " hmph" and kept typing.

"Where?"

"He's in the city. Just a few miles from here. She saw him last week after the attack in the alley."

More typing.

"Sadik? You're sure of it?"

"Who is he? Yes, I'm sure." Malachi leaned in, looking over the other man's shoulder, but nothing on the screen made sense.

"There are a number of Sadiks, but none of them are specialists in anything to do with headaches." More typing. More muttering. Rhys shook his head. "Nothing in the government system… nothing in private. Here's one who is a pediatrician. An oncologist?"

"It didn't sound like cancer."

"That one is a woman, anyway. She said it was a male?"

"Ava referred to 'him.'"

More typing. "I'm not finding anything that would match. Not in this part of the city."

Alarm bells started to go off. "What do you mean? There has to be a record. Maybe he moved his office."

"I'm not finding anything…" Rhys started typing again. "If he's practicing anywhere in Turkey, I should be able to find him. He's not in initial searches. I suppose I can keep looking…"

"Yes," he said. Then quickly added, "Please."

"See? You *can* be taught."

J. Sadik, who are you?

He patted Rhys's shoulder. "Thanks for checking. I may have to look in other directions."

Rhys was still frowning, and Malachi knew the scribe was irritated that he hadn't been able to find the answers his friend was looking for. "She was in Israel before she came here. Maybe the referral came from a doctor there. I'm going to search her medical records. I'll see what I can find online."

For some reason, the idea of Rhys digging into Ava's background irked him. "Is that necessary?"

"Do you want to find out who this doctor is and why she's seeing him?"

"Yes."

"Then why do you care?"

The other man went back to furious typing while Malachi drifted back toward the kitchen. It was a good question.

Why *did* he care?

CHAPTER
FOUR

Ava looked up from her tea when she heard the clanging streetcar moving down İstiklal Avenue. She leaned back and watched it. Pedestrians in the crowded Beyoğlu neighborhood moved around the car. Tourists. Locals. Merchants. She was in the heart of Istanbul, but for the first time in her life, the city was… peaceful. The hum of voices had become quieter, easier to ignore. The manic energy that seemed to envelope her most days was absent. Ava felt grounded.

She took a deep breath and had to admit that, for the first time in her life, a doctor's treatment seemed to be working.

Dr. Sadik's methods were unusual, to say the least. Holistic in practice, the psychologist had prescribed her a diet of mostly Mediterranean foods and was using a kind of pressure-point massage in addition to talk therapy. She'd been skeptical. But one of his nurses assisted with the massage, and when she'd left the office after the first treatment, Ava had to admit the voices were slightly muffled. She'd felt more focused and relaxed. After a few days, the effects had worn off, but the next appointment showed even more relief. She was going in every three days and was starting to wonder whether she'd ever be able to leave.

Glancing over her shoulder at the man sitting a few tables away, she wondered what her mother would do if she decided to stay. Would she and Carl continue to pay her shadow? Malachi had started following her more closely since the cruise but still kept his distance. He was both the least and the most annoying bodyguard she'd ever had. He was more than discreet and carried himself with a quiet confidence that put her at ease. At the same time, Ava sensed he wanted to come closer—to talk to her, to know her more—but he didn't. She supposed that was her own fault. It wasn't his job to keep her company.

Still…

She glanced over her shoulder again. He was sipping tea two tables away from her, lounging in a low chair and pretending to read a paper. Behind his sunglasses, she could see him scanning the street, still vigilant despite the peaceful morning.

Keeping her eyes on him, she spoke in a low voice. "Malachi."

His eyes zipped immediately to her.

"Yes?"

"You have good hearing."

"Among other talents."

She grinned. "Why are you sitting two tables away in an empty café?"

One dark eyebrow lifted. "I believe I was told to keep my distance by a certain prickly photographer."

"Well, that was before we got to be friends."

"We're friends?" There was an amused smile on his lips, and Ava saw the hint of a dimple on his slightly stubbled cheek. He had thick dark hair and would likely have a full beard within days if he didn't keep clean-shaven. Handsome? Not classically. But the man had definite appeal.

"Of course we're friends. Do you think I habitually strike up conversations with random men in foreign countries?"

"I wouldn't even try to guess the answer to that." He had set the newspaper down and leaned back in the plush chair, bringing the glass of tea to his full lips as she watched him, watching her.

"I don't. Strike up random conversations, I mean."

"Is there something you want, Ava?"

She let her eyes wander over him, not caring that he noticed her perusal. "You said you're from Turkey?"

"Yes."

"So why don't you stop following me and just show me around?" She surprised herself with the question. Usually she never asked for company. Prolonged contact of any kind could become maddening. But the treatments had calmed her mind, making the soothing resonance he exuded even more appealing. For the first time in her life, the thought of spending the day with a man was attractive, not overwhelming. "I'm bored by myself."

He put down his glass of tea, almost scowling. "I'm not paid to be your tour guide."

The disappointment was quick and sharp. "Fine."

She spun around and turned her back to him, resisting the urge to get up and flee. It would be humiliating for him to see how his rejection had affected her. Besides, he'd just follow her anyway. She picked up her tea with tense fingers and sipped, grabbing a book out of her bag. She briefly debated taking out her small camera and capturing pedestrian traffic, but she'd been trying to take a day off from work and enjoy her newfound calm.

After a few minutes, Ava heard him rise and approach. She gritted her teeth and kept her eyes on her guidebook.

Damn, damn, damn. He'd rebuffed her. The least he could do was pretend to ignore her existence.

No, instead he was sitting down across from her, all six feet and something; his long legs slid under the table, unavoidably brushing against her own. She refused to move.

"Ava."

"What?"

"My apologies. That was rude."

"Yes, it was."

She was still staring at her book. He continued to sit across from her silently. His inner voice took on an amused tone that made her scowl.

"Ava?"

"I'm reading."

"That's impressive."

She rolled her eyes and finally looked up. "What? Reading?"

He tried to control the smile, but the dimple gave him away. "Reading upside down. I can do it as well, but it took many years of study."

Her cheeks burning, she set down the book. "What do you want?"

Malachi was still wearing sunglasses, but she caught the quick glance he gave her. It wasn't clinical.

So, not indifferent, after all.

Feeling slightly smug, she said, "Well?"

"You asked me to show you around the city. I would be happy to do that."

"Maybe I should just hire someone."

Oh, he didn't like that. She could tell by the tightening in his jaw and the way his voice changed. "You could. But, as you pointed out, I am local, and I know the city well. I am already guarding you. It would make the job more…"

"Friendly?"

The dimple was back. "Yes."

"Fine." She picked up her book, flipping it right side up. "I guess so."

"You guess so?" His eyebrows furrowed together. "That's not very *friendly*. Didn't you just say we were friends?"

"Well, that was before you pissed me off, Mal."

"Mal?" He sneered. "My name is not Mal."

Ava cheered internally, pleased to have found something so convenient to annoy him with. "Oh, it can be."

"When I piss you off?"

"Mmhmm."

"Are you always like this? I think I should be warned ahead of time if we're going to be… friends."

"Like what?"

"Irritable and moody."

She looked up in mock indignation. "This is me in a good mood, Mal."

He closed his eyes and shook his head, but the telltale dimple gave away his amusement, and his inner voice was practically laughing.

"Fine. Put down the guidebook. You don't need it anymore."

"It's a good one, though. And I like learning about the history of the places I visit."

"Trust me, I know the history." She looked up, skeptical, but his voice was confident, bordering on smug.

"So you're a historian as well as a bodyguard?"

"Something like that."

The way his lip curled made her want to bite it. He must have caught her look, because the corner of his mouth turned up even more.

"Trust me, Ava." He leaned forward, resting his elbows on the table. "With me, no guidebook is necessary. I'll tell you everything you need to know."

It was cool and quiet; the echoes of people in the cistern melded together with the whispering voices, creating a mesh of quiet noise Ava glided on in the darkness. Beneath the bustle of the streets above, the Basilica Cistern stretched hundreds of yards into the black underground. Held up by endless marble pillars and dotted by gold lights, the shallow water rested, and Ava watched shadow fish dart over the flash of coins visitors had thrown in its depths.

Malachi followed her, letting her take in the grandeur of the vast room before he spoke in a quiet voice.

"Some people call it the Underground Palace. It's the largest of the ancient cisterns in Constantinople, originally built by Constantine, then rebuilt by the Emperor Justinian in the sixth century. There are hundreds of cisterns beneath the city, but this one..." His voice held a note of awe. "It is the largest. It fed the palace itself."

Ava was at a loss. "It's..."

Stunning.

Eerie.

Otherworldly.

"It's beautiful," she finally said.

"It is that," Malachi said softly. "The city cisterns were fed from aqueducts the Romans built. Some still lead back to their water source or have tunnels leading between them. During its use, the water would have been far higher. Over our heads." They strolled along the raised platform, damp with water dripping from the domed ceiling above. "Modern Istanbul holds pieces of Greece, Rome, the Byzantines, the Ottomans. New conquerors, new rulers, new buildings. Still the same city, just with a different face. The bones remain the same."

"Archaeologists must have a field day here."

He nodded. "There's much to discover still. Istanbul is a puzzle, and I doubt all her secrets will ever be revealed."

"I don't think I want them to be," she whispered. "I like the mystery. I love this place, this Underground Palace."

Malachi's eyes took on a distant stare. "It's set apart. Another world, almost." He walked to the edge of the platform, looking out over the dark water. "There are many places like this in the city. Places where the present and the past seem to coexist at once. As if they live next to each other, only a ripple away."

She watched him as he turned back to her, eyes still scanning the darkness. Who was this man?

He caught her glance. "What?"

"Who are you?" she asked. "You don't sound like any bodyguard I've ever had."

Malachi smiled. "I'm not so unusual. Perhaps you keep too much distance."

"It's necessary."

"Why?"

Was it the darkness? In the quiet underworld, she felt as if she was talking to a shadow. "I just can't be around many people. They make me uncomfortable. It's exhausting."

"Why?"

Ava turned away. "Find a new question, Mal."

Silence fell between them, filled with the echoes of voices in the dark. Ava could feel him—actually feel him—approach from behind. She tried not to tense.

"You have been more at ease than when we first met." He kept the question light. "Is your doctor helping?"

"Yes, he is."

"That's good."

She forced herself to turn and smiled. "I'm optimistic. Istanbul might just become my favorite city."

"Because of the doctor?"

They kept walking, strolling farther through the cisterns. Ava paused at the edge of a tour group, but the guide was speaking German.

"Partly. But I think the attraction was here even before I met him. There's just something about this place, you know?"

"I don't know, I—"

She interrupted him with a laugh. "You're from here, so you probably don't really get that. I mean, I know people love L.A. Love Hollywood, but it never seemed all that special to me because I grew up there. Istanbul is probably that way for you."

"No."

He had stopped behind her. Ava turned to him. "No?"

"I understand. It's part of the reason I came back. This city… It feeds the soul."

A strange fluttering started in her chest. "I didn't know my soul was hungry."

"Didn't you?" He smiled. "Hmm."

"Oh, Malachi…" Ava turned and pretended to read a sign. "The things you say in a single 'hmm.'"

She felt him step closer. Could feel her body react. His lips were sealed, but his voice whispered to her. Taunting, teasing whispers that begged her to come closer. She turned her head, and her heart raced as his eyes dropped to her mouth. He leaned down, parting his lips as if to speak, but before he could say anything, a child bumped into Ava from behind, giggling as she sent Ava stumbling into Malachi's chest.

He caught her elbows, and she heard him suck in a breath.

There was a flash of awareness. A sense and a silence. In that second, his pure voice was the only thing she heard, and the sense of harmony threatened to overwhelm her. Ava gasped.

She needed.

Wanted.

Needed.

Utter and complete peace enveloped her for a brief moment, then it was gone when Malachi dropped his hands. Eyes blinking, he backed away, and she let out the breath she held. Once again, the voices wrapped around her, muffled—like a distant chorus they circled and taunted her.

For a second, they had been gone. Completely gone.

And his voice was the only thing she'd heard.

"Malachi?"

"Hmm?" His face was an impenetrable mask, half-cloaked in darkness.

"I…" What was she going to say?

Touch me.

Hold my hand.

Can you make them go away?

"I… don't feel very well," she breathed out. "I'd like to go back to my hotel now."

"Of course," he said quickly, immediately ushering her toward the exit.

Did he know? Could he feel it, too? Ava shook her head to try to shake some sense into it. Of *course* he hadn't felt it. He wasn't nuts. The odd feeling was probably a result of the strange mood in the underground cistern combined with dehydration and an unexpected—and entirely impractical—attraction to the man.

It had snuck up on her, but she was honest enough to acknowledge it, even as she recognized the futility of the attraction.

What man would want a relationship with her? Her lovers were fleeting. They had to be. Prolonged contact only made her condition worse. Her longest relationship had been during college. It was only three months before he'd been overwhelmed by her, and she by him. She'd flooded him with her energy, her moods, her manic bursts of activity.

"I can't keep up with you."

"You're exhausting."

"Too much, Ava. You're just… too much."

Too much.

It was all too much. She and Malachi walked through a tour group coming down the stairs. Dozens of people brushed past her, almost causing her to stumble. For a second, tears welled in her eyes. She saw Malachi reach for her hand instinctively, then he stopped, drawing his fingers back like a child not allowed to touch. She stayed close behind him, letting his broad shoulders clear a path through the crowd. When they finally reached the outdoors, the sound of traffic overwhelmed the wash of voices. The honks and shouts of the drivers were an unexpected relief.

Ava slipped on her sunglasses and, without waiting for her shadow, started back to the hotel.

• • •   • • •

Her appointment with Dr. Sadik couldn't come early enough the next day. She left Malachi drinking tea at a café across the street and walked up to the office, opening the door on the third floor landing before she made her way down the hall and into the office. The pleasant receptionist greeted her with a smile.

"May I get you some tea, Ms. Matheson? You are a few minutes early. Dr. Sadik should be ready for you shortly." She rose before Ava even answered, moving to the corner where a pot of the tea sat in a clear carafe. Taking one of the modern armchairs, Ava held out her hand when the young woman brought her the drink.

"Thank you. And please, call me Ava."

"Such a beautiful name," the receptionist said with a smile. "Please let me know if there is anything else I can get you, Ava."

"Thanks." She settled in, sipping the tea and listening to the quiet hum of the woman's mind drift over the meditative music that filled the room. In a few minutes, she heard the door on the other side of Dr. Sadik's office close, signaling that his other client had left. A few moments later, his smiling face poked through the door.

"Ava! How are you this morning?"

Immediately put at ease by his presence, she rose. "Doing fine, thank you."

The look in his eyes told Ava that he knew there was more to the story, but he didn't prod in front of the receptionist. She walked to the office and quickly took a seat on the chaise. "Is Rana here yet?"

The nurse who helped with the massage was usually there when Ava came in the office.

"She is running just a bit behind today. I apologize. Why don't we talk for a few moments?"

She took a deep breath. "Sure."

"How have the voices been?" He cut straight to the chase.

"Um... good." She smiled tentatively. "Well, better."

Dr. Sadik nodded, his gold-rimmed glasses flashing in the light from the window. He was sneaking up on middle age, but something about his expression and manner seemed far older. It was probably just a cultural difference.

The doctor said, "I believe I told you to expect that, did I not? We are not attempting to *cure* you of anything, because it is my belief, and yours as well, that there is no mental illness to cure. What we are doing is learning to manage the unique circumstances—an unusual perception, shall we say—under which your mind works."

"Yes." She let out a breath and tried to relax. "I like it. I feel better. And I'm glad you don't think I'm crazy. You're probably the first person to treat me who doesn't think so."

He smiled. "I told you, you are not my first patient with this condition. And the others saw relief with the treatments, as well."

She glanced at the clock on the wall. "Did Rana say how long she'd be?"

"Just ten minutes or so."

Most of the pressure-point massage happened in the head, neck and shoulders, but Dr. Sadik seemed to be very cautious about contact with Ava unless his nurse was present. He'd insisted on it from the beginning, which had put her at ease. Ava was eager to end the small talk and get on with her appointment.

"How are you enjoying Istanbul?" he asked. "You are traveling alone, am I correct?"

"I am. But everyone here is so friendly, I almost feel like I've been here before and they recognize me."

He smiled. "Turks take hospitality very seriously. It is a wonderful part of their culture."

Their culture? She frowned. Ava had assumed the doctor was Turkish. "Yes, well… I'm enjoying it. I'll definitely come back. Someone I met told me that Istanbul feeds the soul. I think he may be right."

She caught a flash in his eyes, as if he recognized the saying. Was it a common proverb in Turkey? The expression fled, and polite interest took its place again.

"Istanbul has been important to many world religions, particularly Islam and Christianity. But even before that, it has always been rich with enlightenment and culture. One could definitely say it is good for the soul."

"Maybe that's why the voices aren't as loud," she joked. "My soul isn't as hungry here."

"Perhaps." He didn't seem to take it as a joke. "There are many beliefs about the soul. Ancient Persians were one of the first to classify the soul as something distinct and eternal. They believed the soul survived death, as do Jews, Christians, and Muslims. The Egyptians believed the soul existed with five distinct parts, one of which was the heart." He smiled and patted his chest. "Others believe the soul is what gives a person their personality and creativity, though we know those are functions of the brain, of course."

"Of course." Why was he on this tangent? And when was the nurse going to get there? She didn't have all day.

Well, actually she did.

"But the mind is where *my* interest lies, of course." Dr. Sadik was still talking. "The mind… such a complicated, wonderful organ. So many mysteries to solve. Perhaps the mind is the seat of the soul. After all, it is the seat of creativity, which many world religions consider a reflection of the divine."

"What is? The mind?"

"Creativity," he said, his eyes gleaming. "Surely, as an artist, you have experienced this. The flash of insight that seems to come from outside yourself. Some would say creativity is the voice of the soul."

His inner voice was muffled, but she could still sense his excitement. "I'm… I'm just a photographer, Dr. Sadik. I don't really create like that. I'm not a painter or anything."

"Ah." He leaned back in his chair. "Perhaps that is not where your true creativity lies."

At that moment, Ava heard the door open and Rana walked in.

"Dr. Sadik, I am so sorry! Ms. Matheson, forgive me. My father is unwell, and—"

"Not to worry, my dear." Dr. Sadik rose from his chair. "Ava and I have just been chatting. But we should begin." He turned to her and held out a hand. "Ava, are you ready?"

She heaved a sigh of relief that the odd philosophical conversation was over. "Absolutely."

CHAPTER

FIVE

I t was close to dawn when Malachi heard his watcher stir. Damien paced outside the locked ritual room the scribes used to write *talesm* as Malachi worked. Candles flickered against walls inscribed with their own unique magic, old protective charms the Irin who built the house had carved into the limestone walls. No electric light was allowed in the room. No windows pierced the web of incantations. A meditation fire burned constantly, tended by the watcher of the house. It was probably why Damien was pacing.

Let him wait.

Malachi didn't look up from his skin. He was working on a new spell for his right arm, a particularly intricate *talesm* to guard against temptation and provide focus. The ivory needle pierced his skin at lightning speed, the sacred ink luminescing with a faint silver glow as the spell worked itself into his body. He could feel it pulse and grow, the new magic twining with the ancient symbols that surrounded it. Malachi, like all Irin scribes, had become inured to the physical pain the tattoo produced. He only stopped to dip the needle into the ink made from the ash of the ritual fire. Within minutes, the characters of the Old Language took shape, twisting and joining the existing pattern of spells.

When he finished, Malachi took a deep breath and focused on the flames. He gave silent thanks to the Creator. To his mother who bore him, and his father who trained him. To his teachers. The council of the Elders. He closed his eyes and let the magic take hold. Then slowly, he opened them and looked down.

On a human, the skin around the tattoo would still be red and weeping, but Malachi wasn't entirely human. The *talesm* was already sealed, a thin layer of ink dried over the old letters; by morning, the scab would be gone. The silver glow surrounding the tattoo would fade until activated by his *talesm prim*, the circular spell inscribed on his left wrist.

As if sensing the waning magic, a soft knock came at the door.

"Malachi?"

"You can come in, Damien. I'm finished."

The door cracked open and Damien entered, clad only in the ceremonial wrap all watchers wore when attending to the sacred fire of their scribe house. The wrap covered his hips and upper legs, allowing the rest of Damien's *talesm* to warn anyone watching of his years and skill with magic.

Malachi, still flush with new power, sat back in the wide chair and let out a long breath. He could feel the magic working within, connecting and bonding with the older characters that marked his body.

"Good morning," Damien said, "You're up early."

"I slept little."

Damien grunted and rubbed his eyes. "You have finished your new *talesm*?"

"I have."

The watcher glanced over at Malachi's bicep, and his eyebrow lifted. "Self-control?"

"And focus."

There was a thoughtful pause before he asked, "Have you given thanks?"

"I have, Watcher."

Damien nodded.

Malachi took another deep breath as the other man kneeled before the fire, lifting his left wrist and tracing the letters of his own *talesm prim*. As the magic rose, Malachi could see the faint silver glow travel over Damien's body, from the newest spells on the man's legs to the family tattoos marking his shoulders and back. Malachi had similar tattoos, the only ones he had not written himself. He'd received the first from his father at the age of thirteen. The first taste of the ancient strength he would spend centuries perfecting.

As a boy, his mother's power had protected him, but at thirteen, Malachi was no longer considered a boy. His eyes were drawn to the first halting letters on his left wrist. The old spells hadn't faded, but the clumsy, boyish work still made him smile. The characters slowly grew more sophisticated as they traveled up his arm, trailing over his shoulder and collarbone before they started their centuries-long journey down his right arm. Wrapped and stacked around each other, each was unique, an expression of the scribe who wrote it.

Spells of protection on his forearm.

Long life over his wrist.

Strength.

Speed.

Keener vision. Steadier reflexes. Immunity to poisons and drugs. An Irin scribe as old as Malachi was practically immortal in battle unless he willingly gave his magic to another. But as Malachi had no mate...

His eyes flickered to the marks below Damien's left shoulder, directly over his heart. The scribe was rising from his knees, finished with his morning prayers, and collecting the ash from the brazier to make more ink.

Malachi asked, "Have you heard from Sari lately?"

Damien shot him a dark look. "Why?"

"Just curious."

"None of your business."

Silence. Malachi should have known better, but the urge to rankle his superior and the flush of magic made him brave.

Finally, Damien muttered, "No."

"I'm sorry."

The watcher shrugged. "I know she's safe. That's the most important thing. I can see her in our dream-walks; she just chooses to ignore me."

The light-headed feeling of new magic finally passed, so Malachi rose to his feet and dropped the tattoo needle in a basin to clean it. Then he gathered the linen cloths marked with ink and blood and tossed them in the fire. He stood, watching the pieces burn as Damien swept up the remains of the ash.

"I am drawn to her," Malachi confessed in a low voice.

"Since I'm going to assume you haven't lost your mind and aren't referring to my mate, I must assume you mean the human woman."

"Ava."

"Ava," Damien said thoughtfully. "It is a good name."

It was an Irina name. Malachi had wondered, but he knew humans used it too. It meant nothing.

"I touched her."

The brush clattered to the table and Damien grabbed him by the shoulder, spinning him around. The watcher's eyes were frigid pools of blue.

Malachi was quick to continue. "It was only a second. An accident caused by an unruly child in the crowd."

"She was not harmed?"

"No. It was only a few moments. No."

The grip on his shoulder relaxed slightly. "You're sure?"

Malachi lifted his hands. "She was tired afterward and asked to go back to her hotel, but I sensed it was the crowd bothering her more than anything. It had become busy at the cistern, and her head was aching again." And he'd reached out to relieve her as if she'd been Irina, Malachi realized later. Luckily, he'd drawn his hand back before their skin could connect. "She had a doctor's appointment the next day. She seemed completely healthy."

"Good." Damien took a deep breath and turned back to his tasks. "Has Rhys made any progress finding information about this doctor?"

"He's found her doctor in Tel Aviv, but there's no record of that man referring any patients to a Dr. Sadik in Turkey. Or any doctor in Turkey, for that matter."

Damien grunted again. "You two trust your computers too much. You think just because it isn't written in some electronic cloud, it cannot exist? Not everything is written, you know. Especially if this does have something to do with the Grigori. They would know better than to leave a record."

"Her doctor is not Grigori. I've seen him. And all his staff are women."

Damien nodded. Both men finished their tasks and walked out of the ritual room, which remained unlocked and open unless a scribe sealed it to mark *talesm*.

"I want you to patrol tonight," the watcher said. "I'll put Leo to watch the girl."

"Leo?" Malachi instantly felt mutinous. "Leo is too young."

"He's over two hundred years old, brother." Damien smirked. "How old do you think he needs to be to watch a tourist sleep in a hotel and go out to dinner? She won't even see him; make sure you're ready to fight tonight. I don't like any of us to go too long without battle."

Malachi wanted to object but knew it was useless. Damien ran the scribe house; his word was final when it came to matters of safety or strategy. Though he deferred to Malachi or Rhys on occasion because of their age, he didn't have to.

"Fine." He walked to his room, wishing he'd gotten better rest the night before.

Damien called out, "She's human. How much trouble could she attract in one night?"

* * * * * *

MALACHI WATCHED THE EDGE OF THE WATER WHERE THE WAVES crashed up against the embankment as a giant freighter glided through the narrowest part of the Bosphorus. It was a normal sunny day along the water, so why was his mood so dark?

"What's with you today?" Ava nudged her foot against his knee. She was relaxed again. The change in her temperament would last for a few days after each appointment before the agitation would start again. It was a curious cycle, but one he couldn't question more without arousing suspicion. He caught the tip of her shoe in his hand, pinching her toe under the leather before he released it. Another curious thing. He found himself finding ways to touch her without contact with her skin. A brush of arms as they passed each other. A hand on the small of her back as they walked through a crowd. It was fleeting and probably unwise, but he couldn't resist.

He didn't really want to.

He frowned when he realized he'd never answered her question. "I'm fine."

"You're being all broody, Mal."

He muttered, "I really wish you'd stop calling me that."

Ava picked up her glass of tea and sipped before she answered. "It's good to want things… Mal."

He couldn't help it; she made him smile. He shook his head, relieved that she hadn't wanted to do anything more strenuous than stroll along the waterfront and shop a bit. She'd bought an embroidered purse for her mother, earrings and a scarf for herself. The earrings were so long they almost brushed her bare shoulders, and the scarf held her hair back, its colors vivid against her dark curls. He felt it again, the pull to put his hands on her. To stroke the skin where the jewelry touched. To pull the scarf from her hair.

They'd retired to a café, one of Malachi's favorites, to drink tea and grab a quick bite to eat. Bread and cold salads covered the table, a mezze platter of eggplant and yogurt and the spicy tomato salad she loved. Black olives and oil-soaked cheese. Ava tore off a piece of bread and dipped it, still tapping her foot against his.

"Have you always fidgeted?" he asked.

"Yes. My mom says it's the reason I'm so thin. Couldn't keep still if my life depended on it."

"Even though you eat constantly."

"Hey, you burn through a lot of energy when you contain this much awesome." She winked, but the smile on her lips held a trace of bitterness.

He fell silent again, thinking about going out on patrol that night. He wondered why Damien was insisting on it. The watcher hardly needed to worry about Malachi being battle-ready. He'd done almost nothing but fight for over two hundred years. First in Germany, where his parents had been killed, then in Rome for a time. Buenos Aires. Chicago. Johannesburg. Atlanta. He'd traveled the world, killing the Grigori who had slaughtered his family, then others—any others—he could find. He'd become known for his quick, brutal killing style and relentless drive. He was focused and disciplined in battle, though reckless regarding his own safety. Nothing and no one came between Malachi and his target once his sights were set.

Her foot just kept tapping…

Hot tea spilled on his pants.

"Oops!" Ava laughed. "Sorry about that."

"It's fine." He picked up a napkin, dabbing at the tea as he watched her from the corner of his eye.

She was jiggling her foot, tapping it to the rhythm of the street musician playing on the corner. The woman burst with life, more than any human woman he'd ever met. When Malachi looked at her sometimes, he wondered how her skin could even contain her personality. Her eyes might have held pain and exhaustion at times, but her body was in constant motion.

For a moment, he reveled in the fantasy that she had enough energy even for his touch.

Fingers linked. Arms wrapping around her slight frame. Drawing her to his chest as his mouth descended to her skin. Laying his rough cheek to the satin of hers. Pressing his lips to her neck. The curve of her jaw. Her lips. Feeling the pulse of life seep into his skin. Her fingers digging into his neck. Gripping his hair at the nape. The touch of her mouth to his.

The touch…

He banished the rebellious thoughts, disgusted with himself. He was no better than a Grigori.

"Hey," she whispered, her own cheeks flushed as if she shared his thoughts. "Malachi, where did you just go?"

He blinked and looked up. Nothing had distracted him in two hundred years.

Who was he kidding?

He swiped a quick hand over his face and shook his head to clear it. "Sorry. Didn't sleep well last night."

"And then I dragged you out."

"It's fine, Ava." He grabbed an orange from a dish on the table, letting the bitter spray from the peel wake him. "I'm just a little tired."

"We could head back," she said. "And don't you have some kind of backup? I mean, not that I don't prefer your company, but surely you have someone who can… fill in for you, or something. If you're sick?"

It was the perfect opportunity. Leo was scheduled to take over for him tonight. Damien was confident Ava wouldn't even notice the younger scribe watching her, but Malachi wasn't convinced. After all, the woman had spotted a Grigori stalking her through a crowded market; he doubted a six-foot behemoth with a mane of blond hair would be hard to pluck out of the crowd. "I… uh… I do have someone, as a matter of fact. His name is Leo. He's very reliable. Maybe I'll call him."

She reached out to pat his hand, but Malachi tensed before she paused and drew back. "That's a good idea. I'm wearing you out."

"You're fine, Ava. I don't mind."

"No, I do it to everyone." Her face had fallen back into its polite mask. He could practically feel her withdrawing. "It's... fine. You should call your friend. Take a break from me."

He didn't want to take a break from her. Leaving her with Leo seemed like an even worse idea than it had only a minute before. Her mask was an open wound to him. The confident, energetic woman was gone, replaced by a cool, carefully contained stranger.

"Ava." He waited until she finally looked at him again. "I enjoy spending time with you. It's no chore. You're intelligent. Funny. I like that you're so curious about everything. And it's my privilege to show you around Istanbul." He allowed himself to smile. "Besides, it makes my job easier when I can keep you within grabbing distance."

Not that I could actually grab you without hurting you.

The sadness behind her eyes still didn't flee, but her mouth turned up at the corner. "You, too. Well, not the grabbing-distance thing. You probably don't want that."

You have no idea.

He cleared his throat. "Better keep it professional, Ms. Matheson."

She took another bite of bread. "Absolutely... Mal."

THE NARROW STREET STUNK OF URINE AND ROTTEN MEAT. MALACHI AND Rhys stalked the edges of the city where the Grigori preyed. Here, a missing girl would go unnoticed. Her family might worry, or they might not. But either way, these were the people the authorities ignored. Missing girls from this neighborhood were quickly forgotten. Girls who appeared mysteriously pregnant were hidden or sent away, even killed by family members convinced the girl had brought dishonor on herself. Foolish humans.

The Grigori didn't care.

Damien had heard police reports of girls going missing in this neighborhood. It was possible the monsters had found a new hunting ground.

Malachi saw Rhys's shoulders angle toward a dark alley.

"Hmm?" They spoke as little as possible on patrol.

A nod was his only answer. Malachi saw Rhys trace the characters along his wrist, calling on his magic. Malachi copied the action. Within seconds, he felt the power creep up his arm, crawl over his shoulders, then down his back. In the time it took him to draw a silver dagger, his vision sharpened; the black became grey. His arms flexed with new strength. His skin pulsed with a web of incantations that made him impervious to human weapons.

Malachi followed Rhys into the alley, alert to his surroundings as his brother focused on a point in the darkness. He heard the scribe utter a soft oath in the Old Language, then he ran and fell to his knees, pulling on gloves before he lifted the broken figure on the ground, making sure his skin didn't brush hers for fear of further harm.

"Too late," Rhys muttered as he stood and started walking. "It's Grigori, and from her condition, he hasn't been gone long. Do you sense anything?"

"No smell. Not even a hint." A seductive smell of sandalwood usually followed Grigori attacks. Malachi followed the other scribe as he rushed back toward the street. "Is she alive?"

"Barely."

As they approached the street lights, Malachi got a better look at the victim. She appeared to be no more than sixteen or seventeen. Her skin was pale and her breathing shallow. The young woman's torn clothing was traditional but new. He saw Rhys's gloved thumb brush her cheek.

"A child." The raw fury bubbled under the surface of the quiet man's voice. "She's a little girl, Malachi."

"They don't care."

Grigori soldiers seduced mercilessly, using their otherworldly charm and beauty to convince a human woman to give them the soul-energy they craved. The women went willingly, joyfully, never aware of the magic that drew them. And when the monsters were finished, they left, the female but a forgotten moment of sexual gratification in their centuries-long lives.

Dead. Unconscious. Drained of their most vital energy, most humans didn't survive an encounter with a Grigori. The rare one who did was often impregnated by the monster. If the survivor was lucky, she would live to bear a very gifted child, one who bore an echo of his or her otherworldly parentage. It was a cruel twist that had resulted in some of history's geniuses. Diluted Grigori blood was laced through the human population, like a black thread through a colorful tapestry.

"Call Maxim," Rhys said. "See if his friend's clinic is open tonight."

Malachi pulled out his phone as Rhys walked back toward the Range Rover they'd parked under the brightest light on the main road. A few curtains flickered, but at two in the morning, not even the nosiest Turk would ask what the two imposing men were doing with the woman they carried. Malachi opened the back door and Rhys slid the unconscious girl inside.

They couldn't take her to a hospital. The human doctors would have no idea how to help her, and her family might be contacted. There wasn't much that could be done except rest, fluids, and oxygen. If the young woman survived, she wouldn't even realize she'd been attacked. Most Grigori survivors went searching for their attackers, convinced they had experienced an act of the purest love imaginable. Often, they became obsessed.

The phone kept ringing with no answer. Eventually, Maxim's voicemail picked up.

"Max, we have a girl here," he said softly. "Grigori attack. She's alive. Young. Call us. We need to take her to your friend's clinic."

Only a few humans in Istanbul knew of the existence of the scribes. Maxim's doctor friend was one. He was discreet, and he and his wife did their best to help any girls who survived Grigori attacks. As they crept slowly through the neighborhood, Malachi rolled his window down. The summer night was cooler, and a breeze blew off the water. Turning a corner, he caught a whiff of the telltale incense.

"Rhys!"

"I smell it." He slowed the car at the corner, glancing between Malachi and the girl in the back. "We've got to get her to the hospital. She's dehydrated. Her breathing is shallow, and—"

"You go." Malachi wrenched the door open. "I'll go after the bastard."

"Be careful," Rhys yelled, but he didn't try to stop him. It would take more than a single Grigori to worry any of their kind. Even a small group of them was considered no more than an annoyance. Their greater numbers were all that made them a threat. Still, Malachi was careful. It was miscalculation of Grigori strength and cunning that had led to the horror of the Rending.

He paused on a deserted corner, closing his eyes to take a breath and trace a few more temporary spells on his forearm. Magic not inscribed on the body would fade in time, but it was enough to give him a quick burst of strength. Just as he finished one set, he caught the scent again, but stronger. The Grigori was coming toward him.

Malachi grinned and ducked behind the corner of the building, a small café that was struggling to remain respectable in the crumbling neighborhood. He could see the graffiti that had been painted over, layers of it, rising to his eyes as the magic flowed through him.

Curses and political slogans. There was an advertisement for Coca-Cola that had been painted over many, many times. Still, the words drifted up, as if reaching for him through the years. In a city like Istanbul, every building held ghostly writing only an Irin scribe would see. Words through the ages, ever and always visible to his kind.

Their gift. Their curse.

The smell of sandalwood and a seductive laugh.

"I will get in trouble," the girl protested weakly. "I don't… No, it's fine. I…I don't care."

"Of course you don't." The monster had his arm thrown around the young woman, who looked up at the handsome man adoringly. He was European; sandy-blond hair gleamed under the streetlights. His accent sounded German.

"Your voice," the woman whispered. "It's so beautiful."

"I know." He gave her a wicked smile. "Do you love me?"

"Yes," she breathed out. "Say my name."

"I don't know your name," Malachi heard the man say as he led her to an alley just as filthy as the one they'd rescued the last girl from. He watched them, waiting to see if the Grigori was alone. Often, they would hunt in pairs or even small packs. This one appeared to be alone.

"Is this all right?"

"Yes. Touch me. Please… kiss me again."

Unwilling to wait another moment, Malachi sprang from behind the building, his dagger ready. He rushed into the alley and grabbed the man's shoulder. Spun him around, only to be met with a silver dagger gleaming in the grey light.

With a grunt, the scribe fell back.

It was a trap.

"You must be the one they call Malachi," the Grigori said with a leer. "We haven't met."

"No need to introduce yourself," Malachi said softly as the two men began to circle each other. "I'll be killing you soon." If the Grigori had been carrying an ordinary weapon, Malachi wouldn't have hesitated. His *talesm* were a living, pulsing armor around his body. But something told him that the Grigori's blade wasn't an average dagger. It shone with a dark metallic gleam.

"I'm sure that would usually be true," the other man said. "I could barely sense you. Your concealment charms must be older than me."

The Grigori *was* old. Malachi hadn't examined the man when he'd been walking down the street, but on closer inspection, Malachi sensed his opponent's age. His scent was deep, not like the lighter scent of a young soldier. His green eyes were calculating. And now that he had drawn Malachi in, he had no interest in the woman, even kicking her away when she tried to cling to the man's legs, desperate for his touch.

"Please," she begged. "I beg—" She cried out when the Grigori flung her into the wall.

He was stronger than the young ones. If Malachi had to guess, he'd say the Grigori was almost as old as Rhys.

Which meant he had taken part in the Rending.

Malachi snarled, curling his lip as the realization struck. As if reading his mind, the other man grinned, watching Malachi with taunting eyes.

"I have killed your kind, Scribe. But please feel free to underestimate me for a while longer. That will suit my plans perfectly."

He was speaking in puzzles. Malachi lunged to the right, taking the man off-balance as he tossed the dagger to his left hand and reached around, trying to pierce the base of the Grigori's skull.

His opponent ducked and countered. The blade slashed along Malachi's stomach, sizzling as it hit the protective spells. Malachi's skin held... then split open with a hiss.

It was no ordinary blade. The Grigori carried an angelic weapon.

His mocking laugh echoed off the walls. "I do love that look of surprise! When was the last time you saw one of these out of Irin hands?"

Malachi grunted as he sucked in the pain, weaving it into the fabric of his armor as he shifted and hooked his ankle around the other man's knee, sweeping his foot out from under him and causing the man to stumble back. The blade clattered away.

The smirk fell from the Grigori's face. He dropped into the fall, rolling over and away from Malachi, reaching for the dagger where it had fallen. Malachi saw his eyes dart into the night sky a second before the footsteps landed behind him. Three Grigori soldiers had joined their friend.

The Grigori with the angelic blade muttered, "Too soon."

Malachi grinned as he spun around. Taking stock of his new opponents, he realized that all of them had human weapons. He kicked out, catching one in the solar plexus as his right arm extended toward the other. In one smooth movement, he had twisted the Grigori's head around and plunged the knife deep into the base of his skull.

The human woman screamed, then passed out as the body Malachi held began to disintegrate. Within seconds, there was only a fine gold dust, drifting up in a column, reaching toward the heavens.

He looked over his shoulder, but the blond Grigori had fled, leaving him with the other two. One was just getting to his feet, and the other one looked like he wanted to run after his friend but was too frightened.

Malachi strode to the Grigori he'd kicked, curious whether the other would take the opportunity to run.

He didn't.

Malachi ignored the glancing blow the gasping man swung toward his shoulder. The dagger hit the scribe's *talesm* and bounced off, no more dangerous than a child's toy. Malachi twisted the man's neck around and ended him, too. Then he waved the second cloud of dust away and frowned at the last Grigori.

The young man was ethereally beautiful, like all his kind. He had curling dark hair and porcelain skin. His eyes were a light hazel green; his scent was designed to entice his prey.

And he was scared to death.

"Why didn't you run?" Malachi asked, stalking toward him. "I'm going to kill you now."

The Grigori couldn't have been very old. His scent was bright and panicked. "I… I know. But I have to stay here. With you."

Malachi halted.

"…*please feel free to underestimate me for a while longer. That will suit my plans perfectly.*"

The second trap snapped shut.

"What does he want?" He lunged at the man, lifting him in a chokehold and pushing him against the wall. "Why are you still here?"

Malachi knew the answer before the man's lips moved.

"The woman," the young soldier gasped. "He's… after the human woman. Had to… keep you distracted. All of you."

"All of us…?"

They had plans for Leo, too.

Malachi twisted the man's neck around, striking quickly, and then he began to run. Behind him, a faint cloud of dust rose to the stars.

CHAPTER

SIX

Leo flipped through channels on the television as he ate another massive sandwich Ava had ordered from room service. His accent sounded Russian, but he reminded Ava of a giant happy Labrador with his gold hair and cheerful disposition. They sat in the hotel's library, which doubled as a lounge. Books lined the walls and a television sat in one corner, streaming international shows from all over the globe. Ava was processing images on her laptop, so Leo had turned on the television.

She'd met her new bodyguard that afternoon after Malachi had called him to meet her in the hotel lobby.

• • • · • • •

"Who's this?"

"This is Leo. He'll be guarding you tonight if you need to go anywhere." He'd handed over a small slip of paper. "This is his number. You already have mine."

Ava had turned to Leo. "Hi."

The blond giant gave her a boyish smile. "Hello, Ms. Matheson."

Malachi said, "She likes to be called 'Ava.' Don't leave her unguarded; you have my number."

Then Malachi had turned and walked away without a glance back. *Asshole.*

Ava turned to Leo. "Care to come inside? I was just about to order room service because I don't feel like going out. I'll buy you dinner since you're on babysitting duty tonight."

She saw Malachi pause at the door. She'd never once invited him into the hotel. They always met in the lobby.

"Sure," Leo said. "Thanks!"

Malachi half-turned, then stopped, meeting her eyes over his shoulder before his narrowed and he spun around again.

"Night, Mal!"

NOW SHE WAS WISHING HER SILENT SHADOW WOULD RETURN. THERE was nothing wrong with Leo; he was friendly as a pup, but he exuded energy, not calm, the way Malachi did. His internal voice bounced and jumped, almost always cheerfully, but much louder than Malachi's did. And though his voice held the same odd resonance, it felt slightly out of tune. All in all, his presence was distracting.

A voice from the television caught her attention.

"What was that?" she asked.

Leo lifted an eyebrow. "What?"

"The TV."

He'd already flipped past the channel. The one he'd stopped on looked like a soap opera set in Topkapi Palace.

"Turn it back."

"Turn it back to what?"

Ava stood and grabbed the remote.

"Hey!"

Not that. Not that. Not that… There.

"Him." She pointed at the TV. It was a news program, and an old man was being interviewed on the screen. "That man. What language is he speaking?"

Leo frowned. "That's Farsi. It's a Persian program; I'm surprised they even have it at this—"

"No." Ava shook her head. "I've heard Farsi. I've been to Iran. That doesn't sound like Farsi."

The bodyguard shrugged. "Well, it is. His accent is odd. Let me..." Leo's voice trailed off as he listened intently. After a few minutes, he said, "He's Assyrian; that's why it sounds different. He's speaking Farsi with an Assyrian accent. They're interviewing him for a cultural program. It's just a different part of Iran. The accent is different."

Her heart sank. "Oh."

"Why did you want to know?"

"I didn't... It just reminded me of a language I heard once. That's all." Ava watched the old man for a few more moments, memorizing the rise and fall of his voice before she handed the remote control back to Leo. It had to be a coincidence, but for a brief second, the man had sounded like he was speaking the silent tongue of the voices she'd heard her whole life. Ava had studied languages. She'd traveled the globe, listening to accents and intonation. The peculiar rhythm of foreign lands. She'd spent years searching for the language that haunted her.

She was never successful.

Leo was still watching her, clearly suspicious of her excitement over the news program. She concentrated on the computer screen, ignoring him, but his silent voice was colored with curiosity.

Ava tried to change the subject. "So how many languages do you speak?"

"I..." He hadn't been expecting the question. "I've never counted, to be honest."

"That many?"

Leo shrugged. "I'm not fluent in all of them, but I speak many. It helps when you travel."

"Have you worked for Malachi long?"

"We, uh, we work for the same company. He's more senior than I am, but we've both worked for the company a long time."

"Oh?" She continued fiddling with the color balance on one file. "You're not from Istanbul, I'm guessing."

"Outside Moscow, originally. But I've traveled a lot."

Ava snorted a little. He couldn't have been older than his late twenties. Of course, she knew firsthand you could cover a lot of ground when you wanted to avoid home.

Leo asked, "How about you?"

"Malachi didn't tell you?"

"No." His answer caused Ava to look up. He'd finished his sandwich and was wiping his mouth. "He wouldn't. He hardly talks at all except to yell at me and my cousin if we drink his beer and don't replace it. He's known for being very focused when he's on a job."

For some reason, Ava found that endearing. It sounded like her shadow was a cranky old man to more than just her.

"I'm from L.A."

"Really?"

"Yep. And I hate it."

Leo laughed, a deep chuckle that filled the lounge and made her smile.

"So that's why you travel all the time? Because you don't like home?"

"Among other reasons." She couldn't concentrate on her work. Leo's silent voice was alive with excitement, like a little kid just begging to play. She finally snapped her laptop case shut. "Why don't we go for a drink? There's a café on the corner. I feel like getting out of here."

"I don't know…"

She could tell he was uncomfortable with the idea, but Ava knew drowning out Leo's presence would be easier in a crowd. Hopefully, he could blend in with the group of people and create a white noise affect that wouldn't pierce her temple.

"Okay," she said, standing. "How's this? I'm going to go for a drink because you're not, in fact, my babysitter. Then you can follow me, like I know Malachi told you to do. You can either sit with me or lurk suspiciously on the edge of the room. It's up to you, but I'm going." She packed her laptop in the case and walked down the hall to her room. Within moments, she was back in the lobby, and Leo was waiting, glancing at his phone like he was expecting a message.

Ava nodded at it. "You already tell on me?"

"It's just… Malachi said you usually stay in at night."

"That's when I've been walking all day. I'm not tired. I want a drink." She brushed past him and opened the door, nodding at the burly doorman on the way out. "See you."

She was barely at the curb when Leo caught up with her.

"Are you always so stubborn?" he asked.

"Yes."

The man was looking around as if he expected commandos to come pouring out of the fashionable doorways of the Sultanahmet. Ava shook her head.

"Seriously, Leo, relax. You're too young to worry this much."

"Haha."

"You're not even going to drink, are you?"

"Not if I want to remain living."

⋅ ⋅ ⋅

AVA WAS HALFWAY THROUGH A BOTTLE OF VERY MEDIOCRE RED WINE when she noticed it. First one had drifted in. Then another.

"Whoa."

"What?" Leo looked up from his phone. He'd been madly texting someone for the last ten minutes. Ava was guessing Malachi was busy. Too busy to worry about her, anyway. Poor Leo. He was tense, poised on the edge of his seat like a dog waiting for a command. He hadn't drunk anything, not even the tea the waiter had set in front of him at the café that looked down to the water. Ava had visited before, but not at night. It was a decidedly different crowd. A football match was playing on the television, and young people of every nationality hung on the score. It was definitely a tourist place, but a friendly one. And that night, it had more than its share of very pleasant scenery.

"You probably haven't noticed unless you're into guys, but this bar has suddenly become hot guy central." She looked around in wonder. It couldn't just be her imagination. Every woman in the place seemed to be under a spell. The whole place was full of wildly handsome men. "Is there some kind of… modeling conference in town? Fashion week or something?"

"I don't know," Leo said tersely, still typing madly on his phone.

"This is so weird. I mean, I'm not complaining—"

"Whatever you do," Leo interrupted as he stood. "Do *not* leave this spot. I need to make a call, and I need to be able to see you through the window."

She sneered automatically. "Hey, buddy—"

"I'm serious, Ava." He did look serious. "Don't leave. And avoid talking to anyone if you can. I'll be right outside."

Her eyes narrowed as she watched him walk away. Leo glared at one of the handsome men who sat in the corner with two women draped over his arms. The man turned and locked eyes with Ava; she glanced away, looking for Leo, but he was already outside. What was with him? Was one of these guys with his ex-girlfriend, or something?

There was the one Leo had passed, sitting by the door with two women. He looked like someone she'd seen in an underwear ad. There were two other men sharing a table on the opposite side of the bar. They might have been brothers with their stunning blue eyes and dark brown hair. They were currently the focus of at least five fawning women. There was a blond by the hallway leading toward the restrooms, and still another sitting directly across from her, giving her sultry dark eyes that did absolutely nothing but make her think of a self-absorbed actor she'd dated once in college.

"Whatever," she muttered and refilled her glass. She was starting to get a perfectly nice buzz that was helping to drown out the voices. The last thing she needed was bossy men ordering her around or coming on to her. She was tempted to leave the place, just for spite. But… She wasn't going to waste a perfectly good—well, adequate—bottle of wine.

One of the men across from the bar winked at her, then the one who'd been standing by the hallway came up and sat in the chair Leo had occupied.

"What's your name?" he asked.

"None of your business." He looked shocked, but the whole situation was giving Ava goose bumps. What was the game here? She didn't get it. There was something going on, but the wine had muffled the voices, making it harder for her to read the intentions of the man sitting next to her. She looked around the place. She was in a pair of old jeans and a T-shirt, hadn't even attempted to dress up. Why was this guy talking to her? She had no illusions about her own beauty. Ava knew she was moderately attractive, but she wasn't the kind of woman who turned heads. Certainly not heads that looked like they belonged in fashion magazines.

"I'm just curious. You're a beautiful woman, and you're all alone."

"Yes. Happily alone."

Keep telling yourself that, Ava.

Stupid wine.

"But you weren't alone earlier."

"Your point, Einstein?"

"Did your boyfriend leave you here?"

"None of your business."

"So he *is* your boyfriend? Do you know what he is?"

What? Ava took another drink. This guy wasn't making any sense. Maybe it was a language thing.

"You know," she said in a low voice, sliding closer. "I'd really like you to…"

He leaned in. "What?"

"Leave."

Hottie's eyes narrowed. "I don't think you know just who your boyfriend is, do you?"

Irritated, Ava blurted out, "He's not my boyfriend! But he will take care of you if you don't leave me alone. Now."

Well, that made him happy.

"So he's not your boyfriend! May I join you?"

She squinted. Yep, buzz definitely getting spoiled. "Are you deaf? No! Are all Turkish men this forward? Do I look like I want company?"

He said something she really didn't listen to. The noise from the television seemed louder. Had the bartender turned it up? Hot Guy was still talking.

Was it some kind of game? A bet? She looked around, but none of the other men were looking at them. In fact, even Mister Wink Wink across the bar was looking away. Ava was starting to get nervous, and she really wished Leo would come back. She pulled out her phone and saw that he had just texted her.

Meet me by the door I left through.

Normally, she'd ignore him. After all, he worked for her—or her stepfather. Whatever. She didn't have to do what he said. She finished the glass of wine and narrowed her eyes at the handsome man who still looked like he expected Ava to fall into his bed. He was watching her like she was the most fascinating thing in the world.

"What are you?" he whispered with barely contained excitement.

"I'm an American photographer. It's really not all that exciting."

"I don't think that's what you really are."

Weirdo. He might have been handsome, but the guy did nothing for her. She was about to pour another glass of wine when she heard her phone buzz again. She looked down. It was Malachi's number.

Ava, go to Leo. Now.

"Ugh." Her head fell back and she groaned. "Bossy men. Damn *bossy* men. Who the hell do they think they are?" She'd tell them off in person.

Ava stood and picked up her purse. As soon as she did, she felt a hand on her arm. It was Hot Guy, who had morphed into Mr. Intrusive.

Okay, not cool.

"Hey!" Feeling bold with wine, Ava rounded on him as she yanked her arm away. "Do *not* touch me, do you understand? Did I give you permission to do that? Did I indicate in any way that I wanted your attention, mister?"

The man's green eyes widened in shock.

"You pulled away from me."

"For heaven's sake, do you really think you're God's gift? Get over yourself, buddy!"

She was starting to draw attention. Luckily three-quarters of a bottle of wine meant she didn't really care all that much. She was only a block from her hotel, after all. And there was always—

"Leo!" She grinned, her annoyance forgotten. She turned to the pushy stranger. "Now this guy? He's a catch. For one thing, he's handsome without looking like he's been airbrushed, because really?" She waved a hand in front of the guy's face. "Are you wearing makeup? I mean, whatever, if that's your thing, but see, Leo here—"

Leo cleared his throat. "We should go, Ava." He was trying to steer her toward the door with a hand on her shoulder, but Ava ignored him, still talking to Hot Guy.

"See, Leo's got the confident-without-being-arrogant thing. You need to learn that. Because girls don't usually go for… a guy who looks in the mirror more than they do." Ava giggled as she looked around the place. "Well, obviously not some of these ladies, but where I come from… that's probably a bad example. Still—"

"Ava." His low voice sounded across the bar. She turned, stilling immediately when she heard it. Heard *him*. Their eyes met.

There you are.

Even slightly inebriated, she was shocked by how the realization hit her.

He was here. And he belonged with her.

Malachi strode into the room, looking rough and angry. His shirt was torn at the collar and there was a bandage across his ribs. He was still the best thing she'd laid eyes on in… ever.

"You're here," she murmured, letting his voice wash into her mind.

Relieved. He was relieved, but worried. She reached out for his hand. She knew if she could just hold it—

He dodged her at the last minute, slipping around Leo's back and standing between the stranger and Ava, pressing a warm hand to the small of her back. She could feel it through her shirt. The heat. The calm. She wanted to surround herself until she lost her mind in his.

"Let's go," he said, pushing her toward the door.

As soon as her feet started moving, she came out of her daze. "Hey, I'm not—"

"You're done. We're going back to the hotel. I'll explain more there."

"You'd better. And I don't appreciate—"

She broke off when the man with two women, who was sitting by the door, leaned toward her as she walked by. There was a snarl, then before she could blink, Leo had shoved her behind his back, and Malachi had the gorgeous man pinned against the wall of the bar, his hand around the man's throat. The girls at the table started shrieking and calling for the owner.

Ava peeked from around Leo's back, and she heard Malachi whisper, "If you want to survive to see the dawn, come no closer. My dagger hungers for your neck."

She gasped. "Holy *shit!*"

Leo spun and almost shoved her past Malachi and the other man, dragging her onto the sidewalk outside the bar.

"What the hell was that?" she yelled.

"Ava, let's get going."

She shook off the hand that had reached for her shoulder. "You people are maniacs! Get away from me!"

Ava was practically running toward the hotel. She could see the doorman sitting outside the door, smoking one of the sweet cigarettes he always carried. She could smell the waft of tobacco reach her nose a second before a hand grabbed her shoulder. Malachi spun her around, then immediately raised his hands in surrender.

"Let me explain, Ava."

"Explain what? How you threatened to stab some guy because he was making a pass at me?" She backed away from him, inching closer to the doorman with every step. "He wasn't even making a pass at me. He *leaned* in my direction, and you—"

"There was a girl almost killed tonight."

"That's horrible." She kept backing away. "But what the hell does that have to do with me?"

"Those men are…" She saw him give Leo a panicked glance. "They're… in a gang."

Liar. She shook her head. He was lying; she could hear it.

"And that gang is the one responsible for this girl's attack. They specialize in… human trafficking, and they're targeting foreign women traveling alone."

He was just making things up as he went along, but his voice… His inner voice was still panicked. Worried. He was lying, but it was out of fear. Something had frightened the big, bad bodyguard, and it had to do with her safety. That reason alone caused her to take a deep breath and stop backing away from him. Logic, even the fuzzy logic she had to work with from all the wine, told Ava that if Malachi wanted to harm her, he'd had plenty of opportunities in the week and a half they'd already known each other. He'd had her alone many times. So obviously something else was going on.

She asked, "What does this have to do with me?"

"There were four of them in that bar, Ava. One attacked me earlier as an associate and I were rescuing a girl they had kidnapped and almost killed. We have a standing assignment from our bosses in Vienna about this organization. They're active all over the world, and for some reason, they're targeting you. We don't know why."

For the first time, his words had the ring of truth. Ava took a deep breath. She still felt like there was something she wasn't seeing, but at least some of what he said made sense.

"Carl," she muttered.

"What?"

"My stepfather, Carl Matheson. He's rich as Midas. Richer, maybe. In addition to being a film producer, he also has all this family money. Shipping. Oil. He's loaded. If it's human trafficking, they probably want me for ransom. It wouldn't be the first time someone has tried."

Or succeeded. She tried not to think about the awful week when she was eight. Routine, they had called it. The monsters who had taken her in Brazil had laughed and called it a routine kidnapping when they teased her. One girl for one million dollars. A respectable week's work. She hadn't slept through the night for a year afterward.

Malachi said, "That must be it. They've become bolder, and I don't know why." He stepped closer cautiously. "I'd like to stay at the hotel. I called already and booked the room next to yours."

And just like that, she was pissed off again. "Didn't ask me, did you? Did you ask Carl? Is anyone going to even pretend to keep me informed?" She spun around and walked toward the doorman. He frowned for a moment before he said something to Malachi in Turkish. Malachi barked back, then the doorman shrugged and opened the door to their group.

"Some security you are," Ava muttered. "I was told this hotel had the best security in the city. I stayed here for that reason. I don't need handlers. I don't want someone watching me eat breakfast and following me to the bathroom, Malachi."

A wave of embarrassment washed over her as she walked to her room. For a few days, she'd almost felt normal. The voices were quieter. She was going out and touring a city she was growing to love. She'd forgotten Malachi had been hired to look out for her. She'd felt like she had a friend who enjoyed her company. Enjoyed spending time with her. Maybe even…

She was foolish to have forgotten. Other people got those things. Not her.

"Ava." His voice was softer, pleading. She refused to turn around. "I'm trying to keep you safe."

"By getting a room in my hotel without even asking me?" she asked in a hoarse voice. She had to get away from him. She was seconds away from crying. "By ordering me around like I'm a child?"

"Please—"

"I'm going to bed now. I don't want to talk to you. I'm tired, and we'll talk more about this in the morning."

He fell silent. She could feel the warmth of his hand inches from the nape of her neck. His breath stirred her hair, then he drew away. "Fine. I'll be in the room next door."

"I don't want to know that," she said. "I'm pretending…"

That you'll meet me tomorrow for breakfast, just because you want to see me.

That we'll tour the city, and you'll joke with me, and the voices will be a little easier to bear.

I'm pretending… that you're my friend.

"I'm pretending you don't exist, Malachi. Stay away from me tonight."

She slid her card in the lock, then quickly walked in and shut the door. She turned the dead bolt and the sliding lock, then she walked to her window and checked the locks there, too. When she was sure her room was secure, she sat down on the bed and waited to hear him leave the hallway. After a few minutes, Malachi moved toward the lobby, talking to Leo in Turkish.

Seconds later, she pushed back the tears that wanted to surface, and her phone was in her hand.

"Mom?"

"Ava!" Her mother's voice was brimming with excitement. "Isn't it late there? I'm so glad you called! How are you liking—"

"These guys Carl hired, Mom. They're out of control." Her voice was shaking with anger. "He needs to dial them back, or I'm ditching them completely. You know I can."

"But Ava—"

"They practically shoved me out of a bar tonight because some guy was making a pass at me. You know me. I can take care of myself, and they went way overboard. I'm surprised no one called the police. Is that the kind of publicity that Carl wants?"

"Who—"

"*And* one of them is staying at my hotel now! He says there's some kind of threat against my life! Has there been a threat and you haven't told me? I mean, I know shit happens, but you've always told me if there has ever been any specific—"

"*Ava, shut up!*"

Her mother never raised her voice. She shut up immediately.

"I want you to listen to me very carefully." Her mother's voice sent chills down her neck. "Are you alone?"

"Yes."

"The man Carl hired quit over a week ago. There was some sort of scheduling conflict, and I convinced him you were perfectly safe since you were staying in the city. Ava… he didn't hire anyone else."

She sat on the edge of her bed, breath coming in small panicked bursts. "Mom…"

"Whoever these people are who *say* they are guarding you, Ava, they were not hired by us. Do you understand?"

She nodded, but no words left her mouth.

"Ava, are you still there?" Her mother's voice was panicked. "Carl!"

"I'm here, Mom."

Lies. Lies. Lies.

It was all a lie. Ava had never felt more vulnerable in her life. The chill at her neck spread. She heard her mother and Carl muttering in the background, then her stepfather picked up the phone.

"Ava?"

"Yeah?"

"This man, he's been following you for a week?"

"Yes. We've… been friendly. He seemed nice. Very professional."

"Does he have any idea you suspect him? Did you tell him you were calling home?"

"No."

There was a pause. "I'm calling my contacts in Istanbul as soon as we get off the phone. In the morning, there will be a package waiting for you at the front desk. I want you to find out who these people are." Ava heard her mother protesting in the background, but Carl's voice was cold and clear. "If you're threatened, if you're in danger at all, use it. I know you know how. We can take care of any fallout after you're safe."

Ava took a deep breath. "I understand."

CHAPTER

SEVEN

"And you're sure she has no idea?"

"With this woman?" Malachi looked around the open-air patio where the hotel served breakfast. He could see Ava's door from where he sat, so he kept his voice low. "I'm not sure of anything with her."

"Leo said she didn't react normally to the Grigori."

"No. She seemed completely immune to them."

There was nothing but silence. What could Damien say? All human women had the same reaction to the Grigori. All women, except Ava. It was inexplicable.

Finally, Damien said, "Rhys is doing things on the computer. Max is out hunting his sources right now. Whatever this is, it's now a priority. Leo stays with you."

"Who was the blond in the alley?"

"It sounds like Brage. I've met him before. He's skilled. I didn't know he was in Istanbul. This is a new development."

"What do you know?"

"He's Scandinavian, but I'm not sure from where. Not one of Jaron's. Older. About four hundred or so."

"One of Volund's?"

"Perhaps. I don't know."

"But he's in Jaron's territory with an angelic blade."

"Yes, I noted that in your report. And I've passed it along to Vienna."

Obviously Damien didn't know any more than Malachi. He heaved a sigh and noticed movement in Ava's room. All the rooms in the hotel opened onto the beautifully tended central courtyard. Tiled fountains and lush potted plants created tiny oases within the scattered tables. A few early morning travelers were already up and packed for day trips. They were eating breakfast while Malachi drank his tea. He'd slept only a few hours; luckily, he didn't need much to be alert. He'd woken with the first prayer call at dawn. The curtains in Ava's room moved.

"Damien, I should go. I'll text you later."

"As long as you don't expect me to text back."

Malachi smiled. "I don't. Have Rhys keep me updated if he finds anything."

"What are you going to do today?"

"Whatever she wants, I suppose. I'm still supposed to be her bodyguard."

"And how long is that going to last?"

"As long as I can manage. I was half expecting the police to storm my room last night, but it didn't happen. So I'm guessing she was too angry to call home."

"Just be prepared for anything. If they make a move—"

"The only one I'm worried about is Brage with that dagger, but since Leo's with me, I doubt he'll show his face. He won't take on two of us at the same time. I think the show last night didn't go as planned. They were supposed to keep me occupied longer."

"Don't underestimate them."

"I won't."

He hung up the phone when he saw her door open. He wondered if she would sit with him. He wondered if she'd speak to him at all, or if they were back to how they'd started. Her pretending he didn't exist and Malachi pretending she was just another anonymous human he'd taken a vow to protect.

She stepped into the morning sun, gold touching her hair and making her skin glow. Her fierce eyes met his and froze.

Malachi decided he was done pretending.

"Good morning," he said as she approached.

Ava sat down, but she didn't speak. A smiling waiter brought her tea and set down a plate of fruit between them. Figs drizzled with honey and fresh green grapes. She pulled at one of the grapes and popped it in her mouth before she spoke.

"You were injured last night. How are you feeling?"

"Fine." She couldn't have sounded more disinterested, but he supposed he couldn't blame her. The woman wasn't stupid; she wasn't buying the story he'd told her the night before, so he'd have to be more convincing this morning.

"All right. Convince me why I shouldn't call my stepfather and have you and Leo both fired for being so high-handed."

A fraction of the tension fled. She hadn't called home.

"I apologize for how we handled things at the bar last night. I was worried, and I overreacted. I'd just come from a confrontation with one of this gang, and I saw one talking to you, obviously trying to trick you into going somewhere with him—"

"Did you also see me telling him off in my somewhat inebriated state? He wasn't really all that appealing."

"I'm glad." He paused to watch her bite into a fig. "But I'd just watched my friend take a half-dead girl to the hospital. I wasn't entirely rational at the thought of the same thing happening to you."

She paused with the fig at her lips, met his eyes for a moment, then looked away, leaning back in her chair and looking around the courtyard as she nibbled on the fruit. Malachi was practically growling in frustration. How could this human woman be so impossible to read? Her calculating stare and disinterested posture ate at him.

Malachi continued to sip his tea as casually as he could as Ava ate breakfast. He had expected a torrent of questions. Anger. Doubt. Instead, there was… nothing. It was maddening. Finally, she put down her fork and looked at him.

"I think I'd like to get out of the city today. It feels like it's going to be hot and the traffic… Are there any places we could go that are close? Day hikes? Maybe some trees? Somewhere with not so many people?"

What was her game? Whatever it was, he could play along. "We could go the islands. They're just off the coast. It's a day trip if you take the ferry. One of the islands has a nice hike up to an old monastery. Very beautiful. There are no cars allowed. On foot or horses only. Some carriages if you don't feel like walking."

"No. Walking sounds perfect. I could use a good stretch."

"Okay." He looked at the clock on his phone. "If you're ready, we could catch the ferry in about an hour. Wear good shoes."

"Sure thing. Meet you in the lobby? I have a couple things to do in my room. I need to clean up. Make myself presentable, even if we're hiking."

She looked fine to him—she looked beautiful, if he was forced to admit it—but Malachi wasn't about to question her.

"I'll see you in a bit."

She stood and turned toward the lobby, heading for the front desk. Malachi followed her. She picked up a small box the concierge slid across the desk, then tucked it under her arm. Malachi intercepted her before she made it back to her room.

"Ava, if that was delivered last night, I might need to check—"

"You really want to go through the feminine-hygiene products my mom sends me, Mal?" She gave him a rueful smile. "I mean, it's possible someone snuck a bomb in with the tampons, but I'm kind of doubting it."

He cleared his throat and stepped back. "If it's from your mother, I'm sure it's fine."

"That's what I thought."

She turned and walked to her room, Malachi's eyes following her every step.

• • • • • •

THE RIDE ACROSS THE SEA OF MARMARA WAS SMOOTH, BUT AVA DIDN'T sleep as Malachi thought she might. She remained quiet and watchful, clutching her bag as they rode the waves out to the Ottoman-style ferry terminal on Büyükada, the largest of the Prince Islands. Once the favored spot for exiled royalty, the islands had become an even more-favored vacation spot for Istanbul's wealthier citizens. Shops and cafés dotted the street leading to the central square, which was dominated by a clock tower. Instead of stopping for lunch in the square, Ava picked a few snacks from one of the shops catering to the summer tourists.

"Okay, which way?" She packed the snacks in her small knapsack and threw it over one shoulder.

Malachi pointed toward the carriages by the clock tower. "Are you sure you don't want to hire someone?"

"Definitely. I could use the walk."

"This way, then."

It was early summer and the middle of the week. There were a number of tourists, but most seemed to head toward the beach or the restaurants. Only a few stopped to hire a phaeton to take them up the mountain, and even fewer looked ready for the steep climb through the town and up to the Monastery of St. George. As Ava and Malachi started out, they were alone. Leo stayed near the terminal, watching for any visitors, per Malachi's request.

"Are you ready?" he asked as they headed up the hill. "It's not a short hike."

Ava took a deep breath as they stepped away from the crowds. "Trust me, this is just what I had in mind."

Her expression began to clear the farther they got away from other people. They walked through a neighborhood filled with luxurious mansions on their way toward Luna Park.

"Your house in L.A.?" He nodded toward one mansion. "Is it grand like this?"

"My mom's house?" She shrugged. "It's bigger. Carl likes people to know how much money he has."

"You don't have your own home?"

"No."

They kept walking. Malachi wondered what it would feel like to live in a grand home. The retreat where his parents raised him in Germany was simple, and scribe houses were more like monasteries. The most well-appointed rooms were reserved for the books, scrolls, and tablets, not the scribes who copied or preserved them. He knew some Irin lived with more wealth, those in cities who worked in human businesses. After all, the retreats and scribe houses had to be supported financially, but Malachi had never had the head for human business. His life had been protecting the accumulation of knowledge until it had been about avenging his parents' deaths. He didn't know anything else.

"Tell me more about this organization you're after, Mal."

He wasn't prepared for the question. Luckily, he'd rehearsed an answer that morning while he was waiting for her to wake. "They're an organized, international criminal enterprise that specializes in human trafficking. They're very secretive; you won't find much about them online. Officially, they don't exist."

"Really?" Her voice had that distant, skeptical tone again. "No international task forces? Interpol? United Nations?"

"Governments don't want to acknowledge things they don't know how to combat. It makes them feel helpless."

She raised an eyebrow behind her sunglasses. "So why are you guys after them? I'm assuming your company is being paid."

Curious woman. Curious, *bothersome* woman. The surge of reluctant admiration annoyed him. "Let's put it this way—they've hurt some very powerful people in the past. Those people want to make sure it doesn't happen again, and they're willing to put their resources behind our company to take care of them."

"You mean kill them?"

"Ava, I don't—"

"'My dagger hungers for your neck.'" She mimicked his voice from the night before. "Who talks like that? I'm assuming you were threatening his life."

They were past the houses now, on the edge of the park. Pine trees lined the road along with fluttering scraps of ribbon and cloth, markers left by the pilgrims who'd traveled the road before them. Ava didn't look at him, but he knew she was waiting for his response.

"Yes, I was threatening him. According to the law, he is not a criminal, but he kills and kidnaps with impunity. What should our response be if one of them threatens an innocent person?"

The color on her cheeks was high, and she was starting to breathe more heavily the longer they climbed.

"But you're not police. You're not military. Basically, you're out for revenge on these guys."

"We're keeping them from hurting more women and children. Is there something wrong with that?"

"Well, when you put it that way..." Her fingers trailed along the brush, twisting around one particularly long ribbon that was tied to a low branch of pine. "What are these? What are they for?"

"They're prayers. Pilgrims tie them as they walk up to the monastery. Most of them are from women who want children. The monastery is associated with fertility."

He saw her pause, her fingers twisting around a ribbon, clutching it for a moment before she released it and continued walking.

Malachi saw the quick crease between her eyebrows, and his fingers ached to smooth it.

"Do you want children, Ava?"

She glanced at him, surprised. "None of your business."

"You're right." He swallowed back a frustrated curse and kept walking. "It is none of my business. I apologize."

"It doesn't matter. I won't have them." Her voice was soft, but he caught the words muttered under her breath anyway.

He stopped, turned. "Is it because of your health? Your… headaches?"

"We're not talking about my headaches," she said with a glare before she marched off the path and into a stand of trees.

Malachi watched her, confused for a second before he followed. "Ava, where are you going?"

She was still walking, ducking under low branches as they walked over the forest floor covered with pine needles. He could barely hear her steps as she headed even farther off the path, toward a rocky outcropping that overlooked a desolate beach.

"Ava!"

She stopped. Turned. And pointed a gun at his chest.

"Why don't you stop lying now, Malachi?" she asked softly, her voice chilling him to the bone. "And start telling me the truth about your 'organization' and who really hired you?"

Slowly, he brought his hands together in front of his body, subtly tracing the *talesm prim* on his wrist. The old spells took hold, covering him with magic. "I can explain."

"Good. Start talking."

"Please put the gun down." He was more concerned about her injuring herself or some random hiker than he was himself. "Ava, please put the gun—"

"You are not ordering me around, Malachi." Her hands didn't tremble on the weapon. She stood in a ready stance, obviously well-acquainted with the weapon. "You're not being honest with me. I can tell when you're lying."

"Really?" he stepped closer. "And how do you know that, Ava?"

"I just do." Her eyes were cold. Nothing remained of the teasing, friendly woman he'd come to know.

"Ava, please," he repeated her name again softly. "Put the gun down. Do you really think I would hurt you?"

For the first time all day, he saw her expression crack. "I don't know what to think."

"I have been with you for over two weeks. If I wanted to hurt you—"

"Who hired you, Malachi?"

"—I could have done it. But I won't, because I don't want that."

"Just tell me who you're working for."

He took another step closer, holding his hands out. "You don't understand."

"No, I don't!" Her voice rose. "Why don't you take this opportunity to explain it to me? That seems like a good idea when I have a gun pointed at your chest!"

"Please, Ava—"

"Stop saying my name like that!" Tears gathered at the corner of her eyes. "You're a liar. And I trusted you."

He shook his head. "I would *never* hurt you."

"You already have!"

"Ava, put the gun down."

"Just tell me what is going on!"

"Don't you understand I can't!" he shouted, then muttered a frustrated curse under his breath.

As soon as the words left him, her mouth dropped open. Ava froze. The hand holding the gun sank and the weapon fell with a soft thud on the pine needles. Malachi dove for it, grabbing it to put the safety on, only to realize it had been on safety the whole time.

"Ava, what on earth—?"

"What did you just say?" she whispered.

"I said *what on earth*—"

"Before." She was taking rapid breaths. He looked up from the gun. Her eyes were panicked; she was reaching for him. He had to back away. "What did you say before, Malachi?"

He shook his head. "What?"

"Before!" she shouted with a choked sob. "What was it? Please!"

She looked ready to collapse. She was trembling, tears rolling down her face, and he didn't know what to do.

"Ava, I don't understand what you're asking."

"Please." Her face crumbled. "Just tell me what language it was. I heard you. Just… just tell me I'm not crazy."

Malachi wanted to grab her. Calm her, but he couldn't. She was wearing nothing but a tank top. She'd taken off her long-sleeved shirt halfway up the mountain. And his touch would hurt her. No matter how much he wanted, he would never—*could* never…

He finally registered what she'd said.

Tell me what language it was.

He'd cursed in the Old Language. Most people never even noticed.

Her eyes pleaded with him, and her shoulders shook. "Tell me I'm not crazy, Malachi."

"Ava, did you…" He drew in a quick breath as the pieces began to fall into place.

The headaches. Her nervousness in crowds. His instincts had warned him, but everyone said it wasn't possible.

'I heard you…'

Malachi shook his head.

Defeat washed across her face. "Please… I've heard it for so long." She fell to her knees. "I just need to know—"

"What language are you talking about, Ava?" He knelt cautiously next to her, still stunned. Ava shook her head, eyes glassy and dazed.

"My whole life…" She wrapped her arms around herself. "They called me crazy. And now I'm imagining it out loud. I *am*—"

"This language?" he asked softly, whispering in the ancient tongue of the angels. "Ava, is this the language you're talking about?"

She gasped and clutched the front of his shirt. "Malachi?"

He continued in soft words he knew she couldn't understand. "Where have you heard this, beautiful one?" Malachi lifted trembling fingers to a curl of her hair, then he asked in English again. "Where have you heard this, Ava?"

She clutched his shirt tighter. "Everywhere," she choked out. "I hear it everywhere!"

He shook his head, disbelieving. "It can't be."

"Every person. All over the world. I hear them, Malachi. In my head. The same language, over and over." Her tears kept falling, and she wouldn't let go of his shirt, almost as if she was afraid he would run. "I'm crazy. I know it. I told myself if I could just figure out what they were saying, it would make sense, but—"

"You're not crazy." Malachi lifted a tentative hand to her cheek. *He had to know.* "You're not crazy, Ava, you're—"

He broke off when she leaned her face into his hand, resting her cheek against his frozen palm.

Ava whispered, "You make the voices go away." Then she closed her eyes, let out a soft breath, and Malachi *felt* her.

The rush of energy filled him, lifted him. His heart raced as the force of it elevated him. Malachi lifted his other hand to her neck, tracing the ancient letters over her skin, watching as the faint golden glow illuminated in the shadow of the pines. A choked laugh bubbled up in his throat and Ava's eyes flickered open. His hand traced lower, brushing over her bare shoulder, down her arm, and everywhere his hand went, her skin gave off a faint, shimmering gold.

"You're not crazy." He couldn't tear his eyes away from his fingers touching—actually touching—her. "You're not crazy, Ava. You're... a miracle."

"I don't know what's happening," she whispered.

"I don't know, either." The contact was intoxicating. Malachi trailed his hand up her arm again, finally cupping her face in both hands.

"Malachi?" The frown was back, but this time, he let his finger smooth away the line between her eyebrows.

"*Irina,*" he breathed out, then his lips lowered to hers. The first brush of his kiss was soft and testing. Reverent. But Ava didn't faint. She leaned closer, and Malachi was lost.

His hand slid around to the nape of her neck to hold her as he let himself linger at her mouth. His other hand slid down her arm and around her waist, pressing her closer as he deepened the kiss. Her mouth moved against his, searching. Then he felt her hands.

He pulled away, groaning, "*Yes.*"

Her hands came around his neck, fingers lacing together as she held him against her. Malachi's mouth fell to her neck, pressing kisses against the soft skin there as she laid her cheek against his and held him close.

"Closer," he murmured. "More."

She left one hand at his neck and brought the other to his cheek, stroking the rough skin there. "Malachi?"

"Touch me, Ava." He kissed up her neck and over her jaw, searching for her mouth. "*Please.* It's been so long."

His rough hand stroked the small of her back, over her shirt, then he let a finger slide under the edge. She didn't faint. Didn't grow weak. Instead, the energy he felt from her seemed to surge wherever their skin touched. He slid his hand under her shirt, pressing it full against the small of her back as Ava let out a breathy moan.

"So good…"

He captured her mouth again, his tongue tracing along her lips until she opened to him. He slid closer. Tongues and lips. Her teeth scraped against his lower lip.

More.

More.

Her mouth was as eager as his when she pressed closer, gripping the hair at the nape of his neck as they knelt under the trees. Her knees buckled and he laid her down on the soft bed of needles, rolling on his side and bringing her with him, never breaking her glorious hold.

"Ava, Ava, Ava," he whispered against her lips. He let one hand trail down her arm, tracing along her skin, feeling the rush of magic that followed. "You're a miracle."

"I don't know what you're talking about, but don't stop."

"I can't stop. I don't want to ever stop."

Her hands were brushing over his cheeks again, her fingernails scraping against the stubble. He'd forgotten to shave that morning. Usually he never thought about it, but he did now. He wanted nothing between her skin and his. He let the hand at the small of her back rise, fingers trailing up her spine as she pulled away and arched her back with a moan. He kissed her neck. Her shoulder. The delicate skin over her collarbone.

"Ava, wait…" He groaned. "We have to stop. I don't want to, but—"

"No." She was trembling in his arms. "More."

"This is—"

Just then, she let out a shudder that racked her whole body. Malachi felt her heave a great sigh, then she stilled, going limp in his arms. He pulled away, panicked for a moment until he saw the deep breaths she was taking. He put his ear to her chest; her heart was strong and steady. There was a peaceful smile on her face. He gently laid her back on the bed of pine needles and pulled off his shirt, tucking it under her head. Then he lay on his side and stared at her.

Malachi brushed tentative fingers over her arm, still disbelieving what he saw with his own eyes. The gold glow was there, if anything, brighter than it had been at first. He scrolled letters over her, brushing spells across her skin to aid in rest and health. To give her peace of mind and sweet dreams. The breeze swept over them both as they rested in the dappled shade that overlooked the sea.

Ava rested, and Malachi watched.

A miracle.

A mystery.

Malachi hadn't seen one in over two hundred years.

Irina.

CHAPTER

EIGHT

Ava woke slowly. Her eyes were stiff and heavy with exhaustion like she'd never known before. She stretched her legs, moving languidly in the cool sheets that smelled of lemon and… Malachi?

She forced her eyes open, blinking as she looked around. Early morning sun spilled across the sheets, crisscrossed by shadows from the wooden blinds. She was alone in the room, but it wasn't hers. A thousand mornings waking in foreign rooms had trained her. Her bag would be in one corner. Her phone by the bed. Shoes set by the door.

This room was not hers.

It was dominated by a wall of bookcases. On the bookcases were volumes of paperbacks, hardcovers, and more. Intricate, leather-bound tomes. Books in boxes. Even a few scrolls. And the walls that didn't have books had art. It was a small room, narrow and long, but packed with traces of its owner.

It was Malachi's room. It had his smell. Even more, there was a certain odd balance and masculinity to it that reminded her of him. Simple and bold at the same time. At the foot of the bed, Ava noticed some books had been pulled out. She crawled that direction, unwinding the sheet that covered her.

How had she gotten here?

She searched her memories, but they were fuzzy. Her whole head was fuzzy, an odd feeling for her, though not entirely unpleasant. Usually, Ava woke restless. She rose with the feeling that she was already behind in… something. Some task had escaped her. Some memory forgotten. If she was in a hotel, early morning voices whispered to her, almost always in a hurry.

Rush rush rush.

Mornings for Ava were manic.

But this morning…

She took a deep breath and leaned against the wall where the large bed had been pushed and looked around again. The room almost reminded her of a dorm room. A small desk was in one corner with a computer on top. Packing boxes were stacked in another. She saw a narrow door she suspected was a closet.

Or a bathroom.

She jumped up and ran to it, disappointed when she saw all the clothes. Luckily, another glance to the right revealed a narrow door open to a sliver of a sink. With a sigh of relief, Ava walked in and took care of her most urgent concern, looking around for a moment as she sat.

If this was Malachi's room—and she was almost certain it was—how did his shoulders fit through that door? Did he walk sideways into his own bathroom? And that shower was ridiculous. Did he crouch in it? His scent was stronger in the bathroom. As she was washing up, she picked up a bar of soap.

Yep, definitely Malachi.

"Think, Ava." Her voice was rasping and hoarse. She needed water. There'd been some in the backpack she took to the island…

"The island." She met her own surprised gaze in the mirror. "We were on the island."

The island. The mountain. The monastery.

The *gun*.

She groaned. Leave it to Carl to send her a .45. He knew she was more accurate with a 9mm. Still, when one was sending contraband handguns to one's stepdaughter in Turkey, Ava supposed one couldn't be too picky. And leave it to Malachi to be more concerned than frightened when he saw it.

She walked back out to the bedroom, head still a little fuzzy.

What was she doing in Malachi's room? How had he gotten her there? The whole time between the hike and waking was a blur. They'd been hiking to the monastery. Ava had confronted Malachi with the gun.

And then…

The memory rang clear as the morning light.

Where have you heard this, Ava?

She almost ran into the door.

Malachi had spoken it! Her unknown language. Only a brief mutter at first, but her mind had latched on to it. Then more. He had spoken the words that haunted her. Not a whispered cadence. His voice had been real, and Ava had…

Well, she'd completely freaked out.

Where have you heard this, Ava?

He'd spoken it. Not in a whispered jumble. Not in a stutter or a whisper as she'd often tried. He'd spoken it like a native.

Malachi knew what her language was.

You're not crazy. You're a miracle.

A miracle of what? She closed her eyes and flushed at the memory of his kiss. More than a kiss. It had been *more*. Right and whole and real and true. Like the realization she'd had at the bar, it struck her soul-deep. Malachi was made to kiss her, and she was made to kiss him. He'd kissed her on the edge of that mountain like it was his purpose in life, and a small hopeful voice whispered to Ava that perhaps it was true.

She looked at the door, knowing that somewhere on the other side, she'd find him. She'd find Malachi, and he'd be able to answer her questions. Questions that had plagued her for twenty-eight years. And Ava had to admit the idea of finding answers was almost as frightening as the unknown. She sat down on the edge of the bed with trembling knees.

"Get a grip, Ava." She clenched her eyes shut and commanded her heart to stop racing. "Focus."

Irina, he'd whispered.

"Who is Irina?"

The sunlight flowed through the window, illuminating a book open at the end of the bed. There was a chest there with more books, but one was open, and Ava moved closer, drawn to the gold-trimmed page that glowed in the slanting light.

It was a manuscript. A very well-preserved one. The illuminations marked it as medieval, but the writing wasn't like any she'd seen before.

Ava had studied enough foreign languages and religions to know it was probably Middle Eastern. Something about it reminded her of Hebrew, but it wasn't. It was older. Simpler. Not hieroglyphics. A simple alphabet that could be carved as easily as written, she was guessing. It had shades of both Hebrew and Arabic but was neither. Phoenician? And what was it doing combined with what looked like Medieval European illustrations?

The art next to the script was exquisite. It was a picture of a couple embracing. The man's upper body was covered in strange, silver tattoos, and his face was a picture of ecstasy. The woman held him, her body also covered in the same marks, but the artist had used gold to draw hers. They twined together, two halves of one whole. Everything about them spoke of completion.

She closed the book and looked at the binding. It was old, but well oiled. The book, whatever language it had been written in, was exquisitely preserved. There were marks in the corners of the vellum and a few pages had been torn at the corner. This was not a museum piece. It had been treasured but used. Finally, she opened it at the beginning.

The first thing she saw was an intricate page of illuminated letters in the unknown language. Text only. Then, there were pictures of men with glowing faces and white robes. Beautiful women embraced them. Ava continued to turn the pages, not understanding the writing, but looking for the story the pictures told. Children were born. The figures showed both joy and sorrow. Then the men with glowing faces left, the women's arms held out to them in supplication. There were more pictures of children. Pictures of young men building what looked like temples. Houses? More men copying books and building fires. Writing on walls. A room full of scrolls. A library?

There were pictures of women. Breathtakingly beautiful and detailed, the pictures of the women were wrought with infinite delicacy and vivid color. Women holding children. Women putting hands on the sick. Overseeing a building project. Tending and drying flowers. A woman standing in front of an assembly, who looked like she was singing. The faces of the audience, each rendered in detail, exhibited awe.

Ava paged through the book, questions flying through her mind until she got to the last page again. The page with the couple embracing. Tears had come to her eyes. Who were these people? And why had this been out for her to find?

From beyond the closed door, she heard voices. For a moment, it didn't register. She was so used to hearing it, Ava hardly noticed. But then, she did. She put the book down carefully and walked to the door.

There it was again. It was real. Low male voices spoke in the language she'd heard from her youth. Not whispers. Not murmurs. They were actually *speaking* it. Out loud.

"I'm not crazy," she whispered with a smile. "I'm really not."

Ava cracked the door open and peeked out. Malachi's bedroom was at the end of a dark hallway, and she could see stairs leading down. The room below glowed with morning light, and that was where the voices came from.

"Don't chicken out now, Ava." She patted her cheeks and left the room, walking slowly toward the stairs. The voices began to rise, and she paused.

They were arguing.

She heard Malachi and another man arguing. Another, calmer voice occasionally chimed in, but mostly she heard Malachi.

Beautiful. Rise and fall. The cadence of his voice in the unknown language drew her closer. She reached the stairs and started down. No one halted the argument as she walked. When she reached the bottom, she realized she was in a large open living area with couches and tables. There was even a flat-screen television surrounded by chairs in one corner, but the voices were coming from a room off the main one, a room with a door half open.

Ava walked toward it. The arguing was getting even more intense, but she told herself to be brave. She had to know what was going on. Where the hell was she? Who did they work for? She was assuming she wasn't a hostage or prisoner, because she could see the front door from where she stood. No one guarded it. No alarms were going off. There was only intense arguing coming from unknown voices. She took a deep breath and walked in.

As soon as she stepped through the doorway, everything stopped. The arguing. Any and all movement. It was as if they had frozen.

She waited for someone to break the silence before she finally lifted a hand. "Hey."

There were five men. Five very large men. She recognized Leo in the corner as he lifted a hand and smiled. Ava smiled back, relieved that someone was acting friendly. There was another man next to him who looked like he could be his brother, but his mouth only gaped in shock. Ava's eyes swept the frozen room. Sitting at a desk, a tall, lanky man with black hair and very pale skin watched her with cautious green eyes. He didn't smile, but he didn't glare, either. And across the room, which appeared to be a library, Malachi stood with another man, braced for a fight.

The other man was even bigger than Malachi, almost a giant. His hair came down to his shoulders, but she could only see his back and bare arms, arms that were covered in the same intricate tattoos she'd seen in the book.

"Oh! The... the men. The ones in the manuscript? They have the same tattoos!"

Ava looked for Malachi, her eyes alight with curiosity, only to realize that—for the first time—his own arms were bare. He'd always worn long sleeves. Always. But he didn't now, and the intricate tattoo work that she knew started at his collar crawled down his arms, covering his forearms and biceps. The words were scrawled at odd angles, like they'd been added and crowded into every available inch of skin. She looked at Leo. To the black-haired man.

"Holy shit, you all have them. Just like the men in the book."

The giant threw up his arms and yelled, "I can't believe you showed her one of the books, too!"

Malachi said, "Damien, she has to know."

"Does secrecy mean nothing to you? Does the safety of our race—"

"She's part of it!"

"She can't be! We've searched the records. We know where she was born. We know who her mother is. There is no trace of—"

"Forget the records and look at her!" Malachi strode over to Ava, who stepped back. He slowed and held up his hands. "Please, Ava. I have to show them."

She gulped. "Show them what?"

"What are you doing?" The green-eyed man's voice was concerned. "Malachi, you mustn't—"

"Trust me," Malachi whispered, meeting her eyes. Ava felt instantly secure, warm and safe, despite the strangers surrounding her. Their inner voices, all alive since she'd walked into the room, were practically shouting now. "I won't hurt you."

"I know," she said. "I know you won't."

The green-eyed man rose to his feet as his hands reached out. "Malachi!"

Malachi stepped behind her, wrapping one arm around her waist as the giant named Damien yelled, "No!" He lunged toward Ava and Malachi, but before he could reach them, he halted, and his eyes went wide with shock.

She felt Malachi's finger trace along her collarbone and she shivered at the sensation. His finger moved up and down along her exposed skin. Was he writing? Her eyes were glued to the reactions of the men around her. Damien, who had been lunging toward them, fell to his knees, suddenly staring up at Ava with a wild expression of awe. The green-eyed man was just as shocked, his mouth frozen in an *O*. Leo and the other blond man grinned in the corner, expressions of sheer joy across both of their faces.

"You see?" Malachi pleaded. "It's true. She does not faint at my touch."

She might not faint, but swooning was a definite possibility if he kept drawing on her skin like that. It felt amazing and oddly intimate. She blushed furiously, aware of all the eyes on them as Malachi held her.

"Malachi, you have to…" She tried to push his arm away, but he wouldn't let go of her. He did, however, stop writing on her skin. She felt his mouth at her ear.

"I'm sorry. I didn't mean to embarrass you."

"It's fine," she whispered as his hand moved down her arm again. She glanced down to see his heavily marked forearm still around her waist, holding her up. His other arm lay against hers, and his finger was trailing… She blinked rapidly. "Holy shit, there are gold letters all over my arm."

Then everything went black.

• • •   • • •

When she woke up this time, afternoon sun shone on the red roofs outside the window, and Malachi sat on the edge of the bed, a cool washcloth pressed to her forehead. In the chair by the desk, Damien also sat, unabashedly staring. Ava pushed Malachi's hand away and sat up.

"What happened?"

"You fainted." Malachi smiled. "And Damien was convinced that

I'd killed you until I picked you up and showed him how deeply you were breathing. Are you all right?"

"Why would you have killed me? And where am I?"

Damien spoke from the corner. "You are in the Irin scribe house of Istanbul, Ava Matheson. And my brother's touch would have eventually killed you… if you were human. But you're not entirely human, are you?"

She blinked and rubbed her eyes. "What are you talking about? Of course I'm human." She turned to Malachi. "And so are…"

You…?

She couldn't say it, because in that moment, Ava knew it wasn't true. Not entirely. The book. The strange tattoos. The language.

"Are you people aliens?" she whispered.

Malachi burst out laughing, and Damien rolled his eyes.

"What?" She was indignant. "What am I supposed to think?"

"Not aliens!"

"Well, I'm glad this is so funny to you, Mal. I'm just rolling with laughter here."

Damien said, "We are not aliens, Ms. Matheson."

"So, what are you?" She pulled her legs up and wrapped her arms around them.

Malachi smiled and put his hand on her bare foot. "We are the Irin. The heavenly race."

"What are you talking about?"

"Do you know history?" Damien asked. "Think about human myths and legends. Genesis. The Book of Enoch. The heroes of Greek myth. You have written about us; you just never knew the whole story. Haven't you heard the myths of those who fell from heaven? Of their offspring?"

"Fell from heaven?" she asked. "You're talking about… angels? Fallen *angels*?"

"Of course."

Her temper snapped. "Nothing is 'of course' about this situation!"

Damien said, "Please calm down, Ms. Matheson. We are trying to explain."

"But you're talking about *angels*."

"Yes."

"Actual angels. From heaven. Coming down and—and sleeping with human women?"

Malachi said, "Angels don't sleep. But if you're referring to sexual relations, yes. The Fallen took human women as mates."

She turned to him. "And you're telling me that you and your… whatever you all are would be their… what? Their sons? Is that what you're trying to get me to believe? That you're the sons of *angels*?"

"Not only the sons." Damien looked offended. "What would that have to do with you, then?"

She frowned. "What are you—?"

"Did you think the angels only had *sons*?"

All the air left her lungs. Ava's eyes were locked with Damien's, but she felt Malachi reach for her.

"Ava, we are the Irin people. We are the descendants of those first children. We are the sons… and *daughters* of angels."

"Daughters?" She looked back to Malachi as his thumb brushed her cheek. "Of angels? You must be—"

"Crazy?" he said quietly. "Is that what you think? Truly?"

"I don't know." She didn't know. Their words made no sense, and yet there was no hint of deception in them. No waver in their silent voices told her to guard from harm.

Malachi asked gently, "Did the humans call you crazy, Ava?"

"Of course they did."

She could tell the knowledge pained him, but he kept his hand on her foot. His fingers on her cheek. Gentle and constant, his touch soothed her.

Damien asked, "Malachi says you hear voices. Is that correct?"

She shrank back. "Yes."

"In the Old Language," Damien mused. "If this is true, then you hear as the Irina do."

"What does that mean?"

"The Irina hear the voice of the soul. It is one of their gifts."

Her chest was tight. She swallowed the lump in her throat. "I don't understand what that means. How can the soul have a voice?"

"How can it not?"

"I don't understand any of this." She was overwhelmed. Part of her wanted to keep firing questions, and the other part wanted to run away.

As if sensing her panic, Malachi grasped her hand in both of his. "We are all confused. None of us understands how this happened, Ava."

"I don't even know—"

"Know this: I believe you are one of us." His grey eyes met hers. They burned with passion. "I know it. We will find the answers. We will help you."

She nodded, keeping her eyes on his. Even if nothing else made sense, some instinctive part of her trusted Malachi. Through all of this, he had watched out for her. He grounded her with his utter and complete confidence. She allowed herself to take a deep breath.

"Okay?" he asked.

"Okay."

"Malachi speaks the truth as he believes it," Damien bit out. "I am not convinced. We know your mother is not one of us."

"My mom?" She looked between Malachi and Damien in confusion. "What about my mom? What do you know about my mom?"

"You look just like your mother," Damien said. "Almost exactly."

"Yeah, so?" She was starting to get irritated. "And how did you get pictures of my mom?"

Damien turned from her and spoke to Malachi. "Irina only come from Irina."

"That's what we've always been told."

Ava asked, "So why do you think I'm one of these Irina?"

Both men ignored her and continued to argue in low voices.

Malachi said, "She's reacting like the Irina. She hears the soul-voice. She can bear our touch. Judging from the color in her face, she even seems to thrive on it."

"It's not enough. We need to know how this could happen. Admittedly, she looks healthier than she did when she first came here, but—"

"What do you mean, 'when I first came here?' Who all was following me?" As irritated as she was, Ava had to admit she did feel great. Malachi was holding her hand and she felt calm. He was like the medication she'd tried once, but without the awful side effects. Holding his hand muffled Damien's inner voice, making it easier for her to concentrate. She felt centered and easy. Relaxed. Her head was clear, and she was starting to remember more about the day.

"She can't go back to the hotel," Damien said. "She has to stay here. Stay protected."

"Hello?" Her voice rose. "I am still in the room."

"The Grigori still followed her yesterday?"

"Leo and I lost them on the way back from the islands, but—"

She squeezed Malachi's hand, trying to get his attention. "Who the hell are the Grigori, and why are they—" Her eyes widened. "Shit."

That one word was enough to silence the two irritating men.

Damien asked, "What?"

"How long was I sleeping? After we…" She glanced at Malachi. "You know."

Malachi ignored her embarrassed flush. "I carried you back from the island yesterday afternoon. I thought you'd wake up after a while, but I think I underestimated your exhaustion."

"So I've been out of contact for over a day?" Ava pushed his hand away and scooted to the edge of the bed. "Where's my phone? I have to call my mom and let her know I'm not dead, or she and Carl will be sending out the commandos."

Malachi went to his desk and opened a drawer. "So you *did* call them the other night. Is that where you got the gun?"

"Carl sent it." Ava glanced at Damien, who was watching her like she was some curious animal at the zoo. "I…" She sighed. "I don't know what to tell her. Last I talked to them, I was convinced you guys were part of some international conspiracy to kidnap me."

Damien murmured, "You might not be far off."

"What does that mean? Does this have something to do with the Grigori guys you were talking about? What's a Grigori?"

Malachi handed her the phone. "There are others related to our kind who are after you. We're not sure why, but it cannot be good."

"Supernatural bad guys? Of course there are supernatural bad guys." She threw up her hands. "I mean, you don't get superheroes without supervillains, right?"

"I wouldn't call them super," Damien said with a frown. "But they do have an interest in you." He rose. "I need to call Vienna. Malachi, can I see you in the hall for a moment?"

Malachi glanced at Damien, then back to her. "I'll be right back."

"And I'll call my mom." She waved her phone. "I guess I'll tell her… something."

• • •   • • •

By the time Malachi returned to the room, Ava had ended the call with her mother after spinning a very elaborate story about

Malachi and the old bodyguard miscommunicating. About how, really, it had all been a huge misunderstanding, and Ava was fine, and it had all worked out for the best.

Because she and Malachi were now involved in a whirlwind romance.

If there was anything that could distract Lena Matheson, it was speculating about her daughter's love life. Plus, Ava figured that it would keep her mom from calling too often if she was daydreaming about the nonexistent grandchildren Ava might someday give her when she found "the right man."

She had the book open again, staring at the entwined couple, tracing the edges of the page and remembering the way that Malachi's touch had lit her skin from within.

"Ava?" His voice was soft and solemn.

"Hey."

"How is your mother?"

"Happy, actually. I convinced her that it was all a misunderstanding, and we're now involved in a torrid affair. That'll distract her." She kept her eyes on the book. Now that they were alone, she didn't know how to act around him. She craved his touch, but the craving put her on edge. Was it natural? Normal? If he was really part of some supernatural race, could he make her feel things she wouldn't otherwise feel? Her heart told her Malachi was trustworthy, but a lifetime of rejection warned her to be cautious.

Malachi said, "That would have distracted my mother, too."

There was a strange sort of sadness in his tone. A tone that told her, somehow, in the moments they'd been apart, something delicate had shifted. He stood a little farther back, and a shadow tinged his voice.

"Your mom..." She lifted the corner of the page and tried to pretend the shadow wasn't there. "She's..."

"She was Irina. Our women are called Irina."

"Ah. And you think I'm one of them." Her finger trailed lightly over the gold leaf on the woman's skin, illuminated just as hers had been when Malachi touched her.

"I think you have to be."

"You think I'm part... angel?"

"It's slightly more complicated than that, but yes." He brought a chair over and sat across from her.

"My stepdad would disagree strongly with that."

"It's not what humans think."

"But you think I'm like you." She pointed to the woman in the book. "Like her?"

"I do."

She paged through the book a bit more but kept coming back to the picture of the couple he'd left the book open to at first.

Malachi said, "You're taking this all rather well. No running and screaming. Part of me expected you to be on a plane back to Los Angeles by now."

"You have to remember"—she closed the book and let out a rueful laugh—"you're talking to a woman who's heard strange voices from people's heads her whole life, remember? I don't think you can classify me as a skeptic."

"I suppose that's true. So you believe us?"

"Sort of. Kind of. There's a lot I don't understand."

She heard him shift in his seat, but he didn't come closer. "Then we will help you find the answers."

"Is that why you kissed me?" she asked quietly. "Because you wanted to know if I was like them?"

He paused. "Partly."

"Of course." Ava nodded. "That makes sense."

Malachi said nothing, and Ava refused to look up. She just stared at the couple. A perfect balance of male and female. Perfect longing. Perfect love. She ached for something always out of reach. She'd thought she felt a hint of it with him, but maybe it was all an illusion. Malachi certainly wasn't making any grand declarations about his feelings. His arms were crossed over his chest; his eyes avoided hers. Ava itched to reach out and trace the intricate letters that were marked on his skin, taste the edge of his jaw the way she had when they kissed, but everything about his body language screamed stop, even as his silent voice coaxed her closer.

"Ava, there is a scribe house east of here, in Cappadocia. One of the oldest in existence. There are scribes there who are far older than me or even Damien. Scribes who might know how all this is happening. Understand why you have the magic you do, even though you weren't born Irina. I think there might be answers there."

"You want me to go with you."

"Yes."

"To Cappadocia?"

"Yes."

"To visit a bunch of old scribes."

He finally cracked a smile. "We're a bunch of old scribes, too. We just don't look it."

And suddenly, she was wondering just how old he was. "I'm almost afraid to ask. So, you really think there are answers there?"

"There's a greater chance of answers there than here. The library of Cappadocia has been preserved for hundreds of years. And it would also be for your safety. To get you out of the city. Damien will continue to investigate why the others are looking for you. But in the meantime, you'd be somewhere much safer."

"I don't know…"

"It's also very unusual." His tone was more coaxing. "You could visit the underground cities and churches. There is nowhere else like it on earth."

She narrowed her eyes, knowing that he was tempting her curiosity, but unable to argue against his reasoning. "I suppose… there'd be lots of time for pictures?"

"As much time as you want."

"So you and me—"

"It won't be just me," he said in a rush. "Rhys will go with us. He's our resident researcher and scholar. He's the one most familiar with our history."

"That's the black-haired guy by the computer, right?" The lanky one with the vivid green eyes.

"Rhys is also a very fierce warrior if he needs to be."

"So Rhys and you and me?"

"I know I'm asking you to trust me. Trust others you don't even know." He cleared his throat. "But I promise you have nothing to fear. You are… a miracle, Ava. Any one of us would guard you with our lives."

A memory of Malachi came to her. Rough and angry. Standing at the door of the bar with a bandage across his abdomen. Ava shivered, knowing there was far more to that story than she'd been told. "I don't want anyone hurt because of me. I'm not worth that."

"Of course you are," he said roughly. "You are Irina. We know how precious you are."

Ava took a deep breath. What were her options? Stay in Istanbul and continue seeing a psychologist for voices that never went away, or go to some place in the middle of Turkey with tattooed people she barely knew in order to research whether she was some obscure form of angel spawn.

Well, she couldn't call it a *boring* vacation.

"Okay. Why not?"

CHAPTER

NINE

Malachi was glad they had decided to drive but wished Rhys hadn't insisted Ava not be left alone in the back of the car. Because of that, he was forced to sit next to her, keeping his hands clenched tightly at his side to avoid touching her as Rhys drove. The old landscape whipped past, familiar and foreign at the same time. So much had changed since he was young.

Ava was napping across from him, and her leg slipped from her side of the Range Rover, stretching out to brush his as they bumped over the eastern roads.

His fingers itched to touch it. The memory of her skin throbbed in his mind, but so did the warning his watcher had given him.

"No, Malachi. Would you take advantage like a Grigori? She has no idea what it means to be an Irina. She has been thrown into this world."

"But—"

"We do not know what any of this means. And neither does she. Any Irina, deprived of an Irin family, would have reacted the same way."

The thought had floored him. Had he taken advantage? Were his feelings an illusion? Perhaps she would have reacted to any man's touch the same way. The memory of her lips haunted him. The memory of her skin underneath his hands was a silent torture.

"What's put you in such a bad mood?" Rhys asked from the front seat.

"Nothing."

"You're a bad liar." Rhys switched to the Old Language. "Tell me, what is wrong. Is it the woman?"

He didn't reply, because Ava shifted and her eyes fluttered open. A beautiful smile spread over her face.

"You guys have no idea how amazing that is."

"What?" Rhys asked from the front seat.

"Hearing it?" Malachi asked. "Out loud, instead of from our minds?"

She nodded, closing her eyes again as she turned her face to the sun.

"I've never understood how Irina handled that," Rhys said. "Hearing the soul of every person you meet? I'd think it would drive me mad."

Malachi smiled. "More mad than seeing the shadows of every word written on something?"

"That's different."

"Is that what you can do?" Ava asked. "You can see writing? Even if it's erased?"

"Erased. Painted over. Plastered over." Rhys glanced at Ava over his shoulder. "An Irin scribe can see beneath the layers to every word ever written. Like your gift, it's a blessing and a curse. We're graffiti experts, I tell you."

Malachi added, "It's also very useful when preserving and copying ancient documents, which is what most of us are trained for. All Irin magic is controlled and practiced through the written word."

"That's why you call yourself scribes?" she said with a smile. "I was wondering."

"Wonder no longer, my dear," Rhys said. "You may ask us anything."

"Really?" She glanced over at Malachi, but he only shrugged.

"Anything you'd like. If we don't want to answer, we won't."

"Oh, that's helpful." She sat up and brushed her hair back from her face. "Okay, my voices. You're telling me the voices I hear are actually souls."

"Yes," Rhys said. "What other explanation would you have for every person on earth speaking in the same language? Humans speak in many languages, but the soul..." Malachi saw his friend's eyes light up in the rearview mirror. "Our souls are the same. All of humanity,

Irin, Irina. Even the Grigori have souls, though they're black as night."

"The Grigori are the bad guys, right? The ones who were following me before Malachi found me?"

"Yes, those are the Grigori."

"They sound scratchy."

Rhys laughed. "What? I've never heard that before."

"You Irin guys sound different than humans. Your voices are… bigger." She glanced at Malachi from the corner of her eye. "More layered, somehow. But you all—well, most of you—sound similar. And the Grigori voices sound the same, except scratchy. Like they're out of tune."

"I suppose that makes sense," Malachi said softly. "Every light casts a shadow. The Grigori are ours. We are the children of the Forgiven. They are the children of the Fallen. Our purpose is to protect humanity and preserve its knowledge. They are predators who have no purpose but to gain power for their masters and indulge their own perverse appetites."

Rhys said, "And reproduce, of course."

Ava paled. "What, really?"

"Grigori will procreate with human women, though it generally doesn't end well."

"And they were after me?" Her voice held a slight note of panic that infuriated Malachi.

"They won't get you," he said. "And they weren't acting normally with you. They were tracking you, but not attacking."

"And by attack, you mean…"

"Not rape the way you're thinking," Rhys said. "They don't have to be violent. Leo said you saw them in the bar. Is that right?"

"Yes."

"Handsome blokes, aren't they? Charming bastards, every one of them."

"They seemed a little full of themselves, if you ask me."

Rhys burst into laughter. "That's because you're not human. Grigori seduce. They don't have to attack humans. Women find them naturally appealing—well, *unnaturally* appealing, really. They go with them by choice. When a Grigori sets his sights on a human woman, she will go willingly."

"So…" Ava frowned. "I'm confused. I thought you said they

attacked women. I mean, they sound like jerks, but that's not really an assault."

"It is when the women don't have a choice," Malachi said. "Human nature draws them to the Grigori, and the monsters take advantage. Is that any worse than drugging someone? To take away their free will? Take advantage of them?" He broke off when he caught Ava and Rhys's shocked stares. "It's wrong. That's all. The Grigori use women and leave them for dead most times. Most don't survive, and if they do, they become infatuated with the very thing that seduced and almost killed them."

"That's horrible!"

"Most humans legends of succubi are based on the Grigori," Rhys said with academic detachment. "If a human woman does bear a Grigori child—it happens occasionally—they're usually quite extraordinary. You can't discount angelic blood, after all."

"And are they… normal? The kids?"

"For the most part, yes. Usually very gifted in some way. Mathematics. Music. Art. Many of the world's geniuses have Grigori blood."

"So I could have met a part-Grigori kid and not even known it?"

"Possibly," Malachi said. "The strongest magic is gone, but most would still have that inexplicable something that makes them stand out in human society. And the majority show no more evil tendencies than the average human."

Ava rolled her eyes. "Thanks so much."

Rhys said, "Hundreds, thousands of years they've been hunting in the world. Grigori blood is laced through human biology like a dark thread by now."

"I feel like I'm taking crazy pills," Ava muttered, and Malachi tried not to smile.

"You're processing all of this very well," he said quietly. "I can't imagine what you must be feeling."

Malachi saw her reach for his hand, then pull back. And he wanted —he *wanted* to grasp it. Wrap it in his own. He felt like a man starved, then given a single bite of bread. She was there. She needed his touch. If he could only—

"So if Grigori and Irin are basically the same with the bloodlines and stuff, why aren't the Irin men predators, too?"

Rhys curled his lip. "We have purpose, conscience, and discipline."

"Don't forget, Rhys." Malachi watched her. "We also have the Irina."

"The Irina," Ava said. "What you think I am?"

"Yes," Malachi said. "The Irina are our other halves. And they are stronger than human women."

Ava shrank back in her seat. "I don't have any super-strength, Mal. I think you guys are mixed up about what I am."

Rhys laughed. "Not like what you're thinking. And, for the record, the more time I spend with you, the more I agree with Malachi. You give off energy like a reactor."

"What do you mean?"

"Irina channel human energy; it's part of their own magic. And if you think about it, you've probably always had an excess. Humans would have called you nervous. Anxious. A bit jumpy and irritable."

"Maybe…"

Malachi knew from the tone of her voice that his brother had touched a nerve.

Rhys continued, "But what *humans* think is nerves or anxiety is normal for an Irina."

"You hear the souls of the world, Ava." Malachi tore his eyes from hers when she looked at him. "You absorb some of their energy. That's why crowds can be so overwhelming for you. It's inevitable."

"But *we* love it!" Rhys said. "We need it, really. Irin are only truly powerful when we're mated. Keeps us balanced. Healthy. Irin and Irina were created to work together."

They stopped at a small crossing to let a herd of sheep pass over the road. Rhys waved his hand out of the car window at the shepherd and continued driving. The terrain was slowly becoming hillier. They'd left the greener landscape near the coast and were heading inland, up the ancient Anatolian plain, not far from his own birthplace near the Sakarya River. The sun was hot, and the temperature was climbing as they drove. Rhys had been driving since they'd left the city, so it would soon be Malachi's turn. Perhaps then he could think about something other than the tempting woman next to him.

Almost as if he'd heard Malachi's thoughts, Rhys said, "I'm going to pull over and fill up. Take a turn driving?"

"Of course."

They stopped at a small petrol station outside Ankara, and Ava went in to use the restroom as Malachi filled up the car. Rhys came back from paying the shopkeeper, giving Ava an appreciative glance on the way back to the car. Malachi gritted his teeth as his friend approached.

"So, what's got you all broody, Mal?"

"Don't call me Mal."

"Only the pretty girl gets to call you that, eh?"

"Be quiet."

"I like it." Rhys snickered. "She's got your number, as the Americans say. Is that why you're in such a foul mood?"

"No."

He narrowed his perceptive green eyes. "I thought you liked this woman. She's intelligent. Funny. Obviously very attractive. What's your problem?"

"She's Irina."

"Yes." His friend nodded. "Hard to explain how, but she certainly bears the most common markers. That's a good thing for you, remember?"

"But she was raised human, Rhys."

"And?"

He lowered his voice. "She was around humans all her life. She's never… She doesn't know about Irin relationships."

"What in heaven's name are you talking about?"

"I touch her, and…" He frowned. "For the first time, she feels one of her own kind. She says I help take the voices away. I can relax her. And *I* feel… well, you can imagine how I feel."

Rhys spoke as if to a small child. "Again, the problem is…?"

"What if it's not *me*?"

A look of understanding dawned. "You mean what if she'd react to any Irin male that way?"

"Yes! If she'd been raised like us, her mother and father would have hugged her and held her. She would have had a normal childhood. Not one where she was starved for contact with her own kind for twenty-eight years. It's not fair for me to take advantage of that, Rhys. How would you react, if it were you?"

A bitter smile touched his lips. "You mean if I'd been denied the comfort and strength of a mate for two hundred years? If I had little to no hope of ever achieving the kind of connection with another Irin that my parents had? I just can't imagine, Malachi. Who would be able to imagine that, except… oh, ninety-five percent of us?"

"You know what I'm talking about."

"And you're being ridiculous. You had feelings for this woman when you thought she was still human, you idiot. This sounds like some nonsense Damien told you." Rhys only sneered when Malachi flushed in anger. "That's right, isn't it? Damien warned you off her. Filled your head with this rubbish."

"You think he's wrong?"

"I think he *has* a mate," Rhys hissed. "Even though they rarely see each other outside their dream walks. And I think he distrusts anything and everything he doesn't understand. I also think Ava has feelings for you, and you're being a right ass toward her."

Malachi stepped back and finished with the gas pump. Ava was still in the building. "I'm trying to do the right thing."

"You think the right thing is leaving her without a friend in this crazy new reality?"

"I think she deserves to find out what all this means for herself without being influenced by what I want!"

"Truly? Well, then…" Rhys smiled. "*Excellent.*"

Malachi's eyes narrowed. "What does that mean?"

"It means the first new Irina seen in two hundred years is riding in the back seat with me all the way to Göreme, and I'm suddenly feeling much happier about the journey. Thank you."

Malachi's face fell. "You wouldn't."

"You seem to think that she might be drawn to anyone, so I might as well give her the option, my friend."

A red haze fell over his vision, but just then, Ava stepped out of the shop, carrying three bottles of water and a bag of oranges. Rhys walked over with a smile, holding out his hands for the bag.

"Here, let me hold that. That was extraordinarily thoughtful, Ava. These look delicious."

She smiled up at Rhys. "Well, I wasn't sure what you guys like to eat, but I'm assuming it's more than milk and honey. Or whatever the myths say."

"Clever girl." He slid an arm around Ava's shoulders, guiding her back to the car. "I assure you our appetites are very similar." He opened the car door and helped her inside. "And we always appreciate sweet things."

. . .

HE WAS GOING TO KILL RHYS. SLOWLY. IN SEVENTEEN DIFFERENT WAYS so far, and they were only two hours past Ankara. The man talked and flirted, drawing Ava out in ways that had her confessing childhood mischief and university adventures. He asked about her travels and told her about his, making himself the hero of every confrontation, the key to every success.

Malachi was going to kill him.

He touched her casually, a brush on the arm, a bump of the knee. Ways that Malachi knew must be killing him. Like most of the Irin, Rhys hadn't had regular contact with any woman since the Rending. He must have been as ravenous for Ava's touch as Malachi had been on that hill by the monastery, but unlike Malachi, he had his control clamped down.

Malachi had been overwhelmed. Even the memory of her lips left him in a painful state of arousal, which was rather inconvenient, considering he had four more hours of driving.

He saw Rhys brush his elbow against Ava's knee as he bent down to get something from his backpack. Malachi slammed on the brakes, sending Rhys's head crashing into the front seat.

"Sorry."

Rhys straightened, rubbing his forehead, murder in his eyes and a book in hand for Ava.

"No problem. Accidents happen."

"I thought I saw a dog run across the road. False alarm."

Ava said, "Rhys, are you okay?"

"I'm fine, Ava. I'm used to Malachi's driving. It's always been quite bad."

"Here, let me take a look."

Then she put a hand on his jaw and pulled Rhys's face down toward her neck so she could see the red bump on the man's hard head. From the corner of his eye, Malachi saw Rhys's eyes close in pleasure as Ava's small fingers traced over the nonexistent wound.

"Does it hurt?"

"Only a little. Did it break the skin at all?"

"Not that I can see, but let me…" She started to run her fingers through the hair at his temple, examining it for any blood.

Eighteen. There were eighteen ways that Rhys could die.

· · ·

It was nighttime when they pulled into the old house in Göreme. The small Cappadocian town was ancient, dug into the soft volcanic rock of the hills. Once an Irin retreat had thrived only a few miles away, but after the Rending, when most of the Irina and the children were gone, the remaining Irin took shelter in the scribe house. They dug farther into the cliffs, scribing spells into the rock that made the compound one of the most secure places in the world. The libraries were legendary, as were the skills of the scribes who had stayed.

Ava crawled out of the car, sleepy and stumbling on unused legs. They'd driven straight through without stopping after the last break for petrol. Rhys was still snoring in the back seat.

"We're here?"

"Yes." He opened the back of the car as she leaned against it.

"Anything I can do to help?"

"It's fine. I can get most of it, and the others are expecting us." Malachi could already see the gates that guarded the compound opening. Lights began to switch on all over the side of the hill and scribes climbed down from their solitary rooms to greet the visitors. "Everyone will be out in a minute. I'm sure they'll have rooms ready for us."

"This place is amazing." She looked up at the terraces and caves that had been carved into the hill. The scribe house had been a work in progress for hundreds of years. The oldest parts were near the base where the library had been dug down into the rock, the dry Cappadocian air perfect for the preservation of manuscripts. The rest of the compound stretched up and back into the hill. A series of gardens, terraces, and decorative metalwork gave the compound a stark beauty.

Ava said, "Rhys told me the scribes here are older."

"Yes." He set some of his bags in the dust, moving them out of the way to get to hers. She would want her things so she could sleep. "Most of the scribes here came after the Rending. Many of them stopped casting the spells that prolong their life, so they are aging. More slowly than humans, but still aging."

"How old are you?"

"Biologically?" He smiled. "Around thirty. But I've lived for over four hundred years."

Her eyes were saucers. "Wow."

"And you will live as long or longer than that." He tried not to think about it. Tried not to see the gold letters forming under his fingers as they trailed down her spine to the small of her back. Tried to block out the rush of desire the image brought. "The magic is shared by Irin couples so they can age together."

"Oh."

Ava stared up at the stars, her skin pale and milky in the moonlight.

"What did I do to piss you off, Malachi?"

"Nothing," he choked out. "You didn't do anything, Ava."

"Are you sure? It seems like you're mad at me, but I don't know why."

"I'm not mad at you. I'm… trying to be your friend."

"My friend?"

"Yes." He forced a smile. "You told me once we were friends, didn't you?"

"I guess I did." She turned her eyes to him, and Malachi wondered whether those dark pools could see through him. See through to the longing inside. "I guess, I thought there was something… I was probably imagining things, right?"

He cleared his throat. "You have so much to think about. So much to consider and learn. It's not that I don't want—"

"Are we here?" Rhys yelled from the back of the Range Rover. The door creaked open and he climbed out, unfolding his long legs from their cramped position. "Oh, Ava, love, do you need help with your bags?"

Malachi bristled. "I've got them, Rhys."

"Good man." His friend slapped him on the shoulder before he grabbed his own bag and hoisted it out.

Malachi saw some Irin walking through the old gates. An elderly scribe raised a hand and waved.

"Ms. Matheson?"

Ava stepped forward and held out her hand as Malachi and Rhys stopped to watch. Watch the old scribe take her hand delicately, then more confidently, his face breaking into a huge smile. Most of the Cappadocian scribes were older, having stopped their longevity spells after the Rending, but a few of the younger men gaped at Ava as Malachi and Rhys followed her into the scribe house with the luggage.

Rhys was still groggy. Sadly, he was also talking.

"She was pressed against me in the car, Malachi. Heaven, I'd forgotten what that felt like. Just to have the weight of a woman—"

"Really!" he burst out. "Just… shut up, Rhys."

Thirty-three. There were thirty-three ways Malachi could kill him.

CHAPTER

TEN

He was avoiding her. It was the only explanation for the fact that Ava had been at the scribe house in Cappadocia for almost a week and had seen Malachi a grand total of two times. Fine. Whatever. If he was avoiding her, she refused to be sorry about it. She had other things to do.

For the first few days, she slept. For once in her life, sleep seemed to come easily. There was something about the inner voices of the Irin scribes that soothed her. Though none had the resonance that Malachi's did, the combined chorus of their souls blended into a soothing tapestry, almost like the white noise of ocean waves. She dreamed vivid dreams where she wandered in a dark wood. Nothing about it was frightening; it was profoundly peaceful.

Her days were spent with Rhys and the oldest scribe at the house, Evren. She'd met Evren the first night, and he seemed to take Ava under his wing. He told her he was seven hundred years old, but he looked around seventy. His dark hair was sprinkled with silver and curled at the neck. His skin was olive-toned, but pale. Ava suspected he spent most of his time among the books.

"And your mother's maiden name?" Evren asked quietly, taking notes with a pencil as Rhys typed on a computer in the library. Small windows, high in the walls, were the only bit of the outside world she saw. Like much of the oldest parts of the scribe house, the majority of the library had been dug underground into the soft volcanic rock.

"My mom was born Magdalena Russell. Lena."

"Ethnicity?"

Ava shrugged. "Honestly, I don't know. Her family has been in America for ages. I don't think I've ever heard her talk about relatives in another part of the world. I think I'm a mix of all sorts of stuff."

Evren nodded patiently, taking more notes she couldn't read. They were in the same rough script that marked his arms and the back of his hands. She could see similar markings peeking out from the collar of the loose shirt he wore. All the scribes were tattooed with what Rhys told her were spells to enhance different senses and control magic.

"You said she was from South Dakota originally. And your mother's mother?"

"Just her mom?"

Evren folded his hand in a way that reminded Ava of one of her favorite undergraduate professors. "When researching the Irina, it is the female line that is important. Irina power stems from their mother's magic. Even when tracing Irin bloodlines, we always start with the Irina. Irin scribes are the preservers of magic and knowledge, but Irina hold the creative force in our race."

"Oh. Okay, my mom's mom was Alice Cook. Her maiden name was Rutner. She was from Missouri. I think. I don't know much about her. My mom and she weren't close."

"Your mother's grandmother?"

"I think her first name was Sarah, but I'm not sure. We're not big on family history. Do you need to know about my dad?"

"Probably not." Evren smiled. "Though I'm sure that seems backward to one used to human tradition, where male bloodlines are more thoroughly documented."

"I hadn't really thought about it, to be honest." At least they didn't need to know about her dad. Jasper's family was a total mystery.

Evren cocked his head. "Do women still take a husband's surname in America?"

"Not always, but it's pretty common. My mom did with Carl. That's why I'm legally a Matheson. He adopted me after they got married."

"Hmm."

Ava squirmed, feeling like she was under a microscope. "How about you guys? What's your last name?"

Rhys turned from the computer. "We don't have surnames in our culture."

"Isn't that confusing? I mean, you guys live a long time."

Both men chuckled.

"Well, I suppose it helps that we don't have many children," Evren said. "They're quite rare. If we were more prolific, I suppose it could be."

Rhys said, "We have our own ways of keeping track of family history." He reached down and pulled off the T-shirt he wore, then he rolled his office chair toward Ava and showed her his back, which was marked with more strange writing along with the first decorative tattoo work Ava had seen. Without thinking, she reached out and traced the intricate knot work that showed a distinct Celtic influence.

"This is beautiful." She felt his warm skin shiver underneath her fingertips, but she didn't take her hand away. Like any casual touch from one of the Irin, the contact was calming. "What is this? Is it magic, too?"

"Yes and no." Rhys cleared his throat. "The writing on my back is the only work I haven't done myself. My father did it. The names down the center are my family's. Mother first—"

"Always the mother first," Evren said. "Because we are protected by Irina magic when we are born."

Rhys continued. "Then my father's name. Then my maternal grandparents and then paternal."

"So it's like your whole family tree, written on your body. And the design?"

"From my mother." His voice was quiet. "It was her gift to me."

Evren said, "An Irin mother always designs something of beauty to add to her son's *talesm* when he leaves for his training at thirteen, then his father does the tattoo. It goes on his back, over the heart. To be matched on the front of his chest when he is mated as an adult." Then Evren's face fell a little. "Though my son has neither, as he was only a child when his mother died."

The look of sorrow on Evren's face was enough to make Ava's heart weep. His silent voice groaned at the mention of his wife as Ava waited for the words.

Vashamacanem, his soul whispered.

At least, that's what it sounded like. Ava had come to think of it as the universal mantra of the grieving. She didn't know what the phrase meant, only that she'd heard the same words from countless people around the globe. Funerals. Hospitals. It was one of the few phrases that was completely universal.

She pulled her hand away from Rhys's back and squeezed Evren's hand. "Where is your son? Does he live here, too?"

Evren squeezed her hand back and took a deep breath, forcing a smile. "He lives in Spain now. In a scribe house near Barcelona."

A young man walked into the library, staring at Ava with the tentative awe she'd come to expect from most of the men. He bent down and whispered to Evren, who nodded and turned to her.

"We will have to take more notes later, Ava. I do apologize, but there is something I must tend to this afternoon."

"Of course," she said. "Don't let me keep you."

"Is there anything you need before I go? There is an English section in the library. Not large, but there are some books about local history that might interest you."

Rhys said, "I'll show her around, Evren."

"Are you sure? I can find where Malachi—"

"I'm sure Rhys can keep me entertained." Ava said, winking at the young scribe, then turning to Rhys who offered her a mischievous smile. Evren smiled knowingly as he and the young man turned to go.

When they were alone, Rhys said, "You know, scribe houses are almost as bad as sororities when it comes to gossip."

"I'm counting on it."

"Bad, tempting woman, you are." He shook his head before he pulled on his shirt. "You're going to get me stabbed. Malachi is not a man accustomed to sharing."

"Well, then I guess he should be the one to keep me company. And you know about sororities, huh?"

"Sadly not through personal experience." Rhys grinned. "But modern movies can be quite the education."

"That was never my scene. Sorry. The popular girls don't hang out with the crazy ones very often. Unless it's to make fun of them."

"Ava, Ava," he muttered, throwing a casual arm around the back of her chair as they sat next to each other at the library table. "Don't you know you're not crazy? You're special." She felt him toying with an errant curl. "You're magic, love. Someday you'll understand how much."

A beam of light came through a high window, flooding the room with sudden light and illuminating a mural on the other side of the library. One old man sat in the far corner, staring at the beautiful scene depicting a village bustling with life. In the six days she'd spent in the library, Ava had seen the old man do nothing else. He looked to be in his eighties or nineties, though like all the Irin, she knew he must be far older. Suddenly, she knew exactly what she wanted to do.

"Rhys?"

"Hmm?" He was staring at the mural, too.

"Will you tell me about the Rending?"

"THERE'S A HUMAN SAYING: YOU DON'T KNOW WHAT YOU'VE GOT TILL it's gone. We Irin should have that tattooed on our foreheads."

Rhys led her past the mural, toward a long hall lit with candles. On the dark wall, more images flickered from a mosaic of intricate design, made with shards of glass and pieces of pottery. Bits of stone, both precious and common, interspersed with paint and cloth and plaster. It was a confusing mixture, but as Ava stepped back, the images became clearer. She said nothing, waiting for Rhys to speak.

"It happened in the early 1800s. Things had been turbulent in human years. Wars. Revolutions. Political and social uprising. But for the Irin…" He shrugged and took a step down the hallway. "It had been an oddly peaceful few decades. Time has always moved more slowly for us. We exist among humans, but separate. We had become isolated in our own communities, for the most part. The council decided it was necessary after the madness of the medieval period in Europe."

"Why?"

Rhys pointed to a section of the mosaic where a long-haired woman was laying hands on someone in a bed. "The Irina have always been healers. Before humans developed modern medicine, the Irina used their magic and their knowledge to help humanity. Herb lore. Wives' tales. Those little bits of knowledge that have passed down in human custom. Much of it came from the Irina. Sadly, many humans thought their magic was evil. Some Irina were captured and executed as witches. Their families were devastated, and their mates often took revenge, killing the ignorant who had murdered their wives. Inevitably, innocents were killed, too. The council finally made the decision to isolate families so the Irina and the children could be better protected."

"The council?"

The two had stopped near a depiction of an ominous Gothic building.

"The Irin council is in Vienna." Rhys smiled and nodded at the Gothic building. "Everyone has their politicians, don't they? They are ours. Once it was made up of seven scribes and seven singers—"

"Singers?"

"Irina." He smiled again. "Their magic is in their voice. The oldest and wisest Irina would sing—" His voice broke. "The most beautiful, powerful music you can imagine. Ethereal. Their voices *are* magic. The council was always even, but once they had decided that families needed to stay in the retreats… there was conflict. Many of the Irina felt as if they were being punished for their sisters' deaths. Many didn't want to be isolated in the retreats. Eventually, though, it settled down. The Irin and Irina who were mated—particularly those with children —would live in retreats. Irin without mates, or with mates who were in study and meditation, worked among the humans or manned the scribe houses that preserved ancient knowledge." He gestured around them. "Like this one. The Irin worked here. The retreats—small villages, really—were for families. There were also other Irina compounds where they went to train and study, but Irin weren't allowed there, so I know little of those. I was raised in a retreat in Cornwall."

"And Malachi?"

"He was born near here, actually." Rhys smiled. "Though I believe his parents moved when he was still a child and were living in Germany when the Rending happened."

"The Rending."

"Yes… the Rending." Rhys nudged her farther down the hall as his inner voice took on a low, desperate tone. "One summer, there was a sudden rash of Grigori attacks in the cities. We learned later that it all happened within just a few weeks, but at the time, we had no idea. I was in London, about one hundred years old. I'd finished my training and was doing guardian work, as we all do. The Grigori, who had been relatively quiet for years, started attacking many human women. It was unexpected, and we couldn't keep up. We'd let our guard down." He let out a shaky breath. "My watcher followed protocol. When we needed help, we called for the mated men to come help us. They left the retreats to aid us in the city, because that was where the threat lay… we thought."

They took another step down the hall, and Ava saw the edge of chaos.

She whispered, "But they left the Irina in the retreats alone."

"Irina…" Rhys's fingers came up to trace the image of a woman, arms stretched out as dark figures ran toward her. "…have frightening magic of their own. Powerful. Deadly. But they were outnumbered, and they had to protect the children." Ava felt the tears wet her cheeks as she watched him trail his hands over the scenes of carnage the artist had rendered in frightening detail.

Bodies broken on the ground.

Homes burning.

Children's toys, bloody and abandoned.

Rhys stopped in front of the depiction of another woman, this one with a fearful gash on her throat. Rhys's finger traced down the woman's face, lingering near her neck as if to cover the wound. "Grigori will go for the throat first. If an Irina cannot speak, most of her magic is rendered mute as well. Their voices are…" Ava saw him blink away tears. "The Grigori soldiers overran retreats all over the world. The Irina protected as many children as they could, but most didn't survive. The girls, especially, were hunted."

A rushing began to fill her mind. Ava could almost hear it. Hear the voices of the women, silenced forever. Their children, cries cut short by murder. A terrible pain began to throb in her chest.

"How many?" she whispered.

Rhys shook his head. "No one knows for certain. Thousands. It was a coordinated effort on the part of the Grigori to render us weak. They know we are most powerful when we are mated. And they have always feared the voices of the Irina. They fear magic they don't understand. So, they killed them. As many as they could, along with most of the children and the men who had stayed behind."

Ava felt the trembling start in her legs.

"The council estimates eighty percent of our women and children were wiped out within a matter of weeks in the summer of 1810. Our race was cut in half. That's why we call it the Rending."

The shaking grew. The horror was too much. The loss—barely comprehensible.

They halted at the end of the hall where a tapestry hung, woven with the same circle of Irin and Irina depicted in the book Malachi had shown her. But instead of a couple embracing, the tapestry was torn down the middle, forming a kind of curtain that Rhys pulled back.

Behind it, there were more words, written in the ancient script.

"These are names of the Irina and children from the retreat nearby," Rhys whispered. He pointed to one near the top. "This was Evren's wife."

Ava stifled a cry. Hundreds of names followed that first one. Column after column of names. Some worn smooth by fingers rubbing over them. Others sharp and jagged, as if the stone still held the anger of two hundred years.

She felt rage bubble up along with a primal grief she could barely comprehend. Words caught in her throat, and her hands clenched, her fingernails digging into her palms till she could feel the skin break and the blood run. She felt powerless. Strangled by her own pain. By Rhys's pain. By the pain lurking beneath every face she'd seen. She shook with it, knowing she was crying, but the tears weren't enough.

"Ava?" Rhys's voice seemed to come from a distance. "Ava, are you all right?"

Don't speak. Can't speak. Never speak again.

Shaking her head, Ava pulled her hair and closed her eyes. She dug her fingers into her temple, relieved by the bite of pain. Her tear-filled eyes rose to the wall of names, but there was only silence.

And Ava knew.

These *were* her people. And they were gone.

"No," she whispered.

The shivering took over, starting in her chest and spreading to her limbs. Her mind flew in a thousand directions as she closed her eyes again and rocked.

"Ava?"

She felt Rhys's hand on her shoulder. He tried to put an arm around her, but she shoved him back.

"*No!*"

"Ava, I'm sorry. I shouldn't have—"

Rhys broke off at the unexpected cry of grief that came from her throat. It was a groan. A shout. It was everything her soul didn't have the words to express. Ava leaned against the far wall, staring at the mosaic, feeling her legs start to give out. She felt locked in a pain she couldn't escape.

And then she felt him. Felt him running toward her. Heard his footsteps coming down the hall.

Closer.

"What did you do?" he shouted.

"She asked! Was I not supposed to tell her the truth?"

A shove. A punch. Ava reached out, her eyes still closed, grasping for something she couldn't name yet.

Hands met hers. Arms encircled her. And the calm followed. The rage fled, and in its wake was a fierce grief for a thousand faces she would never know. A thousand voices she would never hear. Ava held on to Malachi and wept for a loss her mind could barely comprehend. He lifted her and took her away from the hall. Away from the flickering candles and the bloody stones. Ava closed her eyes and let him take her away.

"So many dead." She closed her eyes and whispered into his skin.

"I know."

"Women like me. They hated them. They killed them. Because they were afraid."

They were sitting in a quiet corner of the scribe house, in a room she hadn't seen before. Low lights flickered from sconces on the wall, and the room was lined with comfortable chairs and sofas. There was another mural on the wall, but this one was a picture of the sky, vividly blue against the light stone walls. Malachi was holding her on his lap, stroking her hair as she burrowed her face into his neck.

"Was your mother killed, too?"

He didn't answer for a moment. "Yes. And my father. He had remained behind at the retreat when the men in our village went to Hamburg to help the guardians. He was killed, too. Almost our entire village was wiped out. I was stationed in another city."

She fell silent again, focusing on the quiet comfort of his skin against hers. How could a people survive such a loss?

"You lost your wives. Your mothers. Your children."

"Most of us haven't even seen an Irina since the Rending." His voice held suppressed rage. "We are half a people."

"That's why you called me a miracle," she said.

She felt his arms tighten. "Nothing about your family says you can be Irina, but you *are*. We lost so many, but… I am willing to hold out hope that somehow, if you exist, then others might, too. That our race will survive. We are dying, Ava. We may live forever, but we are dying from the inside. Once there were so many of us. Families. Generations. Now there are almost no children. The Irina who still live hide away, angry with the rest of us for leaving them vulnerable. Enraged at the loss of their sisters and children. And who can blame them?"

"And the Grigori know who I am."

His arms squeezed a little tighter. "They will not get you. I will not allow it. None of us will."

She pressed her face into the skin of his neck and breathed deeply, allowing herself the comfort. Allowing herself to dream for a moment that there could be a future for her that didn't mean loneliness and isolation.

"Ava." She heard the reservation in Malachi's voice and felt him begin to draw away. She held his shoulders tightly.

"Just give me a few more minutes."

His shoulders tensed, then relaxed, and she felt his arms go around her even more tightly, pressing her into his chest as he took a deep breath. His voice was only a soft murmur in her mind, and no other intruded. Malachi began stroking her hair again, tentatively brushing his fingers along her neck and behind her ear.

He finally said, "A few more minutes."

And just like the moment in the hall, when grief and recognition slammed together, Ava knew. However it had happened, whatever strange twist of fate had caught her… these *were* her people.

And however he tried to deny it, Malachi was hers, too.

CHAPTER
ELEVEN

It was getting harder and harder to avoid her. Malachi sat in the corner of the library, watching Rhys and Evren interview Ava about her family again. He'd trusted his brother to look after her, even if Rhys's behavior had irked him, but Ava's collapse in the hallway had been unnecessary. Rhys should have known. Irin scribes still struggled to talk about the massacre that had taken most of their families. How did he think Ava would react?

So Malachi was back to guarding her, this time from his own people. He didn't know why he was so attuned to the woman, but perhaps days of reading her expressions had given him some insight the others didn't have. She was handling her new reality well, but he knew she was still stressed at times. Like when they asked her about her family…

"Listen… Yes, I have a lot of cousins on my mom's side." Her voice was clipped, her hands clenched tight. "But no, as far as I know, none of them hear voices. My mom doesn't hear voices. Her mom didn't either. I don't know why you don't understand this. There is no history of mental illness—"

"Not mental illness," he muttered from the chair at the far end of the table, glancing up at her. "Stop calling it that. You're not mentally ill, Ava."

She rolled her eyes. "Fine. Whatever. Angel blood. Irin blood. Call it what you will. I'm the only one, okay? Lots and lots of girls all over my mom's side, and none of them hear voices. Or souls. Or whatever this is."

The rest of the world might have disappeared. Malachi and Ava glared only at each other.

"Are you always this sarcastic?" he asked.

"Are you always this taciturn?"

He picked up a book again and pretended to read.

Ava said, "I'll take that as a yes." She turned back to Evren. "Okay, next question."

Evren cleared his throat. "It seems improbable, but let's explore all genetic possibilities and look at your father's side."

"Now that could be difficult."

"Because?"

"I barely know my biological father."

Her father was a famous musician, Jasper Reed. He and Lena Matheson had never married. It was a brief relationship that only lasted until Lena became pregnant. From Malachi's research, he knew the father had stayed in the mother's life in a peripheral way, remaining friendly, but not an active part of his child's life. Malachi found little to admire about Reed, despite the human's legendary musical talent.

Children were rare to the Irin. A mated couple would probably only ever have one, possibly two, children in hundreds of years. No one knew why. Perhaps it was simply a divine trade for the unnaturally long life their race had been granted. For that reason, children were unreasonably cherished. Malachi might even say pampered, except for the rigorous magical training that started when Irin children reached the age of thirteen.

The thought of fathering a child and abandoning her was unheard of.

Evren asked questions carefully, but Malachi could tell Ava was becoming more upset. She twisted her ring in a nervous gesture, and the air around her became charged. He had the almost unbearable impulse to shove Rhys from his seat next to her so he could take her hand, just to calm her down. He quashed it. Damien's warning still rang in his ears. Ava wasn't a normal Irina who had been nurtured by a loving family. She had been subjected to the battery of human emotions her whole life. In that situation, any Irin male would be able to offer her comfort. It didn't mean she had a special bond with *him*, even if he felt drawn to her.

But...

Maybe it was more than just a normal attraction. She wouldn't let Rhys approach her when she broke down in the hallway. She'd reached for *him*. Even with her eyes closed, she'd sensed him. Almost as a mate would.

Reshon. The word had become a persistent whisper in his mind.

There had been an overwhelming feeling of comfort as he held her. Malachi knew he was soothing her, but the act of giving comfort fed his soul, as well. Not to mention the intoxicating feel of her skin against his. Then the memories of their kiss on the island—

"Shut up!"

He blinked and looked to her. Ava was glaring at him, and Malachi frowned.

"I wasn't saying anything!"

"Not out loud. But did you forget I can hear you? *You.* You're here, and all the other voices fade, and I just hear *you.* And there's this weird mix of pride and frustration and wanting—" Her voice caught. "And guilt and anger and I cannot take it anymore, Malachi. I can't deal with all this and you, so please just go."

If she had punched him in the gut, he couldn't have been as shocked.

"Ava—"

"*Go.*" He could see a sheen in her eyes. "I can't handle all your complicated shit and these questions, too. So I need you to leave."

He saw Rhys begin to rise, but one look from Malachi had the other man sinking to his seat again.

He set down the book. "Fine." He shoved back his chair and marched from the room, ignoring the voice inside that practically begged him to take her with him. He wouldn't stay where he wasn't wanted, even if everything in him said she was exactly where he belonged.

He called Damien from the garden outside the scribe house. Phone reception was spotty in Cappadocia, but there was a corner of one garden that seemed reliable.

"How is the woman?" his watcher asked, by way of greeting.

"Coping." He paced, frustrated and anxious for some activity after being cooped up in the scribe house for over a week. "Have you learned any more about Dr. Sadik?"

"The therapist seems to be on holiday, from what we can tell. No one is in the office, not even nurses or the receptionist. No sign on the door, either. Considering the summer months, it could be a coincidence—"

"Or it could be that his reason for remaining open left the city." Malachi drummed impatient fingers against his thigh. Part of him craved the energy of the city. Part of him knew he was only looking to escape his own temptation.

Damien said, "Tell me more about the human."

"She's not human, and you know it."

"She cannot have Irina blood. I spoke with Evren yesterday. There is no evidence from family history that she is anything but a normal human woman."

"A normal woman who can hear the voice of the soul? A normal woman who can bear our touch? Who craves it, even?"

There was silence on the other end of the phone.

"To answer the question you didn't ask...," Malachi said, "Yes, I've been keeping my distance. Even though it has been difficult."

There was still more silence.

"Rhys has been keeping an eye on her, though there was an incident where she became very upset yesterday. He told her about the Rending, and she... She became distraught, as you can imagine. I was eventually able to calm her."

"Completely understandable," Damien said quietly. "It is still upsetting for all of us."

"We have been without Irina influence for too long," he said. "We become too blunt. I don't think Rhys expected her to become so upset."

Another moment of silence, until the watcher said, "Rhys told her?"

"I told you, I have been trying to maintain my distance," he snapped. "She was curious, so she asked him."

"But you were the one to comfort her?"

"I sensed her distress."

"And she asked for you?"

"Not exactly. But she wouldn't let Rhys touch her, so… She reached for *me*. I held her until she calmed. Was I supposed to ignore her when I seemed to be the only one who could reach her? The only one who—"

Damien interrupted him with a low chuckle that grew into a longer laugh.

"What's so funny?" Malachi asked.

"You've really been staying away from her all this time?"

"Of course!"

"When have you *ever* followed my orders so precisely, brother? At most, you take them as suggestions."

"I was trying to do what was right for Ava. You told me—"

"I think you misinterpreted my advice."

Malachi stopped the drumming of his fingers. "What do you mean?"

"I only wanted you to slow down. I know how rash you can be. I advised you to give the woman space, not ignore her completely. She'd just had a huge shock, and you were hovering over her like a worried mate. But if you gave her space and she still showed interest in you, then what are you waiting for, you idiot?"

"I thought you said—"

"Do you care for the woman?" Damien asked. "That's the real question. Not just the thrill of a woman who can stand your touch, but *her*?"

Did he? Was it too soon to be feeling as strongly as he was? What did he know about Ava, really?

He knew she was intelligent and funny. She was independent. He knew that beneath the tough exterior lay a vulnerable soul, and he suspected a deeply sensuous nature. She was cautious, but unafraid of him, or any of the other scribes she had met. He remembered her, standing boldly among the Grigori, flush with wine and unafraid of the creatures she challenged. Eyes flashing with indignation. Eyes that swung to him, as Malachi saw…

Recognition.

There you are, reshon.

He'd known in that moment, but it had seemed like an impossible dream.

"Yes." He cleared his throat. "I care for her. Deeply."

"Then, Malachi, see her for the gift she is and cherish her." Damien's voice grew rough. "We know how unexpected life can be."

"You're right." He nodded, feeling a profound peace for the first time in weeks. "Thank you."

"Don't thank me yet. You've probably angered her thoroughly and will have to convince her to let you court her."

"I haven't courted an Irina in over two hundred years." Malachi had begun pacing the garden without realizing it. Thinking of the volatile relationship between Damien and his mate, he asked, "Any advice?"

"You're asking me? My wife hasn't allowed me to see her face outside of our dreams for over ten years. Though Sari is unusually stubborn. Even for an Irina."

"Good point. Why did I listen to you in the first place?"

"I'm your superior. It's required. Now, I have to go."

"Sadik," Malachi said, remembering the reason he'd called. "I want to continue watching him. I'll ask Ava if she's called him. I think there's still something we're not seeing."

"I would agree with you. You said that his visits seemed to calm her? Release some of the tension she'd been having?"

"Yes. She always seemed calmer after a visit with him. She said he used acupressure. Nothing unusual. Mainly around the head and neck." He paused and thought. "If I didn't know any better, I'd say that she'd been in contact with—"

"An Irin."

"Yes."

"Someone siphoned off her energy enough for her to function more easily."

"It's possible."

"But he is not Irin; Leo was watching him. Following the doctor. He said he wasn't Grigori, either. Didn't appear to be anything other than a normal man."

A disturbing thought tickled the back of Malachi's mind. "Appearances can be deceiving, brother. Especially for certain beings."

"Only for…" Damien fell silent.

"Is it possible?"

"Anything is possible, as your human Irina proves. But is it probable? No."

"And yet, it seems there are all sorts of *improbable* things going on lately."

"If you're right, why? Why her?"

Malachi stopped pacing to look at the sun, setting west into the hills and painting the sky in vivid purples and reds. "She could be a miracle, Damien. The first Irina born from human bloodlines the world has ever seen. Why wouldn't she have attracted their attention?"

"It's worth looking into. If you're right, then her description, and Leo's eyes, mean nothing."

"He could be anyone."

"Not anyone… There aren't many."

"Keep me updated?"

"Of course. Keep her safe."

"I will."

By the time Malachi made it back inside, Evren had packed up his notes for the day and Rhys and Ava were chatting by the computer. Ava appeared to be checking her e-mail while Rhys read over her shoulder, laughing about something in a friendly way. Looking up, the scribe spotted Malachi coming into the library and the teasing look fell from his face. Stern grey eyes met narrowed green ones as Malachi approached. He glanced at Ava with a possessive gleam, then looked back to Rhys.

Cocking his head, the corner of Rhys's mouth lifted before he asked, "Hey, Ava?"

"Hmm?" She never turned to look at Malachi, even though he knew she must have sensed him.

"Where did you want to go for dinner tonight?"

"I don't know. You know the town better than I do."

Malachi stopped. Bastard. He'd planned on taking Ava out to dinner in the village to get her away from the scribe house, but apparently Rhys had already thought of that.

Continuing toward them, he took the seat on Ava's other side. "I'll join you. There's a place I know with a beautiful balcony I think you'd like."

Finally turning, Ava sighed. "Malachi, I don't…"

She trailed off as he picked up her right hand, casually playing with the ring on the middle finger the way he'd wanted to for weeks. It was her own nervous gesture, but he'd been fascinated with her hands every time she did it.

"Do you remember that coffee shop you liked near the Bosphorus?" he asked, continuing to play. "The owner of the restaurant is a cousin of the man who owns the coffee shop. We'll get a good table, I promise. And the food is excellent."

He didn't let go of her hand. Her cheeks flushed, and she pursed her lips as if she was holding back words.

Rhys said, "It's Friday night. Are you sure you can get a table for three?"

If Rhys wanted to tag along, Malachi could work with it. "I'm sure. Ava?"

He finally set her hand down, letting his fingers trail over hers as he drew back and crossed his arms across his chest, flexing his forearms and the intricate spells he'd worked over them. He'd seen her looking at his *talesm* many times. He knew she was fascinated by them. Her eyes grew wide before she looked away.

"Yeah, that sounds fine. Table for three?"

"Of course. I should have taken you out before. I'm sure you're tired of the kitchen here. It can be rather simple food."

"It's been fine." Her voice was a bit rough and the color on her cheeks was heightened. "Just give me a few minutes, and I'll put my stuff away. Meet you two in the garden?"

Rhys said, "Good idea."

They both watched as Ava gathered the bag with her laptop computer and left the library. When she was a suitable distance away, Rhys turned on him.

"I see someone has finally removed his head from his posterior. Congratulations. You've thoroughly pissed her off at this point. Hope you like a challenge."

He shrugged. "I've never backed away from one."

"Good." Rhys stood. "Neither have I."

"Rhys." His friend froze halfway to the door. "I'm not backing away again."

The scribe shook his head and grimaced. "You changeable bastard."

"She doesn't feel that way for you."

"How do you know?"

"Because I do." Malachi rose and walked toward him. "The same way I know she's for me."

"Are you sure about that?" Rhys's eyes met his in challenge.

"Absolutely sure."

THE THREE MET IN THE GARDEN AS THE SKY TOOK ON THE DEEP, midnight blue of the evening. It was late, but Malachi had already called the restaurant, reserving his favorite table in a corner of the balcony. They walked toward town, Ava between them, and Malachi forced himself to remain casual, even when the scent of her perfume drifted to him on the breeze. It held notes of jasmine and smoke, a sweet fragrance with hidden depths he knew would be even stronger at the curve of her neck where he had kissed her before. Kissed her neck. Her mouth. He imagined nibbling on the skin that peeked from above her waistband when she wore the green shirt he liked.

Malachi let his mind wander down sensuous paths, knowing she would hear the tone of his thoughts even if she couldn't understand them. Ava turned around, eyes wide and color high. He simply smiled before he shrugged and kept walking, letting their hands brush casually on the uneven sidewalk.

"What kind of food does this restaurant serve?" she asked, obviously trying to ignore him.

"Turkish, along with some Cappadocian dishes that are very good. There is a lamb dish I think you would like."

"I love lamb," Rhys said. "Quite the delicious fluffy animal, don't you think?"

Ava gave him a mock scowl. "Do you dine on kitten, too?"

"Only if they're prepared with the right sauce, love."

The two joked all the way to the restaurant. Malachi tried not to let it bother him, but they had obviously become familiar over the past week. It wasn't that he didn't want Ava to like Rhys. He was one of Malachi's closest friends, after all. But he also knew the look on Rhys's face, and it was one he hadn't seen in two hundred years. The Irin was infatuated with the woman. And Malachi had thrown them together.

He really was an idiot. He could only hope that his gut feeling was correct, that Ava didn't feel for Rhys the same way she felt for him. They had none of the electricity that charged the air between her and

Malachi. When Ava gave Rhys's shoulder a friendly jab, Malachi tried to hide his smug expression.

The restaurant was bustling that night, but Malachi nodded to a waiter he recognized and they were shown to a private balcony looking out over the town. Low lights and candles flickered. It was an unmistakably romantic setting that he hoped would impress her.

It did.

"Oh! This is so beautiful. Look at that view!" Ava's eyes glittered with delight as the waiter held her chair for her. Rhys gave him a dirty look.

The table where they were sitting was private enough that he knew they didn't have to worry about being overheard, which let him relax as Rhys and Ava began chatting about Irin history in the region.

"You were born near here, weren't you?" Ava asked him. "I'm sure it's changed a lot over the years.

He smiled. "This area? No, but I remember visiting here with my father as a child. The cities change more, of course. Cappadocia can almost feel like a time capsule. I was born west of here. It's still a very rural area. The village where I was born in is no longer there."

Malachi thought he saw a troubled look filter across her face. He wondered if she was thinking about the Rending.

"I have many happy memories from that retreat and the one in Germany," he added, hoping to ease her mind. "Both were wonderful places to grow up."

Rhys distracted her with a joke about Malachi, and within moments, the troubled look left her face. He would have been resentful if he wasn't so grateful.

Malachi watched them at dinner, trying to discover her feelings. It was clear she liked Rhys, but Malachi was still convinced that his and Ava's connection was unique. It had to be. Even when he was young, he didn't remember being drawn to one woman the way Ava drew him. Of course, he'd had his flirtations and even a few brief relationships with suitable Irina when he'd been young, but nothing like this. He could spend hours just watching the subtle play of emotions across her face.

They'd been eating for over an hour, and the wine had brought a flush to her cheeks, and then she asked the question.

"Hey guys, I've been wondering. There's this phrase I hear repeated a lot in people's minds. It sounds kind of like... *Vasha*—"

Rhys slapped a panicked hand over her mouth as Ava's eyes widened. In the next second, it disappeared as Rhys's arm was twisted away and shoved to the side. Malachi bared his teeth as Ava gasped.

"You do not silence her. Ever."

"But the magic—"

"Never." Malachi's grip tightened around Rhys's wrist and the man winced. "Warn her if you will, but never attempt to silence her again."

"Let go of my arm," Rhys growled.

"No one is looking."

"They will be if you don't let go *now*." Rhys warned Malachi with a glare.

Malachi released him as Ava let out a breath.

"What on earth just happened?"

Rhys cleared his throat. "Forgive me, Ava. I was concerned and I overreacted." His eyes cut toward Malachi. "As did your defender."

"What did I do?"

"Nothing," Malachi said. "You asked a perfectly reasonable question."

"But you must be very careful, Ava," Rhys added, his voice dropping. "Remember that the words you hear are in the Old Language. The eternal one. It is the same language we use to cast spells. For scribes, those spells must be written down to have power. But for singers—"

"Ooooh." Her own eyes widened. "They speak them, right? So if I say something—"

"You could be performing magic you have not been trained for. Rhys is correct about that," Malachi said softly. "We start to manifest power near puberty. It is why we start training then. But for you, who has no training in magic, even repeating a simple phrase you hear from the mind of a human could be quite dangerous. You do not understand your own power yet."

He saw the curious gleam in her eye.

"But I can learn? Even though I'm older?"

Rhys and Malachi exchanged a look.

"Irina magic is always taught by other Irina," Rhys said. "What we don't know outweighs what we do. Still, there has to be a way. There are Irina in the world, though they are mostly in hiding. We will find a way to let you unlock your power, Ava. I promise."

"As do I." Their eyes met in the flickering candlelight, and Malachi had a vision of Ava, her arms spread, her voice raised in song. Magic poured from her. He imagined her voice whispering secrets in his ear, the ancient words a mate would share. The most beautiful power imaginable that bound two into one. The thought brought a rush of emotion he hoped she heard. From the flush of her cheeks, he was guessing she did.

CHAPTER

TWELVE

F our days later, Ava was still thinking about Rhys's words.

We will find a way to let you unlock your power, Ava. I promise.

Power. They told her the manic energy that had stalked her wasn't illness or mania, it was power. For someone who had spent her life skirting around the edges of insanity, it was hard to fathom.

Excitable.

Emotional.

High-strung.

Hyperactive.

Troubled…

The descriptions from friends and doctors had slowly devolved as she'd gotten older. They'd gone from amusement to awkwardness. And though her mother had always cushioned the blow, Ava had known from the time she was a child that there was something different about her. Something that wasn't good. Something that made her "too much" to deal with. Carl had only confirmed it when she'd reached her teens. His constant stream of classes and camps and internships may have given her a résumé most twenty-somethings would kill for, but Ava knew it had little to do with concern. She was a problem, one he preferred to farm out.

"Evren?" She turned to the old scribe sitting across the table from her.

"Yes, my dear?"

"Would you say that I'm… normal? For an Irina?"

Evren gave her a slow smile. "But what is normal? For any man or woman?"

"You know what I mean."

"I know what you mean." He put down the pencil he'd been taking notes with and folded his hand. "You are who you were meant to be, Ava. I see nothing damaged or wrong with you. How you came to be who you are?" Evren lifted his shoulders in a helpless shrug. "Who can say? In Irin history, there is no incidence of any Irina being born in a human family. But you are here now. You are among your people. You are a wonder to us, not an oddity."

"My whole life, I've never fit in."

"Of course you haven't," he said. "I'm sure in the human world, you would stand out. Here? You are normal. You remind me very much of a girl I grew up with. She was so curious." A dimple touched Evren's cheek. "She was the favorite of our teachers in the village."

Ava was quiet for a long time, staring at the high, glowing windows of the library. When she finally spoke, she spoke softly.

"I thought I was crazy for a long time. My whole life, really. It's hard to leave that behind, even with all of you telling me that I'm not."

"Why?"

"Don't get me wrong." She shook her head. "I know it should be a relief. But there's a part of me that still doesn't believe it. A part that thinks I'm locked in a room somewhere because my delusions have finally taken over. The voices have finally won, and this is all a kind of dream that my mind is using to cope."

Evren opened his mouth, then closed it. Finally, he said, "I think…"

Pain bloomed in her knee when he kicked it under the table. Ava's mouth dropped open in shock.

"Ow! What the heck, Evren?"

He shrugged again. "That wouldn't hurt in a dream, so you're not dreaming."

She was speechless.

"What?" he asked. "You want me to come up with some deep, philosophical answer? You're not crazy. You're part of a race that is descended from the offspring of angels and human women. Is this so hard to believe? Look at your legends and myths. There are bits of truth all over. Pieces of the story that have been told for thousands of years. Wise women. Oracles. Heroes of ancient times. We've always been here. You just thought the stories were nothing more than stories. So your doctors hear you tell them about whispers, and they call you crazy. A thousand years ago, they might have called you a witch or an oracle." Evren curled his lip in disgust and turned back to his books. "Modern humans learn much, but they forget even more."

"Okay," she said. "Got it. Not crazy."

"It's insulting for you to say it."

"Cut me a little slack, will you?"

"You cripple yourself and your own power when you say this, Ava."

"I get it." She tried to turn back to her books, but then she looked up again. "So, these powers…"

"Yes?"

"How… I mean, what do I…" She frowned, unsure of what the right question was.

"What powers do you have?"

"I guess so."

Evren said, "It varies. All Irina have the capacity to speak and perform magic. Other gifts are rarer. A very few have the gift of fore-sight, which is directly from our angelic forefathers. Our magic expresses itself in similar ways. Some Irina spells are exactly like our own. For health and strength. Longevity. Physical or emotional strength for our mates. Others are uniquely Irina. We have no capacity for their magic."

"Like what?"

"Healing of humans. Creative spells. Much to do with the natural world that helps the plants grow or brings health to a baby in the womb. Bearing children—"

"My mom says there's nothing magical about that experience, Evren."

He chuckled. "But of course there is! Though it is not without pain. Irina have a unique talent for anything creative. Wonderful architects and artists. But their greatest magic is *listening*."

"Like the voices."

"It is not only the voices in their minds." Evren pinned her down with his stare. "There are seers, yes, but also those who hear what is unsaid. They listen and they *understand*. As we Irin are able to discern the tiniest marking on parchment, a gifted Irina hears what is said and also what is unsaid. They discern where others do not."

"Well… that makes sense."

Ava wondered if that was one of her gifts. After all, she'd always had a pretty good bullshit detector, because the inner voice, that no one else heard, couldn't lie. Sure, someone could say one thing, but the tone of their silent voice gave their true motive away. It was probably why she'd always had so few friends. It was also why she was still so confused about Malachi.

He had been quietly present ever since the night at the restaurant. She got the distinct feeling he was biding his time. For what? She had no idea. But the tone of his thoughts had taken on a decidedly heated air, even though she couldn't understand what he was saying.

And she could always hear him. Even when others were around, his voice shone through. With a little guidance from Evren, she'd begun to master control over the voices. Even casual contact with the scribes around her helped. Evren made it a point to pat her hand as they worked, and even the shyest scribe in the house, when he met her, greeted her with a warm handshake that enveloped her palm. They were quietly affectionate, all of them treating her like a treasured sister or daughter. Everyone except Rhys and Malachi.

With Rhys, it was a teasing grin, or a tug on her hair. A casual arm thrown around her shoulders as they walked to the village. A flirtatious nudge as they sat next to each other on the couch.

With Malachi, a pass in the hallway meant a shiver-inducing brush along her arm. He continued to taunt her fingers, letting his own linger when he handed her a book or sat next to her at the table. He didn't flirt with her. Didn't even speak to her much when others were around. But Malachi was always there. She could feel his eyes. She could sense his heat. Could feel his irritation every time Rhys came close.

The pressure was building, and Ava had no idea when things might boil over.

THE PHONE FELT HEAVY IN HER HAND. IT RANG AND RANG WITH NO friendly secretary picking up. Finally, she heard the message for Dr. Sadik's office, but hung up. He'd given her his mobile number, so she used it. She had to tell the man something. She'd have missed two appointments by now. She hoped he hadn't worried. She'd already called her mother, and that had been bad enough. Dr. Sadik's mobile rang only twice before he picked it up.

"Hello?"

"Dr. Sadik?"

"Ava! How are you? I've been wondering what happened. I hope you are well. You've missed your appointments for two weeks. Did you go back to the States?"

"No." All of a sudden, the careful excuses she'd rehearsed flew from her mind. "I… I met some friends. We decided to travel for a while. I'm so sorry I forgot to call you."

"I'm only happy to hear you are well. I'll admit that I was worried. Where are you traveling? Are you still in Turkey?"

She took a deep breath and smiled. His calming voice always put her at ease. "I am. Traveling in Cappadocia, as a matter of fact."

"Ah. A very interesting part of the country. How do you find it?"

"Excuse me?"

"Are you enjoying yourself?"

"Yes." She saw Malachi enter the small room where she was using the landline. "Mostly."

"And your friends? Are they Turkish? From that region, perhaps?"

"Kinda."

Malachi stopped and listened for a moment, then his face became a very carefully composed mask.

Dr. Sadik said, "Pardon me?"

"Hey, Doctor, can I call you back? I'm going to return to Istanbul eventually, but I just wanted to let you know where I was and apologize for missing my appointments. If there's a charge, just let me know, okay? I really need to go." There was something wrong with Malachi. He'd gone entirely still, and he was staring at her.

"Ava, is there—"

"Really need to go." She felt her face flush. "I'm fine! I'll talk to you soon."

She hung up. Malachi stood carefully on the opposite side of the room, still staring.

"You called the doctor," he said quietly.

"Yes."

It wasn't a calm quiet.

"From the house phone."

She shrugged. "Um… yeah. What's the big—"

"The one that can be traced?"

Ava frowned. "By my psychologist?"

"We have no idea who he is, Ava."

She rolled her eyes. "Right. But I imagine he's calling the Turkish police to come raid the place right now."

"Don't make light of this."

"Yep! That Dr. Sadik, he's actually a… a spy who's into old—"

"Ava." He took a step toward her. "There is no Dr. J. Sadik operating in Istanbul."

A heavy silence filled the room, and a thread of anger uncurled in her chest.

"Of course there is. You've been to his office with me. You know, if you wanted an excuse to argue with me, how about—"

"He. Doesn't. Exist." Malachi crossed to her. "Do you understand me? He is a ghost. Rhys can find no documentation on him from Turkish medical boards. No trace of his practice. And he left his office in the city the same time we did."

A sick churning hit her stomach. "You were checking up on my psychologist?"

"Do you understand what I'm telling you? We don't even know what his connection is to your psychologist in Israel."

Her mouth dropped open. "You're unbelievable!"

"We're trying to keep you safe, as it's evident we're the only ones who—"

"Shut up!" Ava rose to her feet. "I understand there could be any number of logical explanations why a harmless man who was *helping* me might not be in Rhys's computer searches." The anger took over, begging her to slap at him for the intrusion. The doubt. For making her question everything and everyone she'd allowed herself to trust. "What I *can't* understand is why you felt you had the right to spy on me. What else have you been looking into? Checking out my trash? How about listening in on my phone calls like you did just now?"

"You're missing the point." He stepped closer.

"No, you are!" She pushed a finger in his chest. It hardly budged. "You come into my life. You lie to me. You follow me. You act like you're protecting me, then you… you kiss me!"

"Ava—"

"No! Shut up. I'm talking here, remember? You kiss me, and the next day you act like I don't even exist. You ask me to trust you, but who am I supposed to trust? You're hot and cold. You pawn me off on Rhys, and then you're mad at him when he's the only one who makes me feel slightly normal. And now? You're just *there*. All the time. And don't even get me started on what you've been thinking, because that —" She broke off when she saw a young scribe poke his head through the door. Malachi spun around and barked something in the Old Language that had the man scurrying back.

Ava snapped, "That's right, scare the nice scribe, why don't you? Jerk."

His eyes widened. "You're calling me… a *jerk*?"

"I could call you a lot worse."

"I have a few choice words myself. And everything I've done has been to protect you, so stop bitching at me."

"Bitching at you?"

"Yes, bitching. You kissed me as much as I kissed you. I backed away because I didn't want to overwhelm you, and what do you do?" He stepped closer and glared. "Rhys? After everything? Rhys! Where was he when the Grigori—"

"He's my friend!"

"He wants a hell of a lot more than friendship, *love*." The last word dropped with a sneer. "If you'd pay attention, you'd have figured that out by now."

"So what if he does? It's not like you have any claim on me. You act like you don't want anything to do with me."

"Is that what you think?" His voice fell, and he put his hand on the side of her neck. Immediately, her pulse roared. Her mind went silent. There was only him. His scent and touch. The rest of the world went quiet when his thumb stroked the base of her throat. "You really think I have no claim on you?"

She swallowed with effort; her eyes locked on the stormy grey in his. "None."

"Really, Ava?" He leaned down, his breath whispering across her cheek. "How do you feel when I touch you, *canim*?"

Her mind warred with her body. She ached to have him close the distance. Ached to feel his lips on hers again. But her protective instincts went on high alert.

Too close! Once he had her, he'd tire of her. He'd leave like the others. And if he left…

"You could be anyone," she whispered, the lie bitter on her tongue. "Any… any Irin man would feel like you."

Malachi froze. Then his head drew back and his hand left her neck. When she managed to meet his eyes, they were full of cold anger. His soul, however, whispered hurt. She said nothing, already hating herself for lying to him. No one felt like him. No one sounded like him. But she was tired of feeling jerked around, and her feelings—the depth of them—frightened her.

"I'm going for a run," he said. "We'll talk later about your Dr. Sadik. Don't call him again."

Ava was too bruised to argue. "Fine."

He left, and she was alone again.

"WHAT'S GNAWING AT YOU, LOVE?"

"Hmm?" She looked up. It was dark outside, and she and Rhys were sharing a drink in the garden. They'd eaten at the scribe house, the table a mesh of languages Ava had been able to disappear into. Turkish, English, German, the old Irin language, and a few more she hadn't recognized. Among them all, she'd felt comfortable being silent. Malachi hadn't been there. He'd disappeared in the afternoon and, as far as she knew, hadn't come back.

"Thinking about tall, dark, and brooding again?"

Annoyance flared. "My life doesn't revolve around him, you know?"

"I know it doesn't. Nor should it. So why don't you wipe the frown off your face and enjoy the wine? It's… well, it's not great. But it's not horrible, either." He smiled, a brilliant flash of white in the twilight.

"Don't tell me how to feel. I'll be annoyed if I want to."

"Oh, two hundred years was almost enough to make me forget the churlishness of an angry female." Rhys threw an arm around the back of her shoulder and leaned in. "Nothing quite like it. And all that anger sitting behind so much power? It's a wonder more Irin don't suffer from missing—"

"You talk too much." She pulled him down by the collar and kissed him. Hard. His lips were frozen in shock, and Ava released them almost immediately, pushing him back. "Sorry."

His voice was a rough growl. "Finished punishing him?"

"I said I was sorry."

"Don't be." His arm slipped lower, looping around her waist and pulling her into his chest. Then his mouth met hers in a yearning kiss. Hungry. Biting. Rhys's lips pressed against hers, and his tongue licked out, teasing along her bottom lip until she gasped. He danced along the edge of desire, his hands holding her carefully, his mouth doing wicked things to her own. After a few heated moments, he pulled away, his green eyes practically glowing in the moonlight.

"Well," he said. "That was…"

Her cheeks were flush with embarrassment. "It was definitely…"

"Fine." He sat back and his shoulders slumped a little. "It was fine."

And Ava felt exactly the same. "Totally and utterly… fine."

They both let the silence hang for a moment.

"Why wasn't it more than fine?" Rhys asked.

"It should have been. Good technique."

"Well, that's nice to hear, considering there's been a necessary lapse in practice."

She patted his thigh. "No, you're good."

"Just good?" The corner of his mouth lifted. "Maybe I should try again."

Ava couldn't stop the smile. "Please don't. It would just be weird at this point."

"Totally agree." He squeezed her shoulder.

Silence fell between them again, and Ava felt the depths of her own stupidity. Her kiss had been unfair to Rhys. Unfair to herself. Rhys was her friend. Would this change things? Would he resent her? She was mentally cataloguing her faults when she heard him speak.

"It's all right, love."

She whispered, "I wish it had been more than fine."

"I'm not him," Rhys said. "I think he'll figure it out soon. He's very bright, despite being an idiot. But he holds honor above self-interest, which is both wonderful and maddening."

"I don't know what you're talking about."

"Don't lie. We're past that now. And I'd be lying if I pretended not to know how he feels about you."

"I'm not…" She struggled to put it into words. "I'm not used to expecting happiness, Rhys. I'd probably punch it if it looked me in the face. So really, I'm as much of an idiot as he is."

"His voice sounds different to you, doesn't it?"

She blinked. "How did you know that?"

He seemed to draw away. "I didn't. Just a guess."

"What does that mean?"

A slow smile crept across his face. "I don't think I'm going to tell you. It'll be too fun to watch you find out on your own."

Pounding steps approached in the night. Malachi appeared out of the black, shirtless and dripping despite the cool evening air. His *talesm* seemed to glow when he caught sight of her, a low silver light in the darkness. He said nothing, shooting Rhys a glare as he walked past them and into the house.

"Has he kissed you?" Rhys asked when Malachi was gone.

"Yes. On the island."

"Was it more than fine?"

Her breath left her body in a rush of memories. "So much more than fine."

He nudged her shoulder with his own. "Then don't be stubborn. Go."

Fifteen minutes and another glass of wine later, Ava knocked on his door. Malachi opened it, holding a towel. He'd showered, and a few drops of water still clung to his tanned shoulders. He wore a pair of loose pants and a guarded expression.

"What do you want?"

"I kissed Rhys."

Now she knew she wasn't imagining it. The tattoos pulsed silver in the dim light of the hall. Ava forced her eyes back to Malachi's face, which was locked down tight. Only a tic in his jaw told Ava her words had even been heard.

His voice was low and thick with tension. "Get that out of your system?"

"Felt a little like kissing my brother."

He dropped the towel and tugged her into the room. "This won't."

CHAPTER

THIRTEEN

With one hand, he pulled her into the room, and with the other, Malachi slammed the door shut. He tugged her into his chest and captured her lips with his own. Desire roared through his body, thick with tension after two hundred years of fasting and a lifetime of waiting. For her. For Ava.

Reshon.

Malachi knew as he held her. He could feel the power pulsing through his *talesm*, the bare skin over his heart aching to be marked by Ava's magic. He could feel it singing over her skin, her touch igniting the fierce passion he'd buried for so long.

Backing Ava against the door, he curled his body over hers, bracing his arms on either side of her head, forcing her to look into his eyes.

"Do you want this? Say so now." He dangled on the edge of forever. All he needed was a word.

He saw the edges of doubt cloud her eyes, but behind it was a desperate hunger that mirrored his own. He pressed closer.

"Do you want me, Ava?"

Malachi saw her mouth form the word before he heard it. "Yes."

His control snapped.

Reaching down, he gripped her hips, lifting her against his chest as Ava wrapped her legs around his waist. A fierce possessiveness overtook him as Malachi pressed her against the wall and ravaged her mouth.

He held her with one arm while the other tugged at the back of her hair, baring her neck to his kisses. He inhaled the heat of her skin as he trailed his tongue up the line of her throat, pausing to press a gentle kiss at her neck where he could feel her voice hum.

"More," she whispered.

"Yes."

"I need… Malachi—"

"I know." Groaning with desire, he swung her around and walked across the room. "Bed."

It was small, barely fitting his own tall frame, but it would have to do. He'd find more fitting accommodations later, but for now Ava was tearing at her clothes as he carried her, as desperate for contact as he was. He could feel the heat of her arms branding him. Feel the draw of energy as if touching a live wire. He lay her down and slid next to her, suddenly aware of the manic energy that hummed underneath her skin. It took everything in him to cage his own desire and think of her.

"Ava." He took a deep breath and pressed a hand over her heart, halting the fingers that were fumbling with the buttons. "Ava, wait."

She stopped, eyes narrowing. "You better not be backing out of this. If you've got some noble idea about being cautious or taking things slow—"

"Be quiet and let me undress you, woman." His low growl shocked Ava out of her anger. "I've been thinking about this for over two hundred years."

Brushing her hands away, he slipped open the first button, and Ava watched with wide eyes as he bent down and kissed the newly bare skin. A single finger trailed from her neck down, leaving a faint gold trail in its wake. Malachi traced a calming spell over her skin and felt her pulse stop racing. The urgency was still there, but as the magic took hold, the frantic energy was drawn into his own body, feeding his passion as he slowly stoked hers.

"Beautiful," he whispered, slipping another button open. His lips tasted again as he trailed another charm between her breasts. His tongue followed the gold letters that bloomed there, and Ava's back arched in silent pleasure.

"Malachi…"

"Tell me what you're feeling," he whispered. "I want to hear."

"Hot."

"Yes?" He flicked open another button, spreading her shirt and flicking open the lace that bound her breasts.

"Aches… Keep touching me. Don't stop."

"Never." Her skin bared to his eyes, Malachi stopped for a moment to stare. With a groan, he closed his mouth over one sensitive peak as Ava clutched the hair on the back of his head. He closed his eyes and lost himself in the taste of her. The salty bite of her skin and the lingering scent she wore intoxicated him. He would never get enough.

"Too much!" she finally gasped. "It's too much."

"Shhh." He soothed her, laying his forehead in the smooth valley between her breasts. He forced his mouth away from her skin as his fingers made quick work of the rest of her shirt. Slipping it off, he took a moment to gaze at the beauty spread before him.

Ava's skin still glowed with the traces of magic he'd written over her heart. A small bruise was forming on the rise of her left breast where his mouth had taken her skin. Malachi forced back the urge to mark her. There would be time. For her, he had eternity.

Shaking his head in wonder, he said, "For you? It is never too much."

"Faster," she urged.

"No." He bent his head again, fighting back his own desire to take and claim and spend himself in the cradle of her body. He loosened the button of her jeans before he slid them down over her legs. Each newly revealed limb received the attention of his lips. His fingers. Magic flowed between them. He could feel her energy and smiled, knowing one day she would mark him too.

"When you find your power," he murmured in her ear as he stretched out beside her on the narrow bed, "you will sing to me. And I will feel your magic as you feel mine."

"Is that what I'm feeling?" she said with a smile, throwing one leg over his thigh and pulling him closer. "That's a lot of magic."

He grinned, pleased by the laughter in her eyes.

"Ava," he whispered again. "*Reshon.*"

Her voice dropped to a whisper. "I can hear you. Inside. All I hear is you."

He stilled his hands. "And what do I sound like?"

"Perfect," she choked out. "You sound… perfect."

He saw the tears forming, so he came to her, knowing there was no pleasure she could ask for that he would not give. He ran a hand from the nape of her neck, down her spine, picturing the spells he would mark her with. Spells to strengthen her. Claim her. Mark her as his mate as she would mark him as hers.

"What do you want?" he asked.

"You."

Now it was his breath that was coming faster as she reached down and took him in her hand. His head fell back and Malachi felt Ava press kisses along the line of his jaw as she worked his pants down over his hips. Then her lips trailed over the markings on his collarbone. His shoulder. Her delicate teeth closed over his nipple for a moment before she continued across his chest. He was on the edge of losing control.

"Ava, stop." His head swam with the rush of sensation.

"Really?"

"Uh… no, not really."

He was light-headed with desire. Intoxicated by her touch. She might not have been able to use Irina magic, but Ava had a power all her own. Her energy was mounting again, feeding him, stoking the fire that built between them. They were face-to-face, staring into each other's eyes while Malachi's fingers moved over her skin.

"So warm." He buried his face in her neck and she wrapped her arms around his shoulders, holding him there. "I need you."

"Then take me," she whispered. "And don't let go."

He lifted her thigh and drew her forward, sliding into her body with aching slowness as he drank in the sensations. Heat. Pleasure. His instincts roused, and he groaned into her mouth as they rocked together. Skin against skin. Lips melded together. Push. Pull. He felt the blood rushing in his veins. Felt their breath mingle as their pleasure built. And when he felt Ava begin to fall over the edge, he followed.

He would follow her anywhere.

"What does 'jah-num' mean?"

"Hmm?" He was drowsy after the third time he'd taken her. Sex energized Irin men, but eventually, even the strongest man tired. Ava was like a loose rag draped across his chest. She had tried to move away when she started to fall asleep, but he wouldn't allow it, pulling her closer, still needing the contact.

"You say it sometimes. When we're together. 'Jah—'"

"Oh, *canim*. It means… my darling." He pressed a kiss to her forehead. "My life." More kisses along her cheek, ignoring the slight tension his words evoked. He didn't hold back. "It means 'my soul.'" The shell of her ear. Loose lazy brushes of his lips that soothed her and fed his need. He had forgotten what it meant to be held.

"*Canim.*" She tried the word out, whispering as her fingers traced over the *talesm* on his chest. She circled down to the blank area on the skin over his heart. "There's nothing here."

"I've never taken a mate."

"Never?" A slow smile curved her lips. "You don't make love like a virgin, Malachi."

He could feel the quiet laugh from her, and he reached down, pinching her thigh before his hand spread to soothe the sting.

"There was an Irina… before the Rending, there was someone. We were planning on a union. Our families liked each other. We liked each other very much. We were very compatible. And yes, we had been together. But she broke it off."

"What?" She picked her head up and frowned. "Don't tell me you weren't good enough for her. That's ridiculous."

He shook his head, smiling at her annoyance that another had found him lacking. It made him want to crow with pride. "No. She found her *reshon*. Her true mate."

"*Reshon?*"

He nodded slowly, sliding his hands down to lie along her waist. Ava was extraordinary. He could already feel her energy mounting— even away from humans in the isolation of the scribe house, she shone.

"It doesn't always happen, but it's something we all hope for. She found her *reshon*, so I let her go. It would have been foolish to continue courting her when her heart had already left."

"That cheating—"

He covered her mouth with his own. When he drew back, her eyes were blinking with languor again, and the irritation had fled. "It wasn't like that. It hurt her to break off our relationship, because she did care for me. But I did not fight it, even though it pained me, too. A *reshon* is a blessing. Your destiny in another person. The perfect complement to yourself. Not everyone finds a *reshon*, but those who do are considered doubly blessed. And very, very powerful."

"Why?" Her gaze fell to his chest again, and Malachi wondered what she would ask him to create there. The mating mark was dictated by the Irina, a visible expression of her mate's dedication and love. She traced the smooth bare skin and said, "Why more powerful?"

"Imagine…" He drew her up so they were face-to-face on the narrow bed. "Imagine a person created for you. Another being so in tune with you that their voice is the clearest you've ever heard in your mind." He saw her eyes widen, so he looked away and trailed a finger over her shoulder. "Her touch sharpens your senses. Her lips…" He pressed a light kiss to her open mouth. "…feed your soul. A bond like that strengthens both. One magic feeds the other. Within it, Irin and Irina become who we are meant to be."

Malachi could feel Ava's hands tighten on his shoulders. Knew she was quietly absorbing the words he'd said. He didn't want to push her. He knew she was his *reshon*. Looking back, it had been evident from their first kiss. But he was heeding his watcher's advice in another way. He could give her time. He would let Ava come to the knowledge herself. Patience. He would seduce her body and mind until her soul compelled her to accept him. It would be his most pleasurable hunt ever.

"What are you smiling about?" Ava teased him, snuggling into his chest. "You look like the cat who ate the cream."

His laugh was low and satisfied. "I'm quite sure that I did. More than once."

Malachi laughed again when she elbowed his side, then he pulled her close and said, "Sleep, Ava. Rest with me."

"I don't think I've ever felt this exhausted."

"Sleep," he whispered. "I will see you in your dreams."

When he dreamed, it was of her. A shadow he chased through a dark wood. She eluded him for a time, but eventually a faint outline walked to him out of a fog. He could not see her face, but when her lips touched his, he knew her. And she was his.

He blinked awake. Ava was still sleeping next to him, boneless in her exhaustion. Malachi slipped out of the narrow bed, wishing he had someplace more private to take her. The newly awakened magic did not want to share its mate. And though his room in the scribe house was one of the most isolated, it still lacked the privacy he craved.

He threw on some clothes and left the room, needing some water. Ava, too, would be hungry when she woke. Her metabolism, which was typically fast, would probably wake her with hunger before long. Though expending energy during sex was one of the most effective ways to calm her, it was also draining. They couldn't stay in his room forever.

Not that the idea wasn't appealing.

He ran into Rhys halfway to the kitchens. The other man backed away for a moment, then seeing Malachi's expression, relaxed.

"I was wondering whether you were going to hit me or not," he said. "But you've obviously found another way of marking your territory."

Malachi grunted and crossed his arms. "If she'd been more complimentary about you, I'd be more offended."

"I'm letting that pass since you're in a postcoital haze."

"Ava is my *reshon*."

Rhys was speechless for a few moments, instinctive rebellion evident in his eyes. But finally he said, "Of course she is. I probably knew that before you did, you idiot. Does she know what it means?"

"Not completely. She's smart. She'll figure it out."

Rhys fell silent again. "She's not had an easy time of things, brother. Her relationships, from what I can tell, have been… difficult. She may fight it."

Malachi's lips curled. "She won't win."

"If you expect me to bet against fate, you're wrong." A shadow of sorrow passed over Rhys's face. Then the expression cleared and his acerbic wit resurfaced. "Heaven, you're going to be more insufferable than Damien when Sari agrees to see him. I swear, you even look taller."

"I *feel* taller."

For the first time, Malachi understood why mated Irin were on the front lines in all battles and held the highest positions. Union with his mate had given him the kind of energy even magic couldn't accomplish. He felt stronger. Sharper. The afterglow of Ava's touch made him feel as if he could take on a hundred Grigori and win without a scratch.

"Mated Irin," Rhys muttered. "You're an insufferable lot." He started back in the direction of the library. "I'll see you later. Next month, maybe."

"I want to take her away from here. The research, all the questions… It's been tiring."

"Don't make excuses," Rhys called back. "You're being selfish with the pretty girl." A hint of wicked humor came back. "Besides, these beds… I can only imagine the frustration."

"Don't imagine." He glared. "Even though you're right."

His friend laughed. "Take her to Kuşadası. No one is using the house there. It's not fancy, but it's private. You can blend in with the tourists. She might like the beach."

Malachi frowned, thinking of the crowded tourist port where the Irin kept a small safe house. "It's too busy."

"Not as busy as Istanbul. And she'll be with you. The voices will be more controllable for her now, but other senses will waken. It might be a good idea to ease her into things before you go back to Istanbul. Otherwise, it'll affect both of you now."

"Maybe." He finally conceded, "Yes, that is a good idea."

"I have lots of them. Now go find some food for the woman. She's going to be starving."

With that, the scribe turned and left. Malachi watched him go, a spear of sorrow piercing through his own joy. He wanted his friend to find the same happiness. Wanted it for his people. They had lived in isolation for too long.

Gathering up some water, bread, and apricots, Malachi returned to his room to find Ava sitting up in bed, a thin blanket wrapped around her. Her eyes were still sleepy, but they brightened when she saw him walk in.

"Hey."

"Hello." He smiled. "How do you feel?"

"Amazingly rested. Oooh." Her eyes settled on the bottle of water. "For me?"

"Yes." He opened it and handed it to her, then set the basket of fruit on the small table beside his bed. He sat on the edge while she emptied half the bottle in one gulp. "Make sure you eat, too. Your body will be recharging for some time."

"Mmmm." She smiled. "I'm not going to complain about your workouts."

"I'm glad." He leaned over and kissed her lips, taking lazy pleasure in drawing a satisfied sigh from his mate.

"Oh, you're so good at—" There was a rustle in the hallway outside the room, and Ava's eyes widened in shock. "There's someone close."

He frowned. "There are more bedrooms past mine, but I'm sure—"

"I didn't hear them." He heard her pulse pick up, and she clutched the blanket around her. "I didn't hear their voices, Malachi. What's wrong with me?"

Suddenly understanding, he said, "Nothing." He took care to smooth a tendril of hair away from her face and kissed away the frown between her eyebrows. "There's nothing wrong with you. You're not hearing them because we made love."

"So… sex with you…"

"When we're together, I draw away much of your energy. It's the reason Irin can't be with human women. The energy we draw during sex is too much. But you…"

"I have more than average."

"Far more. For you, your energy becomes balanced. It makes *both* of us stronger. But since our relationship is new, I expect you may not hear voices for some hours, even days. I know older couples have more control over it, but until we become more accustomed to…" Suddenly wary, he asked, "Are you all right? I didn't think to warn you about this."

As much as the voices had tormented Ava, they were still one of her senses. He couldn't imagine what it would feel like if part of his hearing suddenly dropped out. Would he feel vulnerable? Broken? He shouldn't have worried. A glorious smile spread over her face and Ava fell back into the pillows on the bed.

"Best. Afterglow. Ever."

Chuckling, Malachi stripped off his shirt and lay beside her, still craving contact with her skin. He absently wrote on her back as she curled into his body again.

"What are you writing on me?"

"Property of Malachi."

"Haha. Seriously, what is it?"

Well, it wasn't as if he'd lied. "Mostly charms to help you sleep. For good dreams."

"I had the wildest dreams last night. So vivid."

"Really?" His lips curled in satisfaction. She was already dream-walking with him. Soon, she'd know what it meant.

"Mmhmm. I don't really remember what they were, but they were good."

"I'm glad." He paused. "What would you say about going to the sea, *canım*? There is a house near the shore that we use for a retreat. It's safe."

"No Grigori?"

"No Grigori."

"No endless questions?"

"Only you and I would be there."

"Does it have bigger beds?" She wiggled against him, trying to stay on the mattress.

"Most definitely."

CHAPTER

FOURTEEN

Kuşadası was a busy port town home to cruise ships, tourists, and more cruise ships. Ava smiled as she and Malachi held hands, walking down the pedestrian walkway leading to the smaller marina where sailboats moored and nightclubs flourished. It could have been any number of port cities along the Mediterranean. Turkey. Greece. Spain. There was an odd kind of familiarity that was soothing, despite the crowds.

She squeezed his hand and smiled at the family with the sleepy toddler who was nodding off in his stroller. An older couple passed by, holding hands, the woman smiling at Ava after she'd glanced up at Malachi's striking figure. The sun had set and the humid heat of the day had given way to a soothing breeze that wrapped around her, twisting her skirt around her ankles and lifting pieces of her hair. Malachi leaned down and captured one curl that brushed in her face, stopping to tuck it behind her ear and steal a kiss.

"Are you having fun?" he asked quietly. "Do you want to go back to the house for dinner? There's food there. And you spent all day on the beach."

"No," she demurred. "I'm fine. The beach was nice."

"Honestly?"

"Honestly."

For the first time in her life, it was true. Malachi had been right, the days and nights of intimacy notwithstanding, a few days after their first frenzied coupling in the scribe house, she had started to hear the familiar voices again, whispering over her mind and filling her thoughts. Unlike before, she had someone to hold on to. Someone who understood.

Imagine a person created for you. Another being so in tune with you that their voice was the clearest you've ever heard in your mind.

Reshon, he'd called her. He thought she didn't remember, but in the heat of passion, the word had escaped his lips. The thought was frightening and thrilling all at once. Malachi thought she was his *reshon*. Every shield she'd built over a lifetime of solitude rebelled at the thought. She didn't want to be anyone's perfect match. She had no idea what he wanted from her, and a small voice whispered it was simply too good to be true. Eventually, he would grow tired and leave her. Everyone did.

A quick squeeze of his hand made her look up. He was watching her with suspicious eyes.

"What?" There was no way he knew what she was thinking. It wasn't as if he could read her thoughts.

"You're worried about something," he said. "What is it?"

"Nothing." She started walking again, but he wouldn't let her hand go.

"Me?" His silent thoughts were a swirl of confusion and concern. She hated hearing that from him. As big and tough as Malachi appeared, she knew there was a gentle part of him, and Ava suspected she was the only one allowed to see it. The thought of damaging that trust chilled her.

"I'm fine. I just—Whoa!" He picked her up and lifted her in his arms, smiling as the passing tourists laughed. Then he hopped over the rock wall and over to some deserted beach chairs near the lapping waves. He sat in one and positioned her so that her legs straddled his.

Reaching up to frame her face with both hands, he asked again, "What is it?"

"You're being pushy."

"This is new to me," he said urgently. "I worry I no longer know how to care for a woman. It has been too long. I cannot care for you if you don't tell me what is wrong, Ava."

"Malachi…"

"You must be patient with me. And tell me what you're thinking.

You know my thoughts, but I do not know yours." A small smile lifted the corner of his mouth. "You have me at a disadvantage."

She couldn't look away. His grey eyes bored into hers. His skin was illuminated by the full moon that rose over the black Aegean Sea and his dark hair lifted in the breeze.

"It's too good," she finally whispered.

An understanding look passed over his face, but he said, "What is too good?"

"I… This. Us. It's too easy."

"It should be difficult?"

"It always has been."

He took a deep breath, then let it out slowly. "Other men are not me."

"Because you're Irin."

"Because I am me." He kissed her chin. "And you are you." Another kiss at her temple as his hands began soothing strokes up and down her back. She could feel his fingers playing along the delicate skin over her spine. "There are others like us in the world, but they are not us. We decide who we want to be."

"And you really want to be with me?" A thread of doubt worked its way into her voice, even though she willed it away.

A slow smile crossed his face. "Do you think me a martyr? That I do things I don't want to do?"

"No. I can tell that already." She had already seen his stubborn personality—it was apparent. It was hard to argue against it when iron control was so much of who he had to be. She could feel it under her fingers as she began to stroke his arms. Unbelievably powerful, Malachi had to show the strictest control among human beings. She saw it walking with him through the bazaar. At the shops. Among the more gentle scribes in Cappadocia.

She'd recognized it even when they first met so many weeks before in Istanbul. He was one of the most controlled men she'd ever met, his power on a very short leash. The fact that he loosed it when he held her, let his power wash over her in a gentle wave when they made love, caused her heart to soften dangerously toward him. It would be easy to put her heart in his hands. Easy to let him take care of her. But what would he take in return? Ava didn't know if she was hanging on to enough of herself to share.

"Are you worried about the Grigori?"

Sensing an escape, she answered, "Yes. This seems like a place they'd hang out."

He smiled. "Normally, yes. They love the tourist women. But I think so many of them were drawn to Istanbul when you were there, they may have left their usual hunting grounds. I haven't seen a single one since we've been here."

"And what would you do if you saw one here?"

"Kill it."

The flat certainty in his voice chilled her. "But how… They're like you. Not exactly, but didn't you say—"

"The Grigori may have had similar origins, but they chose their path long ago. They are predators. We are protectors. Once, the Irin helped humanity. We shared our knowledge and secrets until it became too dangerous. When we were no longer wanted, we withdrew. The Grigori continued to feed. Now our job is to stop them from killing. It is the only way we can still serve the humans we were meant to guide and protect."

Ava's back stiffened. "You act like humans are inferior."

"Not inferior. Different."

"I'm human."

He stifled a laugh. "No. You're not."

She stood up and glared at him. "My mother is Lena Matheson. A human woman. My father is Jasper Reed. A man. I am human. However this happened to me, I'm still human."

Irritation colored his voice. "Ava—"

"Do you think I'm inferior?"

"Of course I don't!"

"Then why—?"

"Why are you trying to start a fight?"

It brought her up short. What was she doing? She knew Malachi didn't see her as an inferior. If anything, she felt like he put her on some frightening pedestal. He stood and brushed off his slacks, slowly straightening his clothes before he met her eyes. He was angry.

"Do you think I'm going to get tired of you? Walk away?"

He turned with a glare and started toward the pathway while Ava stood frozen in the sand, the ocean breeze unable to warm the chill that reached toward her heart as she watched him retreat. Just before he reached the stairs, he turned and held out a hand.

"You can piss me off and twist me around, Ava, but you're not going to get rid of me."

She started toward him, and when she got close enough, his hand curled around hers. She swallowed the lump in her throat as he carefully ushered her up the steps.

"I want to go back to the house," she said as they reached the path along the main road. "I know you're mad at me—"

"Good."

They were silent on the long walk back, the cars and scooters honking as they darted across the main road. Ava had the distinct feeling that Malachi could have stopped them with a single glare if any got too close. They walked up the hill and toward the small, nondescript house they'd been sharing the past four days. It was nothing fancy, but at the end of a dead-end road, it was private and the beds were more comfortable than the ones in Cappadocia.

They didn't make it to the bed.

As soon as Malachi shut the door, he spun her around, desire and anger lighting up his eyes. Before a word could leave her, he had captured her lips, pulling her to his chest as she grasped the nape of his neck, digging in her nails when she heard him groan.

"Not. Leaving. You," he muttered between biting kisses, backing her toward a gathering of low couches and pillows in one corner.

"Okay." She could barely keep up, overwhelmed by his fierce possession. She held on to his neck, her teeth nipping at the softer skin there as she tore at the buttons on his shirt until he lifted it and pulled it off with an irritated scowl, as if the fabric itself was offensive. He carefully took off the twin daggers strapped to his torso, then he glared at her own clothes and knelt to strip them off.

"Do you understand me?" He pulled off her skirt, her blouse, finally slowing when he reached the fevered flesh beneath. Malachi bent down to the low couch, kneeling before her and pressing his face to the soft skin of her abdomen, his arms wrapping around her hips. Her whole body shuddered in awareness of the power at her feet. "I will not abandon you. I will not leave you. Ever."

She wanted to believe him. Wanted to be worthy of the devotion he offered. She reached a tentative hand out and brushed at the hair falling over his forehead, her pale fingers threading through the thick locks that teased her skin. His breath was hot against her belly when she tilted his chin up to meet her eyes. She traced the tip of one finger around the sculpted beauty of his mouth before she pressed it between his lips, and his tongue darted out to taste her.

"Show me."

HOURS LATER, AVA DECIDED THE FIGHT HAD BEEN WORTH IT. LYING against Malachi's chest in the lone extravagance of the house, the marble-clad bathroom, she looked over his shoulder.

"I think I like fighting with you."

He pinched her ass under the water.

"Hey!"

"I do *not* like fighting with you. Don't start fights."

"Some fights are going to happen."

He closed his eyes and shrugged, the water lapping against his chest. "Don't start unnecessary fights."

After a few silent minutes, she said, "I know you don't see humans as inferior."

"So what were you really worried about? The Grigori?"

She knew she should be. The shadowed hunters were still stalking her, as far as anyone would tell her. Damien, Leo, and Maxim were still tracking them in Istanbul. Rhys said Dr. Sadik was still suspicious and out of contact. They would have to return to the city at some point, and she really had no idea what she'd be walking into.

"Hmm?" He touched her face, tilting it toward him.

"I'm worried... about lots of things."

"The Grigori?"

"Yes."

"Dr. Sadik?"

"Yes."

He paused for a moment. "Me?"

"I can't help it," she said, her shoulders stiff. "Nothing is this... There's a reason I've been alone my whole life, Malachi."

He lifted his hands to her shoulders and Ava knew he was letting his magic soothe her. She'd only suspected it before, but there was a tingling kind of hum that she felt when he used magic.

"Don't use—"

"Shhh." His head dipped down and his lips teased behind her ear. "Just to relax your muscles. I won't touch your emotions, canım. Just let me help you."

Giving in, she leaned back and felt his arousal pressed against her, but he continued massaging her shoulders and arms. Her neck. The base of her skull.

"You're really good at that." He grabbed a silk washcloth from the side of the bath and rubbed some soap on it. The smell of orange blossom and fig filled the steaming room. "The bathroom here is amazing."

Though the house may have been modest, the bath was not. Clad floor to ceiling in grey marble, it was a picture of indulgence. A deep soaking tub filled one corner, and a rain-shower was in the other. There were steam vents and heated floors. Fragrant soaps and oils to condition the skin. Ava decided she might not ever leave as long as Malachi would keep her company.

"We Turks like our baths," he said as he brought the soap to her skin, the bubbles coating her shoulders before he began massaging her again.

"I can tell."

"And for Irin, too, touch is very important. Especially between… lovers."

Reshon. The word whispered in his mind.

Ava cleared her throat and said, "That makes sense."

"We're a very affectionate people," he said, lifting one arm and repeating the massage. Soap. Slick skin. Deep, soothing strokes. He brought her arm up to lie over his shoulder, and she twisted her fingers in his hair as he covered her with the rich scent. "When we are young, we are coddled. Children are so rare, they are fussed over. I was cuddled and played with constantly as a child. I could barely get any time alone." His voice held no resentment, only a hint of laughter.

"I spent most of my time alone," she whispered, her eyes half-closed. "I liked it that way."

"Did you like it?" he asked, washing and massaging her other arm. "Or were you simply accustomed to it? Was it easier without the voices?"

Both her arms stretched around his neck, baring her body to him as Malachi moved on from her arms to brush the silken cloth over the rise of her breasts.

Her voice hitched. "It was easier. I didn't have to concentrate on blocking the voices when I was alone. It was peaceful."

"Are you peaceful now?" he whispered, the cloth ducking lower, stroking over her breasts, circling her navel, until her body was trembling.

"Malachi—"

"Relax," he murmured, leaving the cloth and using his hands to stroke over her flesh. Slowly, deliberately teasing her. His tattooed arm slid under the water and toward the lush heat of her. His fingers dipped to the juncture of her thighs, feathering touch along the crease before he dipped into her slick heat. Her body soft with pleasure, she arched back and felt his lips tracing down her neck.

"I love touching you, Ava." His breath whispered across her neck. "You were meant to be touched and kissed. To feel pleasure."

She felt it rising. His fingers moved deliberately, his other hand on her breast as he played Ava's body, and her sighs echoed off the marble walls.

"You…" She gasped, looking down to see his black-scribed arms cradling her, one hand teasing her breasts as the other disappeared into the water, driving her slowly mad. "Come in me. I want you…"

"I love watching you." He turned her head, swallowing her cries of pleasure in a kiss as she came against his hand. Her skin was alive. She felt him behind her, the hair on his chest brushing against her back, his legs cradling her. Every sense was alive. Every instinct pulled her toward him.

Reshon.

The voice hadn't come from Malachi. The word whispered through her own mind as he kissed her over and over, his arms banded around her, dark ink against pale skin. She could see the faint silver glow as his *talesm* reacted to her.

Reshon.

He slowly worked her down, her pulse calming under his hands. There were tears in her eyes when they slipped closed.

"Sleep, Ava," he whispered as she laid her cheek against his shoulder. "I will hold you."

THE NEXT WEEK PASSED IN RELATIVE PEACE. MALACHI CONTINUED WITH his dogged patience, diffusing the fights Ava seemed unable to stop instigating, even when she tried. Try as she might, she couldn't seem to combat his steady affection. She snapped; he joked. She sneered; he smiled. It was maddening.

It was wonderful.

And with each small conflict, each new resolution, Ava felt a growing current of devotion and loyalty. Their chemistry was undeniable, but every time she turned from him and Malachi pulled her back with a simple hug or teasing kiss, a little bit of her walls crumbled, rolling toward a growing foundation of something she could barely acknowledge.

Love.

She was falling in love with him.

They were sitting across from each other, sipping two beers at a café as Malachi watched one of the cruise ships with amusement.

"There are so many of them." He played with her fingers as he stared at the massive cruise ship that had just docked, travelers pouring off like ants. "How do they even see the country with so many—"

"I'm falling in love with you."

He stopped speaking immediately, a smile teasing the corners of his mouth. "Hmm."

Ava narrowed her eyes. "Hmm? I say I think I'm falling in love with you and all you say is 'Hmm'?"

Grabbing her hand and holding on when she tried to pull it away, he said, "What did you want me to say?"

Her mouth dropped open. "I… Maybe that you… You know what? Never mind. I changed my mind."

"So you're not in love with me?"

"I never said I was!"

"Exactly." He winked and pulled her hand to his lips, kissing each finger deliberately. "If you had…"

"If I had?" She knew she was holding her breath, but she didn't know why.

Malachi leaned closer. "How do you think I feel about you?"

How did he feel about her? She didn't even need to ask, really. She knew without asking that he loved her. It was in every kiss. Every embrace. Every teasing comment. Every patient smile. His dogged affection had worn her down. In that moment, her heart tumbled, and she could feel the flush on her skin.

"I think…" Her eyes were drawn to a man who had just walked around the corner. "Grigori."

He frowned. "You think Grigori?"

She clutched his hand. "Grigori. There's a Grigori coming up the sidewalk. He's—"

"Another one just came in the back. He's by the bar."

Grabbing his wallet and throwing a fifty-lira note on the table, Malachi rose. "Walk calmly."

"He's already looking at me." Her heart raced. "Malachi, he's already—"

"This one spotted us, too. They're not here hunting. They're here for us."

They walked toward the sidewalk, nodding at the host who looked at them in confusion. Malachi muttered something in Turkish as they passed and the man nodded. He kept his hand on the small of Ava's back, walking quickly in the other direction. Ava chanced a look over her shoulder. Both Grigori were following them. Another melted into the foot traffic as they passed another café.

"There's three. Three of them are behind us."

"I'm leading them away from the humans."

"Should I—?"

"Stay with me. Keep yourself behind me when we get there."

"Get where?"

They were speed-walking up the hill until Malachi ducked into a side street. Houses rose on either side, the street dead-ending into a hill covered by pink oleander and trash. Ava tripped over a scattering of cans that littered the ground as Malachi leaned down for a quick kiss, his eyes gleaming.

"I love you. Of course I love you. Now stay behind me while I take care of these nuisances."

He turned his back to her and drew two silver daggers from the sheaths against his skin just as six Grigori soldiers turned the corner.

CHAPTER

FIFTEEN

Six? Where had the other three come from?

No matter, Malachi grinned in anticipation. Playing lovers' games for the past week had been more than satisfying, but the hunter in him craved this fight. He paced across the alleyway, letting the Grigori come closer. Let them grow more confident. It would make them more fun to kill. The one in front could have been his brother, so alike were they in height and physique. But the soldier didn't have what Malachi had—years of experience and the strength of his *reshon* flowing through his body.

Malachi faked to the right, more pleased than irritated when the Grigori wasn't fooled. Their eyes met for a brief moment before the soldier's eyes flicked to Ava standing behind him. He heard Ava let out a small sound of panic.

Enough. He'd forgotten she would be frightened.

Crossing his arms and brushing both hands along his tattoos, Malachi felt the preternatural strength flood his body. His eyes grew stronger in the early evening gloom. His hearing more acute. He could track the soldiers' movements almost as if the men were moving in slow motion. And he could hear the two soldiers the Grigori had stationed at the mouth of the alley to warn away any passersby. Ava's pulse hammered behind him. The rush of blood filled his ears.

By the time Malachi pulled his knife, he'd already darted to the left, pulling one soldier by his arm, spinning him around and plunging the silver knife into the base of his skull. He shoved the body away as it began to disintegrate, only to grab another, his movements so fast he saw Grigori eyes blur.

Spinning around, he caught one with a swift kick to the jaw, sending him to the ground as he knifed the second Grigori in the neck. He could feel the gold, sand-like dust coat his hands before the wind lifted it, shielding him from the view of the fallen soldier's compatriots. Through it all, his senses were tuned to Ava, who continued to stay directly behind him, not cowering in a corner, but shadowing him, keeping Malachi between her and the monsters.

Clever girl.

The Grigori in front came toward him, ignoring the scrambling of the other soldiers. The man's eyes flicked to Ava again, and he moved as if to approach her, drawing Malachi's attention from the soldier he'd been about to knife. He sliced at the man's neck and threw him to the ground, only to have the Grigori's foot whip toward him unexpectedly.

The kick surprised Malachi, causing him to lose the knife he'd used on three of the men. It clattered to the ground, but Malachi did not pick it up, instead shoving it behind him with his boot, toward Ava, while he grabbed for his second dagger with his left hand. In the seconds he was distracted, the Grigori had come within a few feet, attacking with far more skill than the other soldiers.

But just before he reached Malachi, he darted to the left and toward Ava. From over his shoulder, he saw a flash of silver. Then the powerful Grigori stopped in his tracks as the knife plunged into his eye.

Malachi seized the opportunity, grabbing the man as he screamed in pain, spinning him around, then smashing his dagger into the base of his skull. He grabbed the other knife as the man's corpse disintegrated in a river of gold sand before it was gathered by the wind and lifted toward the heavens. The three remaining soldiers stood stunned as their captain drifted away, then one ran while the other made a last attempt at his mission.

It wasn't successful.

Malachi kicked him to the ground with a boot to his knee, then crouched on top of the soldier. Turning the Grigori facedown, he slammed the dagger home.

In the back of his mind, he heard the cries of the children left in his village, hidden by the Irina who had been slaughtered. He blinked at the memory of a little girl, her arm riddled with bites from her own teeth as she forced herself to remain quiet in the hiding space under the floorboards. Her hollow eyes and blood-stained lips haunted him as he moved to the last soldier on the ground, blood still pouring from the gash in his neck where Malachi had slashed him.

The Grigori stared up at the stars, dead eyes unseeing, bubbles of air bursting at his throat. His lips formed the words over and over.

"Please. Please. Please."

With a swift jerk, Malachi flipped the soldier over and ended his life.

Bowing over the corpse as it dissolved, he let his head hang as he opened his senses. The last soldier had fled with the other two who'd been standing guard. He could hear them fleeing toward the main road. Then car doors slammed shut and an engine roared to life before speeding away. Whoever had sent the soldiers would know where they were and that the attempt had not been successful.

He finally turned to Ava, who was standing stunned and wide-eyed, staring at the ground.

Roused from the fight, he blinked and tried to read her expression. "Ava?"

"I…" She swallowed. "I killed it. Him. Well, I stabbed him and you killed him. And then… he melted."

"It's a kind of dust." Malachi wiped phantom sand from his hands. "Irin and Grigori both—"

"I killed him," she choked out. "He was coming toward me and I just…" Tears started to roll down her face. She clutched her arms around her body. "And you killed, like… lots of them."

"There were four." And he could have killed more. He'd wanted to. He still felt high from the thrill of the battle, but his mate's reaction was starting to scare him. It was easy to forget in the heat of battle that Ava was a stranger to violence.

The shivers started in her shoulders but spread down her back.

"Ava." He held out a hand and she just looked at it as if he was a stranger. The pain was swift and sure. "Ava, please."

With a sob, she came to him, and Malachi wrapped his arms around her shoulders while the fist around his heart loosened. "I'm sorry. I'd forgotten. You're not accustomed to violence."

"Were they trying to kill me?"

"No," he soothed her. "Just kill me. I think they were probably trying to capture you."

She cried harder. Perhaps that wasn't the right thing to say.

"K…kill you?"

"Shhh." He stroked her hair, glad that Grigori didn't leave messy corpses. "I only have a few bruises. They'll be gone in minutes." Then he tilted her head up with a smile. "And my fierce love has her own defenses after all. Where did you learn to throw knives?"

"C…circus camp." She hiccupped. "Summer I was fourteen."

The smile grew wider. "Circus camp?"

"I can walk a decent tightrope, too, but knives were my favorite. I liked throwing, so I kept practicing. Mom bought me a set and Carl's gardener made me a big target." Her eyes were wide and glassy. Her lip was still trembling. But Ava smiled through the tears. "It was fun."

"I'll keep that in mind." Sensing the tension in her shoulders had eased, Malachi sheathed both knives before he turned and tucked her under his arm and they started back to the house. They'd have to leave that night. He'd need to call Rhys and let him know. Call Istanbul and tell Damien to expect them back. Call—

"Your knives are much better balanced than my set, though." Her voice was growing steadier as they walked. "Can I get some for myself? They might come in handy."

"Are you going to use them on me?"

"Probably not."

"We'll see. What other camps did you go to?"

"Um… circus camp. Art camp. Surf camp. Photography. Wilderness skills. Horseback riding. More photography. Sailing."

"You're very well-rounded."

"You should see me start a fire."

THE CAR RIDE BACK TO ISTANBUL WAS QUIET. AVA SLEPT SINCE Malachi was still jumping with energy. Even their adrenaline-fueled sex back at the house had done nothing to take the edge off. He was beginning to think the woman had more energy than any Irina he'd ever met. It might have simply been a consequence of too many years with no Irin contact, but he was starting to suspect that, with training, her powers would be formidable. It made him want to thump his chest like a Neanderthal. His woman, his *reshon*, would be a force to be reckoned with.

His phone rang.

"Hello?"

Damien asked, "Is anyone following you?"

He glanced in the rearview mirror, but it was still empty. The only traffic had been scattered, though he knew it would become heavier the closer they got to the city. Here, they sped through countryside populated by more tractors than immortal assassins.

"We're fine. Nothing suspicious."

"Maxim said he's picked up more activity in the last couple of days than what he'd expect for this time of year. More outsiders than he's seen before. Something is definitely happening with the Grigori in the city. And Leo says that the elusive Dr. Sadik seems to be back in his office. Says the secretary showed up this morning, even though no patients came."

"No sightings of the doctor?"

"No, but if the secretary has come back from her holiday…"

"The doctor could be expected soon." He paused, adding the fact to the mosaic of information he'd been building about Ava. "Has Maxim heard anything?"

The young scribe was the best information merchant they had. While Rhys could command the computer systems, sometimes nothing beat having ears to the ground. And the quietly charming Maxim had become a favorite among some of the more… legally challenged elements of Istanbul. His love of gambling probably helped.

"Maxim claims your Dr. Sadik hasn't rung any bells with the human element, though a Grigori he captured went stubbornly silent when the name was mentioned."

"So he is Grigori. Or connected in some way."

"Or the soldier knew he was going to die and didn't feel like giving Maxim the answer to his question. It's all speculation at this point, brother."

He thought for a moment, wishing he could just be back in Istanbul without the long drive. Ava's breathing changed slightly and she let out a soft murmur but didn't wake.

"You and the woman," Damien asked. "You're together?"

"Yes. She's mine."

"You're certain?"

"Yes."

There was a long pause, and when Damien's voice came back, he sounded amused. "It'll be good not to be the only one tormented by a mate. Congratulations."

Malachi grinned, reaching over to play with a piece of hair that was tickling her nose. "My Ava adores me. I don't know what you're talking about."

"Ha!"

He bit his lip to hold in the laughter when she frowned in her sleep and batted at his hand. Adoration, indeed.

"I'll let you off the phone. Drive carefully. Rhys should be back tomorrow night. He left Göreme just a little bit after you left Kuşadası."

"It will be good to see him. Has he made any progress with Ava's genealogy?"

"He sounded like he'd made some kind of breakthrough, but he didn't say what. Just that he had a few more questions for her."

Malachi frowned. "Fine."

"And I'm going to suggest she go see the mysterious Dr. Sadik."

"Not without me."

Damien paused, then said, "We'll talk about it when you get back."

"Not without me, Damien. It's not going to happen."

"She saw him for weeks with no danger."

"We don't know that. How do you think they found us tonight?"

"It's hardly out of their normal hunting grounds. Perhaps it was a coincidence?"

"I don't believe in a coincidence that leads six Grigori to corner me in an alley while I happen to have Ava with me."

"You're newly mated, and thus you're paranoid. It's completely understandable."

"And I'm completely right. She's not going to his office without me."

"We'll talk more tomorrow. Until then, take care."

"I'll see you later."

As he hung up the phone, the question plagued him. How had the Grigori found them? Not just in Kuşadası, but in that particular restaurant at that particular hour? It couldn't be a coincidence. He glanced at Ava, still sleeping securely. He didn't think she'd called Dr. Sadik again, so how had it happened?

He slowed the car and pulled over near a roadside market, then he grabbed her mobile phone from the center console. Could Sadik have tapped into the network somehow? Doing so would indicate he was far more connected than Malachi or Rhys had initially suspected. Perhaps it was simpler. A tracker of some kind. A simple GPS chip would have allowed him to track Ava anywhere she went. He flipped her phone over, looking for any indication it had been tampered with.

"What are you doing?" Her sleepy voice didn't distract him as he looked at the edges of her mobile. No scratches or marks indicated that the case had been manipulated or modified.

"Do you have one of those location apps on your phone so you can find it online if you lose it?"

"No. I turned off all the location services except for maps. Carl put one on and it pissed me off, so I shut all of them off. Why?"

He muttered, "How did the Grigori find us?"

"What?"

"At the restaurant tonight. How did they find us?"

She sat up straight. "I don't know."

"You haven't called Sadik, have you?"

Ava rolled her eyes. "I still don't buy your suspicion of him, but no, I haven't."

Another thought occurred to him. "Did Dr. Sadik ever give you anything?"

"What?" She rubbed at her eyes. "No. I don't think so."

"Think, Ava. It might have looked innocent. Like a trinket."

"Well… nothing he could use to—"

"What did he give you?" His interest spiked. "Something harmless. What was it, love?"

She shrugged and reached into the purse near her feet. "It's nothing. I'd kind of forgotten about it. It's one of those nazar-amulet key chains. To ward off the evil eye, you know? Dr. Sadik told me to keep it with me. For luck."

From a pocket, she pulled out the vivid blue glass. Around four centimeters wide, it looked like any of the tourist trinkets hanging from every shop in Turkey, only it was backed with metal he suspected doubled as an antennae. The white and blue circles stared back at him, accusing him of paranoia. Malachi held it up to the light.

"I thought it was kind of silly, but I put it in my bag and I haven't really thought about it since."

"I'm sure he was counting on that."

In the darkest blue of the glass, there was an almost translucent chip with a wire leading toward the metal frame.

"There." He held it out so Ava could see. "Do you see? I think it's a chip."

She blinked. "Like they put in dog collars to find them if they're lost?"

"A simple GPS chip. As long as you have this with you, he could track you."

He saw the color rise on her cheeks, but her eyes were cold. "Son of a bitch…"

Malachi grabbed her hand. "You trusted him. I know. It's not—"

"That asshole!"

"He betrayed you, and you're—"

"I'm gonna *kill* him."

Now it was Malachi cautioning patience. "We need to find out more before you do."

"This thing—" She tried to grab the nazar, but Malachi closed his fingers over it.

"No."

"Give it to me! I want to smash it to pieces!" She was already opening her car door. "I want it as far away from me as—"

"Do you want him to think you're in the middle of nowhere on the side of the road?" He shook the hand she was trying to pry open. "Think."

Ava blinked, coming out of her rage. "He'd know I found it."

"Exactly. We're not going to take it back to the house, but we don't want him to know we've found it."

She took a deep breath and nodded. "Okay, so what do we do?"

"We're going to take it back to Istanbul, and we're going to leave it someplace very safe." An idea sprang to his mind, and Malachi smiled. "Someplace that will confuse the hell out of him."

It was morning when they walked into the lobby of Ava's old hotel. The streets of the Sultanahmet were almost deserted as they made their way past the sleepy young man at the front desk and toward the courtyard near her old room. The young man raised his head in a quick smile, recognized Ava, then put his head down again, not realizing she no longer had a room there.

"This way," she said softly. "I think this is where they keep the carts."

Malachi spotted a maid turning the corner with one of the narrow cleaning carts, so he tugged Ava toward it, engaging the girl in a conversation about finding a razor because his luggage had been lost. Malachi trapped the young woman in conversation while he passed the nazar to Ava. She palmed it, took out the gum she'd been chewing, and stuck it to the glass-and-metal amulet. Then she pressed the blue circle into a corner, out of the line of sight, but hopefully secure enough to remain on the cart. Malachi saw her stuff a rag under the nazar to hold it in place, then she tugged on his hand.

"You know what? I totally forgot, honey. I have an extra razor in my bag." Ava put on a big smile as she shook her head. "Can't believe I forgot about that. I was surprised they let it on the plane."

Malachi switched to English. "Is that so? I won't bother her anymore then." He turned to the confused maid with an apologetic smile and thanked her. Then he and Ava turned back toward the lobby and slipped out of the hotel.

"Hopefully, the cart will move enough that he won't be immediately suspicious. Plus, you've stayed there before. So while he'll know you're back in the city, he won't realize you're at our house."

"I can't believe I stuck gum to the corner of her cart." Ava shuddered. "The well-behaved schoolgirl in me is appalled by my behavior."

"You were really a well-behaved schoolgirl?"

"Of course not. I was the crazy chick with a reputation to uphold."

"That's what I was hoping for."

CHAPTER

SIXTEEN

By the time they arrived at the scribe house on the other side of the bridge, morning traffic had started. Cafés and shops were stirring, and the corner market near the old wooden house in Beyoğlu was opening its doors. Ava held Malachi's hand as they walked from the car park. She had slept in the car, but not deeply. She needed quiet, food, and warm arms surrounding her while she slept.

I love you. Of course I love you.

He said it like it was the most natural thing in the world. And Ava, despite a lifetime's worth of disappointment, was starting to believe it.

"Malachi." She tugged on his arm a few steps away from the front door. The sun was rising, painting the side of the house a warm red-brown. It touched his hair, and Ava was blinded for a moment by the planes of his face. The warmth in his eyes as he looked down on her. He was becoming the most handsome man in the world to her. Just the sight of him stole her breath.

"What?"

"What happens now?"

He smiled and touched her cheek with a finger. "Now my brothers will greet us, and we will both get some rest. We eat something. We take things one step at a time, Ava. We will find who is after you and what they want. Then, we will make you safe."

"It sounds pretty simple when you put it like that." She felt her head swimming and knew she'd reached the end of her rope. She was five steps from the door, but minutes away from collapse.

Malachi squeezed her hand and reached over to knock, but the green door was already opening. Damien stood in the doorway, a fierce, intimidating figure, his torso bare save for the markings across his chest, shoulders, and arms. A linen cloth hung around his waist, and Ava saw black stains on his hands. His hair hung past his shoulders, and Ava could see the ancient warrior in his eyes as he stared.

"Morning greetings, brother," he said quietly, opening the door farther and holding out his hand. Malachi put a hand at the small of her back and grasped Damien's forearm with his hand.

Malachi asked, "Does the fire still burn in this house?"

"It does, and you are welcome to its light." Then the stern expression melted, and Damien looked down at her. "You and your own."

With that, some kind of wall was breached, and she heard Malachi's thoughts swell with pride and excitement. He held her with one arm while grabbing his friend in a fierce embrace. The two men's quiet laughter enveloped her as they ushered Ava through the door, and she saw Leo and Maxim standing behind Damien, both wearing the same joyful expressions. They lined up to greet her. Damien was first, leaning down to put both hands on her shoulders and kissing her cheeks, right and left.

"You are welcome, sister." Damien's voice held a slight waver. "You honor us with your voice."

Aware that there was some meaning she didn't quite grasp, Ava only said, "Thank you."

Maxim was next. His vivid blue eyes held a devious glint, but his smile was warm. "Welcome, sister." He leaned down and also kissed her cheeks in greeting.

"Thank you."

Leo was the last to say hello, but Ava was grateful to see his familiar, playful expression. "Welcome home, Ava. I'm so happy you're back."

She was almost ready to burst into tears when his lips touched her cheek. She felt Malachi's hand at her back a moment before he pulled her back and into his chest.

"Rhys?" he asked as she tried to recover her composure. She had never felt so welcomed in her life. A small, abandoned corner of her heart sighed and whispered, *Home.*

"He arrived a few hours ago. Still sleeping."

"Is our room ready? We both need sleep."

"Of course," Damien said. "Leo?"

The smiling man stepped forward. "We moved you to the second floor. The east room has the most space, and it's coolest in the afternoon."

"Thank you," Malachi said.

"Wait." She put a hand on his arm. "They moved your room?"

"Our room," he said softly, leading her toward the stairs. "Thank you, Leo. We'll see you later."

"Rest well." Without a whisper, he disappeared, along with every other man who'd been there a minute ago. Ava blinked back the blurriness in her eyes and followed Malachi.

"Wait… so, what? They moved me in?"

"I believe Maxim collected your things from your hotel after we left Istanbul. They simply moved them to a new room along with my things."

"Isn't that—" She couldn't stop the yawn. "—a little premature? I mean, we've been… whatever-we-are for—"

"They don't think like that," he said with a smile. "They see the truth."

"Oh?" She yawned again, walking through the door he held open for her. She entered a dim room surrounded by bookcases on three walls. There was a window shielded by wooden blinds and a beautiful mural painted around it. But all Ava saw was the bed. Low, covered with pillows, with the bedspread turned down. It was the most beautiful thing she'd ever seen. She collapsed face-first onto the pillows, barely registering Malachi's quiet chuckle.

"A little tired?"

"You haven't let me get much sleep the past week, you insatiable man."

"I think you've worn me out, too," he said as he tugged off her shoes and jeans. Then he rolled her over and eased off the button-down shirt she'd worn, leaving her in a lightweight tank and her panties. The cotton sheets were a cool kiss against her skin, and Ava burrowed into the pillows as he pulled the bedspread up to her chin. "Sleep, my love."

"You, too. Come to bed." She pulled at his hand, rolling toward him with her eyes closed when she felt the other side of the bed dip. Then his arm was around her, and his skin pressed against her own.

Leg to leg. Chest to back. His arms encircled her as oblivion descended.

"Malachi?"

"Hmm?"

"Your brothers… what do you mean, 'they see the truth'?"

"About you and me."

"And?"

"We belong to each other," he murmured, his voice growing dim. "The Irin know how precious love is. How quickly it can be taken from us."

"Still, so fast…"

"Perhaps… we have learned not to wait."

Reshon, reshon, reshon.

She didn't know whether the whispers were coming from his mind or her own. And for the first time, Ava didn't care.

She woke slowly, the knowledge of *who* reaching her before the *where*. Malachi was with her, arm still wrapped securely around her waist. As her eyes blinked open, she realized they were back in Istanbul, in the wooden house with the green door, where she'd been greeted like family before falling asleep with the man she loved.

Loved to distraction.

She turned carefully, wanting to watch him as he slept. His face was covered with dark stubble, and his hair fell across his forehead, a frown on his face as he dreamed. His full lips pursed in disapproval at whatever visions he saw, and long lashes curled on his cheeks. He really did have the most beautiful eyes; his lashes would be the envy of women everywhere.

"Angels would weep," she whispered, only realizing after she'd said it how truly ironic it was. Angels probably had wept.

The Forgiven. The angelic ancestors of the Irin. In the story Rhys told her, the Forgiven had been the ones who left. Leaving behind their women and children to return to heaven when they were called. And in return, their descendants had been blessed with knowledge and magic in exchange for their sacrifice. Ava traced the stern line of Malachi's lip.

"I think I'd pull down heaven," she said, "if that's what it took to keep you here with me."

A slow smile curved his lips. "And I'd abandon it if you weren't there." His eyes flickered open. "Good morning."

"I'm pretty sure it's afternoon."

"Oh well." He rolled over, dragging her with him so she lay over his chest. "Let's go back to sleep and forget them all."

Ava giggled and squirmed as he held her. "We should get up."

"I'm well on the way. Can't you tell?"

"Clearly." She managed to wiggle to his side. "But I have some questions."

"Oh…" He groaned and buried his face in her neck, nipping at the soft skin with gentle teeth. "Do I get a prize if I answer correctly?"

"Not those kind of questions."

"What kind then?"

"Last night…" She shook her head. "This morning. When we got here. The things they said… That meant something, didn't it?"

"Yes." His voice held an abundance of caution.

"What did it mean?" When he didn't answer, she rolled over. "Well?"

She started to sit up, but he grabbed her and pulled her down, curling around her as he spoke.

"When we went to Cappadocia, the scribes there greeted us as guests. You might not have noticed, as they're not as formal there."

"You were speaking in the Old Language, too."

"Yes. But here… When we arrived this morning, Damien greeted us as family. In the old way, the way the head of a household would greet a mated couple returning to a retreat. He called you sister. He called you my own."

A quiet suspicion began to take shape. "They moved us into this room. Which is quite obviously intended for two people."

"Yes."

"And all your stuff is here. And my stuff."

"Ava, I—"

"Are you telling me they think we're married or something?" Her heart started pounding.

"Irin don't marry," he said, just a little too quickly. "So, no."

"But they think something."

"They know we're together. That's all. I told them we were together. Aren't we?"

"I guess…" Ava felt like she was trying to find her way in a dark room that everyone could see but her. "Yes, we're together. I just want to know what's going on. This is all happening really fast. Do they think I'm going to live here forever or something?"

She felt him stiffen, and his face went blank. "Are you planning to leave?"

"Not right now. But… I don't know." She knew her words caused him pain, but they had to be said. "I have a life, Malachi."

He drew back, and Ava hated the distance immediately. "Yes, you have a life."

"And I can't just—"

"A life where you travel from place to place every few months, never putting down roots." His voice was brittle. "You don't speak of any close friends. You have a mother who loves you but doesn't understand you. A stepfather who protects you but doesn't love you."

His words stung, even though Ava knew they were true. "You have no right—"

"You were alone," he said, grabbing her hand and stopping her from leaving the bed. "Like I was. Even more than I was. We were alone, but now we're not."

The urgency in his voice, the raw honesty of it, cooled her anger. "Malachi—"

"Why do you want to leave that? I need you, as you need me." He drew her back down and placed a lingering kiss on her lips. "We can stay here. We can go another place. We can seek out the Irina who have hidden themselves and ask them to train you in magic. We can hide from the world if we must. I don't know what we'll do for money, but we'll find—"

"I have plenty of money," Ava said. "Money for a lifetime. I'm not worried about that."

"Then why?" He kissed her again. "Why leave? I don't care where we go, as long as we're together."

Her heart swelled, and she tried to swallow the lump in her throat. "Is this real?"

He smiled a glorious smile and kissed her again. "Of course it is. We can live forever. The two of us. Forever. Have a family. A life."

"I love you." Ava kissed him back, her heart pounding out of her chest with a mad hope. She believed him, and it scared her. "I love you so much."

"I love you, too."

He held her on the bed, rocking back and forth as Ava bit her lip and tentatively allowed the dreams he shared to take root in her heart. She could see it. For the first time in her life, she caught a glimpse of a life that didn't end in loneliness and pain. She wanted to be cautious, but her reckless heart ran toward him.

"To be completely honest, however…" He glanced down. "Some might consider us… mated."

Ava sat up. "That's the Irin version of married, isn't it?"

"It's not exactly…" He was fiddling with the fingers on her right hand in what had become his own nervous gesture. "Yes."

"I knew it!"

Ava and Rhys were looking through old record books, trying to identify the Grigori she and Malachi had seen in Kuşadası. Unlike police lineup books, which Ava had been acquainted with due to her kidnapping as a child, the Irin records were a mix of pictures and sketches. The profiles she paged through were only for the longest-lived and most dangerous soldiers, which meant it read more like an encyclopedia of evil than a suspect book.

Ulrich, son of Grimold. 1734. Took part in Rending near Stockholm.

Finn, son of Volund. 1856. Known kills in Barcelona, Madrid, and Rabat.

Michael, son of Svarog. 1699. Took part in attack of Prague prior to Rending.

Kemal, son of Jaron. 1955. Known kills, multiple victims in Istanbul, Athens, and throughout Romania.

Joseph, son of Volund. 1902. Known kills in London, Edinburgh, Manchester, Brittany, Lyon, and Milan.

Some of the names had been crossed out, usually with a notation about who had killed them. There were also notes about how each Grigori fought or who their associates were. Certain names kept popping up over and over.

Volund.

Jaron.

Svarog.

Galal.

"Hey, Rhys?"

"Hmm?" He looked up from his computer.

"These names—the fathers of the Grigori listed—so are these…?"

"Fallen angels," he said. "The real kind. Not offspring like us, and definitely not the nice fluffy variety you see on the television. The Fallen never left Earth, and they're incredibly powerful. Incredibly cruel. We've killed a few over the years, but it's very difficult. They can shapeshift and cloak their power, so more than one Irin scribe has lost his life thinking one of the Fallen is a harmless old woman or child in need of help. It's more common they kill each other than we're able to kill them."

"How do you kill an angel?" she whispered to herself.

"There are only a few weapons that can do it. Most are in the possession of the Council in Vienna. They have an ancient armory they loan out to very specific people. One of their daggers showed up on a Grigori soldier last month, which has everyone scrambling. Damien was up in arms when he called Vienna, wanted to know how the bastard had obtained it."

"Does anyone know?"

Rhys shrugged. "It's possible an assassin they sent to kill one of the Fallen failed. Brage—that's the one who had it—is one of Volund's most trusted children. Volund controls most of Northern Europe and Russia. He might have given it to him, but if he did, he'd have a very specific purpose for it. It's not something you'd give away lightly or carry every day."

"Is it weird that one of Volund's Grigori is here in Istanbul?"

"It could be, but then, it may be nothing. Most go back and forth despite some rivalry."

"Huh."

"Though… there's a lot of strange happenings lately," he muttered, still searching for something online. "Like your Dr. Sadik."

Ava burned just thinking about him. Bastard. She'd trusted him, and now she had no idea who the doctor was, or even if he was a doctor at all. Rhys was still trying to track him down. They worked in silence for several more minutes, but Ava could feel Rhys's eyes keep coming back to her.

"What?"

"I'm curious about something." Rhys handed her a book written in what looked like Farsi just as Malachi entered the room. Ava tried to push down her own annoyance at seeing him.

"I can't read this," she protested, looking through the book. "I can speak a little Farsi, but—"

"Just look at the pictures," Rhys said. "See if you recognize anyone."

Malachi walked toward her, but she shot him a look. She was irritated about the whole "mated-not-married" thing, and she wasn't going to try to make him feel better. He could have at least warned her. And the fact that everyone around her was so damn happy only irked her more. Would it have killed him to keep her informed?

"If you want to punish him, you're doing a bang-up job," Rhys said when Malachi crossed the room to speak to Maxim about something. The two conferred for a moment before heading toward the library door, leaving her and Rhys alone. Ava turned to him.

"I'll get over it eventually, but right now I'm pissed."

"He didn't mean to anger you. I'm sure of it."

"But he didn't exactly keep me informed, did he? Did Malachi tell *you* we were mated?"

Rhys's mouth did a little gasping-fish thing. "Not in those words… exactly."

"Really? When?"

He muttered something that sounded like "Captain Donkey."

"What?"

He cleared his throat. "Cappadocia."

"Oh really?" She glared at the door. "We were there *one night* after we… you know."

"I think the whole valley knew. Caves echo." Rhys kept talking, even though her face reddened. "Honestly, love, the two of you had been dancing around each other for weeks. Stop being such a fussbudget."

"A…a what?" She tried to hold in the laugh as Rhys blushed.

"Nothing."

"Did you just call me a…a *fussbudget*?" The snicker turned into a laugh.

"I… well, you are. Being very fussy about all this. You're—"

"Showing your age, old man." Ava couldn't stop laughing.

"And you're being annoyed for the sake of being annoyed." At least Rhys was laughing, too. His eyes were lighter than they had been since the disastrous night she'd kissed him. "So just stop." The laughter left his voice and Ava wiped the tears from her eyes. "You two have what most of us have only dreamed of for over two hundred years. A mate. A partner. We can all see it, even when you're annoyed and he's exasperated."

She sighed. "I do exasperate him."

"And he loves it. He loves you. And you're clearly besotted with him." Rhys grabbed her hand and squeezed it for a second. "So stop trying to be sensible about it. Grab love when you can. It doesn't come around for everyone."

"I'll try."

"You'll try…" He shook his head and turned back to the computer screen. "You know what? Keep fighting the inevitable. It makes for very entertaining—"

"Oh my God," she breathed out, staring at the face on the page. The vivid green eyes were rendered in black and white, but the shape was exactly as she remembered. The sketch looked old, maybe from the turn of the century or earlier. It was hard to tell. After all, that particular style of glasses was classic. "It's him."

Rhys whipped around. "Who?"

"Him." She pointed to the angular face on the page. "It's him. Dr. Sadik."

"You're positive, Ava?"

"I'm sure! It looks just like him. Exactly." She looked at the other pictures on the page. Even though she couldn't read the writing, it was clearly an extensive entry. "You're saying my therapist is really a Grigori soldier?"

"No, he isn't." Rhys reached over and closed the book, swiping a thumb over the title. For a moment, the letters shimmered and shifted, then the characters reshaped into the more recognizable Roman alphabet.

"That spell is incredibly…" Ava blinked when she read the title. "Oh. My—"

"Your therapist isn't a Grigori," Rhys said, pulling away the book. For a moment the letters held, then the title shifted back to the original Farsi. But the name was branded onto her mind.

JARON.

"Your Dr. Sadik is a fallen angel."

CHAPTER
SEVENTEEN

Malachi shivered just thinking about it. She had been alone with him for weeks. The monster had touched her. Touched his mate. The fact that she was still so silent probably meant she was in shock.

"Absolutely not," Malachi said, pulling Ava closer as they sat on the couch in the library.

Maxim said, "But surely you can see the value of—"

"You will not put her at risk," he barked, unable to comprehend why they were even considering his brother's suggestion.

Ava's doctor was Jaron. Jaron was Sadik. The fact that his mate was still in the city drove him to distraction. He wanted to board a plane. No, not a plane, the bastard could fly. A boat? Water was safer. A car would do. Anything to get Ava away. Get her as far away from the monster as he could. For the first time, he completely understood why the Irina had fled.

"Malachi, calm yourself," Damien said, standing in the doorway.

"I want to know more." Ava spoke for the first time since the brothers had gathered.

Rhys sat near the computer. Leo sat next to him, looking through more books, everything they had on record about the fallen angel known as Jaron. Maxim was sitting across from Malachi and Ava, and Damien was waiting for a callback from Vienna.

"I want to know more about the Fallen," Ava said again. "This makes no sense. How did Jaron know about me? Why was he even interested? Malachi acts like the Fallen are more powerful than you guys—"

"They are," Maxim said.

"So, what did he want with me? And why didn't he hurt me when he could have?"

The set of her jaw told Malachi he'd be answering questions whether he liked it or not. When his mate set her mind on something, she was impossible to budge. Part of him loved it. The other part wanted to tear his hair out.

But then, there was no such thing as a biddable Irina.

Maxim crossed his arms and leaned toward them. "Ava, the first thing you must understand about the Fallen is this: They are not human."

"I understand."

"No, you don't." Malachi ignored the clipped manner his brother took with Ava. For such a young scribe, Maxim had more knowledge of Fallen and Grigori society than he did. Malachi had a tendency to stab first and question later.

"You don't truly understand what they are," Maxim continued. "It's impossible. The Fallen are angels; beings with no place in this world. Completely and entirely foreign. Irin are at least partly human."

"The Fallen are bad; I know that."

"Don't make the mistake of assigning moral judgment to them," Maxim said. "Good. Bad. These have no meaning to them. They do not live by human mores. They were never intended to."

"But…" He saw her frown. "I thought angels were meant to be good."

"No, they were meant to serve. That is their sole purpose. Servants of the Creator."

Ava leaned forward, away from Malachi's arm. "But the Forgiven…"

"The angels fell from the heavens, tempted by the beauty of human women, curious about the interest their Master had in this new race. Remember that: They *all* fell."

"Because they fell in love?"

Maxim shrugged. "Don't assume so. Don't assume any human emotion when it comes to angels. They wanted and they took. They're curious creatures. Human women would have been stunned by their appearance. They probably thought they gave themselves to gods. Their children were powerful and magical. Heroes and seers. The first offspring were imbued with the powers of their fathers, but they were uncontrolled. Unpredictable."

"So what happened? Where did the Irin come from?"

"We are the children of the Forgiven. Fallen angels who returned to heaven."

"Why? Why did they leave?"

"The Creator offered forgiveness. They took it. We don't know why or how."

"But they left," Ava said. "They left their wives. Their children. How could they?"

Malachi said, "Angels were never meant to live here. The Fallen were heavenly creatures who turned their back on their purpose. And as Max said, their offspring were frightening. Some were thought to be gods. Others became so powerful their own fathers were forced to destroy them. The Irin believe the Forgiven returned to heaven because —though they realized they could rule over the Earth—that power was contrary to everything they had been created for. So they left us and returned. They sacrificed their own power for the good of humanity and were redeemed."

"And their children?" Ava's voice wavered, and Malachi took her hand when her eyes filled with tears. "You said some were destroyed, but the Irin are still here. Even with the Irina mostly gone—"

Damien broke in. "The Creator took mercy on the mates of the Forgiven and on their children. He protected the offspring who were not destructive. Allowed them the strength and knowledge of their fathers, but on the condition they would watch over this new race of humans. That is where we came from, Ava. We are of the race of angels. Neither wholly human, nor wholly heavenly. The Irin were meant to guide humanity and guard it. Servants on Earth as our fathers were servants in the heavens. That became our purpose."

"And the Fallen?"

"The Fallen are an abomination in every sense," Damien said. "Beings meant to serve who repudiated their Creator and desired to rule. They didn't leave, because they sought to conquer. They saw humanity as sheep. Lesser beings. They break every law of the universe, simply by their rebellion. The Fallen cannot be trusted. Their very presence on Earth is evidence of their dishonor. That is why their children are cursed."

"The Grigori," she said.

"Yes," Malachi drew her closer. "They became predators like their fathers, the Fallen. They prey on the humans we seek to protect. It has always been so."

Ava asked, "How many fallen angels are there?"

"We don't know," Rhys said from the desk. "There are nine prominent ones, scattered across the globe. Each rules over an area, but there are minor Fallen as well. They kill each other off occasionally. Fight their own wars, which we only pay attention to when it affects us or the humans."

Leo muttered, "It's not as black and white as you all believe. There are variations. Subtle shifts in power that—"

"We all know your fascination with them," Rhys said. "Trying to understand the Fallen doesn't make them any less evil."

Leo and Maxim simultaneously bared their teeth, and Malachi was reminded, again, how young the two cousins were. Only around two hundred, they were babes when the Rending happened, hidden by their mothers somewhere in the cold North. No one knew how, exactly, the boys had survived. They had been delivered to a scribe house in rural Finland weeks after their families had been destroyed.

"Fallen society is, in its own way, as complicated as ours," Maxim growled. "I've studied it. Jaron is—"

Malachi finally broke in, exasperated by the bickering. "Can we please stop the history lesson and return to how we're going to protect Ava?"

Maxim said, "I'm just saying that Jaron is not easy to classify. The fact is he had access to your mate for weeks when no one suspected him. He could have harmed Ava at any time, but he didn't. Clearly, he has some interest in her that is not wholly understood. It may be beneficial for her to meet with him and try to get more information."

"It's not safe," Rhys said. "He may have not moved then, but how do you explain the clear aggression in Kuşadası? They were trying to hurt her. Or capture her at the very least."

"Malachi," Maxim asked. "You said the Grigori in Kuşadası looked like Brage?"

He nodded. "Not the captain, but the rest of them were lighter skinned and light haired. Most likely not Jaron's children. More Northern-looking. Maybe Volund's or Grimold's, if I had to guess."

"And Brage has been seen in Istanbul," Leo said. "With an angelic blade."

Damien nodded. "In Jaron's territory. He may have other alliances. We may be seeing a move from the North that would upset Jaron's rule here in the region."

Rhys asked, "A coup? Volund moving against Jaron, and using his most trusted Grigori to kill him? He could have been the one to give him the blade. There were rumors he had one."

"They all have them," Maxim grumbled. "Don't let the council in Vienna fool you."

Damien barked out a reprimand in the Old Language, and Maxim shut up.

"If there is a coup in the works, then having Ava collect more information from Jaron could be crucial," Leo said. "She's smart. And she's in the perfect position to—"

"She's not a bloody soldier!" Malachi said.

"And I'm not a china doll, either." Ava stood, looking around the room, glaring at every man in sight. "You guys keep talking about me like I'm not here. Enough."

Malachi stood with her. "*Canim*—"

"I'm going to the garden to think for a while," she said. "Alone. I need some quiet, so don't follow me. Any of you." She left the room, and Malachi could hear her climbing the stairs, all the way to the roof garden that looked toward Galata Tower.

He turned to Rhys. "Are there security cameras up there?"

"Yes." His brother clicked a few times on the computer, then tilted the monitor toward Malachi. "She's covered from every angle. And the alarms will go off if there is any movement on the sides of the house."

He pointed toward Rhys's chair as Maxim and Leo drifted from the room. "I'll watch her. At least give her some privacy."

Rhys looked like he wanted to object, but a quick word from Damien called him from the library, leaving Malachi alone with only the image of his mate in black and white, staring off into the distance with haunted eyes.

· · ·

Maxim crept into the library an hour later, at sunset, as Malachi was watching Ava.

"You have a lovely mate, brother."

"I do."

"An unexpected blessing to our kind."

Malachi had the urge to cover the computer so his fellow scribe could not see her. But Maxim only glanced at Ava briefly before turning to Malachi.

"He was with her for weeks, and no harm came to her."

His voice held a warning note. "Maxim…"

"I believe there is something happening," Maxim said. "There are shifts in Vienna. Then Ava appeared like this. Strangers are showing up in Istanbul. So many rumors among my associates. I hear them, Malachi. I know everyone thinks me a gambler and a rogue, but—"

"Max—"

"Something is happening." He leaned forward. "And I think she is the key. There is something she is or has that Jaron has an interest in."

"Of course he does!" Malachi finally burst. "She's the first new Irina in centuries! However she came to be, she could be the key to restoring our race. And if the Irin are made whole again, the Fallen could be conquered."

"Is that what we're truly fighting for? Don't be like Damien and follow the Council blindly."

Malachi narrowed his eyes. "You speak rashly, Scribe. And you make assumptions that betray your years."

"Just because I'm young doesn't mean I don't see things. Damien is wise, but he never questions orders from Vienna."

"And you question them too often."

"I only seek to see our people whole again," Maxim said. "We are constantly at war, but where are the Irina? Why are there none on the council any longer? When did the future of our race become the will of eight old men? There are too many secrets."

"The Irina retreated of their own will," Malachi said. "Were we to force them to stay?"

Maxim sat back, no argument rising to his lips as he turned his eyes back to Ava. "She is the key. And Jaron showed her no aggression. She should meet with him and find out why. He is not an unreasonable creature."

"He's a Fallen."

"Now who's making assumptions?" Maxim said. "You admitted that the angel was helping her cope with her abilities before we knew what she was. Perhaps there is more to him than you think."

Malachi sat back, staring toward the screen. Ava wrapped her arms around herself as the evening breeze picked up. A slight shiver shook her frame. He immediately rose to go to her. She'd left her sweater in their room.

"I must go," he said. "We'll talk more later."

"It's really rather simple," Maxim said as Malachi reached the door. "Why don't you ask Ava what she wants to do?"

He turned. "She's mine to protect."

The young scribe shook his head. "She's all of ours to protect, brother, but she has a will of her own. Ask her."

Malachi went to their room first, grabbing a blanket from the closet before he climbed the twisting staircase to the tiled garden on the roof. The sun was setting over the city, and the sky was painted a lush golden red. Ava turned when she heard him, then silently held out her hand.

He went to her, sliding behind her on the chaise where she sat and pulling her back into his body as he wrapped the blanket around them both. Ava leaned against him, their earlier argument seemingly forgotten as she took a deep breath and tucked her face against his neck.

"What were we fighting about before?" she asked quietly.

"You going to Jaron's office? All of us speaking for you, instead of with you?" He tucked a curl behind her ear as the breeze tossed her hair into his face. "Or me stupidly not telling you the implications of coming back here together?"

"To be fair, I probably would have run screaming at the thought of a lifetime commitment, so I understand why you didn't."

"I think the phrase 'stupidly in love' applies. I'm very out of practice handling women."

He felt her laugh against his skin, and she turned until she'd wrapped her arms around his waist as he laid back.

"I don't need to be handled. Just informed."

"I'll remember from now on. I promise."

Night descended, cool wind sweeping up from the water and over the city as lights lit up the evening sky. The cries of the muezzin came and went, echoing from all corners before the call to prayer drifted into the night, leaving them in a cocoon of darkness and warmth as they huddled together.

"There's no going back," she finally whispered. "I know that. I...I don't even want to. You were right about what you said before, even if the truth hurt. I was alone. Plus, I'm stupidly in love with you, too, so I guess we'll have to figure this out together."

He thought his heart would beat out of his chest with joy. "I love you, Ava." He squeezed her tighter. *Reshon.*

She tensed for a moment, then relaxed, and Malachi suspected she'd heard his soul speak the word. She'd probably been hearing it for days. Weeks? And despite that, she'd stayed with him. He'd been a fool to doubt her.

"But if these are my people," she started, "then this is my struggle, too. My responsibility."

"Don't—"

"I want to meet with Dr. Sadik. With Jaron. Maybe he knows where I came from. Maybe he knows what this all means. Why those Grigori were after me. I know you always suspected him, but looking back, I never felt unsafe. I could hear his voice, Malachi." She turned her face up to his. "And I know he didn't mean to harm me. So, why? If he was only a predator, why?"

"I don't know."

"I want to find out. And I also want to know if he was telling the truth about there being others like me."

Malachi sat up. "What do you mean, others?"

"He'd said he'd helped others with my same symptoms. Maybe he was lying, but maybe he was telling the truth. I didn't hear any dishonesty in him. And if there are others out there, other women like me..."

"There could be more Irina," he said softly.

"It's possible. We still don't know why I am the way I am. Where my powers came from. But maybe Jaron knows."

"But would he tell us?"

"He might not." Ava shrugged, and a glint of excitement lit her eyes. "But there's only one way to find out."

The waiting room looked like any other waiting room of any other office in the city. Bright. Modern. Framed art on the walls and an efficient secretary quietly making calls.

Malachi thought nothing had seemed as menacing. He abhorred masks. And that, no matter what Ava thought, was what this office was. A few minutes later, a cheerful nurse poked her head in.

"Ava?"

"Hello," she said, rising with Malachi's hand grasped in her own. "Good to see you again."

"So happy to see you back. How did you like Cappadocia?"

The two women chatted as they walked down the hall and were ushered into a comfortable office. Malachi's daggers burned against his skin. He would be able to reach them in seconds, even though they would do nothing against a fallen angel. His brothers surrounded the office building, watching from all angles while Malachi and Ava were inside.

A few minutes later, a seemingly harmless middle-aged man entered the office. His green eyes flicked to Malachi for a moment before he greeted Ava.

"My dear," he said warmly. "So good to see you back. And this is your friend you were telling me about?"

"Yes, my… fiancé." Ava glanced at him, but Malachi didn't take his eyes off the doctor. The disguise was seamless. He could sense no extraordinary power from the creature. No flicker of otherworldly strength. No wonder they'd all been fooled.

The angel, pretending to be harmless, held out a hand. "So good to meet you, Mister…"

"My name is Malachi," he said, ignoring the offered hand. "And you know what I am."

A slight waver in the mask. "You'll have to pardon me, but—"

"We also know who you are," Ava said quietly. "So no more lies. No more disguises. Let's speak plainly… Jaron."

Green eyes widened for a heartbeat before the doctor stepped back. And Malachi watched, never letting Ava's hand leave his own as Dr. Sadik stood behind his desk with a small smile flickering over his lips.

His eyes darkened to near black, then lightened to a glowing gold color as the mask dissolved. Jaron's shoulders grew wide and thick. His frame lengthened before them until the being was at least a foot taller than he'd been before, almost seven feet. There was a faint gold shimmer that covered his skin as the mask of the harmless doctor fell away and the heavenly being emerged.

His hair grew longer until thick ebony strands brushed past his shoulders. His human clothes disappeared, and the angel stood before them in nothing but a pair of loose pants. The bronze skin of his torso glowed in the afternoon light and raised *talesm* rose like shimmering brands on his skin.

He was radiant.

Glorious.

Terrible.

The only other time Malachi had beheld an angel, the creature had been cloaked. Jaron was probably still cloaked, but he was letting Ava see him far closer to his true form, if Malachi had to guess. It was little wonder that early humans had thought the creatures were gods. No classical sculpture could compare with the utter perfection of the angel's form.

And throughout the transformation, Jaron's eyes never left Ava's. He stared at her as if Malachi didn't exist, his eyes glowing with a gold light as he watched Malachi's mate. When he glanced over, he could sense Ava's awe. She stood, her heart racing, clutching his hand, but her eyes never left Jaron's.

"I am Jaron," he said. The Fallen's voice was low and resonant. Malachi could feel it pressing against his mind. It wrapped around his body, and he had to fight the urge to flee. "Now you see my true face. Hear my voice. *Ava.*"

"I…I didn't know." She stammered as tears came to her eyes. "*I didn't know.*"

"Child, you should not have come back."

CHAPTER

EIGHTEEN

Ava couldn't speak. Her eyes locked with Jaron's as image after image flooded her mind. Bright, glaring, as if seen through eyes that took in every shadow and color in preternatural detail. The pictures flickering like an old film reel, she saw herself as a child, stumbling through her first steps. Splashing in a wading pool in front of a tiny house in Santa Monica. Riding a horse at Carl's ranch.

Darkness.

Then images from her first days in Istanbul. Wandering through the spice market. Buying chestnuts from a vendor near Galata Bridge. Drinking tea with Malachi. Their kiss on the island.

Malachi.

Utter black. Pain. Despair.

She clutched Malachi's hand tighter, gasping when the next images flew past.

Two dark-haired children. A girl with a golden gaze, laughing as butterflies swirled around her. A boy, staring back at her with his father's eyes. An ink-black jaguar curled around the children protectively as a wolf and a tiger paced behind. The tiger bent to the girl, opening his mouth. Ava felt her heart race, but the great beast closed his jaw around the girl's nape gently as she continued to smile and pet its cheek. The image flickered away as a great circle rose in the sky, like a sun twisted with gold and silver. Higher and higher it rose, until the sun faded away to stars, a million scattered points of light dotting the heavens, dancing in concert to a growing song.

Darkness.

Ava felt Malachi's arms around her. Heard Jaron's whisper in her mind. Not in the Old Language, but in her own.

I show you what has been. What will be. And what could be. Do not fear the darkness.

Her eyes came back into focus, staring into Malachi's as he looked down on her. She must have stumbled, because he was holding her in his lap, sitting in a chair in the doctor's office.

"Ava?"

She couldn't speak for a moment, still lost in the eyes of the boy as her mate's eyes stared back at her. She reached up, brushing away the dark hair that had fallen across his face.

"I will not fear the darkness," she whispered. Turning her head, she looked at Jaron again, but the radiance had grown dim and the Fallen appeared more human, though no less frightening. "Who are you?"

"You ask the wrong question, child."

"Who am I, then?" She blinked and sat up, trying to fight the wave of nausea that swept over her. The instinctive fear that hummed in her blood.

"A better question, but one I have already answered."

"No, you haven't." She frowned when she saw the angel's lip curl slightly at the corner.

"You're right. It's better to say that I've answered it as much as I want to right now."

"I don't understand any of this."

"You will." He shrugged. "Or you won't. Try to understand, as more fates than yours rest in your song."

Ava stood, vibrating with anger. "Why don't you tell me more, then? What am I?"

She felt Malachi rise behind her, putting a calming hand on her shoulder. "Ava—"

"I'm not scared of you, Dr. Sadik. Or Jaron. Or whatever your name is."

The angel looked amused. "You should be scared. Wiser ones usually are."

Malachi growled behind her, trying to push forward to stand between Ava and Jaron. Ava wouldn't let him; she pushed forward.

"Ava, stop—"

"If I'd wanted her dead, Scribe, she would be," Jaron said, his voice growing more resonant and his face starting to glow again. "If I'd wanted to harm her, she would be gone. Wiped from the Earth and your memory as if she had never existed."

"Impossible," her mate murmured, drawing Ava back to the safety of his arms.

"Very possible," Jaron whispered. "Never underestimate my kind, Scribe. She has chosen you, yes. But I am not convinced you are equal to the task. What darkness have you truly battled?"

She felt him draw one of the daggers from under his arm. It glinted in the light from the window as he held it between Jaron and herself.

"I have battled evil like you before."

In the space of a heartbeat, the angel towered over them. Ava trembled, but Malachi stood firm, his arm across her chest never wavering. His hand on the dagger didn't tremble.

Jaron spoke, and his voice moved over them like a wave. "You have never battled one like me. You will meet the darkness, and it will overwhelm you." His gaze flickered down to Ava. "She knows what could be now. Protect your woman, Scribe. Get her out of this city. It is no longer under my domain. Others seek to take her from you. They will show you no mercy. Even now, your brothers battle children who are not of my blood, and one carries a heavenly blade."

Then Jaron spoke something in the Old Language, and the writing that covered his body, even more intricate and beautiful than Malachi's *talesm*, glowed with a burnished-gold light. Ava had to shield her eyes, and when she opened them, the angel had disappeared.

"We have to get out of here," Malachi said, tugging her away from the gold glow where Jaron had been.

"Where did he go?"

"I don't know. I don't care. We have to move, Ava. Now."

Bursting through the door, Ava could hear them. Silent physically, but their dark minds scratched at her own. Vicious whispers of violence and blood. She ran after Malachi, halting briefly when she saw the blood.

The receptionist and the nurse were dead, their necks split open, blood pooling on the tiled floor and staining the intricate carpet in the waiting room. Malachi cursed under his breath and pulled her from her shocked stupor.

"Th…they killed them. Why didn't Jaron—"

"Tools," he hissed. "I told you. They were nothing to him. He's left here. Possibly left the city. Whatever protection he was granting you is gone. I have to get you away."

Malachi and Ava ran down the stairs, leaving the vicious whispers behind, only to be slapped by shouting voices when they left the building.

"This way!" She pointed toward an alley where she sensed them, running toward it and pulling Malachi with her.

"Ava, no!"

"But Rhys and Leo are there! I can hear them."

With another muttered curse, he followed her, shoving her behind him as they ran. "Stay back, but stay close." He dropped her hand and pulled out his other dagger when they'd left the foot traffic behind. Ava could hear the humans around them, chattering about the man with the weapons. A few wondered if a movie was being filmed. Their inner voices buzzed with excitement and curiosity, but no fear.

As they reached the back of the building, Rhys and Leo emerged. Leo was bent over, holding his side as Rhys held him up.

"Angelic blade," Rhys panted. "Damien distracted him. They're still fighting. There were… so many. Heavens, Mal. Too many. There are too many. Even Max looked shocked. I have to get Leo out of here. He won't heal unless I can get him back to the fire."

"The fire?" Ava's eyes flew to the wound at Leo's side. It was deep and weeping. The blood was clotted and black around the wound.

Malachi grabbed Leo's other arm, and the young scribe groaned as the two men lifted him. "Any Grigori left?"

"We killed the six that were here. That blond bastard, Brage, was leading them, but Damien drew him off after he'd wounded Leo. Maxim has seven or so more on the other side, but none of them carried any serious weapons. He'll be fine."

They stumbled to the car, easing Leo in the back. Rhys pulled out the keys and opened the front door for Ava. "You keep him steady in the back. Ava, in the front seat."

"Why does he need a fire?" Ava asked as she slid in the car. They were only a few blocks from the scribe house, but Leo had fallen silent, and Malachi looked grim as he held him.

"Not just any fire," Rhys said as he drove through the twisting streets. "We need a flame from the ritual fire at the scribe house to cauterize the wound. I can stitch it up, but without that flame, it will never heal. What happened with Jaron? I'm going to assume this is some angelic shite we didn't know about."

"Apparently…" Malachi started speaking the Old Language and Ava tried not to scream. They were doing it again, withholding information she knew was important. She wanted to yell at them, but Leo's low groan interrupted her.

"Malachi…"

"Almost home." He brushed the blond hair from Leo's face, holding the man as he would a child. "You'll feel better soon."

"Hurts." Leo's voice was brittle with pain. "Won't… Tried all my spells. Won't heal."

Malachi held his hand over Leo's forehead, tracing letters Ava couldn't read, then the young man fell silent, soothed into a restless sleep.

"Rhys, how much longer?"

"There's a protest near the square again." More muttered curses as Rhys turned right, then left, trying to maneuver around the crowds gathered near Taksim Square.

"We could get out. Carry him?"

"Too many police. Too many questions."

The smell of smoke drifted through the windows, causing Rhys to look over to her. "Close it! There could be tear gas if there are protests."

Night was descending on the city, and the shops were lit up, taking advantage of the increased foot traffic, even as the police tried to herd pedestrians from the square. Ava could hear the chaotic shouts mixed with laughter and music blaring from the passing cars. The smell of smoke only grew stronger as they turned a corner that Ava finally recognized.

Rhys breathed out. "No…"

"What?" Ava turned her head from watching Leo and Malachi in the back of the car and her stomach dropped.

The scribe house was burning.

"What are we going to do?" Ava asked as they watched the old wooden house being licked by flames. Firefighters were already there, the spray of hoses and shouts filling the already chaotic night. "Malachi?"

Rhys barked something in the Old Language and got out of the car, keys still in the ignition. Malachi followed, the two arguing as Leo began to moan from the back seat again. After a few tense moments, Malachi slammed the back door shut and got in the front seat, putting the car in reverse and backing away from the scene.

"What are you doing?" she said. "You can't just—"

"I'm taking you and Leo to a safe house, but if Rhys can't get a piece of the fire, Leo won't survive the night. Rhys has to save a part of it, Ava. Even if the house survives, the firefighters will douse the fire. He has to keep part of it going for Leo."

"How on earth is he even going to—?"

"He'll find a way," Malachi said. "He has to."

Ava looked over her shoulder, but Rhys had already entered the house, slipping past the crowds that watched in fascination and horror as the old house burned.

"This is my fault," she said. "I brought this."

"This is a war, and it's been going on far longer than either of us have been alive, *canim*. Everything happens for a reason. Rhys will be fine."

Despite his comforting words, Ava couldn't escape the grim tone of his voice.

"You guys are practically indestructible, right?"

"Exactly."

AVA STILL HAD SMOKE IN HER NOSE WHEN THEY PULLED UP TO THE modest carpet shop on the other side of the bridge. It was dark from the outside, but Ava could see a light glowing dimly on the second floor.

"Stay here," he said, pulling the car into a deserted alley.

Malachi got out and walked around the corner, returning after only a few minutes with a set of keys and a determined expression. He opened the back door and started to ease Leo out of the seat. The young man winced and Ava saw the blood start seeping from the wound again, black and thick.

"Help me," Malachi grunted. "You'll need to get the door." He tossed her a set of keys and Ava rushed to pick them up.

A few minutes later, the three were climbing a narrow staircase next to the rug shop. Ava opened the door to a deserted apartment with a small sitting room and a kitchenette.

"There's a bedroom in back." Malachi was carrying Leo, the tall man cradled like a child in his arms. Considering Leo was the tallest in the house, Ava wasn't quite sure how Malachi was even standing, but she didn't question it. She opened the door to the back to see a bed, narrow but clean. She knocked off the pillows and stripped off the covers, clearing the bed for the wounded man. Malachi laid him down gently, and Leo immediately curled to the side. Ava saw him bite his lip so hard that it bled.

"Rhys?" she asked.

"I lost my mobile. Do you have yours?"

"In my purse in the car."

"I'll get it. Stay with him and stay away from the windows."

"Can I turn on some lights?" The house wasn't pitch-black, but close. The windows let in light from the street lamp on the corner, but other than that, the low light in the front room was all that shone in the small apartment.

"Wait for now. There are more in the rooms upstairs and the windows are blacked out on that floor."

He ducked out of the room, and Ava heard him on the stairs as she sat next to Leo and stroked his forehead. His skin was starting to burn with fever, so she got up and looked for a washcloth or rag to cool him. She found a towel in the kitchen and returned to him, placing it on his forehead as he relaxed under her touch.

For the first time all day, Ava tried to gather her thoughts.

Jaron had been protecting her; she was almost sure of it. He might be evil—and nothing about their conversation had convinced her otherwise—but he had been protecting her for some reason.

Something very bad was happening among the fallen angels and the Grigori, and something in the city had shifted. Was it a coup like Maxim had predicted? If so, any protection Jaron had offered her was gone. There seemed to be countless Grigori in Istanbul, and they were bold enough to have burned the scribe house.

Ava had no idea where they would go. Did they have other safe houses? Should she go back to Los Angeles and take shelter in Carl's fortress of a house? Somehow, she doubted even her stepfather's hired guns could get her out of this mess. Besides, the thought of leaving Malachi was unthinkable at this point.

Reshon. She was the one saying it this time. The vision Jaron had given her only confirmed it.

I show you what has been. What will be. And what could be.

"What could be…," she whispered, still holding the cool rag to Leo's forehead.

They were her children. Hers and his. With her dark curls and Malachi's grey eyes.

"Do not fear the darkness."

Jaron's words caused her to shiver, even in the over-warm room. What had he shown her? Was it his vision or hers? And why had she seen her childhood? Had he been watching her since then?

Questions still swirled in her head as she heard Malachi climbing the stairs, talking quietly on the phone. He was just hanging up as he entered the room.

"Well?"

"Rhys is on his way. No car, so he's going to have to walk. They won't let him on a tram carrying coals in a clay cooking pot he stole from a restaurant, but they should last until he gets here and can stoke the fire again."

She heard Leo mutter something that sounded like relief.

"And that will heal him?"

Malachi winced, but his eyes did seem less strained. "How good are you at sewing?"

"Horrible."

Malachi opened the small closet and pulled out a black bag that he tossed on the end of the bed. "You can hold him down or sew him up. Sounds like our stitching's about the same. Leo, you have a preference?"

"I'll hold still," he muttered. "You do it, Mal. I'd rather curse at you than Ava."

Ava's stomach began to churn as Malachi stripped off Leo's shirt, peeling the cloth away from the clotted wound. "Can't we wait for Rhys?"

"He's bringing the fire to cauterize it," Malachi said. "We'll stitch it up, and Rhys will seal it. Has to be done, Ava."

"Just get it over with," Leo said. "If I'm lucky, I'll pass out again."

· · ·

MALACHI AND AVA WERE AS PALE AS LEO BY THE TIME RHYS SHOWED up. The wound was over eight inches in length, and it seemed like it took Malachi forever to stitch it after Ava had helped clear the blood as much as she could. According to Malachi, infection wouldn't be a problem. Once the fire cleansed the wound, Leo's own magic would heal him, and having Ava's hands on Leo during the stitches would boost his energy, since she was Irina.

"Irina are the best healers," Leo said, gritting his teeth as Rhys placed glowing coals on the mottled skin at his side. "My father said my m…mother could heal any wound. She studied medicine at university, even." A tight smile. "She dressed like a man so she could go. My father said he laughed and laughed, but really, he liked her wearing pants."

Malachi smiled, brushing back the young man's hair. "That's a good story, Leo. When did your father find you?"

"When Max and I were seven, he just showed up." He closed his eyes as a growl of pain rumbled from his chest. After another gasping breath, he said, "He didn't know we'd survived the Rending. He'd been in Russia killing Grigori. He was… a bit mad, to tell the truth. But he got better eventually."

"Ava, put your palm on his neck," Rhys said, grabbing her hand and placing it over Leo's rapid pulse. "Hold it there."

"What else can I do?" she asked, tears threatening. She felt helpless in the face of the young scribe's pain.

Rhys shook his head, singed hair falling in his eyes. "I don't know how it works. Think about making him well, maybe? I don't know Irina magic."

"There's a song," Leo said, his voice sounding dazed. "My father sang it when we were young. A song to make you feel better…" He started mumbling under his breath as his eyes drifted closed.

"She can't sing it yet," Malachi murmured. "Not yet, Leo. Soon she'll know the words. It's too dangerous for her now."

Too dangerous because she couldn't control her magic. For the first time, Ava felt the sting of resentment. Maybe if the Irina hadn't run away, she would know. If they hadn't run away, Leo wouldn't be suffering as much. Maybe she wouldn't have spent years thinking she was a freak for hearing voices. A bitter seed took root in her heart as she thought about all the Irin had lost.

"Ava," Malachi whispered, pulling her hand away. "He's sleeping now. Enough. You need to save your strength, too."

She was feeling it. For the first time since her night in Cappadocia with Malachi, the voices around her were completely silent. She must have expended far more energy than she realized, helping Leo to heal.

"Take her upstairs to rest," Rhys said. "I'll stay with Leo and keep the fire burning."

"Have we heard from Damien and Max yet?"

"Not yet. I'll keep Ava's phone, if that's all right. Hers is the only one working."

She nodded and let Malachi lead her up the stairs to a tiny bedroom with a small lamp. He turned it on and began to peel off her clothes as she sank into the mattress. She felt Malachi lay behind her as she curled on her side.

"Sleep, my love. Leo will be fine, and you need rest."

"Sleep with me," she said, half asleep before her head hit the pillow. "*Reshon.*"

CHAPTER

NINETEEN

eshon.

She called him *reshon*, and his heart soared. Despite the fear. Despite the loss. She called him *"reshon,"* and he was content. Malachi slept a few hours by her side, hand planted firmly on her soft skin, drawing and offering strength as she rested. But by the time he woke, he couldn't ignore the words Jaron had whispered in the Old Language before he shimmered out of sight.

"Thousands of you, Scribe. One of her. Remember."

Remember? How could he forget? The angel's meaning had been clear: Protect the Irina at all costs.

Whatever Jaron had showed her, Malachi hadn't seen. But clearly he'd been communicating with his mate in some way. The scene in the office flashed back to him. Jaron's transformation. Ava's awe. Their locked gazes held a secret that teased the edge of his mind. There was something…

"I didn't know. I didn't know…"

What had Jaron told her? Why had he been protecting her? There had to be a reason, but Malachi couldn't see what it was. As always, the motivations of the Fallen were incomprehensible. He wished Damien were here to counsel him, but he knew if the Watcher still lived after battling Brage's angelic sword, he was probably in a different safe house. It was better that they weren't all in one place. Had Damien already contacted Vienna? Did the Council know what was going on?

He had to get Ava out of Istanbul. He could drive across the country to Cappadocia, but getting her to Vienna would be better. He wished he knew where Sari was hiding. There was no fiercer Irina than Damien's mate. She would help him protect Ava; he knew it. Would Damien take them to Sari? Malachi felt like he was wandering in the dark forest of his dreams, stumbling through the fog and chasing answers to questions he didn't know. The house was utterly silent, but his mind was filled with disturbing and conflicting thoughts.

Ava stirred beside him.

"I can hear you thinking," she murmured. "Go back to sleep."

"Can't."

She pulled his hand up to her breast. "Then do something more entertaining than brooding."

Despite everything, she still made him smile. He bent down, kissing along her neck and caressing the skin of her breast, toying with her as his energy built.

Reshon.

A thought occurred to him. Ava wasn't in control of her magic, but there *was* a way to make her stronger. To lend her his own. She wouldn't be able to perform her half of the ritual—she didn't know the songs—but he could perform his half, lending her his power and protection. She would heal faster. She wouldn't tire. Her mind would be clearer and her sight better. If they were attacked again, it could mean the difference between life and death for her.

But not for you..., a small voice whispered. It would weaken him, because Ava couldn't lend her own magic.

Thousands of you, Scribe. One of her.

She turned to him, lifting her face for a kiss. He met her mouth with eager lips, delving in to taste and tease. She responded by pulling him closer, melding her body to his in the small bed as his skin sang where she touched it. More. He had to have more of her. Malachi pulled off his shirt and hers until their bodies were pressed together. He'd never felt more whole. More alive.

Reshon.

He pulled away with a gasp. Protecting Ava was imperative. He knew she was the key. And as her mate, Malachi was the only one who could offer her the strength.

"Malachi?" She sat up, her hair spilling over her shoulders in the low light.

"Wait here. I'll be right back." He whispered a kiss across her mouth before he stood and walked downstairs, all the way to the old rug shop. He walked past the showroom, looking into the back room where they stored the new pieces for shipment and also the tools to do repairs.

There, on the workbench, he found what he was looking for. He grabbed the dye and then looked for a brush but couldn't find one. Just then, he spied a child's painting in the corner, sitting on top of a small wooden box. Opening it, he saw a mess of watercolor paints and… He smiled. A brush. Not the best quality to touch his mate's skin, but it would have to do. Someday, they would complete the ritual, then he would brush her skin with sable and decorate her from head to toe. The mental image was unspeakably arousing, so he grabbed the vegetable dye and the child's brush before he headed back upstairs.

When he entered their small room, Ava was sitting in bed with a frown on her face.

"Where did you go?"

He placed the brush and dye on the side table and knelt beside her. "I wish we were not here. I wish we were someplace beautiful where I could stand with you before my mother and father and speak the old vows declaring you mine."

Her eyes filled with tears, but they didn't look sad. "Malachi—"

"I can't do that, Ava. But I want you to know, I would. I will, some-day. And before another hour passes, I want to say the words I can. Words that will mark you as my mate." He ran the tips of his fingers up her bare spine. "Write on your skin the spells that will bind us togeth-er." His fingers reached the nape of her neck as he bowed his face and kissed over her heart. "Will you let me, *reshon*? Will you take me, wholly and completely?"

"Tonight?"

"Right now."

"Your… mate?" She still hesitated at the word, but Malachi smiled.

"Yes."

"Forever?"

He looked up. "Forever. No turning away until death parts us."

A tentative smile crossed her lips. "I thought you guys were immortal."

He kissed her. "We're all immortal, Ava, as long as our stories are told." A small frown creased between her eyebrows, so he kissed her again. "Say yes."

"Yes."

"Yes?" He smiled.

"Yes, *reshon*." She placed her hands on his cheeks, stroking them despite the rasp of stubble. "You're mine. I knew it weeks ago. So yes."

Desire roared to life, but Malachi clamped down on it and said, "Take off your clothes. All of them."

"Every stitch?" The teasing light came back.

"Every. Single. Stitch." He pulled back the cover and reached for the jar of dye.

"What is that?" she asked as she pulled off her underthings.

"Henna dye. It's actually what we've always used, but I apologize for the brush." He shook up the dye and then uncapped it, dipping the rough brush into the jar before he looked up. "It should be much nicer than this."

"What do I do?" she asked, her voice tentative in the silence.

"Turn around," Malachi said. "Hold still. And let me mark you."

Ava pulled up her legs and turned her back to him. Malachi sat on the edge of the bed and took a deep breath. He'd dreamed of this moment for hundreds of years. Granted, the surroundings were usually a little more luxurious, but the sight before him…

Ava's smooth back, pale and glowing in the lamplight. The fine bones of her spine guiding him from the base of her skull to the swell of her buttocks. She was more than he'd dreamt. More than he deserved.

Malachi leaned forward, whispering the ancient vows against her skin, and his breath cast a golden glow as the magic took hold. He lifted the brush and began.

He wrote the spells across her body, the dye taking hold as the magic did. And though the henna would fade with time, the magic would remain, imbued in her skin. Protecting her. Strengthening her. For the rest of her life, his words would mark her. He took care as he wrote, hundreds of years of practice suddenly making sense. Countless hours of instruction. No mistakes were allowed in this; it was the most important *talesm* he would ever scribe.

Protective spells formed down her back. Whispered aloud as he felt the magic leave his body and enter hers. His lips trailed after his brush, kissing along her backbone as her heart raced beneath his mouth.

"Is it…" She arched her back when she felt the brush trail low. "Is it supposed to feel like this?"

He couldn't stop the smile of satisfaction. "This is the ritual performed on the mating night. Does it please you?"

She gasped as the brush moved over the base of her spine. She said, "That would be a yes."

Ava's scent bloomed and Malachi had to pause, breathing deeply as his forehead rested on her shoulder. "*Reshon.* Ava…"

"Keep going," she said, desire lacing her voice. "Don't stop."

Minutes turned to hours. She turned when he told her, baring the front of her body when her back and neck were covered with spells.

The spells for longevity were next, arching along her fine collarbone. Malachi groaned when he saw the golden flush across her throat. Her breasts. Her belly. The brush dipped and traced over and over, the ink darkening and drying as the magic glowed beneath it. She appeared lit from within. He bent his head and let his mouth suckle her breast, giving in to the arousal that had become almost unbearable.

She moaned and leaned back. "Malachi?"

"Almost done."

Spells for increased strength along her arms. Speed on her thighs. Spells for healing across her breasts and belly. He felt the magic leave him, knew he was giving almost dangerously of his own power, but he couldn't stop.

Her energy spilled over, and he felt the hum begin to build in the air.

"Soon?" She panted.

"Soon."

The last spells were over her heart, circling around as he pledged himself to her. He dipped in the dye again, then the brush met her skin as Malachi marked her as his mate. The balance of his soul. The bearer of his young. No other would mark her like this. No one but him. The possessive instinct swamped him as he finished the last stroke of the mating ritual. He braced himself over her, allowing the ink to dry as he drank from her lips. Over and over, she met him, as hungry for him as he was for her.

Patience.

Malachi was aroused to the point of pain. His breath came in rasps as her kisses drugged him, making his head spin. He clenched his hands in the loose sheets, allowing the magic to build and grow until her body was covered in a gold glow answered by his own *talesm*, which shone with a low silver light in the darkness. His magic swelled in recognition of its twin, even without the songs the Irina usually sang. Though untrained, Ava's magic was powerful. It called to him as their mouths met in aching hunger.

"Do you hear that?" she said, tearing her lips from his, bracing her hands on his shoulders.

"What?"

"That note. I…" Tears touched her eyes, but she smiled. "It's beautiful. Perfect. It's… us."

Complete.

Silver met gold when he tackled her to the bed.

Finally.

His body sang in recognition. Here was desire. Here was beauty. Here was completion. He reached down to test her, but Ava was as ready as he was, her body primed from hours of waiting.

"Yes!" She gripped his arms. "Now, *please.*"

He entered her with one thrust, halting when he was seated to the hilt, his forehead pressed to hers as they groaned in unison.

"Yes," she whispered. "Like this. Always like this."

He took her mouth again, leisurely tasting as he began a slow rhythm. She embraced him, arms wrapped around his chest, legs around his hips. The urgency was there, but Malachi didn't want to rush.

"Faster," she said.

He smiled. "No."

She dug her nails in his shoulders, and he bit back a moan. Then he reached down, gripping her hip and changing the angle until her head fell back and her body bowed. He took his time, ignoring her pleas to rush, delighting in her response as he tested their new connection. Her pleasure was his own. Her desire fed his. He held back— barely—when she came the first time. Then his body picked up a faster rhythm as the world narrowed to her.

"Again," he whispered.

"Can't."

"Yes, you can." He could feel it. Feel her body around him. The slow tightening. The catch in her breath. The pressure built as he flipped them over, letting her arch back over him as he watched her skin luminesce gold, alive with the ancient magic of their race.

This.

There was no greater beauty in heaven or earth.

"Again."

"Yes!"

Ava cried out as she came and Malachi's mind flew, her body pulling the long-awaited climax from him as he came in a roar of heat and light, his hands gripping her hips as his own back arched. His *talesm* shone bright silver in the darkness, then his mate fell forward, panting against his chest as he wrapped his arms around her and closed his eyes.

This is why the angels fell.

H E WOKE SLOWLY; THE SUN SHINING THROUGH THE BLACKED-OUT windows cast eerie shadows in the room. Ava was still draped over his torso, exhausted by their lovemaking. Most of the dye had rubbed off during the night, leaving the red-brown henna patterns that mirrored his tattoos. His immediate reaction was to wake her and claim her body again, but he knew she needed sleep. He covered her with a light blanket and wrapped a towel around his body before he walked downstairs.

"Any change?" he asked Rhys, who still sat by Leo's bedside, drowsy in the brighter light of the second-story room.

"He's cooler. The wound is healing. He started getting some real sleep after you two quieted down."

"We weren't that loud."

"It wasn't the sound, it was the energy, for heaven's sake. You forget how young he is. If his body had let him, he would have gone charging into the night, desperate to find a woman."

"Sorry." Malachi pulled up a chair opposite his friend.

"No, you're not." Rhys's gaze flickered down to Malachi's hands, still stained from the henna dye. His eyes widened. "You marked her."

"I did."

"Malachi—"

"It was necessary."

"No, it wasn't. She doesn't know the other half of the ritual. You've given her half your magic with nothing in return."

"Don't say that." He glared. "Don't ever say that. If she was yours, you'd understand."

Rhys opened his mouth to speak but closed it again. After a few tense moments, he said, "You'll be weak."

"And she'll be strong."

"This is the worst time for you to indulge in sentimental—"

"It was necessary, Rhys." He bit back the urge to yell. "When we spoke to Jaron, he said something."

"What could he possibly have said that would make you risk your life—?"

"It was a warning. One of her, Rhys." His friend fell silent as Malachi spoke. "One of her. Thousands of us. She was sent to me for a reason. I have to protect her."

"We will all protect her, brother."

"I'm counting on that. If anything happens to me… I'm counting on that. Do you understand?"

Rhys's eyes finally met his intense gaze. "I understand. I would treat her as my own blood. You know this."

"Thank you."

"But seeing as you're her one true love, you'd better make this promise unnecessary. Do *you* understand?"

Malachi grinned. "You think I want to give her up after I've just found her? Think again. You'd have her forgetting me in no time."

His brother cleared his throat and forced a smile. "No, I wouldn't."

"No, you wouldn't."

"You need to get her out of the city."

"Has Maxim called?"

"No, but I know he keeps an extra car not far from here. With unknown Fallen activity and so many Grigori in the city, that's probably the safest route. If you can just get her out of the city, you'll buy yourself some time."

"Vienna?"

Rhys shrugged. "For now? Yes. But she needs to find someone to train her. After her safety, that's the first priority. Even untrained, her magic is powerful. She's like a loaded gun. She's been good about not speaking in the Old Language, but with your magic running through her veins now, the temptation to use it is going to be stronger. She might not even be able to control it."

"Irina, then."

"Irina. You need to find a group of them. Sari's faction would be the best, if Damien would tell you where they are."

"She's forbidden it. You know how she feels about males now."

Rhys nodded toward the stairs. "But you're not a lone male looking for a woman. You're bringing your mate with you for help. She won't leave an Irina unable to use her magic. It goes against everything she stands for."

Malachi nodded, thinking about their options. "She's rumored to be in Scandinavia somewhere."

"Somewhere. It's a big region."

"And Brage is on the hunt. He's Volund's offspring. If Volund is behind this aggression, Scandinavia may be the last place I want to take her."

"Or it may be the last place he'd look." Rhys leaned over and wiped at Leo's brow, which was still dotted with perspiration. "If you get her out of the city, you two will have time to think. You'll have to find documents for her, anyway. Though if you can find Maxim, it's possible he already has them prepared."

"He's cautious like that."

"He is."

As if called by the gods, Ava's phone rang. Rhys smiled and handed it to Malachi. "Speak of the devil."

Malachi took the phone and saw Maxim's number on the screen. "Hello?"

"Finding unlisted mobile numbers is a pain in the ass, Malachi. Add her to the contact list, will you?"

He let out a sigh of relief and walked upstairs. "As if you already haven't."

"You are correct, old man. How's my cousin?" A slight hitch in his throat was the only clue how worried Maxim was.

"He'll be fine. Do you know about the house?"

"Yes. Did anyone retrieve the fire for him?"

"Rhys managed, but his hair's a bit shorter."

"We both owe him a debt."

"Which I'm sure he'll collect. How badly damaged was the house?"

"Not as much as we thought. The firefighters did an excellent job. I'm guessing whoever set it was trying to scatter us."

"So they succeeded."

"To an extent. Damien and I got hit with tear gas of all things after we got away last night. He's mad as hell this morning, but not damaged."

"We're lucky."

"You need a way out of the city. Damien has already called Vienna about the house, so they know some of what is happening. He was very closemouthed about your mate, though."

For some reason, Malachi was relieved. He didn't know why, but he felt like the less people knew about Ava, the better. "I'm not sure where we should go. Rhys said Scandinavia, but I need to speak to Damien about that."

"You're looking for Sari?"

"If she'll allow us sanctuary."

Maxim's low whistle was all the response Malachi expected.

"I'd tread carefully there. Luckily, I have obtained new documents for both of you. British passports, so you'll have no trouble traveling, but you'll have to be quick about it. Tonight. The row of hotels by the Theodosius Cistern. Go there. I have a spare vehicle at the Antea Hotel, right across from the entrance. The cistern is closed for renovation, so that area is quiet. Your keys and documents should be waiting at the front desk by seven o'clock."

"And if they're not?"

"Find a room. I'm sure you two will be able to keep yourselves occupied."

Malachi smiled when he saw Ava's eyes flicker open. "You'd be correct."

"You're not nice when you gloat, brother. I have to go."

"Wait, Maxim. Is Brage still in the city?"

"As far as I know."

Malachi sat on the edge of the bed, and Ava leaned over his shoulder, her ear to the phone.

Maxim said, "Damien wounded him, but not seriously. He'll be healed by tonight, if not sooner."

"Does he still have the blade?"

"He does," Maxim said. "Damn thing nearly hit one of my arms. I really have to go. Keep this phone with you. Tell Rhys to keep the fire burning. We'll find him and Leo later."

"I will."

He hit the End Call button and tossed the phone on the bedside table, turning so that Ava was pressed against his chest. Then he lay back, taking her with him.

"You've got to stop wandering off after we have mind-blowing sex," she said, snuggling into his chest.

"So… every morning then?"

She pinched his arm. "Cocky."

"Yes." Malachi pressed a kiss to her hair. "Did you hear Max?"

"Yes." Her eyes widened. "Every word, actually. My hearing is super strong right now."

"It's super strong forever, *canım*."

"And my eyes…" She looked around the dark room and frowned. "What did you do?"

He shrugged. "It's part of the mating ritual. I gave you some of my magic. And you'll give me yours. Eventually."

"But until then?" Ava sat up, eyes racing over his chest. "What do you mean, you gave me your magic? Does that mean you're not as strong?"

He reached for her cheek, but she pushed his hand away. "Ava—"

"No! Is that what it means?"

"I'm still very, very strong. We'll be fine. Do you really doubt me?"

Her face fell, and her eyes took on a faraway look. "I can't lose you, Mal."

"You won't."

"Trusting you—trusting *us*—was it for me. If something happened to you—"

"Nothing will happen to me. I'm too greedy. I'll never leave you." He sat up and pulled her into his arms. "We're almost there. Max has a car for us. Documents. We'll leave the city tonight. Sleep today and leave tonight. We'll be away before they can find us, and then we'll be safe." He brushed a hand over her curls, soothing her as she trembled in his arms. "Trust me, Ava. You'll be safe."

CHAPTER
TWENTY

The Antea Hotel sat on the corner of the Piyerloti Caddesi, just at the end of a quiet string of hotels. A few hundred meters from the tourist center, the old street was sheltered by tall trees and staid municipal buildings. A quiet street in the Sultanahmet, but still central enough to the main thoroughfare, it was the perfect place to store an emergency vehicle.

Malachi held Ava's hand as they crossed the intersection, passing the empty cistern and the fountain in the center of the square. Pigeons startled from the sidewalk, but no other pedestrians interrupted them as they made their way into the lobby.

The young woman at the front desk eyed Malachi, causing an unexpected flair of possessiveness in Ava that caught her by surprise. Since the night before, she'd been on edge, bristling with borrowed energy and heightened senses. The passing cars distracted her. The lights were too bright. But her voices, thankfully, had become easier to ignore. The only one she heard clearly was Malachi.

"Good afternoon, sir," the woman said in perfect British English. "How may I help you?"

Malachi lowered his voice and switched to Turkish as Ava took in the gold-accented lobby. It wasn't the fanciest hotel she'd seen, but it was clean and bright. The ground floor was quiet.

Almost too quiet.

Instincts pricked when Malachi took her hand and led her out toward the sidewalk.

"The car is here, but she said our package hasn't arrived yet. She suggested waiting in their restaurant, but I'd rather be out here."

"Me too." Ava looked around at the peaceful street that suddenly seemed ominous. "I don't like it here."

He frowned and smoothed a hand over her cheek. "What do you hear?"

"Nothing specific."

"Then we have to—"

"Not enough," she said in a low voice. "It's too quiet. Where are the other guests? There aren't even any tourists around here."

"It's the middle of the week, *canm*. I think you may be overreacting." He raised a hand when she opened her mouth. "Which is completely normal considering your new senses."

She shook her head but couldn't find anything to argue with in his reasoning. He was probably right.

Since the mating ritual, Ava had been flooded with power. She was stronger. Quicker. She healed faster. She'd deliberately taken a knife to her forearm that afternoon while Malachi had been napping, just to see what would happen. The cut she'd made on her forearm had healed within minutes.

He was stroking her hair, leading them to the bench by the locked cistern. Ava looked at the sign announcing the renovations. It was in Turkish, but she could see the future plans for the new tourist attraction around the historic site.

"Did you get the car keys?" she asked when they'd sat.

"Yes. She said the messenger already called to say he'd be late. She said he'd probably arrive in the next half an hour."

"And Damien? Max?"

"Headed over to the rug shop right now. We'll call them once we get on the highway."

Ava nodded, a sense of unease still heavy in her belly.

"It's fine, *reshon*. Everything will be fine."

MALACHI WATCHED HER, WONDERING WHAT HAD HAPPENED TO THE confident, fearless woman he loved. Since the night before, she was jumpy. A cloud seemed to hang over her shoulders. Was she truly that worried, or was their new intimacy making him more aware of her moods?

It wasn't uncommon for Irin mated for years to be almost telepathic with each other. Though they couldn't speak to each other's minds, the awareness of mood was hard to ignore. He'd know when she was angry or happy. Upset. Worried. He felt them all now as her emotions flooded the magic he'd given her. It was both intoxicating and distracting, and for the first time, he wondered whether the ritual had been the right thing to do.

Too late to second-guess himself.

Malachi watched the front of the hotel as two men exited. They looked up and down the street, then sauntered off in the direction of the Sultanahmet tram station. A few minutes later, a couple entered the hotel from the opposite side. Normal traffic on a quiet afternoon.

And still Ava sat, a silent knot of tension at his side.

"Tell me a story," she finally said.

"What kind of story?"

"Something not serious. What's your favorite childhood memory?"

He broke into a smile. "Swimming at the beach. We'd go to the North Sea in the summer when we lived in Germany."

"Wasn't that cold?"

"Freezing." He put an arm around her, thankful for the distraction. "My father had a good friend with a cabin there. I think it's still there, probably. It was quite old, but very nice. My mother and father and I would stay for two months in the summer. Living in a retreat can be very hectic sometimes. Families live in their own homes, but the children go to school together, the adults all work together. Even meals are communal. So my parents tried to make some time for only the three of us. That was our family time. I would play in the water even though it was frigid. My mother thought I was crazy."

A tentative smile crossed her face. "You were."

"We should go there," he said. "When we have children, we'll take them there."

There was a smile on her face. "We should." Ava took a deep breath. "We'll really have children, Malachi?"

"Hopefully." He squeezed her. "Irin don't have many children. One is normal. Two is fortunate. But I hope we have two."

· · ·

The vision of children Jaron had sent her flashed in her mind again. A dark-haired boy with his father's eyes. A golden-eyed girl laughing. It should have warmed her, but there was a dark side to the vision, as well. The animals had stood at attention, prowling around the girl and boy. Clearly guarding them, but from what?

"Do not fear the darkness."

The memory of Jaron's voice calmed her as she sat. Then she tensed again when she felt Malachi's arm tighten.

"What is it?"

"Grigori," he said, freezing as he watched two men enter the hotel lobby. "Two of them just walked in. Damn it."

Ava looked around them. They were completely exposed in the center of the square. There were no barricades to hide behind, no buildings they could duck into without being conspicuous.

"I can't kill them in the hotel lobby or out in the open here," Malachi said. "We'll have to wait for them to come out. Draw them somewhere isolated."

"Is it just the two?" Ava's eyes landed on the grated door of the Theodosius Cistern. Though it was locked, it was only with a simple padlock. No guards stood nearby. And the dark passageway had a view of the hotel.

"More coming this way," he murmured, taking her hand. "From the direction of the mosque."

Looking uphill, Ava spotted two attractive men strolling down the street toward them. They were looking toward the hotel, not at Ava and Malachi, but Ava knew as soon as they saw their friends leave the lobby, the Grigori would start looking for them.

"More from that street, too." Malachi pulled out Ava's phone and sent a quick text to someone. Somehow the drop location had been compromised.

"We have to get out of here," he said.

"How?" Ava's heart raced. Six streets converged at the cistern park, and from each direction, a group of men strolled toward them. There were two there. Three there. "Malachi, they've cornered us."

"No," he muttered. "There has to be a way…" His eyes landed on the locked grate leading to the cistern entry just as the call to prayer started and birds scattered in flight. The Grigori converging on the square turned their heads toward the mosque on Divan Yolu, and

Malachi used the distraction to drag Ava toward the cistern. "This way."

"That goes underground!" she hissed. It was one thing to stroll through the Basilica Cistern with its dramatic columns and modern walkways, but the Theodosius Cistern looked like nothing but a black cave. "Malachi…"

"We'll watch and wait for now," he said, twisting off the lock that held the grate closed. He opened the door, and Ava was grateful the calls of the muezzin hid the rusty groan. "We can see the entrance of the hotel from here. There are too many to fight alone while I'm not at full strength. If we run, they'll catch us. Until Max and Damien get here, we need to hide."

She knew that ritual had been a bad idea. The thought of a weakened Malachi sent her heart into overdrive. "Did you text them already?"

"Yes." He shoved her farther into the shadowed passageway, and Ava almost tripped over the heavy rubber boots covered in mud that the workmen had left on the platform. "They should come soon. They'll create a distraction, and we'll grab the car. We can figure out documents later. Right now, I just want you out of this city."

"Okay."

Malachi sucked in his breath and darted back from the door. "Brage."

Ava's heart sank. From the darkness of the metal walkway, she could see the blond Grigori soldier walking out of the Antea Hotel and turning his head to look up and down the street. His eyes were narrowed with purpose.

The soldiers knew they were nearby.

MALACHI SHOT OFF ANOTHER TEXT TO MAX, WHO HAD YET TO respond. Where the hell was he? Annoyance and worry competed in his mind. What had happened to the documents? Had Maxim been set up? And further, how could Malachi get the car from the hotel while avoiding the dozen or more Grigori who had taken up residence at the intersection?

When he realized who the blond Grigori outside the hotel was, thoughts of the car fled. He had to get Ava away. Eyes darting into the blackness, he racked his memories for everything he knew about the cistern where they were hiding. It was an old one, and he suspected it connected to the Valens Aqueduct, the ancient waterway the Romans had built to transport water throughout the city. Many of the cisterns still had tunnels leading between them. Was the Theodosius one of them?

Malachi tossed one last look toward the square. The sky was growing dim, and the street lights in front of the hotel had switched on. He could see Brage and the other Grigori milling in front of the hotel. He could wait for them to leave the square, or he could look for another way out.

He looked down to the boots at their feet, then bent down to slip on the biggest pair, handing another to Ava.

"Put these on."

"Where are we going?"

"Down." He saw a small flashlight near the edge of the platform. Flicking it on and hoping the light wouldn't be seen from outside, he peered over the edge. "We're going to see if there's a tunnel."

"What?" Ava squeaked. She might have protested, but she was already pulling on the boots. "We're going farther down? Shouldn't we wait here for Max and Damien?"

"And wait for Brage to notice the broken lock on the gate?" Standing in the boots, he tested them, finding himself not unbearably clumsy in the yellow rubber footwear. "There could be a tunnel out of here. There often are in these old places. And if they do find us in here, I want a wall to my back and you behind me. It'll be easier to kill them if I don't have to worry about them coming from all directions."

He didn't mention Brage wielding an angelic blade. That was the real problem.

"I knew you shouldn't have given me a bunch of your magic," she said, pulling on the second boot.

Malachi was doubly glad that he had. If she was injured in all this, improved healing could be the difference between life and death for her. And with Ava's improved eyesight, they barely had to use the flashlight.

"Come on." He took her hand and started down the creaking staircase.

"Are you sure this thing is safe?"

"Workmen have been climbing up and down on this for months, so I hope so." He paused when one of the steps wobbled under his feet.

Then he started climbing at a slower pace. "We're not that heavy. We'll be fine."

Once they'd safely reached the bottom, Malachi turned on the light. Sweeping it from side to side, he could see the soaring columns belted by steel bands for reinforcement, marching like grey soldiers into the black. The domes of the cistern towered over them, the ancient brick causing the slightest noise to echo. He could hear water dripping overhead and the splash of muddy water as Ava walked behind him.

"They're renovating it right now," he whispered, "but it used to have as much water as the Basilica Cistern."

"Looks more like mud to me." She almost tripped over a shovel leaning against the wall. "Holy cow, it stinks."

"People throw all sorts of things down here. Try not to think about it."

Malachi carefully led them around the periphery of the cavern, but he couldn't spot a tunnel or other exit. If there had been one, it was closed off or under mud or brick. The water grew deeper the farther they went, and thick mud sucked at their feet.

"Anything from Max or Damien?" she whispered behind him.

He glanced at the phone. "I can't get any reception down here. I told them where we were hiding. I just hope they get the message."

"If they don't... then what?"

Then what? He had no idea.

Ava's sense of dread grew with every step they took into the dark cavern. The water sloshed at their feet, and the flashlight seemed unbearably bright in the pitch-black underground. She was certain anyone looking in from outside would see it.

"You know," she whispered, glad her voice didn't waver, "of all the sights for us to see, this is one I probably could have skipped."

"I did promise to show you an authentic side of the city." He scooped up a dead fish and tossed it to the side.

"Malachi?"

"Yes?"

"I love you, even though you're dragging me through really stinky water and mud right now."

He turned and she could see his smile even in the darkness. "I love you, too. I say we deserve a vacation after this is over. Didn't you mention you were rich?"

"Extremely."

"Know any places with better water and less dead fish?"

"I just might."

She saw his shoulders shake with laughter as they continued working their way around the walls of the cistern. Despite careful inspection, no tunnel appeared. No alternate exit presented itself.

Finally, Ava sighed and said, "It's been a while. Maybe they're gone. Or some have left and we could sneak away. We should go check to see if they're—"

The sound of the door creaking stopped her. All ease fled as she heard the whispered voices from the platform above.

It wasn't Damien or Max.

HEART RACING, MALACHI TRACED OVER HIS *TALESM PRIM*, ACTIVATING the magic that remained. He was still strong. Still able. He would be able to defend her. He felt the creep of magic and took her hand, slowly moving behind one pillar and out of the line of sight from the door. He listened.

"—gate open."

"Is this cistern linked through the tunnels?"

"I don't think so."

They were speaking German, the rough syllables echoing over the water as he and Ava stood as statues in the dark. Even a ripple in the water would give them away. She was pressed against him, her heart racing against his chest, but her breathing was deliberately slow. She was concentrating on not panicking.

Good girl.

If they could just remain silent enough...

"There are lights."

Malachi heard a fumbling on the platform, and then the cistern was flooded with work lights hanging from various pillars.

Damn.

Another, heavier step sounded on the metal platform. The other Grigori fell silent.

"I can smell your fear, Scribe."

Brage's deep voice didn't boom. It curled and twisted in the darkness, seeking them where they hid. Malachi felt Ava tremble.

"The scribe and the woman are here," Brage said. "Spread out. Find them."

As soon as he heard the splashes, Malachi moved. Carefully stepping in the shadows, he went farther into the cistern, toward the deeper water where the mud lay thick on the bottom of the floor.

The Grigori were as slow as Malachi and Ava were, their normal speed negated by the pulling mud. He wrapped an arm around Ava to still her so he could listen.

One.

Two. Three.

Four in the water.

Splash!

Five.

A louder splash as one jumped from the railing and into the water.

Six.

"Matteus. Alfred. Stand watch with Mikael by the fountain. If any of the others scribes approach, alert me."

Brage. Three by the fountain. By Malachi's calculations, that meant eight in the cistern. Two more splashes confirmed his estimate, then the water fell silent, save for the isolated curses as the Grigori tripped over each other and the detritus of the work site.

Ava's hand squeezed his own, and he had to force her to release it so he could grab the silver daggers he wore under his shirt. He frowned. Weaponless. His mate was weaponless.

That is, she was weaponless until he saw her pick up the crowbar from a niche in the wall.

He smiled proudly.

"I think I saw some ripples in the water over there!" one said.

"Where?"

"Are there fish in this water? It could be fish."

"Yes. I feel them."

They moved deeper, Ava had sunk to the waist, but was still moving slowly, deliberately, behind him. He'd spotted a corner earlier where he thought she'd be best protected. A round, half dome carved into the wall. He suspected it had once been a walled-off exit, but nothing remained except a few steps. He didn't have time to investigate more.

Once they got there, he drew up her arm and started writing with his finger. The low luminescent writing was hidden in the shadows.

He hoped.

Stay here. I'm going to even the odds.

She shook her head violently, but he kept writing.

Use the crowbar.

He had to wait for the letters to fade before he wrote again.

Swing for the neck and the groin. Don't hesitate. If you can sink the clawed end into a neck, PULL. Do as much damage as possible and stay as quiet as you can. I'll be back.

She shook her head again, tears at the corners of her eyes. Malachi bent down, kissing them away before he whispered, "Don't worry. I told you, I'll be back."

Then he slipped into the darkness.

AVA WANTED TO SCREAM. SHE FELT HELPLESS. CHOKED BY SILENCE, mysterious words whispered in her mind, teasing her as she waited in the darkness. The Old Language called her, the magic begging at her lips.

Powerless.

She was stronger. Faster. Healed more quickly. But she knew nothing about how to protect herself or make her mate stronger. She gripped the cold, gritty handle of the crowbar and lifted it against the dark, tensing when she heard the first sounds of struggle.

CHAPTER
TWENTY-ONE

Malachi slid through the shadows of the cistern, sneaking behind the first soldier and sliding a hand to cover his mouth as the dagger plunged into the monster's spine. The Grigori stiffened, arched, then began to dissolve. The dust lifted in the darkness, pulled by an unseen wind. He spun and darted behind the next pillar, waiting for the other Grigori to react.

"I see dust!"

"He's here."

"Where?"

"In the cistern."

"We already knew that, you idiot."

They were speaking a mix of German, Turkish, and Danish, with muttered curses in at least two other languages. These Grigori were not from Istanbul. Who had sent them? Who was pulling Brage's strings?

Malachi hid behind another pillar, darting out to grab another. He quickly dispatched him as the others scrambled in the water. Two down, six to go. His legs, long used to the strength of his immortal power, ached in the cold water, but pure adrenaline pushed him. He had to keep them away from his mate.

"Work along the walls," Brage said. "You idiots! Forget him. We want the woman. Drive her to me."

Eyes narrowing, Malachi stepped into the light, drawing their attention to him and away from Ava.

"There!"

Two Grigori rushed him, and Malachi was soon lost to the battle. Splashes sounded from overhead as more soldiers fell into the water, heading toward him. Then more shouting as he slashed and stabbed.

Another to dust. Another.

He ducked and twisted, using them against each other in the confusion of the dark water. Many ended up stabbing each other, their blades diverted from his skin by the spells that still protected him. The ones that did land hurt, but not enough to make him pause. It was their numbers that overwhelmed him. As more poured in, Malachi lost count of how many he fought. His only thought was to move toward the exit, drawing them away from Ava.

"One of her. Thousands of you, Scribe."

Protect Ava.

He ducked under the water, crouching down, only to burst up, blades flying, catching two Grigori under the chin and throwing them back as their blood sprayed the slick pillars of the cistern.

He slashed again and again until the muddy water was black with spilled blood. And still the corner where Ava hid was silent.

She watched, lip clenched between her teeth, biting back the screams as she watched him battle. Four Grigori were on him, one slashing his back, another diving for his neck, only to trip over something in the water and fall down, taking out another who approached him.

He fought like a raging beast, his muscles straining, his *talesm* glowing in the harsh light and shadows of the underground cavern. Blood poured from a gash at his temple and she cried when a soldier pierced his side.

Still he fought.

But he wasn't healing.

She'd seen him. Seen the cuts heal in Kuşadası. Seen the unflagging energy. But she knew as he wavered after throwing off an attacker…

He was going to lose.

There were too many. No help came. And a seemingly endless

stream of attackers approached. No sooner had he dusted one than another fell on him.

Ava bit back a sob. He was going to lose. He wasn't strong enough. Because of her.

Furious music pulsed in her head. Ancient songs beat at her.

A low humming chant echoed in a latent part of her mind.

Ava opened her mouth just as shouts echoed from the top of the cistern.

"Malachi?"

She let out a cry of relief when she heard Damien's voice, and two soldiers turned to the dark corner where she hid. Their eyes lit up with predatory glee as they turned to her, and Ava raised the crowbar again.

"Get to Ava!" Malachi shouted, still throwing off his attackers, some of whom had turned to the door. Ava's eyes scanned the darkness. She moved back and forth, trying to see beyond the forest of pillars.

Where was Brage?

The pale Grigori with the angel's blade was her greatest fear. She had no idea what would happen to Malachi if he was hit by the weapon in his condition. Would he be able to hold on as long as Leo had?

"Do you see her?"

"I think so."

The two soldiers drew closer. There was no avoiding them. They were headed straight for her. Ava didn't wait.

Throwing herself into the light with a guttural shout, she flung herself at the first one, swinging the crowbar down where his neck met his shoulder. She felt the bar sink in as the man's eyes went wide with shock; then she pulled. He tumbled forward with a splash, and Ava gasped at her own strength. A chunk of flesh ripped from the man's neck, and his collarbone was slick with blood, sticking out from the top of his chest as he flopped in the water like a wounded carp.

The other Grigori stood still for a moment, then raised a sword, only to look at it with wide eyes and lower it again.

They aren't supposed to hurt me, Ava realized with grim satisfaction.

She plunged forward, eyes focused on the man's neck, but he dodged to the side and grabbed her, tearing the crowbar from her hands as he tried to lift her from the water. She resisted for a few moments, her boots stuck in the thick mud, but eventually he tugged again, and her feet came free.

"No!" she screamed as he threw her over his shoulder. "NO!"

"Ava!"

MALACHI SAW THE GRIGORI LIFT HER, TOSSING HER OVER HIS SHOULDER like baggage. He started trudging toward the exit, moving as quickly as he could in the heavy water. He was fighting two soldiers, feeling weaker by the moment, but he saw Max spot Ava as Damien sliced his way through the Grigori who swarmed them.

"Max, get Ava!" he yelled as loud as he could. The cistern was filled with the sounds of splashes and grunts, blades ringing against the stone pillars and men crying out in pain. Through it all, Malachi didn't think. He kept going, his single focus to move toward the soldier with his mate.

Get Ava. Escape the cistern.

Something tugged at his leg, but he kicked it away, losing one of the boots and a shoe at the same time. Sharp stones dug into his foot when he set it down again, and he could feel them pierce his flesh.

Damien moved toward him, throwing off the soldier who had attached himself to Malachi's back and was trying to grab his weapons. Most of the Grigori had lost their knives in the fight, the blades falling into the water as they struggled.

Malachi held on.

"Max, she's there!"

"I see her!"

He saw his brother head toward Ava, slicing through two Grigori, dusting one and throwing another into the darkness with a roar.

Almost there.

The lights flickered. Went out.

Ava screamed.

On again.

She'd been stabbed in the fighting. Blood poured from her belly, and he saw her face pale.

"Ava!"

Their eyes met in the flickering light as Malachi raced toward her as fast as he could, his heart beating out of his chest and blood dripping into his eyes.

"Hold on!"

"Malachi, no!"

Just then, a large soldier tackled him from behind a pillar. He knocked Malachi down. The water enveloped him as a painful scream filled the air.

THE MAGIC RAGED THROUGH HER, CLOSING THE WOUND ON HER BELLY, and Ava's soul rose in fear and fury. Through the pain, her voice lifted, echoing against the ancient stones.

The songs rang in her mind. The magic called her.

Speak, the seductive voice whispered.

More. Higher. Louder.

Ava's voice rose in pain and anger. She screamed out against the voices in her mind.

The soldier holding her faltered. One hand came up to his ear as he stumbled. She saw others clutching their heads. Blood poured between their fingers.

The lights went on. Then off. On again.

Finally, the one holding Ava dropped her, and she splashed in the water as the soldier ran. Everything was dark and silent for a moment before she surfaced, spitting out the foul water that had filled her mouth. She blinked her eyes, looking for danger. The Grigori who had captured her was pushing for the exit even as Max cut him down. She couldn't see Malachi, but she saw Max. Blood ran from his eyes and ears, but he kept coming toward her.

More Grigori ran past, two scrambling up the stairs as she brushed the damp hair from her face and blinked the mud from her eyes. Max finally reached her.

"You're fine, Ava. You're all right."

"Where's Malachi?"

A voice from the darkness. "I'm here, Ava." He emerged from the shadows, wading through the waist-deep water with a crooked smile. "What was that, love?"

Ava burst out with a sobbing laugh. "I have no idea."

She saw Damien and Malachi on the other side of the cistern. Damien smiled, even as he killed another Grigori with a dagger to his spine. The dust hung like a fog over their heads, wafting toward the exit where the rest of the soldiers had fled. Malachi stood, clutching his side, leaning against a pillar and panting. Blood ran from his eyes and nose, but he smiled anyway, staring across the water.

Come to me.

For a split second, she could hear the thought in his mind.

Ava stood and started running toward him as fast as she could, barely noticing the shadow moving in the corner of her eye.

The shadow rose from the water, blue eyes gleaming in the darkness and blade glinting in the light.

Ava's heart stopped.

Silence.

Malachi stilled as the blade pierced his spine, his eyes locking with hers.

Grey eyes wide in the darkness.

She fell. Her knees gave out.

Cold water rose to her chest.

Her mate's mouth dropped open with a silent cry as Brage's blade plunged in, then his face shone gold.

"NO!" Max's voice behind her.

Gold. He was gold. Shimmering in the darkness. Beautiful. Radiant.

Malachi's visage flickered as the dust began to rise.

Ava's heart beat once, then she heard another long scream.

Silence as her eardrums burst. Her vision went black as the gold dust rose like a ghost in the darkness.

Then the water enveloped her and everything was gone.

CHAPTER
TWENTY-TWO

Blackness. Silence.

She heard groans and knew they came from her throat.

Her chest ached. Her ears hurt. Everything hurt.

Someone was carrying her, but it wasn't him.

"What happened? *What happened?*"

"Gone," she whispered when she heard his brother's voice.

She saw it again. Her mate's radiant face before it dissolved into gold dust and drifted to the sky. The hollow feeling in her chest rose and enveloped her.

She closed her eyes.

Ava ran through a dark forest, thick with fog. He was there. He had to be.

Where was he?

She tripped over roots in the path and the ground rushed toward her. Black leaves slapped her face.

Darkness.

"Do not fear the darkness."

She slept.

She was in Cappadocia. She didn't know how. They put her in a bed that smelled of him, and she slept.

Warm, wrinkled hands forced her up in the bed.

"Drink. You must drink."

No.

"Please, Ava."

SMALL HANDS LED HER THROUGH THE FOREST. SOFT HANDS CLUTCHED her fingers. Childish voices whispered in her mind.

"Come back."

No.

"We need you to come back."

CHAPTER
TWENTY-THREE

Ava woke in the blackness, in the cave where they'd first made love. She was wrapped in his scent, but not his arms.

Everything was gone.

She lay still, staring at the chisel marks in the ceiling, wishing the mountain would close in and crush her.

"I know you're awake."

It was Rhys. She turned her head to the side and he was there, sitting in a corner of the room, staring at her with bloodshot eyes. They filled with tears as he watched her.

"Ava."

He reached over and caught her when she started to sob. The cries wracked her body, wringing her out as he held her. She shouted into his shoulder, beating at his back, but he only gripped her closer, rocking back and forth.

She cried for hours, and then the blackness enveloped her again.

DAMIEN WAS THERE THE NEXT TIME SHE WOKE.

"You need to eat, sister."

"I don't want to."

"He wanted you to live." Damien continued, even when she curled into herself, trying to shut out the words. "More than anything, he wanted you to live."

"Go away."

"Not till you've eaten."

"No."

"It's been over a week. You're dehydrated. Evren is hours away from putting you on an IV if you don't drink something."

"I don't care."

Damien knelt beside her, holding out a soft roll and a cup of water. "Do not let his sacrifice be in vain."

She started to cry again, silent tears rolling down her cheeks, but she sat up. Damien helped her, placing more pillows behind her back after Ava took the roll from his hands. She bit down, and it tasted like dust.

WHISPERED THOUGHTS CIRCLED HER MIND AS SHE STARED AT THE MURAL in the library, the bucolic scene of families in the village. The ancient scribe she remembered sat across from her, staring silently with pale blue eyes.

She was his companion now.

Ava sat in the library for weeks, staring at the painting as the scribes fed her, forced her to drink. Her body grew strong again.

She slept in the bed she and Malachi had shared. The sense of him lingered for a time, and when it started to fade, Rhys showed up at the door with a blanket that held her mate's scent. Ava silently took it and wrapped it around her before she shut the door.

"YOU GRIEVE," THE ANCIENT SCRIBE SAID ONE AFTERNOON AS THE SUN lit the rich colors on the wall.

"Yes."

"As do I."

She glanced over. "How long?"

He shrugged. "Just a little while longer."

"You're immortal."

"She was supposed to be, too."

Ava whispered, "We're all immortal, as long as our stories are told."

The old scribe smiled, nodded, and turned back to the painting.

. . .

She stared at the fire someone had started in the sitting room. It didn't warm her. She was cold to her bones.

"Brage?"

"Gone," Max whispered. "You fell in the water, and you didn't come up. He escaped when we ran for you. He's not in Istanbul. We don't know where he went. But we have his weapon. He lost it in the fight."

"I want to kill him."

"Good."

"You don't sound fine," Lena said.

"I am. Or maybe I'm not." She twisted the phone cord around her finger as she sat. "But I will be."

"I want you to come home."

"No, I'm fine here. I like it here. I'm staying with friends."

"Do you need—?"

"I'm not the only woman in the world who's had her heart broken, Mother." She didn't try to stop the tears, knowing her mother believed the lie. "Give me some time. I'll be fine."

It wasn't a lie. He'd left her.

She told the truth. Just not all of it.

Damien came to her room one night. She was looking through the pictures on her laptop, which had miraculously survived the fire at the scribe house in Istanbul. Pictures from her time with him before. When she'd still been human, and he'd still been her bodyguard.

There weren't enough.

He knocked on the door she'd left cracked open, then slipped in the room, sitting in the corner chair where Rhys, Maxim, Leo, and he had all watched over her.

Like brothers. His brothers.

Damien sat and watched her in silence until she spoke.

"What's up?"

"I'm going to take you to my mate. To Sari."

Ava swallowed the lump in her throat. "I don't want to leave yet."

"You need to."

"Are you going to force me?"

Damien took a deep breath and leaned forward. "Ava, when you screamed in the cistern, you burst your own eardrums, along with Max's and mine. Blood was pouring from your nose when we dragged you out. We were crying blood. The only reason you survived the wound to your abdomen and healed yourself was because Malachi performed the mating ritual. Otherwise, I know you'd be dead."

She choked back the cry. "I told him he was an idiot for doing it."

"Even now, I can tell you struggle to control the power. The songs press against your mind, don't they?"

She could do nothing but nod. The music had grown louder each time she slept. The whispering voices more persistent. Ava worried that she cried in her sleep, that she said the words that haunted her, but she didn't know what she said.

Damien ignored the tears that dripped down her nose. "Your magic is growing stronger, but you have no outlet. You must learn how to control it. You could hurt yourself or someone else without even meaning to. I can't teach you, but Sari can. You must go to other Irina."

For some reason, the thought of leaving the scribes angered her. "So you're just going to dump me with strangers?"

"No," he said. "I will not. I will stay with you. Though Sari might be angry, my mate will not turn me away. Malachi was my brother, and you were his mate. From this day, I vow to protect you." He paused and took a deep breath. "As a brother guards his sister, Ava, I will watch over you. You will *never* be alone."

Her shoulders were shaking when Damien crossed the room and closed the computer on her lap, taking her in his arms as she cried in loss. Relief. Confusion.

You will never be alone.

He finally whispered, "Will you go, sister?"

"I'll go."

CHAPTER

TWENTY-FOUR

She packed her things in a bag Max had found for her. Leo would drive Damien and Ava to the airport, but even she didn't know where they were going. Damien trusted no one. He only told Max to find warm clothes for her, and somehow, the clever scribe delivered, even at the end of a Turkish summer.

She had new documents, a new name, and a new mobile phone with an untraceable number, according to Rhys. She was Ava Sakarya, the name Malachi used on documents when he needed them.

The dreams still haunted her. She stumbled over and over through the dark forest, trying not to be afraid. On the wind, whispers in the Old Language teased her.

But one refrain, the mourning cry, echoed over and over again.

It was the cry she'd heard since childhood. The voice of every heart who had lost. Only now, it was her soul that spoke it.

The day before she and Damien were supposed to leave, she wrote it down as best she could on a piece of paper and went looking for Rhys in the library.

Ava found him working on the computer. She stood behind him, watching as he typed an e-mail in some language she didn't recognize. Farsi, maybe. It didn't matter.

She placed her hand on his shoulder, taking comfort from the contact. She'd learned not to hold back. Malachi's brothers needed to hold her hand. To hug her. To offer her whatever comfort they could. She knew their hearts ached, too.

Rhys leaned over, pressing his cheek to the back of her hand before he turned. He pulled over a chair, taking her hand as she sat in it, and pushed up her sleeve. With soft fingers, he brushed them over her forearm to reveal the glowing gold spells Malachi had written on her during their mating. They lay hidden in her skin until the touch on another Irin made them visible.

Weeks ago, the very sight of them caused her to burst into tears, but now, looking at the soft smile on Rhys's face, she forced herself not to cry.

"Malachi always was messy about that letter," he said, rubbing his thumb over a twisting character near her wrist. "Never practiced enough. Always in a hurry to go beat something with a sword."

"I think it looks perfect."

"So do I."

He kept her hand in his until she tugged it away and reached into her pocket for the slip of paper where she'd written the words. She knew writing the letters wasn't dangerous for her, only speaking them. Still, she felt like she'd done something forbidden when she handed them over.

He took them with a frown. "What's this?"

"I just…" She cleared her throat. "I need to know what this means."

He looked at them, then he cocked his head. "Why?"

"I hear it." She swallowed the lump in her throat. She wouldn't cry. She was out of tears. "This phrase. All the time, I hear it now. I've heard it for years. When I pass a funeral. When I hear someone who's grieving." She lowered her voice as she nodded toward the old scribe who still sat in front of the mural. "I think it's the only thing I've ever heard from his mind. I just… I need to know what these words mean."

"Ava, I'm not your teacher."

"But you are my friend." She forced out a smile. "Please? Please, just tell me. It's not that long, right? And it's driving me crazy."

Rhys shook his head. "You're right, of course. There's no reason you can't know what it means. It's not even complicated. It's just…" He cleared his throat. "*Vashama canem.* In the Old Language it means 'Come back to me.'"

"That's all?"

"That's all." He squeezed her hand and tossed the paper in the wastebasket under the desk. "I guess that makes sense for someone who's lost someone."

She nodded. "Yeah."

"Still leaving tomorrow?"

"Like you said, you're not my teacher." She smiled. "But I know I need one."

Rhys knit their fingers together, palm pressed to palm. "I'll see you again someday, Ava."

It wasn't a question.

Damien and Ava drove to Nevşehir the next day, leaving the last pieces of the familiar back in Göreme with Evren and the remnants of the Istanbul scribes. She stared at the twisting rock formations as they drove, then closed her eyes as the plane took off, trying to imagine Malachi's arms wrapped around her as she slept.

That night, Ava stared out the window of her hotel room near Atatürk Airport, watching the moon shine over the city. She draped herself in the blanket that barely held his scent and remembered the night they'd watched the moon rise behind the Galata Tower, huddled under the blanket on the roof of the old wooden house.

"There's no going back. I know that. I...I don't even want to. You were right about what you said before, even if the truth hurt. I was alone."

She wasn't alone anymore. No matter what. She knew that.

"Plus, I'm stupidly in love with you... so I guess we'll have to figure this out together."

"I love you, Ava."

Then the whisper from his mind. From his heart.

Reshon.

Ava buckled over, and sobs wrenched from her gut as the pain hit her again. She was walking through darkness, having lost the one love she'd ever dared to trust. Rage battled with grief as she knelt on the floor of the sterile hotel room, clutching the last piece of him she had.

"I hate you tonight, *reshon!*" She sobbed and curled against the bed. "How could you leave me like this? How?"

Ava beat her fists against the floor, pressing her tears into the rough blanket that had wrapped around them in the garden that night. The scent of her mate filled her nose, but he wasn't there. No arms held her. No touch soothed her. No familiar voice filled her mind.

"I love you," she choked. "I hate you. I love you. Come back to me, Malachi. What's the use of all this if you're not with me?"

His spells glowed in the darkness, and Ava stared at them, the old words whispering in her heart. Her soul wept, reaching for its other half.

In the darkness, Ava cried out. The words slipped from her lips, reaching up to the heavens.

"*Vashama canem, reshon. Vashama canem.*"

COME BACK TO ME.

CHAPTER

TWENTY-FIVE

Hundreds of miles away, he woke with a gasp, his lungs filling with the night air as he lay cold and naked on the Phrygian plain. Grey eyes gazed into the heavens, staring at the full moon, and grass pressed to his back on the deserted riverbank. Night cloaked him, bare and unmarked as the first night he'd been born into the world.

He knew nothing and no one.

But a million stars danced over him, and a familiar voice whispered in his mind.

"Come back to me."

THE SINGER

IRIN CHRONICLES BOOK TWO

For my mother
A remarkable, powerful woman,
and an inspiration to her family.

PROLOGUE

T he Fallen appeared on the summit of Mt. Ararat. Golden eyes reached west, settling on some point unseen by the hawks circling overhead. The wind whipped past Jaron, brushing the black hair that fell to his shoulders. He wore his human form, content to cloak his true nature and enjoy the sharp pleasure of the sun on his skin. Ancient *talesm* covered his shoulders and chest, gold against bronze. He was a vision of glory, resting against the snow.

His brothers appeared beside him: Barak with his wolf-grey hair, gold eyes watching the birds overhead; Vasu, already pacing, his lean human form dark against the snow.

"You gave up your city, brother." Vasu stared down as he spoke, seemingly mesmerized by the tracks his bare feet made in the snow. The angel chose to reside in warm climates, though none of their kind were truly bothered by either heat or cold. They commanded their senses at will.

"You imply defeat. I simply chose not to fight for it. It no longer interested me."

Barak murmured, "And the rest of your territories? Are they secure?"

"Volund knows better than to challenge me. I allowed his child to overrun Istanbul because it served my purpose. No doubt, he was confused to find my people withdrawn."

"Where are they?" Barak asked. "And do not underestimate Volund. I thought the same about him until he attacked. Now my children think me dead. They hide, afraid of their own shadows." Barak's lip curled. "I would cleanse the earth of their presence if doing so wouldn't give away my continued existence."

"I am watching," Jaron said. He couldn't take his eyes off the city. Something was churning there. Some pain reaching out. The sun fell in the west, slipping below the clouds to shine pink over Asia Minor. "I am always watching."

"But for what?" Vasu asked. "I hope your visions sing true."

"Have they ever not? I warned you of Galal's attack, didn't I?"

Gold eyes flashed from behind Vasu's curtain of black hair. His *talesm* sparked gold. Black and gold, the Fallen glared at his brother. "And I allowed you to persuade me. Now my children think their father murdered by a foreign god. They fight to remain true, even as Galal's soldiers slaughter them."

"Tell them to be more careful then." Jaron shrugged. "When the time comes, you will breed more."

Vasu curled his lip. "I have not consorted with human women for years. You know I tire of their attention."

"I hear sorrow," Barak growled, rising to his feet and looking west to the ancient city. "What is this? I thought the female was unharmed."

"She formed a bond with one of the Irin scribes. He sacrificed himself for her." Jaron's voice held a faint note of admiration. "She mourns."

"Does this change anything?" Vasu asked.

"No."

Barak cocked his head. "Why did you allow the sacrifice? Did you foresee it?"

"I did. I was… curious."

"And she mourns him?" Barak's voice held no pity. His gold eyes were impassive as he stared into the distance, the evening sun flushing his pale skin a gold-tinted rose.

"She does."

"You were curious?" Vasu asked, his voice holding more judgment than Jaron expected. Then again, Vasu was younger than his brothers, a mere boy when the Fallen had left their home. He had lived longer in the human realm than the heavenly. "Toying with humans is beneath you."

"His sacrifice was necessary for the pieces to be put into place."

The three angels rested at the peak of the mountain, the hawks circling above them, screaming at their intrusion. Jaron, bronze and gold in the light, eyes watching the distance, seeing beyond time and space. His children, when it served him, bore traces of his foresight. Vasu stood slightly behind him, dark and brooding. His physical presence dwarfed his brothers, not in size, for the tall, lean human form he donned was not imposing; but his energy, the tightly chained physicality of his presence, marked him as different, more terrestrial, than his brothers.

Barak sat next to Jaron, his brother's mirror in eternity. While Jaron saw, Barak heard. His solemn presence was the eternal and constant punctuation of Jaron's curiosity. Friends. Brothers. The two angels had existed in tandem for millennia. And now they struggled to attain what others thought was lost.

"Do you truly think it possible?" Barak asked, rising to his feet. "After all this time?"

Jaron continued to stare. Something was stirring in his vision. "Seven years or seven million, brother. He does not see time as we do. It has to be possible."

A flicker. A wavering in the heavenly realm as the stars danced above. Jaron stood and walked to the edge of the cliff.

Barak asked, "What is this I hear?" His eyes sought Jaron's, which were wide and filled with a long-lost emotion.

Wonder.

"A… complication."

Vasu darted to his side. "What? What do you see?"

"Look, my brothers."

Then Jaron opened his vision, sending it to the two angels at his side. All three looked curiously at the woman crouched in a hotel room. All three heard the words she uttered, then the tearing of the heavenly realm.

Vasu blinked. "Unexpected."

"Does this change anything?" Barak asked.

"No. He was necessary to keep her alive. Other than that, he is incidental."

"The female did this," Vasu said.

"So it would seem."

Barak said, "We knew her powers would be unstable."

Vasu lifted an eyebrow, a decidedly human gesture Jaron wondered if he was aware of. "Is it any wonder our sons fear them?" he murmured.

"She is a means to an end," Jaron said. "That is all."

Barak and Vasu exchanged a look but did not argue with their brother.

Vasu and Barak asked in unison, "Does this change our course?"

"No," Jaron said, his eyes narrowed on a dark riverbank. "We do what we always do. We watch."

CHAPTER
ONE

Anatolia, Turkey

He stared at the whirl of stars overhead, feeling their loss even as the soft grass caressed his back. They danced, tremulous in his vision, as her voice floated away on the night breeze.

Come back to me.

As the words drifted away, he caught flashes of another life.

Dark curls lifting in the breeze as the sun flashed on water. Rocking. Snatches of foreign voices and scents.

"Do you like to travel alone?"

"What?"

"Am I not allowed to ask you questions?"

"It's unusual."

"Call me unusual, then."

He closed his eyes to the stars. Another vision. Arms and legs tangled together. Sun-darkened skin against milky-white. She arched above him, her hand pressed to the carved wall of the cave as she sighed a name.

His name.

"Malachi…"

Her face flush with pleasure.

Her face.

Gold eyes and fair skin. Her mouth parted. She was speaking.

Speaking.

Screaming…

Hidden in the shadows, he saw her. Surrounded by grime and the scent of foul water. Saw her eyes widen in horror. Then…

Black.

The man sat up with a gasp, looking around with wide eyes. The river was familiar. But not. The air didn't smell as it should. There was an acrid tinge of smoke in the breeze and lights in the distance. He pushed to his knees, his legs feeling stiff and uncertain, as if he hadn't used them in days. He stared down at his bare chest and arms, frowning. Something was missing. Something lacked. But he couldn't find it in the jumble of his thoughts.

Everything was confusion.

He finally stood and, ignoring the rocks on the riverbank, made his way downstream. There were always humans if you followed the water. His father had taught him that.

He *thought* his father had taught him that.

The man walked for what could have been hours. He had no sense of the passing time. There was only night and one foot stepping in front of the other. The sound of water and the occasional low of a cow. Step by step, he made his way toward the lights.

The lights appeared from behind a grove of olive trees. As he approached, he realized it was a home, but not like any other in his hazy memory. A dog began barking at him, so the man hung back near the edge of the trees, not wanting to frighten the humans.

Humans would be afraid of his kind.

There was a slamming door, then a man walked out, calling something in a foreign tongue. He looked like a farmer, his pants were stained with the mud from the fields, and his grey hair was mussed as if he'd worn a cap all day. The farmer's voice rose as he shushed the dog and looked into the dark orchard.

The man stepped forward, holding up his hands to show he wasn't dangerous. As the farmer caught sight of him, he stopped. He shouted, gesturing for the stranger to go away, no doubt alarmed by the man's nakedness.

The farmer couldn't understand him, and the man knew that was wrong.

Shaking his head, he held out his arms, trying to make the farmer understand he wasn't a threat. That he needed…

What did he need?

Come back to me.

He needed to get back to the woman.

He didn't know her name, didn't know where she was or *who* she was…

Then he realized he didn't know who *he* was, either.

I don't know who I am.

He felt as if the air had left his lungs. His arms dropped, the farmer's anger forgotten. The dog's barks faded into the background as he closed his eyes and tried to control the panic.

I don't know who I am.

Something in his expression must have given the farmer pause, because he stopped shouting and stepped closer. He said something else the man didn't understand, but this time it sounded like a question. He ignored the human, clenching his eyes closed, trying to remember. Remember anything. Even his name—

"*Malachi,*" the woman had sighed.

His name.

Her soft voice had named him Malachi.

If he knew nothing else, he knew his name.

Malachi opened his eyes and took a breath to center himself.

The old farmer stepped through the gate. He'd grabbed a bedsheet from the line in the farmyard and held it out, speaking in a lower voice. Malachi took it, wrapping it around his body and cutting the chill of wind that had begun to bite his bare skin. The farmer motioned him closer, obviously concerned. He waved for Malachi to bend down, so he did. The farmer ran a hand along Malachi's scalp, turning his head back and forth, muttering under his breath.

Malachi realized he was looking for injuries. Moved by the human's kindness, he instinctively stepped away from the farmer's hands.

He wasn't supposed to touch humans. He did remember that.

The farmer spoke again, motioning Malachi through the gate and pointing at an outbuilding that looked like a metal-clad barn. Then he raised his voice again, shouting at the house until the door slapped open and a female voice yelled back.

There was a confused exchange as the old farmer led Malachi to the barn and flipped a switch on the wall that illuminated the interior with blinding false lights.

No, not false. Malachi knew what they were. They were the electric lights the humans had invented, fed by the manufactured energy they used to power all sorts of things. Lights. Musical players. Machines. Malachi caught sight of the machine at the end of the barn.

A tractor. The name popped into his mind before he had a chance to catch the source. Snatches of knowledge kept bubbling up, unpredictable and elusive. Disconnected from one thing to the next, he realized he knew the name of the tractor and what it did but had no idea what language the man was speaking. And some instinctive part of him knew that he *should* know. Knew that if he could just find some of the language written…

There.

Malachi blinked, ignoring the old man who ushered him to a chair by the workbench. He didn't even notice when the farmer walked out; his eyes were glued to the paper on the table. He grabbed it as his heart began to race. Letters and characters always made sense. He sat down in the old chair and traced his hands over each one, learning its shape, letting his mind unlock its secrets.

The curve of an *S*, like a serpent in the grass, hissing its tongue.

The circled perfection of the *O*.

The slashing strength of the *V*.

His mind drank them up like a beast deprived of water. The letters turned into words, the words jumped into sentences. And as the meaning of the letters crept into his mind, Malachi felt a surge of power. The shouts on the other side of the wall began to make sense.

"—could be!"

"…looks hurt, not dangerous."

"…no head wounds. …if he was attacked? Do you want…?"

Malachi glanced at the front of the paper. Then at the date. He understood the date, even if it didn't make sense. The year seemed wrong, but then, what did he know? He read the headlines.

Protests Spread to Ankara

Economic Forecasts by the EU Favorable into 2014

Tourism Down in Istanbul for Summer Months

The letters soothed his mind, ordering the chaotic thoughts that tumbled and twisted. More pieces fell into place. He was in Turkey, in Anatolia, where he had been born. But it was hundreds of years later, and he knew his family was no longer here. But others were, and he needed to find them. Others of his race would be able to help him. Perhaps they would know why he couldn't remember anything. Did he need to go to Istanbul? Part of him latched on to that idea while a darker whisper warned him to avoid that ancient city.

The woman.

Where was the woman? He continued flipping through the newspaper, and every picture jogged different memories. Rush-hour traffic in Ankara. An airplane crash. Charts showing the ebb and flow of commerce. His brain registered it all as he read, but nothing pointed him toward the woman. Nothing jogged the memories he was so desperate to find.

Malachi looked up when the barn door opened. The old farmer and his wife stood side by side, the man concerned, the woman obviously suspicious.

"Thank you," Malachi said softly, not wanting to frighten them. "I must have been… I'm not sure. I may be in shock. I don't know how I came to be in your field."

The old man blinked. "So you are Turkish? We thought you might be a tourist who was robbed. Who are you? What happened?"

"I… I'm not sure, exactly. I know my name is Malachi, but my memory…" He frowned and rubbed a hand through his hair. She'd told him he needed a haircut. He cocked his head at the bubble of memory. "I'm remembering more and more. But nothing makes sense. I was born here, I think."

"Tell us their name. We will find them for you."

"No… no, they're all gone now. I just… I need to find—"

"Who?" The farmer's wife spoke. "Is there someone we can call for you? Perhaps we can take you to the hospital in Polatlı? Your name is Malachi? What kind of name is that? English? You don't look English."

Malachi shook his head. "I don't need a hospital. I feel fine, just confused."

The cave. There was a place with many caves. A place he and the woman had been. They'd been safe there. He remembered the feeling of safety. Was the woman still in the caves?

"But if you don't remember anything, then shouldn't you see a doctor?" the farmer asked. "That is not normal. You are a young man. Perhaps there is some illness in your mind that—"

"I need to find a place with caves," Malachi said, standing abruptly, suddenly confident in his destination. He heard the farmer's wife gasp and her eyes widened as she glanced down. Malachi realized the sheet he'd tucked around his waist had fallen off. Clearing his throat, he reached down and wrapped it around himself again.

The farmer only looked amused. "With caves? A place with caves? There are caves all over Turkey."

Malachi's heart sank. "I remember being in a cave. I have this memory of my…" *What was the human word?* "Wife. My wife and I. There was a house in the caves."

The old woman cocked her head. "You were living in a cave with your wife?"

"I think so. Or… we were staying there. There was a bed and… a desk. A washroom, even. I… I don't know more than that."

They exchanged a look, and the old woman shrugged. "Cappadocia, maybe?"

"One of the cave hotels?" the farmer asked. "Perhaps they took a holiday."

"I can't think of any other place. Who lives in the caves these days?"

"Cappadocia?" Malachi said, searching his mind. There was a faint memory… Yes. His father had gone to Cappadocia to study when he was a boy. There were scribes there—

Scribes.

He took a quick breath as another bubble of memory rose. He was a scribe. That was why the letters spoke to him. He was a scribe and others of his kind were in Cappadocia.

"Yes," he said in a more confident voice. "In Göreme. I have people there. People who will pay you if you bring me back. I need… I need to find her. I think she is there."

The farmer's eyes narrowed. "Are you sure? I still think it might be a good idea for you to visit a hospital. You can always call them—"

"No." Malachi realized the farmer was talking about using the telephone. "I… don't remember any telephone numbers." The more he searched his mind, the more he remembered. Odd things. He had crystal-clear pictures of his childhood, but couldn't remember his mother's name. He knew he wasn't human, but also knew he couldn't tell the humans what he was. He could picture faces, but not in context. He'd traveled the world—he knew that—but he wasn't sure if he could drive a car. It was as if he'd been put back together from pieces, but too many of them were missing to create a clear picture.

And he couldn't remember her name. He desperately wanted to remember her name. Remember more about her. But other than a few brief memories, his mind was silent.

"I have a friend who could take you," the farmer said. "He has a truck going to Kayseri tomorrow. I can ask if you can go along."

"I don't have any money to pay…"

The farmer shook his head. "I can sense you are an honest man. I know these things. You will pay him when you get there. Or send money back."

The wife's raised eyebrow told Malachi she was more skeptical, but she didn't argue. Instead, she said, "I will get you some blankets. You're welcome to sleep on the cot over there." She pointed at the corner where a small pallet lay. "Are you hungry?"

He nodded. His stomach had been aching since he woke. "I don't remember the last time I ate."

"I'll get you a plate then. Osman will bring it out after he's called Ibrahim."

"Thank you." Malachi sat again. "I cannot thank you enough. I promise I will repay your kindness somehow."

The woman's voice softened. "I hope you find your wife. Sleep well. I'll send extra blankets. The nights are getting cold."

• • •   • • •

He slept deeply that night. Malachi dreamed he was running in a dark forest. He knew he was searching for her, but no matter which way he turned, the paths all led to dead ends. He could hear her crying somewhere. The sound almost brought him to his knees. She needed him. She was as lost as he was, but so far away.

Come back to me.

He heard her whisper it again. His soul raged in pain and anger, and Malachi knew he would hear her his whole life. She would call and he would answer. He belonged to her as surely as she belonged to him.

• • •   • • •

W HEN HE WOKE, THE SKY WAS STILL BLACK, BUT HE WAS MORE determined than ever.

The truck came at dawn, the honk of the horn answered by the old farmer's friendly yell and the smell of breakfast wafting from the house. Malachi dressed in the too-small clothes the farmer named Osman had given him, apparently left from a cousin who'd lived there briefly. The pants were too short and a little baggy, but the T-shirt fit him well enough. He kept looking down at his arms, sensing something was wrong… but they were fine. The skin was smooth and unmarred by injuries or scars. He shook his head and went out to meet the driver.

Osman's friend, Ibrahim, was a delivery driver for a shipping company out of Ankara. He was taking a load of wool to Kayseri and bringing back finished textiles. As he was an old friend of Osman's, he was more than happy to do the favor, though he couldn't promise how fast Malachi would be delivered. They took off as the sun was rising, Malachi shaking Osman's hand briefly, conscious of his growing strength, careful not to hold the farmer's hand too long.

Malachi could sense some energy growing. It made him edgy. Uncomfortable.

Luckily, Ibrahim didn't ask many questions; he mostly wanted an audience. Ibrahim liked to talk. Malachi sat back, amused by the humorous old man, smiling for the first time as he listened to the raucous jokes and fantastic stories of the truck driver. Two hours later, he drifted into a fitful sleep, only to wake when the truck jerked to a halt.

Ibrahim was smiling. "What was that?"

"What?"

"That language you were speaking! I've never heard it before, even in Istanbul."

What language had it been? Probably the language of his thoughts and dreams. The one he knew the humans weren't supposed to know about.

Malachi decided to play dumb. "I have no idea." He smiled. "How could I? I was sleeping."

Ibrahim laughed. "Fair answer, friend! Well, we're here."

Malachi looked around the dusty town, but nothing seemed familiar. "In Cappadocia?"

"Osman said you had people in Göreme. I brought you to Göreme."

Cars and pedestrians were scattered around a lively intersection, but Malachi could tell it was a very small town. Surely, once he was walking, he'd recognize something.

"Where are the caves?"

Ibrahim laughed again. "It's Göreme! There are caves everywhere. Are you sure you don't want me to take you to a hospital?"

"No." Malachi sat up, spying something out of the corner of his eye that looked familiar. It was a restaurant with a balcony. Red umbrellas shaded the tables. There was something about the balcony… "No, I just realized where I am."

"Are you sure?"

He nodded, reaching for the door handle, suddenly eager to explore. He halted when Ibrahim's arm shot out.

"Wait." The old man reached for his wallet. "I like you. Take a little money, just so I'm not so worried, eh?"

"I don't—"

"Please, take it." He held out some notes. "I'll give you my card. If you want, you'll pay me back when you find your people. But Allah would not be pleased if I sent you away with nothing. Take enough to be safe for a day or two, okay? And you'll have my phone number, too."

Touched by the man's generosity, Malachi smiled. "You are a good man, Ibrahim. And you tell very good jokes, even though I didn't understand all of them."

Ibrahim roared with laughter. "Well, you have brain damage! What can I expect?"

A few minutes later, Malachi waved as Ibrahim drove down the road, then he turned and searched for the restaurant. He walked slowly, hoping that, somehow, things would start to make sense. As he passed the restaurant, he caught the edge of a sign for a rug shop and knew he'd walked by it before.

She swung her arms as she walked, and Malachi let his brush against her. Just the brush of contact. Just so she knew…

He turned right, then right again at a cafe with a cracked window.

She stopped, her cheeks flush with embarrassment as she caught the tenor of his thoughts. Embarrassment, but desire, too. He knew she wanted him…

Up the hill he climbed, until he'd left the shops behind and the streets were filled with stone houses. A striped cat walked along the top of a wall, following him as he searched for clues. At each intersection, he'd see something.

An orange tree that tilted to one side.

A wall with colorful graffiti no one cared to paint over.

An abandoned cupboard with grass growing through the bottom.

Each turn led him up the hill and farther away from the town center, but with each step, his sense of familiarity grew.

She was chatting about something with a dark-haired man. Laughing at some joke he wasn't a part of. He was irritated by their ease together.

At the end of the road, a house rose into the cliffs. Or, he should say, a group of houses. There were buildings stacked at the base and rooms carved into the cliffs with stairs leading up. A wall surrounded the old compound, but no graffiti covered it. Trees grew over the walls and he could hear voices whispering within. He didn't recognize the language.

Here.

She was here. She had to be.

Malachi stepped up to the large wooden door in the wall and lifted the knocker, banging it down as the voices beyond the wall stopped. There were shuffling steps, then an old man opened the gate.

"Yes? How can I—sweet heaven!"

Malachi stood speechless as the old man's face paled. His eyes were like saucers.

"Hello?"

"It can't be…," the man breathed out.

"I'm sorry to disturb you, but I… I think I—"

"You're dead." The man stepped back, and fear rose in his eyes. "You're *dead.*"

"I don't know what you're—"

"What are you?"

"What?" Fear twisted Malachi's heart. Perhaps he'd been wrong to come here.

The old man's hands shook. "You wear the face of a dead man."

"I don't understand—"

"What *are* you?"

Anger rose up. "I don't know what you're talking about! I'm *not* dead, obviously. I just don't remember—"

"Malachi?" The awestruck voice came from behind the old man.

Malachi raised his eyes to see the dark-haired man he'd seen in his memories. "I remember you."

The other man's eyes were also filled with fear. But it was a fear mixed with hope. "They said you were dead."

"Who did? I don't know what's going on. Who—"

"It can't be." The dark-haired man stepped forward, his arm raised. He reached for Malachi, confusion written wide on his face. "They saw you die. Your dust rose. She felt your loss…" The man's fingers touched Malachi's shoulder and gripped. "You're real. How are you real?"

A thick emotion filled his throat, and his eyes burned. "I don't know what happened to me, but I need to find her."

Another voice rose in a shout. "No!" The sound of running steps, then a tall blond man stood in front of him, mouth gaping. "No, I saw you die."

"Maxim," the dark-haired one said. "Are you sure?"

"How can you even ask me that?" he cried. "We all saw him die, Rhys. You saw her grieve. This is something… This is not our brother!"

She grieved… For him? Fear and shock and anger wrestled within him. Malachi said, "I don't know who your brother is, I just need to find her. Where is she?"

"You will not hurt her!" the blond man yelled. "Whatever *thing* you are, you'll keep away from—"

"But Max"—the dark-haired man named Rhys stepped between his friend and Malachi—"if it *is* him—"

"It can't be!"

"What if it is?" He held the blond man back by the shoulders. "What if some miracle—"

"*Miracle?* Is this the time of the ancients? This is evil. Evil wearing the face of our—"

"I need to find my wife!" Malachi roared. "I don't know what's going on. I don't know who I am. But I know I heard her. Heard her calling me to come back to her. I just need to—"

"What?" Rhys had frozen, turning to look at Malachi, even as he continued to hold Maxim back. "What did she say?"

"I said, I need to find—"

"No," he hissed. "What did *she* say?"

"I don't—"

"When you heard her"—Rhys stepped closer, looking Malachi in the eye—"what did she *say*?"

Malachi tried to calm his racing heart. "*Vashama canem.* She said, 'Come back to me.'"

All the color drained from Rhys's face. "Heaven above."

CHAPTER

TWO

Ava was still sleeping when the car came to a stop. She clenched her eyes shut, holding on to the safety of silence for as long as she could.

"Ava."

Damien knew she was awake. The man had preternatural senses that never switched off. Ava had decided he was like a weird combination of the most overprotective dad and big brother in history. Which, being the only child of a mother who saw her more as a peer than a child, was a new and interesting experience.

She snuggled into the down-filled jacket under her cheek and ignored him.

"Open your eyes. I know you're awake. It's going to rain in about fifteen minutes, and I'd like to start up the trail before it pours."

She lifted her head and turned to him, speaking in a scratchy voice. "I never would have let you talk me into this in Turkey if I hadn't been such a mess."

"But you did, and now we're here. Get your jacket on."

She caught him looking at his reflection in the rearview mirror. "Looks like someone's nervous to see the wifey," she muttered.

"Ah, look. Acid-tongued Ava is back. I missed her so much while she slept." Damien gave her a droll look. "Wait, no I didn't."

"You're the one who dragged me out here."

"Would you like to go back to Oslo?" He pulled the keys out of the ignition and tossed them to her. "Go ahead. Hope you can outrun Volund's Grigori. Maybe you can scream again if they get close. Or maybe not. You'd pass out and hurt yourself if you did that."

"Shut up."

"Or maybe you can follow me and stop acting like a child."

"Stop trying to manage me," she croaked, her voice dry from sleep.

"For now you need to be managed."

She licked her lips and Damien held up a bottle of water. Ava took it, drank, then handed it back, noticing the extra-grim expression on his face. Slightly mollified by the water, she softened her tone.

"Hey, Captain Sunshine, shouldn't you be happier than this? You're going to see your wife at the end of that trail."

Damien only stared into the thick trees that surrounded them. "A piece of advice—Sari doesn't like the word wife."

"Why not?" Ava knew the Irin used the word "mate" more than wife, but she'd heard the scribes in Turkey use both on occasion.

"She was born in a time when the human term 'wife' implied property." Then a rare smile flickered at the corner of his mouth. "And Sari is no male's property. Now get your shoes on and lace them up tight. I don't know everything that will meet us on that trail, but I do know this: there will be mud."

They were somewhere in rural Norway, surrounded by blue and green. Steep green mountains laced with waterfalls cut against the clear blue sky. Blue-green water from the glacier melt. Ava knew they were somewhere in the fjords, but she wasn't sure where.

The plane had taken them to Paris, then Berlin, then Damien had found a car and started driving. He didn't tell her where, but she could read the signs. They'd headed west, then north. Through Hamburg and into Denmark. They'd taken a ferry that landed them in Bergen, then after a brief sleep in a small hotel, they'd started driving again.

Through mountain highways and on smaller ferries, they'd driven farther and farther into the Scandinavian countryside. Towns were quickly overcome by wilderness and an utter sense of isolation that Ava found comforting and frightening in equal measure. As she stepped out of the car, she felt as if she and Damien were the last two people on earth.

There was nothing but trees, sky, and a biting wind that carried the promise of rain.

She shivered, not only from the cold but also the memories of her dreams. Every night she dreamed of a dark forest. She thought she heard him, calling for her, running through the trees, trying to get back to her. In her dreams, she'd call for him, but no one would come. And then she'd weep the tears she no longer allowed herself in her waking hours. When she woke, they were cold on her face.

Ava locked away her grief and focused on the task ahead. Damien was pulling a backpack from the trunk of the small car they'd pulled over to the side of the road. She looked around into the forest.

"Is the car going to be safe here?"

"It will be fine. She'll send someone down for it if she decides to let us stay. I know they keep some cars there, so they must have a place to park them out of the weather."

"What do you mean, 'if she decides to let us stay'?"

He shrugged. "She'll allow you to stay, I'm sure, but she won't want me." He couldn't hide the pain that crossed his face as he said, "She'll be angry I showed up without an invitation."

"But you said that you wouldn't leave me here." A wild flutter of panic filled her chest. Damien might have been the grumpiest travel companion she'd ever had, but she knew him. And she knew he'd saw off his right arm to keep her safe. "You promised—"

"Yes, I did." He narrowed his eyes. "You let me worry about Sari. I'm not going anywhere."

He buttoned up his jacket and threw on the pack. Then he walked over and tightened up the drawstring around her neck. "It's colder here than you're used to."

"I've been in cold weather before."

He shook his head. "Not like here."

Ava batted his hand away and sneered. "Actually, exactly like here. A magazine sent me to the fjords a couple of years ago to cover a new luxury hotel that was built to be completely self-sustaining. And that was in November. I get it. It's cold and wet and the weather changes in five minutes. Now stop fussing and let's walk."

"Fine."

"Good." Ava couldn't let his concern weaken her. She'd allowed herself to be soft and trusting with one man. She'd given him every-thing and he'd died. It wouldn't happen again.

*   *   *   *   *   *

THE PATH WAS STEEP, CLIMBING UP ONE OF THE NARROW VALLEYS CUT BY glaciers at the dawn of time. Thick forest surrounded them, and the well-worn path quickly turned muddy when the rain began to fall. Ava saw no signs of life. No tire tracks or footprints. The only indication they weren't completely alone was the occasional rustle in the forest that could have been an animal… or something more.

Damien walked with grim purpose, never ceasing, turning only to check that she was still with him. Luckily, Ava had always been a good hiker. Her years of work in remote places left her as comfortable outdoors as she was in the city. The boots she wore were almost a carbon copy of the ones she kept in her room at her mother's house, only less worn. She marched with Damien, never slowing as they climbed.

They'd almost reached the crest of a hill when she saw him stum-ble. Damien halted for a second, then took a step back, his foot sliding in the mud.

"Damien?"

"Keep walking." His voice sounded strained. "Just keep walking, Ava."

She walked closer, noticing that the strain in his voice was evident on his face, too. "What's going on?"

"You can't hear it?"

"I don't hear anything."

"Good. Keep walking." He looked as if every step he took pained him. A vein began to pulse on the side of his forehead. With a low grunt, he picked up his feet, the mud sucking at them as he forced himself farther up the hill.

"What's going on?"

His jaw clenched, he said, "She knows we're here."

Ava looked around but could see nothing. The hill they'd climbed led into a small meadow, then the muddy path led up another hill.

"How?"

"With her magic, she knows. This is her land."

Ava thought she heard a howling sound whip through the wind, like the cry of a bird high in the air. The rain fell harder, soaking her collar, even though her hood was drawn up. Damien grabbed her hand, pulling her along the path. The forest seemed to close in the farther they walked. The green meadow narrowed as they approached another rock-strewn hill, the path twisting back and forth up the mountain. Ava pulled back, worried that Damien was hurting himself. His face had gone pale under the dark stubble he hadn't bothered to shave.

"Ava, we have to keep walking."

"You're hurt."

He shook his head and said under his breath, "I'll hurt worse before this is through."

The cry on the wind died away, and Ava heard what Damien had been talking about. A low hum drifted down the mountain and brushed along her body. Goose bumps rose on her skin, and the hair at the back of her neck prickled with sudden cold.

"What is that?" she asked. "Where... where is it coming from?"

"Irina," Damien whispered, his eyes rising. "Now you'll see why they are feared."

Ava followed his gaze to see three grey figures at the top of the hill. They strode with purpose; the one in the center carried a long staff that struck the ground with each step. Another carried a sword, and the third held nothing, hands tucked out of sight. All three wore heavy coats in dark colors, but as they approached, Ava could see they were women.

The one in the center was tall, with strong, square shoulders and legs that ate up the ground beneath her. She pushed back her hood and the wind whipped long blond hair across her face, but Ava could see her eyes, vivid blue as the northern sky, piercing Damien where he stood. The woman's stunning features were frozen in anger.

He stepped forward and took a ready stance as Ava saw the woman's mouth open. Her lips moved, and a second later, a whisper wrapped around Ava, forcing her to the side as Damien was flung back, tumbling down the hill.

"Damien!" She started toward him, only to be held back by one of the woman's companions. The dark-skinned woman with the fearsome sword grabbed Ava's arm, and when she looked up, it was into cold black eyes and a face scarred from the cheek to the throat, as if the woman's neck had been ripped open by a wild animal. She said nothing but only gave a small shake of her head. Ava tried to loosen the woman's hold, but she might as well have been struggling with the mountain itself.

"Calm yourself," the other woman said, putting a hand on Ava's shoulder. She was shorter and her soft brown hair curled around her cheeks, but her grip was still firm. "Let them… talk."

Damien had come to a stop in the meadow below, rolling to his feet as the tall blond woman strode toward him. He reached to the ground, taking up a thick branch of a tree that had fallen a moment before the blonde's staff struck.

They parried for a moment, Damien forcing her back with quick blows before the woman's superior weapon cracked the branch and swept Damien's feet from under him. He rolled away a moment before the staff would have come down on his skull. He jumped to his feet, shoulders braced as he locked eyes with his opponent.

She was almost as tall as he was, a formidable woman who was clearly familiar with the weapon she held. She circled Damien, her eyes never leaving his. Another movement of her lips, and her staff split in half. She tossed one half to him, and they began again.

The two crashed together, their weapons evenly matched as they dueled, using arms and legs to try to trip each other. Yet even as they battled, Ava could sense the connection.

This was Sari.

She swung the staff at her mate's head, only to be stopped by Damien's forearm. He winced but grabbed her weapon, pulling it toward him and forcing her closer. But Sari countered, sweeping her leg between Damien's and hooking one of his ankles, causing him to stumble back and release her staff. They went back and forth, both falling in the mud over and over again, only to rise and continue fighting. Ava, standing between the two strange women, felt as if she'd stepped into a battle older than time.

Damien was physically stronger, yet he held back when Sari aimed a punch at his face. His lip was split and his eye bruised, but he leashed his power, refusing to hit back. The wind whipped around them and the rain fell harder. Both were slipping in the mud, and though the humming had stopped, the chilling power had not dissipated.

With a hoarse cry, Sari struck his knee and Damien fell with a grunt. Dropping the staff, he held out his arms in supplication, looking up at his mate with such obvious adoration that Ava felt her breath catch. Sari halted, her staff at his neck, as Damien watched her with bruised face and bleeding lips. Mud coated his hair and cheeks, the rain making tracks as he knelt before her.

Ava heard the woman at her right whisper something in the Old Language, just as Sari dropped her staff and went to her knees. She grasped Damien's hair and pulled him into a searing kiss.

They clutched each other, and Ava could hear Damien's low groan even from up the hill. He wrapped his arms around his mate, grabbing her coat and pulling her closer, as if his life depended on her touch. Sari was just as voracious; she pulled at Damien's neck, holding his lips to hers in a ravenous kiss. Then, just as abruptly, she shoved him back and stood, spinning around and reaching for her staff. Ava could see the tears rolling down Sari's cheeks as her lips moved again, and she held her staff out. The piece she had given to Damien flew through the wind and melded itself to the piece in her hand.

She marched up the hill, eyes flickering to Ava's once before she barked out an order to the two women and walked past, up the hill and into the driving rain.

The woman at her right turned to Ava. Rosy lips parted in a small smile. "English?"

"American." She glanced over her shoulder at Damien, who was still kneeling in the mud, looking as stunned as Ava felt. He finally looked at her and gave her a small nod before he struggled to his feet and walked back up the hill.

"My name is Astrid," the short woman said, giving Ava a small push as she began to lead her up the path. "Mala and I will escort you and Damien to Sarihöfn. You are welcome here."

"Am I really?"

Astrid's eyes held laughter, but her voice was serious. "Yes, really."

Damien was only a few steps behind, and Ava saw the woman named Mala nod respectfully as he fell in step beside her.

Ava glanced at him. "So that was Sari."

He shrugged and wiped the blood from his lip. It had already healed. "It went as well as I'd expected."

"Why did you fight with her?" Ava asked from her chair in the small sitting room that connected her and Damien's bedrooms. They'd been put into a cottage with two rooms, a small kitchen, and a bathroom they'd have to share, all situated away from the main house. She'd slept in worse.

"Because she needed a fight." He stepped out of the bathroom, holding a towel to his hair. "And I give my mate what she needs."

He was dressed in jeans and a short-sleeved T-shirt, despite the cold. Ava had noticed in the car that Damien seemed to run hot. She'd never noticed in Istanbul, but walking around in long sleeves to cover his extensive *talesm* must have been irritating. The tattoos reached from his collar to his wrists, with some spells even crawling down onto the backs of his hands. She knew he had them on his legs, too, though she'd never seen them. The scribe was very powerful, yet Sari had beaten him to his knees. And even though Ava knew he'd been holding back, it hadn't been by much.

There was a fire already burning in the grate when they'd arrived. Damien insisted that Ava get cleaned up first, then took his own shower to get rid of the caked-on mud. It was only five o'clock, but the sun was starting to disappear, sinking behind the mountains that surrounded the narrow valley.

"Where are we?"

"Norway."

"Yeah, I figured."

He took a seat by the fire. "We're in the Nordfjord. Sari's family has had this property for hundreds of years. It used to be just a small cottage they used for holidays. Very private. Her family was always very private. They liked their own space and never took well to living in retreats. After the Rending, after we lost... so many, she left me and came here. I knew she'd gathered other Irina but didn't know how many."

"This is your first time here?"

"Since the Rending, yes. I came here before. When we were first mated." He looked out the window at the lake in the base of the valley. "We spent time here together. I'm one of the few Irin scribes who even knows this place exists. We're safe here; I'm sure of it."

"When was the last time you saw her?" Ava asked as Damien bent his head, holding his shoulder-length hair near the fire.

"It's been years. We used to try to meet in other places." He frowned. "But it was too… It's complicated, Ava."

She nodded, still not really understanding. She could sense how painful the topic was, despite his natural stoicism.

"Does she really hate you so much?"

He looked up, his elbows propped on his knees, and his eyes burned with pride. "She hates me as she loves me. Wholly and completely. Sari never does anything by halves."

"Are they all angry? Are all the Irina angry like Sari?"

"No. Maybe." He took a deep breath and sat back. "There's not a simple answer. And there are so few Irina in most places. I am… not the best person to explain."

"Try. I need to understand."

He absently rubbed his cheek where his mate had struck him. The wound had already healed, but a faint shadow remained.

"You can see how powerful they are. The Irina, I mean. An Irina singer at the height of her power, trained by her elders, can wield frightening magic. With a word, they can change the course of the wind. Render a strong man weak or a weak man strong—"

"Break a stick in half and then mend it?"

He nodded. "All Irina have different powers. Seers. Healers. Elemental magic. Some of that is natural and some depends on how they train. In the past, they used their magic for mostly creative endeavors. Healing. Building. Teaching the young. Scientific discovery. These were always their greatest strengths. The more… martial magics… were not valued." He smiled. "Many of the older Irina derided offensive spells. 'Male's work,' my grandmother would sneer at my father and me. All Irina knew some protective spells, of course. And many to help themselves blend in with the human world, but it was the Irin scribes' job to protect them. And for our part, we didn't encourage our mates to learn offensive magic. Why would they need it? They had us. And we…" His voice grew hoarse. "We would never leave them unprotected."

A low anger began to smolder in her gut. "Except you did."

"We did." He braved her eyes. "And we learned how desperately wrong we were only after we lost everything."

"Not everything," she said, trying not to taste the bitterness on her tongue. "You and Sari still have each other. Lots of people—most of the Irin—lost their mates."

"I'm one of the lucky ones." A sad smile lifted the corner of his mouth. "We aren't exactly a peaceable pair, but then, we never have been."

"Will she ever forgive you?"

"I don't know." Then his eyes gleamed and his smile spread. "But I'm tired of being patient. And as I give Sari what she needs, so she will give me what I need. If meeting you has taught me anything, it's that change is possible. And there are powers at work that we may never understand. We lost half our race during the Rending. Then we—Irin and Irina—allowed this wound to fester. We're dying from within, and it must stop. Change is no longer only possible, it's necessary for survival."

"Do you think they're ready for it?"

"I don't know. But look at you, Ava." He leaned forward, bracing his elbows on his knees. "Everything in our writings, in our history, tells us you shouldn't exist. And yet, you do! Though your mother is human, you hear the voices of the soul. Your words hold power. You mated with a warrior in my house. You *are* an Irina." Damien turned and stared out the window toward the large house that dominated the valley. "Change has already come. They just don't know it yet."

CHAPTER

THREE

Cappadocia, Turkey

"I'm a what?"

Malachi was sitting in a room with Rhys and the old man called Evren. Both wore looks of confusion as they tried to ascertain what had happened to Malachi.

"An Irin scribe," Evren said patiently.

"And the Irin are descended from… angels."

"We are the race formed when angels fell from heaven and mated with human women. Heroes of old. Some would call us demigods, though we are not. We are half human, half angel. There have been generations of us. A separate people, so to speak. The angelic race."

"But we're not angels."

"No," Rhys said. "Angels are frightening creatures, and you don't want to meet them."

"But…" The memory jolted him. "I think I have met one."

Eyes darkened to near black, then a glowing gold as the human mask dissolved. Jaron's shoulders grew wide and thick. His frame lengthened… almost seven feet.

"Yes," Rhys said, sliding forward in his seat. "You have. Do you remember?"

A faint gold shimmer covered his skin as the mask of the harmless doctor fell away and the heavenly being emerged. His hair grew longer… thick ebony strands brushing past his shoulders. The bronze skin of his torso glowed in the afternoon light, and raised talesm *rose like shimmering brands on his skin.*

Malachi's eyes blinked back into focus. "I was with her. I had to protect her, but he didn't hurt her, and I was confused."

Rhys narrowed his eyes. "We were all confused. What else do you remember?"

Thousands of you, Scribe. One of her. Remember.

"He told me there were thousands of us and only one of her." He looked up in confusion. "There's only one of her? What does that mean?"

"We'll explain that another time," Evren said. "Is there anything else?"

"Yes and no. There are pieces I remember. Odd things. I knew I was something different as soon as I woke up. A… scribe, I suppose. I knew my father— Is my family still living?"

Rhys shook his head. "No. You have no siblings and your parents both died many years ago. Ava is your only family other than us."

Ava. The name fell into his mind and filled it. It brought the memory of air tinged with cloves and roasted hazelnuts.

"Who is she?"

The old man looked at him, pity in his eyes. "She is your mate. You remember nothing of her?"

"My mate?" Not a wife. More than a wife.

"Your mate. Your *reshon*. It is a sacred union."

"*Reshon?*"

"Your souls were created for each other. And when you marked her with magic, they bonded."

"Where is she?"

Evren and Rhys exchanged a look. Rhys said, "We don't know, but we're going to try to find her. We *will* find her."

She wasn't here. He felt as if he were stumbling through the dark, looking for something just out of his reach.

"Malachi," Evren asked. "When you woke, you were like this?"

Malachi frowned. "I was by the river. There was nothing around. But I followed the water and found the farm."

"The old retreat," Evren said. "He woke near the old retreat. I think when he came back, he was reborn in the exact place he was born the first time."

Rhys said, "You think Ava—"

"It must have been. I don't know how, but it is the only explanation."

"No Irina has the power to—"

"No Irina is like Ava. She has no training. She has never been told what she may *not* do, so who knows what she is capable of?"

Malachi broke into their quiet conversation. "You're telling me I died?"

Evren and Rhys turned to him.

"I died?" he asked again. "Truly? I died. And I came back to life?"

"What do you remember?"

"Nothing. I remember *nothing*. Just her voice on the wind and the stars overhead. I've been getting flashes here and there, but I don't remember her. How could I forget *her*?" He felt torn. Incomplete. And it wasn't just the memories he was missing. "And you think she did this somehow?"

Evren said, "We don't know. Not really. But there is no other explanation. Your brothers saw you die. Saw your body turn to dust. Your mate saw you die—*felt* you die."

"But why would Ava be able to—"

"She said the words," Rhys said. "The words she had heard her whole life. From the souls of everyone who mourned. She came to me before she left. Asked me what it meant. *Vashama canem.* Come back to me." He turned to Evren. "I had no idea. How could I?"

"There was no way of knowing she could do this, Rhys. No way—"

"Wait!" Malachi felt a chill creep along his skin. "You're telling me she spoke this command and I answered. Even from beyond death?"

"He's telling you words have power," Evren said. "Ava asked you to come back to her. And you did."

◆ ◆ ◆   ◆ ◆ ◆

THE TWO MEN STOOD ACROSS FROM HIM, STARING. MALACHI REFUSED to sit down after being introduced to Max's twin, Leo. He felt restless. He wanted to do something. Go somewhere. Sitting around a library made his skin itch. Rhys had left, along with Evren. The two men with him claimed to be his friends, but he had no memory of them.

Leo leaned over to Max and asked, "What happened to them?"

Max shrugged. "I don't know."

"Did he—"

"He died and came back to life, Leo. Who knows what happened to them."

"Will they come back?"

"How should I know?"

Malachi suppressed the urge to punch them both. "What are you talking about?"

Leo rolled up his sleeves to reveal intricate tattoos all over his arms. "Your *talesm*. Your spells. Tattoos. You used to be covered with them like us. More than us, because you're quite a bit older."

Of course. That was why his arms felt wrong. He'd sensed a lack of... something since he woke. He rubbed his hands over his forearms, wishing he could rub away the unwanted attention. "I don't know what happened. And you don't look much younger than me, so how old am I?"

Leo said, "You used to be around four hundred. But do we start over now?" He grinned. "Am I not the youngest anymore?"

Max tapped Leo on the back of the head. "Stop. He's obviously still Malachi. He's just different. You're still the youngest in the house."

"Damn."

Malachi looked toward the door. "Where did all the others go?"

Leo said, "Evren sent the scribes in the house searching the archives to see if there are any records of Irin coming back to life after death. Rhys went to search Damien's phone and credit card records to see if he's still traceable. I'm guessing he won't be, but we can hope."

"And Damien is with..."

"Ava."

"Yes, Ava." His woman. His mate.

"It must have been her." For the first time, Max's eyes softened as he watched him. "Somehow... We thought we'd lost you, Malachi. I watched you die. Saw the dust rise to heaven when he killed you."

Leo put his arm around his brother. "There was no question. She felt your loss."

"Ava was... torn in two when you died," Max said. "I've never seen —I don't remember the Rending, so I've never seen grief like that before."

Malachi swallowed a groan. She was out there, grieving his loss, and he was unable to comfort her. Even though he couldn't remember her, Malachi bristled in awareness of her grief. "I need to find her. Why did this man take her from here?"

Rhys opened the door, face grim. "Damien took her away because her power was unpredictable and growing stronger every day." He glanced at Malachi. "Obviously."

"You're saying she didn't mean to bring me back. This was some kind of mistake?"

"Not a mistake," Rhys said, his voice breaking. "Never a mistake, brother."

"Then why—"

"No trained Irina would have done it. They have rules. Boundaries. As we do. Set in place thousands of years ago by the Forgiven when they gave us the gift of magic. To do something like this—to tear a soul from heaven—is… not done. I didn't even know it was possible."

"There probably isn't even a spell for it," Leo added. "But Ava grew up among humans. She has power, a lot of it—especially since the mating ritual between you two—but she has no idea how to use it."

"Whatever happened to bring you back was instinctive," Rhys said. "She's probably unaware she worked magic at all."

His heart thudded. "So she doesn't know I'm alive."

"I very much doubt it."

Max asked, "Did you find Damien? Is there any way—"

"Damien and Ava dropped out of sight a few days ago. There's no telling where they are now. The last point of contact was a car he picked up from the scribe house in Berlin. He didn't say when he'd be returning it, though he asked the watcher of the house for something with all-wheel drive. There was GPS in the car, but it was disabled outside Hamburg. They haven't used credit cards, and Ava left her old mobile phone here. The ones they have now are burners. Damien made sure of it."

Max crossed his arms. "So he's gone to Sari."

"It appears so. We knew that was probably where they were going." Rhys sat on the edge of the sofa, which seemed to give all the men permission to follow his lead. Malachi joined them as they sat.

Leo said, "Which means he's in Scandinavia somewhere."

"Wasn't Sari raised at a retreat near Gothenburg?" Max asked.

"Yes, but her family isn't from there," Rhys said. "Her mother was a dissenter and only brought Sari there when she was ready for school."

Malachi asked, "A dissenter? And who is Sari?"

"Sari is Damien's mate. Ava will be safe with her."

"Why?"

Rhys sighed. "This is so strange. You really don't remember any of this?"

Malachi crossed his arms and shrugged. "Bits and pieces."

"I just... don't understand."

Of course you don't. You haven't lost every bloody memory that matters. Malachi pushed back his own annoyance and tried to explain. "Sometimes it's like being reminded of something. Some of the things you've said, I remember immediately. As if I had always known them. Like my *talesm.*" He leaned forward with his elbows on his knees. "Almost as soon as Leo mentioned them, I knew what he was talking about."

"That's so strange," Leo said.

"What?"

"The way you're sitting. You always sit like that. And your expressions. They are exactly the same. Sorry. Not important."

Max frowned at his cousin, then turned back to Malachi. "Please. Continue."

"Now I remember them in detail," Malachi said. "I remember how they felt. I remember... scribing them. Is there any way of knowing whether or not they'll return?" Hundreds of hours of careful work had vanished from his skin, and he felt the loss of power keenly.

"None," Rhys said. "Not unless Evren's scribes find something in the archives that mentions Irin returning from the dead."

Max was looking at Malachi with narrowed eyes. "The more important question is are they still working? If they're not, you're aging right now. Your magic is channeled by your *talesm.* If they're gone—"

"You'll be weak," Leo's face was pale. "Unprotected. Like... a human."

Max said, "Not to mention, you look a bit naked. It's unnerving."

Rhys patted Malachi's shoulder. "At least we know his natural powers are still intact. Language seems to come normally, otherwise he'd not be able to speak Turkish like he did at the gate."

"I thought I was born here," Malachi said.

Rhys shrugged. "You're Irin. The Old Language is our first tongue, the only one we're born knowing. The humans who found you, did you understand them at first?"

"No. I had to find a newspaper. I could read it. After that... the pieces of the language just seemed to fall into place, and I could under-stand them."

"See?" Rhys said to Max. "His natural magic still works, which means he can build his other magic from there. He'll have to relearn his spells and rescribe his *talesm*, but he should be able to recover."

"And who knows?" Leo said. "Maybe when you find Ava, she can help."

Rhys nodded. "Agreed. The first step is to find Ava and Damien. One, she shouldn't grieve any longer than necessary. Two, she's his marked mate. She may be able to heal him."

"Do you think she could give me back my memories?"

The hollow corners of his mind mocked him. Malachi knew he had lost his past, but he didn't know where to find it. Or even where to look. Isolated knowledge and bits of the past kept popping up unexpectedly, tucking themselves into pockets in his mind. But with each new revela-tion, the depth of his loss only became more disturbing.

"She might be able to help," Max said. "You remembered her? Immediately?"

"No—yes. I remember her voice. Her face." He grasped at the fragments, as if his very existence depended on holding them. "Hers was the first face I saw in my mind. I saw us here. Together. We were…" He looked around at the curious faces of the men. "None of your business."

Leo grinned and Max shook his head.

"Still a lucky bastard," Rhys said. "Even half-alive and naked."

❖ ❖ ❖   ❖ ❖ ❖

Rhys led him out of the sitting room where they'd been enjoying the fire, up to a terrace that led to a series of stairs, which twisted and crawled up the hill. The sky was deep blue and the first stars were beginning to shine. Lamplight flickered along the face of the cliffs, and Malachi stopped. Looking up, his eyes hung on the majesty of stars that littered the sky. Pure white against the deep blue and purple night, he blinked and caught a glimpse of a dark sun rising in his mind.

"Malachi?"

He shook off the vision and continued to follow Rhys down a narrow corridor carved into the rocks.

"My rooms are all the way back here?"

"You like your privacy. You always pick rooms that are isolated if you can."

The green door flashed in Malachi's mind a second before they turned the corner and saw it.

"This was my room. Was Ava here, too?"

Rhys's voice was thick. "Yes. She stayed here after you died. Her things are still there. She wanted... Well, she wanted to sleep where you had been."

His heart tripped as he put a hand on the door and pushed it open. Her scent hit him immediately, and traces of her were scattered around the room. The shoes tucked under the bed. The large suitcase in front of the wardrobe. This was the room he'd seen in his mind. There was the spot on the wall where she'd braced her hand as they made love. He walked around the room, willing more memories to come, but his mind was stubbornly silent.

"These are her things?"

"She needed warm clothes wherever Damien was taking her, so she left her other things here. Said she'd just come back for them. She even left her computer."

Malachi frowned, picking up a sweater that lay draped across the chair by the door. He held it up to his face and inhaled.

"Did she take her camera?" he asked, his face still buried in her scent.

"You remember."

Rhys was wearing a huge smile when he looked up.

"What?"

"Her camera. She's a photographer. Did you remember?"

He walked over to the bed and touched the edge of a pillow. "I don't know. The question just popped into my head."

"Hmm." Rhys watched him taking in the room. "To answer your question, yes, she took her camera. I don't know why she left her laptop. Maybe where they're going there's no Wi-Fi."

Malachi looked for the small silver laptop and found it on the desk. He walked over and opened it.

"I'm fairly sure it's password protected," Rhys said. "So I doubt..."

Malachi let his fingers type without thinking.

F-R-E-A-K

"I hate that password," he muttered, staring at the picture of him and Ava that popped up as the background.

"How did you know her password?"

"I don't know."

The picture had been taken near the ocean in the early evening. Malachi thought it might be near the pier in Kuşadası. There were lanterns floating in the background and the two of them stood smiling with the purple sky behind them. He remembered the faint perfume he could still smell on her sweater.

"Rhys," he said, trying to mask the tension in his voice. "Can you please—"

"I'll go," the other man said quietly. "Let me know if you need anything. I'm down the stairs and to the right. The red door with the lion character on it."

Malachi hardly heard the door close. He grabbed the laptop and took it to the bed, leaning against pillows tinged with a faint floral scent that might have been her shampoo. He turned his face to the side and inhaled, pressing his cheek where hers might have lain.

He scrolled through her pictures, looking at the stunning images she must have taken in Istanbul. Boats on the water. Children laughing at pigeons. Old men catching fish. He skimmed through her albums from Cappadocia until one miniature caught his eye. The album was entitled "M is a thief." He clicked on it.

The first pictures were more bedding than anything else. Blurry. Out of focus. He frowned, then let out a choked laugh the farther he clicked through the scene. He'd stolen her camera. She was hiding in the sheets, but she was laughing. He'd managed to capture the top of her head in that shot. Her nose in the other. The edge of her smile as he tickled her ribs. Then…

His breath stopped.

The last picture in the set was off center and crooked. Snapped as he held the camera away from them, capturing their kiss. Her fingers were pressed into his inked shoulders, and his mouth took her swollen lips.

"Ava," he breathed out, touching the computer screen before it blinked out. Malachi tried to turn it on again, but the battery must have died. He sat up and carefully placed the computer back on the desk, plugging it in before he stripped off his clothes and returned to the bed. He wrapped himself in sheets that he knew smelled of his mate and closed his eyes.

Why couldn't he remember her?

Malachi felt broken. His memories. His lost *talesm*. Confusion and weakness. All of it paled in comparison to the gut-deep awareness that his mate was in the world, grieving him, and he could not ease her.

He closed his eyes and searched for her in dreams.

THE FOREST WAS MIDNIGHT BLACK, SHROUDED IN A THICK FOG THAT curled and twisted around his ankles. The path he followed was not clear; wet branches slapped his face as he stumbled in the dark.

Where was she?

He could hear her in the distance. Her cries ripped through his chest. Every time she grew louder, he was forced to turn again as the path diverted him. The dark maze wove through the forest, teasing him. Frustrating him.

He would not be defeated.

The dark mass rose before him, looming over his head as if trying to block out the stars. Damp branches laced with thorns twisted in on themselves, blocking him from going farther. The maze urged him to turn again, but he stopped. Held his hand up.

Her voice was audible now.

"Please. Please come back."

With a frustrated roar, he pounded on the thorns. Then he spun around, looking for a way out or around or through. It was a dead end. There was nowhere to turn but away from her again.

But his mate needed him. She called for him, and he'd left her alone too long.

He plunged his hands into the thick brush that separated him from her voice. He ignored the pain as he forced his way forward.

"Please," she whispered, her voice thick with tears. "I need you."

He tore at the hedge, ripping away the thorns and branches that tore his skin, ignoring the pain in his chest, ignoring everything except her voice. Finally, his bloody hand reached through and felt the cool air on the other side.

Pale moonlight streamed through the fog as he forced his bleeding body the rest of the way through the brush. There, on the far side of the clearing, he saw her.

Broken and bent with grief, she curled into herself, her arms wrapped around her legs. She wore a pale robe, streaked with mud, which pooled around her feet. She rocked back and forth as he approached. He approached cautiously, kneeling in front of her where she sat. Then he reached out a tentative hand and pushed a damp curl from her face.

She looked up.

"You left me."

"I found you."

"Why did it take so long?"

"I was lost."

Her gold eyes didn't glow as they should have. They were dull with sorrow. Exhausted with weeping. He could see the tear tracks glittering on her cheeks.

"I found you, *reshon*."

She held out her arms like a child asking for comfort. He reached out and picked her up, lifting her from the cold ground and cradling her against his chest. He felt her fingers tracing over his scratched skin.

"What happened to you?"

"I told you. I was lost, but I came back."

"You found me."

"Yes."

"And you're not leaving again?"

"No. I promise."

"I'm so tired." She laid her head on his shoulder, and he felt his heart swell with purpose.

"Then rest while I hold you. I promise I won't let go."

CHAPTER

FOUR

Sarihöfn, Norway

When Ava woke, she felt rested for the first time in weeks. Her head was clear. The tension that seemed to burn under her skin was gone. She felt fresh. Renewed. So renewed she didn't even scowl when she heard the knock on the door. By the time she was up and presentable, Damien had already let the visitor in. It was the woman she'd met the previous afternoon.

"Good morning," the visitor said with a smile. "I hope you slept well. My name is Astrid."

"Yeah, I remember."

She was definitely the most welcoming woman Ava had met so far. Without the heavy clothes and aura of magic, Astrid looked like a teacher or a doctor. Smart and friendly, she exuded calm welcome. Sari and Mala hadn't made the greatest impression the day before, and Ava had gone to bed with second thoughts about the remote enclave where Damien had brought her. Astrid's appearance put her at ease.

"So, what's up?" She looked between Damien and Astrid.

"Sari and Damien thought it would be good for you to tour the retreat today and get a feel for where things are since you'll be here for some time."

Ava asked Damien, "How long?"

He shrugged. "As long as you want."

"As long as it takes," Astrid said, "for you to be able to control your magic. Letting you roam the world untrained would be too dangerous."

Ava bristled. "I've managed for a few years on my own."

"The Grigori hunt you. The humans do not understand you. And Damien says you mated with an Irin scribe who bonded with you and lent you his power. Your magic will be stronger now."

"I have it under control."

Barely. The voices pressed on her. Damien's presence might have been soothing, but it did nothing to dull the soul voices as Malachi had done. They crept up on her. She had no shield from them. And worse, she seemed to have tapped into other voices, voices that were unlike the others. Dark and twisted, they haunted her dreams. At times Ava thought she was losing it.

Astrid's eyes were narrowed in suspicion. "Remember, you might not even realize you've worked magic. Without training, you'd have no idea. Here, you will be protected, and so will the rest of the world."

"You're acting like I'm some loaded gun."

"In a sense, you are. I started learning to control my magic as soon as I could talk. My mother guided me until I went into formal training at thirteen. For scribes"—she nodded toward Damien—"the act of working magic is far more deliberate. No child is born writing. It is learned. But for Irina, our magic comes like breathing. It is our first language. The fact that you've been able to exist without hurting those around you is somewhat astonishing."

The steady woman's voice grated on her, killing the peace she'd woken with. "I would never hurt any—"

"You need our help. You burst Damien's eardrums when your mate was killed." Astrid's voice was no longer soothing. She stepped closer to Ava, and though the woman was even shorter than Ava, Astrid's presence dwarfed her. "You hurt yourself, three Irin, and countless Grigori—"

"You're worried about the Grigori now?"

"I'd kill every one of them if I could," Astrid said calmly. "But that is not the issue."

Maybe Astrid wasn't so unlike Sari after all.

"Maybe it is," Ava said. "Maybe I don't want to hide in a village somewhere and lick my wounds. Maybe I want to fight with the scribes instead of—"

"You have no idea what we do here."

"And maybe I don't want to!"

She stopped shouting when Damien put a hand on her shoulder.

"Sister," he said quietly, brushing a hand down her arm.

Ava felt the calm immediately. She took a deep breath and tried to focus on the peace she'd felt that morning, but it was wrapped up in dreams of Malachi and it hurt as much as it helped.

Astrid had backed down, too.

"Stay, Ava. We can't force you, but we can help you. I promise."

She said nothing, but relaxed when she saw Astrid smile a little.

"So, you want to kill Grigori?" the woman asked.

"They killed my mate."

"And how do you know we don't kill Grigori?"

Ava frowned. "But the scribes said—"

"Irin scribes say many things, hidden away in their scribe houses or lecturing in council meetings." Astrid glanced at Damien and winked. "But they can be frightfully blind when it comes to reading things other than books."

Ava hadn't considered it, but it was true. Most of the scribes she'd met had admitted to not seeing an Irina in two hundred years. Why on earth was she taking their word for anything?

"So, what you're saying is—?"

"Have you seen how the scribes fight?" Astrid asked, stepping closer.

"Yes."

"They are the world's finest warriors. None can match them in strength or grace. They are ruthless. Strong. Fast." There was a fierce pride in Astrid's eyes when she spoke. "Their *talesm* is like a living armor around them. A trained scribe could take on a dozen Grigori soldiers and walk away with their dust on his shoulders. Do you want to fight like that?"

She wanted to scream, *Yes!* But Ava flashed to the image of Malachi as he battled Grigori in the alley in Kuşadası, the graceful thrusts and twisting combat. The powerful way his muscles moved under his shirt. She didn't think she'd ever be able to match that. What was she thinking?

"I… I don't know if I—"

"You can't." Astrid cut her off. "You never will. You are not Irin. You will learn physical fighting—we learned our lesson two hundred years ago—but Irin have their strengths"—her eyes flickered to Damien—"and we have ours. To fight as an Irina, you must learn to use magic. And we can teach you that. The scribes think we withdrew?" She shrugged. "That just shows you how well we can hide."

A surge of desire shot through Ava. The dark voices whispered in her mind and a ripple of power teased her lips.

Kill them, they whispered. *Take them. Hurt them as they hurt you. Hurt them more…*

"You want that," Astrid said.

"Yes."

"I can see. But before any of that happens, you must do something else."

"What?"

Astrid's voice softened. "You must rest, sister. You must grieve. And you must heal."

The Irina's words were sour in her ears. An ache rose in her heart, and she tried to push it back.

"I'd rather just kill something," Ava whispered.

"You try to forget him, but you can't. You never will. He is the other half of your soul."

"Astrid," Damien said softly, but the Irina ignored him.

"Half of you died with him, Ava."

"Shut up."

"Half of you died, but you must understand, *half of him still lives.*"

She could feel the tears welling. Tears she'd shunned. Tears she forced herself to battle back. If she let them loose, they would fall forever.

"He lives in you."

"Shut. Up." She choked on the lump in her throat. "You have no idea—"

"I have every idea." Astrid took a hand and put it to her throat. Then a whisper came from her lips in the Old Language, and the marks on her skin began to glow. Her mating marks were intricate, like gold lace covering her skin. When she pulled her hand away from her throat, Ava saw a band appear. Duller than the other marks, it crossed her collarbone and disappeared over her shoulders.

"What is that?" Ava asked.

Damien put his hand on Astrid's shoulder, leaning down. "Too soon, sister."

Astrid blinked and her mating marks disappeared. "Of course. Forgive me, Damien. I forget myself."

"A rare occurrence, if I remember correctly."

"Not so rare as before," she said with a smile. She turned back to Ava, all friendly business again. "Shall we meet in an hour? That will give you time to dress and eat some breakfast. Did Karen bring a basket?"

"Yes, it's in the kitchen."

"Good." Astrid nodded brusquely. "Eat something, dress warmly. Good shoes. I'll be back in an hour to show you around."

"I'll be ready."

"And if you need anything, if you're not sleeping well… Just know that's very normal when we lose a mate. I can help if you wish it. I'm the resident healer here."

Damien stepped to the door as Astrid walked toward it. "Thank you."

Ava saw him grasp Astrid's hand in both of his. Saw the gentle hold she knew must be easing some of the other woman's tension. Then Astrid smiled sweetly at him and left.

"She's a widow," Ava said a few moments after the door closed. "Astrid. She's a widow."

Damien nodded. "Yes."

"What was that band around her throat? Does that happen when…"

"No," he said softly. "Nothing has changed with your mating marks, Ava. Astrid wears a mourning collar to show respect for her lost mate, but it's not permanent like a mating mark."

"How long?"

"He was killed during the Rending. He was a good man. A friend."

Ava looked out the window. She could still see Astrid walking along the pathway to the large colorful house where most of the Irina lived. Her soft brown curls bounced cheerfully and she saw her stop another woman and exchange some words that made both throw their heads back in laughter. Would she ever laugh like that again? Would she mourn for two hundred years, as Astrid had?

Half of you died with him.

Only half? It felt like more.

As if he could read her mind, Damien said, "You will take your own path to healing, Ava. Don't ever look to another to rule your grief."

She didn't want to think about Malachi. Didn't want to think about her dark dreams and the dull pain that lived in her chest.

Ava slid on a facade and turned from the window. "I heard someone brought breakfast?"

• • •   • • •

Hours later, she was walking through the valley with Astrid, drinking in the beauty of the water and the sky. The hills rolled softly up from the fjord, and the houses dotted the green meadows that rested in the shadow of the mountains. The retreat was far from just a collection of houses. There were greenhouses, workshops, even animals the community kept for milk and eggs.

"We're mostly self-sustained. We try to keep to ourselves. The people in the nearest town think we're hippies." Astrid smiled. "They leave us alone, for the most part."

"How many women?"

"It varies. Some of the older Irina, those Sari trusts the most, come and go. Living here full time, there are probably fifty or so."

"The ones who come and go, what do they do?"

"Various things. Some maintain ties to the human world. A few have mates in active service in a scribe house somewhere relatively close. Most do other things that protect this haven and a few others like it around the world. So much of the world is run on the Internet now. We're hardly isolated at all."

"So there are other places like this? Where?"

Astrid glanced at her. "Sari doesn't know you that well."

"And everyone just follows Sari?" Ava found that hard to believe.

"At the end of the day," Astrid said with a smile, "this is really her house. Her land. She doesn't force any of us to stay, but where else would we go?"

"What about the scribe houses? Or that council they told me about in Vienna?"

"The council?" She sneered. "Old men who think Irina shouldn't leave the house. The council of the elders thinks the only thing Irina are good for is breeding little scribes and inventing things to make them rich. They're the ones who isolated us in retreats to begin with. They're the ones who allowed the Rending to happen."

Ava was shocked by the ire in the woman's voice.

"Okay, then what about the scribes? The ones in Istanbul—"

Astrid stopped walking. "The Irin are far from one mind about this. You've seen Damien and Sari. You know they're equal partners. I'm sure your mate was the same. They keep to the old ways. Many of the scribes are just like that, because that's the way it's supposed to be."

"So—"

"But that's not the reality. Before the Rending—even now—many Irin wanted the Irina powerless. If we were their equals, then that made the scribes less, in their eyes. Twisted, I know, but some of the sickness of the human world has crept into the Irin race, as well."

"So why withdraw?" Ava asked. "You can't change things if you just disappear."

"We didn't have much of a choice at first. And now?" Astrid shrugged and continued walking. "We change things. In our own way."

"In secret. So that no one knows what you're doing or where you are?"

"If that's the way it needs to be? Yes. Do you think we want to paint another target on our back?"

"Why can't you work *with* the scribes? Work together? Malachi said that Irin were most powerful when they were mated."

"Yes, because we can loan them Irina power when they go into battle," Astrid's voice was acid. "Why do you think the Grigori decimated us as they did? Most of the Irina were weak from loaning our mates magic. So when we were attacked ourselves, we were vulnerable. You think we will chance that again? Think we will put our sisters and the few children we still have at risk so that the Irin gain glory?"

"Malachi loaned me his power," Ava said. "And I gave him nothing. He went into battle weak so that I could be strong. And he died because of it. He sacrificed his own safety for mine."

Astrid said nothing for a moment.

"Your mate will be rewarded in the heavens." Astrid spoke quietly as she continued walking. "The Creator values nothing more than love. And what is love that does not sacrifice?"

"But you're acting like he's the only one." Ava shook her head. "Malachi and his brothers treated me like some sort of royalty when I was at the scribe house in Istanbul. Don't you realize? There are men —*good* scribes—out there. Fighting against the Grigori who harm people. Fighting against the Fallen. And they're doing it alone. They're mourning mates and children, *alone*." Ava thought of the devastated faces of the scribes in Cappadocia. The longing she'd seen in Rhys's face. In all of Malachi's brothers. "They would give anything to have the Irina back."

"*They* might, but you know little of the Irin world, Ava. One group of good scribes does not mean that we are safe from all. There are still those who want us silent. And that is something we will not be."

Ava said nothing. Astrid was right. She knew little about the Irin world outside her own narrow experience. It was an argument she couldn't win. At least, not at the moment. Plus, she was tired. The time change, the travel. Her restless nights all seemed to be catching up with her. It must have shown on her face.

"Come," Astrid said. "You're tired. We'll go to the house for lunch. Then you can rest."

"I thought I wasn't allowed in the house."

"No." Astrid smiled. "*Damien* isn't allowed in the house—for now—and he insisted on staying close to you. Which is why you're in one of the cottages. You're Irina. You're always welcome in Sari's house."

"But her mate isn't?" Ava shook her head. "I gotta meet this woman."

Astrid's smile was mischievous. "You will."

• • •   • • •

WHEN AVA WALKED INTO SARI'S HOUSE, THE ENERGY OF THE PLACE almost knocked her over. Her exhaustion fled immediately, even before Astrid led her to the dining hall.

Far from institutional, the dining hall in the house was attached to the kitchen. So while some of the women cooked, others sat at the table, some chatting and keeping company with the cooks, others working on their own projects. Ava saw one black-haired woman working on a laptop and slugging coffee back, seemingly oblivious to the chaos around her. Another was knitting an intricate scarf. Still another was playing a guitar in one corner while two others listened.

The whole mess created a lively hum over Ava's skin that echoed the sudden jolt of power in her blood.

And sitting at the end of the table, braiding the hair of a girl no older than twelve, was Sari. Her long blond hair fell almost to her waist, and her face was softer than the first time Ava had seen her. The girl tilted her head back and Sari kissed her forehead before she shooed her away. She wore a soft blue sweater that brought out the color of her eyes. She noticed Astrid and Ava, and her eyes narrowed a bit as she waved them over.

Sitting down on the bench to her left, Astrid motioned to the chair across from her that backed up to one of the stoves.

"Sit there," she said. "It's the warmest spot."

"I'm fine."

"Sari, this is Ava. She's not a dumb human." Astrid waved her hands between the two. "And Ava, this is Sari. She's as mean as she looks, but she won't bite unless she has to."

"Ha ha," Sari said, rolling her eyes at the woman who was obviously a close friend. Then she turned to Ava. "Damien told Astrid that you've traveled to Norway before?"

"Yes, for work."

"You're a photographer?"

"I am."

"Welcome to my country. And to my home."

"Thank you."

The woman looked amused at Ava's terse answers. "Have I offended you in some way?"

Ava decided that Sari would respect the direct approach. "I showed up and you tried to bash in the head of the guy who's been protecting me. Even though he's your mate. What do you think?"

The room fell almost silent around them, but Ava never let her eyes leave Sari's. Sari said nothing, but the smile never left her lips.

"And how is this your business, Ava Sakarya? Did I attack you?"

Ava supposed she had a point. It wasn't her business. Not really. So why was she so resentful of the woman? "No, you didn't attack me. I just think… you're lucky to have him," Ava said in a low voice, her eyes flicking to Astrid. "Not all of us do."

Was it her imagination, or did a hint of guilt cross Sari's face?

"I suppose you're right. Then again, he's quite lucky to have me, as well."

"I'm sure he'd say the same thing."

Sari's eyes gleamed. "I know he would."

There was a pause, then attention shifted away from Sari and Ava as the voices in the room resumed their quiet hum.

Sari stretched her arms up. She was an immensely tall woman. Her body and presence both made Ava feel like a child. Her muscles were hardened and lean. In the human world, people would assume she was a serious athlete. To Ava, she simply looked lethal.

"Are you comfortable here?" Sari asked.

"Yes. Thank you."

"And how are you sleeping?"

Astrid barked something in a language Ava didn't understand, then exchanged a few sharp words with Sari.

But Sari only smiled at her. "Astrid tells me that this is none of my business, and that she is the healer. I disagree. You're in Sarihöfn—which was named for my great-grandmother, by the way, not me—so that makes your sleep part of my business."

"My sleep? What does sleep—"

"Sleeping. Dreaming," Sari said. "For us, these are not the same as for humans. Sleep is when our souls reach out. We can perform magic in dreams if we're not careful. Didn't they explain that to you?"

"No. There was a lot the scribes never explained."

Sari sighed. "Well, that is… sadly typical. They do love their mysteries and cryptic puzzles."

"There also wasn't much time."

Astrid said, "Sari, move on. I'll talk to her about sleeping. I think she's fine."

"Very well," Sari said. "Astrid tells me you are a mystery. Were you truly raised among humans?"

"Yes."

"Very curious. I assume your mother lost her mate. Why did she not seek shelter with her family?"

The focus of the room was back on them both, and Ava tried not to cringe under the scrutiny. She felt like she had every time she entered a new school. Her stepfather's money and connections meant that people had certain preconceived notions about who Ava would be. Their notions always exceeded the reality.

"You're not crazy. You're a miracle."

His voice whispered to her, reminding her to sit up straighter. "My mother is human, not Irina."

Sari frowned. "I know a human raised you, but who is your *real* mother? A nanny? A servant? It wouldn't be unheard of after the Rending to hide among the humans, but someone must have shielded you as a child. Didn't they ever find out? Surely the scribes with all their voluminous records could find your real mother. Even in America, they have archives."

Why hadn't Damien explained it better? "No. Lena Matheson *is* my real mother. And my father—"

"So she *is* Irina." Sari looked as frustrated as Ava. "And mated to a human?"

"No, my mother is *not* Irina. I told you—"

"But she has to be."

"She's not," Ava said through gritted teeth.

"But you're Irina!" Sari said, grasping Ava's wrist. She tried to pull away but couldn't. "I can feel you. So powerful. You're like a shot of pure energy. And mated, as well. Marked, Astrid said."

"Yes."

"So there must be some mistake." Sari squeezed her hands tighter. "You must not have known. Your real mother—"

"Lena Matheson *is* my mother," she said. "Now let me go."

She didn't. "But your mother must be Irina."

"Well, she's not. And before you ask, I look exactly like her. Everyone knows I'm her daughter. A single look would tell you."

The whole room had fallen silent, and Ava fought the urge to crawl under the table or run screaming from all the eyes on her. She trained her eyes on the scarred grain of the wood table, trying to block out the room.

"How is this possible?" Sari's voice soft and searching. "Sister... how did you survive?"

The sudden softness in Sari's voice startled her. "I just did. I knew I was different. Always different. Obviously, the scribes were looking—"

"But how?" Sari lifted a hand to her cheek. "Who shielded you? Who taught you to silence the voices?" She turned her hands to weave Ava's fingers with hers, her grip strong. When she did, Ava felt safe, like a blanket of protection covered her, and she understood why all the others followed the woman. In that moment, Ava knew that Sari would fight to the death to protect her, no matter where she had come from. Because she was Irina.

She was like them.

"No one taught me anything," Ava said. "I've heard voices my whole life. I just thought I was crazy."

The collective gasp from the women around the room made Ava want to run. She would have, if Sari's hands hadn't held her in place. She chanced a look up.

The color had drained from Astrid's face, and she held her hand to her throat.

"Oh, Ava…," she murmured.

Sari looked murderous.

"I'm not hungry." Ava tried to push back from the table, but Sari locked her foot around the leg of Ava's chair. "Let me go. I want to leave now."

Sari looked around for a moment, then she barked out something in another language and the women around the table bustled back to their tasks. When she spoke again, her voice was chillingly calm. "So the humans thought you were mentally ill?"

Ava shrugged. "What were they supposed to think when a little girl told them she heard voices no one else heard?"

That was a question none of them seemed to be able to answer. After a few moments, a rich bowl of steaming soup was placed in front of her along with a basket of sliced bread. As the food was set down, Sari removed her foot from Ava's chair.

"Eat, sister."

Ava had the urge to leave again, just because the woman's commanding tone rubbed her the wrong way. But the scent of the soup was enticing, and Astrid's hopeful eyes met hers.

"Please, Ava. Stay and eat with us."

"Fine." She picked up a piece of the bread and dipped it in the soup.

Astrid and Sari both murmured something under their breath, then they began to eat.

"I'm glad Damien brought you here," Sari said after a few minutes of silent eating. "It is not good that you were in the world for so long on your own. You could have easily hurt someone, including yourself. Not to mention, I'm amazed you're not locked up somewhere, rocking in a corner."

"I'm rich enough to avoid padded rooms," Ava said. "So that helps."

"I imagine it does." She paused and looked out the window toward the cottage. "And then you had to go and stumble into my mate's scribe house."

"He wasn't very happy to have me."

Sari rolled her eyes. "He's a suspicious old man. The Creator has plans he doesn't always share with his scribes, no matter what they'd like to think. The folly of men is pride."

Astrid said, "And the folly of women is resentment, sister."

"I didn't ask you, Astrid."

"I think Malachi said something similar once," Ava added after a minute of quiet staring between the two. "About Damien being a stubborn old man."

At that statement, Sari and Astrid exchanged a look that Ava couldn't decipher. Then Astrid said, "It's good that he brought you to us. We can begin your training immediately."

"And what kind of training will that be?"

Ava looked up when they didn't answer. Astrid looked amused, and Sari's eyes were glinting.

"A very thorough training," she said. "My grandmother will enjoy meeting such a mysterious Irina."

The knot of dread settled in Ava's belly. "Oh. Goody."

CHAPTER
FIVE

"Tell me what this says."

Rhys pushed a clay tablet across the table, then leaned back into his chair. Malachi tore his eyes away from his knuckles, which were inexplicably scratched. He didn't remember hurting himself, but his hands looked like he'd fought his way through thorns. He took a deep breath and looked down at the library table, frowning when he saw the smooth clay in front of him.

"This says nothing."

"Look again."

"Rhys, there's nothing…" He felt, rather than saw, a tremor from the corner of his eye. "Wait. There *is* something—"

"Don't look at it."

He looked, growling in the back of his throat when the shadow disappeared.

"I told you not to look," Rhys said. "Take a minute to close your eyes, then look again. This time, don't try. Let your mind absorb it without conscious thought."

Malachi closed his eyes, took a deep breath, and looked again, staring at the center of the tablet as ghostly figures teased the edges of his vision. He didn't focus on them. The letters seemed to take on a life of their own, crawling tentatively from the edges of the tablet until they formed beneath his gaze. When the letters seemed more solid, he let out the breath he'd been holding and allowed his eyes to finally focus on the top of the tablet, looking first right, then left. Instinct guided him as the characters turned into syllables in his mind. The syllables turned into words he translated instantly.

"'And Leoc, giver of visions and bearer of prophecy, returned to the heavens,'" he began, reading aloud. "'His daughters bear his mark, the mark of the seer, though their eyes now glimmer only faintly with their father's gift.'" The story went on, talking about the gifts of prophecy some of the female of his race were given. The tablet was old, and though the writing had been completely worn away, he could still read the words that had been written by an ancient hand. When he finally looked up, Rhys was watching him with a measuring stare.

"Your natural magic is as strong as it ever was. In fact, I think it's actually stronger. A young scribe just starting his training would have had to meditate on that tablet for hours before the writing revealed itself."

"What language is it?"

"Greek. Medieval period. It's one of the earliest tablets this scribe house produced. Most of the older documents were taken to the master libraries in Vienna many years ago when human interference became more of a concern."

"And I can read it because…"

"Because you're a scribe. We can see and decipher any written language with little to no practice." Rhys slid another document in front of him, this one a sheet encased in a clear plastic sleeve that held tiny rows of black characters. "Try this one."

Malachi frowned for a moment, then said, "It's a tax record. Of… barley?"

"That's a Sumerian tax ledger copied from the original clay tablet three hundred years ago."

"Why would we preserve a tax ledger?"

Rhys frowned, as if he'd never considered that before. "Why wouldn't we?"

"Well…" He frowned, not wanting to offend.

"Irin scribes preserve knowledge, Malachi. It's our mission." Rhys scooted forward and leaned over the table, clutching the edges of the tablet. "Battling the Grigori. Protecting humans. These are all secondary pursuits, and a necessary evil of this fallen world. But preserving knowledge is our purpose. It is what we were born to do."

"But why is a tax ledger important?" Malachi picked up the plastic sleeve that contained what must have been hours of work.

"Maybe it's not important to you," Rhys said. "Or me. Maybe it won't be important for one hundred years. Or five hundred." Rhys shrugged. "Maybe it will never be important. But if it is, it will be there. If the knowledge is needed, it will not have been lost. To lose knowledge is a tragedy. As you learn more about yourself, about our world, don't forget that. This"—he motioned to the shelves of books and scrolls around him—"is our purpose. Beyond the fighting. Beyond the struggles. This is what scribes were born to do."

Malachi nodded and ignored the voice in his head that told him sitting in the library with Rhys was most definitely *not* what he'd been born to do. What he'd been born to do was help his mate, who was somewhere in the world, suffering without him. The urge to get up and leave the library was hard to resist.

"I know you must be feeling stifled," Rhys said. "Frustrated. But until we have some direction on where to look for Damien and Ava, it's no use rushing off. We'd be just as well to stay here and try to figure out what you can and can't do."

Malachi pushed the Sumerian manuscript back toward Rhys. "I can read ancient languages and understand them. So useful. What else can I do?"

Rhys ignored the sarcasm and held up his hand. On the inside of his left wrist was a swirl of ancient letters, almost too small to read across the table. They curled around in a spiral until the words crawled up his forearm, then twisted and wrapped around his arm like a snake.

"You can do this."

A low hunger started in his belly. Something in the dark corners of his memory told Malachi that this was something he wanted. "*Talesm.*"

"*Talesm.*"

"Our magic." Malachi rubbed hands over his bare forearms.

Rhys took a deep breath before he spoke. "Irin have two kinds of magic. Natural magic, which we are born with—the kind that lets you read any language in front of you and see words even after they've been erased from the physical eye—and learned magic. Both were gifted to us by our fathers."

"The angels?"

Rhys nodded. "Our books say that when the Forgiven left the earth, the Creator allowed them to hide a shadow of heavenly magic within their children. But not everything. That had been their mistake with their first children. They had given them too much power. So much that some had to be destroyed. Before they left, they divided their magic. To their sons, they gave the gift and power of the written word. To their daughters, the songs of the ancients, along with gifts of healing, foresight, and discernment."

Malachi remembered the story on the clay tablet. "The daughters of Leoc?"

"An old name for those Irina who are gifted—or some say cursed—with visions. Different angels bore different gifts, depending on their role in the heavenly realm. Their children bear a fraction of their fathers' powers, but it is still formidable. For Irin, we learned over time that we could work magic—control it, mold it for our own uses—through the written word."

"And the Grigori?"

Rhys shook his head. "The Fallen were not gifted as the Forgiven were. Their children are more than human, yes, but they cannot wield magic as we can. A Fallen may loan some magic to a Grigori occasionally, but it is not really theirs. When we Irin tattoo spells on our bodies, we permanently make that magic a part of us."

"It's like armor," he said.

"That's one way of looking at it. We use it to strengthen our bodies. Make ourselves stronger. Increase our longevity. A mature and trained Irin scribe is practically immortal."

Malachi rubbed the back of his neck. "But not entirely."

"Clearly."

Silence fell between them, with nothing but the tick of a mantel clock filling the air. Rhys watched him with some unspoken question burning in his eyes.

"What?" Malachi finally asked. "Are you tired of telling me all these things? We should take a break. I feel like running."

"You generally do after a day cooped up inside. Or when you're irritated."

For some reason, Rhys's knowledge of his habits irked him. Why did this stranger know more about him than he did?

"Will my *talesm* come back?" he asked. "Or are they lost? Will I have to tattoo them all over again? How long will it take to be strong enough?"

"We have no idea." Rhys shrugged a single shoulder. "You need to do basic protection spells, at the very least. Once we find Ava—"

"And when will that be?"

"I don't know." Rhys's eyes flashed. "I told you, we don't know where Damien took her. We're doing our best, but you're going to have to be patient."

"I am being patient," he growled.

Rhys made a disgusted noise at the back of his throat. "You're still so… you. Even when you're not."

"What's that supposed to mean?" His shoulders tensed.

"Never thinking ahead. Rushing into danger with no thought to—"

"I'm thinking of my mate," Malachi bit out, rising to his feet. "She needs me, and I must go to her."

"To do what? Protect her?" Rhys stood up, glaring at Malachi from across the table. "You can hardly protect yourself right now. You need to—"

"I need *her*," Malachi said. "And she needs—"

"She needs her mate back!" Rhys snapped. "Right now, you're only a shadow of who she needs."

Malachi bit back the rage on the tip of his tongue and narrowed his eyes at the man who had called himself his friend. Or, he'd called the old Malachi his friend. Perhaps the two were no longer the same.

"You are angry with me," he said, crossing his arms. "Resentful. Why?"

His old friend's head snapped back in surprise, and his green eyes widened. "I…I'm not."

"You are. Why?"

Rhys's mouth dropped open, but he did not speak. When his words finally came, they were almost inaudible. "I love her, you know. Maybe not like you did, but I do love her."

He shoved back the instinctive anger and spoke calmly. "She is my mate."

"She is." Rhys looked down, shuffling the papers they'd been looking at into a pile. "She is, without a doubt, your *reshon*. A true soul mate. I saw it even before you did, I think."

Malachi didn't know how, but the emotion was there, wrapping his mind with certainty. "I love her."

"I believe you," Rhys said, before clearing his throat. "You love your mate. But… you don't love *Ava*. You can't, because you don't know her anymore."

The hollow loss rang in his chest, and he knew, in part, that Rhys was correct. As much as he hated it, Malachi knew the other man spoke the truth. And there was nothing he could do about it.

"She needed you back. And you are. But you're not the same man. I don't know if you ever will be. And that—*that* is why I am angry."

• • • ✦ • • •

MAXIM, LEO, RHYS, AND MALACHI MET IN THE SITTING ROOM THAT evening. The outside air had taken on the snap of autumn, but in the house in the caves, the fire warmed the small room where they sat, drinking tea and talking.

"It's clear we're not going to find any written or electronic records," Max said. "Damien is too savvy for that. What we need is a personal connection."

Rhys scowled. "Damien doesn't have any personal connections. Why do you think he made such a good watcher?"

"Watcher?" Malachi asked.

Leo was the one who answered. The friendly scribe had been the one person with whom Malachi felt at complete ease. "All scribe houses in cities are organized in teams of five to eight men. A watcher is the head of the house. He tends the sacred fire and makes the most important decisions. Damien's your boss, in other words."

Max said, "Watchers also watch. Don't ever forget that. They're the ones who report to our main council in Vienna. It's very structured. Damien reported to the lieutenant of a councilor. That councilor reported to his elder. Every area is tightly controlled. The Irin council has ears everywhere."

"You don't have to make it sound so sinister," Rhys said. "Damien knew when to keep a confidence."

"He did." Max nodded. "Why do you think he was still a house watcher, as old and experienced as he is? If he were more politically savvy and less loyal, he'd be a lieutenant or even a councilor in Vienna now."

Leo said, "It's true, and you know it, Rhys. Damien became a problem for them when he mated Sari."

Malachi asked, "Why? She's the Irina he took Ava to?"

"His mate," Leo said. "And Sari was a problem because her parents were well-known to the council as dissenters ."

"What does that mean?"

Max continued, "It means they didn't agree with the steps taken when the retreats were formed. They didn't believe that women and children should be isolated or that Irina should withdraw from the human world."

"But Rhys said the Irina were being attacked by the humans for practicing magic. Wasn't it wiser to protect them?" Malachi frowned, remembering the painful history lesson he'd been forced to sit through. As always, once he'd been told, he could remember some things, though they mostly came in the recollection of feelings. Horror over the Rending, pain from the loss of his parents and village. A dull, burning anger toward an enemy he couldn't remember. The memories were shadowed and fleeting.

"True, they were being attacked," Max said. "But the dissenters didn't believe in turning from the old ways. Didn't believe in separation. They were proponents of the Irina being trained in more offensive magic and not focusing on only creative and healing work. Sari's parents were some of the most outspoken."

"Isolating half our population was never a smart idea," Leo said. "It left them too vulnerable."

"Be careful," Rhys said in a low voice. "You and Max were both children during the Rending. You don't remember before. You may not agree, but there were reasons the retreats were formed."

Max frowned. "I know—"

"No," Rhys continued in a quiet voice. "You think you know, but you don't. Not really. Try to imagine the pain of losing your mate and child because an ignorant human thought she was a witch sent by the devil and your child the devil's spawn. Imagine the rage you'd feel, then multiply that by the Inquisition. It wasn't only the Irin males who proposed the retreats, many Irina did, too. They didn't want to worry about their safety or the safety of their children. Didn't want to live as we do now, constantly battling against the Grigori and looking over their shoulder for humans, too. The retreats were not concentration camps; they were communities. There is no black and white here."

"The Irina left their protection in the hands of others," Max said. "How was that wise?"

"They left their protection in the hands of their *mates*." Rhys said. "Their fathers and brothers. How were we to foresee the Rending? Yes, there was fault, but our race's tragedy wasn't born from hate, Max. It was born from love. And the fear of losing what we loved."

"But now our race is dying because of it," Leo said. "And the council does nothing. Younger Irin want change—we know how much we need the Irina back—but no one will listen to us. Damien wouldn't listen to us."

"Maybe not as much as you'd wish, but he did listen. To me. To Malachi. He wasn't some puppet of Vienna, so don't make him out that way. And do you read *any* news? Vienna is churning with proposals to get the Irina back. You have to remember change comes slowly, Leo."

"Who did Damien trust?" Malachi asked, uninterested in the politics they were caught up in. "That's the real question, isn't it? Who else would know where his mate has hidden?"

Max and Leo exchanged a look Malachi couldn't decipher, then Max said, "I've heard Sari has a haven somewhere in Norway with a large group of Irina, but no one knows for sure. Her family was very secretive about their land after the retreats were formed, so only other members of the family knew about it."

"But Damien would have known?"

"Yes. I'm sure of it."

"And Gabriel," Rhys said under his breath. "Gabriel would know, too."

"You can't possibly think Damien would go to Gabriel," Max said. "Even I know the bad blood there. And there's no way he'd take Ava to Vienna."

"Of course Damien wouldn't go to him," Rhys said. "I'm just saying Gabriel might know where Sari is."

"Gabriel?" Malachi asked. "Who is… Are you talking about the angel?"

Max looked at Malachi as if he'd just spit on the floor between them. Leo laughed, and he could see Rhys trying to stifle a smile.

"Do you think archangels go for jaunts on the earthly realm?" Max said. "Of course not the angel Gabriel."

"Then who—"

"Gabriel is Damien's brother-in-law," Rhys said. "Or he was. His mate was Sari's twin sister. She was killed during the Rending."

"But why does he hate Damien? You said many scribes lost—"

"Sari's sister was killed during battle," Max said. "Not an ambush on a retreat. Damien took Tala into battle because of her foresight, and Volund's Grigori killed her."

"Oh." Suddenly, the bad blood between Damien and his brother-in-law made more sense.

Leo cleared his throat. "As you can imagine, they don't really get along."

• • •   • • •

IT WAS LEO WHO WAS LEFT TEACHING MALACHI THE NEXT NIGHT. THE two scribes were practicing Malachi's writing in the library, practicing the spells in the Old Language, which he would scribe on his hands and arms to give himself the most basic protection before they left. Max and Rhys were still arguing about the best way to approach Gabriel, who was an assistant to one of the senior elders on the Irin council. They were going to Vienna, but everyone agreed that Malachi needed more strength before they left.

"Your *talesm prim* will be much better this time," Leo said with a smile, holding up his hand. "For scribes, our first tattoo is always the shakiest, because we do it when we're young and first starting. Nothing can really prepare you for the pain of jabbing an ivory needle into your own skin over and over again."

Malachi tried to remain stoic. "I suppose not."

"We get better with practice, of course. But your writing is very good. Muscle memory, I imagine. We'll have to see how you do with the needle."

Malachi wrote carefully, always stopping short of completely finishing a sequence. Leo told him he must only finish the spell when he was casting it on his body. For now, he would simply practice. He looked at the book the other man had given him, a scribe's primer with dotted lines instead solid, to train the boys who would become warriors and scholars.

"What was your first spell?" Malachi asked. "After your *talesm prim*, what was your first?"

Leo smiled bashfully. "To be taller."

Malachi laughed. The man towered over everyone in the house

except his cousin, who matched him in height. Yet, despite his great size, there was a playfulness about Leo that Malachi found endearing.

"Well done. It worked."

"You think it's funny now, but the summer I started scribing my *talesm*, Max had shot up a few inches on me. I was worried."

"You're cousins?"

He nodded. "Our mothers were twin sisters. Most Irin couples only have one pregnancy, but twins do happen. It's considered a great blessing. Our mothers were very close. Max and I were born within months of each other, so we're really more like brothers than cousins."

"Always a competition?"

"When we were younger. Not as much now. We're very different."

"Max is… intense."

Leo smiled. "He's very passionate about the future. He questions everything, especially the politicians."

"It's good that someone does."

"And I know he desperately wants a mate," Leo said in a quieter voice. "We all do."

"It must be frustrating." Malachi knew that Irin males couldn't touch humans. He had no desire for anyone except Ava—even though he barely remembered her—but for unmated males like Leo and Max…

Malachi saw a faint tinge of red on Leo's cheekbones. "I believe that heaven has already chosen my *reshon*. I must simply be patient and wait for her. Though human females are… tempting. I cannot lie."

Malachi stopped his practice and put a hand on Leo's shoulder. "She will be worthy of your patience, brother."

"Thank you." Leo pointed back to the paper he'd been using. "Your letters are well formed. I really can't help you any more with them. I can answer any questions you have about the tattooing, but I suspect your muscle memory will hold true in the ritual room, as well."

"And you'll be there?"

"I'm not your father, but we don't do our first *talesm* alone, so yes." Leo smiled. "I'd be honored to witness for you. It won't be too much. Just the *talesm prim* to activate your magic and call on our forefathers' magic, then the basic protection spells and a few others. You're a good runner already—very fast—so I'd focus on eyesight, reflexes, and protection from blades. Those would be the most important if we encounter any fighting. After that, you can improvise spells as you need them. You'll find all the basics in that book."

Malachi paged through the book for a moment, then looked up. "Thank you, Leo. You've been very patient with all this."

"You're welcome."

They both read in silence a bit longer, then Malachi said, "Rhys told me when I first started watching Ava, before I knew she was Irina, that you were the one to help me guard her."

"I was."

"Would you tell me about her? Can you?"

Leo smiled. "Of course. I liked Ava very much. Even when we thought she was human."

"What is she like?"

"She's… unpredictable. She never really does what you expect."

Malachi frowned. "Oh?"

"But then, looking back, you aren't surprised at all."

"Why not?" He listened, rapt to hear any crumb of who this woman was. She'd captured Malachi's heart without him knowing anything about her. He wanted to. Desperately.

Leo continued, "I think it's how she throws people off. By being unpredictable. She likes to keep others off-balance so they don't look too closely."

That made him smile. "She doesn't like being the center of attention?"

"No, definitely not." Leo grinned, then his smile fell. "Ava is, more than anything, a survivor."

"What do you mean?"

"She had to be. She heard voices her whole life—like the Irina do —but she didn't know what they were. Her parents thought she was mentally ill. I think she still thinks that sometimes. She makes jokes about being crazy."

"I think I remember that," he said, recalling the password he'd typed into her computer.

"You hated it; I could tell. Max and Damien say she's actually very powerful. They think it's because she has so much power bound up from living a life away from magic. I always thought it was because she's not like other Irina."

Malachi frowned. "What do you mean?"

Leo shrugged. "Her parents are human. We never did figure out where she came from, but biologically, she shouldn't be Irina. I mean, Irin are not entirely human or angel. We're different. And Ava is definitely like us, but we can't figure out how a human could become Irina."

The answer seemed obvious to Malachi. "A lion doesn't become a wolf, Leo, no matter how it might want to be."

"So?" Leo crossed his arms and raised an eyebrow. "What do you mean?"

"It means her parents are Irin. They have to be."

The blond man smiled. "Our records—everything we could find about them—say they're not."

Malachi frowned. "But humans don't give birth to Irin children."

"No, they don't."

"So if they produced Ava, then they're not human."

"But they're not Irin. We have a record of every Irin child ever born. If there's one thing we're good at, it's keeping records."

"You're forgetting something," Malachi murmured.

"What's that?"

Malachi looked around the room filled with scrolls and tablets. Books and boxes were hidden in every corner. He turned back to Leo and said, "We're an ancient race of angel and human hybrids that has lived under the nose of humanity for thousands of years."

"And?"

"We may be good at keeping records, but we're also good at keeping secrets."

1.

I t wasn't often his father called him to appear in person. But given the task Brage had just accomplished, it could hardly be said he was dreading the appearance. He strolled through the Götaplatsen, ignoring the human women who cast longing looks in his direction. The package his father was expecting rested safely at his side.

The blade from Istanbul had been found. A heavenly blade. It was one of only three that Brage had ever seen. The only one that had been in his hand. It would be nothing to human eyes. Dull. Devoid of decoration or flourish.

But to one of heaven's children, it was a treasure beyond price.

Countless hours searching through mud and shit, through rotten food and human waste, and he'd found it. Or, his brothers had while he directed the search. They didn't question him; few Grigori lasted as long as Brage. At nearly three hundred years old, he was almost as strong as one of the Irin he despised.

Fucking scribes with their fucking honor. Their fucking magic and mates and foolish sentimentality. They, like he and his Grigori brothers, could rule the humans if they wished. Rule as the ancients had.

Brage stopped in front of the Poseidon statue and waited to feel him. He only waited moments.

There.

The soldier's eyes closed, and his mouth dropped open as the wave of fear and adoration swept over him. The cynical soldier disappeared, and the child leapt to the surface. Brage wanted his father's approval. Needed it. Would do anything, kill anything, steal anything to get it. He longed for the love of this creature, as if the lack of it would damn him.

He took a deep breath and opened his eyes.

"Hello, Father."

"Brage." The stunning man appeared at his side. The humans around him would notice nothing. They would have no memory of the angel appearing, for he had always been there. No side-glance or double take. The handsome man in the double-breasted suit and overcoat stood next to another man who could be his brother.

Brage knew Volund appeared that way purposefully. If the angel had been speaking to one of his Russian or Turkish brothers, Volund's appearance would have reflected their appearance, just as his blond hair and vivid green eyes reflected Brage in that moment. It appealed to the human side of the Grigori. Their vanity. The younger and more foolish soldiers believed this resemblance indicated some particular favor when they saw it. Brage had thought so himself when he was young.

"Do you have the knife?"

"Yes, Father."

"Good. I want you to keep it."

Brage worked to conceal his surprise, but it was useless. Volund knew him intimately. Like any of his blood, the angel could read his children. Read their moods, feel their fears, find them if they tried to hide. There were no secrets between the Fallen and their offspring. There was no place that Brage could hide, and for that reason—and many others—he didn't even try.

"I assumed you would want it back."

Volund turned to him, the edge of a sneer twisting his perfect lips. "That was when I thought it had done its job."

Brage said nothing at the harsh words. He did not know what his father spoke of, but knew Volund would offer no more information than was necessary. It was useless to ask. Brage would be told only enough to complete his task.

He bowed his head and said the words that had kept him alive for three hundred years. "Father, I am yours to command."

There was a pause as Volund considered him. In the silence, Brage listened to the hum of the humans around him. The cheerful chirp of women and children. Music played in the background. It was a sunny day, even if it was cold. The humans were enjoying the weather.

Brage had no part of their world. He existed in it as a predator. A lion culling the weakest of the herd.

Volund tilted Brage's head up with one finger. "The female's Irin mate is alive, Brage."

Brage dared not contradict the angel, though he wanted to. He'd felt the knife pierce the scribe's spine. Saw the golden dust rise in the air. He had fallen in the water when the woman had screamed. The woman, he'd been told, was "only a human," but valuable for some reason. He knew his father lied. The burst of magic when the "human" woman had screamed was unmistakable. She was Irina.

Or something far more frightening.

"I do not know what to tell you, Father. I killed the woman's mate. I did not lie to you."

"I know you didn't." Volund's voice was no longer angry. His hand stroked over Brage's cheek, soothing his child. "She is quite unexpected, isn't she? I'm trying not to kill you for failing to bring her to me. I know you are the most skilled of my children."

"Thank you, Father."

"But you still failed."

"Forgive me, Father."

"I want you to find her mate. Find the one they call Malachi. He is of the angel Mikhael's blood. A warrior by birth and destiny. And he has taken the female as his mate."

The fiercest Irin scribes were from Mikhael's line, and Brage knew from experience they were intensely protective of their mates.

"Do you have any information for me?"

Volund's mouth formed a pout. "Jaron has concealed her from me, but if you find the scribe, you will find the woman."

"Yes, Father."

"Kill the scribe… again. Bring the woman to me. Do not fail this time."

Tears of gratitude slipped down Brage's cheeks. "I will find her and kill him."

"Or die trying."

Brage bowed his head and made the vow. "I will kill the scribe and bring the woman to you, Father, or I will die in the effort."

CHAPTER
SIX

"She wants to know what you can do."

Ava blinked away from the aching memory of her dream the night before. She looked between her translator, the blond girl whose hair Sari had been braiding the previous afternoon, and her tormentor, the fearsome Irina named Mala whom she'd met the first day.

There couldn't be two more opposite females on the planet. The girl, who had introduced herself as Brooke and sounded American, had the kind of blond hair that almost looked silver. Her eyes were a clear crystal blue, and she couldn't have been more than twelve. She was slim and tall for her age, but her face still carried the rounded cheeks of youth. Her figure was just starting to develop, but she still sported lean muscle that marked her as an athlete.

"What do you mean 'what I can do'? Like… my résumé?"

Brooke snorted and looked at Mala, who was running in front of them. Mala's smooth skin glowed with perspiration, her long legs pumped up the hills and over the meadows as they ran through the countryside. She was dark-skinned and fiercely lovely in a way that made Ava envious. Her skin was the color of rich teak, and her hair was shorn close to her head in a cap that showed off her graceful neck and shoulders. She looked like she could have been featured in a fashion magazine, except for the vicious scar that ran from her jaw, across her neck, and down to her collar. But it was her eyes, twin pools of black fire, that made Ava want to photograph her.

Ava couldn't help but feel thin and drawn between the two females who were pulsing with life. One young and delicate, the other vibrating with old power, they were opposite in every way the world might see. Yet something intangible bound them together. Brooke had been sent with Ava and Mala as a translator since Ava wasn't fluent in signing.

"Not like your résumé," Brooke said.

Mala didn't even stop, just raised her hand over her shoulder and flipped through signs so fast that Ava could scarcely pick them up. Brooke didn't seem to have a problem, though.

"She wants to know what sports you played in school. If you've taken any martial arts. Things like that."

"Uh…" Ava tried not to gasp as they jogged. She'd thought she was in shape. She was wrong. "I didn't really… play sports in… school."

More signs tossed into the air from Mala.

"She says you're in good shape for someone who doesn't play sports."

"Sure doesn't feel that way right now."

Brook laughed. "You'll get used to it. You're keeping up and she's not going easy on us. Mala's the hardest trainer here."

"I hike a lot with my job," Ava said. "Go to remote places like this. And usually I'm carrying a lot of equipment. So it's probably from that."

"High altitudes?"

The question had come from Brooke, not Mala, which caused Ava to blink and look over at the girl. "What?"

"Did you hike a lot at high altitudes? That probably helps. Even though there are mountains here, we're actually not that high up, so the air is thicker."

"Oh… okay."

"What places did you go?" The girl's eyes were alive with curiosity.

Ava managed a weak smile. "Almost everywhere. I've been to every continent on earth."

"Even Antarctica?"

"Yep, even Antarctica."

That drew a surprised look from Mala, who turned briefly with curious eyes.

Ava continued. "I'd been through most of Europe by the time I was sixteen. School trips. My mom took me places, too. Then, when I got to college, I traveled in South America for a few semesters. I minored in Spanish, so…" She paused to catch her breath. "I took some pictures in Venezuela one summer and my mom showed a friend of hers. She was an editor at a travel magazine, and… she asked to see more."

"That's so cool," Brooke said, her own breath coming harder the longer they jogged. "So you started working for a magazine?"

"I did what you could call freelance work in college. Just for my mom's friend. Any time I traveled for school, I let her know where I was going, and she'd let me know if she wanted pictures. After I graduated, I was on staff for a while there, then I started doing freelance work again, only this time I got paid more and I got to pick what jobs I wanted."

Brooke's blue eyes were wide. "So, are you really rich?"

Ava snorted, wiping the sweat from her forehead. Mala might have been glowing, but Ava was dripping. "Not from my photography work. I make enough to get by on that, but not by much. I have money, but it's from my father. He's really rich and he set up a trust fund for me when I was a baby. I got control of it when I was twenty-three. So I can kind of go wherever I want as long as I don't get too crazy."

The girl grinned. "Nice."

Ava attempted a shrug. "I think I'd rather have had my dad than the money. But what are you gonna do?"

"Nothing," she said flatly. "There's nothing to do." Before Ava could question her, Brooke continued. "I don't have a dad, either."

Ava remembered Malachi telling her how precious children were to the Irin. "Where is he?"

"I was born in Virginia. My mom and dad… they lived on their own. The closest scribe house was in Arlington, but we never went there. They would have made my dad patrol and fight, and he didn't want to leave my mom and me. My mom was really paranoid. She lost all her family in the Rending. So we were just living with the humans, trying to blend in."

"What happened?"

Brooke shrugged. "We don't know. Not really. You can want to be left alone, but that doesn't mean it will happen. One night, my dad just didn't come home. Didn't call. My mom was frantic. Then later that night, she started crying." Brooke drifted off, and Ava could see the haunted grief in her eyes. "I was only eight, and I've never heard anything like it."

Mala's eyes caught Ava's as they ran, and Ava nodded in silent understanding. Brook's father had been killed, and her mother only knew when she felt their connection snap. As Ava had known when the knife struck Malachi's neck. She didn't want to hear any more, but Brook kept talking.

"My mom woke me up the next morning, and her face was just… wrong. I knew he was dead. We were gone before lunch. We left every-thing there but some clothes and pictures. We came here."

"And you never left?"

"We're safe here."

"With Sari."

"Yes," Brooke said. "Sari makes everyone safe."

She saw Mala glance at the girl. Grief had joined the fire in her gaze, but she didn't pause or slow down their run.

Ava had finally reached the endorphin high of running. Her legs felt looser and longer. Her heart pounded. The air was clear and biting, and the breeze felt liquid against her skin. She lifted her head and ran along the path with the two women, one old, the other painfully young, and suddenly she didn't see their differences. Not a single one. The three ran together, bound by something far beyond the external.

• • • • • •

"Hey, Damien." She pushed the damp hair from her forehead as she walked into the cottage. Damien was sitting in the kitchen area, reading something and taking notes in a big notebook. "You know, I don't think I've ever seen you doing scribe stuff."

He blinked and looked up. "Hmm?"

"You know, scribe stuff. Book stuff? Not like the others." She pointed to the books and notebook on the table.

"What are you talking about?"

"In Istanbul, it seemed like you were always on the phone or talking with one of the guys in a very solemn voice. Or ordering people around. You did a lot of that. I don't think I've ever seen you doing any scribe kind of work."

His face cleared of confusion, and he shrugged. "When I am a watcher, I have more pressing concerns. I don't have time to spend with texts. Bringing you here, having this time when I'm not on guard, it's probably good for me. It's easy to forget what's important."

"Books?"

She saw him run both hands down his forearms. "Yes. Books. Stories. Our families. Our history." Then his fingers ran over the dagger he wore at his waist. "Those are the reasons for living."

"And fighting?"

"Yes, and fighting."

Her sweat was beginning to dry, and the northern air was starting to chill her, so Ava started toward the bathroom. "I'm going to take a shower."

"Sari has you training with Mala." It wasn't a question.

"Yep. She's… well, so far we've just run a lot."

He nodded, frowning in concentration. "Mala is a fierce fighter. Before the Rending, she often accompanied her mate into battle. She'll be an excellent physical trainer."

Ava hesitated but asked anyway. "What happened to her?"

"Her scar?"

"Yes."

Damien looked hesitant for a moment, but finally he said, "Mala and her mate never had any children, so during the Grigori attacks prior to the Rending, they both fought in the area around Lagos. The humans there…" He shook his head. "Mala and Alexander were fighting, and he was killed in battle. They were overwhelmed."

Ava's heart had clenched in her chest. "They killed her mate?"

"Yes. And she killed them, over ten Grigori, according to Zander's brothers, but not before they clawed out her throat." He lifted a hand to his throat, curling his fingers like claws as he scraped from his jaw down. "That's what the Grigori do to Irina in battle. If they take their voice, they can't work magic. If you silence an Irina, she's far easier to kill."

Ava shivered, but it wasn't from the cold anymore. "And then she came here."

"Sari and Mala had been friends a long time. I imagine Sari had to convince Mala to come, otherwise, she'd still be out there, hunting. But she's very protective of her friends. If Sari asked Mala to come and help protect this haven, she'd do it."

And that was the woman who was going to be her trainer. Fire-eyed

Mala with the scarred throat and the battle-hardened muscles. Ava only hoped she didn't die of exhaustion. Or embarrassment.

"Take your shower." Damien motioned toward the door. "Astrid asked if you would have lunch with her after you got back. I imagine she's in the medical clinic I saw near the road."

"Yes, sir, Captain Watcher, sir." She mock-saluted and scurried to the bathroom.

"Ha-ha."

Ava shut the door and pulled off her sweaty shirt, turning to toss it in a small hamper before she froze.

Grief struck at the oddest times. Like a cat, it waited to pounce. She could go about her day, even talk about Malachi, ignoring the black hole that lived inside, then something little would swallow her up.

It was nothing, really. Just a man's shirt hanging on the towel rod. A shirt like the ones he'd worn. The ones she'd teased him about not putting in the hamper. He left them draped on the clean towels or tossed on the ground. She'd found it irritating.

She pulled it off the towel rack and put it to her face, but it smelled wrong.

Ava buckled as if she'd been punched in the stomach, sliding down to the floor as her back scraped along the counter. A wretched sob tore from her throat, and she heard footsteps pounding.

"Ava?"

She shook her head, gripping Damien's shirt that smelled wrong. His voice sounded wrong. And his arms felt wrong. She couldn't stop another sob. Or the next. Or the next.

Damien opened the door. "Oh, sister…"

Wrong. Wrong. Wrong.

As kind as Damien was, he wasn't who she wanted to see.

She threw his shirt at him shouted, "It's not fair!"

"I know," he whispered, sitting next to her and gathering her in his arms. "I know it's not."

"We didn't have time." Her body shook with rage and grief. "We should have had time."

"I know."

"No, you *don't* know. Sari may hate you, but she's still here." Tears were hot on her face and she hit his shoulders with clenched fists, even as he held her closer. "I just found him. I finally found him. And then he was gone."

"I'm sorry, Ava." He held her close. "I miss him too."

"Everything is wrong. Everything hurts more."

"I'm sorry."

"I thought it would be better if I left. If I left Turkey, I thought he'd stay there. But he didn't."

"Of course he didn't."

"I see him everywhere. He's everywhere. And he always will be."

"Ava—"

"And I *hate* him for that. For leaving me," she choked out. "And for *not* leaving me."

Damien didn't say anything for a while; he just let her cry. And when the worst of it had passed, Ava whispered, "I know that doesn't make sense."

"Yes, it does." He held her close, pressing her cheek against his shoulder. "He would have moved heaven and earth to stay with you, Ava. You know that."

"But he didn't, Damien. Of all the things he could do, he couldn't do that."

Damien ignored his lunch that was growing cold on the counter. Ava ignored her growling stomach. She sat on the floor of the maple-paneled bathroom with Malachi's brother and allowed herself to feel more than she had in months. Until finally grief slipped away to hide its face until the next time.

◆ ◆ ◆ ◆ ◆

HOURS LATER, AVA FINALLY HEEDED THE CALL OF HER RUMBLING stomach and went to look for Astrid. There was a road leading into the isolated valley, but a visitor clearly needed to know where they were going to find it. Ava had seen a few cars come and go, along with a truck that delivered boxes of supplies on Wednesday morning and took some of the milk and vegetables the haven produced.

In addition to the Irina, there were also a few Irin families. They seemed to keep to themselves, but Ava had seen a few men hanging at the edge of the compound and even a small child. The families lived in a group of cottages half a kilometer or so deeper into the valley and away from the main house and the road. Clearly, protecting them was a priority since Ava had only caught glimpses.

To any visitor driving in, the compound would seem like a commune of sorts, with animals and greenhouses to grow food. Low buildings housed workshops and storage units and a small clinic that Damien said was open to any emergency since Astrid was the only trained doctor for miles around. What the average visitor wouldn't see was the interior of the brightly painted barn where women fought and parried with sticks, staffs, and knives. The archery range was hidden behind innocuous greenhouse fronts. Ava doubted many would see the cameras so expertly hidden among the buildings or understand them if they did.

Ava saw everything. And far from just being a haven for wounded Irina, she could also see what the Irin scribes hadn't known.

This was a training center, and it might have been isolated, but it was far from idle.

She knocked on the door marked with a bright red cross. She heard shuffling, then the door opened.

"Welcome," Astrid said with a smile. "Come in, come in."

"Thanks."

If Astrid caught Ava's swollen eyes, she said nothing.

Astrid's clinic looked just like a small cottage with a sitting area and kitchen in the main room, then three doors leading off a small hall in the back. Her desk was in a corner of the living area, and a kettle was on the stove. Ava wandered around the room, which was decorated with pictures of women, children, and families.

"I didn't know there were so many families left," she said as Astrid went to the kitchen. "How many are there?"

"More in the last few years."

"I thought most of the Irin and Irina lived apart."

"Most, but not all. The girls who weren't mated after the Rending mated quickly, if they were still interested. Many weren't. But some. So there are still a few families." The smell of pepper and red meat filled the air. It smelled like Astrid had made chili. "There are more in Vienna since it is the safest Irin city. But even there, Irina live very quietly. A very few live in scribe houses with their mates. Some live in places like this. But most Irina have hidden in the human world."

"Does the council know about them?"

"They do and they don't. They know we exist. From the news that leaks out of Vienna, there are as many solutions to the 'Irina problem' as there are elders."

"I can imagine."

"I doubt that," Astrid said, but she didn't seem condescending. Just tired. Her movements were deliberate as she set out the cups for tea. "So, only a few families. And of course, there were some children left."

"How many—"

"Fifteen… maybe twenty percent of the children survived."

It seemed impossible that any people could endure so much tragedy.

"Can the Irin survive, Astrid? Really?"

Astrid cocked her head. "Biologically? Yes. There are enough of us to survive. But will we? Who knows? Things are still very fresh for us."

"But the Rending was two hundred years ago."

She smiled. "It seems strange to you, I know."

"More than a little."

"Life didn't stop for us, Ava." Astrid waved her toward the table and Ava sat. "But it did slow down. For many years we all just… waited."

Astrid's eyes had drifted off; she stood at the stove, but was looking out the window over the sink.

"For what?" Ava asked.

"I think I spent ten years after Marten died, waiting to wake up and realize it was all a horrible dream. Life seemed to stand still. It was easier for those with children to move on, because children don't stop growing. But there were so few children left. The villages were destroyed. No one even wanted to try to rebuild. The council was… unbelievable."

"How?"

"Immediately after the attack, there were some who blamed the Irina for letting their guard down. 'They should have been more prepared,' they said."

Ava gasped. "But—"

"Most who took that view were condemned, of course." Astrid shook her head. "What a horrendous thing to say! One elder was attacked and killed by scribes from a house near Leon. They'd lost everything. Not a single survivor from their village. It had been burned while the scribes were fighting the Grigori attack in Paris. They blamed the council for ordering them away."

"What happened?"

Astrid shrugged as she ladled stew into deep bowls and set one in front of Ava. "I don't know. It wasn't like now with instant communication. Letters would take weeks or months to arrive. There was so much confusion. Those of us who remained went into hiding. We didn't know if more attacks were coming. None of us felt safe anymore. Many of the scribes whose mates *had* survived left with them and hid, even though they abandoned their posts at scribe houses and libraries."

"They could do that?"

"No. Even now, if they came out of hiding, they would be punished by the council, so it's not worth it to them to try to reenter Irin society. They'd rather remain with their mates." Astrid's eyes glanced toward the window again, and Ava got the distinct impression that more than one of the males she'd seen was a fugitive.

"But not everyone joined their mate," she said, thinking of Damien and Sari. "Some of the Irina here, they have mates in the outside world, don't they?"

Astrid nodded as she sat. "Yes. Some do. There are three Irina here who have mates who fight in houses away from here."

Ava couldn't imagine Malachi being in the world and not being with her. "How do they… I mean, don't they need—"

"Contact?" Astrid smiled a little. "Of course they do. Emotionally. Even biologically, Irin and Irina need physical contact. Mates dream walk, of course, but the mated Irina here often leave."

"And Sari lets them?"

Astrid smiled. "We're not stuck here. We can go anytime we want. Most of the women with mates meet them when they can get away. They go to the city for a while, or places in the country where they can be alone."

"And children?"

Astrid shrugged. "I'm sure a scribe would be given leave if his mate was pregnant. Children are rare for us, and Irin men seldom leave their women alone when they are pregnant."

"So how does nobody know where this place is?"

"Orsala."

"Who's Orsala?" Ava asked. "And… does she have tentacles and a great singing voice?"

Astrid threw her head back and laughed. "Singing voice? Yes. Tentacles, no. Orsala is Sari's grandmother. She's very old. The oldest singer I know. She's letting herself age now because her mate was killed during the Rending. But she's still with us. And Orsala is the one who'll talk to you before you leave. After you talk to Orsala, Volund himself couldn't make you give up the name of this place."

She felt a shiver creep up her spine. "Magic?"

"*Strong* magic."

AVA FELL EXHAUSTED INTO BED THAT NIGHT, HOPING TO LOSE HERSELF in dreams. She suspected she was sleeping too much—and had spoken to enough psychologists to recognize the symptoms of depression—but something drew her. Some instinct tugged her to darkness and rest. She huddled under the thick down blankets and closed her eyes.

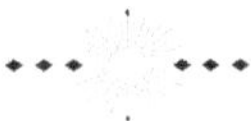

SHE WANDERED THROUGH THE FOREST, BUT SHE NO LONGER WEPT. SHE waited. He'd said he would be there, and she knew he would come.

"*Reshon.*"

She turned toward his voice, smiling. "You're here."

"I told you I would be." He approached cautiously, one hand lifting as she drew near. "You're not crying anymore."

"I don't need to." She took his hand and led him toward a low bed that had appeared at the edge of the clearing, butted up against the hedge he'd torn through. The gash had closed, and now the dark leaves were lush, no longer forbidding. The forest surrounding them was a shield and not a barrier. It hummed with life, and the meadow where they rested was lush with grass and dotted with white flowers that glowed under the half moon.

The two lay down on the bed and he wrapped her in his arms. Her body hummed in awareness as he traced over the marks he'd painted on her neck and shoulders, and everywhere he touched, her skin turned gold.

"You're not as tired as you were before," he said.

"No. I'm sleeping better now that you found me."

"I'm glad." He nestled his face in her neck and took a deep breath. "I miss your scent."

"And I miss yours."

"Jasmine and smoke. We met in the market; it smelled like cloves."

"I think… I remember that."

She held on to the arm that banded around her waist. He'd rolled her onto her back and kissed softly along her collar and neck, his mouth lingering on her skin. His tongue tasting. Teasing. She closed her eyes and let her senses take her away, losing herself in the feel of his skin against hers, his energy aligning with her own. She felt calm. Content to her bones. But slowly, with every nip of his teeth against her neck, desire rose.

Her grip on his arm tightened. "I need you."

"As I need you."

His arm slid around her waist, and suddenly the clothes she'd felt against her skin and his were gone. In their place, a warm breeze wrapped around them as his mouth met hers. Their tongues touched, and he swallowed the low sigh that came from her throat.

"I missed this," she whispered. "I missed you so much."

"So did I. I don't…" He pulled away for a moment, frowning. "I don't remember what happened."

"I don't either." Her hand went to his cheek, and she rubbed her thumb against the coarse stubble on his jaw. "Kiss me. It doesn't matter. You're here now."

A slow smile—the one she loved that made his dimple stand out—spread over his face.

"I'm here now," he whispered. "I love you."

"I love you, too."

He murmured it over and over again as he moved over her in the dark. The forest protected them; no danger hovered nearby. Soft night birds called in the trees as they held each other, and that moment was all she knew. They made love under a blanket of stars.

And it was enough.

CHAPTER
SEVEN

Malachi woke slowly, keeping his eyes closed to hold on to the edges of the dream. He could still taste her skin. Still smell the jasmine in her hair. He rolled over, eyes slowly opening, and the bedclothes were damp, as if they'd been left out in the night air.

"Ava…," he whispered.

A knock came at the door.

"Wake up." It was Rhys. "We've got work to do in the library. Leo wants to start your *talesm* tonight."

He glanced at the clock. It was just after six. Malachi took a deep breath and stretched up from the bed, his body refreshed and relaxed despite the hour. He stretched his neck to the side and reached over his left shoulder to stretch the muscle in his arm. As he did, his fingers brushed against something that made him wince. He frowned and stood, going to the mirror near the closet door.

Curved into the tan skin of his shoulder were three scratch marks.

"More."

He blinked at the memory of her voice. Was it a dream or a memory?

"It's been too long. I need you. Harder."

He could feel the bite of her nails. Hear her breath. There was a low rumble in his throat as he remembered her nails digging in. The tug of her hands in his hair.

Malachi looked at his reflection in the mirror as Rhys banged on the door again.

"Malachi, wake up."

"I'm awake," he called.

There was a pause, then the sound of shuffling feet. "Meet me in the library."

He pulled on a pair of pants and, with one last glance at the nail marks, threw a T-shirt over his head. Then he looked at himself in the mirror.

"It was just a dream."

He gave a last glance to the bed, then he shook his head and walked out, down the hall, and toward the library.

Dawn was breaking over Cappadocia, and the rocks of the cliff where the scribe house was built glowed pink in the morning sun. Birds called from the olive trees near the gate, and a lazy cat stretched on tiptoes atop the wall. Two young scribes were sitting near an outdoor fireplace, drinking tea and arguing quietly over a book. Both of the men looked to be in their twenties, though Malachi knew they were probably far older. Vivid black *talesm* crawled up their wrists and under the sleeves of their sweaters.

He'd been practicing his characters with Leo for almost a week. Like anything having to do with writing or reading, it came easily. Once he'd practiced a little, reading was no struggle, whether it was a blank wall that had once held Roman graffiti or an ancient Chaldean manuscript, which Rhys claimed was the human tongue most closely related to the Irin language. His writing had become almost rote. He could copy characters with ease except for a few that Leo had said he'd always had a problem with. Malachi already knew how his *talesm prim* would look.

So he supposed it was silly to be nervous about it. Still, the knowledge that he would unleash ancient magic solely by writing words on his skin was a bit intimidating.

The library door was open, and he could feel a cross breeze from the high windows in the back of the room. Even though it was November, the air was still dry, so the scribes were airing out the library, which could become stuffy with the fires burning in the hearths. The chill in the air nipped at his neck, and he shivered as he approached the table where Rhys sat.

"Hope your blood thickens up," Rhys said. "Or you're going to be miserable when we head north."

Malachi sat down. "Is that where we're going?"

"It appears so. I found surveillance footage of them on the ferry from Denmark. Once they reached Norway, we lost them again."

"But they're in Norway?" He felt his heart pick up.

Rhys didn't look as optimistic as Malachi hoped.

"Norway is a big country. Huge. And with over twenty-five thousand kilometers of coastline and thousands—*thousands*—of islands, do you have any idea how easy it is to hide there? We can't just go stomping off to the great north and expect to find them. We need to speak to Gabriel. If we don't get some clue from him about where Sari's home is, it could take forever."

Malachi tried to look on the bright side. "But we know which country they're in."

"Or they could have gone to Sweden. It wouldn't be unlikely for Damien to anticipate me finding the ferry footage and heading in a different direction, just to throw us off."

"He is very distrustful, isn't he?"

"You have no idea," Rhys muttered. "He's paranoid. But then, since he's been alive longer than either of us, I suppose there's something to be said for that."

Rhys was still checking things on the computer.

"What are you doing?"

"Just checking e-mail."

"Electronic mail?" He'd heard Leo and Max talking about it and wondered, "Do I have any of these e-mails you talk about?"

The other scribe's mouth lifted in the corner. "I doubt it. You hate e-mail because you say it's impersonal. Though you text on your phone like a madman."

Malachi pulled out the mobile phone Rhys had given him. Apparently, it was an exact replica of his old phone, including all the information and contacts on it, though Malachi had no idea how the man had accomplished that. He pushed a few buttons and scrolled through the texting conversations like Rhys had taught him.

"Texting seems to be a very efficient way to communicate."

"It is." Rhys kept typing.

Malachi touched Ava's name, bringing up their conversation history. Scrolling up, his eyes widened, and he shifted in his seat. "That is… unexpected."

"What is?"

He quickly turned off his phone while making a mental note to explore more of his very… *stimulating* texting history with Ava later. "Nothing. You had more books for me to read?"

"Yes." Rhys reached over a hand and shoved a box toward Malachi. "More Chaldean. It's a minor language now, but its similarity to the Irin language in grammar and morphology is startling."

Malachi took a deep breath. "Sounds just fascinating."

"It is." Rhys ignored Malachi's sarcasm, frowning at the computer screen. "Impossible."

"What's impossible?"

"There have to be records." He scowled at the screen, obviously caught in his own thoughts. "There have to be. It's the California foster-care system. There have to be records. There has to be… something."

At the word "California," Malachi's head jerked up. "What are you talking about? What's in California?" Ava was from California. According to Leo, she'd been born in Los Angeles.

Rhys waved a hand. "Just some leads I've been trying to follow regarding Ava's background. We still don't know how she's Irina. According to everything we know about her, she can't be."

This was far more interesting than old manuscripts. Malachi shoved the box to the side. "I know it would be unheard of, but could an Irin have fathered her?"

"No." Rhys seemed sure, but Malachi kept pressing.

"But is it possible? I know she is her mother's daughter. I've seen the pictures of them together, but could her father—"

"No."

"Some Grigori victims survive, Rhys. And biologically speaking—"

"Malachi, I'm telling you no."

"Maybe artificial insemina—"

"That's not possible either." Then he cocked his head. "Well, I suppose it might be possible for an Irin male to… hmm… But in Ava's case"—he looked back at Malachi—"no."

Malachi let out a frustrated breath. "How can you be so sure? I know we're not meant to touch human women, but we're not perfect, either. You're saying it's not even possible that some Irin and Ava's mother—"

"I'm saying in this case, it's not possible."

He glared at Rhys. "How can you know for sure?"

"Because—" He lowered his voice. "Because there was a paternity test, Malachi."

He frowned. "A what?"

"A paternity test. To prove Jasper Reed was Ava's father. She doesn't know about it. The records were sealed, and her father and mother never wanted her to know."

Malachi felt a flare of anger. "Why would he question it?"

Rhys sighed. "Reed regretted it, but there was a time when Ava was a baby, and his manager… His career had already taken off. He'd been successful before, but he was starting to attract worldwide attention. Awards were coming in. And—to be completely honest—Jasper Reed has always been a bit of a mess. Some of the media suspect he's bipolar. Some say he struggles with depression. He takes cocktails of drugs. There's no doubt he's incredibly talented, but I don't know how *smart* he is. His manager at the time convinced him that Ava's mother might be lying about the baby. Convinced him to ask for a paternity test. Her mother objected; it went to the courts. There's a record of it, though I had to dig to find it."

"There's a record," he repeated, furious at Ava's biological father on her behalf. According to everything he could find out from Leo, the only support Ava had received from her father was financial in nature. Jasper Reed hadn't held her when she cried or protected her in any way. Those jobs had belonged to Ava's mother, and later, nannies and other household staff.

"Reed's an ass, but the test proved he *is* her biological father. And Lena is her mother. They're *human*, Malachi."

"But she's not."

"Well, no. Clearly not." Rhys took a deep breath. "We have no idea."

Malachi frowned. "So what were you talking about earlier? Why were you looking at the foster-care system in California?"

Rhys frowned at the screen, then snapped the laptop closed. "It's probably nothing, but I'm trying to find out more information about Ava's parents. Her mother is fairly easy. Easily traceable history for over one hundred years. Her father, however…"

"What?" There it was again, that stirring in his gut. The awareness that there was something beneath the surface that he needed to find. It wasn't unlike the feeling he had when looking at a blank piece of paper or clay tablet where he knew words had been. There was something on the edge of his mind that told him Jasper Reed, Ava's do-nothing father, was the key to her identity.

"He's a black hole, Malachi. He grew up in the foster-care system, but that's as much as I can find." Rhys crossed his arms. "And I can find a lot. But for him? Nothing. No records at all. It's as if the man didn't exist until he started waiting tables at a beach bar in Santa Monica when he was eighteen. No mother. No father. I can't even find a record of the last foster home he was in."

"No one just appears out of nowhere, Rhys."

"You're right." He crossed his arms. "And Irina aren't born to human parents. Irin magic always stems from the female line. And there are no human Irina, Malachi. Except…" He leaned forward. "There are."

They fell silent as three scribes walked past, arguing in French.

"Does the council know about her?" Malachi asked Rhys when they had passed.

"No. I've been trying to keep it as quiet as I can while I dig through the online archives. I have a friend in Los Angeles who's been making local inquiries for me. I've asked him to be discreet."

"Is it just me? Why do I feel like the fewer people who know about her, the better?"

"It's not just you." Rhys leaned back but kept his voice low. "Because if there's a way for some human women to become Irina, then that changes everything, doesn't it?"

"It might not be just Ava."

Rhys nodded. "Ava told you, and you told me and Leo before you… died, that Jaron had helped others with 'her condition.' Had helped other humans who heard voices. Malachi, if that's correct, then—"

"There might be more human Irina out there."

••• •••

THE IDEA OF LOST IRINA LIVING IN THE HUMAN WORLD WAS SHOVED TO the back of Malachi's mind when he entered the ritual room with Leo. Both men wore nothing but the traditional linen wrap used during ceremonies. Malachi's unmarked skin was stark in the shadowed room, which had been decorated with countless spells and enchantments dug into the soft rock. Some were scribed in different colors. Some surrounded intricate mosaics and paintings in vivid hues. The entire room, from the polished floor to the ceiling, was covered with Irin magic.

Evren followed them. He and Leo spoke words over the fire that was burning in the center of the room. Then Leo waved Malachi over, and the ritual began.

First, he prepared the ink, made from the ashes of the fire Evren tended every morning. Mixing the powdered ash with oil, he carefully poured the ink into an alabaster bowl that had been stained black from hundreds of years of use. Then he reached for the needle that Leo held out.

Leo was murmuring under his breath. "…and for the blessing of this power, handed down to us from our fathers. For the right use of our magic. For the balance of our race. We ask the Creator's blessing on this scribe."

Evren echoed Leo's words with a few of his own, but Malachi heard little. There was only the ivory needle in his right hand. The ink in his left. He sat down on the stool with the small table before it and imagined in his mind the characters he would write. He closed his eyes and felt a slow curl of power building up from his chest, clearing his mind, and steadying the hand that had been shaking.

Then Malachi opened his eyes and began to write.

The first prick of the needle pierced the fog of magic that had covered his mind. It hurt. He dipped into the ink and made a few more rapid strikes the way Leo had shown him. It still hurt, but slowly he reached past it. The first character formed under his skin, glowing with a dull, pewter-like shine. Malachi started on the second. He felt the magic unfurling within as the pain reached a clarifying plateau.

By the fourth letter, his muscle memory awakened, and the magic took over.

Dipping from the ink to his hand, over and over again, Malachi steadily scribed the ancient words, calling on his angelic ancestors, his mother, his father, and the long line of Irin before them. He claimed his power in black ink as the spells circled the inside of his wrist, slowly curling like a snake around his forearm and crawling up his elbow. They twisted and shone as he marked himself, calling on the powers of Uriel, for longevity. On Rafael for swift healing. He harnessed Mikhael's magic for swift hands in battle and Ariel's for protection from blades.

Malachi focused on the oldest of the Irin spells, those given to the earliest scribes by the Forgiven. Other, more nuanced, magic could come in time. The power flowed over and through him. His skin was alive with it. His hand never wavered.

Behind him, he felt Leo's hand on his shoulder, his brother sharing the magic and grounding him as he wrote. He took deep, steady breaths that Malachi copied when he realized he was holding his own breath, gritting his teeth against the constant pain.

And there *was* pain.

Through the endorphin rush and the magical high, Malachi could feel the sharp ache as his skin closed around the ink, red and angry from the ivory needle.

He didn't stop.

Finally, Leo squeezed his shoulder and leaned down.

"Finish this spell, and then enough, brother."

Malachi blinked, not halting in the repetitive tapping that dug the needle into his flesh. "Enough?"

"It's been seven hours, Malachi. That's enough."

"Not finished…" He knew—an ancient, aching part of him knew that this magic only touched the edge of what he'd once owned. He wanted more.

More power.

More strength.

More.

"Enough." Leo squeezed again, and Malachi finally paused. "Enough, brother."

"Enough for now," Malachi said, finishing the last character on a spell that he knew would help him see more clearly through deception.

"Fine." Leo sounded amused. "Enough for now. And you better not eat anything for at least a day. You'll be sick from it. It's well past midnight. Go lie down and let your system even out."

Malachi knew what he needed and, though his skin was still bloody and raw, he'd never wished more fervently that his mate was nearby.

Evren must have come back to the ritual room sometime in the previous hours. He took one look at Malachi's expression and raised an eyebrow.

"Shower, then lie down. Leo's right. You're flush with magic. How do you feel?"

Malachi's voice was rough. "Strong."

And hungry. He'd never felt more hungry.

He rose and put one hand on the wall to steady himself. His left arm ached where his new *talesm* shone, glowing in the candlelight. The spells had reached halfway up his arm before Leo stopped him. He slowly walked toward the door, leaning against the wall for another moment to let a wave of dizziness pass.

Leo laughed and slapped his right shoulder before he hefted an arm around Malachi and led him toward his room.

"This, my brother, is as close to intoxicated as we get. Enjoy."

All Malachi could think was he'd enjoy it a lot more with his soft mate under him.

He managed to make it into his room and get cleaned off before he fell into bed, exhausted, wired, and aching.

"Come to me," he whispered before he fell into dreams.

* * *   * * *

SHE WAS THERE WHEN HE OPENED HIS EYES. THE FOG LIFTED JUST enough to reveal her form, standing on the edge of the dark wood. The misty air nipped at his bare skin as he ran to her. She must have heard him a moment before he reached her, because she was already turning and her mating marks gleamed gold in the low light.

He didn't speak. He simply picked her up at the waist and walked to the edge of the wood, laying her down on a bed of leaves that appeared before him. She opened her mouth, but he covered it with his own, catching her gasp as he spread her legs and lay in the cradle of her body.

He kissed her over and over again. Her fingers twisted in his hair and dug into his neck, pulling him closer. Her legs wrapped around his hips.

"More," she murmured when his mouth left hers and he buried his face in her neck, biting the soft skin there as she arched beneath him. "More."

"Yes." He hissed out in pleasure when his hips surged forward and his body breached hers. The sharp bite of her nails in his shoulder reminded him of the needle in his arm and the heady pleasure and pain of his new spells.

He pulled back to meet her eyes, and the naked desire in them fed his own. She bit her lip, then pulled his head down, sinking her teeth into the full curve of his lower lip as he moved faster and harder within her.

More.

The magic surged through him and into her, linking them. Every mark on her body was lit up, and her eyes glowed gold in the darkness.

More.

She cried out when she came, pulling him closer and wrapping her arms around his shoulders as he continued to drive into her. Inextricably, eternally linked. The other half of his soul, reaching for its mate. He found what he'd been searching for in the darkness, and he pulled her with him over the edge.

And still he craved more.

CHAPTER

EIGHT

Ava woke in the pitch black, her body aching in awareness and his voice whispering in her mind.

"I love you, reshon."

She pressed her eyes tight, holding on to the dream. She could sense his phantom touch. Smell his scent. Feel the rough stubble along his jaw as it brushed over the sensitive skin on her belly. Her stomach was in knots and she ached.

Ached.

As if her muscles remembered loving him, even though months had passed. As if she could turn over in her bed and he would be there. She forced back the tears in her eyes, shutting them in the darkness and holding on to the shadowy images that haunted her nights.

"Reshon…"

Ava sat up, pushing back the down comforter and letting the cold bite her skin. She rubbed her arms in the brisk northern air and swung her legs over the edge of the bed. She'd get no more sleep that night. Dressing in the warm clothes Max had found for her in Turkey, she crawled out of bed and headed toward the kitchen. The clock in the corner told her it was only three a.m.

Amazingly, when she got to the kitchen, she saw a lantern set on the counter and a woman's figure bending over the table.

Ava halted, trying not to be alarmed.

The woman must have heard her, because she turned and held up her hands, smiling. "I'm sorry. I hope I didn't wake you."

"You didn't."

"I'm Karen. I woke very early this morning, and I just knew you would need breakfast."

"Hi." She relaxed. She'd heard Karen's name before. "I'm Ava."

The woman gave a rosy smile. "I know."

She was short and curvaceous, exactly what Ava would have pictured for the woman who made the delicious breads and pastries that were delivered fresh every morning. Her blond hair was tucked under a wool hat, but Ava could see spun-gold curls poking out around her ears. She was bundled against the cold morning air, and a basket of steaming baked goods was sitting on the table.

"I was just going to tuck these in the oven and leave a note. It's getting so cold in the mornings I don't like leaving the bread outside."

"Thanks. That's really considerate." Ava's stomach growled to life. "You're an amazing baker, by the way. I've been meaning to thank you."

"You're welcome!" A dimple popped out on Karen's cheek just as Ava heard a rustling and stomping at the door. "Oh, that's Bruno. He's probably wondering what's taking so long."

The door cracked open, and a bear of a man poked his head through. He had to have been six and a half feet, with a long brown beard and shaggy hair that hung over his ears, as if he were overdue for a haircut. His shoulders filled the doorway, and his flannel shirt hung open at the neck, revealing dark *talesm* that stood out against pale skin.

"Sweet, what is taking so—oh, hallo!" His eyes swung toward her, and Ava pulled on her sweater as she lifted a hand in greeting. The bear grinned. "How did my sweet girl know you would be awake? But that's her gift, yes? She just knows these things, my Karen. A touch of Chamuel's blood in her."

He stepped through the door and seemed to get impossibly taller.

"Bruno," Karen hissed. "It's early. Ava might not want company."

Bruno's eyes turned toward hers, wide and blue, as if shocked by the thought of a neighbor not wanting to visit at three in the morning.

"Sorry. Would you rather we…" He motioned to the door.

"No." Ava was quick to smile. Something about the giant man

reminded her of Leo. "No, that's fine. I'm not going to get any more sleep."

"Well sit, then." Karen began bustling around the kitchen. "I'll make coffee. I'm sorry about this, Ava. You were probably hoping for a quiet morning."

All her mornings were quiet now. There was no teasing Malachi trying to keep her in bed, whispering delicious secrets and making her laugh. There was nothing.

"No, it's fine." She forced a smile. "I like the company. I haven't met many people yet."

"Oh." Karen waved a hand as she filled the electric kettle. "They don't want to overwhelm you. Sari warned them your mind isn't protected yet. But you'll learn the spells soon, and then they'll introduce themselves. Everyone's excited to meet you. We don't get many new people."

Bruno crossed to her and reached out his hand. Ava took it, and the immediate wash of comfort almost broke her control. Bruno held her hand in both of his big paws and bent down, smiling. "Welcome, Ava. I'm Bruno, and this is my mate, Karen. It's very nice to meet you. We're glad you're here."

"Thank you."

"And I'll try to be quiet, huh? So we don't wake your guard." He winked one blue eye, and Ava had the sudden image of Bruno in a red cap and coat.

"Do you ever play Santa at Christmas? Because you'd be awesome."

Bruno threw his head back and laughed, patting his flat stomach. "I've been trying to fatten up, but it doesn't seem to work."

"Shh! You'll wake Damien." Karen shook her head and turned back to the kettle.

Ava shook her head, smiling as she walked to the table. Bruno slipped behind Karen at the counter, bending down to wrap his arms around his mate.

"Did you hear, sweet? Ava says you're not feeding me enough."

Karen said something Ava didn't understand; it made Bruno growl low in his throat and pull Karen closer to drop a kiss on her neck. Ava turned her head from the easy intimacy between them. She pulled three plates from the cupboard, then turned back and got another.

There was no way that Damien would be sleeping for long, not with Bruno's booming voice filling the kitchen.

In fact, by the time the coffee was poured, dark and steaming from the French press on the counter, Damien was wandering out of his room, hair mussed from the night but already dressed in warm flannels.

"We took down a tree yesterday, and he's still awake at this hour," Damien said, eyeing the steaming cup that Karen was already pouring cream into. "Bruno, you've scribed a spell I don't know."

Bruno winked at Ava again and pulled Karen's chair closer. "Yes, but I'm not sharing. You'll have to figure it out on your own."

"Damien, how is Sari?" Karen asked. "Any progress?"

Bruno guffawed as Damien closed his eyes. "Woman, don't you know he gets that question in some form or another ten times a day?"

Karen shrugged. "That's because we all know she'd be far less… cranky if they reconciled."

"We'll be fine," Damien said, sipping his coffee. "I'm not leaving until we've resolved some things."

"Good," Bruno said, reaching for some of the spiced nut bread that Karen had set out. Instead of grabbing a piece for himself, he reached across the table and put a piece first on Ava's plate, then Karen's, before passing the basket to Damien. "What I want to know is when Ava is meeting with Orsala." He looked at her, wiggling his eyebrows. "We're all very curious what you can do."

Ava tried to smile. From the first day here, she'd felt and heard the probing curiosity. She wasn't convinced there was anything special about her other than her mysterious parentage. Certainly nothing like Sari's elemental powers or the healing she'd witnessed Astrid perform the day before. Even Karen seemed to have some sixth sense regarding baked goods.

"I can take really good pictures," Ava said. "But that's not very supernatural."

"Hmm," Karen mused. "But *why* are you such a talented photographer? Practice and training, I'm sure. But often, we hone our gifts without realizing their full potential. I wouldn't be surprised if something about your chosen profession relates to your talents as an Irina."

Bruno winked again. "See? Chamuel's blood. My sweet girl has a sense about these things." His eyes flicked to Damien. "I have a feeling our friend here has his suspicions, as well."

Damien shrugged when Ava turned to him. "You'll meet Orsala this afternoon. She'll be able to read you."

"How?" Ava asked.

Karen said, "Bruno teases that I have a touch of Chamuel's blood."

"Chamuel? Is he an angel?"

"He's our forefather who gifted the Irina with empathy and mental influence. My mate is probably right—"

"Say it again." Bruno sighed. "It's music to my ears."

Karen gave him a wry smile. "I have a touch. But Orsala? She has Chamuel's gift, only far stronger than me. She's a very potent empath and she'll be able to read you."

"Empath? So, she can actually… feel what I'm feeling?" Ava was reluctant to vent her own emotional roller coaster on another person, even one who was supernatural.

"She can feel what you're feeling and influence your mind, though she won't unless it's necessary."

"I don't want her in my mind." Forget it. She'd run away before she met this Orsala person. She'd rather take her chances with the Grigori.

Karen reached out a hand. "She won't do anything. Not unless it's necessary. And she'll always tell you ahead of time. Our songs say that is why empathy and influence go hand in hand. Only those with extreme empathy for another can be trusted not to use that influence to manipulate."

Damien said, "In short, Ava, Orsala *could* influence your mind to do almost anything, but since she would feel your emotions—feel the consequences of forcing you to do something against your will and the mental agony that would produce—she would never do it. Does that make sense?"

"I guess." Ava felt herself start to relax.

"It's the reason that Sarihöfn is protected," Bruno said. "Orsala gives everyone a mental prompt—a safety—so we are unable to reveal its location. This is what keeps us safe from Grigori who might try to kidnap one of our people and make her talk."

"Has that happened?" A chill went down her neck.

"Yes," Karen said softly. "A number of times. The Grigori finally realized that kidnapping us wouldn't work. So now they just kill us on sight."

"Orsala will give you that mental prompt when you meet her, Ava," Damien said. "You *won't* have a choice about it."

"I'm fine with that."

"Good."

The thought of being forced to lead the Grigori to this peaceful place made Ava want to throw up. Instead, she steadied her hands on her coffee cup and took another bite of bread, deciding to steer the conversation into less dangerous waters.

"So, Karen, if I baked, I'd ask you for this recipe. But I don't, so I'm just going to ask that you bring it by a lot."

Karen gave her a bright smile. "Would you like to *learn* how to bake?"

"Unless you want your kitchen in flames, it's probably a bad idea."

AVA WAS WALKING BETWEEN SARI AND DAMIEN ON THE PATH TO Orsala's house. The older woman lived about a mile away from the main house and surrounding cottages. The energy between the two mates crackled despite their silence, and Ava tried to ignore the rush of voices that flew from their minds. Both obviously had a lot to say, but they had no intention of sharing.

Finally, Ava had to break the silence, if for no other reason than to stave off the approaching headache. "So, why does she live so far away? Is it because of the empath thing?"

"Hmm?" Sari looked over her shoulder, as if surprised that Ava was still there.

"Orsala. Why does she live away from everyone else?"

"She can shield herself from the emotions around her, but it costs energy she knew she was going to need to read you the first time. So she went to her house. She likes her solitude, but she's often in the main house."

"That's why you haven't seen her," Damien said. "After today, she'll be around more."

"I feel bad she had to keep away."

Sari shrugged. "She doesn't *have* to do anything. She chose it. It's no responsibility of yours, so don't feel bad."

"Still, I'm sorry—"

"Don't apologize. My grandmother hates it when Irina apologize too much."

Ava bristled at Sari's tone but bit back her reply. The woman was brusque, to be sure. Probably more so than Damien. Ava found herself on the "get Sari and Damien back together" train, despite her initial dislike of the woman. Both of them obviously needed to get laid.

Finally, Sari spoke again, but this time it wasn't to Ava. "You didn't need to accompany her."

"I'm paying my respects to your grandmother, Sari. It would be rude of me not to see her."

"She's not your grandmother."

"No, but she's yours. And, unless you've forgotten, I am your mate. Therefore, she's my family, too."

Their inner voices were practically shouting at each other. Ava wanted to put her fingers in her ears and sing something. Sadly, that didn't really work.

"Trust me," Sari said. "I have not forgotten."

"Are you sure about that?"

Ava groaned. "You guys are impossible. You should hear yourselves."

Sari cut her eyes to Ava. "Then stop listening. It's rude."

"Don't you think I *would* if I could?"

Ava saw Damien fighting a smile, but he didn't say a word.

She practically cried in relief when they crested the hill to see a cheerful blue house tucked into the hills. It was low to the ground with a white porch and a traditional turf roof. A few flowers still bloomed in buckets on the porch, though most of the garden around the house was dying for the season. As they approached, a willowy woman opened the door, raising her hand in greeting. She wore a thick blue sweater and her blond hair hung loose around her shoulders. As Ava approached, she could see the woman's temples were touched with silver, and crow's feet creased the corners of her vivid blue eyes. But her round face was still stunning, and her smile was wide.

"Damien," she called, holding out her arms. "Oh, my son! I was wondering when you would come visit me."

Ava could practically feel the waves of annoyance rolling off Sari as Damien embraced her grandmother. They exchanged words in what Ava guessed was Norwegian, then Orsala turned to Ava and held out her hands. "And you must be Ava."

She smiled, and Ava tried not to stare. Damien had told her that

Orsala was close to a thousand years old, but the woman barely looked older than Ava's own mother.

"You are so very welcome. Thank you for coming to visit me."

It was amazing how cordial she made it sound, considering Ava knew she really didn't have a choice in the matter. Orsala's smile only got wider the longer she held Ava's hands.

"You have a wonderful sense of humor," the older woman said. "I can tell." Then she squeezed Ava's hands and dropped them, motioning them all inside.

Within minutes, they were all sitting at the round kitchen table, drinking a fragrant herb tea that made Ava think of the spice market in Istanbul.

"Damien keeps me supplied with tea," Orsala said, sitting down next to Damien and patting his hand. "I can only get the plain teas here. The ones from Istanbul are the finest."

"I'm glad you enjoy them," Damien said quietly, holding back another smile as Sari carefully avoided meeting his eyes.

"So much drama," Orsala said under her breath, looking between the two. "On to other things." She turned her attention to Ava. "Evren sent a letter with Damien. He says that they cannot discover where you've come from! What a delicious mystery, huh? Perhaps reading you today will give us a clue."

"How?" Ava asked.

"How much do you know about Irina blood?"

"I… a little. Not much. I know that Irin and Irina magic is different. Related, but different."

"Two sides of the same coin, is the saying, I think." Orsala smiled. "We speak the same language they write. But unlike us, Irin can grab the magic. Hold on to it with their writing. We can't do that."

"Has an Irina ever tried?"

Sari said, "Yes. Some try. It doesn't work for us."

"No more than an Irin speaking magic works for them," Orsala added. "We are different. We were designed to be."

Sari grimaced. "And you just end up with messy tattoos and no extra magic."

Damien leaned toward her. "They're not messy. I actually think they're rather attractive, my dove."

"*Don't* call me 'my dove.'"

Ava tried not to laugh. Was there anyone less dove-like than Sari?

Orsala was smiling at her granddaughter before she spoke again. "So, Irina speak our magic in the Old Language as the Irin write it. But we also have other gifts. Again, no one knows why. I'm assuming you haven't heard any of our songs?"

"Songs?"

Damien said, "Our history. Most of the books we have written—like the one Malachi showed you when you first came to the scribe house—are written records of Irina songs."

Orsala waved a dismissive hand. "Written songs are not songs. There is no way of capturing the true nature of our history on the page. It must be heard to be understood."

Damien smiled indulgently and turned to Ava. "This is a very old argument."

"It's true," Sari added. "The songs were never meant to be written. The act of writing them diminishes the power of their meaning."

"I'm not going to get into this argument, my dove."

Sari slapped her hand on the table. "Stop calling me that!"

Orsala barked out something in Norwegian that made both Damien and Sari sit up straight. For a moment, they both looked like chastised children, then Orsala switched to English.

"So, while I am working with Ava and teaching her beginning spells, you two will continue to research her background. We have records, too. And you can speak to Candice."

Sari's jaw had clenched. "But—"

"Candice's father was a historian and genealogist. One of the first in the Americas, so it's possible she might know something about the families that Ava might have come from. Once I get a feeling for her blood, you'll have more to go on."

"And you want us to work together?" Damien asked quietly. "Are you sure?"

"I am quite positive," Orsala said. "Why don't you both finish your tea and start right now?"

"Together?" Sari seemed limited to one word answers forced out between clenched teeth.

"Yes. In fact, just take your tea with you and leave Ava and me alone."

Damien couldn't hide the pleased expression on his face as he rose and held out his hand. "Shall we, my dove?"

Sari was muttering under her breath. She ignored her mate's hand

and put her cup on the counter, then without a backward glance, she walked out the front door.

Damien turned to Orsala and smiled. "So good to see you again, *matka*."

"Don't thank me yet, *Damjan*. You have a long way to go."

* * *   * * *

"WILL THEY MAKE UP?" AVA ASKED AFTER THEY'D FINISHED THEIR TEA and been left alone in the cottage. The fire crackled in the hearth, and Orsala added wood to the flames before she settled in the chair across from Ava.

"Yes. There was hurt on both sides. They both made mistakes, and I understand why Sari feels the way she does. But now?" Orsala shook her head. "It is time. Damien is a different man than he was during the Rending. Sari needs to learn that some Irin grow from their mistakes, and that forgiveness isn't something to be withheld from your mate, not even in grief."

"Was it that bad? Really?"

Shadows flickered in Orsala's eyes. "Yes." Then the old woman shook her head and asked, "Are you ready to listen?"

"Do I need to take notes?"

Orsala smiled. "I imagine you'll be sick of this history by the time we're done. You have a lot to learn, but everything draws from this, so it will be repeated."

"Okay, hit me."

"There were twenty-one cardinal angels who fell to the earth from above. Twenty-one who defied the creator and took humans as mates. Had children. Many of them. Seven returned. Seven were killed. Seven remained. Others followed them, but they were the first. The seven who returned, we call the Forgiven. They are the fathers of the Irin race."

"The ones who left their children," Ava said.

Orsala cocked her head. "They were not creatures of this world. They had no business here. Sometimes leaving is the right thing to do."

Ava ignored the twist of anger in her belly and asked, "And these seven gave their power to their children."

"Uriel gave us the gift of life. Male and female, we can harness his magic to extend our lives. Gabriel gave Irina the gift of hearing so that we might hear the souls of the world around us to aid in their protection. The other powers are more specific and more rare."

"Like empathy?"

Orsala nodded. "Chamuel gave a few of his blood the gift of empathy and influence. Rafael gave others the gift of healing, and also the ability to read the history of objects."

"You're talking about touch telepathy?" Ava was starting to get excited. It was real and unreal at the same time.

"In a sense." Orsala continued without further explanation. "Mikhael gave his daughters the gift of strategy. Sadly, not a developed gift for far too long. It was not as respected as some of the others."

"Why not?"

"Irina revere creation and prophecy. Seeing the connections between things is not creative. It is, however, one of the more potent offensive gifts that we have learned to wield."

"That makes sense."

"These are also not exclusive. After so many generations, our blood has mixed. So Sari exhibits some of Mikhael's blood traits, though her primary talent comes from Ariel."

"Which is…"

"Those of Ariel's blood exhibit elemental magic. He was the oldest of the cardinal angels. Some songs say he was present with the Creator at the dawn of our world, though we have no way of knowing this. Ariel's children can control the elements to varying degrees. Primarily wood and metal. In the past, Irina of Ariel's blood were our chief architects and builders. Very highly respected."

"Okay. By my count, that's six angels."

"Yes."

"So who was the seventh?"

Orsala leaned forward and peered into Ava's eyes. "The seventh was Leoc, the seer. *And Leoc, giver of visions and bearer of prophecy, returned to the heavens, but his daughters bear his mark, the mark of the seer…*"

Ava's skin began to prickle. She could feel the swell of power coming from the old woman.

"*…though their eyes now glimmer only faintly with their father's gift.*"

Her heart beat a rapid rhythm as the whispers in her mind grew louder.

"Leoc's daughters are seers?" she whispered. "They have… visions?"

"And golden eyes, Ava. Angelic eyes."

The images she'd seen in Jaron's office flipped through her mind.

Malachi.

Utter black. Pain. Despair.

Two dark-haired children. A girl with golden eyes, laughing as butterflies swirled around her. A boy, staring… The ink-black jaguar curled around the children protectively as a wolf and a tiger paced behind. The tiger bent to the girl, opening his mouth. The great beast closed his jaw around the girl's nape gently as she continued to smile and pet its cheek. A great circle rose in the sky, like a sun twisted with gold and silver. Higher and higher it rose, until the sun faded away to stars, a million scattered points of light dotting the heavens, dancing in concert to a growing song.

Darkness.

"I show you what has been. What will be. And what could be," Ava whispered Jaron's words. "Do not fear the darkness."

Orsala's voice came as if Ava was deep underwater. "Tell me, Ava. Do you see visions?"

She couldn't speak. Did she? Or was that something that Jaron had projected to her mind? Could angels do that?

"Your eyes are gold, Ava. To human eyes, they would seem only a beautiful light brown, but they're not. I haven't seen eyes like that since I was a child. They belonged to the oldest woman in my village. A daughter of Leoc who was very, very strong."

"I don't know…," Ava whispered. "I don't know what I see."

She didn't. She only knew that she needed to get away from Orsala's piercing gaze. The darkness hovered at the edge of her mind, and the frightening whispers grew in strength.

Orsala didn't hear them. The old woman leaned forward and put her fingers on Ava's temples. At her touch, Ava fell calm.

"Tell me what you see with your golden eyes, Ava, daughter of Leoc."

11.

Istanbul, Turkey

It was amazing how much was left after the fire. Brage kicked through the wreckage of the old wooden house in Beyoğlu, following the muffled screams of the young scribe they had captured on the road out of Göreme.

He slid into the room that had been carved with protection spells. Useless now that the Irin fire was gone. Foolish Irin put too much stock in magic. Brage's fingers trailed over the cryptic script of the Old Language that had been carved into the walls. It was a mystery to him, just as the Fallen intended.

Bitterness twisted his heart.

Unlike the Irin fathers, Volund and the other angels did not share knowledge with their children. They didn't trust them enough. Didn't believe them worthy. After all, they were half-human. They were servants and soldiers, not true sons.

The young scribe before him was fair-skinned and dark-eyed. Handsome enough to human eyes, though not stunning as the Grigori were. The angelic blood had been tempered by time and distance. The Irin were mere shadows of their forefathers. But the mysterious script marked the young scribe's arms and shoulders, though the glow of power was gone. Blood covered the young man's chest and face. Pieces of his *talesm* were missing. Strips of skin had been gouged from his arms.

Brage's brother handed him a flap of skin they had carved from the scribe's left wrist.

"*Talesm prim*," Brage said softly, kneeling beside the scribe who was tied to the chair.

The man looked at him with disgust, but Brage knew that he was growing weaker by the minute. These Irin could not last long without their magic. And by carving off the spells, the Grigori had neutralized the scribe's only advantage.

"That's what you call it, correct?" Brage held up the skin. "Your very first spell? The one that all the others draw from. Did they warn you about this? Or were they too arrogant?" He stood and shook his head, as if chastising a child. "They didn't, did they? Your elders teach you that you are superior to us. Your *magic*," he spat out. "It makes you so *blessed*. You are the favored of heaven. The weak Grigori with little magic have no power over you. But, of course, we do."

Brage leaned down and brought his knife to the young man's neck. He winced when the knife cut in and the blood welled around the wound. "Tell me where the Istanbul scribes are," he murmured, "and I'll kill you quickly."

The scribe's throat worked to respond. "No," he choked out.

Brage slid the knife under the skin of the young man's neck. It stretched and slowly stripped the flesh away as he screamed.

"Tell me," Brage whispered.

"Never."

It went on for hours, the slow interrogation. Brage was forced to revive the young man a number of times. By the fourth time he woke, the scribe's eyes were swimming, and Brage knew he was delirious and close to breaking.

"This is not your battle, child." He placed a cool cloth on the scribe's bloody forehead, gave the man a sip of cool water. "You are one young Irin scribe. How old are you?"

"For…forty-three."

"See?" Brage said. "You are practically a child. You are alone. Tell me where they are. Let them fight. They are armed and strong, with their brothers at their sides. They will not condemn you for telling me."

Tears slipped down the young man's cheeks, making paths in the crusted blood and sweat.

"Tell me," Brage whispered.

"Vienna," he finally choked out. "Th…they were driving to Vienna."

Damn.

Brage let out a breath and sat back on his heels. Of all the cities they could go to, Vienna was the one that Volund had forbidden. The Irin were too strong in that city. And making an appearance in the heart of the Irin power structure would alert too many people that Volund wanted lulled into complacency.

He stood and walked behind the bleeding man. Half the skin of his upper body was gone, and he was barely recognizable. Brage could feel the eager bloodlust of his brothers, but he had made a promise. And he did not break his promises.

The young scribe was weeping when Brage put the blade to his spine and drove it in.

He walked away as the gold dust rose behind him.

Vienna.

They were going to Vienna—

He stopped and smiled at the realization. No, they were *driving* to Vienna.

Driving to Vienna would lead them through several cities where the Grigori presence was strong. Though that heretic, Kostas, ran Sofia, more friendly elements made their home in Budapest. Svarog was a powerful angel, and his children were numerous, but the angel had friendly relations with Brage's father. A well-timed visit might be in order.

He made his way from the scribe room and to the bathroom on the second floor.

"New clothes," he said to the soldier guarding the door.

Brage took a quick shower, careful to wash the blood from his pale hair. He needed to feed, and a human woman would most likely be put off by blood.

Or possibly not. Some humans were delightfully perverse.

Smiling, he dressed in the immaculate clothes his brother had laid out for him, then he left the house and found his way into the night crowds of Beyoğlu. It was nothing to the rowdy atmosphere of Amsterdam or Berlin, but it would do. All he needed to find was a human woman who wanted the company of a good-looking man for the night. A tourist, he decided. Someone with a clean, comfortable hotel room where he could rest after he fucked her into unconsciousness and fed his ancient soul hunger.

Brage was more than capable of giving a woman an unforgettable night. He was old enough that he didn't need to draw much energy for his hunger to be fed.

Perhaps, if she survived, he would give her an unforgettable morning, too.

It was the least he could do.

CHAPTER
NINE

Sofia, Bulgaria

The man gave up his knife after the second attempt at Malachi's neck. It clattered to the stones in the alley as the Grigori lunged toward him. Catching him in midair, Malachi hugged the soldier to his chest and felt the magic coursing through his own body. He grabbed for his own silver dagger, ignoring the chokehold his opponent was attempting. The man twisted around, realizing too late that Malachi was armed. He loosened his hold and tried to flee, but by that time, Malachi had a firm grip on the man's long hair. He twisted it around his wrist and pulled up, letting the Grigori dangle and scream as he kicked.

"They said you were dead!" The man tried to break Malachi's hold, tried to pry open the fingers that held him, but the scribe's grip didn't falter. "They told us—"

"They were wrong," he said, jerking the soldier closer and plunging the blade into his spine.

In the blink of an eye, the body shimmered and turned golden. Malachi stared into the man's black eyes as they met his own. He was gold. Shimmering. Translucent in death. And for a moment, the soldier was gone and Malachi watched his own face dissolve as a piercing scream shattered his ears.

"No!"

He blinked away the echoing scream and came back to the alley. From the corner, a young woman held her arms out toward the dust that rose.

"What have you done, you monster?" she shouted at him, tears streaming down her face. "Ciril!" she sobbed, rocking back and forth.

Malachi went to her, bending down. "You're safe now," he said. "We'll keep you safe."

The woman kept rocking, clutching her arms around her body and sobbing into her knees. Malachi looked up, wondering what to do with the woman in the back streets of Sofia. They'd stopped in the capitol of Bulgaria to eat and stretch their legs before they continued driving to Budapest. Leo, Rhys, and Malachi had been taking turns, but they all needed sustenance. The fact that they'd happened to find a Grigori preying on a human woman at the restaurant was simply a coincidence. He'd run from them immediately but had grabbed the woman and taken her with him. They'd all given chase; Malachi was just the first to catch him.

Within seconds, he heard his brothers' scuffling feet near the mouth of the alley. Malachi was trying to soothe the sobbing human without putting his hands on her skin. Rhys had said Grigori victims often mourned their attackers' deaths, not knowing how dangerous the creatures truly were.

"Please," Malachi said. Rhys had handed him a Bulgarian dictionary as soon as they'd crossed the border, so Malachi had already absorbed most of the language. "Please, miss, who can I call for you? Surely, there is someone—"

"There was Ciril," she choked out. "There was only Ciril. And now there is no one." She clutched her head, pressing her palms to her temples as she wailed.

"He would have hurt you," Malachi said, speaking softly as Rhys and Leo approached. "You're safe now."

Finally, the woman's eyes lifted to his. His stomach dropped when he saw them. Blank. Dead. There was nothing behind the young woman's gaze.

"You know nothing," she whispered.

Then she lunged forward, bashed her forehead into Malachi's nose, and scrambled up, darting between Leo and Rhys and out of the alley before Malachi had time to recover. Blood streamed down his nose and into his mouth. She was gone by the time he reached his feet.

"What was that?" Leo asked with wide eyes.

"I have no idea." He wiped the blood from his face with the corner of his sleeve. "I killed the Grigori, and she went crazy."

Rhys shook his head sadly. "It's horrible. They become obsessed. I only hope she has someone she can go to."

Malachi narrowed his eyes. "She knew his name. Do they usually tell humans their name?"

Rhys shrugged. "He told her *a* name. I doubt it's his. Let's go. Who knows who that woman is calling right now? She could be running to the police. We need to get back on the road."

Leo was staring at the spot where the woman had been crouched, his eyes lost in thought. After a second's silence, he shook his head and said, "Rhys and I will grab some food from one of the corner shops. Malachi, you get back to the car. Your face would draw too much attention right now."

"All right."

As they walked, Rhys slapped Malachi's shoulder. "How do you feel? No trouble with the new spells?"

"I feel fine," he said, rolling his shoulders as he felt his nose start to knit together. "Actually, I feel amazing."

It was true. Nothing about the fight had been a struggle. It was as if his muscles knew exactly what to do, from the way to immobilize his opponent to the exact angle at which to stab the knife. Like so many things, he only consciously thought about his actions after they were over, not unlike watching a movie on rewind, wondering how each point connected to the last.

Leo asked, "Did you remember anything more? Rhys and I have been debating whether or not tapping into your magic and scribing some of your old spells would help your memory."

"I don't remember anything more about Ava," he said, "if that's what you were wondering."

No, he didn't remember anything from the past, but his dreams— the intimate communion he reached for in sleep—those, he decided, they didn't need to know about. Perhaps he was falling in love with his subconscious memories of the woman. He knew her without question in his dreams. He only wished he had something to hold on to when he woke.

"TELL ME WHERE YOU GO," SHE ASKED AFTER THEY HAD SATED THEIR bodies on the forest floor. "When you leave me here, where do you go?"

The moss was a thick green carpet at his back, and the night birds sang overhead as he cradled her on his chest.

"I'm not sure," he said. "I don't remember, exactly. I only know you're not there. But you're here when I sleep."

"Hmm." She closed her eyes and traced her fingers along his collar. "I miss your markings."

"I have some back." He raised his left arm and she trailed her fingers along the black ink. "I will write more for you."

"Okay."

"Are yours still there?"

She smiled up at him. "Of course, silly. They're always here." She lifted his hand and put it over her heart. "And they always will be. Kiss me."

He kissed her, and her lips were honey to his tongue. Far too soon, she pulled back, and in the low light of the misty forest, he could see them—his own marks—glowing in the darkness. Gold magic swirled on the skin over her heart. It shone on her shoulders. He sat up, twisting her until she sat in his lap with her back to his chest. Then he leaned back on his arms, staring at the intricate letters that trailed up her spine, over her neck and shoulders.

"So beautiful," he murmured, stroking the magic that he'd used to claim her. "I love seeing these on you."

"I know." She was smiling as she looked over her shoulder. Her gold eyes, he realized, were almost the same color as her mating marks.

"Extraordinary."

"Hmm?"

"Nothing." He kissed her again, pulling her closer before he laid them down again on the moss.

"*Reshon?*" she whispered against his chest.

"Yes?"

"Come back to me."

"Come back now, brother." He felt the hand slapping his cheek and he bolted awake.

"Ah." Leo was grinning. "There you are. You were dead to the world."

"Hmm," Malachi grunted, blinking the image of his mate's bare shoulders away.

Dream. Just a dream.

"Come back to me."

"Where are we?" he asked in a rough voice.

"Twenty kilometers outside Belgrade. You've been sleeping for almost four hours. Rhys is stopping for petrol, then it's your turn to drive."

He nodded his head, swiping a hand over his face to rid himself of the misty dream. Then he slapped his cheek and said, "Get me some tea and I'll be fine."

The three men stopped at the all-night petrol station, stretching their legs as they walked to the small shop to get coffee for Malachi and a bottle of water for Rhys.

"Don't you want anything?" Malachi asked Leo.

"No." The blond man shrugged. "If I sleep, I sleep. I'm not tired though, so I'll probably keep you company."

"That would be good," he said. It was true. There was still an underlying tension between Malachi and Rhys, as if the man resented Malachi for the loss of his memories. With Leo, however, there was only a cheerful acceptance. Malachi decided it would take more than death, resurrection, and amnesia to rattle the goodwill of the optimistic scribe. Plus, Leo was a font of information.

"Tell me more about the council," Malachi asked when they were back on the road and Rhys was snoring.

Leo frowned. "I'm not sure where to start."

"How was it formed? Has there always been one?"

Leo nodded. "Well, for as long as anyone knows. The stories say that before they returned to heaven, the seven cardinal Forgiven chose seven scribes and seven singers to guide their children. So, that's where the council came from, according to tradition. They say there are written records from the beginning, but no one ever sees them, of course. Maybe the Chief Scribe in Vienna. According to Max, he sees everything. If there is one Irin scribe who knows the whole of our history, it would be the Chief Scribe."

"The written history, that is."

"Hmm?"

"Well… the Irina would keep an oral history, wouldn't they?"

Leo looked as if he'd never considered the question. "Of course. I suppose they would."

"So, the Chief Scribe wouldn't know all the history. Just what the scribes had written down."

"Yes." Then Leo grinned. "But we write everything down."

"And the council. Can they see it?" Malachi was wondering whether or not there was some clue about Ava's past in that great library. Perhaps, if they asked the Chief Scribe, there might be some other incidence of a human turning into an Irina somewhere in the past.

"I suppose they could see whatever they want, but they're hardly historians, are they? The council is made up of politicians. No avoiding them, no matter what race you are. But the Irin council… it has a spiritual purpose, too. Or it's supposed to."

"You said there were seven singers on the council. What happened to them after the Rending?"

Leo's face paled. "No one knows. I mean, we know that some were killed. The others? There were no official reports, only rumors. Some say they were all killed, but I don't think that's possible. Most lived in Vienna and they were highly guarded. Others say that they withdrew when the retreats were ransacked. That they took their most trusted singers and formed havens around the world. Havens like Sari's, where the remaining Irina could hide."

"What do you think?"

"I think some were killed. Some formed havens." Leo crossed his arms. "Anything is possible. All I know is they're gone. Now the council is only old men."

Malachi narrowed his eyes, trying to measure Leo's mood even as he drove the car. "You're… resentful of them? The Irina?"

"What me?" Leo's eyes widened. "No, I—"

"You are. You blame them for leaving. Or, at least, a part of you does."

Leo stared at him, stared at his profile so hard that Malachi could feel his eyes. Finally, he said, "They left us alone. Irin and Irina were never meant to be separate. We were always meant to fight together."

"So many had been lost, Leo. It must have been a huge shock. They were frightened."

"We're all frightened sometimes." Leo's voice was barely over a whisper. "But you don't run away. You never run away."

* * *   * * *

THEY DROVE FOR ANOTHER THREE HOURS. RHYS SNORED IN THE backseat, and Leo and Malachi had turned to more pleasant topics of conversation.

"You must remember some of this," Leo said with a laugh. "She was so angry with you."

Malachi grinned. "I don't. She really stood up, drunk in a bar full of Grigori, and told them you were a catch?"

"And criticized their grooming. Don't forget that part."

Both men burst out laughing.

"And there was some comment about makeup, too."

"Was I laughing this hard then?" His sides ached with the vision of the tiny human woman he'd seen in pictures telling off six Grigori while Leo looked on, helplessly wondering what to do.

"Are you joking?" Leo wiped tears from the corner of his eye. "You were furious. Ava was ready to call the police when you threatened to stab one."

"It sounds like she didn't like me very much."

"Well, she didn't know the truth then. She still thought you were an out-of-control bodyguard. Trust me, she liked you very much." Leo couldn't contain his smile.

"What did she do after that? She didn't call the police?"

"No, she took you out to an isolated monastery on the Prince Islands and pulled a gun on you."

His eyebrows shot up. "What?"

"Then she kissed you. Or you kissed her. You were vague relating that part of the story."

He couldn't laugh anymore, but he did smile. "I should think so."

"When you brought her back to the scribe house, Damien was livid. But you stood up to him. You were certain of her identity. Even though it took some convincing, you were certain. And you were right. You and Ava belonged together. I knew it."

"I loved her, didn't I? Even when I thought she was human, I loved her."

Leo opened his mouth, but no sound came out at first. Then he said quietly, "I believe you did. Even when you thought she was out of reach."

"Come back to me."

Malachi nodded, ignoring the tight clutch in his throat. "I, uh… I dream about her, you know?"

"About Ava?"

He just nodded.

Leo angled his shoulders toward him. "What do you dream?"

"Just that we are together. We speak. We… we're together. I don't remember everything, but she's there. Every time I close my eyes, she's there."

Leo said nothing, just blinked in surprise. Finally, he faced the road again. "Well, no wonder you didn't want to wake up earlier."

They fell silent for another few kilometers, but when they saw the lights of Budapest in the distance, Leo reached back and shook Rhys's knee. "Wake up, old man."

"What?" Rhys muttered. "I'm awake. I'm up."

"We're almost to Philip's," Leo said.

Malachi could see Rhys shaking his head and rubbing his eyes in the rearview mirror. The scribe patted his cheeks and grabbed his water bottle to take a drink.

"So, what have you ladies been gossiping about without me?"

"I was telling Malachi some of the funniest stories about Ava."

"Oh really?"

"Like the time she told the bar full of Grigori that I was a catch."

Rhys's eyes gleamed mischievously in the light of a passing truck, then the corner of his mouth curled into a smirk.

"Did you tell him about the time she kissed me?"

Malachi hissed, *"What?"*

"There was tongue."

He slammed on the brakes to avoid hitting the back of a red van, and Rhys went flying into the passenger seat, smashing his nose on the headrest.

"For heaven's sake," Rhys yelled from the back. "This again?"

* * *   * * *

Malachi didn't know what Rhys was griping about. By the time they'd arrived at his friend Philip's scribe house on the outskirts of Budapest, his nose had completely healed. Other than the smear of blood on his collar, he looked none the worse for wear.

They grabbed their bags out of the back of the Range Rover and walked toward the entrance.

"We'll rest for a couple of days here," Rhys said. "I'm still waiting to hear from Max. He should have a meeting with Gabriel by tomorrow at the latest. After that, we'll know more about what's going on in the city and what the political climate is like."

"Do you still think we should keep quiet about what happened to Malachi?"

"Damien said not to tell anyone about Ava unless we absolutely had to. If that's the case, I say we avoid talking about Malachi as well. Unless the word has spread from Cappadocia, we should be fine."

Leo said, "I don't think the scribes in Cappadocia have much communication with the houses in the city."

Malachi had realized that if no other descriptor was given, "the city" always referred to Vienna. According to Leo, it was the center of the Irin race. Everything, from finances to art to government, centered on Vienna, where the Irin had lived for centuries under the noses of the human population. Malachi couldn't remember it at all.

"Rhys?" Malachi tried to get his attention as they walked up the block to the nondescript building on the corner that looked like it housed a bar on the first floor.

"What?"

"Leo said there are no Grigori in Vienna."

"It's true. The Fallen abandoned that city long ago."

"But why? If it's the center of the Irin race, wouldn't they have focused their efforts there?"

Rhys gave him a grim smile. "Of course not. How could they lull the most influential Irin into a complacent state of greed if they hung around and caused trouble?"

"You mean they don't think—"

"Vienna hasn't seen a concentrated attack from the Fallen or their

Grigori since the Rending, Malachi. According to many, the Grigori are a nuisance, nothing more."

Malachi was stunned.

Leo only nodded. "It's true. We may be fighting all over the world, but in Vienna… they dance."

CHAPTER

TEN

Ava had spent a week being mentally poked and prodded by Orsala and physically beat up by Mala. Sure, Mala might have called it "training," but Ava was fairly certain she was just working out some deep-seated resentment at Ava's expense. The fact that Brooke, the twelve-year-old who looked like a fairy princess, was her training partner was just another blow to the ego.

"She wants us to do it again," panted Brooke, tossing the short staff to Ava, who had collapsed on one of the benches that lined the barn where they practiced.

Mala was teaching them how to use the Irina short staff. It was hardly glamorous-looking, but according to Astrid, it was the traditional weapon for all Irina because it was so practical. Ava did see her point. The staff Mala had chosen for her was about the length and width of a broomstick, though it was much stronger because of spells that had been laid over it. She'd doubted how much damage the innocent-looking piece of wood could do until Mala had demonstrated by taking off the head of the training dummy.

"Again?"

"Yes." Brooke didn't look any more pleased than Ava. The days of training were even taking a toll on the child's natural optimism.

Ava pushed to her feet and grabbed her staff, then walked with her partner to the center of the ring. Mala stared at them from the edge of the barn, making a clicking noise with her tongue to get Brooke's atten-tion. Once she had it, her hands formed a flurry of signs that Brooke took in, nodding while Mala spoke.

"Okay." Brooke turned to her. "Mala says you need to practice your approaches. Focus on keeping your shoulders more…" She looked back toward Mala, who repeated herself with a sigh. "Oh. You're kind of… showing me what you're doing before you do it. Does that make sense?"

Ava glanced at Mala, who was rolling her eyes. "I think so." She tried not to smile. "You want me to keep my shoulders looser?" she asked her trainer, and Mala nodded. "So I don't let Brooke know what my attack is going to be?"

Mala gave her a thumbs-up and sat back down to watch them, clapping for them to start.

She tried to do what Mala had asked, but it was difficult. Her instinct was to lean into an attack, not keep her shoulders loose and fluid. Brooke seemed to take to the practice more easily, getting in more than one good strike to Ava's side or knee. More than once, Ava was convinced that Brooke was going easy on her.

"Sorry," the girl said with wince after she'd struck another blow, this time to the back of Ava's thigh.

"No, don't apologize." She grunted, straightening up. "But seri-ously? How did you get so good?"

Brooke smiled. "When I was young, I played with sticks as often as dolls. I remember watching my mom and dad spar with staffs when I was little. Mom always had one around. Humans don't even notice them. They think it's a broom handle or a walking stick. Mom says it's the best weapon in the world."

There was a whistle and they turned their heads toward Mala, who shot off a few signs.

Brooke smiled again. "Mala agrees. She said that throughout history, Irina have used the short staff as a primary weapon because we could take one everywhere. They're very easy to overlook."

"And very effective."

"Yep." Brooke went back to her ready stance. "Don't worry! You'll get the hang of it."

Ava took a deep breath and rolled her shoulders, trying to remember to keep them loose. Ready. She was an Irina, after all. She'd get this. It was probably genetic or something. She lifted her staff in both hands and angled forward at her right shoulder like Mala had shown her. Brooke stood across from her in the same stance. Her face showed nothing. Ava shifted to the right, and Brooke leaned forward, just a little. Ava leaned with her right shoulder, deliberately hinting that she would strike from the right, only to have Brooke shift with lightning reflexes to the left, and then her staff circled down, hitting just below Ava's left knee.

"Shit!" Ava hopped back, her previous plan of attack forgotten as the pain radiated down to her ankle and up her thigh. "Damn—*oww*! How did you—"

"Sorry, sorry! Your shoulders looked great, but then you did this thing with your leg and you shifted back, so I knew you were going to attack from the left, so I—"

"Yeah. Okay. Got it," Ava groused, ignoring Mala, who was smiling wide and clutching her stomach. If the woman had been able to laugh, it would have filled the barn. "I know, all right? I'm completely transparent."

"But your shoulders looked better!"

Great. A twelve-year-old was kicking her ass and trying to make her feel better about it.

"It's fine, Brooke." Ava glared at Mala. "Can we take a break now? I think I need to ice this leg."

An unfamiliar voice sang from the door. "You're never going to get better if you keep taking breaks."

Ava turned to stare. The woman was tall and dark with olive skin and black hair that streamed down her back. Everything about her— from the black clothes to the wary expression—screamed "Danger!" Ava stepped in front of Brooke, but the girl shot out from behind her and rushed forward.

"Renata!"

"*Ciao, bella mia*," the woman named Renata murmured, holding out her arms to the girl and enclosing her in an embrace. She looked up at Mala. "Who's the new girl?"

Mala signed quickly, and Renata lifted one hand, signing back while still holding Brooke with her other arm.

"No," Brooke said, clearly understanding the silent conversation. "She's from Los Angeles. She was only visiting in Istanbul when Damien met her. She's not Turkish."

Renata said, "I was thinking Persian, actually. Welcome to Sari-höfn, Ava."

"Thanks." She lowered her staff and stepped forward. "Your name is Renata?"

"Yes." Renata eyed Mala. "Are they done for today?"

Mala shrugged, then signed something that seemed to indicate Brooke could go, because Renata turned and started toward the door with the girl still curled under one arm.

"I'll see you later, Ava."

"Bye!" Brooke called.

Ava lifted her hand in a wave, then started toward the bench where she'd left her jacket, only to be stopped by a staff across the belly. Groaning, she lifted her eyes to Mala.

"Let me guess. I'm not done yet."

The corner of Mala's mouth lifted, and Ava didn't need to understand signing to read her expression.

Not even close.

• • •   • • •

SHE WANTED NOTHING MORE THAN A BATH AND A BED BY THE TIME SHE finally made it back to the cottage. Mala had drilled her for another three hours after Renata had shown up and taken off with Brooke. Luckily, Ava was picking up some signs from Mala and communication was starting to get better. And so, despite her reservations, were her attacks. Mala was a patient teacher and seemed to understand instinctively where and how Ava was struggling. By the end of the session, she was parrying with a fair amount of success instead of simply fending off blows. And, if she'd read Mala's signs correctly, the next week they were going to add daggers.

Ava liked daggers.

"Wash up," Damien called from the kitchen. "I'm fixing tea and I'll make you a snack."

"Thanks, mom."

"Then we're going to a sing. There will be a dinner before at the house." He glanced at her. "I'll get you an ice pack, too. Do you need two?"

"A sing? What's a sing?" She tried to sort through the barrage of information. "And yes. I probably need two."

"I'll get three. There's hot water for your shower, but don't take too long. I don't want to be late."

"What's a sing, Damien?"

"It's a ceremony. With singing." Damien walked over and patted her head. "Hence, it's called a sing."

"You're the only person I know who uses 'hence' in everyday conversation."

"Aren't you fortunate that you know me, then?" He waved toward the door, unusually chipper. "Go. I'll get the tea going."

"Why are you so happy?" Then it dawned on her. "Oh, this 'sing' is going to be at the main house, isn't it? *Sari's* house?"

"Yes." A smile teased up the corner of his lip.

"And it's like a party?"

"It is."

"And you're invited?"

"I am."

"Ahhhhh." Ava was smiling.

"What?"

"Damien's making progress," she sang.

"That's enough." He shoved her shoulder. "Go clean up. I don't want to be late."

"Mr. Cranky is gonna get some," she sang some more, then ducked in her room after the kitchen towel smacked the back of her head. Ava slammed the door and yelled, "Maybe you won't be Mr. Cranky after tonight!"

"You are childish and you stink. Take a shower, Ava."

She gathered her things and went to the small bathroom, still smiling. Ignoring the tug in her heart. Ignoring the quick twist of pain at the thought of her friend's happiness. Damien was a good friend. A good man. He deserved his happiness, even if she'd lost her own.

"I will not abandon you. I will not leave you. Ever."

But you did leave me.

Would her heart ever stop bleeding?

She heard Damien banging cupboards in the kitchen, no doubt looking for the tea, which he could never seem to find. Maybe he would go to this party tonight and Sari would talk to him without scorn in her voice. Maybe they would make up. She could hope. The world didn't stop just because she'd lost Malachi.

With that thought, Ava stepped into the shower and let the warm water wash away her tears.

⁂

AVA DIDN'T KNOW QUITE WHAT TO EXPECT FROM THE PARTY THAT night. She tried to imagine, but she kept coming up blank. Her lessons with Orsala had been minimal. The old woman had focused on teaching Ava the magic to block the soul voices from her mind. It was a simple spell, designed for a child to be able to master. Orsala had helped Ava create a door in her mind, and for the first time in her life, that door was slammed shut.

It had been a revelation. Salvation. At first, the voices stopped all together, but the door cracked open after an hour or so as voices tried to push through a familiar hall. The next time she spoke the words, the door stayed closed a little longer. Then a little longer. The first day that she heard little to no voices at all, Ava had shown up at Orsala's door, almost weeping with relief.

Since then, the spell had become a mantra. The voices never disappeared entirely around other people—Orsala said they weren't meant to—but a quick recitation of the words was enough to shut the door so the whispers were only murmurs that came from a great distance. Her tension headaches disappeared. Her agitation lessened. Now when Damien took her hand and squeezed it, she felt happy and content. There wasn't the desperate relief she'd once needed just to get through the day.

And for that she was grateful. Because though the weeks with Malachi had been a profound blessing, Ava knew she would probably never take another mate. Orsala had told her she might eventually find another partner. It was more than acceptable for Irin and Irina who had lost a mate to find love again. But Ava had a hard time imagining settling for anything less than what she and Malachi had once had, even if it had been brief. It was more than love. He was her soul mate. She didn't want another.

And if she looked forward to sleep a little more than normal, well, that was understandable. There was comfort in dreaming of him, even if the waking reality tore her heart.

"Are you sure this shirt is acceptable?" Damien tugged at a brown shirt that brought out the color of his dark eyes. Ava had suggested it instead of the dull black button-down he'd been about to put on. They were walking to the main house, and Damien was as nervous as a teenager on his first date.

"Yes. Stop fussing."

"I feel like I should have shaved."

Ava rolled her eyes. "Will you stop? The beard looks good. She likes it. Trust me."

"How do you know?"

"Do you seriously not pick up on the 'I want to lick you' looks that woman sends your way every time you're in the room?"

"I…" Damien blinked rapidly. "No. Mostly I'm trying to not irritate her."

"You need to irritate her more, not less."

"That makes no sense whatsoever."

"Sari's a busy girl, and she's filed you away under 'things I'll deal with later.' You need to make her deal with you *now*. I'd suggest pissing her off. Like you said, she hates you the same way she loves you. The love is there, Damien. You guys just have to sort out your shit."

He halted, forcing Ava to stop next to him when he held on to her arm. "I tried to rush her once. I tried to push past her grief before she was ready. And it caused more harm than good. I don't want to do that again. I can be patient for her."

Her heart warmed at his words. "I know you can. But you shouldn't waste time. Trust me. You never know how much time you'll get."

Damien frowned and squeezed her hand. "I am sorry you didn't have more time with Malachi."

"I don't… want to talk about that right now." She couldn't. Not if she wanted to get through this party without crying.

"I understand." He started back up the path and deliberately changed the subject. "Are you curious what the sing will be?"

"I'm trying to release my expectations, or something like that. Whatever happens, happens."

"You don't want to know?"

"Nope. I'm getting my zen on."

"Your 'zen'?"

She could hear the smile in his voice even as they approached the house, which was lit up in every window, with more people spilling out in the garden. The fall air made their breath fog, and frost crunched under their feet. Soon, everyone told her, it would snow.

As they entered the house, calls came from every corner, and Ava pressed on the door Orsala had built with her, making sure it was shut. She closed her eyes, let the magic take root, and then she opened them. The women around her smiled in understanding. There were many she was beginning to recognize, but a lot of them still looked unfamiliar. There were also more Irin men than she'd seen before, standing in small groups or holding their mates. It was, quite obviously, a party. The smell of savory meat filled the air, and spices tempted her nose. Someone handed her a glass of what looked like cider, and she took a sip. It was delicious.

Damien nudged her shoulder. "Can I leave you with Astrid?"

Ava spotted her friend in the corner of the sitting room, waving. "Yep. Go find your woman and irritate her."

"Wish me luck."

"Somehow, I don't think you'll need it."

He disappeared into the crowd as Astrid approached.

"Come," her friend said. "Let's get you some food. People eat quickly, then we head over to the barn for the singing."

"What—" She caught herself before she could ask for explanations. "No, don't tell me."

Astrid smiled. "You don't want to know what it is?"

"Nope. I want to just… experience. If you have no expectations, you can't be disappointed with reality."

"Fair enough."

They made their way to the kitchen, where more people were gathered. Mostly women, but again, a few scribes. One man, whom Ava vaguely recognized, held an Irina on his lap. She squinted when she noticed that he had no *talesm* on his neck.

"Wait." She tugged on Astrid's arm. "Is he…?"

"Human?" She nodded. "Yes. Orsala is not pleased with the relationship, but then, Cam does what she wants."

"But how do they… you know?"

Astrid frowned. "Didn't you say you had lovers before Malachi? Irin can't touch human women, but we don't have the same problem. Most human men just can't handle our energy or intensity for prolonged periods of time. Johan doesn't have that problem, apparently."

"But aging? Won't she stay young as he gets old?"

"Yes." Astrid shrugged. "It's her choice, Ava. And his."

They pushed past the group gathered around the table and made their way to the food that was spread out on the counter. Soon her plate was piled with meat pies and sausages made in the haven, as well as roasted turnips and carrots. There was a soup made out of pumpkin that smelled like it was spiced with chilies. She and Astrid stood in a corner, eating their dinner and chatting with a few visitors whom Ava hadn't met yet. As Orsala had warned her, most were very curious about the new girl. The crush of people was more than Ava was used to, and she sighed in relief when people started filtering out of the house and down to the barn.

Astrid and Ava followed the steady stream after they finished their food. By the time they entered the barn, it was half-full. The training equipment had been taken away, and benches filled the room, along with heaters to chase away the cold. At the front of the room, Orsala sat, along with Sari, Renata, and another older woman with a cap of silver-grey hair. Murmurs and laughter filled the air as everyone took seats on the benches.

"Do you want to sit near the front?"

"No." She felt conspicuous enough.

"That's fine." Astrid found a spot near the back wall. It was cooler, as the air leaked in from cracks in the wall, but there were enough people and heaters that Ava wasn't uncomfortable.

"How much of the Old Language do you understand?" Astrid asked.

"Not much. Just a few things, though I've heard it plenty, of course."

Astrid's eyes lit. "You might understand more after tonight. The songs might help your understanding."

"What does that mean?"

"Just listen."

After a few more minutes, everyone seemed to have arrived. Ava even spotted Damien across the barn, near the side door, standing by himself but staring at his mate. Ava also noticed Sari sneaking glances at him and trying to hide nerves.

"Hmm. Something definitely going on there."

Astrid followed her eyes. "It's about time."

"Right?"

Orsala stood, and immediately everyone fell silent.

"We are here to celebrate a new sister among us and a sister returned home." Orsala's eyes met hers, but luckily she didn't ask Ava to stand or single her out in any way. She continued, a smile spread across her face. "As is our custom, we welcome our sister Ava with the songs of our fathers. It is with our voices we remember, with our ears we understand. For our fathers gave us the gift of their songs, and it is our duty to sing them. It is our joy to remember. And as we create new life and preserve the safety of those under our care—" Orsala nodded to Sari. "We hold in our hearts and minds the stories of our past and the power they give us. For as we create and protect, we reflect the will of heaven on earth."

Ava felt a chill travel down her spine. Goose bumps rose on her arms as the room seemed to fill with a humming noise. It wasn't unlike the hum she'd heard on the first day approaching Sarihöfn. It was a low thrum that traveled along her skin and seemed to settle on the back of her neck. Then her mouth dropped open in surprise as she realized some of the hum came from her own throat.

She barely felt it, but it was there. And as her voice joined the others in the room, a single tone rang out, high and clear at the front of the room. Astrid gripped her right hand, and another woman reached for her left. Ava felt no urge to pull away. No discomfort. She realized the hum that had started in her throat had traveled down each arm and was linked with the same resonance coming from both Astrid and the woman to her left. The noise surged with life and magic. The air grew electric, snapping around her as she felt the hair on her arms rise.

Ava was one and part of everything in that moment. Tears came to her eyes as she watched the small older woman with the silver hair stand in front of the room, her arms lifting as her voice rose.

Then the Irina began to sing.

Some joined with the woman in front, others rang out at different times, harmonizing as they joined, until the room was filled with the tapestry of sound. She did not understand the words, only the clear purity of voice. Ava continued to hum, along with the women she held on to. But as she sang, she felt it. She was connected. She was one with the Irina in the room. Irina long passed. The ones who had been lost. Others still hiding in fear.

As the song continued, images washed across Ava's mind. Gold and light. She closed her eyes and a twisting kind of rainbow filled her vision. When it faded away, she not only heard—she *saw* what the old woman sang.

The glory of the angels on the mortal plane. Songs of love and joy.

New life.

Sorrow.

Joy.

Purpose.

Flashes like the images in the book that Malachi had shown her, and behind it all, a chorus of voices rose and fell, filling the air with a magic that elevated her soul. Fed her heart. In that moment, there was no sadness. No heartache. She had not lost Malachi, for she would see him again. In the blink of an eye, they would be together as the angels welcomed them home.

Tears streaming down her face, she opened her eyes to look for the singers. All four women stood at the front of the room, and three of them glowed with gold light. Orsala, Sari, and the old woman's mating marks shone in the candlelight. Renata's face was lifted in song, a single circle of magic on her forehead. When Ava looked down, she saw her own arms glowing with Malachi's marks, saw Astrid's mating marks lit up as well.

All around the room, the magic swelled and rose, coursing over the company of Irina and their mates. Damien stood across the room, his dark eyes fixed on his mate, his *talesm* lit up like burning silver. For a moment, she saw their eyes meet.

There it was.

Tears fell down her face when she recognized it. It was the look she'd seen in the manuscript. The expression of perfect completion.

Then the image that Jaron had shown her rose again. The great circle in the sky. A sun twisted with gold and silver. Higher and higher it rose, and Ava realized in the back of her mind that her own voice rose with it. She closed her eyes as the sun faded away to stars. She rose to her feet as a million scattered points of light dotted the heavens, dancing in concert to a growing song.

Then a single voice rose above the others until it was all she could hear.

And Ava realized the voice was hers.

III.

At the edge of the valley, Jaron watched. Opening his mind's eye, he saw the circle of voices as the daughters of the Forgiven lifted their song. And in his frozen soul, he heard the chorus of angels, calling out in joy as the heavens rang. A gold sea, as calm and clear as a mountain lake. His heart swelled with longing. For peace. For purpose. For home.

Then Jaron heard her. Her voice was different. And yet, somehow, it wasn't. It lifted over the others as she sang powerfully of the vision he had sent her. It was a song of longing and strength. It was, to the ears of the Fallen, a song of hope.

Jaron closed his eyes and allowed his heart to join the song he had given her.

Barak appeared beside him.

"Can he see her here?" the grey-haired angel asked, always alert to danger.

"Normally he can see her everywhere, as I can. But I cloaked the valley when I knew she would be coming. She's safe. For now."

The two stood silently in the darkness as the magic rose in waves, flowing over the land. Elsewhere, the trees had lost their leaves. The ground was harder and the wind more bitter. The haven the daughters of the Forgiven had created was as gentle a place as the harsh Earth could be. When the snow finally fell, it would lie soft on the ground.

"If he sees your fingerprints here, he will know."

"He will."

There was silence between them until Barak heard the words that Jaron had not spoken.

"You have distracted him in some way."

"I have."

"With the scribe?"

Jaron shrugged. "I was not expecting to have an ally as convenient as him. Even an unwitting one."

"You call him your ally?"

"He is my ally as long as I can use him."

The Fallen narrowed his eyes. "The scribe is no ally of mine."

"We both believe it was her magic that rent heaven, brother. It was her magic that brought him back."

"So?"

"She *tore the fabric of heaven* with her magic, brother."

Barak was silent.

"There must be a reason. And if her magic needed his, then we will use him. Perhaps there are possibilities we have not considered."

Barak crossed his great arms, covered with the raised *talesm* of their kind. "He is our ally for as long as he proves useful, and no longer."

Jaron shrugged. "Of course."

Then the two Fallen turned their eyes back toward the Irina song and watched the sunrise.

CHAPTER

ELEVEN

He saw her as soon as he opened his eyes. She was waiting at the edge of the trees with a glorious smile spread across her face.

"You're happy," he said.

"Supremely."

He walked toward her through the mist, and she wrapped her arms around him. He lifted her and swung her around, her joy spreading into his own soul. She nestled her face in his neck, and he could feel her smiling against his skin.

"I understand now," she said.

"Understand what?"

"That you're not gone. Not really."

"Of course not," he said, smiling. "I'm right here."

"No, in the other place. When I'm not with you. Even there, you're not really gone."

Something tickled the back of his mind. There was something he needed to tell her. Something he desperately needed to share, but it drifted away like the mist that hovered over the ground. Her happiness took over his body, and he laughed.

"I miss this, though," she said more softly. "In the other place. I miss this."

"Miss what?"

"Being near you. I miss your smile. Your laugh."

"You could always make me laugh," he said. "Even when things were bad, you made me laugh."

"I'm glad."

The joy was dimming; he sensed it. Felt it, as if her soul and his were knit together. He didn't want that. He set her down and held her face in his hands as his lips touched her skin with light, teasing kisses. Soon she was smiling again.

"I can sing now," she said, almost shyly. "I'm learning."

"Show me."

She blushed. "I don't know…"

"Please?" He sat down on the mossy ground, leaning his back against a tree and pulling her down to straddle his lap. They were face-to-face. He liked this. Her eyes met his, and she couldn't hide what she felt. She never could if he could see her eyes. Not anymore. Once, she'd hidden from him, but he had conquered her fears. Conquered the shadows that had haunted her. He could sense them again, hovering in the corner of his vision.

"Sing to me," he whispered. "*Reshon.* My soul. Show me your secrets."

She began, halting at first. Her eyes flickered away from his, and he pulled her closer. She laid her head on his shoulder, but he didn't mind. She could hide in him if it made her brave. She still sang, her voice growing as she wove a story for him. She sang of lonely stars across a black sky. Of a great circle divided. Souls reached toward each other but slipped away. And as she sang, he could see it, see the circle in his mind. He saw the sun and moon rising as one, and the stars beat against the sky.

Then her song changed, and his heart ached. There were no words, only a barely audible whisper of longing that spread along his skin. The vision in his mind changed, and he saw them in another place and another time.

"You're so beautiful. Please, Ava…"

Ava.

She smiled and hid under the sheet as he turned the lens on her. "No! No pictures of me."

"Just a few. It's only fair. You're constantly taking pictures of me. Don't deny

it," he said when she started to protest. "I catch you all the time. I just don't say anything about it."

"Do you mind?"

"Do you need to take pictures of me?"

"Yes."

"Then I don't mind."

Ava, he mouthed silently.

He opened his eyes and looked down at the woman in his arms, brushing her hair to the side. Her skin was glowing with the mating marks he'd placed there. His arms wrapped around her back as her song drifted into a soft hum. He felt it, spreading over his body, and as he held her, he saw the silver *talesm* start to glow on his wrist. Then a faint shimmer began on the bare skin above the *talesm* he'd inked.

The marks crawled and spread, as if an invisible hand wrote upon him.

"Ava," he said, his arms tightening.

"Hmm?" She stopped humming, looked up, and the spell was broken. "What did you call me?"

"Your name."

She closed her eyes, a frown between her eyebrows, then they relaxed and she smiled again.

"Oh," she said. "Of course. I didn't remember until you called me."

"Like you called me."

"I did?"

"You told me to come back to you. So I did."

Tears shimmered in her eyes. "You did." Her hand lifted to his cheek. "You're here. You'll always be here."

"Reshon—"

"Kiss me, love."

He could deny her nothing. His mouth touched hers and she clung to him, deepening the kiss as she pressed her body to his.

"I want to stay here," she murmured against his lips. "Forever."

"We can't." There was that tickling at the back of his mind again. He needed to tell her. Needed…

"I need you," she said. His body responded to the grip of her hands on his shoulders. And then all he thought of was her.

When Malachi opened his eyes, he was staring at the peeling paint on the ceiling of the scribe house in Budapest. He blinked to clear his eyes. The dream still lingered in his mind; he could taste her on his lips. Just then, flickers of the dream came back to him, and he lifted his arm.

They were still there. On his left arm were the spells he'd inked. But below them, faint shadows of other, older spells lay like smudges beneath his skin.

"Ava," he whispered. "What did you do?"

There was no doubt in his mind anymore. The dreams were not dreams. He was reaching her somehow. On some plane they were linked, even though she thought he was dead. How was it possible?

A knock sounded on the heavy door to his room.

"Are you awake?" It was Rhys.

Malachi cleared his throat. "I am."

"Come down for coffee. They've made breakfast."

He could smell it. The spicy scent of peppers and sausages drifted in the air. His stomach growled and he sat up.

"I'll be right there."

"Hurry if you want to eat. Don't forget, Max may not be here, but Leo is."

Malachi dressed quickly, grateful that the weather had turned cold enough that long sleeves would not be questioned. He didn't know what to make of the *talesm* that had bloomed on his arm, and he didn't want to try to explain them. As far as he knew, none of the scribes in the house were mated. The house watcher, Phillip, had lost his promised Irina in the Rending, according to Rhys, and the other scribes in the house were young.

Phillip, Rhys had also explained, would need to know what happened to Malachi. According to his friends, Malachi and Phillip had been brothers in the Berlin house years ago. There was too much history for Malachi to pretend to be who he was. Luckily, Rhys also said Phillip was trustworthy.

He followed his nose down the narrow staircase. Unlike the scribe house in Cappadocia, the one in Budapest was showing its age. Frayed carpets lined the hallway, and Malachi could see stains on the walls. Even the lights seemed to flicker with uncertainty.

Luckily, the kitchen showed no such deterioration. Food was spread over the table, with a stocky man at the head. He was sandy-haired and fair-skinned, but his eyes and smile showed faint traces of the city where he lived.

"Good morning," he said. He was American. Malachi didn't know why that was surprising.

"Good morning."

"I'm going to assume you still like a big breakfast," Phillip said. He nudged the shoulder of the younger man sitting to his right. "Victor, move. Let my friend sit down."

Victor didn't seem offended. The young man simply picked up his plate and moved a few chairs down at the massive kitchen table, which was spread with all manner of food. Steaming plates of sausages and bacon. Thick slices of brown bread and cheeses, along with the stuffed peppers he'd smelled from his room upstairs. Eggs. Pâté. It was a feast fit for the group of massive men who filled the room.

Phillip waved to the chair and Malachi sat down. Rhys took the chair opposite him.

"My mother would be proud," Phillip said with a grin. "That is, she would be if I'd cooked any of it."

"Who cooked?" Malachi asked, immediately beginning to fill his plate. For some reason, he felt as if he hadn't eaten in days.

Phillip nodded to another man who stood at the sink. "You can thank Tas. He may be from the country, but he knows how to cook."

Tas shrugged and reached for a pack of cigarettes by the window. "I know how to cook *because* I'm from the country, you American idiot," he said in thickly accented English. He lit up the cigarette, scraping a hand over a jaw that looked like it hadn't seen a razor in days.

Phillip smiled again. "I'm smart enough to make sure you're the one cooking for guests, aren't I?"

Rhys and Malachi shared a smile as the Budapest scribes laughed. Even Tas gave what Malachi guessed was as close to a smile as he ever reached, then he turned back to the stove. Phillip spoke again as the quiet hum of morning conversation filled the room.

"You got in so late last night we didn't get a chance to catch up."

Rhys said, "Life has been… interesting lately."

"I heard about the fire," Phillip said, shoveling eggs onto the edge of his toast. "And that Damien went to the city to petition funds to rebuild." Phillip cast his eyes around the room and shook his head. "Good luck to him; he'll need it. I've been struggling to get promised funds for years now. The bureaucrats are not very receptive. I'm assuming you're on your way to join him."

"Not exactly," Malachi said, exchanging a glance with Rhys.

Rhys said, "It's a bit more complicated than that, Phillip." He directed his eyes toward the younger scribes at the other end of the table. Phillip caught the glance and barked out something that sounded like an order. Within minutes, the men had filled their plates with food and abandoned the room, leaving Malachi, Rhys, and Leo alone with Phillip and the sullen Tas, who grabbed an ashtray and joined them at the table, a cup of black coffee in front of him.

Phillip said, "Tas is my second. He's very trustworthy. Anything said to me can be shared with him." Then he turned to Malachi. "What's going on? You seem different. What's happened to you?"

Leo said, "You don't miss much, do you?"

Sharp green eyes met Malachi's. "No, I don't. And I've known this one longer than you've been alive, boy."

Malachi slowly chewed the bacon in his mouth, swallowed, and set down his coffee cup.

"Technically," he said, "that might not be true anymore."

Phillip's mouth still hung open. "So… you're telling me—"

"I was dead. And now I'm not."

"And your *mate*—congratulations, by the way—your mate actually…"

"Brought me back." Malachi and Rhys looked at each other. "We think."

Rhys said, "We're not sure. We're not sure of much, to be honest."

"And you don't remember who you are?"

"I'm starting to," Malachi said. "It's coming in pieces."

"Certain things don't seem to be a problem," Leo said. "When he scribed his new *talesm*—"

Phillip and Tas hissed out simultaneous curses, and Phillip said, "You lost your *talesm*, brother?"

"Yes."

Tas said something unintelligible under his breath, but it didn't sound good.

"No, I can't even imagine," Phillip said to him before he turned back to Malachi. "And your mate has disappeared with Damien?"

Malachi nodded.

"Taken to Sari," Tas said, the cigarette hanging from his lips as he reached across the table to help himself to another sausage. "He took her to his mate. Fierce woman. She'll be fine."

Phillip frowned. "Only she still thinks he's dead, you idiot."

Tas shrugged his wide shoulders. "But he's not. It will work out." He sucked in another lungful of smoke, then exhaled, saying, "Why are you going to the city when she's not there?"

Rhys said, "We think Gabriel knows where Sari is."

Tas let out a grim chuckle. "He probably does, but he won't tell you. No one can tell you."

Malachi's eyes narrowed on the dark man, who seemed to know even more than the watcher of the house. "Why do you say that?"

Tas's hooded eyes gleamed. "Old, old magic over that place. Even Irina who have lived there can't tell you where it is." Then the corner of his lip curled up. "Trust me. If she could have told me, she would have."

Rhys leaned toward Tas. "Wait, you've met an Irina from Sari's home?"

A secret smile played along his lips. "More of Sari's Irina around than most scribes know. They avoid Damien's territory for obvious reasons, but they're out there."

Malachi looked to Phillip.

"It's true," the watcher admitted. "And these are not the Irina we remember. They're ruthless. As far back as I can remember, the scribe mandate has been clear: Protect the humans. Kill the Grigori when they attack, but keep away if they're not interfering, so as not to provoke the Fallen." He nodded to Malachi. "I believe you and I had words over that policy more than once. But the fact is, unless they're attacking humans, scribes leave Grigori alone."

Tas said, "But that's not the Irina mandate. I doubt they even have one. If they do, it's much more brutal than ours. We found a Grigori house here in Budapest five years ago with not a soul in it."

Leo asked, "What do you mean?"

"I mean the beds were slept in. The lights were on. But there was nothing but dust in the air."

"All dead?" Malachi asked. "And you're positive it wasn't a scribe?"

Tas gave another one of his infuriating shrugs. "It might have been a rogue scribe who defied protocol… Or it might have been the long-legged beauty with the Italian name I met the next night, drinking alone and looking mad at the world." He grinned. "She wasn't mad all night."

Leo spoke in a low voice. "What was her name?"

Tas's eyes rested on Leo, measuring him, as he lit another cigarette, inhaled, and let out a long stream of smoke. "Renata. Her name was Renata. And she was one of Sari's Irina. That's all I know."

Rhys said, "But you said she would have told you… if she could."

"Well, that's what she said. She might have been trying to let me down easy when she left the next morning." He glanced at Malachi. "Women, eh?"

"I wouldn't say."

"Or are you one of those scribes who think your mate descended from heaven itself?"

Malachi's eyes narrowed. "I'm a scribe who doesn't presume to make judgments based on limited experience." Then he smirked. "Even though my mate *is* a glimpse of heaven."

Tas muttered something in Hungarian as Phillip's hand clapped down on Malachi's shoulder. "This is interesting! So, we have a scribe raised from the dead by his mate—which as far as I know, hasn't happened before—and an Irina who seems to have come out of nowhere and has now disappeared into nowhere, though I imagine she's very safe with Damien. We have Grigori who are now being hunted on two fronts—Irin and Irina—and that might account for the escalation we're seeing here and other places—"

"What escalation?" Rhys broke in, but Phillip only raised a hand and continued.

"And we still have an elder council in Vienna who believes that nothing is wrong except the health of their pocketbooks!"

"They know something is going on," Tas said. "Why do you think some of the Irina have returned?"

"What?" Leo said. "What do you mean? They're back?"

"In the city, yes. Only a few," Phillip said. "Mostly mates of prominent council members or businessmen. It's all very…"

"Calculated," Tas finished. "And very quiet. They're not seen much. Only when their mates need them to be seen. The idiots in the city are planning something."

"What could the Irin council be planning about the Irina?" Leo asked. "And what about this escalation?"

Phillip stood and walked to the counter, refilling his coffee before he turned. "It's not in Vienna, of course. That city is still a bubble of peace. But here, it's bad. I was speaking with Yakov in Odessa just last week. He's feeling pressure from the Russian territories. And Poland. Slovakia."

"That's not good," Rhys said.

"No, but the bigger surprise is the West. England and Scandinavia are still relatively quiet, but there's more activity in France and the Netherlands than there has been since the Rending. Some in Germany."

Malachi said, "But not Vienna?"

"There's a reason that Irin society is based in Vienna, Malachi. It's in the very heart of Europe. Surrounded by scribe houses and strongholds in the East and the West. There have always been Grigori in Europe, but not nearly as many as other parts of the world."

"So it's protected?"

"It has been. That's part of the reason the Irin living there are so complacent. They don't see Grigori attacks every week. If they see one a year, it's shocking."

"That makes sense," he said.

Tas asked, "Is it true Jaron is no longer controlling the Grigori in Istanbul? Not that there's anything like a good Fallen, but he wasn't as bad as Volund. And he didn't breed Grigori like rabbits."

Leo shook his head. "We don't know what Jaron is doing. We're fairly sure the attack that killed Malachi was from Volund's people, not Jaron's."

Phillip mused, "If Volund is making a concentrated push to expand his territory, he'd go for the outlying territories first. Turkey doesn't fit with that."

Malachi said, "But if he's reaching down from Russia and into the Ukraine, then Turkey isn't that far off."

Rhys said, "He'd run into Svarog."

Phillip shook his head. "Volund doesn't fear Svarog."

"He should."

"What does he want?" Malachi muttered, picturing a map of eastern Europe in his mind. He pulled back, looked at all the continent. Not as the humans did, with their constantly changing borders. He pictured the slowly shifting spheres of power, ebbing and flowing with the centuries. One Fallen rose, another slowly toppled. Where was Volund in that cycle? And why had Jaron ceded power of Istanbul when he had held it for centuries?

Irin presence shone through Europe, a bright glowing thread that wove through most of the major cities; its brightest star being Vienna.

"What does Volund want?" Malachi asked again.

Phillip shrugged. "Power. To control as much territory as possible. And wipe out the Irin, of course. It's always been the theory that Volund was the primary force behind the Rending."

Malachi's eyes narrowed. "So…"

Rhys said, "But you said there's more activity in the West, too. It's not just coming from one direction. Volund has little influence in western Europe."

"We all have allies," Malachi said, more and more of the picture snapping into place. "Volund's strongest area has always been Russia, correct?"

"Since he destroyed Barak." Leo smiled. "How did you know that?"

"I just did. Concentrate." He spread his hands over the table, using cups and silverware to mark his mental map. "Volund wants to expand his influence from his base in Russia, but he doesn't want to be noticed. What does he do?" He grabbed a saltshaker near his right elbow. "He gets Jaron out of Istanbul."

"Or Jaron leaves," Rhys said. "Either way, he's gone."

"And with him, the strongest competition for dominance in the east. Svarog is cunning, but he does not hunger for power."

"And how did you know *that*?" Rhys asked.

"I don't know! It doesn't matter." Malachi's left arm came up and rested on the table, across from his right and on the opposite side of the map. "Now Volund comes from the north and the east. He needs help from the west, but according to you, Phillip, he's getting it."

Phillip nodded. "There are more Grigori popping up in France and Germany. Spain is still relatively stable. Grigori leadership there is fractured. It used to be controlled by Barak, but Volund killed him. Now we don't really know who controls it."

"But we know something is happening there." Malachi's left and right arms began to move closer together, showing the direction of movement across the map. "Volund controls the Grigori in the north. He's moving in the east"—he lifted his right arm—"and someone else is moving in the west." He lifted his left. "Volund wants to wipe the Irin from the earth. And where is the center of the Irin world?"

"Vienna," Leo said. "But—"

"Exactly. And why would Volund send an arrow to Vienna when he could give them…" His arms closed in on a mental point in the center of the table. "A nice, slow hug?"

CHAPTER
TWELVE

T he words Orsala had taught her slipped from her lips, an ancient incantation that set Ava's blood humming.

"Shanda vash…"

This was Power.

She could feel it welling up, stirring under her skin as the words took shape on her tongue. A spell to distract and disarm an enemy. Ancient words. Holy words. Dangerous words…

Bruno winced and closed his eyes. "Yes. She's definitely hit it."

"What do you feel?" Orsala asked.

"Like if she doesn't stop I'm going to lose my lunch on your lovely Turkish carpet, Orsala."

"Details, Bruno. I need to know the effects."

"There's a—a piercing pain in my temple. A—and my limbs feel weak, as well."

"Excellent. She's only been practicing this one for a few days."

His voice was strained. "I'm serious. I'm about to throw up."

Ava barely heard him. The magic was too heady. Like wine, it seeped into her blood and went straight to her head. It wasn't the painful jolt of power she'd felt in the cistern. Orsala had taught her control, so the words she spoke flowed from her belly, up her throat, and left her mouth softly. Weaker magic, perhaps, but magic she could hold far longer.

Speak.

The dark voice called her.

Yes…

"Ava." She felt the hand on her shoulder as if in a dream. "Enough."

Bruno's hand was at his temple. "Orsala," he forced out the words. "I can't—"

"Ava, you need to stop." Orsala's grip was firmer. Her words more clear. "Now. Release the magic."

Not yet…

Bruno was barely standing. His face was pale. "Orsala…"

"Shanda huul!"

The old woman's words hit her in the stomach like a punch. Ava gasped, rocking back on her heels as the force of her own spell was turned against her. She could feel the pain in her head, like the high whine of a piercing whistle. It turned her stomach inside out, and she almost fell down when her knees buckled. Bruno caught her before she hit the ground.

"There you are," he said. His eyes still carried hints of pain, but he was smiling. "Got a taste of your own medicine, did you?"

"How were you even standing through that?" she choked out.

Orsala said, "He's a bear. And a very good-natured one at that. Thank you, Bruno."

The great man enclosed her in an embrace, pressing his hand to her cheek. The warm affection flowed into her like a hug against her soul. "That was a lot of magic you were wielding. Not even my Karen at her angriest has hit me like that."

"I'm so sorry." With the heady rush of power dissipating in the room, Ava felt the guilt rush in. She'd caused him pain, and she'd held it for long minutes. She'd only felt a second of her spell turned on her and it made her want to curl in a ball and sleep for a week.

He laughed. "It's fine! I'm happy to help you practice. How do you feel, sister?"

"Tired. You?"

"Hungry."

"Hungry? How can you be hungry after that?"

"I am a scribe of tremendous appetite." He set Ava on her feet and stepped back. Then he patted his belly and looked toward the door. "Are we done here? I need to find my woman."

"You are a beast," Orsala said. "Go. And thank you, Bruno."

He left Orsala's cottage whistling.

Ava watched him through the window. "That is the most cheerful man I've ever met."

Orsala smiled. "He is a treasure to us. Gentle as a dove and strong as an ox."

She turned and looked at some of the pictures scattered over the walls. Family pictures. Friends. A few paintings.

"He and Karen don't have any children?"

Orsala shook her head. "They lost a daughter during the Rending. They have not had another."

Ava said nothing. There was nothing to say. It was easy to be caught in her own grief until she remembered that all of the Irin had lost someone. Mates. Children. Siblings. Parents. Her own grief, as heavy as it felt to her, was only a drop in an ocean of sorrow.

"Well done." She broke out of her reverie when Orsala patted her on the shoulder and led her toward the chairs by the fire. "That was very well done. That spell is your most basic disarming spell. I imagine it's a more controlled version of what happened in the cistern when you were being attacked. So obviously it's very instinctual for us. If a Grigori is trying to attack you, use it. It won't kill them, but it should give you enough time to escape."

"Okay." Ava paused before she asked her question. "Are there spells that *can* kill them?"

Orsala stared at her with measuring eyes. "Be careful, Ava."

"What?"

The old woman leaned forward. "There is a dark thread to your power. One I've not encountered before."

Ava said nothing, because she knew Orsala was right. She could feel it. She didn't know what it meant, but she remembered the dark whisper in her mind as she held the magic over Bruno.

Not yet…

It had *wanted* to hurt him. Or maybe it had just not wanted to let go of the power.

"A part of you liked it, no?"

Ava said nothing.

"Your magic is very strong," Orsala said. "Untrained, yes. But also untapped. It will be greedy. I don't know what you'll be capable of. It's clear to me that you are not like other Irina—"

"You knew that already."

"I'm not saying it's a bad thing." Orsala met Ava's growing anger with calm. "I am only saying you must be careful."

"Fine," Ava said. "I'll be careful. Are we done?"

"I want you to try to sing again."

She let her head fall back. "Again? I told you, it only happened the one time. There's no way—"

"Just try." The tension drifted away like smoke up the chimney. If Orsala had wanted to remind Ava she still had a lot to learn, trying to tap into her supposedly supernatural vision was the surest way to accomplish it. Ever since the sing, she had tried to recreate the experience, but nothing had come of it.

"I'll try. But no guarantees."

Orsala nodded. "Nothing in life is guaranteed, daughter."

Ava closed her eyes and focused on the blurry memory of the ceremony. She tried to remember the words that had slipped out of her mouth, the song that had risen from her chest until it burst over the gathering. A song that, apparently, everyone could understand with perfect clarity. Everyone except herself. She'd sung in the Old Language, but she couldn't remember a single detail.

She held the memory of that night in her mind, turning it from every angle until she could almost see herself standing in the old barn, her arms raised, her mating marks gleaming. Minutes passed. Hours, maybe. Ava could feel a soft cradle of power around her, as if Orsala was feeding her magic, but no words would come.

She let out a frustrated breath. "I can't. There's nothing."

Orsala sat back in her chair, looking frustrated beyond what Ava had ever seen her. "This makes no sense. I heard you with my own ears. You sang perfectly, as if you'd spoken the Old Language as a child."

"All I get are images. I can remember the images I saw perfectly, I just have no idea what the words were."

"You sang a vision. It was..." She struggled to formulate her thoughts. "Unlike anything I've experienced. It was as if, with your words, you made real the vision in your mind. I've never met a seer with that power before. I've never even heard of it. But when you sang, we all saw it. And we all saw the same thing. Irin and Irina alike. I've asked everyone. The only ones who didn't see it were the humans. And even they said they could feel something going on."

Ava frowned. "But isn't that what you do, too?"

Orsala cocked her head. "Explain."

"You have empathy. *Profound* empathy. And with that, you've developed your magic to the point where you can create emotional reactions in other people. Like the spell to guard this place. It's not like your spell makes people physically unable to speak, they just have such a strong emotional reaction to even speaking the name of Sarihöfn that they would never consider revealing its location, even under torture."

Orsala's mouth turned down as she leaned forward. "So, what you're saying is you think that—not only do you have these visions— but you can make others see them as well? Project them, not just with words, but actual images?"

"Why not?"

"Because—" Orsala's mouth dropped open. "I have no idea. Because I've never heard of it before. According to legends, this is something Leoc could do, but I've never heard of even the strongest Irina seers having the ability to manifest their visions to others the way you did that night."

Jaron had done it to her, but then, he was an angel like Leoc.

"Is it really that far a stretch?"

"No." She finally smiled. "It isn't. It does make me curious about your mother, though."

"I told Evren, my mom—"

"I know, I'm sorry." Orsala waved her hand. "It's habit. We all automatically assume our magic comes from our mothers. I really meant that I was curious about your family. Sari tells me that she and Damien are trying to investigate your father now."

"Good luck with that."

"Why do you say that?"

"Foster kid," she said. "He doesn't know much about his birth family. I mean, it's not something we've really talked about. We talk about... nice stuff. Stuff that won't stress him out."

Orsala frowned. "But he is your father."

"He's a mess." Ava shrugged. "He loves me, but he's a mess. Jasper has had drug problems for as long as I've known him. He never stays in one place long. His house in LA is nothing more than a place to keep the stuff he collects while traveling. He's... like me, kinda."

Orsala's eyes widened. "He hears voices?"

"No voices. Music." Ava smiled. "He may be a mess, but he's a brilliant one. I remember once finding him in my mom's study at home when I was a child. He was sleeping and humming a song at the same time. Like, he was hearing it in a dream. A year later, I heard it on the radio. My mom was listening to it, smiling."

"I thought he wasn't in your life when you were a child."

"He was. A little. I just thought he was my mom's friend who would crash at our house occasionally. My stepfather didn't mind, and my mom… Well, they've always had a complicated relationship."

"It sounds like it. He must be a fascinating person." Orsala's eyes were unfocused. Thoughtful. "And he never talks about his family?"

"Not really. I know he knew his mother, but she died when he was young. No idea who his dad is. That side of my family tree is a total mystery to me."

Orsala murmured, "So that's where it must be."

"What?"

"The Irin blood. I've never heard of it before—and how you're as powerful as you are is a mystery, but it must have come from somewhere."

Ava decided she liked the idea of *not* knowing where her Irin blood came from. The mystery was frustrating, but a knot in her gut told her that some secrets were better left hidden.

"Does it really matter?" she asked. "Does it matter where I come from?"

"I don't know."

* * *   * * *

Brooke let out a joyful whoop as they ran.

"Try again!" the girl said.

Ava had had far more success in her training with Mala and Renata. She was jogging along the path by the lake, and the frosted hillside sloped up to her right. Mala ran ahead of her and Brooke at her side. Renata was with them, but hiding on the hillside and in the woods, testing Ava's range.

Ava opened her senses and stretched. Now that she could turn off all the voices, it took more effort to listen in a controlled way. She pictured the door Orsala had taught her to focus on in her mind. Slamming that door shut had been her salvation. Now, she was learning to crack it open in a way that would leave her in control of how much she heard. Isolated places like this were easier, and the mental exercise stirred her blood.

"She's on the hill again, ahead of us." Ava looked up, opening the door a bit more. "There." She nodded toward an outcropping of rocks shielded by a stand of cedar trees. "Behind those rocks."

Mala looked over her shoulder and shook her head, a grin on her face.

"Renata, come out!" Brooke called, and the woman stood up from her hiding place.

Exactly where Ava had pointed.

Mala whistled approvingly and Renata ran nimbly down the hill. "Did she hear me?"

"Yep!" Brooke was grinning. "She's awesome."

Renata fell in step behind them. "I've never seen range like yours. It's so strong. I wonder if it's because you didn't know how to shield for so long."

"Maybe," Ava panted. "I never really had any control over it until I met Malachi. And most of the time, he made the voices go away completely."

They all fell silent at his name, and the knot around her heart twisted again.

"It's okay," Ava said after the silence had dragged on too long. "Part of me wants to talk about him. Part of me worries about forgetting."

Mala threw a look over her shoulder and signed something.

"You won't forget," Brook translated. "Don't worry that you'll forget."

"Thanks, Mala."

Renata changed the subject. "I want to take you into the field."

Mala wheeled around and immediately went to run beside Renata as Brooke and Ava took the lead on the trail. Neither she nor Brooke could see the other women; they could only listen to the one-sided conversation.

"I know that."

A pause.

"Can you imagine, though? With her range and accuracy, she'd be a huge asset. Plus, she's a *seer*. Once she's had more training, she'll—"

A much longer pause.

"I haven't forgotten, but it's been two *hundred* years. Sari is going to have to get past her—"

Another pause and a few disapproving clicks of the tongue.

"I know, I know." There was silence, and Ava chanced a glance over her shoulder, but Mala and Renata were both jogging and *not* looking at her.

"I still think it's worth suggesting," Renata said. "She wouldn't even have to be close to help. She'd be… advance intelligence. And once she can understand more of the Old Language, she'd be invaluable. We could protect her. Partner her with someone with more field experience. And as she gets stronger—"

Mala made more disapproving clicks and Ava could hear her grunting slightly as she signed.

"Fine. I'll wait."

Ava looked over her shoulder again but didn't see anything. Brooke caught her eye and grinned. Ava seized on Renata's words. *With her range and accuracy, she'd be a huge asset.* Could the voices that had driven her near to insanity be the key to avenging Malachi's death?

It sounded like Sari wouldn't approve of her joining, for some reason, but then it wasn't only up to Sari, was it? Ava let the idea churn in her brain while the four women ran back to the compound.

* * *

"WAIT, WAIT," THE LAUGHING ITALIAN WOMAN SAID, THROWING A perfectly manicured hand over Astrid's mouth before she could speak. "You have to let me tell it."

"No!" Astrid was indignant. "You always make it sound so much worse than what it was."

Karen and Bruno both burst out laughing, obviously having heard the story that Renata wanted to share. Ava and Damien only exchanged confused looks over the kitchen table where the six friends had gathered to share coffee, wine, and a chocolate cake Karen had baked.

Bruno was right, the woman was a supernatural baker. It was the only explanation for how good that cake was.

"I am the only one who knows the truth!" Renata shouted, her grin huge. "You always try to hide how bad—"

"It wasn't that bad!"

"Oh…" Renata's eyes turned to Ava's. "It was bad. I will never take her into the field again. She was flapping her arms like a bird that had been trapped in the rafters. 'Renata!'" The woman's voice took on a high-pitched tone. "'Dust! Grigori dust all over me! I have to shower.' Blood. Bones. She can put the most wounded body back together from pieces, but she couldn't handle the dust."

Damien even cracked a smile as Karen and Bruno laughed again. Ava was trying to control herself, but Renata's imitation of Astrid's voice was too good.

"It was my first time in the field," Astrid protested.

"And the last time," Renata said. "How can you be so squeamish?"

"I can handle blood and guts, not evil fallen angel remains." The healer gave a dramatic shudder. "They're… gritty. They get every-where. You can *inhale* them. Disgusting."

Even Damien was chuckling at that point. They'd been telling stories for hours. It had started with Damien and Renata catching up and then devolved into battle stories. Renata was more than willing to share her exploits. The others had to pry them out of Damien. But eventually, all of them were adding their tales, except for Ava.

Everyone knew her battle story, and no one wanted to dwell on it.

Ava finished her wine and pushed back from the table. "I should get to sleep."

Astrid and Damien exchanged a look. Damien reached for the bottle of wine and filled her glass again. "Stay up and visit."

"I'm tired." Ava was lying. She just wanted to sleep and hopefully dream about Malachi. Still, she smiled and nodded at Renata. "Someone likes jogging way more than me."

"I'm trying to toughen you up, California girl."

"Come," Astrid said. "Stay up. It's dark, but not too late. Only nine o'clock. We want to hear your stories, too." She blinked a little and smiled. "From LA! I bet you've met celebrities, haven't you?"

What was going on? If Astrid actually wanted to know about celebrity gossip, Ava would eat her favorite lens. She narrowed her eyes at Astrid, then she opened the door in her mind. As she'd suspected, from the tone of her inner voice, the other woman was hiding something.

"I'm just tired," Ava said carefully. "There something going on?"

Damien shrugged. "We all have a rare night free of obligations.

Catching up. Getting to know people. It's better than watching television."

Bruno looked around, more than a little bleary-eyed himself. "Wasn't there a game on tonight?"

"Want me to look?" Damien stood up, as if to turn on the television in the corner of the room. Damien never watched television. Ever. Not even football.

"That's it." Ava stood too. She pointed to Astrid and Damien. "What's up with you guys? Why are you being weird and why are you trying to keep me awake?"

Damien's eyes never wavered. He crossed his ink-covered arms over his chest, reminding her too much of Malachi's disapproving stance. The pain was quick, like a knife jab. "You sleep too much."

"What?"

"You do," Astrid said. "I've noticed it, too. Other than the night of the sing, you're in bed almost right after dinner. You don't come to the house to play games or read in the library. We hardly see you at all before you go to your room."

Ava shrank back. "I like privacy."

Renata was watching with quick, assessing eyes. "I think, Ava, that your friends are worried about you."

"Well, I'm fine."

Silence fell over the previously boisterous table.

Astrid finally said, "Yes, we are worried about you. The sleep. The lack of appetite. You barely eat anything except for a few of Karen's cakes."

"You think I'm depressed."

Once again, no one said anything, but Ava recognized the signs of awkward concern. She'd lived with them her whole life. From her mother to her stepfather to every friend or boyfriend she'd ever attempted to retain.

Her throat tightened. "I'm not depressed."

Of course she was depressed.

"You're not?" Renata asked. "I thought you just lost your mate."

Karen winced visibly, and Bruno put a hand on Renata's arm.

"Rennie," he said, "we're trying—"

"What?" Renata said. "It's not like she's forgotten. Of course she's depressed."

Damien said, "We just want Ava to know we're worried about her."

"We want her to know she's not alone," Karen said. "That we're here to listen if—"

"Let her be depressed for a while if she wants, damn it. It happened just months ago. And they'd barely met." Unexpected tears shone in Renata's eyes. "She had a glimpse of happiness, then it was taken away." Her voice was hoarse, matching the lump that had risen in Ava's throat. "If she wants to sleep, let her sleep."

"I'm fine," Ava managed to choke out. "I appreciate you're all worried about me, but really, I'm fine."

Renata's eyes cut to her. "Of course you're not fine. What a ridiculous thing to say."

This time it was Astrid who put her hand on Ava's arm before she opened her mouth in anger. "The important thing is everyone grieves in different ways. I think Ava knows we're worried about her. She knows we care. And she can take as much time as she wants to come to terms with the loss of her mate."

"Malachi," she whispered.

"Hmm?"

"His name was Malachi." She blinked back tears. "You don't have to avoid his name or pretend he was just some faceless guy." Her eyes met Damien's. "He was your friend. Your brother. And you never say his name. I know you miss him, too."

Damien's eyes burned into hers. "I'm sorry, Ava."

"And I sleep…" Ava cleared her throat and decided to just tell them. "I sleep because, in my dreams, he's there. And for a little while, I'm happy."

Astrid said, "That's very normal, Ava."

"So if I want to sleep a little more, then it's my own business. I had nightmares for months, and now they're gone."

"Good." Astrid squeezed her arm. "That's good. I'm glad you're sleeping better."

"Thank you." She paused and took a deep breath, trying to see their interference for what it was. Concern. Caring. Even love. Part of her acknowledged that the pattern she'd developed wasn't healthy. But most of her didn't care a bit. Still, she decided to throw a line to the people she'd come to know as friends.

"I guess… since you're all here, I'll stay up a little later."

She didn't want to. She wanted to sleep. Wanted to feel Malachi's arms, even if it was only a dream. Ava sat down again, but there was silence for a few moments until Bruno spoke.

"I could eat more cake."

Karen said, "You can always eat more cake."

"Then I was smart to fall in love with a baker."

A knock came at the door. Ava took the opportunity to distract herself and walked to answer it. She cracked open the door and saw the unexpected sight of Sari on the other side. Sari never came to the cottage, and she certainly never did it looking nervous. But there she was. And she was definitely nervous.

"Um…" Ava blinked and opened the door wider. "Hi."

"May I come in?"

Ava felt Damien behind her. She backed away and let him hold the door.

"Sari?"

He looked as shocked as Ava felt. Even after the sing, when they seemed to stop antagonizing each other, she never visited.

"Sari!" Renata, clueless to the tension or deliberately ignoring it, called out to her friend. "Come in! Wine or coffee?"

"*Kaffe,* thank you."

"Of course."

Karen rose to fill another coffee cup as Damien stood motionless at the door. Finally, Ava stepped forward and closed it.

"What's the matter with you?" she asked under her breath. "She's not the queen of England."

"She came to my door," he said, his voice tinged with confusion. "With… all of you here."

"I have no idea what you're talking about. Get over it."

"I'll explain later." He nudged her toward the table where Sari had sat. "Maybe."

Damien's eyes burned into Sari as he sat across from her; Ava saw a smile lifting the corner of his lip.

"My dove," he finally said, and Ava could almost see Sari flinch at the endearment. "What brings you here—to my door—tonight?"

"You know…" Sari sipped the coffee Renata put in front of her. "This is *my* land. My guesthouse. So technically, I don't think this is your door."

"I believe that's what they call 'splitting hairs.'"

Astrid looked amused. "Well, this is entertaining, but I do think there might be some larger purpose to this visit than just coffee and cake."

"There was a group of Grigori spotted in Bergen," Sari said.

An entirely different tension fell across the table.

"How many?" Damien and Renata both asked at once.

"Three that we know of. But I'd not be surprised if there were more. There's an Irin couple who lives there, among the humans. No children. They watch for us."

Ava leaned over to Karen. "Bergen is the closest town to here, right?"

"The closest one of any real size, yes."

Renata said, "I'll go."

"I'll go, too," Damien said.

"No," Sari said. "This is our territory. Renata will take care of them."

"Sari, this is no time for—"

"Besides"—she held up a hand—"I'd like you and Bruno to start doing patrols around the perimeter of the haven. Orsala has sensed some outside magic, and she wants us to be careful. Some protective spells written on the trees would be appreciated."

"Fine," Damien said in a clipped voice. "And Bruno and I will start patrols. It's only three Grigori. I'm sure Renata can handle that on her own, anyway."

"You just wanted to steal my fight," Renata said with a grin.

"Obviously."

Sari glanced at Ava. "I don't suppose you've seen any threats?"

"Uh…" Ava looked around the table, confused. "Should I have?"

Sari shrugged. "You're a seer."

"I'm not any good, though."

Bruno snorted.

"No really, you can ask your grandmother," she said. "I was trying to do… the thing I did the other night at the sing. And I couldn't. So I don't know if I'll see any trouble coming. If there is any coming."

Everyone just kept looking at her.

"Is there… some trouble coming?"

"Trouble is always coming," Renata said. "I'll take care of it."

"Don't be too eager," Sari said. "We don't want them to know they're close to anything important. Draw them away from the city, if you can."

Damien said, "And try to find out who they belong to. I know Grigori in the territory generally belong to Volund, but we had some surprises in Istanbul. Powers may be shifting."

"Powers are always shifting," Sari said.

"Change is constant." Damien stared at his mate. "And healthy."

"According to you."

"You can't stop this," he said quietly. "You never could."

"I can try."

His voice was low and coaxing. "You shouldn't."

Ava said, "Well, obviously we're not talking about Grigori anymore."

Renata piped up. "I want to take Ava to Bergen."

"Absolutely not," Damien and Sari both said at once, then turned to each other in shock.

"You don't think she should go?" Sari asked.

"No."

Ava was tempted to butt in. They were talking about her like she wasn't in the room, and she really wanted to go. Killing—or helping to kill—more Grigori soldiers was what she'd been waiting for.

But she was too curious about the exchange to interrupt. Sari and Damien both stood and glared at each other.

"But she'd be a tactical advantage," Sari said. "I've heard about her range."

"She's too young. And untrained," Damien countered.

"She'd be with Renata."

"She would still be vulnerable."

Ava said, "Wait, I'm confused. Is Sari arguing for or against me going with Renata?"

"Shh!"

That came from at least three people, but Sari ignored everyone except Damien. "Are you telling me it wouldn't be worth the risk?" she hissed, her face pale. "To have an intelligence advantage like her skills in the field—protected and at a distance from combat—are you telling me you wouldn't risk that?"

Astrid slapped a hand over Ava's mouth before a word could escape. *"Do not say a word,"* she whispered.

"I wouldn't risk it," Damien said quietly. "I wouldn't risk *her*. Not anymore, Sari."

"But..." Sari's eyes shone. "It makes the most tactical sense."

"*Milá…*," he breathed out. "I learned the hard way. Not everything is about tactics."

Ava didn't know how to describe Sari's expression. It was pain. Anger. Relief. Rage. It was everything rolled into one, but Ava had cracked open the door to Sari's inner voice and listened. And the voice inside cried out.

Vashama canem.

Reshon.

Reshon.

Reshon.

The pain of Sari's yearning was like a punch to the chest. Ava gasped and felt Astrid flinch. She wondered if the healer could sense Sari's pain, too. It didn't matter, because in the next moment, they were gone. Damien had walked around the table and grabbed Sari's arm, marching them both out into the cold night. The door to the cottage slammed closed.

Silence.

"So, I'll take you to Bergen," Renata said. "Mala can come with us and guard you. It will be a good first mission."

Karen glanced nervously at the door. "But Rennie, don't you think—"

"They'll sort it out." She waved a careless hand toward the door. "And I'll convince them both. You don't really think they were talking about Ava, do you?"

Ava didn't. Not for a minute.

She was running through the forest, laughing. Running. Playing. He was behind her, and he was laughing too. She darted to the left, but he caught her, grabbing her with both arms and tackling her to the soft forest floor. They rolled across leaves and moss, which were verdant with life. The birds sang overhead and the new light of a crescent moon shone down.

"Can we stay here forever?" she asked.

"No."

"Why not?"

He looked confused for a moment. "I… don't know."

"What if we didn't wake?" she whispered, smoothing a lock of hair from his forehead as he braced himself over her. "What if we stayed here?"

"We can't, Ava."

"But why?" Something dark lurked at the edge of her vision. Some sadness waited there. She knew if she woke it would find her.

"I have things to do." He frowned. "I think. When I am not here, I have things I must do."

"Things more important than me?"

"No. I think… I must find you."

She smiled. "You already found me."

"No, Ava." His eyes were clearer. His mouth firmed. "I must *find you*. So you know."

"So I know what? I don't understand," she said.

He lost focus. Confusion swam in his eyes. "Kiss me, my Ava."

"Always."

Their lips met, and everything fell away beneath the moon.

CHAPTER

THIRTEEN

The blood pumped in his veins as he ran through the eerily familiar streets of Budapest. The scent of sandalwood trailed after the fleeing Grigori, and he followed it, turning down dirty alleys in dark corners of the city where the smell of humanity stained the air.

The soldiers had been attacking four nameless girls. Leo and Phillip had dragged the women away, allowing them to escape, while Malachi subdued the four Grigori. By the time the first was dust, no human was there to witness it.

It was the fifth that Malachi was chasing.

The brown-haired soldier had slashed at the sensitive skin near the small of Malachi's back and then made his escape, and the blade had almost found its mark. But Malachi dodged at the last minute and his *talesm*—including the new ones he'd inked the night before—pulsed as the adrenaline flooded his system. The scent of his own blood mingled with the stale odor of beer, cigarettes, and urine. He ran, his legs eating up the ground, his feet pounding over the cobblestones.

He ran, and he felt alive.

A flash of his dream the night before.

Ava.

Now that he knew her name in his dreams, he couldn't seem to stop saying it.

Ava.

She said nothing, gasping when his mouth left a trail of kisses down the center of her body.

Her taste…

Hands gripping his hair, twisting the roots as he feasted on her. He felt the pain dimly, so focused was he on the pleasurable task in front of him.

Her pleasure, for as long as she could stand it. He felt it build in the tension of her hands, the quiver of her belly, the soft cries that escaped her lips. He was relentless, pulling away to watch her fall over the edge, only to return and chase her back up the hill, pushing her toward another climax.

Finally…

"Come back to me," she panted. And he came, sliding up her body, taking her mouth with his as he surged inside her, following her ecstasy.

The grip of her flesh on his. Her hands still twisted in his hair. Her thighs held his hips captive as they moved together.

Fast.

Faster.

Her grip didn't loosen. She arched back, baring her neck as a breath tore from her throat.

"Ava," he groaned, hiding his face in her neck.

"You…" The grip of her fingers loosened in his hair, and he pulled back, bracing himself over her as her fingers stroked his forehead, curling around his ear, tender in their exploration as he slowed the relentless pace of their lovemaking.

"You," she whispered again. Their eyes met, gold and grey. The tips of her fingers traced his lip.

It was a dream. But not a dream. A dream had never felt so real.

"Blast!" The pipe caught Malachi in the face as he turned the corner. His cheek sliced open, and he saw stars as the Grigori swung again. Malachi ducked and decided he was tired of running. The Grigori danced in front of him, his clothes still rumpled from the human women's hands and his quick flight. His hair hung over his eyes and a deep cut was already healing on his unearthly face. He had the thin, ethereal beauty of so many of his kind, ironically so like the angels the humans depicted in art. Delicate, almost boyish.

Malachi was not fooled.

The soldier danced in front of him, quicksilver over grit. Malachi felt like a slow brute with his heavy fists and thick muscles. The Grigori was faster than him. He'd have to be to get the jab in that he had, even now, when Malachi wasn't at full strength.

They said nothing, both taking the measure of each other. The Grigori's glance flicked over Malachi's shoulder, then he feinted right. Malachi caught the look and slammed into the man's body as he tried to slip to his left.

The Grigori might have been faster, but brute strength still won when it found its target.

Slamming the soldier into the cobblestone street, Malachi tried to flip him to his belly so he could pierce his spine, but the man proved as stubborn as he was fast.

"No," he hissed, finally starting to panic. "Not like this!"

Malachi could not turn him, not while he had to hold his dagger with one hand and straddle the man to keep him from running. Irritating little bastard.

"Why don't you just cooperate and die like a good monster?" he grunted, holding the man by his hair.

"Fuck you!"

"That's not nice." He grinned as an idea came to him. "Maybe you're too much trouble after all."

Malachi slid to his right knee, letting the man lunge up, desperate for escape, but the scribe's heavy leg still lay over the Grigori's waist. With a quick twist, Malachi slammed his opponent's face into his braced knee and felt the nose crunch. The back of the Grigori's neck suddenly bared, Malachi brought the silver blade home, piercing the man's spine. The only sound was the sucking gasp as the soldier began to dissolve.

For a moment, Malachi saw her face. Felt the cold water at his waist. He was in the cistern again, and he heard Ava's scream.

"No!"

Then the memory was gone.

And so was the Grigori.

He sat in the dirt of the alley and stretched his back. He could feel the deep gash over his kidneys mending. He pushed up his sleeve and traced over the healing spell again, letting his fingers linger over the new marks that had bloomed as Ava sang to him in his dream.

She did this.

Malachi pushed his sleeve down when he heard Leo and Phillip coming down the street. But he still sat, rubbing his knee a bit where the Grigori's nose had left a spurt of blood. That was irritating. He didn't have that many clothes, and he hated asking Leo for things.

The two scribes turned the corner, chuckling when they saw him sitting in the center of the alley.

"Did you get tired?" Leo asked.

"Just taking in the sights."

Phillip glanced around. "Well, if you were looking for a scenic corner of Budapest to loiter and people watch, you did not find it." Then he grinned and held out a hand.

Malachi grasped it and pulled himself to his feet.

"Take care of the runner?" Leo asked.

"Yes."

"He was fast."

"Faster than me." Malachi twisted his neck to the side, feeling the joints release. "Luckily, big guys get lucky sometimes."

Phillip said, "More than luck, my friend. If you don't remember Chicago in '72, then I'll remind you someday."

"Maybe later." He wanted a shower; he could still feel the dust on his skin. And then they needed to get on the road. He and Leo had only run out for a quick hunt when Tas decided they needed a different car. The irritable scribe had gone out to procure one from questionable sources while Leo and Malachi helped Phillip on patrol.

"Tas should be back by now, huh?" Leo asked.

Phillip shrugged. "Probably."

"And where is this car coming from?" Malachi asked.

"It won't be stolen," the watcher said. "Not recently, anyway. But he's right. If any of the Fallen have you on their radar, it'd be good to change cars occasionally. How are you doing on funds?"

"We're all right," Leo said. "Max left us some money."

"He still playing cards?"

Leo smiled. "He calls it supplemental income."

"The boy has rich tastes," Malachi said. "Always has."

Both of them stopped and looked at him expectantly.

"What?" Malachi said. "I remember bits and pieces. Most of it is still a blank."

"If you say so," Phillip said.

"Besides, Max's taste is obvious. How many scribes do you know who wear a five-thousand-dollar watch?"

"It didn't cost me five thousand dollars, Leo."

"But Malachi said—"

Leo held the phone out. Max was on speaker, calling from Berlin.

"If he bought it in a store, it would cost that," Malachi said, eyes on the road.

"But you didn't buy it in a store, did you, Max?"

"Where I buy my watches is no one's business but mine. Now, can we talk about Vienna, or did you want to discuss my shoes?"

Leo bit back a laugh. "You do have a pair of grey loafers that—"

"Vienna," Malachi barked. "Please. What have you found out about the Irina?"

"Phillip is right, there are definitely more Irina in the city, and they're becoming more visible. One of my sources was watching an interview with Edmund's mate—"

"Edmund?"

"British council member. He's become very pro-compulsion."

Malachi glanced to Leo. "Explain."

Leo said, "There is a movement to solve the Irina problem. Critics are calling it 'compulsion.' Basically, some elders want to force the Irina back into retreats."

Max said, "They claim it is for their own protection and to protect the future of the Irin race. It's gaining popularity among younger scribes who want the opportunity to find a mate—as slim as that chance may be—and among scribes who see our race dying off if nothing is done."

"Our race *is* dying off," Malachi said.

"Yes," Max said, "but trying to force the Irina back into the retreats where they were all but slaughtered isn't exactly the wisest way of coaxing them back, is it?"

"All the elders want the Irina back," Leo said, "but they don't agree how to achieve it. Gabriel works for Konrad, who is more traditionalist. He says the reason Irina fled was *because* of the retreats, so it's useless to try to force them back. He's proposing to reform the full council. Irin *and* Irina elders, the way it used to be. That way the Irina would know they have a full vote by their own elders and not just a bunch of old scribes."

Malachi narrowed his eyes, watching the road as he mulled over what Leo and Max had told him. "Max, how are the elders chosen?"

"By the watchers," Max said.

"But I thought the watchers were chosen by the Council."

Leo said, "It's not a perfect system. Irina elders were chosen more democratically. Singers voted based on regions. Seven regions for seven council members."

"Keep in mind," Max said, "it was easier for the Irina, because they were more centralized. Most singers were in retreats and didn't move around much, whereas the scribes were scattered. Different cities. We move much more. Having the watchers choose the seven elders does make a kind of sense."

"Yes, but it also leaves a lot to be desired, considering there is no check on the council's power," Leo said. "Corruption is inevitable."

"It's inevitable in any government, Leo." Malachi took the turnoff from the highway. They were only half an hour outside the city that governed the Irin people. He knew that he must have been there before, but he didn't remember it. It all looked foreign. He felt as if he were stepping into an alien world, and he had no idea who was a friend and who was an enemy. Instinct told him that nothing in Vienna could be taken at face value, including the intentions of the scribe they were meeting.

He knew little about Gabriel except that he was Damien's brother-in-law, and it was possible that Damien's actions had led to the death of Gabriel's mate. Hardly surprising the two didn't get along. Gabriel also worked for Konrad. And Konrad sounded like someone Malachi might agree with.

But then, politicians were liars. That, he knew, was true of every race.

Compulsion.

The very word made the hair on the back of his neck stand on end.

"Tell us more about the Irina in Vienna," Malachi said.

Max and Leo had been chatting in Russian, but they switched back to English. "The Irina who have been out publicly are those whose mates are very pro-compulsion. They've been talking about 'tradition,' but there's little traditional about their conversation. They're talking about other Irina as if they were the enemy. Talking about 'the good of our children' and 'meeting the needs of our scribes.' Acting like all they want is to be protected. The few Irina I've met would spit in their faces."

"So the Irina are back, according to them, and eager to go into retreats again? I find that hard to believe."

"Those speaking publicly claim to speak for their sisters, but we have no idea where they've even been hiding for the last two hundred years."

Max said, "There are rumors that some of the old council hid their wives and wouldn't let them leave their homes. Claimed it was for their own protection. This happened for years. Then a few started coming back to the city. Now, there is a small Irina presence, but it's still very quiet. Out of the public eye. Nothing like what it used to be, according to the older scribes. But it's Vienna, so they're safe."

"And now we have the complication of Ava, as well," Leo said.

Malachi glared. "Ava's not a complication."

"She is in the sense that we still don't know where she comes from." Leo's voice was logical, but his words scraped Malachi's nerves. "And the council will want to know. Have you heard from Rhys?"

Rhys had rented a car and driven ahead to Vienna days before. He'd told Malachi and Leo he needed to check in with a few "associates." Plus, he was the one arranging a meeting with Gabriel since the two scribes had always been friendly.

"No."

"I need to go," Max said. "I'm meeting with a few people here. I think Ava and Damien came through the city on their way to Sari. I'm going to try to get more information in case Gabriel can't or won't tell you what he knows."

"Good luck," Malachi said. "Keep us updated."

"Call me after you've spoken to Gabriel."

Leo put the phone away and silence filled the car.

After a few minutes, the lights of Vienna shone in the distance and traffic started to thicken.

"You know I didn't mean 'complication' in a bad way, don't you?" Leo finally asked.

"I know."

"It's more hopeful than anything else, isn't it? Finding Ava."

"What do you mean?"

"Just that if Ava was out there for so many years, then that could mean there are others we don't know about, too." The longing in Leo's voice was almost painful. "There could be other Irina out there. Not only the survivors of the Rending, but others."

Malachi shrugged. "It's possible. They'd be outsiders, though. Different from the humans around them."

"Ava said that the humans thought she was mentally ill," Leo said quietly. "They thought she was crazy."

The mere idea infuriated him in a way he couldn't articulate.

He said, "If there are other Irina out there—*lost* Irina—"

"We need to find them."

• • • ✦ • • •

THE CALL CAME THROUGH ONLY MINUTES AFTER THEY'D CHECKED INTO the Irin-friendly hotel near the city center. It was a boarding house, set over a handsome *kaffeehaus* lined with wood panels and buzzing with activity from young patrons. There was a message from Rhys telling them that Gabriel would meet them at a different coffee house near the archives. Leo and Malachi quickly stowed their weapons and made their way across town.

Most of the Irin buildings were in the oldest neighborhoods of Vienna; handsome baroque facades hid offices that most humans would simply assume belonged to one of the many corporations or international organizations that made Vienna their home. It was a diverse city, the perfect place for the Irin to hide. And the archives themselves, where Rhys was doing research, were mostly underground, centralized during the late medieval period when the city walls were built.

Leo spotted Gabriel the moment he walked in, and Malachi followed his gaze. Nothing about the Spanish scribe was familiar to him. He had average looks, and his dark suit gave the impression of an ordinary businessman out for a late lunch. Only those who looked closely might notice the edges of tattoo work that peeked above his collar, which was hardly unusual anymore for a man who appeared to be in his late twenties.

But Gabriel was far older. And the wary dark eyes that finally met Malachi's over the French newspaper made that clear.

Leo and Malachi sat down at Gabriel's table, which was in a corner, isolated from the busier tables in the room. Still, Malachi looked around cautiously.

"The owners are Irin," Gabriel said quietly, putting down the newspaper and leaning back. His English was softly accented but precise. He did not offer any greeting. "You are some of Damien's scribes."

"We are," Leo said. "I am Leo. This is Malachi."

"The Istanbul house burned," Gabriel said. "It was noted with some interest here in the city, even though the cause was determined to be accidental."

Malachi spoke. "It wasn't."

"We didn't really think it was," Gabriel said.

Malachi wondered who the "we" referred to. Gabriel and his employer, the Elder named Konrad? The council as a whole?

Leo said, "Our house was targeted by a group of Grigori that belonged to Volund."

A reaction, finally. One eyebrow lifted. Leo might have been the one speaking, but Gabriel was looking at Malachi when he said, "Istanbul is Jaron's territory. It has been since he spread from Persepolis."

Malachi answered the unspoken question. "Not anymore."

"Where is my brother-in-law?"

Leo and Malachi exchanged glances.

Finally, Malachi said, "We don't know."

"The watcher of a scribe house lets his house burn, set on by Grigori outside their known territory, and he does not report it." Gabriel's voice almost sounded amused, but Malachi could sense the man's tightly leashed tension. "In fact, he doesn't report in at all. He disappears with the previously unknown mate of a fallen brother, and no one knows where they are."

Malachi's heart raced. Apparently, Max was right. The Irin council really did have eyes and ears everywhere.

"Needless to say," Gabriel continued, "I am surprised to see you looking so very much alive, Malachi of Sakarya."

CHAPTER

FOURTEEN

"I'm still surprised she let me go."

"*Let* you go?" Renata's eyebrow lifted. "She's not some despot. You wanted to go. You went. We're not military, like scribes."

Mala signed something and Renata interpreted. "Mala says we're also not as organized or efficient."

Ava leaned back in her chair as they sat in the small restaurant beneath the room Renata kept in Bergen. "It probably also helped that Sari and Damien appear to have reconciled."

Mala snorted and began signing again.

"Yes," Renata said with a laugh. "Very loudly."

"I don't even need to speak sign language to get *that*," Ava said. "But yes, I don't think they're noticing much about anything except each other at the moment."

It was nice to see. Painful, but nice. Everyone was happy for them. Damien hadn't slept a night in the guesthouse since the night they'd argued there. Argued and not returned. Now Ava's nights were guarded by a series of friendly scribes and singers who watched over the house while she slept. She could hardly begrudge Damien his time, and it made her early nights less noticeable to the others. She escaped into dreams. It was none of their business how often.

They sat near the window, not chancing the freezing temperatures outside. The window was cold enough. A few tourists still wandered the streets of the charming Norwegian town, taking pictures of the bright houses and soaring, snow-covered mountains.

Winter had descended on the fjords, and though the small valley where Sarihöfn lay was protected from the worst of the elements by Sari's magic, Bergen was not shielded. It was a bone-chilling cold that Ava hadn't experienced for a few years, though it wasn't anything she could forget. She looked with longing at the visitors loading skis into cars, wishing she had the time to join them.

But, as Renata reminded her, this was work. Not fun.

Mala and Renata had fallen silent, sipping their coffee and allowing Ava to listen. Other than brief snatches of conversation, she'd been scanning voices for hours. Most of it was still meaningless babble to her, but she was beginning to recognize a few common words and phrases in the Old Language.

Humans, she realized, were more than a little repetitive.

Worry. Worry. Longing. Joy.

A frustrated man stormed past. His voice felt like anger. She caught the word for "wife" in his thoughts, but not much else.

Worry. Worry. Joy. Contentment.

Love her.

Happy.

Stop. Must stop.

Understanding came in flashes. The drone of the whispers never ceased. Adults were anxiety and longing. Children were laughter, but simple worry was still there. Names flashed. Voices rose and fell.

Ava rubbed her head. In the safety and silence of Sarihöfn, she'd forgotten how exhausting people could be. Luckily, both Mala and Renata hummed low repetitive tunes that blended into a kind of white noise. If she'd heard them in isolation, they would have driven her crazy. But among the throngs of other voices, the background music helped her focus.

…he comes…

Where? Here? Now?

…pretty, pretty human…

Her ears perked at the odd tone of the whisper. She closed her eyes and tried to focus on the single voice that had mentioned the human.

…work… morning…

So much meaningless babble. She couldn't wait to understand more than just—there!

...human ...want...

It was faint and scratchy. Discordant. Just like the Grigori she remembered from Istanbul.

"I've got one," she said softly, closing her eyes. Mala and Renata were silent, but she could hear their humming stop. Their inner voices jumped, alive with curiosity. Excitement.

"Shut up!" Ava said. The humming started again as she tried to track the voice. It was moving away. Ava stood and grabbed her jacket, desperate to find it.

I've got you, asshole. No humans for you today.

She bumped into two people near the door, but she didn't apologize. She walked out into the snow-covered streets, searching for it, hoping that Renata and Mala were following. Not paying attention to anything but—

"Got you," she whispered when her eyes fell on him. Like all his kind, he was beautiful. Golden-brown hair shone in the low sun. He was laughing, flirting with a woman in front of a hotel who looked at him as if he'd hung the moon in the sky along with all the Northern Lights. If Ava didn't know what he was, she would have stopped and stared, too.

Ava paused at the corner and turned to Renata and Mala, who hung back, careful not to get too close. "Him. On the corner in the blue sweater."

"Oh yes," Renata said with glee, "I see him now."

Mala signed and Renata said, "Do you hear any others?"

She tried to focus again, narrowing her mind to the area around the small hotel. "I think... there are some in the hotel, too. Two more voices. It's hard to say for sure."

"That would make the three Sari heard about. Hunting on the ski slopes, it looks like. Tourist areas are always popular. Makes women disappearing much harder to find if they're not in their regular routine. This is good, actually. It means they're not here because of anything but the tourists. It's no wonder with this mild weather we're having."

Ava said, "This is mild?"

Mala just grinned and shook her head. Renata said, "Only in Norway."

Ava murmured the shielding spell and happily slammed the door shut. She took a deep breath and felt immediate relief. The world around her muffled and her vision cleared. Her eyes returned to the Grigori, who was helping the woman load two sets of skis onto the top of her car.

"So, what are we doing with Prince Charming there?"

Renata and Mala exchanged a flurry of signs before Mala nodded and Renata said, "I have all my gear at my place. I'll follow them up the mountain. Skiing is the perfect cover." She smiled. "Snow. Dust. It's easy to lose yourself on the trails."

"You're going after all three by yourself?"

"I'll be fine. You and Mala hang out here until I get back. Then we'll return to Sarihöfn in the morning."

"You have my number if you need help?"

Renata gave her an indulgent smile. "Trust me, I'm looking forward to this. Humans have their fun…" She waved at a car full of skiers as they walked back to Renata's flat. "…and we have ours. Mala's just jealous right now because she doesn't ski."

Mala gave Renata a sign that needed no interpretation.

◆ ◆ ◆   ◆ ◆ ◆

"WHAT DO YOU DO WHEN YOU'RE NOT HERE?" HE ASKED.

She stared into the dark branches overhead. Her head still ached, but she couldn't remember why.

"I don't know."

He took his arms from around her waist and put both palms at her temples. She closed her eyes and felt the soft whisper of his power as he traced spells on her skin. Slowly, the pain began to recede.

"Whatever you are doing, it hurts you." There was disapproval in his tone.

"But then I come here, and you make me feel better. I'm fine now."

She was. The pain was gone, and in its place was a reassuring warmth. The sounds of the forest began to creep in. Low rustles and bird calls. Wind in the trees. They were lying on a bed again, but this time it wasn't in the meadow. It had been drawn farther into the forest. She could hear water flowing in the distance.

He tucked her head on his shoulder and lay back, looking up into the trees as they rested. He lifted one arm, and she could see the marks there, silver and gleaming in the moonlight.

"You made more."

"What?"

"When you sang to me. They grew. I noticed it later."

She lifted her head and frowned. "Is that a good thing or a bad thing?"

"Good, I think."

"Oh." She lay back down again. If it was good, then she'd sing some more. "What do you want me to sing for you?"

"What do you remember?"

She closed her eyes and let her mind loose. The pictures fell into her memory, like photographs scattered across a table. She focused on one and smiled.

"We were near the ocean once. There were lanterns, and they floated into the sky."

She sang softly, and as the old words left her mouth, she could see them take flight, winging their way to his mind. She reached down and felt for his hand. She knit their fingers together, and she could feel the warmth and magic flow between them.

"Ava, look."

Her eyes opened and she looked down to where their hands joined. She saw it. The spells on his arm creeped up and over, curling into themselves as if drawn by an invisible hand. She watched them, still singing, and when she finally fell silent, the marks remained.

"I remember when you sing to me," he said. "My mind. My heart." He smiled before he kissed her. "You're bringing me back to life."

She smiled and leaned forward, craving another kiss.

There was a rustle in the forest and a blast of cold air.

His eyes narrowed and swung toward the disturbance.

The sound came again. Louder.

He squeezed her hand. "You need to wake up."

"What?"

He sat and pulled her up with him. "Wake up, Ava."

Fear clutched her throat. His name came to her. "Malachi?"

He shook her shoulders. "I'm not there. I'm not there, and there's danger."

"I don't understand."

"Wake up, Ava. Wake up *now*!"

• • •   • • •

"MALACHI!"

She gasped, calling out his name as she sat bolt upright in bed. Renata's flat was pitch-black, but Ava could hear someone struggling in the corner. Hissed voices and the rasping whispers that haunted her nightmares.

Grigori were in the room.

She heard a crack and a thud, then Mala stepped into a shaft of light, brandishing twin daggers that seemed to glow. She stalked toward Ava with death in her eyes.

"Mala?"

The Irina opened her mouth, but no sound came. It was enough to make Ava open her senses and listen.

Ava scrambled away from the hissing whisper she felt at her back just in time to escape the grip of the soldier who snuck from behind. He muttered a curse before he rolled away, dodging the silver daggers Mala threw at him. Ava kicked out, catching his knee with her heel. He grunted, still trying to remain quiet. The Grigori rolled into the darkness and Mala followed.

Ava yelled out, "Mala, lights?"

Two clicks of Mala's tongue told her yes. She felt for the switch on the wall and flipped it up.

The smell of sandalwood filled the air, and the window to the bedroom was open. A flicker of the curtain as freezing air blasted into the room. Then another flicker as a shadow darted in the corner of her eye. The Grigori attacked silently, grabbing her neck as he tackled Ava to the ground. He forced a hand around her throat and pressed, cutting off both her voice and her air. She could hear another soldier climb in the window and run toward Mala.

The helpless rage filled her. His body trapped her on the ground. For all her training and preparation, she was no match for the large male. Her heart raced as his palm pressed harder. Her breath was running out. She would pass out soon, and there would be nothing to stop them.

Black spots danced in front of her eyes. Then the blackness grew and spread as the whispers in her mind grew louder.

Do not fear the darkness.

Ava closed her eyes.

A rush of wings and feathers from the corner of her vision. A rising shadow. Tall, as if a dark mountain had come to life, he loomed over her, cloaked in the void. A soughing breath stirred the black feathers that drooped over his hood. He was nothing. As if the stars had been snuffed in the night, he bore no face behind the droop of his black cloak. A nightmare. A monster. He leaned closer, forcing her to look. Forcing her to face the secret—

Her eyes flew open with the screaming.

No hand clutched at her throat. It had fallen away, and the Grigori soldier was screaming in her ear. She rolled over, shoving him off, but he kept up his hoarse cries, even as the building began to come alive. Someone pounded on the door. Ava heard shouts and running steps. All the while, the soldier rolled on the ground, clutching his hands to his temples, his eyes frozen on some invisible terror, his pupils dilated so his eyes appeared pure black.

In a blink, Mala rolled him over and speared her knife into his neck, ending the screams and releasing the creature's dark soul. Then she turned to Ava with fear in her eyes.

There was a muffled conversation at the door, then the voices died away and Ava heard the deadbolt turn. She closed her eyes and breathed deeply, enjoying the bite of the winter air that still poured into the room.

"What happened?" It was Renata. "The neighbors thought someone was being murdered!"

There was silence, so Ava knew Mala was signing the answer. She simply rolled over, making no attempt to rise. She watched the two women who stood at the door. Mala was almost naked. She was only wearing a T-shirt and underwear to sleep. Two empty knife sheaths were strapped to her thighs. Renata looked exhausted. Covered with a dusting of snow, her hair was almost grey. Mala's explanation went on a long time, then Renata finally turned to Ava as Mala went to snap the window closed.

"Ava, are you all right?" Renata knelt down and shook her shoulders. "Why are you crying? Are you hurt?"

She hadn't realized she was crying.

"I'm fine."

"What did you do to the Grigori?"

"What?" Ava sniffed. "Mala, how do you sleep with those on your legs?"

"Pay attention." Renata swatted her cheek, not hard enough to bruise but hard enough to notice. "What did you do?"

"I don't know." Ava curled up on her side, shaking with cold and not caring that she was lying on the floor. She reached for a blanket that had half fallen off the bed. She was freezing and she shook so hard she felt as if her skin might fly off her body. "Maybe h…he was scared of the black angel, too."

Renata looked at her like she was crazy. Maybe she was. Adrenaline coursed through her system. She felt hopped up, despite the tears on her face. "I didn't even get a punch in. Not even a kick. Need to practice more. And my magic—"

"She's rambling," Renata said. "Ava, sit up. Take deep breaths."

She could breathe now. She hadn't been able to when the Grigori had his hand on her throat. Hadn't been able to say anything. The black spots danced across her eyes again, so she sat up carefully.

Renata stood and crossed the room to the window.

"Three sets of prints below the snow." She secured the blinds and turned. "Just those three?"

Mala nodded and signed some more. She also kept her distance from Ava.

Renata said, "Mala says thank you for turning on the lights. And she doesn't know what you did to the Grigori, but whatever it was incapacitated both the one she was fighting and the one who had you."

"Oh…" She sniffed. "Well, that's good."

"And she always sleeps with her daggers. Her mate thought it was sexy."

Somehow, an Irin scribe thinking sleeping with a deadly woman was sexy didn't surprise Ava at all.

Mala was still signing and Renata watched her with a frown.

"No," she said. "I have no idea."

More signing as Ava climbed to her knees, smoothing the sheets on the beds and wondering if she would ever sleep again.

Renata said, "I told you, I don't know. Orsala said she sees visions. You said their eyes went black?"

If Ava couldn't sleep, then when would she see Malachi?

"Wake up, Ava. Wake up now!"

He'd known. He'd warned her.

She shook her head. No, of course not. She was being absurd. It wasn't Malachi. Her subconscious had sensed danger and used her dream to wake her. Her quivering hands pulled on another sweater.

"I'm not there."

The pain in his voice… It was almost as if he was speaking from far away. As if he could swoop in and protect her. Impossible. Fresh grief threatened to swamp her, and Ava thought she heard a flutter of wings in the air. She shoved the grief to the back of her mind.

Mala and Renata were still speaking.

She felt like climbing the walls. Her skin crawled. Were shadows moving in the corner of the room? There was something just beyond her perception. Some instinct needled her. She couldn't pinpoint the threat, but she could feel it.

Run.

She started packing up, throwing her things into the small bag she'd brought, scanning the room for other belongings.

"What are you doing?" Renata asked.

"Packing."

"Oh?" Ava could hear the humor in her voice. "And where are you going at three in the morning?"

"I don't know. Away. I don't want to be here." The threat might have passed, but she could still feel it, like eyes on her back.

Someone, *something* was watching. She could sense it.

"You're not going anywhere. Mala and I will take turns watching, then we'll leave in the morning."

"No." She shook her head, hands trembling. "I can't stay here. Not here."

"Ava, there's no——"

"I will not stay here!" she yelled. "It is not safe. Maybe you don't feel it, but I do. We are not safe here. *Someone* can see us!"

Mala stepped closer. She put her hands on Ava's shoulders and stared into her eyes. Mala's eyes were deep brown, like the darkest coffee. Ava didn't flinch when she held her gaze. Something shifted in the Irina's expression, and she nodded. She stepped away and signed to Renata.

"What?"

More signing.

"So you're just going to drive back to Sarihöfn in the middle of the night because——"

Mala interrupted her with two clicks of her tongue, then a long stream of signs passed between Renata and Mala. Ava was frustrated, catching only the occasional word or phrase, but they seemed to be arguing.

"Fine," Renata finally said. "Ava, you and Mala are going back to Sarihöfn right now."

Mala walked to the sofa where she'd been sleeping and pulled on a pair of pants.

"You're not coming?"

"No," Renata said, her mouth twisted in irritation. "There is someone I need to contact. I'll go to Oslo and meet him there. He's… very well connected and he knows more about Grigori politics than most. Mala thinks that one of the Fallen may have eyes on you. That may be what you're feeling. How that could be is a mystery to me, but I haven't studied them. This scribe has."

"But we'll be safe in Sarihöfn?" The creeping feeling still stalked her. She could sense it, like darkness outside a lit room.

"Did you feel this way in Sarihöfn before?"

"No."

"Then it's possible that Sari and Orsala's shields work to protect you from… whatever it is you're feeling. Either way, it's the safest place for you."

"Okay." She let out a breath. "Okay. The ones today, on the ski slope—?"

"Dust," she said. "Gone now. They were from the city. Just looking for easy prey. No one else with them that I could see."

"So the ones that came here tonight—"

"Coincidence."

Ava thought that was about as likely as Mala giving up her knives. Still, she had no other explanation to offer. She just wanted to go.

They packed quickly and Renata brought her car around. She'd catch the train to Oslo, then stay in a safe house she kept. She promised to call within a week to check in. Sooner if she had news.

Within an hour, Mala and Ava were back on the road, heading into the countryside. It was quiet in the car, but Ava didn't sleep. And the feeling of being watched never went away.

IV.

He hadn't expected to be welcomed into Svarog's home. The angel's residence in the small town near Budapest was not nearly as grand as the most humble of Volund's homes. The entryway was light and airy, with potted plants and many windows facing an interior garden that was a riot of colors, despite the cold air. Svarog must have put an enchantment over the garden to keep the springlike look of the place, even in the dead of winter. Still, it was doubtful the angel truly lived here any more than was necessary to breed with the human women Brage had seen passing. They greeted him with friendly and aloof smiles but did not speak to him.

Most appeared to be pregnant or nursing. The pregnant had the healthy glow he recognized in those carrying angelic offspring. The nursing mothers were in various stages of slow decline, no matter how they adored their beautiful sons. Eventually, their children would drain and kill them.

A small boy skidded into the entry and almost ran into Brage's legs.

"*Szia,*" Brage said to the Grigori child.

"*Jó napot,*" the child replied politely.

"English?" He hoped an adult would appear. He did not speak more than the most cursory Hungarian.

The little one shook his head.

The boy was beautiful, as all Grigori children were. His skin had a faint glow and his eyes were clear blue, the color of a summer sky. He started babbling at Brage, who only watched him with pleasant indifference. It wasn't unheard of for an angel to keep their offspring near, but it was unusual. Volund had sired Brage, but he'd never met his father until he was ready to serve. Children were not welcome in Volund's house.

A harried-looking soldier appeared in the entryway and barked at the child. Despite the harsh tone, the child turned to his keeper with a mischievous gleam in his eye that told Brage he wasn't afraid in the least. He waved at Brage and then trotted off after the grim man, grabbing his hand as he skipped toward French doors that led to a garden.

"He lost his mother only a month ago."

Brage turned toward the sad voice of the woman who carried an infant. They were wrapped in blankets on a chaise near the windows.

The woman continued, "He seems to be doing well."

Brage gave her a polite smile. "They always do."

"Are you here to see the master?"

"I am."

"He'll be here soon."

"I'm sure he will." Brage didn't want to speak to the woman anymore. He hoped she'd lose interest in him. They were broodmares to the Fallen, nothing more. It was useless to converse with something so ephemeral. The child she held and nursed was far more valuable than the mother.

The woman's face broke into a glorious smile when Svarog appeared. "*Aranyom!*"

The Fallen put an absent hand on the woman's cheek and smiled at the child in her arms. Then he turned to Brage. "Come."

The angel led him down a hallway lined with books, then past another sitting room and a large dining room where more women ate and chattered. It was not unpleasant, but Brage wondered how the Fallen lived with so many around him. It was like living with livestock, to his mind. The Fallen led him to a small library where a fire burned. He'd taken the guise of a middle-aged man with steel-grey hair and vivid blue eyes. He was wearing a sweater and slacks, the picture of a successful human in his country retreat, but Brage knew better. Svarog, for all his affection toward his offspring, was a vicious killer who had no regard for any but his own. Humans he didn't breed with were nothing to him. It was one of the reasons he and Volund had always been allies.

"So," Svarog said, closing the door behind them, "what does Volund's oldest son want in my territory?"

"I am looking for someone." No subterfuge was necessary. Svarog, like all fallen angels, understood vendetta. "An Irin scribe my father wants me to kill."

"And you know he is here?"

"He was driving from Istanbul to Vienna. I am hoping to catch him before he enters the city."

Svarog nodded. "Fine. Hunt if you like. But I have a message for your father, and I expect you to deliver it. Your mouth to his ears, do you understand?"

"I do."

Cautioned by Svarog's tone, Brage waited.

"Tell him I know what he is doing, and I want no part of it. If he thinks I will roll over as Jaron did in Istanbul, he is mistaken."

Brage blinked but showed no other outward sign of surprise. "Why do you ask me to deliver this message?"

The Fallen had ways of communicating with their own kind that surpassed human or Grigori understanding.

Svarog stepped closer, letting the human mask fall. The angel's eyes shone gold and the automatic terror froze Brage in place.

"I want you to deliver the message," he said, "because I want Volund to know that his most valued son was in my house, near my children, and I let him live. Do you understand?"

"Yes."

"Go. And do not bother telling your father where I dwell. By the time you leave my city, this house will be gone."

"I understand."

Brage left the house quickly and drove toward Budapest, more confused than ever.

"I know what he is doing…"

What *was* Volund's plan? Brage was reminded of his early years as a soldier. The years just before the Irina slaughter had been like this. Mixed messages and mysterious errands. Half-truths and outright lies. He'd understood nothing until the order had come from the oldest soldiers in their house in Berlin. They were leaving the city for some tiny village in the country. They slaughtered women and children, ripping out their throats so they were defenseless.

He'd told himself it was no different from killing humans.

He still told himself that.

"If he thinks I will roll over as Jaron did in Istanbul, he is mistaken."

He tried to drive the doubt from his mind. Volund would sense it. Doubt was death to the Fallen. Nothing was accepted but utter and complete loyalty. After all, there were hundreds of brothers waiting to take his place if he stumbled.

Brage would not stumble.

A chirp from his mobile phone. It was the number for one of the Grigori who ran Volund's house.

"Yes?"

"Our father has a message for you."

"What is it?"

"Come to the house in Göteborg immediately. He will meet you there."

Brage stopped the protest on his lips. The scribe was in Budapest, he was sure of it. To pull him away now—

"Do you understand?" his brother asked.

It didn't matter. He was a weapon, nothing more. Volund's to command, like the blade Brage wore under his shirt.

"I understand. I will be on a plane tonight."

CHAPTER

FIFTEEN

His roar of frustration finally brought a pounding at the door. Malachi had been pacing for hours. It was the middle of the night, but somewhere his mate was in danger. Someone had attacked her. He'd woken from his dream with sweat pouring from him, his heart racing, and adrenaline pumping through his system. He'd bolted from the bed, ready for battle.

But there was nothing to do.

He was in one of the secured guest rooms at Gabriel's townhouse. Leo was in the room next to him. They'd followed Damien's brother-in-law there after their meeting.

"How did you know? Who told you?"

"Evren called me when he found some information he thought you should know. He knew my father, and he trusts me. You really ought to be better about checking your messages, Leo."

"What—?"

"It has to do with Ava's father. And… an impossibility that is looking more possible all the time."

Gabriel had tucked them into his black chauffeured car and hidden Malachi and Leo away in his spacious home. Gabriel, along with being Konrad's right hand, was a financier in the city and had accumulated more than his share of wealth. They'd left a message for Rhys to meet them there. As much as Malachi distrusted everything around him, Leo was certain that Gabriel was an ally. Max—who seemed to know just about everyone—confirmed it.

Leo called, "Malachi?"

He said nothing. He couldn't stop the animalistic growl that left his throat. She was out there, and he had no power to help her. He didn't even know where she was. Every night since he'd realized his dreams were more than dreams, he went to sleep commanding himself to ask her where she was. To tell her that he was alive. Truly alive. And every night, his mind hazed and he could focus only on her. The outside world fell into shadow. His conscious demands drifted away.

The pounding came again.

"Malachi." It was Gabriel. "Open the door, or I will break it."

Something in the scribe's voice told Malachi he wasn't joking. He opened the door.

Leo and Gabriel stood there, both dressed in pajamas, both with clenched fists.

"What the—"

"She's in danger."

Gabriel's eyes narrowed. "How do you know?"

"I know! We were there, in the dream, and I felt it. Like a shadow surrounding us. Then it came closer. It was searching for her. For Ava."

"Where?" Gabriel stepped into the room. "Where were you?"

"In the dreams…" The truth tumbled from his lips. "I've been dreaming. Well, I thought they were dreams at first, but they're not." He held out his arm. "She sings to me and they grow. She's… healing me. But I can't talk to her. It's so—"

"Dreamy?" Gabriel raised an eyebrow. "Yes, I could have told you. That's how the dream walks work."

"Dream walking?" Leo slapped his forehead and followed Gabriel into Malachi's room. "Of course! Why didn't I think of it? She's his mate! How could I be so stupid?"

"Since you've never been mated, it probably wouldn't be the first thing you thought of." Gabriel sat on the bench near the foot of the bed and rubbed the sleep from his eyes. "And there was no way of knowing how Malachi's death would affect their bond. Tell me more details. Well… not *all* the details. But there might be clues."

"Are you listening to me?" Malachi said. "She is in *danger*!"

"And there is absolutely nothing you can do about it," Gabriel said, rising to his feet. "It's frustrating, isn't it? To know that your mate is threatened. To know her fear. Her panic."

"You have no idea."

"I have *every* idea." The cold words cut through the room, reminding all of them that Gabriel had lost his mate, Tala. Damien had taken her into battle, and she had perished.

Gabriel continued in his chilling voice. "But there's nothing you can do for her right now. If she was dead, you would feel it."

"Does it hurt?" The fire went out of Malachi's belly. The pain twisted in his chest. "When I died, did it hurt her?"

He wasn't sure whether or not Gabriel would even answer. But the scribe raised his chin and said, "Yes. It hurts. Physically. Emotionally. If she was gravely injured, you would feel it. Not in an incapacitating way, but you would know. Do you feel anything like that?"

"No."

"Then she was in danger, but the danger has passed. Tell me about your dreams."

He could feel the heat in his cheeks and Gabriel gave him a knowing look. "We don't talk much."

"That's normal. Most Irin couples who are physically parted don't spend their dream walks in conversation."

The three men settled into seats near the fireplace. Clearly, sleep was a memory.

"Why can't I ask her questions?" Malachi asked. "Every night, I go to sleep, and I tell myself I will ask her where she is. But when the dream starts…"

Gabriel crossed his arms and took a deep breath. "I've heard it said by scholars far more intelligent than me that the Forgiven gave Irin mates their ability to dream walk in order to feed the soul. It is not conscious life, though it still feeds us physically. Otherwise, our tactile need for each other when we were separated would become a liability."

"So even though I'm away from her, I'm still caring for her?" It helped. To know that he was at least doing something.

Gabriel nodded. "She's probably sleeping better than most widowed mates would. She'd be more calm. Centered. Physically, she will be stronger because of the walks."

"But why can't I ask her anything? Why can't I ask her where she is, like I always tell myself to."

"You don't understand. You're not meeting on a conscious level.

Dream walks are your souls speaking to each other. And the soul isn't concerned about worldly problems. Day-to-day worries never enter into a dream walk. You don't chat about the children or work. If you're fighting, your souls would reach for each other *more*, not less. Dream walks are the place Irin mates connect on the most spiritual level, where your soul reads your mate's and gives it exactly what it needs. Connection. Comfort. Pleasure. It's not like a normal conversation."

"So her soul doesn't need me to find her?" That couldn't be correct. He had reached for her even when he didn't know her name.

"Don't you see?" Gabriel asked. "Her soul has *already* found you, Malachi. Within her dreams. Your souls have found each other. It is only your bodies that have not."

Leo asked, "Do you think she knows they're more than dreams?"

"Probably not. After all, why would she even consider it?" Gabriel's voice was rough. "She thinks Malachi is dead. They all do. After Tala died, I dreamed of her almost every night. For years. I knew it wasn't the same because I'd experienced dream walking, so *I* knew the difference. Ava does not. She probably thinks her walks with Malachi are only that. Very vivid dreams."

Malachi cursed silently. Then he held out his arm. "And this? My *talesm* returning?"

"That, I have no idea about." Gabriel shook his head. "It's not like we've seen many resurrected scribes. It must have something to do with her particular magic. The scholars would drool over this."

Leo said, "And the reason we're not consulting them is…?"

"I finally spoke to Rhys last night," Gabriel said. "He's been here for a week now, doing research. Based on what he's seen, he thinks there is too much division in the archives. He wants to keep Ava and Malachi as quiet as possible, at least for now. All the elders have their own scholars doing research into the Irina problem, trying to find writings or visions that back up their own position." He shrugged. "Konrad does. And he's one of the most honorable elders on the council. But he's not going to actively support research that could favor compulsion any more than Edmund is going to support research in favor of restoration."

According to Gabriel, the Irin Council had become fairly evenly divided into two camps: those elders supporting compulsion, which would hunt down the Irina and force them back into heavily guarded retreats "for their own safety and the future of the Irin race"; and restoration, which would petition the most respected Irina to reform the Irina Council so that Irina could come back to public life with full protection.

It was more complicated than Malachi had expected. Compulsion grated on his instincts, but the arguments were compelling. The Irin *were* dying off. Generations of Irin children had been lost. The Irina needed to be protected. In fact, some of the most pro-compulsion elders on the council had lost mates and daughters during the Rending. They were passionate about the safety of the Irina. Passionate about the need for them to be protected from the Grigori. And most did not downplay the Grigori threat.

On the other hand, many of the elders who supported restoration clearly had no idea just how much the Grigori were spreading. They dismissed the Fallen, almost as if they were something out of a myth. They claimed that those in favor of compulsion were fear-mongering bigots, that there was little threat to the Irina. They needed to simply step back into public life and everything would sort itself out.

Vienna was a city riddled by politics, confused by its own safety, and flush with more money than Malachi had ever imagined. It was lazy and indulgent. The city stank of greed.

"We should try to get some sleep," Leo said. "Rhys will be by in the morning, and Max is supposed to call around noon."

"Where is Max?"

"I don't know," Leo said. "He mentioned a message from a contact the last time I talked to him. I think he was in Berlin."

"Berlin?"

Leo grinned. "They asked after you. If we're going to keep your story a secret, we may need to avoid the city. You spent many years in Berlin."

• • •　• • •

By noon, Gabriel had gone into his offices and Leo, Rhys, and Malachi met with Konrad in Gabriel's library.

"So you are the scribes that nobody and everybody is talking about," Konrad said. He was a gruff man. Not handsome in the least, he appeared to bear the weight of the world on his stooped shoulders. He was barrel-chested and gray-haired, clearly having cut back on the longevity spells after he'd lost his mate, Catherine. She had not died in the Rending but, of all things, a traffic collision while they were on holiday. It was a shocking reminder to Malachi of how dangerous the world could be, even in ordinary times.

"I don't know about that," Malachi said. "I'm not much for gossip."

"Oh, we eminent politicians don't call it gossip, Malachi. We call it 'intelligence.'" He lifted the corner of his mouth in what could almost be a smile. "I knew your father for a time. You look like him. When we were young, we trained together near Jerusalem. Of course, that was very long ago."

"Yes, sir."

"You lost him during the Rending?"

Malachi looked at Leo. He was trusting that the story the scribe had told him was true, since he didn't remember much about his parents. "They were in the conflict in Berlin. They were living in a retreat near there and both went into the city to fight."

"And I suppose that is why the Grigori call you the Butcher of Berlin, eh?" Konrad sniffed. "Good work there. We need more soldiers like you."

Malachi blinked, unaware of the nickname. Leo smiled nervously. Clearly, he'd forgotten to give Malachi all the details of his past life.

Ignoring it, Malachi steered the conversation in another direction. "It's good to know that not all the elders are unaware of the escalating Grigori threat."

"No, not all of us are unaware."

Rhys muttered, "But enough to make it a concern."

Konrad said, "Well, it doesn't help convincing people when things like Grigori burning down scribe houses are left unreported."

Rhys said, "That, I do not understand. I know Damien reported it. I heard him make the call."

"Oh, we knew it had burned, but it was ruled accidental by the Turkish authorities."

"No." Rhys shook his head. "Damien was on the phone with someone in Vienna. He told them it was a Grigori attack. He *told* them that Volund's soldiers were in the city. That Jaron has ceded control."

Konrad said, "We never got that message. I only heard rumors and innuendo. Someone died. Someone found a mate. It was never clear what had happened to whom." He nodded toward Malachi. "And now the story you tell me? If I hadn't seen his *talesm* so depleted, I'd think you were liars. But no scribe reaches his age with so few spells. It's unnatural."

"Did Evren call you?"

"No, but he called an associate I trust. A genealogist from America." Konrad raised an eyebrow. "This theory they have about your mate's identity is… unorthodox."

"Everything we know tells us that it should be impossible," Rhys said. "But I agree with Evren, no other option makes sense."

"Irina have taken human lovers over the centuries," Konrad said. "This has always happened, because they are not bound by touch as we are. It's not something a family would talk about. As far as I can tell, no children have ever come from those unions. Biologically, we've never understood why, but—"

"But Ava's father is the only possibility at this point. If Jasper Reed's mother was Irina—who somehow had a child by a human—it's possible she could have hidden it."

"And who is his mother? Your mate's grandmother? Do we know? She must have been extraordinarily powerful for her granddaughter to control so much magic with only a fraction of Irin blood."

Rhys said, "That's the problem. We're having trouble finding anything about her. We found Reed's medical records from the American foster-care system. Her name had been erased, but that's not a problem for us, of course." Rhys glanced at Malachi. "Her first name was Ava, and that's the only name listed. We have no other evidence of her. No paperwork. She disappeared from the system after she surrendered her son."

"Is she alive?"

Leo said, "Ava says she isn't. That her father told her his mother died when he was a child."

Konrad said to Malachi, "And your mate was named after her grandmother."

"Apparently."

"Ava is a very common Irina name," Rhys added quietly.

Konrad sat back in his chair and looked between the three of them. He looked for a long while as a smile teased the corner of his lips. "You think this is bigger than one misplaced Irina," he finally said, smiling at Malachi. "You think there are more."

"If we didn't know about Ava, maybe we don't know about others,"

Malachi said. "If one Irina had a child with a human lover and hid it, others could have as well. Maybe there are lost Irina out there. If there are, they need us to find them. They are not at home in the human world."

Rhys added, "And if there are more Irina, if our race was not in danger of dying out, it would change the balance of the council, would it not? If there are lost Irina out there, Grigori would be drawn to them. Perhaps some unity of purpose could be sought. Contain the Grigori *and* find our lost sisters."

"It would be a goal all would be able to support, even the most hesitant members of the council. An interesting theory," Konrad acknowledged as he rose to his feet, coffee finished. "But it is only a theory right now. The more pressing issue is the Grigori problem. We don't need our focus shifted from hunting Grigori to hunting Irina who may not want to be found. It's foolish and useless. Find Damien. I need to speak to him. If he reported the details of the Grigori attack to someone in Vienna and the report was hidden, I need to know."

"And you need to know whether whoever he spoke to has suppressed other reports of Grigori aggression," Leo said. "Communication may have broken down. And if protocol isn't being followed…"

"I will look into this," Konrad said. "But now, I must go."

Malachi, Leo, and Rhys stood to walk Konrad to the door.

"The scribe house in Budapest says that requests for funds are being ignored," Malachi told him. "They feel they are fighting Grigori without support. Is he the only one?"

Konrad shook his head. "No. But I'm one of the lone voices in the wilderness on this issue." He waved his arms around the room. "We are in Vienna! Jewel of the Irin crown. Grigori attacks are almost unheard of. They happen… elsewhere. More scribes are concerned about their empty houses and empty beds than the human population. They want mates and families, not war in far-off places."

Leo snorted. "Budapest is not so far away."

"Nor is Istanbul. Paris. London." Rhys frowned. "Do Irin here really not know?"

"Some do. Some don't. They ignore it if it's convenient for them."

Malachi shook his head. "Vienna is slowly being surrounded by increasingly aggressive Grigori. The Fallen are showing their face to us. Powers are shifting. Vienna will not be able to bury the truth for long."

Konrad said, "Bring Ava and Damien to the city. Give me proof to show the council. Without proof, without testimony, I am speaking to deaf ears."

 ⋆ ⋆ ⋆ ⋆ ⋆ ⋆

"Has Max called yet?"

"No."

Leo was sitting near the window, staring out into the quiet street when Malachi walked in. He felt restless. There was nothing to do in the city. Rhys was continuing his research at the archives, trying to track down the families and genealogies of other Irina who were known to have taken human mates. Gabriel was at his office, putting together more funds for their search, which Konrad had quietly approved. Leo and Malachi were stuck at the house with nothing to do and no Grigori to fight.

Malachi sat down across from him. "Ava was named after her grandmother," he said. "It can't be a coincidence that Jasper Reed named his daughter his biological mother's name. He was put into the system when he was very young, but he must have known her name."

"I'm surprised Ava's mother allowed Reed to name her," Leo said. "I thought she didn't have much to do with him."

"Lena Matheson might not have known the significance. And Ava is a common enough human name."

"There's no other record of the first Ava?"

"Not that Rhys has found. Or Konrad's contact in America."

Leo was silent for some time. Then he said, "If he knew her name, is it possible he knew more than that?"

"What do you mean?"

"He's a very famous musician, isn't he? He has a lot of money. Do we know if he was wealthy when Ava was born?"

Malachi said, "Rhys said Reed was already famous when Ava was born."

"So he probably had money. And if he had money, he could have found his mother. Maybe as an adult, even. Reed might be the reason her records don't exist."

"Why would he make his own mother disappear? Especially if she was dead?"

Leo shrugged. "I don't know."

"But if he has her records, or knows where they are..." Malachi was starting to see where Leo was going. "There's no way we could talk to him. He has bodyguards. Handlers."

"But he only has one daughter."

"He would tell Ava. Probably."

"Maybe."

The phone rang. The loud electronic buzz filled the silent library. Leo picked it up. "Max?"

Malachi could hear his brother's voice from across the room.

"Get to Oslo, Leo. Get Malachi and get on a plane *now*."

Malachi's heart raced. "Oslo?"

"I've found them," Max said. "I've found Ava."

CHAPTER

SIXTEEN

The feeling of being watched continued into Sarihöfn. It continued during her lesson with Orsala the next day. It hung over her shoulder and she could not rest, even when she tried.

"Something is coming," she said to Orsala, who was fixing tea during a break in their lessons.

"Have you seen something? What is it?"

"Something dark. I see it in my dreams. I've brought something dark here."

Orsala narrowed her eyes, then closed them, and Ava knew she was taking a gentle scan of the emotions around her. It was part of the shields that Sarihöfn held. The scribes who lived there wrote their magic on the trees and walls of the compound. Sari manipulated the very elements that surrounded them. There were patrols and guards. Video monitoring and electronic sensors. And Orsala could feel the emotional temperature of any inhabitant when she wanted to.

"Nothing feels wrong, Ava. Except that you're worried. For the first time in many years, our wards here are stronger because Sari is complete."

At least one good thing had come from her visit. Damien and Sari's reconciliation had strengthened the whole community and put both of them in a far better mood. By the time Mala and Ava had returned from Bergen, there were flowers pushing up through the snow. Playful ribbing might have reddened Sari's cheeks, but the aura of contentment was evident all through the valley.

Except for Ava.

She could feel it. Something dark shadowed her. It lurked in the trees.

"I dream of dark things, Orsala." Her voice was barely over a whisper. "Even when Malachi is there, there's a darkness, too."

The old woman put a hand on her arm as she sat next to Ava at the table. "That's normal, daughter. I dreamed of my mate after I lost him, too. It's normal that your dreams of him would be troubling. He was taken from you in the most violent way. Don't hide from that. Your soul must grieve."

"They're not always dark."

"Good."

"But there's something…"

"What?" The kettle began to whistle, and Orsala rose. "What is it?"

"I feel like it comes *from* me. Or it's tied to me, but separate. I don't want it… but it's part of me. Like when I didn't let go of Bruno. It wasn't that I couldn't. Part of me didn't *want* to. I *liked* the power."

Ava could smell the aroma of tea rising from the cheery brown pot Orsala always used. It did nothing to cheer her.

"You're angry," the old woman said.

"At myself, yes."

Orsala finally sat again, putting the tea and two cups in front of her, closing the book of spells they'd been studying.

"Ava, you spent much of your life in the human world, not realizing who or what you were. For years, they told you that your mind was wrong. That could easily have created the shadows I see within you. Yes, there is darkness. But none of us are completely dark or light. We are, none of us, perfect beings. Not even the angels are perfect. We fail and fall like the humans. We have rage. Greed. Violence against each other. But we seek the light. That is what makes us different from the Fallen." Her lip curled. "From their Grigori spawn. Our souls seek the light."

Her mouth turned up at the corner. "You don't feel the darkness in me?"

Orsala hesitated. "I do."

"I do, too."

"But I see far more light than dark. Yes, your magic has… a

shadow. I've seen it just as you have. But I truly believe the longer you are with us, the longer you know who you are and what you are meant to be, that shadow will lessen. It will never overpower you."

"Are you sure of that?"

"Are you?"

"No."

"Be sure, Ava." Her voice dropped. "Summon the will that kept you sane among the humans and fight it. If you aren't sure of yourself, then the darkness *could* win."

"And the shadow I'm feeling? The one surrounding me?"

Orsala shrugged. "We'll watch. But Sarihöfn is protected, Ava. Very protected. We know Volund is after you, but it is doubtful even one of the Fallen could find you here with all the shields in place."

"Okay." She took a deep breath and let it out. "Okay."

"Shall we study more?"

"Yes."

Because if there was anything she could learn that might help hold back the darkness, then Ava needed it.

"Do not fear the darkness."

• • • • • •

SHE SLEPT, BUT HE WASN'T THERE. SHE STOOD AT THE EDGE OF THE forest, looking out. There was nothing there but blackness, and the birds did not sing.

"You shouldn't have left."

The voice came from behind her. She turned and saw the soft-spoken man in glasses.

"Who are you?"

"You shouldn't have left. He's coming now. His children found you, so he can, too." The man sighed. "Blood. It's very difficult to stop blood magic."

"Where is he?"

"That, I cannot tell you. Perhaps he does not sleep."

She blinked and the image of the man wavered.

"Take off your mask," she said.

He smiled. "You are bold in dreams. I do not find offense in this."

"Then take off your mask."

"Are you sure you want to see me as I am?" He must have read the uncertainty in her eyes. "I will show you a shadow of my face in this world, but that is all."

The man grew. Expanded. His soft face shimmered away and a harder one took its place. A beautiful face. Unearthly. His hair was black and shining as a raven's wing. His eyes were a glittering amber gold. Smooth tan skin was marked by raised letters she recognized. They were like her mate's, but more. This being's magic was not written on him, it was part of him. She knew he would not hurt her. He was frightening, but she felt no fear.

"You're beautiful."

"You are not the first to say so."

"Your spells…" She stepped forward and put a hand on his arm. The skin was warm under her fingertips. The raised letters glimmered with a faint, silver sheen.

"They are not spells."

"What are they?"

"Magic that is part of me."

"Like my magic is part of me?"

"No. They are more."

"I don't understand."

"You're not meant to, child. It is a thing beyond your ken."

She looked around the forest. The darkness crept closer. Around the glowing being, it was held back, but it did not seem afraid of him any more than she was.

"Why does it find me here?"

"He finds you because he can. Just as I can."

She looked up into his glowing face. "Will it hurt me?"

He cocked his head. "I do not know his purpose. Only that he would thwart mine."

"And what is your purpose?"

He smiled. "That is not for you to know yet. I gave you my vision once. I will give you others when you need them."

"When will I need them?"

He shook his head. "Not now."

"Why not?"

"Wake up, or the darkness will find you."

She frowned. "I don't want to leave yet. You don't answer my questions."

His smile turned sad. He lifted his hand to her cheek and trailed a warm finger there. "I had hoped… You look nothing like your mother. But your voice reminds me of her."

She felt tears on her cheek, but he brushed them away. "I don't understand you."

He vanished from her sight, but his whisper came from the trees around her.

"Wake, Ava…"

She woke, and the tears were cold on her cheeks. There was a commotion outside the cottage. She could hear shouting and car engines roaring to life.

Ava bolted up in bed, throwing on her clothes and racing from the bedroom. Damien burst through the door a moment later.

"Two Grigori. Both dead. But they found us, Ava." His cold voice turned Ava's stomach. "They found Sarihöfn."

◆ ◆ ◆　◆ ◆ ◆

"This is my fault," she whispered at the kitchen table, listening to Sari plan the evacuation of the entire community. Orsala sat on one side. Damien sat on the other. Irina bustled around, listening for instructions and then setting about tasks as Sari gave them.

"No." Damien gripped her hand. "You did nothing wrong. Mala is sure you were not tailed from Bergen. This is from some other crack in our defenses. It was… surprising. But we had become too complacent. It was probably inevitable after so much time. There have been so many who have used Sarihöfn as a refuge over the years. No magic is impenetrable. And with the Grigori becoming more aggressive, we should not be surprised."

Far from chaos, a quiet urgency lay over the house. There was no shouting or panic. The Grigori soldiers the guards had apprehended in the woods had been killed, but plans were underway to empty the haven. If there were two, there would be others. Listening to Sari give instructions to Mala and Astrid, Bruno and Karen, she realized that this had always been planned. As secure as Sarihöfn was, the Irin were a people constantly at war. No place was truly safe.

And Ava realized it would always be this way.

Even before the Rending, they had hidden. Hidden from the

humans. From the Fallen. The Irin lived as a people under siege. It was frightening. Exhausting. And this was her future.

No mate. No family. Constantly on the move. Half of her reasoned it wasn't all that different from how she'd lived before she knew she was Irina. The other half just wanted to run like she had in Bergen.

Run from Istanbul.

Run from Turkey.

Run from Sarihöfn.

Where would she run next?

Families were evacuated first; multiple backup plans were already in place. Irina with mates were calling them, finding places to meet. There were other havens around the world. Other havens could be formed in out-of-the-way places. Some Irina would go to them while others would scatter. For many, Sarihöfn had provided a place to train and grow. Now they could fight their own battles.

"What will they do about money?" Ava asked. "And the farm?"

"There are humans Sari trusts who will take care of the farm. And they have saved money for hundreds of years. They will give money to families and individuals as they need it. They have enough."

"I have money. More than I need. If any of them—"

"Keep your money, sister." Damien placed a hand on her shoulder. "They will be fine."

"They planned for this."

"Yes," he said, a note of sadness in his voice. "After the Rending, we knew no place would be safe forever."

Within hours, cars and trucks were already leaving the barn. People took only what they needed. Furniture would be left behind. Perhaps, at some point, it could be retrieved, but safety was more important than sentiment.

"We'll stay here a few days with Sari," Damien said. "We're still deciding where our family will go. Sari and I have different ideas about what should happen now."

"And me?"

"You're coming with us, of course." He smiled. "That we all agree on. You still have many lessons with Orsala. And you're part of our family."

Her throat tightened. "I'm not sure I'm a very safe person to be around right now."

"Good!" Sari's voice sounded from across the room. "Then my plan it is, Damien."

Damien shook his head. "*Milá…*"

"I know you want to go someplace safe and hidden, my love." A wild smile crossed Sari's face, and there was fire in her eyes. "But I cannot agree. I have taken care of my sisters. I have sheltered those who needed it. I have been peaceful too long. Give me an enemy to bloody my hands on."

"The Irina need—"

"We know what we need." Ava hadn't expected the soft-spoken Karen's voice to be so strong. "And that is not to have others dictate to us. Bruno and I can take care of those who need shelter. There is a house that belonged to my mother outside Prague. It has been empty for many years. Bruno and I will create a safe place and let you know when it is ready. I am not a warrior." She looked up at her mate. "And my Bruno knows this. But your mate is, Damien. And you know that."

"I will go with Karen and Bruno," Astrid said, looking at Ava. "And know that you can always come to my door if you need healing. Any of you."

Mala signed something to Sari.

"Mala will go with them, as well, at least for a time," Sari said. She looked around, frowning. "Has anyone been able to call Renata?"

Ava said, "Candace was trying to call her mobile. She's not at her apartment in Bergen. She might still be in Oslo. Candace and Brooke are going to the scribe house there with Chelsea. Her mate is stationed there."

Sari nodded, then she took a deep breath and closed her eyes. In that moment, Ava could see the years on her face, though it remained the smooth porcelain of youth. The kitchen was almost empty. Within hours, the evacuation would be complete.

"We always knew this place could not last forever," Sari said, reaching for her grandmother's hand. "Change has come. We are ready. Now let this quiet war end."

CHAPTER
SEVENTEEN

They debated flying to Oslo, but in the end decided that a plane would be too problematic. And traceable. Malachi, Leo, and Rhys decided to drive. Borrowing a new car from Gabriel, they left as soon as Rhys made it back to the house. The scholar was going in circles with his research into Ava's family background, so he decided to join them. Max hadn't given them much information. He didn't know Ava's exact location, only how to find her, and he claimed that Oslo was the starting point.

"Be prepared," he had warned. "There is something going on here. Something big. Grigori are swarming the city. The local scribe house has been inundated and has even called on neighboring houses to help. It's dangerous. Volund's soldiers are everywhere."

There was, of course, no talk of Grigori aggression in Vienna. Gabriel quietly took note of the information, then procured a car for the three scribes to borrow indefinitely. It might have been cramped in back, but it was enough for Leo to stretch out while Rhys took a turn during the eighteen-hour drive.

The modern highway sped past as Malachi watched out the window, alternately disturbed and comforted by how familiar and yet foreign the drive turned out to be.

"I've driven this route before," he said to Rhys. "Many times, I think."

"Probably." Rhys reached for the cup of coffee he'd been nursing. "You were in Berlin for a long time. I imagine you drove this way when you went to Vienna."

He frowned. "Would I have gone to Vienna much?"

"You were second to the Watcher in Berlin. I imagine you spent plenty of time there."

Malachi shifted uncomfortably. "Konrad called me something when we met with him."

"What?" The corner of Rhys's mouth lifted. "The 'Butcher' thing?"

"Yes."

The other scribe chuckled. "You loved that nickname. Cultivated it, once upon a time."

"Why?"

"Because fear is as potent a weapon as fists or knives," Rhys said. "Think of how many Grigori avoided Berlin knowing that a scribe known as 'The Butcher' was there."

"So they simply went someplace else. What made Berlin more important than any other city?"

"It's not more important or less, Malachi. But… we all have places that are significant."

"And my parents died in Berlin." He remembered what Konrad had said.

"Yes, they did," Rhys said. "And when you returned to the city, you painted the walls red with Grigori blood."

"It sounds like I was very angry."

"You were. For hundreds of years, you were angry. Until you met Ava, I think."

Ava. His heart ached with unknown longing. He hungered for something but couldn't remember the taste.

"We all grieve in different ways," Rhys said quietly.

Malachi tried to control his frustration. His past was a giant empty wound that would occasionally offer up a bubble of insight. But for the most part, there was nothing. Flashes of knowledge. An image. A scent memory. Most of what his mind offered him came from his childhood. His training. There were occasional flashes of Ava, but nothing concrete.

"You weren't getting anywhere with the research into her family?" he asked Rhys.

"I've run into a brick wall. Her mother's family is transparent. Grandparents. Great-grandparents. Ava told me once that her mother's family didn't talk much about their history, but it was relatively easy to find. French and German, mostly. Midwestern immigrants who came in the middle of the 1800s. Nothing about them stands out as having any supernatural origins. It's her father who is the problem."

"So it must be there."

Rhys opened his mouth. Closed it. Finally, he said, "It goes against everything we know about Irin biology, but yes, it must be on her father's side."

"So her grandmother must have been Irina?"

"She must have been. And for Ava to be as powerful as she is, her blood must have been potent. Old. To not be diluted in the third generation, her grandmother must have been extraordinary."

"But we know nothing about her."

Rhys shook his head. "Her father is a musical genius, obviously, so the angelic blood shows there. But he had a normal—well, normal for him—relationship with Ava's mother, so he's not an Irin male. Not like we are."

"Does he have any other children beside Ava?"

"Not that we know of."

"Curious."

"Or just careful," Rhys said. "He doesn't seem like the fatherly type."

"No." Though from what Malachi had learned of Ava's father, perhaps his absence had been a blessing in disguise.

"So, Ava's magic must come from her paternal grandmother, whom we have no records for except a single note on her father's file that his mother was also named Ava."

Malachi said, "Leo and I think that Reed hid her records. As an adult, we think he paid to have them disappear."

"Why?"

"Why do we think so?" he asked. "Or why would he hide them at all?"

"Both."

"He named his only daughter the same name as his mother. Do you think that is a coincidence?"

Rhys took the turnoff, concentrating on passing a large truck and ignoring Malachi's comment. "I hadn't considered that," he said after traffic had cleared. "You're right, a coincidence like that is highly unlikely."

"So Jasper Reed knew his biological mother's name. And he had money before Ava was born. He'd already made several records at that time. He would have had the money to make her records disappear if he wanted to and knew the right people."

"And from what I've heard, there is more than one person in his employ who has a questionable relationship with the law."

Malachi said, "So he knew his mother's name and she has disappeared from the public record. It's not hard to make the connection that it was deliberate."

"So the other 'why' remains? Why would he hide it? I've read interviews with him. He's very open about being raised in the foster system. Even seems proud of it, in his own way."

"Maybe she was a criminal."

"She blackmailed him?" Rhys offered. "And he didn't want anyone to know?"

"Is she even still alive?"

"The secrecy doesn't seem consistent with his public persona."

Rhys nodded. "He's very well-known. Most of his adult life has been lived in the public eye, and he's notoriously unstable. He's been arrested. Publicly intoxicated. Repeated stints in rehabilitation clinics for drugs and alcohol. He doesn't seem to hide anything."

"Except..." Malachi's voice dropped when he realized what Rhys had missed. "Except Ava."

"What?"

"Ava. He hides Ava. Have you ever heard of him having a daughter?"

Rhys thought for a moment. "No. He doesn't speak about her in interviews."

Malachi grudgingly acknowledged, "He seems to be very protective of her, as far as keeping her out of the spotlight. And from what you've said, it was his money and his influence with Ava's mother that kept her independent."

"Ava said her father was adamant that nothing was wrong with her mentally. Even..." The car slowed as Rhys's thoughts drifted. He was blasted to awareness by an angry honk behind them. "Blast."

"Do you want me to drive?"

"No. I'm not tired. I was just thinking of something Ava told me once."

"What?"

"Her father set up an independent trust fund for her to access when she was twenty-two. Her. Only her. Her mother had no access, though she had other child support while Ava was growing up. But it was the trust fund that made Ava independent. She even owns a house in Los Angeles that Reed bought her in the hills near Malibu. Very private. She never stays there, but he bought it for her."

"So—"

"Reed knew her as a child. She thought he was only a family friend, but she *knew* him. Quite well. And Ava said he was one of the few people who never treated her any differently, even when she had massive anxiety and mood swings. Even when the doctors were telling her mother to commit her. At her worst—which sounded like puberty—Reed was one of the few adults in her life that Ava said she didn't have to guard herself around."

The light began to dawn. "You think he knew she heard voices? Did she tell him?"

"No. But if his mother was Irina, maybe he did know, Malachi. Maybe in some way, he knew his mother was different. Knew his daughter was different in the same way."

"He named his daughter after his mother, then hid both of them from the world."

Rhys nodded. "We know what he was hiding with Ava. Or maybe what he thought he was hiding."

"Maybe he hid his mother for the same reasons."

· · ·　· · ·

It was close to midnight when the three finally arrived in Oslo. They hadn't warned the scribe house there that three traveling scribes were coming. Rhys knew Lang, the Watcher of the house, and was certain they would be welcomed. Max said he would contact them the next night with more information.

They knocked on the door, knowing someone would answer even at midnight. Lights were on all over the house, and he could hear voices, even past the formidable old door. The cold wind whipped down the vacant street, and the air was bitter with snow. Malachi drew his jacket closer around him.

Rhys knocked on the door again, louder, and Malachi finally heard footsteps. The door was yanked open by a harried-looking man with shaggy blond hair and hard blue eyes. He frowned for a moment until his gaze settled on Rhys.

"Rhys," he said, a smile cracking the hard planes of his face. "Thank heaven. I didn't know if London would send anyone. Then… I didn't know whether I should cancel the order for help. To see a trustworthy face is more than I could have asked."

"Lang," Rhys started, "what are you—"

"Your friends"—the sharp eyes grew cold again—"can I trust them?"

"Of course. These are my brothers from the Istanbul house. We've just come from—"

"Istanbul?" Lang stepped toward them, and Malachi realized how tall the scribe was. Standing next to him, Malachi almost felt like a boy. Lang had to have been at least six and a half feet, and though his build was lean, he was hard-muscled and quick. His eyes narrowed on Rhys. "That's right… you're not in London. Not anymore. You've been in Istanbul for years now."

"You know this, Lang. I didn't call before because—"

"What are you doing here?" The watcher crossed his arms, and Malachi could see a hint of old *talesm* at his wrists. All friendly welcome had dropped from the scribe's face, and he reached back to bang his hand on the door in three sharp, rhythmic raps. Within seconds, two more scribes were there, one even paler than Lang, the other with skin dark as the night around them. They stood, two ominous counterpoints, behind Lang's suddenly hostile stance.

"Lang?" Rhys's normally pale face went even paler. "What is this?"

"I received no word that scribes from Istanbul would be coming to my city. What is the meaning of your presence here?"

Malachi tried to keep his voice low. "Has the hospitality of Oslo house fallen so far that three Irin brothers are not even given welcome on a freezing night?"

Lang's attention shifted to Malachi. "The night may be frozen but my mind is not. You come here for some purpose. I can read it in the Englishman's face. Who sent you?"

"No one sent us."

"Really? Then state your purpose. Or leave."

"Really, Lang!" Rhys was indignant. "What kind of nonsense—"

"Perhaps before we state our purpose," Malachi said, "you should tell us why you called for help from London."

"That's none of your concern. If you will not state your business, leave now."

He turned and the two scribes behind him stepped forward. Both would be formidable adversaries. Malachi's palms itched for his knives.

"We're looking for my cousin." Leo, who had been silent during the whole exchange, stepped out of the shadow. Lang turned toward his voice. "You know him. Everyone knows Maxim."

Lang blinked in surprise, then said, "If you hadn't said cousin, I would have thought twin. Yes, I know Max."

"He called us. Told us to come to Oslo. We are searching for some-one. A woman."

Lang's eyes narrowed. "What would a woman be doing in a scribe house?"

Far from allaying suspicion, the three Oslo scribes became even more hostile.

"We don't know," Leo said. "Max told us to come here, so we did."

Rhys said, "Lang, our house in Istanbul was attacked. Our watcher left with an Irina who had taken shelter with us."

Lang's eyes narrowed. "There was an Irina in your house? In *Turkey*?"

"An Irina who Volund's Grigori were targeting. It's a complicated story, but we have been looking for them. Max called and told us to come here. I don't know why, but—"

A flurry of Norwegian broke out between the three scribes. Malachi could follow only parts of it, but one word stood out.

"*Sarihöfn*," Malachi said. "What does Sarihöfn mean?"

The argument stopped, and Lang's eyes swung toward him. "Who was the watcher who took the woman?"

Rhys said, "Who is the watcher of Istanbul? The same scribe for the last two hundred years, Lang! Damien, of course."

"Sarihöfn… Sari's haven? Is that what you're talking about?" Malachi asked, slowly stepping toward Lang. "Do you know where she is?"

"I don't know what business you have with Sari, but—"

"For heaven's sake, Lang!" Rhys broke in. "You know Damien.

Think! You know I've been serving under him. I am looking for my watcher, and I don't understand why the hell you're being so…"

It was a little sound that stopped him. Such a little sound, Malachi thought, to stop six grown men from almost coming to blows. A delicate sound, drifting from the warmth of the open door.

A child's laughter.

A *girl* child's laughter.

Lang barked out, "Close the door!"

But before he did, Rhys and Leo had both stepped forward.

"Who are you guarding, Lang?" Rhys asked. "What is going on here?"

"Can I trust you?" he asked Rhys.

"I can't believe you're even asking that."

"Yes," Malachi said. "You can trust us. All of us. We're looking for Damien. I need to find him."

"Why? I don't even know your name, scribe."

Malachi took a deep breath and fought the roar of anger that burned in his chest. "My name is Malachi of Sakarya. I am a bound scribe of Istanbul. And I am looking for Damien, because he is guarding my mate."

"Your *mate*?"

Rhys said, "They met in Istanbul. Were mated there. Volund's Grigori overran the city, and Damien took Malachi's woman to Sari to keep her safe. But we need to find her. We need to find them both. That is the only reason we are here."

Leo said, "Though I'd like to know who exactly you're guarding behind those doors, Lang. That was no scribe's laughter."

"It is none of your concern."

Rhys asked, "What do you know of Sarihöfn?"

"What is Sarihöfn?" Lang asked with a blank look on his face.

Malachi forced himself not to assault the scribe. "Why do you refuse to help us? What are you afraid of?"

The dark scribe who guarded the door stepped forward, putting a hand on Lang's shoulder before he could lunge at Malachi. He was just as tall as Lang, but with an even broader build. "My name is Jeremiah," he said, his accent marking him as American. "You must forgive our caution, but we do have reason. Lang—all of us—received a shock a few days ago when my mate returned from Sari's haven, saying it had been compromised. We don't know more than that."

"Sari's home has been compromised?" Leo asked. "When? How?"

"The Irina are here?" Malachi asked, his heart racing.

"Only a few," Jeremiah held up a hand. "My mate, along with a widowed Irina and her child. They are only passing through the city."

"We don't know the details," Lang said. "We've known Sari's haven was somewhere in the Nordfjord region for centuries. Jeremiah and one other scribe had mates who sheltered there while they worked in the city."

"You've been there?" Rhys asked Jeremiah.

"No. Chelsea and I met in other locations when we could. Away from the city and the haven. It was the safest way for her and the others."

Lang said, "None of us—not even me—knew the location. The younger scribes didn't even know it existed."

"Vienna had no idea?" Leo asked cautiously.

"No," Jeremiah said. "The havens are secret for a reason. They are the last places the Irina feel safe."

"Vienna didn't need to know," Lang said. "The council would have the remaining Irina forced back into retreats and breeding like livestock. I would guard Sari's location with my life, were it necessary. Any of the havens."

"We have no quarrel with you," Leo said. "I only ask because we are avoiding the council's attention, as well."

Jeremiah and Lang exchanged looks, and Malachi felt some of the tension lessen between them.

Lang said, "We have had no word from Istanbul. Your house burned in a Grigori attack?"

"We have had little news of any kind from Vienna," Jeremiah said. "When did this happen?"

"Months ago," Rhys said. "We know it was reported to the council, but someone is keeping it quiet."

Leo stepped forward and said, "Please, brother, does the fire still burn in this house?"

The ancient plea for hospitality must have moved the watcher and his scribes. Or perhaps they were as cold as Malachi. Lang exchanged a look with both the men at his side, but especially Jeremiah, who gave a small nod.

"Yes," he finally said. "The fire still burns for our brothers. You may shelter here."

Malachi and Rhys responded at once. "We offer our strength to defend this house."

"Your offer is accepted."

Lang opened the door and let them in.

*   *   *   *   *   *

"I don't know what to think," Lang said, his shoulders slumping a little as the four scribes warmed themselves by a large fire in the front room. Jeremiah and the other scribe, who introduced himself as Ari, had retreated to the back of the house.

"Why did you call for help from London?"

"The Grigori have been swarming the city. In the last week, we've had a rush of attacks. I have six scribes here at the house, and they've all been patrolling every night, yet we're still losing human women to the attacks. Then a few nights ago, Jeremiah's mate, Chelsea, arrived with the other Irina, so I've kept Jeremiah and Ari here at the house guarding them while the others are out trying to cover even more territory. We're overwhelmed."

"So you called to London?" Rhys asked. "Stockholm would be the closest house, wouldn't it?"

"We normally have a good relationship with Stockholm house, but for some reason, they haven't returned my e-mails or calls as they normally would. Something is going on, but I don't have anyone to send to them."

"So you called London. They said they were sending help?"

Lang nodded. "Then, when Chelsea showed up, I almost considered calling them back and canceling, but I know the Watcher in London. We've… discussed some of the council debates in Vienna, and we're of the same mind. I thought I could trust him. I hope I can, especially with Irina here now. Forgive me, Rhys. I didn't want to be suspicious, but you have to understand how—"

"Please." Rhys raised a hand. "Your brother's mate brought others here for safety, including a child. Extra caution is understandable."

"There is no need to apologize," Leo added.

Malachi asked, "Did Chelsea say what was happening with the other Irina who'd been at Sarihöfn? Did she know where any were going?"

"She didn't. I'm sure the less each knew about the others' actions, the safer they all were. She did say Sari was staying back with her mate and a few others to secure the compound before they moved."

Leo turned to Malachi. "I'm sure Ava would stay with them. Damien wouldn't let her leave without him."

"Ava? Is that your mate's name?" Lang asked. There was a frown on his face.

"Yes, that is my mate's name. Why?"

Lang was still frowning. "That name seems familiar."

Rhys, Leo, and Malachi exchanged looks.

"Jeremiah?" Lang called.

They heard footsteps, then Jeremiah's head popped around the corner. "Yes?"

"The American Irina. The one Brooke and Candice were talking about. What was her name?"

"Um… Ana? No, Ava. It was Ava." Jeremiah's eyes swung to Malachi. "Is she your mate? No, she can't be."

Lang asked, "Why not? How many Irina named Ava would be at Sarihöfn? It has to be her."

"No…" Jeremiah stepped into the room, suspicion clear on his face. "Brooke said that Ava was widowed. That she was grieving her mate."

Lang sprang to his feet and Rhys stood to meet him, holding up his hands.

"There was a mistake. He's not lying. Malachi *is* her mate, but he's not dead. It's… hard to explain."

"Try," Jeremiah said. "Because if he is truly her mate then she would know beyond a shadow of a doubt if he was living or dead. That is not something any Irin could confuse."

Rhys looked at Malachi, then at Leo. Both of them nodded. "You have trusted us. Taken us into your home, even as you shelter your own Irina here. We give you our trust, in kind."

Malachi rose, pulling up his sleeves to reveal his arms. He'd added to his *talesm* in Vienna, but they still only reached to the bicep on his left arm. A shadow of his old *talesm* could be seen on his right arm if he looked closely, but they were barely visible. Lang and Jeremiah halted, their aggression fading at the unexpected sight.

"I… I don't understand," Lang said. "How old are you?"

"That," Rhys said, "is a somewhat complicated question."

Malachi spoke, keeping his voice low. "I am over four hundred years old. This body, however, is… somewhat newer."

Silence. Neither Lang nor Jeremiah were able to say a word.

Leo said, "We don't know how it happened. He was killed. Max and Damien saw it with their own eyes. Ava did, as well. We saw her grief, and it was horrible. He was dead. But then… he came back. We don't know how."

"I heard her voice," Malachi said to the stunned scribes. "It said, 'Come back to me.' And for some time, that was all I knew. My memories are coming back, but slowly. I dream walk with Ava, but—"

"She doesn't know," Lang said, his voice rough. "She would think they are only dreams, like we all experience after we lose a mate."

"I didn't even realize what was happening until we spoke to Gabriel."

"Because I'm an idiot," Leo said. "Sorry."

"So, she is with Damien and Sari," Jeremiah said. "If this Ava is the one who the girl speaks of, she stayed with Damien and Sari. As a sister. Brooke said she had no other people. She was alone."

"She grieves for you," Lang said, his voice still hoarse. "And you are alive. Heaven above, we have to help you find her."

"Max called us," Leo said. "He said to come here. He must know where she is."

Jeremiah shook his head. "The location of Sarihöfn is guarded by very powerful magic. I do not know how he could have discovered it."

"But you said it had been compromised," Malachi said, pulling down his sleeves. It was still freezing cold in the room. "Perhaps he knows where they've gone now."

Lang nodded. "It's possible. Max knows all sorts of interesting types. He's not the most conventional in his company." He glanced at Leo. "No offense."

"None taken," Leo said. "My cousin claims to have gambled with the Fallen themselves. I'm hardly shocked by anything at this point."

"Still," Jeremiah said, "if he's in the city, he's keeping a low profile."

"Is he keeping a low profile, or has he just not left his flat?" Jeremiah asked. "With Sarihöfn compromised, you know Renata is probably here."

"Renata?" Leo asked. "Who is Renata?"

Lang smirked. "That, I'll leave for your cousin to answer. Come."

He waved them toward the door. "Now that you're here, we'll feed you, then I'll map out a section of the city for you to patrol tonight. You may have a mate to find, but until you do, you're working for me. Oslo is a city under siege at the moment. We need as many hands as possible." He looked over his shoulder at Malachi. "Even if they're attached to bare arms."

CHAPTER

EIGHTEEN

Ava stared out the window into the snow that fell over Bergen. She tried to ignore the tension in the small flat, tried to focus on the book of the Old Language that Orsala had given her before she went to the market, but she couldn't.

Damien and Sari were fighting again.

"It's not a good plan. We would be too exposed in Oslo, and Vienna is out of the question."

"I'm not going to hide like a little girl, Damien. You're the one who said change had to come. I'm only agreeing with you!"

Damien clenched his teeth. "Yes, change needs to come, but right now—"

"I don't need to be protected."

"But Ava does."

"Whoa!" Ava held up her hands and spoke up. "Do not pull me into this argument. This is between you two."

"Exactly," Sari agreed. "And I think we head to Oslo first, before we make our way to Vienna."

"What exactly do you think you're accomplishing, exposing yourself this way?" Damien shouted.

"Who is debating now?" Sari said. "Old men? Those who know nothing of the reality around us? I have been hiding for two hundred years and I know more about what's going on in the world than some of them do."

"The council will not understand. They'll try to take you away from me. Try to punish me for abandoning my house. If we're exposed now, *milá*—" His voice broke. "I could not bear it, Sari. Not now. Not when we've finally…"

Sari went into his arms, and Ava turned her head away. She could still hear them.

"They have nothing to condemn you. Your house burned. You reported it. You took shelter at a scribe house. You went to your mate, but you did not abandon your duties. Evren will confirm this, and you know how he is respected."

"He's a scholar, not a politician."

"Gabriel will vouch for you, as well."

"He hates me, Sari." Guilt layered his voice. "As he should."

Sari's voice was muffled, as if she was speaking against Damien's skin. Ava glanced over her shoulder. They were embracing, despite their angry words.

"You told me yourself, Tala insisted on going into that fight. I know my sister. Gabriel knew her, too. He knows this. He may be angry with you, as I was, but he knows his mate would not be held back from battle, whether she was carrying a child or not."

"He lost so much more than we did, Sari. I have never blamed him for his hatred."

"Even if he does hate you, he is pragmatic. My presence in Vienna will only bolster the voices on the council who call for the Irina to return."

They drifted into a quieter argument, and Ava turned back to the book, still trying to concentrate. It was only three in the afternoon, but the sun was already fading. Soon it would be dark. She longed for sleep. Her dreams had been even more vivid in the last nights. Her memories of Malachi gave him life, even if it was only in her own mind. She knew it wasn't healthy. Knew she was only holding on to an illusion. But for those few precious hours, she wasn't alone. She'd take them. She'd take anything that let her feel his presence.

She hadn't seen Jaron again, but the dream of him was far more vivid than any other she'd had. She'd awoken from it feeling perfectly alert. She remembered every word.

"He finds you because he can. Just as I can."

Who was Jaron talking about? Volund? There was no way of knowing who the Grigori who had found Sarihöfn belonged to because they'd been killed immediately. But Volund was the most powerful Fallen angel in the region, so it seemed logical. But why could Jaron and Volund both find her so easily? According to Orsala, the Fallen had never seen past the spells Sari had worked on the land to shield Sarihöfn. What had caused them to fail?

"I do not know his purpose. Only that he would thwart mine."

"And what is your purpose?"

"That is not for you to know yet. I gave you my vision once. I will give you others when you need them."

Why would Jaron give her visions? Despite who he was and how he had lied to her, Ava couldn't help but sense the Fallen angel did not mean her harm. If he had, he'd had too many opportunities to hurt her and nothing had happened. What did his visions mean? And why could she show them to the other Irina through her song?

"Ava?"

She heard Sari's voice but didn't turn from staring out the window. "What's up?"

"We've decided to stay here for a few more nights. I know it's crowded in Renata's flat, but—"

"It's fine." She closed the book and turned. "I'm fine. Have we decided what to do after that?"

Damien had disappeared to who-knows-where, but Sari sat next to her.

"He's still voting for the scribe house in Cappadocia."

"It is very isolated. I felt very safe there."

"And I'm sure they would welcome us. They're very old-fashioned, and Orsala would be highly regarded."

"But you don't want to go there?"

Sari shook her head. "No."

"Why?"

"I'm tired of hiding. This struggle between Irin and Irina, it has to end. I can see that now. Just like my anger with Damien, we have let it fester until we are dying from the inside. If we continue like this, sunk in bitterness, anger, and willful misunderstanding, then the Grigori don't have to kill us. We'll die anyway."

"What do you want to do?"

"I want to go to Oslo and see some friends. Contact a few allies. Then I want the Irina to return to Vienna."

Ava's eyebrows rose. "I don't see you as much of a politician."

She smiled. "I'm not. But my grandmother once sat on the council. And our elders' seats have been empty too long. We are the ones who stepped away. For us to come back, we must be the ones to return. Then we will no longer be silent."

"The other Irina—the others in hiding—they may not agree with you."

"Then I will find them and convince them. If I can convince my stubborn mate," Sari said, "I can convince anyone."

"What about me?"

"You need to go to Vienna, too. It's time to show yourself to the Irin world."

Ava's heart began to race. "I... I don't think that's a very good—"

"He was right, you know?" Sari nodded. "Malachi. You are a miracle. It was a miracle that you survived in the human world as long as you did. It was a miracle you found Malachi and Damien in Istanbul."

"They kind of found me."

"And if they found you, they can find others. Don't you think there are others out there, Ava? Sisters lost in the human world? I don't know how, but I do think they're out there. We have to find them. Show them who they really are."

"I have a feeling that not everyone is going to like that idea."

Sari gave her a rueful smile. "Then it's a good thing I've never cared much about being liked."

* * *   * * *

"WHERE ARE YOU?" HIS VOICE WAS URGENT, EVEN AS HE BRACED HIMSELF over her, covering her body with his as they lay under the forest canopy.

"Right here," she breathed out.

Her heart raced. She held on to him, pulling him down until the broad planes of his chest pressed against her. Her lips tasted the skin of his neck. Her teeth caught his ear.

"Where... where are you, Ava?" He almost sounded like he was in pain. "I need to know."

She frowned, confused, then pushed him back so that she straddled his hips. "I'm here. With you." Leaning down, she pressed a kiss over his heart. "Always with you."

"I came back to you, Ava."

She felt a phantom pain shoot through her chest. "I know."

"Truly." He pulled her down, capturing her lips with his own, their breath mingling in the cold night air. It misted around them, though she didn't feel the cold. The fog was only a blanket, concealing them from the shadows of the forest. "I came back to you. And I must find you. You need me."

"So much." The tears stung her eyes and she tried to focus on his presence. The energy she felt between them. It was everything—everything—she needed. She only had it here. Fleeting. She knew it wouldn't last. She closed her eyes, desperate to hold on to the comfort of his touch.

He kissed her again, gripping the back of her hair with one strong hand. A sharp pain shot through her.

Pain?

He pulled his lips away. "I need to know where you are, Ava. You need me to find you."

The pain distracted her from the pleasure of his kiss. "I don't understand."

"Where are you?"

For a moment, the voice came from outside. From another place that chilled her. An echo of his voice, then another, layered on top of it. She stilled, pulling away from him.

"What is this?"

"Dream..." He clenched his eyes shut, shaking his head. "It's a dream... but not a dream. It's... it's more, Ava. I can't... I don't know how to tell you."

For the first time since he'd found her, dread touched her heart. "No."

"Don't pull away." He reached for her, but she was already across the meadow. "Ava!"

Fear and confusion filled the space between.

"I don't understand." Tears slid down her cheeks. Hot. Painful. Cold wind bit her ankles.

"I'm trying to come back to you!"

"Why am I afraid?"

"Because *I* am! I need to find you, Ava."

She blinked as the memory came crashing down. His face, dissolving into gold dust. She looked down, and muddy water swirled around her feet.

"You left me," she whispered into the darkness. "And you can't come back."

"No," he said, running toward her. But no matter how fast he ran, he could not come any closer. "I came back! You brought me back, Ava!"

She shook her head, pulling the darkness around her like a cloak. "No."

His eyes turned desperate. "Ava, come to me."

"You're gone."

"You must come to me."

She sank to her knees on the cold ground. "It hurts now."

"Please!"

"It hurts."

A hedge sprang up between them, circling her, guarding her. Keeping him away.

"Ava, no!"

The pain that had pierced her heart faded, and his panicked voice grew dim. Faint whispers came from the trees.

"Safe."

"Careful."

"Safe, safe, safe."

"Shhhhhh."

She closed her eyes and sat on the cold ground, pressing her forehead to her knees and ignoring the small hands that tugged at her shoulders.

"Go back," the small voices said. "You need to go back."

No. It wasn't safe. Something… something was different. And wrong. Something had hurt her outside the hedge.

"We need you to find your way back."

• • • • • •

WHEN AVA OPENED HER EYES, IT WAS DARK. SHE CURLED TO HER SIDE and tried to stem the flood of silent tears that washed down her face. For the first time in weeks, there had been no comfort in dreams.

"Not real," she whispered. "They aren't real."

Malachi died again in her heart.

Ava let the darkness take her. She closed her eyes, and she did not dream.

THE NEXT DAY, SHE WALKED THROUGH THE FLAT LIKE A ZOMBIE. SARI and Damien were gone. Orsala was in the apartment with her, but the old woman was studying a book and paid her no attention. She sat near the window, scrolling through the news on Renata's computer. She recognized a familiar name that brought the hint of a smile to her lips.

"Huh."

"What is huh?" Orsala asked.

"My dad. He just started a European tour for the New Year. Might try to see him if it works out."

"Hmm." She was distracted, flipping through the pages of the book with a frown on her face. "You'll have to speak to Damien and Sari. See if one of them can go with you to meet him."

The thought of having to ask permission to see her own father grated on her nerves. "If I want to see Jasper, I'll see him."

Orsala's only answer was a raised eyebrow.

The more Ava thought, the more it seemed like a great idea. Jasper might have been a mess, but he did have lots of security. In fact, she liked his security a lot better than most of the nameless bodyguards her stepfather had hired over the years. Jasper's guards were big and mean-looking, but they usually had a sense of humor. They'd have to, to work with her father. So what if they were mostly for show? It wasn't as if Grigori were going to break into a suite at the Four Seasons and kidnap her. No one got kidnapped at a Four Seasons.

She sighed and contemplated calling her mother. She'd have to if she wanted Jasper's number. Her phone had been left in Cappadocia, and she didn't know anyone's number from memory except for her mom's. If she wanted to see Jasper, she had to call ahead. Most of his people didn't know that Ava existed. Only his manager and head of security knew her by name.

She had time. Looking at Jasper's website, it seemed like he'd be in Europe through the beginning of summer. Then she noticed movement out the window. It was Sari and Damien, arguing again.

"Cranky and Crankier headed back," she told Orsala. "Estimated time of arrival, four minutes, unless they start arguing on the stairs."

Orsala sighed. "They were always like this. For the life of me, I do not understand why."

"They like it."

"You're not wrong."

A few minutes later, Damien walked through the door with no Sari in sight. But the color was high on his cheeks and his lower lip looked distinctly… bitten.

He cleared his throat. "Sari went to call Renata. She finally got a message from her."

"Oslo?"

He nodded and hung up his scarf on the back of the door. "I think so. Yes."

Ava checked her work e-mail for the first time in weeks. Mostly junk, but there were thirty messages from her usual clients. A dozen or so from magazines she'd worked with occasionally. And another from an online publication she'd been considering approaching on her own. She liked their subscription numbers, and one of their regular photographers had won several prestigious awards last year. Things were moving online, and she didn't want to be left behind.

A few months ago, she'd considered leaving her human job behind and following Malachi around the world. She didn't know what they would do, but they'd be together. That dream was over. She'd have to find another. And with the knowledge she'd been learning from Orsala, the skills she'd learned from Mala, with a little preparation and a lot of caution, Ava thought she could probably have her old life back. At least a little bit. After all, what else was she going to do? Hunt the Grigori who had killed her mate? The attack in Bergen had shown her the foolishness of that. Join some war she didn't understand for a race of people she barely belonged to? She had no ties here. No family.

She'd been living in a dream world in more ways than one. That wasn't real life.

She needed her cameras, her computers, and an assignment that took her far, far away. Maybe going back to Antarctica was an option. The Galapagos. The Brazilian rain forest was probably Grigori-free.

And if it wasn't, oh well.

"Damien," she asked, "where are my cameras?"

"In Cappadocia, I believe. Didn't you bring a small one with you?"

"I need my full-sized—never mind," she muttered. "I'll just buy new gear in Oslo."

Maybe instead of taking one of the assignments the magazines were offering, she'd tag along with her dad on his tour. Take pictures of the rock music world for a while. He'd offered during his last tour of Asia, but their relationship had been too new. Too raw. It was still awkward to think of him as her father. But a few years had passed. They talked regularly… well, if every six months or so with the occasional e-mail between was regular.

He said he wanted to know her more. This might be the perfect opportunity.

Damien sat down beside her. "You seem…"

"What?"

"Distant. Did anything happen?"

I woke up from a dream. I realized the love of my life is really gone. I gave up pretending I was anything special.

"Nothing much. Just checking mail. I need to call my dad."

"You talked to your mother last week, didn't you?"

"She informs on me, but I should call him directly. He's in London right now."

"Hmm." He was eyeing her with suspicion, but Ava ignored him. She ignored the pang of guilt. Damien would probably go batshit insane if she talked to him about following her dad on tour. But he wasn't her boss. Sure, they said she was family, but she wasn't. Not really. They had a political war to fight that didn't include her. She didn't even want to get involved. There were other girls like her out there? Fine. She'd survived. They would, too.

"I know you've been cooped up in here. Do you want to go out for a walk?"

And scope out Grigori soldiers for you, so you and Sari could kill them? Make myself even more of a target?

"No thanks. I'm fine."

He was on to her, but Ava didn't care. She was just… done. She could rebuild the wall Malachi had pulled down. She'd have to. Then she'd move on with her life. And if the Grigori caught up with her?

She didn't really care anymore.

There were pounding footsteps on the stairs. The door burst open, and Sari rushed in. She stared at Ava, then her eyes darted to Damien. Then back to Ava.

"What's the deal?" Ava was trying not to feel freaked out, but something was obviously wrong.

Sari blinked and closed the door behind her. "We need to get to Oslo."

Damien frowned. "Why?"

"I'll explain more in the car. But… we need to go."

"Now?" Orsala asked. "The sun is almost down. It's a six-hour drive. We'll go in the morning."

Damien was more cautious. "What is happening in Oslo?"

Sari glanced at Ava again, but Ava looked back to the computer. She'd follow along to Oslo, there was a large airport there. After that, she'd catch a plane to London and make her way from there. She was done with the Irin fantasy world. She needed to get back to her own.

"Some of the Istanbul scribes arrived at the Oslo house. There is… news you need to hear."

Her heart twisted a little. Part of her would have liked to see Rhys, Leo, and Max again. But even the thought was too painful. They looked at her and saw Malachi's mate. She looked at them and saw his brothers. It was too much.

Too much.

She was done.

"Pack up," Sari said. "I promise I'll tell you more in the car. I'm… not sure of everything that is happening. Renata is meeting with them tonight. We'll talk to her after we get there. She'll know more. Ava, are you ready to go?"

She closed the computer and shrugged. "I don't have much stuff. I'll throw it in a bag and we can disappear."

Damien shot her another suspicious look, but she ignored it and started packing.

Oslo. She'd get to Oslo. And then she'd be gone.

V.

Göteborg, Sweden

"Oslo," Volund said, stroking the neck of the woman who lay naked across his lap. "The woman is in Oslo."

"What woman?" the human asked, blinking sleepy eyes.

"Shut up." Volund looked up at Brage. "She was spotted in Bergen by one of your brothers. Pure coincidence. Jaron had been concealing her there in one of the Irina communities."

"The Irina?"

"The compound has been found. It's empty now. They killed the soldiers I sent, but the Irin left anyway. They're not unintelligent."

"How do you know they're in Oslo?"

The sound of the woman gasping was the only clue that Volund was angry. His grip had tightened on her throat and she kicked and flailed while Brage stood in silence, considering his mistake. He'd had too many questions swirling in his mind, and he'd made a foolish error. Volund wouldn't send him there unless he was certain.

"Forgive me, Father."

The angel released the hold on the woman's neck, but she only lay there with tears running down her face. Volund tossed her to the side and stood, growing as he stepped closer to his child and his human mask fell away.

"Find the woman."

"Yes, Father." Brage fought to control his physical response as the angel towered over him and the woman whimpered on the couch.

"Find her and kill the scribe. They are stronger together. But do not harm the woman. She is mine."

Brage trembled before the Fallen.

"Yes, Father."

"Do you have any messages for me?"

A trickle of urine ran down his leg as he remembered Svarog's message.

"A message from Svarog, Father."

"Yes?"

"His words were 'I know what he is doing, and I want no part of it. If he thinks I will roll over as Jaron did in Istanbul, he is mistaken.'"

Brage stood motionless before Volund, bracing for a reaction, though he could not predict what it would be. There was only the whimpering of the woman, the stink of his own urine, and the white tile that covered the floor as he kept his eyes trained down.

Finally, Volund threw his head back and laughed.

"Svarog...," he muttered, stepping away from Brage and sinking back into his human facade.

Volund lifted the woman on the couch and passed a hand over her neck, healing the red marks before he gave her a smile and kissed her on the lips. His fingers brushed away the tears on her cheeks and he cupped her flushed cheek in his palm. "Look at you," he said. "What a pretty one."

Brage said nothing, waiting for his Father's leave to speak. Volund never gave it, but he spoke to Brage over his shoulder.

"Go to the house in Oslo. I've already sent some of your brothers there. Kill the scribe. Capture the woman and bring her to me. No harm must come to her. Do not fail me this time."

"Yes, Father."

"Feed from one of the women in the house before you go."

"I will."

"And tell someone to clean up your piss. It stinks."

Brage pinned the woman down with his body as she moaned in pleasure, keeping as much skin contact as possible between them. It was heady, the rush of energy that flowed from her limbs and into him. He drew from her as he thrust in and out. She gasped and moaned in pleasure, but he could feel her weakening under him. He needed more.

He needed everything.

He captured her lips, breathing in the rush of her soul's life. It was the only magic he owned, this terrible hunger. The woman's soul fed him, filled the hollow in his chest. He could almost picture it. A great black hole that lived where his heart should be.

Hungry. It was so hungry.

He came in a rush after the woman peaked, giving up her climax to the greed of his body. It was the final ecstasy for her, and the closest that Brage would ever feel to satisfaction in anything. For the seconds it lasted, he felt alive.

The woman was unconscious when Brage pulled out of her. He lay back on the bed and pulled her body over his, spreading her arms across his chest to maintain contact.

She would die. But then, she would have died anyway. Humans were fragile. One this beautiful should have been a delicacy to be savored. But he'd been hungry. He hadn't fed since Budapest, and the visit with his father had drained him.

A soft sigh escaped her lips as he felt the last of her energy soak into him.

For a moment, he recalled the woman and the scribe. Remembered how he'd seen them in Istanbul, embracing. He'd held her against his body and, instead of fainting, she'd grown stronger. He fed her as she fed him.

"Find her and kill the scribe. They are stronger together."

As the Irin always were with their Irina. It was the reason his father had led the attack that had almost eradicated the females of the race. They were stronger mated with their own kind. Mating was a privilege never given to the Grigori. They could only take and take and take until there was nothing left.

The woman's heart stopped and Brage pushed her body to the floor, ignoring the bitter taste on his tongue.

CHAPTER

NINETEEN

T he streets of Oslo later that afternoon were just as cold as Malachi expected. Unfortunately, that didn't seem to keep the Grigori inside.

"Another one," Rhys grunted, turning down an alley behind a bar on the outskirts of town, following the scent of sandalwood.

Malachi and Lang slipped into the alley behind the other scribe, and Malachi pulled down his leather glove to trace the edges of his *talesm prim*. Within seconds, he could feel the surge of power. He'd slept fitfully that evening, and his dream walk with Ava was murky. He'd woken from a brief nap with a feeling of dread and loss that chased him out of the scribe house and on patrol with Rhys and Lang.

Urgency stalked him. Some instinct warned him that something very dark and very dangerous was heading toward the cold city on the edge of the fjord. The sky hung bitter and grey, and the clouds were low.

They reached the end of the alley to see two Grigori with human women wrapped around them. The women moaned with pleasure, but as the Grigori turned their heads, the twin expressions on their faces chilled him.

Dead. Malachi had never seen colder eyes. No smirk of pleasure. No vengeful gleam. They were animals, feeding from prey. They shoved off and stepped away from the women in unison, turning to the Irin scribes as they zipped up their pants and pulled out their knives.

"Rhys," Lang called, "get the women inside somewhere. They'll die of exposure with this wind."

Rhys waited until the two soldiers were distracted by Malachi and Lang, then he bent down and tried to help both of the humans up with gloved hands, careful not to touch their skin for fear of harming them further.

The Grigori didn't stop. They didn't charge. They walked steadily toward Malachi and Lang, no expression on their pale faces, no caution in their steps. Their dead faces were eerie. Malachi and Lang spread to opposite sides of the alley and the two Grigori split to mirror them.

Malachi raised his dagger, feinting right before he lunged left, flipping the dagger to his left hand and trying to slip under his opponent's arm, which had lifted to stab him. He felt a quick slice along his shoulder, but within seconds, the Grigori was shoved up against the wall of the alley, and Malachi's blade was piercing his spine.

The soldier said nothing in his last breaths. Then his dust rose to heaven and the silent monster was gone.

Malachi turned to see Lang with the other soldier propped against a wall. The Grigori's face was bloody and his hands hung limply at his sides.

"Who sent you?" Lang didn't yell, and his voice was all the more frightening because of it. "Hmm? I understand what you need. Do you think I do not pity you? To have to touch these... humans, just to feel alive. No one pities you more than I. But tell me, who sent you to my city, eh?"

The Grigori soldier said nothing, perhaps sensing Lang's false sincerity. He looked exactly like his brother. Pale and ethereally handsome, the two could have been runway models. Their light brown hair was close-cropped and their skin unlined. The two humans would have been entranced by the sight of them, Malachi was sure.

Undiluted by generations, Grigori were bred from the Fallen themselves. Direct descendants of the ancients, and their looks proved it. Not even the Irina were immune to their unnatural charm. But for Malachi, Grigori perfection prompted an instinctive revulsion.

"There are more of you this past week," Lang continued to speak softly, but the Grigori still had no expression. "Is there a master in the city? Has Volund come for a visit?"

With any luck, Rhys would have both of the women at the hospital. Human medicine couldn't do much for them if the Grigori had drained too much of their energy, but the doctors would provide a safe place for the women's bodies to heal themselves if they were able.

"Tell me what is happening," Lang said, "and I will let you go. You can chase after the human again. She probably didn't go far."

Finally, the Grigori's expression changed. The corner of his mouth lifted. "Why run after the humans, scribe, when far more delectable flesh awaits those who please my father?"

The air might have been sucked from Malachi's lungs.

"We know…" The soldier grinned, the smile of a predator assured of his prey. He sang, "They're baaaack. We know—"

He broke off when Lang's fist met his mouth. But the Grigori only spit out blood and smiled again.

"My brothers look forward to welcoming the Irina home."

Lang did not hesitate. He pulled the soldier forward by the ear and smashed the monster's nose into his knee. Then the silver knife plunged in, and the Grigori dust rose.

The watcher said nothing, staring at the grimy wall while music and voices from the bar filtered through the alley.

"It's happening again," he said. Spinning around, Lang walked quickly, his long legs eating up the length of the alley while Malachi hurried to keep up.

"Find Rhys. Keep hunting. I need to make calls. We'll not be taken by surprise again. Look for Max and Renata. If anyone knows what the Grigori may be up to, it will be Max. And Renata will be able to contact Sari."

"I'll keep hunting," Malachi assured him, halting near the car while Lang opened the door.

"This will not happen again," Lang said. "Not in my city."

Then he got in the car and shot out into the street. Rhys found Malachi only a few moments later.

"Hey." Rhys's breath froze in the night air. "Where did Lang go?"

"The Grigori know the Irina are back," he said. "He went back to the house."

"Damn."

"We need to find Max."

Rhys shrugged. "No need. He keeps a flat downtown. He's not nearly as secretive as he'd like to think."

"Is it far?" It was cold, and Malachi didn't relish trudging through the dark streets, though it was possible they would pick up a few more Grigori kills along the way. The two they'd just hunted had been their sixth and seventh of the night. The city truly was flooded with the creatures.

Rhys watched the taillights of Lang's car turn left at the light. "Does it matter? We're walking, whether we like it or not."

"Lead the way."

They turned in the opposite direction and began walking. Silent, at first, then remarking on the streets they passed and the human traffic, which didn't seem to slow, even so late at night. They passed many young people, but no other Grigori crossed their path. By the time they made it to the nondescript apartment building where Max kept a flat, Malachi was ready for a drink.

"Do you think he has beer?" he asked Rhys.

"You know, even without your memories, you're still remarkably you."

"And even though I don't remember you, I know that statement should annoy me, and yet it doesn't."

The two scribes entered the building smiling, only to be met in the lobby by a muttered curse. Malachi lifted his eyes to see a stunning, dark-haired Irina, as tall as he was, though far better dressed. He didn't know how he knew she was Irina. Some instinct drew him. Her aura radiated power.

"Ren, do you know where I put my—" Max stepped out of the stairwell, breaking off when he saw them. He halted in the act of wrapping a dark red scarf around his neck and practically shouted, "You're here!" His smile made no mystery of their welcome. "We were just about to drive to Oslo house to find you."

Max walked over and embraced Rhys, slapping him on the back, but Malachi's eyes never left the woman that Max had called Ren.

She stared at him, her face growing pale. He could see her hand trembling and knew just by looking at her that the gesture was uncharacteristic. Max went to her side.

"Renata?"

"You told me… I didn't believe you. Not really. But it's really him."

"I told you."

"He's really alive."

Malachi might have been mistaken, but he thought he saw tears in the corners of the woman's eyes. She walked over, tentatively reaching out a hand.

"I've seen you, scribe. In pictures. In her visions. Her memories of you. She sang them to us. Her grief… To see you here, I cannot—"

"I told you," Max said quietly, putting an arm around Renata's waist.

"You tell me many things, Maxim." Her voice held a note of irritation, even as her hand lifted to Malachi's cheek. It rested there while he met her wondering eyes.

"She thinks you dead, Malachi."

"Please." He fought back the hitch in his voice. "Where is she?"

• • •   • • •

THEY SAT AROUND THE TABLE IN MAX'S STYLISH APARTMENT, WAITING for Renata to finish her phone call. Malachi looked around warily.

"You live well, Max."

The scribe crossed his tattooed arms and smiled. "I've never been very comfortable with the communal life. I serve my scribe house, but that doesn't mean that other… projects do not interest me."

Rhys said, "Max has always been an excellent gambler."

"And investor." He shrugged. "Sometimes interesting opportunities present themselves. I'd be a fool not to take advantage of them."

"This is all very interesting, but why can't Renata just tell us where Ava is? We know Sarihöfn was compromised. Surely Renata knows where they would take her."

"That was a surprise to her. I can tell you that much. She'd not checked her messages for a few days as we were busy. She's contacting Sari right now. They have a system, and I'm not privy to it. No scribe is."

Rhys said, "They're very cautious."

"They've managed to stay hidden for over two hundred years. Of course they're cautious."

"Have you ever been there?" Malachi asked. "To this haven where Ava was?"

"No. And I've no idea how to find it. She couldn't tell me if she wanted to. Which she doesn't."

Rhys shifted in his seat. "Renata doesn't seem like your average Irina."

"She's not."

"What does she do?"

Renata walked into the dining room, phone still in her hand. "Whatever I want to, scribe." She looked at Max. "I left her a message with this number. May I keep this phone for a while?"

"Of course."

She sat down, plainly staring at Malachi.

"How?" she finally asked. "Max said he saw you die."

"We don't know," Malachi said. "Her magic. I don't remember much."

"I've seen her do many things," Renata said. "None of them close to bringing someone back to life."

Rhys said, "Maybe she didn't know she was doing it."

"Obviously." Renata rolled her eyes at Rhys. "She thinks he's dead."

"Well, I'm not."

"The question is," Max broke in. "How are we going to tell her that you're not dead without her going into shock?"

"Would she think it's a trick?" Renata asked. "Not that any of us would be that cruel, but she's going to have a hard time accepting it."

"Maybe not as hard as we think," Rhys said. "They've been dream walking."

"I know they have!" Renata said. "They've been giving her a hard time about sleeping so much. They think she's depressed. Of course, we all thought they were only dreams. There was no way of knowing he was actually… you know."

"Alive?" Malachi said. "Is it that hard to say?"

"It's that hard to believe, and I am not your mate."

What was she, exactly? Malachi looked between Renata and Max. There was clearly some intimacy there, but Malachi was too weary to try to decode it.

"When will they be here?" He sighed. "I just want to see her. We can sort out what to say later. I just… I need to see her, Renata."

Her hand slid across the table and enveloped his. Malachi chanced a look at Max, who had his eyes locked on Renata's hand, clearly displeased.

Oh yes. There was something there.

"I cannot imagine what the two of you have been going through," she said. "But we will make it right. You will be together again. I imagine with the message I left Sari, they will be here by tomorrow. Then you will see your Ava again."

"Thank you," Malachi said. "I know this is all hard to fathom."

She smiled, lifting a hand to tug on the front of his hair. "You're a miracle. Her miracle."

"I hope she thinks the same."

Rhys went back to the Oslo house to let Lang know what was happening. Malachi stayed in the spare bedroom at Max's. Renata had given Sari that address. When Ava came to the city, she would meet them there.

Malachi tried to sleep, but his dreams troubled him. He was once again walking through a dark forest. Ava was nowhere in sight, and she no longer called for him. In fact, the air was dead silent. No birds sang. It was as if all life had left the place. He walked through the shadows, softly calling for her, but she did not answer.

When he woke, he stared at the ceiling, wondering what it meant. From the beginning, his dreams of her had kept him sane. Was she simply not sleeping? Had she withdrawn? Was that even possible between mates?

It was early morning, but the moon was still out. He stared into the blackness outside Max's flat, ignoring the city lights and looking at the stars. A soft knock came at the front door, and he sat bolt upright in bed.

His heart raced, but the only voice he heard was unfamiliar. And male.

Malachi threw on a shirt and walked to the door. Cracking it open, he saw an Irin couple standing in the entry way. The woman was embracing Renata, the man was shaking hands with Max.

Damien. This must be the Watcher they spoke of. He was imposing. Commanding. His presence filled the room, and keen eyes swept the apartment. Malachi opened the door a few more inches and watched as Damien finally saw him.

Shock. Grief. Disbelief. Awe. The emotions flickered through his eyes though his expression did not change. "Impossible," he whispered.

"Not impossible," said Max. "He's here. It's him."

Malachi stepped into the room and saw Sari watching him.

"It's him. It's…" She grabbed for her mate's hand. "Damien?"

"Yes." The first hint of emotion hit Damien's voice. "It looks like him. Brother?"

Malachi approached. "It's me, Damien."

An exclamation of praise in the Old Language, and then Damien walked to him, grabbing his shoulders in a tight embrace. All taciturn soldier forgotten, he hugged Malachi as a brother.

"Praise heaven! I don't know how this is possible," Damien choked out. "It's you. Your voice— It's truly you. How?"

Max said, "We don't know. Evren thinks it's Ava's power. That she somehow brought him back."

"I heard her," Malachi said quietly. "In the Old Language. She called me to come back to her. And… I did."

He heard Sari say, "She can project her visions. Can she actually will them to be?" Her voice bordered between awe and fear.

Damien slapped Malachi on the back and stepped back, wiping his eyes. "No miracle like this would occur without the will of the Creator himself. Who are we to question this, *milá?*"

Sari was still eyeing him with some suspicion. "This will be a shock to her."

Damien nodded. "We will be cautious. But this could not have come at a better time. She has been drawing away. She bought plane tickets to London on her phone."

"What?" Max said. "London?"

"Her father is there. I think she was planning to go to him. Not that I'd have allowed it, of course."

Malachi bristled at Damien's tone, even though he knew the watcher was guarding his mate. "Where is Ava?" he asked. "Is she with you?"

"Heaven, no," Sari said. "We needed to make sure Renata hadn't lost her mind first. She's at Lang's house. She was happy to see Brooke there."

"And Rhys," Damien added. "Though we warned him not to say anything about you yet."

Sari said, "I think she and Orsala were going to get some sleep. Neither was able to rest in the car."

"So you know she was planning to escape to London, yet you left her in an overwhelmed scribe house with only a few guards?" Max asked. "That seems… prudent."

Malachi walked to the door, grabbing for his jacket. "Take me there."

"Brother, hold." Max put a hand on Malachi's shoulder.

"Take me to my mate!"

"Give her time to rest," Sari said. "This is going to be a massive shock. I know you need to see her—you must be going out of your mind with it—but give her time. Otherwise your reunion could go very badly."

Malachi vibrated with need. His heart was racing just knowing she was within reach. He ached for her, but he tried to think of Ava's needs before his own. She thought him dead. It was going to be a shock no matter how much they prepared her. He slowly released the grip on the doorknob and stepped back.

"When?"

"It's not even dawn," Damien said. "Stay here. We'll bring her to you later today. But let us give her time to prepare. Don't forget, Malachi, *she felt you die.* You don't remember that pain, because you were gone, but she lost half her soul that day. She barely ate. She has grieved, brother. This may be far more difficult for her to accept than any of us can know."

"And you are not yourself," Max added, squeezing Malachi's shoulder. "You barely remember her. You barely remember any of your past. You love her, but you don't know her anymore. You will have to learn each other again."

"Give us time, Malachi." Sari, the Irina whom so many regarded with frightened awe, came to him and embraced him. "Give your Ava time, and we will bring her to you."

CHAPTER

TWENTY

As much as Ava enjoyed seeing Brooke at the scribe house in Oslo, she was anxious to get away. It only made her decision to go back to the human world that much harder. She didn't want to witness the easy camaraderie of the Oslo scribes, which reminded her so much of Istanbul. She didn't want to recognize the open adoration the men showered on Brooke and her mother—whom Ava had finally discovered was named Candace. They delighted in every childish story the girl told and answered any question Candace put to them. The older scribes were obviously more accustomed to Irina—one of the men was mated to Chelsea, who had been at Sarihöfn—but they doted on the women no less because of it.

They were exhausted from patrolling but still had time to cook breakfast for all of them and make them welcome in the large old house in the middle of Oslo. They welcomed Orsala with wonder, clearly honored to have the elder Irina in their home. They greeted Damien and Sari with respect. One young-looking scribe clearly had to hold himself back from openly embracing Ava when she walked through the door.

"They've come back," she heard him whisper to his brother. He didn't even try to hide the tears in his eyes. "Do you think... they've really come back?"

Ava tried to ignore it all. She hid in the small room they'd given her, ignoring their kind eyes and welcoming voices. She tried to sleep but couldn't, even though she was exhausted. When she finally dozed off midmorning, she woke to see a familiar figure sitting near the foot of the bed.

"Rhys? What are you doing here?"

"No one had seen you for hours," Rhys said quietly. A bashful smile was on his lips. "I'm sorry to intrude. It's just... very good to see you, Ava."

"What are you doing in Oslo?" Her voice was hoarse, and she reached for the bottle of water near the bed.

"Max called us. He's in the city."

"You left Turkey?"

He nodded. "Things happened. We needed to go to Vienna. I went to the archives there. Tried to find out more about your family. I... uh, I did find out a bit more, but where you come from is still a mystery."

"It's not important." Not anymore.

He just nodded. "I met Orsala. She says you're doing very well with your lessons. Says you're going to be very powerful. A daughter of Leoc? That's wonderful, Ava. Such a gift."

"She's a good teacher." What would she do about living in the human world again? Would she continue to have visions? Would the spells Orsala had taught her continue to shield her? If so, she could live a far more normal life than she had before. Sure, she wouldn't be in physical contact with the Irin again, and her anxiety would probably skyrocket, but she could deal. She'd dealt before. The drugs were improving all the time.

Awkward silence descended. Part of her was ecstatic to see Rhys again. Even with the friends she'd made at Sarihöfn, she'd still felt different. Set apart. She wondered if part of her would always think of Istanbul as home, simply because he'd been there.

But the other part of her—the pragmatic one—didn't want to see any of Malachi's brothers. Especially Rhys. She didn't want to remember his grief or hers. Didn't want to remember his friendship. After she left for London tomorrow morning, she wouldn't see him again.

A clean break from everyone was better. She just hoped she could get to the airport without Damien finding out.

Rhys was still staring at her. "How have you been?"

She nodded. "Fine. Good."

"You're being very…"

"What?" She rubbed her eyes.

"I don't know." He smiled. "Sorry. It's been so long since I've seen you."

"Only a few weeks, really."

Was it only a few weeks? Her days and nights had run together in one long ribbon of confusion, revelation, and grief.

"I suppose it only seems longer. We missed you very much."

"Max and Leo are here, too?"

He nodded. "Max keeps a flat here in the city. Which no one knew about. Get him out of Istanbul and he's quite the man of mystery. I suppose we know part of where he goes when he leaves town. We just assumed it was Monte Carlo or Las Vegas."

She smiled. Somehow, it wasn't all that surprising. "And Leo?"

He hesitated. "Out patrolling right now. Helping the scribes here. There's been an unexpected influx of Grigori and no one knows why."

Ava's eyes narrowed, and she opened her mind to listen to his inner voice. Rhys was lying. But why? What was Leo actually doing, if not patrolling?

"Good of him to help out. I heard about the Grigori. I mean, we didn't get all that much news in Sarihöfn, but once we got here, everyone was buzzing."

He didn't say anything, just continued watching her with those solemn green eyes.

"What's going on, Ava?"

How could he even tell?

"Nothing. I'm fine."

"You're different. Something is different."

"I'm tired, Rhys. It's been a crowded few months. Everything in Turkey… and now I've had to run from the one place everyone told me I was totally safe. I'm… tired."

She *was* tired. No, more. She was weary. Weary of running. Weary of struggling through a world she didn't know anymore. Weary of having tasted happiness only to have it violently yanked away.

"Don't give up on us yet, Ava." His voice was so soft, his words so poignant, it was almost as if he could read her mind. "There are things you haven't seen yet."

"Rhys, I…" She felt her throat closing up, and her eyes started to tear.

Why was he still there? Why couldn't they all just leave her alone? Didn't they understand she didn't want to be protected anymore? The grief was too much. The pain was exhausting. Her whole life… "I'm just really, really tired, Rhys. Can you let me sleep?"

"Sweet dreams, Ava?"

She blinked away the tears and looked up in shock. "What?"

He cleared his throat. "Have you been having good dreams? No nightmares, I hope."

"They're fine." Or they had been until she'd forced herself to remember she couldn't live in a dream world anymore. "I don't remember my dreams much, to be honest. Never have."

Rhys's eyes narrowed. "You're lying. About having good dreams or about remembering them, Ava? Hmm?"

"Why are you still here?" Anger spiked through her sadness. "You can leave now."

"Fine." He stood, his eyes never leaving hers. "Get dressed. Get washed up. I'll meet you downstairs. We have someplace to go."

"I don't want to go anywhere with you."

He rolled his eyes before he turned. When he got to the door, Rhys called over his shoulder. "Don't create a scene, darling. Wouldn't you rather keep a low profile before you try to sneak off?"

Bastard scribe. He always saw too much.

•••   •••

Ava decided to act like the interlude in her bedroom hadn't even happened when she finally made her way downstairs. Rhys was at the counter, speaking with Orsala. It sounded like they were debating the interpretation of some story or myth.

"But the St. Petersburg manuscript—"

"Manuscripts?" Orsala said. "Manuscripts are always influenced by the scribe. There is no avoiding it. What you must look for is the common thread running through all the historical accounts. That is where the truth lies."

Rhys shook his head. "I… I can't believe you're discounting the oldest known account of Deandra's vision. Carbon dating has placed that manuscript within a hundred years of her life. No other existing document comes close."

"But that is only one document. You must look at more than just the documents, Rhys. You must—"

"This sounds like an argument that can't be won," Ava said with a false smile. "Hey, Orsala. I see you met Rhys."

She smiled until her eyes creased. "Such fun to debate with a knowledgeable partner. I met Rhys's mother many years ago. She would be proud of his good mind."

Ava saw the blush at Rhys's neck, but she ignored it and said, "I heard we have some place to go?"

He nodded and finished the cup of coffee in front of him. "Sari and Damien are over at Max's house. During the day, the Grigori activity seems to be slow. I thought we'd head over for lunch."

"Sure. Why not? Orsala, you want to come?"

"I have something to speak to Lang about when he wakes, then I believe I will spend some time with Brooke and Candace." She smiled and patted Rhys's shoulder. "Conversation with the young is a joy to the old."

"Okay." She nodded toward the door. "I'm ready when you are."

He stood and grabbed a jacket that was lying over the back of a chair. They walked to the door and Rhys grabbed her hand, bending down to speak quietly in her ear.

"I'm sorry about before. In your room. Your dreams are none of my business, Ava."

She didn't want to think about her dreams. Or his apology. "It's fine."

"No, it's not. We all grieve in our own way. I just hope… I hope you'll be better soon."

"I'll be fine."

Rhys smiled, and there was a knowing gleam in his eye. "I think you'll be more than fine."

She opened the door and walked out into the glowing white of the street. It was cold—according to Orsala—even for Oslo. It usually didn't reach the lowest temperatures until later in the winter.

"Just lucky for me, I guess," she muttered to herself.

"What?" Rhys closed the door, testing to make sure it was locked.

"Nothing." She heard the complicated alarm system Lang had tried to explain to her beep in their wake before she and Rhys started walking.

"Do you have a car?"

"It's at Max's. They dropped me off earlier. We can catch a taxi up the street. It's not far."

They walked in silence, the air frosting their breath as Ava tucked her scarf closer around her neck. Something itched under her skin. She'd noticed it that morning in the shower. It was almost as if she could feel her mating marks moving. The skin along her spine and neck crawled with energy. It wasn't painful, just an awareness of the marks he had left on her. The marks that would never go away. She wondered if she would feel them less and less as the years went by. Maybe, if she wasn't around other Irin, she wouldn't notice them as much.

Rhys walked in silence. Suspicious, she opened her mind. His inner voice was a confused jumble, but she could pick out a few words. Her knowledge of the Old Language was growing.

Stop.

Pain.

Malachi.

Mate.

Malachi.

Malachi.

Malachi.

Her soul welled in grief at the sound of his name. Rhys's thoughts circled until she locked down her mind with a few whispered words.

"What?" He looked down.

"Sorry. You were… loud."

He blinked at her, startled. "And you used a spell to shut me out. You can understand my thoughts now?"

"Not much. Just… It's never the way people think, you know? Now that I can understand bits of the Old Language, I realize people don't think in complete sentences. Or their souls don't, I guess. It's more like… impressions. A word here or there. A phrase. It's more emotion than distinct thoughts."

"Oh." He turned at the corner and headed toward a taxi stand. It was the middle of the week and traffic was light, but it still took a few minutes for a car to show up. They slid in the back and Ava rubbed her hands together, happy to be in the heat again.

Rhys leaned forward. "Pardon me. English?"

"Of course."

He gave the driver an address, then sat back and looked at her. Then he looked away and stared out the window.

"I know you're worried about me, Rhys."

"You have no idea."

"I'm fine. Really. This is normal, right?" She tried to explain it in a way that would leave him unconcerned about her future. "Like you said, we all grieve in different ways. This is a step. It's hard for me to be around you, because you remind me of… Malachi." She forced herself to use his name. "That will pass in time. God knows, I'm not the only woman in the world to lose a partner. I'll be fine."

She was surprised when he grabbed her hand.

"Just… wait," he said. "Don't shut down on me. Don't draw away."

The intensity of his voice rocked her. What was going on? Did Rhys have feelings for her? There had been a flirtation at the beginning, but she could have sworn they were past it.

"Rhys, you know I only think of you as a friend, right?"

He shook his head. "It's not that. I mean, yes, of course I know—"

"I'm not even thinking of anyone that way right now. I can't." Her concern for him broke through her resolve. The last thing she needed was to break a friend's heart before she cut him—all of them—out of her life. "And I don't want you to think—"

"Ava!" He pressed his lips together when he saw the driver looking back at them suspiciously. "I'm not talking about my feelings for you. Which are only of friendship, of course. I'm talking about—"

"Then what's all the talk about me shutting down and drawing away?"

"I just…" He almost looked as if he was in pain. "There are some things… some mysteries—"

"Here!" The car jerked to a halt in front of a large, modern apartment building. The driver looked at Ava. "Are you getting out with him, miss? Or can I take you to another address?"

Ava smiled at his concern. "I'm fine here. Thank you."

Rhys paid the driver and slid silently from the car, holding out a hand to help her on the icy sidewalk. As the taxi pulled away, he put both hands on her shoulders and dipped his head down to meet her eyes.

"There are some magics—some destinies—we can only guess at. As much as I study, as much as I revere science and strive to be a *rational* scholar, I can never forget this. We are"—he let out a rueful laugh—"descended from *angels*, Ava. There are some mysteries only heaven knows. Remember that."

She frowned. "I know."

"*Remember that.*"

"Will you just tell me what the hell is going on, Rhys? I'm starting to worry."

He grabbed her hand and pulled her into the lobby. "Welcome to my world for the past few weeks."

•••   •••

As soon as Ava walked through the door, her senses were assaulted. There was something seriously… other about Max's place. She ignored Sari and Renata's warm greetings. She ignored Damien's obvious concern. She felt like she was going to jump out of her skin. She flinched when Max put a hand on her shoulder.

"What's wrong?" he asked.

"You tell me." She crossed her arms and stepped away from him. "I don't… I don't feel good. What's going on?"

All five of them exchanged worried glances, but Ava had a hard time focusing on anything but the crawling feeling beneath her skin. She took a deep breath and tried to calm down, but it was difficult. Her instincts urged her to flee.

"Ava," Damien started.

"Where's Leo?"

She rubbed her arms. Her skin was going crazy. She whispered another spell to shut out the souls in the room that were practically shouting at her. The tension caused her stomach to pitch.

"I think… I need to go."

"Ava, why don't you sit down?" Sari said.

Her breathing picked up. "What's going on here? What's wrong with this place?"

Rhys stepped forward and raised his hands. "Remember what I told you, Ava. Remember what I said."

"What?" She didn't remember anything. She felt battered. There was too much going on. Too many thoughts. Too many emotions. And threading through the chaos was the echo of a voice that couldn't be. Malachi's voice. She hadn't heard it in months. Not since she'd started lessons with Orsala. The memory of it shoved her back painfully. Ava felt the tears come to her eyes, but she blinked them back.

"Rhys, I want to go."

"No!" Renata almost shouted. "You can't."

"Please," Max said. "Ava, if you'd just sit down and—"

"Where's Leo?" she asked again. She would see him, then leave. She couldn't stay in this apartment any longer. "Where is he? I just want to see him and then I'll go back. I don't want to be here."

A door down the hall burst open and Leo came charging out with a smile. "Hello, sister." He rushed over and picked her up in his arms, swinging her around. She buried her face in his chest and took a deep breath.

"I missed you, Ava."

"I missed you, too." His arms were warm and steady around her, a familiar comfort. "I'm sorry, Leo. I... I need to go."

"No. Please, stay. Everything will be all right."

"It's not you. I just don't feel good."

"There is someone here, Ava. Someone—"

"Your shirt." She picked at the button on the front, frowning. Something about it.

"You need to sit down. We don't want to shock you, but... There's no easy way to say this."

There was something about the scent of his shirt. Ava took a deep breath as Leo's hand smoothed over her head.

"We all missed you so much."

"What is that?" she murmured, staring at the warm flannel that covered his chest.

"What?"

Her head reared back when she placed the smell. "What the hell?"

Ava shoved away from him, holding up her hands, backing away from all six of her friends.

"Your shirt, Leo." She didn't want to be mad, but months of suppressed anger reared up. She'd tried. She'd tried so hard to keep going. And no matter what she did, Malachi followed her. In her memories. Her dreams. Now, even the scent of him crept up on her from his brother's clothes. It was wrong. So wrong.

Leo only looked confused. "My shirt?"

"It smells—that smells like Malachi's shirt! Are you wearing his shirts now? Why would you do that?"

Leo grabbed for her hand, but she was already heading toward the door. Whatever sick intervention they had planned was over. She was done. Gone. She never wanted to see them again. She needed to get as far away from their twisted world as she could. Ava was getting off the Irin roller coaster, and she never wanted to—

"Ava, please!" Rhys cried out. He ran to her, wrapping his arms around her before she could open the door. "We didn't know how to tell you. We didn't know what was right."

She whirled around in his arms. "What the hell are you talking about?"

The memory of his voice grew louder. It pressed on her. Without her volition, she saw the mating marks at her wrists begin to glow.

Rhys saw them, too. "Open your mind, Ava. Remember what I said. Look at your arms and *listen*. Don't you hear him? Don't you feel him?"

The memories crashed through her. "Why are you doing this?" she said, tears falling from her eyes. "Why?"

Leo stepped forward and raised his hands in supplication. "He's alive, Ava."

"No."

"We didn't know how to tell you."

"Shut up. *Shut up!*" She could feel it. Her heart was actually breaking in her chest. "Why would you even say that? I saw him die! Let me go, Rhys. This is sick—"

"We don't know how," Rhys whispered. "He's alive. Your magic. His. Malachi is alive."

"What the fuck are you talking about?" she yelled. "I saw him die! *I felt him die!*"

Leo pointed down the hall. "He's in the bedroom, Ava. I'm not lying. It's been killing him not to come to you."

She shook her head and wiped the tears from her red, angry cheeks. "I'm leaving. Now. You people are crazy. Rhys, let me go."

"Listen," Renata commanded. "Listen to him! I can hear his voice, and I'm not even his mate."

"Ava, please!"

A muffled shout echoed down the hall, and everyone fell silent.

Her heart stopped, and her mind went blank.

It couldn't be.

She'd finally broken. She'd been expecting it for years. Maybe it had all been an illusion. Some desperate construct of a sick and lonely mind. Her knees buckled and she went limp as Rhys lifted her.

"Take her to him," Leo said.

"No." Ava shook her head.

Rhys carried her down the hall. Ava fought the urge to vomit. Her head swam. The crawling feeling came to her skin again, and the dark voices fluttered at the edges of her mind.

"Rhys," she whispered, eyeing the door with painful dread. "Don't. Please, let me go."

"You have to see," he said. "You have to see it's real."

"Don't. Please don't."

They were at the door. Rhys set her down and pushed it open. Ava drew back but could not stop her eyes from peering into the dimly lit room.

A dark figure was pacing in the lamplight, his hands tearing at his hair. He turned to her, and tortured grey eyes met her own.

A ghost. A dream.

"Ava."

She slammed the door and ran.

CHAPTER

TWENTY-ONE

He shot out of the room. Waiting in the bedroom while she cried had almost broken him. He couldn't lose her.

"Ava!"

They all got out of his way. He caught up to her before she could make it to the door.

"Ava, please!"

"No! No no no no no…" She said it over and over. She closed her eyes when his arms wrapped around her. She shook her head and turned her face away.

"I'm alive."

"No."

"It's me." He buried his face in her neck, inhaling the sweet smell of her skin. She was shivering, but her mating marks glowed against his. Gold on silver. Shining as he held her back from bolting to the door.

"You're dead," she whispered. "I felt it. I can't—"

"I'm not dead. I came back."

There was nothing from her but a sob. The tears leaked from her closed eyes, and he sank to the ground with Ava in his arms.

"I came back to you," he whispered, his lips pressed to her temple. "*Vashama canem, reshon.* I heard you. It was the only thing I heard."

She had stopped struggling, but her eyes were still closed.

"Look at me, Ava."

She shook her head.

"You think you're crazy, don't you?"

She nodded, still silent.

"You're not crazy." Malachi forced his voice to harden, even as he held her as softly as he could. "Ava, look at me."

Her head did not lift.

"Look at your mate."

He felt her shoulders begin to soften. And the fists he gripped in his hands tentatively turned their palms to his.

"I saw you in the spice market," he began, thinking back to the dreams he thought had only been illusions. The flickers of memory his mind had recovered. "It smelled of cloves and honey."

Her head lifted a little.

"And you were carrying an old leather case. I followed you because… you fascinated me."

She finally opened her eyes but didn't look directly at him. Their friends stood, surrounding them, holding their collective breath, but Malachi pretended they weren't even there.

He leaned down to her ear and whispered, "I met you in the forest. I found you, and I picked you up off the ground. I held you, and I loved you under the stars. You thought they were only dreams. I did, too."

Ava finally turned to him, her eyes wide and wet with tears.

"I tried to ask you where you were. From the moment I woke, all I have searched for is you."

She lifted a hand, tentatively touching his jaw. He saw her lips form his name, but no sound escaped.

"I was helpless in the forest. I lost you again, and I thought I would lose my mind."

"This is real?"

He nodded.

"This is *real?*" she asked again, her voice rising. Her other hand joined the first, touching his face. Tracing his lips, then moving down his body. She turned in his arms, but her hands never left his face. His neck. His shoulders.

"It's me, Ava."

She laughed once. Sharp. Painful to his ears. Then she buried her face in his neck and inhaled. "Your smell," she said, her lips pressed against his neck as his arms tightened around her. "It's you. I smelled you on Leo's shirt, and I thought——"

"It's me, Ava. I promise. It's not a trick."

"It's… impossible!"

"I know."

She burst into tears again, but this time he heard relief, not panic. He felt their friends relax, and he saw Damien pull Sari into an embrace.

"It's not possible," she said again, sniffling.

"I know it's not. It just… is."

She picked her head up, narrowed her eyes on him, then leaned forward, shocking him when her lips met his.

It was everything. So much more than the liquid quality of their dreams, Ava's lips were heat and life. His mouth opened to her tongue as she forced her way inside. Tasting him. Drawing back to bite the edge of his lip as he groaned in pleasure. He buried his hands in her hair, pressing her closer. Their teeth clashed. She drew back, only to have him pull her forward again.

He could live on the taste of her tongue in his mouth. The reality of her. The bitter edge of coffee and the salt of tears. And the taste of her. *Her*. It was no dream. She was real beneath his hands. Her flesh gave, and the sharp crescents of her fingernails dug into his shoulders.

Malachi heard murmuring around them, but he ignored it.

Ava finally pulled back, her lips swollen and red. Her eyes wide. "It's really you."

"Would you like to test some more?"

She blinked. "Maybe not while we're being watched."

For the first time, Malachi broke into a smile. The relief coursed through him. Ava smiled tentatively, lifting a hand to touch the lips she'd just kissed.

He closed his eyes at the tender touch and whispered, "Hello, Ava."

"Hi."

✦ ✦ ✦ ✦ ✦ ✦

"I think I'm going to hold off on flying to London for a while."

He frowned, looking down at her as they sat on the couch and drank coffee with Max and Renata, Sari, Damien, Rhys and Leo. Half of them were sitting on the floor, allowing Ava to stretch out at Malachi's side. She had her arm around his waist and he had his around her shoulders. They spoke quietly to each other as the others made small talk and pretended not to watch them.

"You were going to London?"

"I was not in a good place a few days ago."

He frowned. "That dream. I tried so hard to ask you where you were that I frightened you."

"It didn't make sense to me. I still thought they were only dreams. How could a dream feel so real? I guess my mind rebelled against it."

"It still doesn't feel real, does it?"

She shook her head and turned her face into his shoulder. "No."

"It's real. I'm really here."

"I don't care. If I've finally lost it and this is all a hallucination in the loony bin, I'm just going to go with it."

"Maybe we both died," he whispered. "Maybe this is heaven."

Rhys leaned over and slapped the back of Malachi's head so hard his teeth rattled. "That feel heavenly, brother?"

Ava fought back a smile and drew her legs up and over his so she was almost sitting in his lap. "Don't damage my mate, Rhys." There was the first spark of playfulness in her eyes. "I just got him back."

Rhys smiled at her, a smile so full of love and relief that Malachi was almost jealous. Almost, but not. It was his lap that Ava sat in. Her skin against his. He could feel the calm energy between them. It would occasionally heat when he flashed to a memory of their dreams, and he wondered when he would be able to have her alone. He needed her. Almost desperately. But hers was the greater shock, and he was wary.

"You're waiting for me to start crying again, aren't you?"

He cautiously said, "There was a lot of crying."

"I'm fine. For now."

He pressed his cheek to the top of her head. "It was understandable. It was very difficult for me to listen to them try to tell you. We thought it would be best if I didn't just..."

"Walk up and say, 'Hey, how's it going? By the way, I'm not dead'?"

"Your reaction might have been somewhat violent."

"I don't think you're wrong." She let out a sigh and he felt more of the tension leave her shoulders. "Rhys?"

"Hmm?"

"What now?"

Malachi and Rhys exchanged glances. It was the hardest question to answer, past the mystery of how Ava had managed to call him down from heaven.

"I don't know, darling," Rhys said. "We didn't plan much past this moment. He was a bit of a mess in Turkey."

"I was fine." Malachi bristled.

"You didn't even remember your name," Leo said from the other side of Ava. "You've years to go before your *talesm* are back to normal, and—"

"What?" Ava's head shot up and clipped the bottom of his chin. "What's wrong with his *talesm*?"

Would it change how she saw him? Malachi had never felt the loss of his powers more keenly. Was it possible she would no longer find him a worthy mate? He glared at Leo, who did not get the message.

"They disappeared. It was like the day he was born," Leo told her blithely. "Well, not completely, of course. But not a single spell remained. All his scars are gone, too."

"What?" He could feel Ava tense in his arms.

"Leo," Rhys started. "Perhaps you should let Malachi—"

"He used to have this great nasty gash across his ribs—I'm sure you noticed it, Ava—and it's completely gone. Of course, it's possible that when his memory comes back—"

"Wait, what?"

The whole room fell silent.

Ava turned to him. "What about your memories?"

"I don't… I can't—"

"You don't remember… what? The fight in the cistern?"

He swallowed, trying to pull her closer, but she leaned back, eyes intent. "It's not just my death, Ava."

"So… what? What don't you remember?"

Leo and Rhys had wisely fallen silent, and Malachi felt the weight of the room on him.

"I don't remember much, Ava. About… anything. My family. My life."

He could barely hear her when she spoke. "Me?"

"I remember a little."

She pulled away and stood, taking a deep breath. "Oh… shit."

"Ava, it's—"

"All of it?" She stared at him, but he couldn't read her expression. It was confusion. Sadness. Guilt? "But... the market. You remembered the market and the dreams and—"

"They're coming back to me." He grabbed for her hand. "Please, Ava."

There were the tears again. "Do you even remember who I am?"

"Of course I do."

"Do you? Or is it just this—this mating instinct? If you don't even remember what we were, or how we fell in love..." Her voice fell away before she whispered, "Do you even love me anymore?"

Everyone was staring, but no one was offering to help explain. Of course, what was there to explain? None of them knew anything.

He stood and took Ava's hand. "If you would excuse us, I don't think we need an audience."

He'd pondered how he would approach this since the day he and Rhys had talked in the library.

"You love your mate. But... you don't love Ava. You can't, because you don't know her anymore."

But he did! He'd hoped his memories would have returned by the time he found her. He'd hoped, but it was in vain.

"You don't," she whispered. "You don't remember me. You feel the same bond I do, but it's instinct. You don't remember Cappadocia or Istanbul. When you showed me the Basilica Cistern... or the way you used to scold me when I would talk about being insane—"

"I still don't like that, so don't start," he snapped.

He closed the door and spun toward her, suddenly angry. With her. With himself. With the whole damn confusing maze. Didn't she realize? He was as lost as she was. Ava looked shell-shocked, standing in the center of Max's bedroom, staring at a wall.

"You don't remember the island or the kiss. The first time we made love. You don't remember any of it?"

"Stop reminding me of everything I've lost. Trust me, I know."

She crossed her arms over her chest, and he could feel her withdrawing. "How could you not remember?"

"It's not like I had a choice, Ava!"

"But..." She worked to speak. "It was... our time together, Malachi. It was—"

"Brief. I know. They told me it was only a few months. But we are *bound*. Marked. So it's possible—"

"It wasn't brief," she said softly. "It was everything."

He stopped speaking, and the anger drained away.

"It was everything," she repeated. "The happiest time of my life. The first time I felt like I belonged anywhere. With anyone. With you."

He reached for her, glad she didn't pull away. He'd known he loved her, but until that moment, he'd had no concept of how much she had loved him. It thrilled him. Malachi wanted to roar in triumph, but Ava was still trembling.

"I'm remembering more every day. I do remember some things, and—"

"Do you remember any of the things I just mentioned?"

He paused. Malachi ached that those moments were a blank in his mind. "No, Ava, but—"

"So you don't. This isn't just about me." She shook her head stubbornly. "And if you don't remember me—"

"Are you serious?" He was angry again. "I don't remember you?"

"You just said—"

"Ava, you are the *only thing* I remember!"

She said nothing, but he could see the doubt in her eyes.

"When I woke... there was nothing," he whispered. "Nothing. I *was* nothing until you called me. I *heard* nothing until I heard your voice. I didn't remember my name until you named me. I do remember a few things. It's coming back. And each memory is like a beacon—a marker —of the life I lost. *You* were the first one. I *will* remember more. And we will make new memories together. So many that the life I lost will be nothing to compare to it."

The doubt still lived in her eyes. He wanted to battle her doubt and fear the way he battled a physical enemy, but he couldn't.

"Please, Ava. You have to understand."

"I love you." She spoke so softly he almost didn't hear her. "I never stopped. Even when you died. But do you love me?"

He knew it without question.

"Yes."

"But how—"

"I love..." He stepped closer to her and spoke firmly. "I love *you*."

How could he make her understand when he hardly understood himself?

"I don't remember the first time I kissed you," he said. "I don't remember the first time we made love. And Ava… I may never remember those things. But I know I love you the same way I know that… I'm right-handed." He tried to smile, but he knew it came out forced. "I love the taste of oranges because they make me think of my mother… who I also don't really remember. The same way I know that… I will have to shave twice a day for the rest of my life or resign myself to a full beard. I don't like guns, but knives are like an extension of my own hand and axes are highly underrated."

"Malachi—"

He just kept going. "I like beer and not vodka. I get restless when I'm too long indoors and want—*need* to go running."

He saw her eyes start to soften, so he stepped closer and prayed she didn't retreat from him.

"I don't remember a fraction of what I was taught in my training, who is on the council in Vienna, or what singer is popular on the radio. But I can tell you what foods I like and what music makes me want to tear my hair out. And I can tell you, beyond a shadow of a doubt, that I love you."

She lifted a hand and clenched it above her heart. "Please—"

"Because loving you is part of *who I am*. It's not a memory or a moment. It is in my soul. And I will never—*can* never—forget my soul."

Ava said nothing. His heart raced. But finally she went to him, embraced him, and Malachi let out a relieved breath. He wrapped his arms around her and pressed his cheek to her temple.

"I don't understand it either. I just know it's true."

"I love you," she said. "And part of me thinks it's not fair of me to love you when you don't remember—"

"Don't say that. Don't ever say that."

"I don't care!" Her voice was fierce, and he reveled in it. Reveled in her possession. The way her arms tightened around him, claiming his body as her own. "I lost you once. And I pulled you down from heaven to bring you back. You're mine."

"Completely." He kissed her temple. Her cheekbone. "Completely, Ava."

Working his way down her face, he searched for Ava's lips.

"Some days—"

He found them. Kissed her silent, but she pulled away to say, "Some days I thought I wouldn't breathe again. That I didn't even want to."

"I need you." He was rock hard and aching for her. Like her kiss, her body was heat and substance. Not the thin shadow of a dream, but flesh and blood and skin and life.

She began to pull at his shirt. He stepped back and tugged it over his head. Her hands spread out over his chest and dug in, her fingers gripping him almost painfully. Malachi threw his head back and groaned.

"Ava."

She kissed his chest, licked at his skin, tugged at the hair that grew there and scraped her teeth over a sharply aroused nipple. His hands pushed her shirt up her waist to feel the heat at the small of her back as she painstakingly undressed him. The button on his pants, then the zipper. Then she slipped her fingers down the back and pushed down, taking all his clothes with him. He was helpless under her small hands.

Walking him back to the bed in the corner, she waited until his knees hit the edge, then she came down with him, stripping him of his socks, running her hands up his legs. Her mouth followed everywhere.

"You're real," she whispered, over and over again. "Real."

"Come here."

"Your face…" She stood and traced a finger over the arc of his cheekbones. The curve of his lips. "Real." Her warm palm opened on his skin. "Your shoulders…"

Bare. His body hummed with energy, and he tried to ignore the burn of shame at the reminder of his bare skin. He was naked before her in every way.

"Your hands." Her voice was thick with emotion. He could hear the tears she battled as she reached down and linked their hands together.

"Ava, please. I need you."

She ignored him, kneeling on the ground between his legs. "Your feet…" Her nails scraped up the sensitive flesh of his ankles. "Real." Her fingers followed up his calves to his knees. She bit the skin on his inner knee as her fingers tickled the sensitive flesh behind. "Legs. Real. Knees. Real." Her tongue traced a line up the inside of his thigh.

She brought him back to life only to kill him slowly. Malachi couldn't tear his eyes away from her lips. She bent down and kissed the very real arousal that was staring her in the face.

"I need you too," she whispered.

The heat of her mouth enveloped him. She took him deep, and he twisted his hands in her dark hair.

"Ava," he groaned again, his head falling back and his eyes closing in ecstasy. He wanted to keep watching, but… "I can't."

Her mouth left him. "But—"

"Not that." He would spend himself like a virgin if she kept going, and he needed to be *in* her, connected more deeply than just her mouth. "Come here."

He pulled her up and grabbed her waist, tossing her on the bed as he began to undress her.

"Too many." The shoes and heavy socks were gone. "Clothes." The pants, history. "In Norway." The delicate lace-edged panties could be replaced, along with the stockings.

Half undressed, she arched back and fumbled to remove her sweater, long-sleeved shirt, and bra. Malachi took the opportunity to bend down and taste her as she had tasted him.

"Malachi," she moaned, halting her movements to enjoy his tongue. "I thought…"

"I missed your taste," he murmured, pausing to lightly bite the inside of her thigh. "The scent of you. Dreams were not enough."

"Real," she whispered again. "Not a dream."

He spread her legs wider, kneeling down on the floor to take the edge off his hunger. Beautiful. She was utterly beautiful in her pleasure. Her legs thrown over his shoulders. His arms holding her down. He felt her shirt hit him in the face.

"Come up here," she whispered. "Kiss me."

He kneeled on the bed, bracing himself over her, feeling the heat from her body. Their breaths mingled together when their lips met, and he pulled her leg up as he slid inside, seating himself to the hilt. He thrust his hips when he felt her clench around him.

Real.

Now he understood why she said it, over and over again. Everything paused in that moment, as he looked in her eyes.

Real.

"I love you," he whispered.

Ava smiled, and there were tears in her eyes. "I believe you."

"I love you, *reshon*."

"I love you, too." She held on to him as he began to move. "So much it hurts."

"Don't hurt. Please, Ava. Not anymore."

She was always the one who wanted faster, but this time, she didn't have to beg.

"Too long." He was going to come apart in her arms. Fly to pieces when her legs wrapped around him and her heels dug into the back of his thighs. "Ava!"

"Yes," she breathed. "There you are."

"I'm here." He was very, very there.

"Not a dream."

He reached down, changed the angle of his thrusts until she let out a hitched breath that told him—*how did he know?*—she was close.

"Yes," she chanted again. "Yes yes yes…"

He felt her go over the edge and he followed, moving through the rush of her climax and closing his eyes as the lights flashed in his mind. He saw them before, making love in a cave, thousands of miles away, her mouth falling open in pleasure and her head thrown back. The images overlapped in his mind, and he saw them.

The first time.

Again.

Always.

His body met his soul, and Malachi *lived*.

CHAPTER

TWENTY-TWO

T he forest was warmer, but darkness still hovered around the edges. The hedge was wide and high, and though she could hear him on the other side, she did not try to find her way to him. She sat in the center of the dark meadow, knees drawn up to her chest, listening as he paced.

"Why do you keep him away when you brought him back?"

She turned her head and the radiant creature was with her again. "Did I?"

He sat down on the grass next to her and stretched his legs out. "Bring him back? Yes. It was unexpected."

"How?"

The Fallen glanced up. "I am no longer privy to the whims of heaven. Nor do I fully understand your power."

"I'm not really sure I have that much power to begin with."

"If I did not feel your uncertainty, I would think you were jesting." He grimaced. "Your soul rears in rebellion, even in this place."

"Rebellion against what?"

He ignored her and turned his face back to the sound of pacing outside the hedge. "Tell me. Why do you keep him away?"

Her heart stuttered. "I… don't know him."

"Yes, you do."

"I could hurt him."

"Yes, you could."

She could feel the frown creasing her forehead. "I don't understand this place. Is it a dream? I thought it was a dream. It didn't seem real, but now I think it was. It is."

The Fallen sneered. "Foolish child. Dreams are more real than you know. It has always been so. What is the world around us but a dream?"

"What do you mean?"

He shifted quickly, and she saw before her a nondescript human in glasses, then a giant black cat, then a pure gleam of light. Or had she? Before she could blink, the shining creature was sitting next to her again.

"What do you think I mean?"

"Are you real?"

"Very real."

Their eyes met, and she felt a thread of connection that surprised her. "Who are you?"

"You know who I am. You will wake this time and remember it." He lifted an eyebrow. "Unless your human mind rebels against that, too."

"Rebellion," she murmured, remembering what he had said before. "What am I rebelling against?"

"Who you are. Who he is." He nodded toward the sound of the pacing man beyond the dark hedge, then the creature leaned forward and dropped his head to hers. "You will always rebel," he whispered in her ear. "Against power. Against control. Against the will of others. It is in your very blood, Ava. I may have fallen, but you ripped the threads of heaven itself to get what you wanted."

"I didn't mean to."

"It doesn't matter." His voice vibrated with a peculiar resonance. It was excitement and dread. Curiosity and pride, all at once. "Or maybe that is all that matters."

Her heart began to race. The angel pulled back and narrowed his eyes at the sound of the pacing man beyond the hedge.

"He does not understand yet," the creature murmured. "Not yet. But soon."

"Was it bad? To call him back?" Panic was a fist around her heart.

"You don't ask the right questions, child."

"What do you—"

"What is bad, what is good? These things are unimportant. You must only ask, is it *necessary*?"

He was necessary. Not the angel. The man beyond the dark hedge was necessary. She could feel it in her bones, though her head ached with confusion as she listened to him pace.

She wanted him, but he frightened her.

"Are you frightened *of* him or *for* him?" her companion wondered. "I don't know. I know so many things about you. Where you sleep. When you dream. But I cannot interpret the emotions I feel."

"Can you ever?" she asked. "With humans?"

"I don't know that I ever tried." He shrugged. "Maybe. Or perhaps I simply do not remember. I have existed longer than your mind can fathom."

The man beyond the hedge continued to circle, growing ever more agitated. She could sense his desire to come to her. His desire to protect her from the creature that sat at her side. She knew this, just as she knew that she could not let him in.

"Not yet," she whispered.

The Fallen smiled. "No, not yet."

"What do you want from me?"

He placed a hand on her temple and whispered, "It's time to listen."

But it wasn't a song she fell into. The images shot to her mind in glittering, violent life. Two dark eagles with golden eyes, wings spread as they screamed. They flew at each other, colliding in midair as blood dripped over her eyes. A wolf paced at her feet and a tiger lounged in the distance, watching with a lazy, glowing stare.

Only watching.

Jackals circled and laughed, but the laughter held fear, not glee. All the while, the great birds screamed as feathers and blood filled the air.

They tore at each other until one, claws dripping with blood, plunged his bladed beak into the chest of the other, ripping its heart until the great bird fell at her feet, staring into her eyes as she screamed.

"I will tear the threads of heaven to return. And you will help me, Ava."

• • • • • •

Tears were hot on her face when she woke. Ava gasped and sat up, but Malachi did not stir beside her. His bare shoulders twitched as if he was still dreaming. She looked at him, scooting away until they no longer touched. She had slept pressed against him, and her body revolted at the loss.

But her mind…

Somewhere in his sleep, he reached for her. He stretched his arm across the expanse of the bed until his hand lay resting against the skin of her ankle. His fingers closed around it, he took a deep breath, then he relaxed into sleep again.

"Why do you keep him away?"

She remembered everything from her dream. Unlike the misty visions she'd clung to when she'd dreamt of Malachi, her vision of Jaron was glaringly clear.

"You will always rebel… It is in your very blood."

The thought made her shiver, so she stared at the broad expanse of Malachi's back, mentally tracing the patterns that were no longer there.

In the silent darkness, a wave of doubt washed over her.

What had she done? It was Malachi, but it wasn't. She had made love to a dream but woken with a man she no longer knew. A stranger who claimed to love her but had no memories of their brief life together.

"Imagine a person created for you. Another being so in tune with you that their voice is the clearest you've ever heard in your mind."

Would she still hear him as she had? Or had their connection been permanently severed in death?

Had she heard his voice the night before? Had she imagined it? Maybe she'd forced herself not to listen for it, but a tiny voice whispered to her that maybe…

Maybe Malachi wasn't truly hers. Not anymore.

"I think I'd pull down heaven if that's what it took to keep you here with me."

"And I'd abandon it if you weren't there."

The memory of his words brought tears to her eyes, because as precious as that memory was to her, he wouldn't remember it. He wouldn't remember their first kiss or the soft laughter after they'd made love. He wouldn't remember her anger and confusion or his quiet way of reassuring her with just a look and a hand. He wouldn't remember the stories she'd told him about her family or the rambling memories of four hundred years of life that he'd shared with her.

Mind-boggling. Wonderful.

Gone.

He wouldn't remember the night he mated her, drawing his magic onto her body or the passion that had united them as one. The stranger who'd come back to her had found the other half of himself, but Ava's soul still felt torn in two.

Her hand reached out, tracing the curve of a bare shoulder. She tried to remember exactly what had once covered it, but she couldn't. At her touch, his twitching body stilled, and she cautiously opened up her mind to his voice.

It was the same, but different. And just like before, it was startling in its clarity. Words tumbled over each other as he dreamed. She could hardly keep up with his mind. But one phrase whispered to her, over and over.

Vashama canem, reshon.

Come back to me.

This time, he was reaching for her. The dark hedge in her dream flashed into her memory, and Ava started to sniff. Malachi woke at the sound and immediately sat up, wrapping his arms around her.

"What is it?"

She shook her head but could say nothing. She'd never felt more confused in her life.

"Ava, please." His voice was strained, and he rocked her back and forth. "I need to know how to help you. What's wrong?"

"I don't know."

"You don't know what is wrong?"

"I don't know… anything. You're here, but I still feel alone."

He went completely still.

She forced the words out of her mouth. "I'm so confused, Malachi. You were dead. I felt you die. I still feel that ache. But you're here. And I was—I *am* so happy. I don't know how to explain it."

His arms dropped from around her, and he leaned away. His voice came to her so low she could barely hear it.

"I am no longer the man you love."

She grabbed his hand, willing him to understand, even when she didn't. "But you are. And… you aren't."

He rolled his shoulders. "I am not as strong as I was. My *talesm*—"

"Have nothing to do with how I feel about you," she said quickly.

"They never did. I didn't fall in love with you because you were strong or fast or a good fighter."

She couldn't see his eyes in the low light of the early evening that filtered into the room. There was a lamp in the corner, but his back was to it.

"Why did you fall in love with me?"

She melted at the vulnerability in his voice, so different than the reckless confidence he'd always worn before.

"I fell in love with your mind, which understood me. Your humor. The way… you would look so stern, then just the corner of your mouth would turn up when you smiled."

His face was still in shadow, but she thought she saw a smile tilt the corner of his lips, so she continued.

"I love the way you would take care of me. Of anyone you cared about. You were—*are*—one of the most thoughtful men I've ever met. And I loved how confident you were, because it gave me confidence. I thought you could protect me from anything."

"But I didn't."

"You *did*. There were dozens of Grigori in that cistern, but I'm alive. You protected me. Even though it cost your life." She could feel some of the tension leave his shoulders. "I'm just confused."

"Are you sorry we made love?"

"No," she whispered. "When I touch you, it's like being home."

"I feel the same way."

She blinked hard to force back the tears. "But you don't remember me. Or why you fell in love with me."

"But I do love you," he said urgently. "I don't understand either, but when you're in pain—as you are right now—I ache with it. I felt incomplete until I found you. Half-alive. Now you're telling me you *still* feel that way, and I don't know how to fix it."

She couldn't stop the tears that fell. She could hear the panicked sound of his inner voice, but she closed her eyes and whispered the spell to quiet him.

"Ava—"

"I need time, Malachi."

"Don't push me away." His voice was low. Pained. "Please."

"I won't." She admitted it to herself, "I can't."

As much confusion as she felt, she knew she needed him. She

wanted the comfort of his body desperately, wanted the soothing sound of his voice. She wanted more than memories.

"This is going to take time." She tugged him closer and leaned against his shoulder. Whatever her mind was telling her, Ava's body shouted loud and clear that her mate was home. Wounded, but alive.

Her soul recognized him. Her body did, too. Her mind and heart would just have to catch up.

"A wound doesn't heal," she whispered, "just because it stops bleeding."

"But it does heal." He put a finger under her chin and tilted it up, so she looked into his familiar grey eyes. Pure calm. Pure determination. It settled her in a way she couldn't put into words. It was as if her soul took a breath after holding it for too long.

"It will heal."

THEY SAT ON THE BED TOGETHER, WRAPPED IN BLANKETS, ENJOYING THE silence of the apartment. Ava had no idea where the others had gone. If she had to guess, they'd taken off right about the time things got interesting. And loud.

The clock on the small desk read 01:11. Midnight had crept by and dawn was far off, but Ava was wide awake. Sleeping next to Malachi had settled her energy and she'd rested better than she had in months.

The sex probably helped, too.

Her mind was clear, and her magic ran like a fluid line down her back. She could feel the mating marks he'd given her as if they were a living thing. She'd had so little time to get used to them after he'd marked her, and then he'd been gone and their power had dulled, though not disappeared, in his absence.

In his presence, she could sense them again, like a living coat of magic.

She felt his palm at her neck.

"They're glowing," he murmured. "Your marks."

"Do you remember giving them to me? At all?"

"No." He hesitated. "It's very hard to explain. With some things, once people tell me something that has happened, then it pops into my mind, like a puzzle piece fitting, and it's as if that memory was never gone. Other times…"

"What?"

He shook his head. "There are blanks that refuse to be filled. Maxim tried to explain to me what happened in the cistern, but none of it seemed familiar. The only flashes I have seen so far have been of you. I can… hear you, sometimes. Hear you scream. Smell the water. But other than that—"

"Maybe it's better you don't remember."

"I could find the scribe house in Cappadocia, but I had no memory of Evren, Max, or Leo. Only a little of Rhys. I had a single memory of us there. The rest came in pieces. Many of which I still don't have."

She rubbed his arm soothingly, tracing the new spells he'd written there, which were also glowing softly as he touched her. "And these?"

"I had nothing when I first woke. I've scribed these only in the last month or so."

"They're different."

"How?"

Ava smiled. "They're neater, for one thing. You did the first set when you were what? Twelve? Thirteen?"

"I would have started when I was thirteen."

She nodded. "So they were messy. But… it was kind of endearing."

He smiled back. "How?"

"You were this big badass, right? You always were. But then you had this kind of childish writing on your left wrist and forearm. Almost like a kid drawing on himself." Her finger ran up his arm, over the sensitive notch of his elbow and the delicate skin there. His powerful body shivered under the touch.

"Ava—"

"There were certain letters I could tell you'd exaggerated. Made more elaborate, like a young man would show off." Her finger trailed up the curve of his bicep and over his shoulder. "Then, as you grew up, you could tell you'd matured. The letters became neater. More economical. No boyish flourishes, just… utilitarian, I guess."

"Did you like them?" he asked, his voice hoarse.

She laid her lips on the swell of his shoulder, where a particularly beautiful *talesm* had once lived. Now the area was bare, but the flesh pulsed with life.

He was a miracle. A gift. But not a gift without cost.

"Your *talesm* were beautiful and frightening. They were *you*."

She closed her eyes and her tongue flicked out, tasting his skin. A noise left his throat, and he closed his eyes, letting his head hang down as his skin shivered under her touch.

"I could stay here for days, Ava. Talking to you. Touching you," he said. "Making love to you and learning you again. But I don't think we should."

The thought was tempting, but she reluctantly agreed, so she pulled her mouth away from the salt of his shoulder and shifted away. "I know. We should get back to the Oslo house."

"I don't like the coincidence of Sari's haven being compromised right when there is an influx of Grigori into the nearest major city."

"You don't think it's a coincidence at all, do you?"

"No."

She sighed. "I'd like to stop running. Just for a little bit. Think that'll ever happen again?" She scooted forward, but he grabbed her hand before she could leave the bed.

"We went to the ocean once, didn't we?"

She smiled. Nodded. "Do you remember?"

"I remember you, standing near the waves. It was dark, and someone had lit lanterns that flew into the sky."

She nodded, and her heart swelled. "Yes. That happened in Kuşadası."

"See?" He kissed the palm of her hand before he smiled. "It is coming back to me even more now. Soon I will remember every moment."

She tried to lighten the mood so she wouldn't cry. "When you get to the part about remembering you need to put your towels in the laundry basket, focus really hard on that one, okay?"

"What?" He frowned, but she could see a familiar gleam of mischief in his eyes. "I have a habit of not putting dirty towels in the laundry? This is… shocking."

"I'm guessing that bit hasn't changed at all, has it?"

He grinned, and in that moment, he was the cocky warrior she hadn't been able to keep away from so many months ago.

"Real," she murmured.

Ava bent down to lay a searing kiss on his lips before he could stand. He held her head, fisted a hand in her hair to hold her close, before he finally let her catch a breath.

"Real," he breathed out. "And yours. Everything else, we will work through. Together."

"Okay," she whispered, closing her eyes and nodding slightly, though he still clutched her hair in his hand. "Okay."

It was more than a wish or a hope. It was a commitment. He'd been taken from her, but he was given back. A gift and a miracle. She didn't know why or how, but he was alive.

There would be fights. Misunderstandings. But those were inevitable, weren't they? Her heart knew him. Her soul did, too. They would learn each other again. And in the meantime, there would be no secrets.

"Malachi, in my dreams, when you're not there... There's someone—"

"Who?"

"Jaron." The hand in her hair tightened, and he held her even closer. "He's been there, Malachi. In my head. And he's shown me things."

He said nothing for a while, but he relaxed his hands and stroked the hair back from her face, soothing her. Touching her. As if to reassure himself that she was still there and unharmed.

"Tell me everything."

VI.

Oslo, Norway

Brage lounged on the cold roof of Volund's house near the waterfront. He watched the cruise ships come in and saw his brothers head out, following the scent of a human female as a shark scented fresh blood.

He waited.

He'd fed again when he arrived in the city. There were already forty brothers in the house, which had been converted into apartments decades ago before the waterfront redevelopment. Normally, it was mostly empty. Now it held the burgeoning swarm of Grigori soldiers Volund had sired. Soldiers who were beginning to make waves among the human authorities.

Police had come by the house the day before, responding to complaints from the neighbors. Loud parties and women's screams. Brage had been able to assuage them. After all, it wasn't as if the women were screaming in pain. The officers left with embarrassed grins, and Brage had taken out his anger on the back of one of his younger brothers. They were all told to be more cautious, but Brage knew it was useless.

He wondered why Volund had sent so many. After all, he'd killed the scribe the first time in Istanbul with half the men he had here. It was only a matter of herding the woman and her Irin mate to the right location. He knew they were in the city somewhere.

"Brother?" A young soldier shivered at the door to the stairwell.

"Yes?"

"There is someone here to see you."

Brage frowned. "Who?"

The young soldier blinked in confusion. "I… I don't know."

"What?" Brage stood, walking toward him, but stopped when he saw the unassuming man coming up the stairs. The middle-aged man in glasses put a hand on the Grigori's shoulder and the young man turned, leaving Brage alone on the roof with his visitor.

He sat, recognizing the angel's disguise from Istanbul. If Jaron wanted to harm him, he would already be dead.

"I know who you are," Brage said.

"It's good that Volund has some intelligent offspring," Jaron said as he tossed back the cover on one of the patio chairs. A flurry of ice fell to the ground.

"What do you want?"

"Why are you still hunting her?"

Brage frowned. "Why do I do anything?"

His father asked it of him. It was not within his power to refuse.

"Fine." Jaron sat back, still wearing his human facade. He walked in the guise of a fatherly middle-aged man in spectacles. Not too old. Not too young. A confessor. Trustworthy. Despite knowing it was false, the facade still put Brage at ease.

"Tell me why Volund hunts her," the angel said.

"I do not know."

"Don't you?"

Brage shrugged. "He says she belongs to him. Other than that, it is none of my concern."

Jaron smiled. "In a way, he is not wrong."

"Then why do you protect her?"

"Why does your father only tell you half-truths?" Jaron countered. "For though the woman is his, she is also mine."

He closed his eyes and forced himself not to sigh. It would be taken as a sign of disrespect toward the angel. Talking in circles. Why did the damn ancients have to talk in circles so much? Was it too much to ask that one of them give him any kind of answer?

"Half-truths?" Brage said. "I am sure Volund tells me as much as you tell *your* sons."

"I tell my children only what they must know."

"Then we understand each other."

Jaron laughed. "No. You do not understand me at all. But then, you cannot. Is it true that he gave you Grimold's blade? A heavenly weapon to kill an Irin scribe? It seems excessive. But of course, you failed last time, did you not?"

The spike of anger was quick and hot. And Brage knew that Jaron had caught it, for the human facade wavered in that moment, and the glowing gold eyes of the angel flashed.

"Why are you here, Jaron?"

"I want you to leave the woman alone."

"You know I cannot."

"She is something you would not wish to harm."

Brage narrowed his eyes. He had his own suspicions about what the woman was, but they were based on whispers and rumors, like so much in his world. And if both Volund *and* Jaron claimed her...

"What is she?" he asked.

There was silence. Brage wondered if Jaron would respond at all.

"She is under my protection," the angel said. "You will not harm her."

"I don't intend to. Volund wants her alive. Though I will kill her mate. Again."

"Her mate interests me only so far as he benefits her."

"Then you will not interfere?"

"No."

"Do you vow it?"

Jaron leaned back in his chair, smiling. "Does your father appreciate your audacity?"

"I doubt it."

"Then he is a fool."

Brage said nothing.

"Fine," Jaron said. "I will not interfere with your mission, as long as you do not harm the woman."

It was the best that Brage would do under the circumstances. Jaron did not rise, so he dared another question.

"Is she what I think?" he asked. "What the heretics claim?"

"Yes."

His cold heart quickened. "Truly?"

"And no."

Fucking angels.

Brage curled his lip and closed his eyes. When he opened them again, Jaron was gone.

CHAPTER
TWENTY-THREE

She was still cautious around him. Still hesitant as he held her hand and walked into the scribe house.

Was the caution a result of his reappearance or because of the encounter with the frightening creature who had given her a vision? He couldn't read her well enough to know yet. Some things were achingly familiar, but others still confounded him.

Wary smiles and respectful nods greeted Malachi as they walked past the dark entryway and back toward the kitchen. It might have been the middle of the night, but the house was clearly on alert. Malachi spotted Damien, Rhys, and Lang strategizing over a map of the city, which had been spread out over the kitchen table. Sari and an Irina elder he didn't know were with them.

Rhys and one of Lang's scribes were putting red and yellow dots all over the paper. The rest of the gathered company nodded at them but did not interrupt the conversation.

"Ava," the old woman said softly, walking over to greet his mate. "I heard. I am… astonished."

And pleased, from what Malachi could gather. Her eyes crinkled at the corners as she smiled and grabbed Ava into an embrace.

"Thank you, Orsala."

"Have you told Brooke yet? Does everyone know? I only heard from Sari a few hours ago."

"It just happened yesterday. And we…" He saw her cheeks flush a little. "We needed some time alone."

"Of course, daughter." Orsala turned to Malachi and took his hand in hers, though he kept one hand firmly anchored in his mate's. "A blessing," she said. "A miracle sent from heaven." There were tears in the old woman's eyes. "How can we know the purpose of the Creator? And yet we rejoice in it. I am so happy for you both, Malachi."

"Thank you," he said quietly.

The others were still quietly arguing over the map.

"—follow what I'm trying to say, Leo. The red is a confirmed attack and kill," Rhys said. "The yellow are for attacks that were stopped, but the Grigori wasn't eliminated."

"So many," Sari said. "Lang, this is far more than average, correct?"

"Yes. Activity has picked up over the past year, but the majority of these attacks have been in only the past couple of weeks."

Damien asked, "Do we think there is any chance this increase in activity and the exposure of Sarihöfn are not related?"

Everyone was silent.

Malachi stepped forward. "There are few coincidences in the world. It's possible, but I don't think it's likely." He glanced at the map and moved closer, still holding Ava's hand. "Tell me more about Volund." It was Volund's child, Brage, who had killed him, but there was little Malachi remembered about the powerful Fallen angel.

Lang said, "As far as we know, Volund still has one of his primary bases near Göteborg, which gives his soldiers easy access to the continent and a steady stream of tourists, whom his men usually target. He's been building in power for centuries. We believe he took out the major power in Russia in the 1920s, and he appears to have connections with the lesser Fallen in Spain and France."

Leo leaned forward and frowned, staring at the map. "Have you talked to Maxim about what he's heard?"

Lang nodded. "Your brother has been an unexpected font of information over the past few years. I don't know who he knows—"

"It's better you don't ask," Damien said. "I never did when he was in my house."

"I wasn't planning on it," Lang continued. "The sudden absence of

Grigori last summer fits what you and Max have said about him making a move in Istanbul."

"The Istanbul offensive makes no strategic sense to me," Sari said, still staring at the map. "Why Istanbul? It's far away from his power center. It would make more sense to approach from the north, in Russia. Or from the west."

"Remember, *milá*, in some ways the Fallen are as unpredictable as the humans. They're often creatures of impulse."

"Particularly Volund," Lang said. "And from what we know of him, he is a grudge holder. Istanbul could have been a personal vendetta."

Damien shrugged. "From what I know of Jaron, I can imagine the two did not get along. Jaron was vicious, but deliberate. A planner."

"The complete opposite of Volund, in other words," Rhys said.

"And Jaron has a connection to Ava," Malachi said. "We don't know why or how, but he protected her in Istanbul, in his own way. And…" He glanced at his mate, but she nodded at him, so he continued. "And he appeared to her again more recently. In a dream."

"When?" Damien stepped forward. "At Sarihöfn? Was he able to find you there? Is that why—"

"I don't know," Ava answered. "I haven't remembered the details of my dreams about him until the one last night, though I'm fairly sure I've seen him before. He was… cryptic."

"How surprising," Rhys muttered.

"I've been talking over the vision with Malachi to try to make sense of it, but a lot of it is confusing. I… I can try…" She was clearly uncomfortable with so many eyes on her.

Malachi gave her hand a squeeze, and she looked to him again. He nodded to her, offering encouragement. After she had explained what happened at the sing with the other Irina, he'd been awed. But the vague memory of her voice singing to him crept into his memory. It had been the same night he'd noticed some of his *talesm* had reappeared under his skin. There was power in her voice. She was only touching the edges of it. He hoped, now that they were together again, that she could reach her full potential. That they both would.

"Tell them. Show them," he said. "There is no shame in trying."

"I can try to sing you the vision so you can see what I saw," she said, almost as if she were running out of breath.

"Like you did at the sing?" Sari said. "That was amazing."

"What is this?" Lang asked.

"Would you sing for us, sister?" One of Lang's scribes asked from the edges of the room. He appeared to be quite young and more than eager to hear Ava's song. "Would you?"

Lang smiled at Ava. "Most of our scribes are young. They have never heard Irina song before. Only heard stories."

Orsala smiled. "Ava's song is like no other. You would be spoiled by her vision."

Malachi could feel her turning in on herself, shrinking from the attention.

She said, "I don't know if it will work again. It might not."

"This was a vision from Jaron?" Damien asked. "Like the one you had in Istanbul?"

"Yes," Malachi said. "It might have something to do with what is happening now."

"Try, Ava," Orsala urged her. "Only try."

She was pale and nervous. Malachi stepped behind her and put his arms around her waist, holding her to his chest as she faced the room of staring people. He could hear her before she started. Could feel the wave of power pass through him as she opened her mouth. There were no words at first. There was a soft hum and an unsure melody, simple and achingly beautiful. He closed his eyes and tried to breathe slowly and steadily, willing the calm from his own body into hers.

It grew in his chest and moved down his arms. He could feel the marks he'd given her alive beneath him. Malachi dropped his head down, eyes still closed, and put his lips against the back of her neck as she sang. The moment his lips touched her skin, he felt it.

Like a current connecting, power surged from him and into her. She'd told him what was in the vision, but this time, he saw it for himself. It flashed in vivid color across his mind.

Two eagles, circling and attacking each other.

Hot blood sprayed down along his skin. He could hear it. He could feel *it.*

He heard the growls of the wolf at his feet and the eerie laughter of jackals in the bush.

Watching. All were watching as the fierce birds ripped at each other, screaming in rage.

A plummet to the earth.

He felt the wound as if the bird had ripped open his own chest. A blade of sheer agony pierced his heart as he heard the echo of the words in her mind. Jaron's words, not hers. The voice of the Fallen gave him chills, and his new marks pulsed in warning.

"I will tear the threads of heaven to return. And you will help me, Ava."

The monster called his mate by name, and the vision broke off when Malachi felt a roar erupt from his chest. His eyes flew open and she was there, holding his cheeks in her hands and shouting—

"Malachi!"

Rage washed through him like a churning river, like a flame ripping though dry brush. He wanted to hunt what stalked her. Wanted to wipe it from the earth and bathe in its blood. The fury coursed through his veins until Ava put her lips on his.

He took them. Digging his hands into the soft curve of her waist, he clung to her. He banded his arms around her body.

Malachi felt hands on his shoulders, breaking into the trance between them. Voices became clear.

"Leave him. Leave her. There's no way—"

"Did you see that? I've never seen light like that. It looked like fire from the inside out."

"Malachi." Someone pulled at his arms. "Let her go. She can hardly breathe, Malachi."

"No." Ava pulled away from his kiss with a gasp. "I'm fine. He's fine. Malachi?"

He snarled at those surrounding them, and they stepped back. Then she pulled his face down to hers and pressed her cheek to his.

"I'm fine," she whispered. "Fine. Safe. You're here. We're safe. It was just a vision. Not real, Malachi. It wasn't real."

He reached down and pressed her hand over his heart where a phantom pain still lingered. "Hurts. Did it hurt you?"

"No. I didn't see it that way. I'm not hurt."

"He wants you." His voice was hoarse, as if he'd been screaming. "Wants to use you, Ava."

"You won't let him, will you?" Her voice was calm, and he clung to that. "We won't let him use us."

"No."

"And neither will our friends."

As violent as his reaction was, Ava was safe. They were surrounded by allies. She was safe. He forced himself to take a deep breath. His *talesm* still glowed with light, as did Ava's mating marks. In fact, as he glanced around the room, every one of the Irin was lit up like a Christmas tree.

Rhys grinned. "That was different."

Sari said, "It was similar to the vision she shared with us at Sari-höfn, but this one was far more violent and powerful. I would guess that having Malachi back is multiplying her power."

"Two birds…," Lang said. "Volund and Jaron?"

Damien nodded. "I think it's clear that some war is between them now. There were others there, watching. Did anyone else see that?"

Orsala nodded. "And there were jackals. Scavengers. Waiting to see who the winner is? To pick at the bones of the defeated?"

"Is this what is happening in Oslo right now?" Lang asked. "Is all this Grigori activity a result of two of the most powerful Fallen angels in history fighting? That… can't end well."

"And I hardly think the council will be much help," Damien said. "According to Leo and Rhys, there are increases in Grigori activity all over the continent and they are being ignored. Who knows what's happening in the rest of the world?"

"Whatever is happening in Vienna, we need to deal with the problem in Oslo right now," Rhys said. "Analyze Ava's vision later. If so many Grigori are hunting in the city, they have a base. They stay together when they're not feeding. They would have… a house. A warehouse, possibly. Somewhere that a lot of them could be hidden. We need to find it and destroy them in their nest. Fighting all these individuals as they attack is not solving anything."

"So you're proposing aggression?" Lang asked. "Not just defense, but offense?"

Rhys paused. "I know it's not the official policy, but—"

"Just clarifying, brother," Lang said. "You won't get an argument from me."

"Nor me," Damien said. "And technically, I'm still your superior."

"So we find them," Leo said. "Take them out where they sleep."

Malachi said, "And we do it now. It's near dawn. They'll be hunting right now, but they'll be sleeping at dawn. If we pull everyone in, find where they're taking shelter and strike quickly, we might be able to stop this."

Orsala said, "They won't expect it. This is one of the things the Irina have learned. The Grigori expect Irin to be defensive, not offensive. They won't be expecting an attack from you because it's not officially sanctioned."

"And we are oh so very good at following rules," Rhys said.

Everyone moved closer to the map. Malachi took Ava's hand again, leaning in to survey the red and yellow dots. It was true, there were many. Too many. But somewhere in the forest of attacks, they would find a nest of enemies.

Which was good. Malachi was more than ready to kill something.

"An apartment building in the city center?" Sari said. "Would that be too conspicuous?"

"A hotel?" Leo offered. "If many of them have come in very recently, they might not have a house big enough. But a hotel…"

"It's possible," Lang said with a nod. "They would be inconspicuous. And there are many hotels near the larger tourist sites where they've been hunting."

"A group of supernaturally attractive men all in one hotel would be pretty *darn* conspicuous," Ava said. "I mean, it might still be an option, but I have a hard time believing they'd be able to hide for long. It would look like a convention of male models taking over downtown Oslo."

Leo added, "I'll try to get in contact with Max and his friend."

Sari said, "We'll start without them. Send out scouts. Find the Grigori. Find their base. We find it before dawn, and then we kill them all."

Only three hours later, Leo received the call from Max.

"We've found them. It's not good."

CHAPTER

TWENTY-FOUR

Ava had spent little time in Oslo, usually only using it as a jumping-off point for treks in rural Norway. The waterfront was something new. The normally bustling sidewalks of the Aker Brygge were silent at dawn. None of the tourist traffic was out, and the few boats that sat in port bobbed quietly in the frosty air. Tall buildings rose on one side while the frigid expanse of the fjord stretched out before them. It was foggy and near freezing, and Ava stood as close to Malachi as she could while they huddled in the alley with Maxim and Renata. Jeremiah and the other Oslo scribes were cautiously strolling through the area, trying to spot any lingering Grigori or humans. They'd found the body of one girl, dead from attack or exposure, they couldn't tell.

"The police are noticing," Max said. "The girls who are disappearing are not just prostitutes and drug addicts anymore."

Lang said, "Grigori attacks prior to this have been unnoticed—mostly because the women survive and don't remember exactly what happened coupled with the fact the Grigori prey on the most vulnerable on the streets. But this many in the city? I'm surprised it's not raised a public panic yet."

"The house is two blocks down," Renata said. "We haven't been able to get inside, but we've been watching. I would guess there are around sixty soldiers."

"I'd guess more," Max said. "And I think some came in on a ferry today. I'm not positive—I was too far away—but they looked right for Grigori and the human women were reacting to them."

"We never knew about this place," Lang said. "They've kept it very quiet."

"And you've been reactive, not proactive," Renata said with a shrug, clearly not caring if she pissed off the tall scribe who glared at her. "It's nothing to be ashamed of. All the scribe houses are."

"Renata," Max said with a warning tone. "It's not important now. What is important is that they're here now."

"We've been watching," Renata said.

"And most of the Grigori are in for the night. Saturday night is easy hunting for them. They get their prey early, so the majority will be in the house."

"Ava," Sari said in a low voice. "Do you hear anything?"

"I haven't been trying. Do you want me to?"

Sari nodded.

Ava took a deep breath and let go of Malachi's hand. He didn't want to, but she needed to lose the connection before she could open the door.

"Okay," she said quietly. "All of you hum or something."

"Hum?" Rhys frowned at her.

"Yeah, hum. Sing a little ditty. That seems to be the best way to keep your inner voices quiet when I scan for static."

"Clearly," Lang said, "there is much to learn about how the Irina fight."

"Not Irina," Renata said. "Just Ava."

"And thank you again for pointing out how weird I am, Ren. Much appreciated."

"You just have better range and accuracy than anyone else," Sari said. "It's not a bad thing."

Unlike Renata with her quicksilver knives, Sari had brought the traditional staff she'd fought with in Sarihöfn. Ava, however, only had her mind and Malachi's hovering presence. She could feel him at her back. Could hear him. She took a deep breath and tried to push past the clear sound of his voice. Stepping into the street, she opened her senses.

"It's quiet," she said. "I don't… there's not much. There's kind of a murmur. I can't tell if it's human or Grigori."

"If they're sleeping, there won't be much," Renata said.

Max added, "And it's definitely Grigori in the house. We didn't see any humans come in. The buildings around the house are offices, for the most part. They'd be empty right now."

If no voices meant sleeping, then they'd picked the right time to come. The only inner voices Ava heard were those of the Irin scribes and singers behind her.

Wait.

She stepped closer. There was something…

A faint echo. Familiar and eerily calm.

"There's someone…" There was one voice. One that lifted over the others. It was old. Powerful.

"Ava, do you recognize—"

"Brage."

She breathed out his name on a gust of frosty breath. She was certain of it. Brage was near. And he was waiting.

"Brage? Who?"

She wasn't sure who spoke. Chattering erupted around her, but Ava closed her eyes, focusing on his voice until the rasp of it cut into her mind and his presence flooded her senses. Old memories from Istanbul rose up, and a wave of black swept over her. Anger. Fear. Disgust. She could feel it all in his voice. His soul was a black pit, but instead of backing away, Ava stepped closer.

"Come…"

She heard his soul whisper to hers.

"Come to me…"

The black pull of his voice called her, and the dark edges of her heart reached out to the voice.

"Yes…"

She didn't realize she had moved until she felt Malachi's hand on her arm.

"Where are you going, *canım?*"

Malachi was behind her, holding on to her arm while the others argued in the background. His softly spoken endearment snapped her back to her senses.

Canım.

"I loved it when you called me that."

He bent down, and the arm that held her wrapped around her waist as he bent down and whispered in her ear.

"Then I will call you that every day, *canim*. But do not leave this place without me."

"Do you know?" she asked, turning in his arms. "Do you know who Brage is? What he did?"

"He is the one who killed me, yes?"

She nodded.

"Then I have a debt to repay," he said. "Don't I?"

He glanced over Ava's shoulder at the group of arguing Irin who were all debating how to attack the building.

"He's waiting for me," Ava whispered. "For us."

"What does he want?"

"For me to go with him."

Malachi's eyes narrowed. "Do you want to?"

She blinked, shocked that he had picked up on the dark compulsion. "A part of me wants to. I don't understand why."

His eyes narrowed, then he bent to brush his lips across hers before he said, "He cannot have you. You're mine."

Ava looked over her shoulder. Sari and Lang were arguing while Rhys tried to referee. Damien was rubbing his temple, clearly aggravated. Maxim and Renata, Leo and the others waited with impatient expressions.

"They're sleeping right now," Sari hissed. "It doesn't matter how many there are. We go in—quietly—and we will wipe out the house within minutes."

"You're right," Lang said, "so there is no need for you, Ava, or Renata to come into the fight."

"You are really arguing this with her?" Damien asked.

"I know she's capable. But there are few Irina left. There are thousands of Irin. It makes no sense to risk the few when they are so—"

"If you say precious or dear or rare or anything of the sort," Rhys said, "you know she will rip out your throat."

"Then rip it out," Lang said. "This is battle. Not politics."

Renata broke in. "This is useless! We need to go. Now! If Ava can hear Brage, then he is awake. If he is awake, he will wake the others and our advantage will be gone."

Ava spoke under her breath. "But he's not waking them. He's waiting."

"For you?" Malachi asked.

"Yes."

Malachi looked over her head, then down the dark alley where they were hiding. Fog hung low to the ground, and no stars shone overhead. He looked back toward Damien, then at her. Ava felt his grip on her hand tighten a moment before he tugged them away and into the night.

"Do you have your staff?" he asked, once they had slipped away.

"No. Do you have a knife I could borrow?"

He didn't answer, just slapped a heavy hunting knife into her hand as they continued jogging. She didn't hear anyone coming after them but knew the others would be loath to draw attention to themselves by shouting after them.

"Can you track him?"

Ava forced him to stop, then closed her eyes and searched for it. It was still there. Distant. Fainter than it had been. Brage's voice was moving.

"He's moving."

"Can you track him, Ava?"

"Yes." She pointed in the direction of the Grigori voice and opened her eyes. "That way."

She was pointing at the side of a brick building, but Malachi only nodded and urged her forward. When they came to the end of the alley, he stopped again.

"Which way?"

It was easier to find now that she recognized it.

"There." They ran to the left.

Ava and Malachi continued to thread their way through the narrow alleys and streets of the waterfront. Sometimes climbing over fences, a few times dodging humans or dogs they encountered.

"He's moving away from the others," she said.

"He wants to get you alone."

"How did he know I would follow him?"

"I don't know."

"If he wants to get us alone, we're playing right into his hands."

Malachi grunted. "We'll manage. Is it still only him you hear?"

"Yes. He's alone."

They continued to follow, Ava listening for the Grigori's harsh whisper, leading Malachi in what felt like circles. Every street looked the same in the darkness.

"We're heading back," Malachi said. "He's going back to the house."

Ava nodded, her breath catching in a panic. "And he's not alone anymore."

Malachi stopped and grabbed her shoulders. "There are more?"

"He's heading back to the house," she said. "And the others. They're awake."

WHEN THEY REACHED THE HOUSE, IT LOOKED EERILY CALM. ONLY AVA could hear the tumult inside. Bright Irin voices, male and female. Grigori whispers scraping through the air. The soldiers' voices were softer, but more painful to Ava's mind. The Irin voices rose over them, shining and clear. One thread suddenly cut off without warning, and Ava knew a scribe had lost his life.

"We need to go, Ava." Malachi tugged her hand.

Ava froze, and the smell of fetid water filled her nose.

"Ava!"

Brage's body bursting out of the water. Malachi's face shimmering gold before it dissolved.

She could hear her own voice screaming.

"Ava." He squeezed her hand. "*Canim.*"

"I don't want to go in there," she gasped. Her heart pounded, and the still-seductive whisper of Brage's black soul called her toward the house.

"Ava?" He bent down and captured her eyes. "Look at me."

"I don't want you to go in there, either."

"He's waiting for you. He wants you. Which means that I am going to kill him."

"No."

"Ava." His voice was implacable. "He will not hurt you."

"But you—"

"Or me."

She didn't say anything. The terror muted her.

"He will not rob us twice. Do you understand?"

Ava shook her head.

"I will not allow it, Ava."

Tears welled in the corner of her eye. She'd imagined killing Brage so often. Had yearned for it. But Malachi had been dead then, and the thought of risking her life was nothing. Now, the sheer terror of loss paralyzed her. She wanted to live so badly. Wanted her mate to live.

"I can't lose you again," she said.

He gripped her chin and laid a fierce kiss on her lips. She drank it in. Drank in the heat and the life and the burning presence of him. His arms wrapped around her, and his voice rang in her mind, brighter and stronger than the others. Stronger than it had been. A song whispered in the back of her mind and she breathed it into his mouth, her lips moving against his, not in passion, but in words she barely recognized.

Malachi breathed in the magic, and his skin heated under her hands. She pulled away and looked down; his *talesm* were glowing.

His head had dropped back, and she could see his throat working to pull in air.

"Malachi?" Had she hurt him?

He shook his head, his eyes closed. "Wait."

The silent furor in the house behind him continued unabated. Grigori voices snuffed out over and over. Irin voices. And threading through it all, Brage's seductive whisper.

"Come…"

Malachi's eyes opened, as if he'd heard the call, too. They were bright with magic, and she blinked in surprise.

I gave him that.

Ava knew it without question.

He took a deep breath and released her, holding out a hand that she clasped with her own.

"Take me to him, Ava. Now."

Once they entered, Ava could see that the old house rose four stories, with rooms branching off the stairwell and going back into the house. More like an apartment building than a house, and silent voices filled every corner, Grigori and Irin mixing together in almost-silent chaos. A low hum filled the air as singers worked magic. She could feel it like a tremor along her skin.

A low scuffling from the left.

The door burst open and Damien tumbled into the hall, bashing the head of a Grigori soldier into the ground, over and over. Gold dusted his shoulders, rising when he reached the open air of the stairwell. It drifted toward the doorway, escaping like a ghost. Another soldier escaped the apartment and leapt on Damien's back before Sari walked out, sweeping her staff under the soldier's abdomen and flipping him off her mate.

Malachi ignored them and tugged Ava's arm. "Where?"

"Shouldn't we help—?"

A choked gasp cut off Ava's words as Damien plunged a knife into the back of a Grigori soldier. Almost immediately, Sari kicked another to her mate's feet, and he killed that one, too. Gold dust rose around them, filling the air as Damien claimed Sari's lips in a ferocious kiss before they plunged back into the dark room they'd come from.

Malachi looked down at Ava. "I think they're fine."

"Up," she said. "He's up. I think."

"You're not sure?"

"Too many!" She was already becoming overwhelmed by the clamor and resisted using the spells that would close the door, still hoping to be able to track Brage.

They started up the stairs but had to stop on the second landing when three Grigori burst out of a doorway, knives bared. Malachi pushed Ava behind him and attacked. Ava pulled out the knife he'd given her and looked for a target, but the crowded landing made positioning herself difficult.

The three Grigori had come from above and they had the advantage. Malachi was just as fast as he'd always been, but she noticed he didn't heal as quickly. The cuts they gave him were open and bleeding. Blood splattered from the throat of one soldier as Malachi sliced his throat, then used him as a shield to attack the others.

The scent of urine, sweat, and blood surrounded her. From the corner of her eye, she saw a hand shoot out as a Grigori ran from below and reached for her. Ava grabbed his arm on instinct and pulled, jabbing the knife into the cord of muscle on his bare skin. When the knife pierced his flesh, a shot of pure adrenaline lanced through her system. Her heart sped. Her vision cleared. The thrum of voices dropped to the back of her mind, and Ava could hear him again.

"Yes…"

A low laugh cut off by Malachi shouting her name.

"Ava!"

A strangled curse and shout. She was shoved back into the banister as Malachi pulled the Grigori closer and plunged a silver knife into his spine. The dust rose, clouding her vision. Then Malachi was there and pulling her with him.

"Come."

"He's upstairs," she choked out, blinking the dust from her eyes. "I can hear him again."

"This is a madhouse."

"We're killing more of them than they are of us."

He didn't ask how she knew.

They climbed the stairs. One flight. Two. Three.

"He's above us," she said. His voice was no longer whispering, but a thin thread of his presence lingered.

"There has to be a roof," Malachi said, sweeping his eyes from one hallway to the other.

The majority of fighting was going on below them. Ava could hear Renata shouting for Max. Then she screamed and a man roared in anger.

Ava ran toward the stairs, searching for her friends.

"Ignore them!" Malachi shouted. "We need to find Brage."

He grabbed her hand and pulled her down one hallway, but there was no exit. They went back the way they came. At the end of the other hallway, there was an exterior stairwell and a pocket of frigid air. The door had recently been open. Malachi ran through it and Ava followed. He held knives in both his hands, loose and ready at his sides. Ava watched him with pride. Possession.

Her mate.

Broken. Lost. And still every bit the warrior that he had been. With his *talesm* glowing in the dark and a shot of her own magic running through him, Malachi did not hesitate.

Snow dusted the rooftop. It swirled in fat flakes as salty wind blew off the fjord and twisted around them. It was a rooftop garden, bedded down for winter. Heavy furniture lay covered with thick canvas, tied off against the weather. A few evergreen trees sat in pots, their branches a festive white.

Oblivious to the cold, Brage lounged in one of the chairs, its canvas cover thrown off. He was impeccable in a pure white shirt and black slacks, his sleeves rolled up to the elbow as he balanced a dark metal blade on the back of his hand.

"It's about time you arrived."

TWENTY-FIVE

"It's amazing, isn't it? So perfectly balanced," the Grigori said as they approached. "But of course, it was forged in heaven. Or hell. I'm honestly not sure what I believe at this point."

Malachi said nothing, trying to place the blade. He knew he should know what it was. There was something…

"Don't recognize it? I'll admit, it was dark in that shit hole of a cistern," Brage said, flipping the blade from the back of his hand to rest in his palm. "Maybe you couldn't see it clearly."

The knife pulsed with power. Its metal was dull, almost black. There was no decoration on it. No leather wrapped the hilt. Nothing to detract from the purpose of such a grim weapon.

Death.

"Your silence intrigues me," Brage said.

Malachi realized that the Grigori wasn't speaking to him. He was speaking to Ava. And Ava couldn't take her eyes off him.

"You killed him with that," she said softly, the air fogging as it left her lips.

"Yes, I did. Apparently it didn't take." Brage glanced at Malachi, then back to Ava. "My father wants you."

"He can't have her," Malachi said.

"Was I talking to you, scribe?" Brage continued to stare at Ava, flipping the knife in his fingers. Handle. Tip. Handle. Tip. He didn't fumble once. "Will you come with me? Or will I have to take you?"

"I'm not going anywhere with you, you creepy asshole."

Malachi approved of the disdain dripping in her voice. He stepped between Ava and Brage, his knives ready, his heart eager. Her power coursed through him. He could feel her song whisper in his mind.

Brage's eyes flickered to Malachi. Then they closed briefly as a whisper left his lips. "Boring."

He pounced.

The Grigori took Malachi by surprise, knocking him off balance and trying to slip behind him, the blade already raised to strike. Ava stuck her foot out and tripped Brage, distracting the Grigori and causing the blade to nick the side of his forearm as he stumbled back. There was a hissing sound as the smell of sulfur filled the air, then the wind swept it away.

Malachi sheathed one of his knives and circled his opponent as Ava braced her back against the brick wall of the stairwell. Brage swept a foot out and punched Malachi's knee, causing him to slip on the icy bricks. He fell, the snow and slush soaking his back and side.

"Do you even know what she is, scribe?" Brage taunted Malachi as he climbed to his feet. "I'll admit, I didn't at first. I'm still not sure of the details. I do know that your kind won't know what to do with her."

Malachi rose with him, keeping himself between Ava and Brage. The Grigori's lip was cut and the wound on his arm seeped a steady flow of blood. It was black and thick. When the snow hit it, it sizzled.

Brage continued to stare at Ava, cocking his head as if he were puzzling over a specimen in a laboratory. Malachi lunged in, hoping to catch him distracted, but Brage grabbed his wrist and pulled, switching the black knife to his left hand and trying to slice up at Malachi's elbow. He could feel the pulse of magic as his *talesm* repulsed the Grigori's strike. Stepping closer, Malachi hugged Brage to his chest and plunged the silver blade into his side. Blood gushed over his hand, but Brage pushed back, pressing a hand to his waist to stem the bleeding but never lowering his knife.

His lip curled. "I was told you lost your *talesm*."

"Don't believe everything you hear."

Brage lunged again, but his movements held an edge of desperation. Malachi knew he couldn't let the black knife touch him. The cut on Brage's arm was growing. The flesh around it was gray and the veins stood out black against his pale skin.

"You're dying," Malachi said. "Tell us why Volund wants her."

Brage only laughed and dropped to the icy brick, sweeping a leg out again, catching Malachi's ankle with his foot. He brought them both down and scrambled over to him, trying to climb atop Malachi.

Shit.

The Grigori had the upper hand, and Malachi couldn't find purchase on the icy bricks. He was close to panic before a clang sounded through the air. Malachi blinked and Brage fell to the side. Ava was standing over him, clutching a copper urn smeared with blood.

"I couldn't just stand there!"

"Good!"

Climbing to his feet, he almost slipped again, but Ava held him. Brage was shaking his head and blinking at Ava. A frown creased his eyebrows. Still, he persisted.

"Come with me," he pleaded. "You can change everything. You have no idea—"

He stopped when she threw the urn at him.

"Are you nuts?" she shouted. "Why don't you just die?"

Malachi ran and slipped across the roof as the snow swirled. There was a scream on the wind. Nothing human or even animal. Brage looked up, past Malachi. Over his head and into the black night. His mouth fell open in horror and Malachi halted.

A great gold eagle landed on the roof, and the snow exploded around it. It stepped forward and grew into Jaron. He glowed with light, and Brage raised a hand, pointing at him.

"You promised! You said you would not interfere!"

Jaron lifted the Grigori up by the neck. "I lied."

Malachi turned to run to Ava, but found his feet were frozen to the ground.

"No," he gasped. "Ava!"

His body was frozen. He could not reach her. Malachi twisted his neck around, but could barely catch a glimpse of her over his shoulder.

She stepped closer, her eyes locked with Jaron's. Her face held no fear, only a grim fascination.

Malachi shouted again. "Ava, no!"

She didn't turn toward his voice. And she didn't stop.

It was quiet. So quiet.

Peaceful.

One minute she was frightened, watching Malachi and Brage slip across the frozen roof as they tried to kill each other. It held none of the terrible grace she remembered from Istanbul. It was dirty and bloody and cold. Then Brage had looked at her. Malachi was only steps away from killing him, and Brage looked at her with a terrible hunger.

Longing.

For a second, his voice smoothed out. The whisper did not rasp. It curled and twisted, seducing her. Softening her. Then—

Quiet.

Quiet like in her dreams. As if the world had been wrapped in cotton wool and the only sound she heard was his voice.

She saw him, holding the Grigori out to her like an offering. And when he spoke, the whisper came to her ear.

"Do you want him?"

There was nothing and no one on the roof except the three of them. The wind was silent. She was warm. Comfortable. She stepped closer.

"Why?"

"He is yours if you want him," Jaron said, his voice for her ears alone. He held out the black knife as he raised Brage in the air. In his hand, the blade was not a dull black, but a swirling crystalline jewel, glowing with heavenly power.

"Why would I want him?"

The angel frowned. "Don't you want to kill him?"

Of course she did. She'd imagined it countless times. But somehow, the thought of plunging a knife into the limp Grigori that Jaron held out felt wrong.

"I… I don't know. Was he going to kill me?"

"No. In his own way, he very much wants to protect you."

"Then wouldn't it be wrong?"

Jaron cocked his head. "Does it matter?"

Did it? Ava blinked and tried to remember. In front of her, the glowing knife beckoned. She knew it would be warm in her hand. It would fit perfectly. She could feel it sink into the Grigori's spine, and a soft voice whispered in her mind.

Yes…

Come with me…

Take what is yours…

She stepped closer. Brage hung limp in Jaron's grip, like an offering presented to her.

An offering.

To her.

"He would kill your mate," Jaron said. "He would take you to his father, but he would kill your mate to do it."

He *had* killed her mate. In that moment, Ava remembered. The Grigori had killed Malachi. Ripped him from her. Torn Ava's soul in half. The fury rose up and the black whisper grew louder.

Yes.

Kill it.

This is yours.

Ava looked into Jaron's eyes, which held a softness she'd never seen before.

"Tell me what you wish, my daughter," he spoke to her mind. "Tell me, and I will grant it."

She didn't know what to do with such a gift. It was too terrible to offer.

Ava was tired. She only wanted Malachi.

Jaron said, "I cannot grant to you what you have already taken."

"If he would kill my mate," Ava said, "then let my mate kill him."

The angel smiled and closed his hand around the black knife. "I offer you a gift and reap an unexpected reward. How very interesting."

In a blink, he was gone, and Malachi was there, holding Brage by the neck, plunging his silver blade into the Grigori's spine as the monster screamed.

Then the screaming stopped as Brage's body dissolved. The wind snatched his dust, whisking it away from Ava and Malachi, sweeping the snow off the roof in a violent flurry until there was nothing under their feet but black ice and cold brick.

The storm stopped, and everything was silent.

MALACHI KNEW HE HAD EXPERIENCED IT BEFORE. CHANGE HAPPENED slowly and in the blink of an eye. The filthy smell of old water in his nose, the chaos of splashing and shouts and a sharp pain in his neck and Ava's scream—and nothing. Sheer black, as if a veil had dropped over him. Then from nothing, he'd woken with a gasp and a need and the sharp yearning of unremembered dreams.

He was frozen in place, staring helplessly at his mate while she walked toward the fallen angel and the Grigori soldier.

And in the next breath, his hand was on the soldier's neck, the silver blade plunged into his spine. Dust rose, and Brage was no more.

Jaron was gone. Ava was there, staring with haunted eyes at the place Brage had been. And Malachi had no idea how or when he had crossed the roof to kill his murderer.

The furious wind had stopped, and the moon reappeared.

"Ava?"

She blinked, as if coming out of a dream, but she did not speak.

"*Reshon?*" Malachi dropped his knife and put his hands on her shoulders to draw her close. He pressed his cheek to the top of her head and hugged her, but she did not respond.

"*Canim,*" he whispered. "Please."

He finally felt her arms go around him and he let out the breath he'd been holding.

"I don't hear them."

Her voice was so soft he barely heard it, even on the now-silent rooftop.

"What?"

"The Grigori below. I think they're all dead."

"And the others?"

She paused, and he felt the tension leave her shoulders.

"I'm missing three. But none of our friends."

He said nothing. His relief would be silent, for three of their number had been lost. Malachi might not have known them, but they had died—in part—protecting his mate and humans who would never know their sacrifice.

After a few more minutes, he asked her, "What happened?"

There was a pause before she simply said, "Jaron."

"He was here, and I couldn't move, Ava. I couldn't hear. Then he was gone and Brage was in my hands. And I don't—"

"He offered him to me," she said. Her arms went tight around his ribs. "Like… a present. He offered me the knife and asked if I wanted to kill him."

Malachi had killed hundreds of Grigori. Possibly thousands. They were predators. Monsters. In service to their Fallen fathers, they thought nothing of preying on human women, reducing them to nothing more than food for their unnatural hunger. Brage had murdered hundreds. Had even killed Malachi.

And yet the angel's offer to Ava chilled him.

"You refused?"

"Jaron told me Brage didn't want to kill me. That he wanted to protect me, but he would kill you to do it."

"He would protect you by killing me?"

"And so I told him… I told him to let you kill him." Her voice caught. "So you killed him, not me."

"Good."

"No, it's not. I'm sorry, Malachi."

He hugged her closer. "Don't. You did the right thing."

She started to sniff. "Then why do I feel like a coward?"

"Ava—"

"And the worst part… I *wanted* to. I wanted to kill him. So much. Not just kill him, I wanted to make him *hurt*. It was there, Malachi. It's still there inside me. No one understands. There's this black voice that wants me to kill and hurt and keep going until—"

"Stop." He crushed her to his chest, whispering against her cheek and tasting her tears. "Stop."

"Who am I?" she asked, her tears making her voice rough and swollen. "*What* am I?"

"You're my mate," he said, pushing her away so that her eyes met his. His hands cupped her cold cheeks, forcing her to keep her eyes on him. "Mine. My heart. My soul. That is all that matters to me."

"But—"

"That is *all* that matters." He pressed a kiss to her lips, but she froze.

Distant. She drifted away from him even as he held her in his arms. Malachi kissed her, but she was not there. She was lost in her own mind, wracked with needless guilt for the death of a predator. Fearful of her own power.

Vashama canem, reshon.

He could feel his soul reach for her.

Come back to me, Ava.

Tentative hands came to his waist, then reached around and pressed to the small of his back. Her lips softened under his and she allowed him to pull her closer. He wanted to take the kiss deeper. Wanted to spirit her away from the cold killing ground where the scent of sandalwood and sulfur still lingered in the air.

He held her long after they broke the kiss, tucking her head under his chin before he steered her down the stairs, past their friends and the wondering eyes of Damien and Sari. He ushered her into a car someone had brought to the front of the building. It was near dawn, and shopkeepers were beginning to show themselves. Humans called to each other near the docks. The city was waking from the darkness of night, unaware that the silent threat that had been stalking it was gone.

For now.

Malachi took Ava to the scribe house and up the stairs to the room where he found her things. He lay down next to his silent mate and held her until she fell into fitful dreams. Then he followed her into sleep and held her there, too.

• • •　　• • •

It was silent in the meadow, but the dark hedge was gone. Flowers dotted the edges where the forest stood, silent and watchful over its residents. He cradled her in the grass, her arms twined around his neck.

"There's a darkness," she whispered. "And it scares me so much."

"Do not fear the darkness."

"And when the darkness is in me? Should I fear it then?"

"No," he said, lifting her hand from his neck, knitting their fingers together. "Look, my love, there is light, too."

Glowing silver letters pressed against gold. Their arms linked in the moonlight. His dark skin was lit from within by pure white light. And her pale skin—almost white in the moonlight—was touched by burnished gold. Glimmering black lined the edges of her mating marks, and they burned with frightening beauty.

"We were meant to be like this," he whispered. "Two halves of the same soul. Dark and light together."

"How do you know?"

"I know because you told me."

"I did?"

He bent to her ear and whispered, "Remember…"

CHAPTER

TWENTY-SIX

The city of Oslo would never understand why the sudden rash of attacks against women suddenly dropped off with no arrests by the police. There were whispers of organized crime but no complaints. The collapse of an old apartment building near Aker Brygge was only one more mystery that no one tried to solve. There had been rumors about the place for years. Suspicious men coming and going. Strange noises. Rumors of corruption during redevelopment.

The column Ava read in the English edition of the online paper held no answers, only question after question that she knew would never be answered. Not if the Irin had anything to do with it. She sat in the kitchen of the scribe house, drinking coffee and relaxing while everything was still quiet.

"What are you reading?" Malachi asked, sitting next to her with a mug of dark tea.

She snapped her laptop shut. She had no idea why Malachi had carried it while he ran around Europe looking for her, but she was grateful to have it back. "Nothing. Just some news online."

"Anything that will give Lang a heart attack?"

She smiled. "Lang is paranoid."

The watcher was convinced that Irin exposure was imminent. He'd been on the phone with every contact he had in Vienna, trying to figure out what was going on, but he was getting nowhere. The lines of communication were only getting more tangled, and Sari and Damien were no longer debating going to the city. They were planning on it.

"May I?"

Malachi held out his hand, and she passed him the computer, curious what he would do. It was password protected, after all. It wasn't as if he could—

He typed in the password with rapid fingers.

"Hey!"

Malachi shrugged. "Remember how I said that some things just came to me? Well, that was one of them."

"I don't remember giving it to you in the first place!"

"I suppose I must be very observant, *canım*."

She ignored the sweet rush she felt with his endearment and tried to scowl. "That is *my* computer, Malachi," Ava protested as he pointed and clicked. "You don't have any right to—"

"This," he said quietly, angling the screen toward her. "Will you tell me about this?"

He had the photo gallery open. Pictures of Topkapı Palace littered the screen. There were hundreds of thumbnails, but he'd opened the one she'd taken of him while he sat near the cafe, drinking a cup of tea and watching her from behind his sunglasses. He was wearing a linen suit and the sun caught streaks of red in his hair. She put her fingers to the picture, touching his serious face. It was when he was still pretending to be her bodyguard. Before she knew… anything.

"Why this one?"

"I've looked through them all. I tried to start at the beginning, but I still don't remember much. Will you tell me?"

"Yeah." She blinked back the tears. "I can tell you about it if you want."

"I want."

He looked like her mate. Felt like her mate. But in many ways, Malachi was still a stranger to her. This quiet man held only hints of the arrogant, reckless warrior she'd fallen in love with. He was different. More serious. But then, Ava imagined that she was, too.

"You kept following me around the city." She started to smile. "I was pissed, but I can't deny I was enjoying the scenery."

He smiled back. "And you weren't suspicious?"

"You have to understand about my stepfather. I thought he'd hired you."

"Why would your stepfather hire someone to follow you?"

"Carl… he has this accountant who worries…"

He peppered her with questions until she started yawning. Then he guided her up the stairs and into their small room. She let him hold her because she slept better in his arms. So did he. Because, even though her mind didn't know him, her heart and her body did. She let him hold her because Malachi kept the worst of the darkness away.

It still haunted her. She worried about using her magic for more than the most basic protection. Worried about the marks on Malachi's arms that he told her appeared when she sang to him in their dreams. She worried about the strange visions Jaron had given her. And she worried about going to Vienna.

Malachi didn't like the idea either, but if Damien, Sari, and Orsala were going, they both agreed they should follow. She still needed lessons from Orsala. They both needed the protection of friends. Vienna was a hotbed of politics, but it was also the repository of ancient secrets Malachi felt sure would shed light on Ava's origins.

Plus, her father had a concert there in two months. And according to Rhys and Malachi, Jasper Reed might be the one human who could answer questions about the strange blood that made her an Irina.

And why she'd attracted the favor of a powerful fallen angel.

"Tell me what you wish, my daughter. Tell me, and I will grant it."

Ava worried. But for the first time in months, she also hoped.

She drifted to sleep in Malachi's arms, surrounded by the comfort of her mate. And as she drifted, her shields fell. His soul's voice whispered to her, soothing murmurs of love and desire. They wrapped around her heart, fed her soul, and carried her when the darkness beckoned. In her mind, she saw them as they'd been in her dream, light and dark, bound together by heaven.

Not even death had been able to part them.

In her dream, the great circle rose, like the sun after a long night. Gold and silver twisted together, it climbed the sky until it shattered and a thousand points glistened in the darkness. Endless stars lost in blackest night.

And Ava stood below it, staring into the darkness, with Malachi at her side.

EPILOGUE

Nearly a thousand miles away from Ava and Malachi, Jaron sat in a corner of the cell, staring at the woman with tangled hair. Like all her kind, she possessed an ethereal beauty. Her unlined skin was the color of sunset over the desert. Her hair was black and streaked with ribbons of red and gold. When it wasn't tangled, it lay in sumptuous waves over her shoulders. Her lips were the color of ripe berries, and her gold eyes were rimmed by thick, curling lashes.

The woman in the cell knew none of her own beauty. Not anymore. She was lost in her mind.

The humans didn't call it a cell, but that's what it was. They'd given her paints with no brushes, because she would use the brushes as weapons if she could. But she'd used the paint to decorate the bleak walls with the visions that still came to her. Vivid hues surrounded her even though her clothes were an offensive white.

At one time she would have scoffed. As a child, she'd hated any dull color, and he had indulged her.

He'd indulged her audacity, and it had led to this.

She blinked her eyes open in a moment of lucidity and stared at him. "You."

She spoke in the familiar language of her childhood, but her voice was hoarse from disuse. Jaron hadn't visited in a long time.

"Yes. It's me."

"Imagining?"

"No."

She closed her eyes and let out a sigh of relief. He assumed it was difficult to distinguish reality from fantasy. But then, fantasy had always been real to her.

He felt the energy before she started to hum, and he flashed to her side, putting a finger over her lips.

"Shhh," he soothed. He put an arm around her waist and pulled her to his side. "No singing, remember?"

"Why not?" Her voice held the petulance of youth.

"You know why."

She laughed, but there was no joy in it. It was a dark laugh. Strange and frightening. If Jaron had been human, he imagined it would chill him to his bones.

"I sing sometimes when you're not here." She taunted him.

"You should not."

"But I do." She kept giggling until the laughter turned to tears, and she was rocking back and forth with it, knees pulled up to her chest.

"Quiet," he whispered. "No more tears. If they come, I will go away."

She sighed again and curled into his chest. "Tired."

"Then sleep."

"Okay."

He put a hand on her head and held the woman to his chest. Jaron held many powers, but the ability to heal her broken mind still eluded him. The injustice raked his pride, but he put it aside, knowing the feeling would disturb her.

"No dreams," she murmured. "Don't want to dream about him."

"Sleep, Ava." Jaron sent a calming wave of power over her, and her twitching limbs fell still. "I'll keep the dreams away."

• • •　• • •

Continue reading for THE SECRET, the next volume of the Irin Chronicles and the conclusion of Ava and Malachi's story.

THE SECRET

IRIN CHRONICLES BOOK THREE

They took and brought me to a place in which those who were there were like flaming fire,
  and when they wished, they appeared as men.
  They brought me to the place of darkness,
  and to a mountain, the point of whose summit reached to heaven.
  And I saw the places of the luminaries and the treasuries of the stars,
  and of the thunder,
  and of the uttermost depths.

— THE BOOK OF ENOCH

PROLOGUE

S he walked as she always walked in these dreams. Slowly. With no thought of where she was going. She only knew that, within this forest, a dark angel walked on her right and her mate walked on her left. Sometimes she could smell the soft damp rot of the forest; sometimes she couldn't. Sometimes she could hear her footsteps as she walked over leaves. Often the birds chirped and called, but this night they were silent.

She might see his shape, but often the angel was only a presence lurking on the edges of her mind.

This night, her mate was beside her and the angel's dark form walked at her side, his presence tangible. His power muted.

"Why do you visit me like this?" she asked him.

"Because I want to."

"There is another reason."

"If I am here, then the other cannot be."

She glanced at the warrior beside her. "But *he* is here."

"He belongs here. The other does not."

A tendril of anger threaded through her dream. "I don't understand you."

"You will."

"Why can't he hear you? See you?" She glanced at the warrior. In the low light, his *talesm* glowed with a silver sheen. He didn't touch her, but she felt his presence as if the whole of him were wrapped around the ephemeral thought of her, anchoring her mind to her body.

She would drift away without him.

"Your mate is not mine as you are."

"I don't know what that means."

"You will."

"When?"

The dark angel paused. "Soon. You will know soon."

They walked, and the night grew darker. Colder. She shivered, and her *reshon* reached out, taking her hand in his. That was all he did, but the cold fled and she was drawn into his light. The mating marks on her arms lit. Her shoulders grew warm, and the fog that surrounded them grew thinner.

The angel stopped, so she did too. He stepped closer, until his face was lit by the light that glowed from her body. Her own marks. Before her, he grew. And he was not a man. He was more, but she was no longer frightened.

"This is how it should be," he said, one hand hovering over her rune-marked shoulder. "Thousands of years, and I finally understand."

She felt her mate draw closer, but the dark angel held up a hand. He was forced to retreat. The scribe said something she did not hear because her eyes were locked on the familiar gold gaze of a man who was not a man.

"I want you to remember now."

Remember what?

He sent an image to her, but it was not one of the visions that were familiar and frightening. It was a narrow room, and two men were there with a woman. With *her.* One sat next to her. The other in a corner.

This is a memory. This is mine.

"Remember, Ava."

"You are… Irin scribe house."

"Istanbul."

"What are you?"

"…angels."

Angels? Her eyes closed. Her mind focused. Angels.

"Did you think the angels—"

"Ava!"

*   *   *   *   *   *

SHE WOKE WITH A SHARP BREATH, SITTING UP AS HER EYES FLEW OPEN. Malachi was beside her, his hand on her arm. It was early morning, and grey light shone around the corners of the curtains in the house by the sea. The room was cold, but she was covered in a sheen of sweat.

"Ava?"

"I'm awake." She cleared the rasp from her throat. "I'm okay."

"Was it Jaron again?"

"Yeah."

She took a soothing breath as he pulled her into his arms. She no longer had to ask. He no longer hesitated.

In the month since he'd come back to her, they'd grown more familiar, though they still handled each other with care. Malachi was cautious about certain topics. Their past in Istanbul was safe. Their months apart were not.

Part of Ava felt as if she'd woken from a nightmare when Malachi came back.

The other part waited in terror to wake from the dream of him being alive.

"Better?" he whispered into her hair.

"Yes." She breathed again, closing her eyes and listening to the steady surf in the background. "Yes, better."

He held her against the solid wall of his chest, anchoring her to his body, holding her in the circle of his arms.

Safe. Safe.

Some mornings Ava woke feeling as if she could drift away. She was smoke on those mornings. The thin fog that hung over the ocean in the moonlight. They clung to each other in sleep, no matter what had happened during the day or how distant she felt.

Sometimes she woke and he was watching her, frowning as if he was trying to remember.

On the best mornings, she woke and Malachi was the man he had been, light in his eyes and a teasing smile at the corner of his mouth. They made love on those mornings with playful passion. The joy of new lovers in familiar skin, hiding away in his grandparents' house on the edge of the sea.

On those mornings, they didn't speak of the other times he woke her. The hours when she cried in her sleep. Stifling screams. Weeping with remembered loss. In the bleak darkness of those nights, they held each other desperately.

"I'm here," he'd whisper. "Ava, I'm *here*."

Once, she bit his shoulder hard enough to break skin, and the taste of his blood had lingered in her mouth for days.

"I'm here." He said it over and over again.

And in the mornings, she believed him.

But the nights always came. The dark angel walked with Ava in her dreams, and she woke crying, seeing Malachi's face dissolve into gold dust that rose in the damp air of the cistern where he had died.

◆ ◆ ◆   ◆ ◆ ◆

"HOW IS SHE?"

"She grieves."

Rhys paused on the other end of the phone call. "But you're back."

"Her mind knows that. But there are moments when I think her heart forgets."

Malachi held the phone to his ear while he watched his mate take pictures near the shore. His grandparents' house sat on the ocean north of Hamburg, hugging the edge of the North Sea. It was bitterly cold in the middle of winter.

Malachi craved the warmth of southern waters, but Ava resisted a return to Istanbul no matter how Rhys and Leo reassured her.

His brothers called every week and asked the same questions.

How was Ava?

Had Malachi remembered more?

Had any more of his *talesm* returned?

Malachi continued to remember in scattered bits, but nothing like the full recovery they'd hoped for when he and Ava reunited. His *talesm* were stalled. They were nowhere near a scribe house where he could perform the rituals correctly, and none of his previous tattoos had reappeared as they had for a while during their dream-walks.

Ava refused to use her magic.

"Have you asked her about going to Vienna?"

"She keeps saying 'later.' She'll go later. We were going to go when her father performed there, but she changed her mind at the last minute. Said she wanted to have more time with just the two of us."

"That's understandable."

Malachi shook his head. "That's not the reason, Rhys."

"No?"

He took a deep breath and debated confiding in the scribe who had once been his closest friend. Though he couldn't remember all of it, moments came to Malachi when he remembered how close he and Rhys had been. Years of history tied them together. He'd had to learn to trust the man he had been, even if he couldn't remember the whole of himself. Even if it was possible he'd never remember it.

He watched Ava as she looked out to sea. She hadn't moved in minutes. She was letting the icy surf lap her feet as the wind picked up. It whipped her hair into a cloud of black waves. But even as the cold crawled up her legs, she didn't break her gaze on the horizon.

"She won't use her magic."

"What do you—?"

"She's reading a lot. Has me help her with translations sometimes. She's read through everything Orsala sent at least twice."

"But she's not practicing spells?"

"No. She mouths the words, but she won't say anything aloud."

"Do you ever see her marks glowing?" Rhys's voice was concerned. "Any sign?"

"Dreams. Only in our dreams."

"And the visions?"

"Nothing like what happened to her in Norway. She dreams, but she doesn't remember it clearly."

Both men paused in the conversation, and Malachi looked up and down the beach as Ava continued to walk and take pictures. Scanning for threats. Always scanning. She was his to protect and always would be, even now that she had her own power.

Ava looked up and smiled at him once before she went back to taking pictures of something in the water.

Other than when she was reading, she was rarely without her camera, and he often glanced up to see her taking a picture of him with a shy smile.

He loved it when she did.

"Do you think she's feeling unsure of using her magic?"

"I think she's terrified."

"Of what? You're more than capable of shielding her at this point, even with your *talesm* diminished. Your bond with her—"

"She's terrified of what she can do. She hasn't said anything, but you know she feels different."

Rhys was silent.

"She's not like the others, Rhys. Even Sari and Orsala know. They don't say anything, but her magic feels… different."

"We've never understood where it comes from. That has to be disconcerting."

He squeezed his eyes closed for a moment. "Disconcerting" didn't even touch the surface of it.

"Is there any sign of her grandmother?"

"If the older Ava is still alive, Jasper Reed has hidden her so completely that not even I can suss out her location. We've torn through his financial records. Other than being ridiculously wealthy and spending money on enough drugs to intoxicate a small country, everything lines up."

"He's that much of a junkie?" Malachi curled his lip. He'd spoken to Ava's mother on the phone, even spoken briefly to her stepfather. They were polite. Her mother was warm but cautious. Her stepfather, disinterested. But it was difficult to imagine them allowing an addict— even a rich one—into Ava's life.

"I don't know that I'd call him a junkie," Rhys said. "He has many of the signs of bipolar disorder. The drugs he takes could be a form of self-medicating. He's mostly functional, other than the typical artistic excesses."

Ava's father was a world-famous musician and composer, but his offstage antics were legendary. He'd been a peripheral part of her life when she was a child, but they'd developed an affectionate, if distant, relationship as Ava had become an adult. Malachi knew they e-mailed regularly and were planning to meet when her father was on tour in Europe.

"Any word from Vienna?"

"Nothing since last week."

Orsala and Sari were in the city with Damien, quietly taking stock of the fallout from their confrontation with Volund's Grigori in Oslo. The rumbles of discontent from the watchers over Europe had grown, and the Scribe Council in Vienna had been forced to take notice. But for the almost-immortal elder scribes on the council, change did not come swiftly. It would take more than the concern from soldiers in charge of the scribe houses to make the politicians take action.

The stated policy of the Irin Council had not changed.

Protect humans from the Grigori, but do not engage further.

Do *not* provoke the attention of the Fallen.

Defense, not offense.

But though the Irin Council remained silent, formerly hidden Irina around the world had been roused by the attack on Sarihöfn.

Irina who had hidden themselves since the Rending were making their way to scribe houses around the world.

And the Irina weren't interested in defense.

• • •   • • •

SHE WATCHED HIM AS HE ATE, MARVELING AT EVEN HIS SIMPLEST gestures. The way his full lips closed around the tines of a fork. The movement of his throat when he swallowed. The shadow of stubble that grew every day, only to disappear each morning when he shaved. It would rasp against her lips when she kissed him at night, an edge of coarseness against the soft strength of his mouth.

He looked at her, the corner of his lips turning up. "What are you thinking?"

She smiled back and took another bite of the stew he'd made. Ava was pleased to discover that Malachi was a very good cook. He'd never cooked for her in the scribe house in Istanbul. The quiet routine they'd fallen into when they came to the sea was nothing like what they'd ever had before. There had been the tumult and the ecstasy of their time in Turkey. The agony of their separation. The uncertainty of their reunion in Oslo.

They had never just *been*.

"You know what I'm thinking," she said. "What are you thinking?"

"I'm thinking we should finish dinner and clear the table."

"We could leave the dishes until later."

"We could, but I have other plans for the table." He patted a hand on the edge of the sturdy table where he'd eaten as a boy.

Ava smiled. "Your grandmother would be scandalized."

He laughed, and the rich sound of it filled one of the cracks that still riddled the tentative foundation they were building.

"If you knew her and my grandfather," he said, "you'd know how false that is."

"What were they like? Do you remember much?"

He nodded. "I've remembered a lot since we've been here. Stepping through the door. Hearing the ocean… I remember much more about my childhood with the anchors here."

Malachi never said it, but she knew he wanted to go back to Turkey. Wanted to try to jog his memory where they had first met.

According to Leo, it was safe. He and Rhys had been put in charge of rebuilding the Istanbul scribe house, and with so many of Volund's Grigori dead from the attack in Norway, there was little supernatural activity in the city.

It was quiet, but Ava sensed it was the stillness before a violent storm. Jaron's visits had not lessened, and the darkness she sensed around the edges of her dreams only grew deeper.

"Tell me," she said. "About your grandparents. What were they like? They were married—mated?"

"Yes, but not as we are."

"How?"

He took a sip of red wine and refilled her glass from the bottle on the table. "They were mated, but they were not *reshon*."

"What?"

He smiled. "I told you not every Irin couple has that connection. They met when they were both young. They fell in love and took mating marks, even though they knew they might meet their soul mate later."

"What would happen if they did?"

He shrugged. "Nothing. They were bonded. They had shared their magic. They loved each other very deeply and were committed for life."

Ava blinked. "Did they dream-walk?"

"I imagine so. That's a consequence of mating, not because a scribe and a singer are *reshon*."

"But…"

Malachi hooked his ankle around her leg. "What?"

"I guess I can't imagine it. To *not* have that connection… You make everything weird about me make sense."

"I'm glad." His eyes warmed. "Even though I don't think you're all that weird."

"I am. You just don't remember."

He smiled, even as his eyes drifted to the fire they'd started earlier. It crackled and popped in the cold air. "Are we more than soul mates, Ava?" His voice was pensive. "I wonder sometimes. If you are here—with me—from only that obligation."

"I'm not with you out of obligation."

"Are you sure?"

"I'm positive." She blinked the tears away. She was done crying, and he deserved more than her doubt. He deserved his life back. His memories. His mate. "I love you."

"I love you too." He waited for her to speak, but she said nothing. "Come here."

Ava stood and slid into his lap as he pushed away from the dinner table. His arms came around her, and she laid her head on his shoulder, pressing her cheek to his neck. Skin to skin. The comfort was instant. The voices swirling at the edges of her mind were silent. The terrible energy that crawled under her skin calmed.

"Do you want to go back to Istanbul?" she asked.

"I want to be where you feel safe. And happy."

She opened her mouth but paused before she gave him an automatic answer.

He deserved honesty too.

"Happy may still be a ways off. But… I'm content with you. I feel complete."

"You're still frightened."

"Yes. But being with you makes me feel safer. It's going to take time."

"Do you want to go to Istanbul?"

"I want you to find yourself again. To get back to your life. With me in it, of course. But you need to have a purpose again. To help your brothers. I know you're restless here. And I can take pictures anywhere."

"I'm fine."

"You have chopped enough wood in the past month to heat a castle for a year."

"I have not." He ran a hand through her hair. "I've worked off energy in other ways too."

"And I'm a fan of those ways." She kissed his neck. "We can go back. If you want to."

He held her tighter. "Are you sure?"

No.

She took a deep breath and said, "I will be."

CHAPTER
ONE

Malachi watched the traffic crawl by as they eased onto Atatürk Bridge before crossing the Golden Horn in the taxi Ava had flagged down outside the airport. She'd resisted telling anyone they were returning to the city, still wary of any communication that could put them at risk. They'd flown from Frankfurt to Istanbul during the night, arriving just as the sun was rising. It was rush hour, and the familiar shouts of drivers and vendors filled the air along with the smell of the water.

He glanced at his mate, who was sitting quietly next to him in the back of the car. Her phone was out and her fingers danced over the small keyboard, but her leg rested against his.

Touch. Connection. He suspected in the tumult of the busy city she needed as much as possible.

"What are you doing?" he asked.

"Answering e-mails." She tapped faster. "Checking… stuff."

"Anything interesting?" Malachi might have lived longer, but in some ways, he was far more ignorant of the world at large. Ava was independent. She managed her own finances. Ran a business. He knew she had a home in California, but he didn't think she'd been back for over a year.

"A few things from my mom. Two from my agent. One from my dad's manager. A couple from… from my financial adviser."

"Are you still ridiculously rich?"

"Yes." She looked up. "Are you still okay with having a rich wife… mate? Whatever I am?"

"Yes." He smiled. "It's good that one of us knows something about money."

Ava shook her head. "What did you do without me?"

"I don't know." His smile turned into a grin. "Honestly, don't remember a thing."

She shoved his arm. "Don't joke about that."

"Why not? There's nothing else to do."

"You'll remember," she said. "Eventually."

"I have you back." He reached over and squeezed her knee. "There are worse places to start."

She grew silent, but he could see the shadow of worry fall on her.

"What about work?" he asked. "You said there was something from your agent. Is there anything interesting? Any new jobs?"

Ava hadn't worked a proper photography job since the one in Cyprus a few weeks before they'd met.

Through scattered conversations in the past month, Malachi had been able to put together a timeline of what had happened to him and his mate, even though he only remembered pieces. Only a year had passed, and Malachi's world had taken over Ava's with no end in sight. She'd been running from Grigori. Hiding from fallen angels. Learning who and what she was in the world, as much as any of them knew.

A human job might seem like a vacation.

Ava shrugged. "There's an offer from a magazine, but nothing tempting."

"Where is it? Would it be possible for us to go? I can go with you."

"No." She curled her lip. "I mean, it'd be possible. I just don't want to do it."

Malachi frowned. It bothered him that her life had been so disrupted. He couldn't remember what they had planned before they'd been separated, but he knew that she had a life outside of him, and he didn't want her to lose it.

"What would you be doing now?" he asked. "If you'd never met me? If all this hadn't happened."

Ava shut off her phone and looked at him. "I don't know. Traveling. Taking pictures. Going to more doctors? Hiding somewhere remote so I wouldn't go crazy."

His voice dropped, not that he thought the driver was eavesdropping over the pulsing pop music blasting on the speakers. "Is it better than last time?"

"The voices?" she asked softly, reaching for his hand. "Yes. Much better."

"Good."

At least she was using her magic to shield herself. It hadn't been an issue in Germany, but they'd been in the country. He'd worried about her being back among humans, especially in a crowded city like Istanbul. Her refusal to use magic could be a liability to her safety, and no matter how much he could protect her body, there was only so much he could do to help her mind.

"Being with you has always helped. Any kind of contact…" She threaded their fingers together and picked up her phone again. "It makes life much more bearable."

Malachi tugged her toward him, and she rested her head against his shoulder. It was a small thing for him to do. A small thing for her to give him. But she let herself lean on him, and he was content. She continued scrolling through her inbox, reading and deleting things as he turned back to watch the city inch by.

Istanbul was achingly familiar. In the puzzle of his mind, he still had more blanks than complete pictures.

A few things were clear. Summer holidays as a child. Portions of his schooling. Running with his father in the evenings. He remembered that his father had loved to run.

But so much was still empty. He occasionally caught pieces when Ava would say something or he recognized something familiar, but he hoped being back in Istanbul would jog more memories. Especially those of when he and Ava had first met.

"How does it feel?" she asked. "Being back."

"Good." He smiled. "And warmer."

"No complaints about that."

They'd spent the Christmas holidays in Germany. The Irin didn't celebrate Christmas as the humans did, but he'd bought Ava a tree and hung some lights. The Irin *did* celebrate midwinter holidays, but Malachi had little memory of what to do. They were supposed to sing songs, but he didn't remember them. They were supposed to hang lights too. There should have been candles and laughter. But all those memories peeked into his mind before running away.

So they'd celebrated Christmas, and he'd made her a dish that he thought his mother had made, though he'd had to look the recipe up online. It hadn't tasted right, but it was better than nothing.

Heavy clouds hung over the city, and he was glad that Leo had told him the roof of the scribe house was already repaired.

"Jasper sent me an e-mail," she said. "Or his manager did."

"Oh?" Malachi honed in on any mention of her father. They still needed to talk about Jasper Reed. He had been reluctant to bring the subject up, but he knew Rhys wanted Ava to get in contact with Reed to ask about the grandmother she'd been named after.

Her bloodlines were still a mystery.

Irin tradition told that magical ability passed through the mother's line. Only an Irina could give birth to someone with Ava's power. And from what the Irina of Sarihöfn said, Ava had plenty of raw power.

But her mother wasn't Irina. Not in any sense. Rhys had even asked a friend in Los Angeles to trail Lena Matheson in order to confirm what Ava had told them. Malachi hadn't told her yet, but the scribe in California was certain Lena didn't have even a hint of angelic blood.

Ava's paternal line was the only option.

"What did your father say?"

"I talked to his manager. Luis said the usual. Jasper's really busy. Blah blah blah. Crazy tour schedule. He'll call when he can. You know."

"No." He frowned. "I don't. I thought you said you hadn't seen your father in a year and a half."

"I haven't," she muttered, still scrolling through her phone. "We probably should have gone to that concert in Vienna, but…"

"Forget Vienna. Your father is still in Europe?"

"For the next few months. He'll be in Italy, I think. Then France. There may be a concert or two in Spain. I'm not sure. Then he'll go back to his recording studio in LA."

"But right now, he is in Europe?"

"Yeah."

"And you are here."

"Obviously."

Malachi still didn't understand. "But Istanbul is not far. He is traveling anyway. Why doesn't he simply fly to see you?"

She only shrugged.

It baffled Malachi. Irin children were rare and treasured because of it. Fathers and mothers both doted on them, especially when they were young. Scribes were expected to stay close to their families when a child was small, even if they were warriors, as Malachi's father had been. The few memories he'd recovered of his parents were precious.

But though Ava had a close relationship with her mother, her father and stepfather were both distant.

It was something he would never understand. Should they have children, Malachi couldn't envision being disinterested. The thought of Ava bearing his children brought only feelings of excitement.

"Did we speak of having children?"

She looked up from her phone. "Not… specifically. You told me Irin children were rare."

"They are. But most couples are able to have one or sometimes even two."

He saw her color rise. "Are you saying you want children with me?"

"Of course." He had the privilege of a mate when few other Irin males did. Of course he wanted a family as well. "Do you not want children?"

"I…" She glanced at the driver. "Could we talk about it another time?"

"If we must." His stomach felt like lead. He'd never considered that Ava might not want children, though he knew many human women chose not to have them.

"Hey." Her voice softened. "It's not something I thought about. Before, I mean. When I thought… you know."

When she thought she'd been mentally ill. Malachi nodded. Ava probably would not have considered herself a suitable mother then.

He put an arm around her. "We have time."

"I know."

They had centuries if they wanted them. A thousand years to be together. Maybe longer. Many Irin mates broke up the centuries of life by spending significant time apart. It only made reunions sweeter, and they always had their time together in dream-walks.

Malachi didn't want to be apart from Ava. He guessed he could have centuries and still hunger for her.

If they managed to survive.

As if thinking the same thing, she asked, "Still no sign of Grigori in the city?"

"None. Volund depleted his forces in Oslo, and there don't seem to be any rushing to fill the void. Have you had any more visions?"

"Still the same."

Jaron walked with her at night. He could sense the fallen angel's presence but not see him. Not hear him as Ava did. Malachi had never said anything to Ava, but it infuriated him that he was powerless to stop the intrusion of the Fallen into her mind. He could protect her body— would protect it with his life—but he could do nothing to guard her mind.

In that, she was completely alone.

THEY PULLED UP TO THE HOUSE IN BEYOĞLU FIFTEEN MINUTES LATER. Leo was standing at the front step, enjoying the morning sun with coffee in hand. He grinned when he spotted them turn the corner in the cab. The old house stood in the background, scarred from the fire Volund's Grigori had started, but slowly coming back to life.

"Sister!" Leo held out his arms as Malachi helped Ava out of the taxi. She ran to him, and the big man enfolded her in his embrace. Malachi felt no twinge of jealousy at their contact. His brothers had been the ones to take care of his mate when he'd been gone.

But he did envy their familiarity.

"I can't believe it!" Ava said. "You've gotten taller."

"I have not. I promise."

"No, you have. I know it."

Leo smiled at Malachi. "You've just been spending too much time with this midget."

Malachi chuckled. He was above average height for most Turks due to his mother's German heritage, but Leo and his cousin Maxim were from Northern blood. They towered over all the other scribes in the house at well over six and a half feet.

Rhys appeared at the door, and Malachi walked over to him after paying the driver and grabbing their bags.

"We didn't know you were coming," Rhys said.

"She worries." Malachi stopped and set down their bags before he spoke a question that popped into his mind, as familiar as please and thank you. "Does the fire still burn in this house?"

"It does." Rhys's mouth spread into a grin. His eyes darted between

Malachi and Ava, who had come to stand at his side. "And you are welcome to its light. You and your own."

"Rhys!" Ava held out her arms, and Malachi let her go and watched as the dark-haired scholar embraced her.

"Welcome home, sister."

"I missed you guys."

"We kept the fire burning."

The fire that burned in the ritual room of each scribe house was sacred. The fire of Istanbul had burned continually since the house had been founded during the Byzantine era. The scribe house had been torn down. Moved. Rebuilt. But the fire remained the same. Combined with magic, Irin fire could heal, and it was necessary to the scribes who tended it. Rhys had risked his life to save coals from the hearth when the wooden house had burned the year before, knowing the human firefighters would extinguish it with their modern equipment.

The fire still burned. The history was intact. And Malachi felt another key turn in the vault of his mind.

Visions of shadows and light. Candles flickering against carved walls. The tight burning pain as the needle hit his skin. He hissed, looking down at the intricate *talesm* that rose on his right forearm.

"Malachi?" Ava turned to him and noticed it. "Your arm. What—?"

"I just remembered writing it," he said quietly. "In the ritual room here. It was right after I'd met you. I'd been tempted, and I still thought you were human. I wanted to touch you, but…"

Rhys looked down, his scholar's eyes keen on the mark. "It's a spell of focus. To enhance self-control. Very well done, brother."

"Thank you."

"Is it painful?"

He nodded. "Like I've just tattooed it."

"Hmm." Rhys cocked his head and pulled Malachi and Ava into the foyer of the house. Leo followed them until they were away from prying eyes. "It's very likely that your *talesm* will reappear with your memories. They may be tied to specific places. You had the memory here, and the spell reappeared. It seems to be complete, though I don't know if you'll be able to access this magic since it is not connected to your *talesm prim.*"

Malachi's newly scribed *talesm prim* was on his left wrist. The original it replaced had been the first spell he'd ever tattooed on himself, the one that tapped into his natural magic and let him control it better. As he'd grown older, more spells had been added. But when he'd died, they'd died with him. When he'd returned, it was as if he'd been reborn.

To date, he'd only recovered a portion of the magic on his left forearm; the recovered spell was on his right.

"There are these as well." He pushed up his sleeve and showed Rhys the spells that had first reappeared during his dream-walks with Ava. Shadows of his former magic, lurking like smudges beneath his skin. They were sporadic. Patchy.

Leo's eyes narrowed. "You didn't show us these? When did this happen?"

Malachi glanced at Ava. "When she sang to me," he said. "In our dreams."

She bit the corner of her lip. "But I'm not singing to you anymore."

He pushed Rhys and Leo away from examining his arm and pulled Ava to the side. Speaking quietly, he said, "When you are ready, you will sing to me."

"But—"

"There is no rush, *reshon*. We are protected here. My strength is returning on its own. Your magic is *yours*. You must make the decision to use it when you feel safe."

She nodded, but her mouth was still downturned.

"Smile, Ava." He touched her chin. "We are home."

"Don't tell me to smile when you're still not whole."

He swallowed the pain. He wasn't whole. He wasn't the man she'd once loved. He was different. Damaged.

"Do you love me?" he asked.

"Yes."

"Then I'm whole."

A wound doesn't heal just because it stops bleeding.

They were both still wounded, but her love had stopped the bleeding. Malachi knew everything else would come in time.

• • •　• • •

HE walked next to her in the forest, the trees towering over them and the moon high and full. He could hear the birds. Feel the grass beneath bare feet.

She walked with the dark angel at her side, but he could not hear them. As much as he strained, no voices reached his ears. It was as if the dark one had wrapped Malachi's mate in a fog, shielding her from him. From the forest around them. From the night.

From everything.

For a heartbeat, his grey eyes met the golden gaze of the Fallen, and a whisper came to his mind.

Thousands of you, Scribe. One of her.

The warrior scanned the forest with newly woken senses. No longer did he reach for his mate wrapped in the fog; he reached outward.

Darkness surrounded them. And though the light from the full moon shone overhead, it did not illuminate the forest, save for the path they walked. A heavy presence pressed against his skin, and at once he perceived the truth.

Do not fear the darkness.

The dark angel was shielding his mate as she dreamed. Hiding her.

But from what?

◆ ◆ ◆   ◆ ◆ ◆

MALACHI woke when her lips met his. The black night was a cloak around them as she moved over him, covering his body with her own. His magic reached for her but only brushed against the cool of her skin. Whatever barriers fell in the nighttime, she still held her soul back. His *talesm* glowed in the cocoon of their bedclothes, lighting their skin as they moved together.

She was silent as they made love. Their bodies spoke for them.

Kiss me. Hold me. Mend me.

Make me whole.

He felt his soul reach out, straining for hers. Ava sighed as he entered her. His breath became hers.

Again.

More.

Again.

Tighter. Higher. Faster.

When they came, it was together; he felt her pleasure as his own.

She held him over her, her arm wrapped around his neck so their cheeks pressed together. He panted into her neck.

"Ava, let me—"

"No," she whispered. "Stay. Just like this. Need you. Need this."

"Too heavy."

"No." He was still buried in her. She wrapped her legs around his hips and held him tighter. "Stay. I need to feel you."

He said nothing more. Only held her. Kissed her. Over and over. Soft lips brushing her cheeks. Her lips. Her eyelids. Her neck.

"I'm here," he murmured.

"Not a dream." Her voice had become frantic again.

"It's not a dream. I'm here."

"Okay."

"Ava."

"Hmm?"

He pulled away just far enough that their eyes could meet. "Let me in, *reshon*."

Her eyes darted to the moon shining high through the narrow window of their bedroom. "What are you talking about?"

He looked at her for a moment, then he reached up, bracing his arm at her side so that his other hand was free to trail up her body.

Over the curve of her hip. The dip of her waist. The rise of her breast.

His finger settled over her heart and he wrote there, scribing the ancient words she had used to call him back. Dips and swirls of angelic runes over her skin. The incantation glowed gold under his hand.

Vashama canem.

"Malachi?"

Come back to me, reshon.

HOURS LATER, AVA STILL WOULDN'T REST. HE WONDERED IF SHE WAS afraid to dream.

Malachi only dreamed of her.

He could see the dawn begin to break. Birds sang in the small garden below them.

"I need to find out who I am," she said, her voice barely audible in the quiet room.

"What do you mean?"

The first crackle of the muezzin's call to prayer echoed through the air as Malachi rolled to his side and traced a hand over her shoulder, letting his magic flow over her. Her skin flushed gold as her mating marks came alive. She shivered at the contact.

"Stop," she said. "Don't distract me."

He smiled. "But I'm so good at it."

She turned toward him, capturing his hand between her own. She laid them beneath her cheek, and he was content.

"I need to find out who I am," she said again. "*What* I am."

Jaron. Hiding her in dreams. The Fallen protecting her from… something.

Do not fear the darkness.

"You want to find your father."

"Yes."

CHAPTER

TWO

"I'm being straight with you, Ava. Your dad—"

"When are you ever straight with me, Luis?" Ava paced in the living room.

Her coffee sat cold on the end table, and Malachi read the newspaper silently in the corner, keeping one eye on her and the other on the subtitles at the bottom of the television screen. The paper he was reading was Arabic. The news was in French.

She'd once thought herself fairly adept at languages. She had nothing on an Irin scribe.

"Do I need to remind you that I don't work for you?" Luis was starting to get pissy. "I work for your father. And his interests—"

"Are your only interests. I get it. I'm not asking for much. I just want to know where he is because I need to ask him a question."

"Is it something I can help you with?"

She clenched her fist so hard her fingernails dug into her palm. "Is there a reason why you're blocking me from him?"

"I'm not blocking you. Who said I was blocking you? Don't you have his mobile number?"

"He's not answering it."

"What about e-mail?"

"Not answering those, either."

Luis was silent. Her father's manager wasn't usually this big an asshole. He *was* an ass—he worked in the music industry, after all—but it wasn't usually this bad. Which meant something was going on with her dad.

She still had a hard time thinking of Jasper that way, but when she learned the news as a teenager, she hadn't been all that shocked, either. He'd been a part of her life since she was a kid. She just didn't realize he was her father. Jasper and her mother had remained close, despite their past relationship. In fact, Ava had always suspected that Jasper still held a torch for Lena. She was one of the few constants in his life.

The other was Luis.

"Luis…" She rubbed her eyes. "Tell me what's going on."

"Nothing is going on. Your dad is in the middle of a tour, and you know how stressed he gets about that."

"Bullshit. He loves performing. The bigger the venue, the better."

"It's tiring, Ava. I imagine he's exhausted."

"You imagine *nothing* with him," she bit out, her patience at an end. "You are in his business every single day. That's why you have very nice houses in LA *and* Maui. So you know where he is. You know why he's avoiding me. And you know what he's been doing."

Luis said nothing, because there was nothing to say. Ava had paced over close to Malachi, and he put out a hand, absently hooking a finger in her waistband and running his thumb across her skin. The small contact soothed her, and she took a deep breath.

"Ava—"

"Is he using again, Luis?"

"You know he—"

"Dumb question. He's always using. Is he *crashing*?"

Luis was silent again. Ava took another deep breath and sat down on the couch. Malachi reached out and took her hand. She clutched it and could think again.

"Okay, I'm taking that silence as a yes. Where is he?"

"I can't tell you that, honey."

Luis only called her honey when he'd taken off his manager hat. Just like her and Jasper, she and Luis were still figuring out the boundaries of their relationship. He was her father's right hand, but according to Lena, Luis had been the one to discourage Jasper from having a relationship with Ava when she was a child. For her sake or for Jasper's? It could be argued either way.

The man had no life outside her father's career. And Jasper would say he'd be useless without Luis herding him. He respected Ava. Respected her role in Jasper's life. But her father was still the man's first priority, and nothing she said would budge that.

"Has he hurt anyone?" Her voice was rough. She wished she didn't care so much, but she did. She'd always loved him. Even before she knew he was her dad. It was like her mother always said—*There was just something about Jasper.*

"Has he hurt himself?"

"No. Nothing like that. Just… a little worse than normal. He'll be fine."

"I need to talk to him."

"Not the best thing right now, Ava."

"It's important. It's about…" She racked her brain. "It's a health thing. I have some questions about family stuff on that side."

Luis paused. "He's not going to be able to give you much. You know that, Ava. Besides, your father's healthy as a horse."

"Other than the drugs?"

"Despite them." Luis's voice dropped. "Listen, I don't know what deal he made with what devil, but the man has never been sick a day in his life, other than the shit he ingests himself. I've seen guys do… a *tenth* of the shit he's done and ruin their bodies. What's going on with your health? Lena said you were staying in Turkey with friends the last time I talked to her. Are you sick?"

Malachi must have heard the question. She kept forgetting that his *talesm* gave him enhanced senses when he activated them. No doubt he'd been listening the whole time.

He frowned and shook his head.

Luis hadn't earned their trust.

Ava decided to go with attitude because being reasonable wasn't working. "Like I'm going to tell you what's going on with my health when you're not even willing to tell me where my own father is."

"Don't be like this, Ava. If he hears that you're sick—"

"He'll be pissed. We both know it. So why are you keeping me from him?"

More silence.

"He's going to hear one way or another, Luis. And I don't think you want to be the one standing between him and his only kid. Do I need to call my mom?"

It was her one trump card, and Luis still wasn't budging.

"Yeah, why don't you have Lena call me, Ava?" His voice was frosty. "She's not an immature little girl throwing a tantrum. Your mother knows what Jasper's limits are."

"His limits?"

"I'm done with this conversation. I'll call you next week."

Ava hung up her phone when Luis's end went silent and resisted throwing it against the opposite wall.

"So," Malachi said, "that went well."

"Asshole."

He raised a single eyebrow. "Is he always like that? I do not like the way he talks to you, and I'd be more than happy to make that clear."

"Luis?" She huffed out a breath. "He's usually pretty cool. But he's in protective mode right now, which tells me my dad is holed up, trying to see just how many drugs he can ingest without killing himself."

Malachi folded up the paper and pressed his lips to her knuckles. "I'm sorry."

"It's the way he is. The way he's always been."

"But you don't know where he is?"

"No."

"Where was he last seen?"

Ava turned on her phone and pulled up the app she used to keep track of her father. The mobile application was fan-created and borderline creepy, but it had become a convenient way to keep track of Jasper and his schedule. "He had that concert in Vienna on the twentieth of last month. Then another in… Budapest. Then it looks like he went under." She scrolled back up the page and mentally counted down. Four weeks. Six…

"Yeah," she finally said. "He was due."

"Due?"

"It's just the way he is. Every eight weeks or so, when he's touring, he'll crash. Luis works it into his schedule. His next show isn't for three weeks."

"He takes a three-week vacation to get high?"

"Among other things. It's better when he's recording. Seems to work some of the energy out for him to be creative. I can relate," she muttered. "I was kind of the same way before we met. Not with the drugs, but…" She shook her head. "He'll be fine for a while. Using but functioning. Then every now and then he'll go off and get really wasted. It varies how bad it is."

"How bad does this seem?"

"If he's not answering my calls or e-mails? Pretty bad."

"Drugs?"

"Drugs. Vodka. Lots and lots of women."

He narrowed his eyes. "Really?"

She shrugged. "It's sad, but it really is typical music-industry stuff. A lot of these guys are like that. You wouldn't believe the excess. Probably one of the reasons he allowed my mom and Carl to raise me without much interference."

"Hmmm." He was rubbing a hand over his chin, scratching at the thick stubble that had already appeared. It was his usual sign that he was mulling things over.

"What are you thinking?"

"I'm thinking…" He pulled out his own phone. "We should call Max."

That hadn't been what he was thinking about, but she let it pass. "Where is Max?"

"I don't know. But he *is* answering his phone, and if you want to find someone, I think he'd be the one to ask."

"You think?"

"I do."

It wasn't a bad idea. Malachi was clearly remembering more about his brothers after being back in the scribe house. He was easier with Leo and Rhys. Seemed more comfortable in his own skin every day that passed. And Ava knew Max was the one the others turned to when they needed information.

"You think Max could find my father? He won't be at any of his usual houses. Probably won't even be using his name."

Malachi shook his head. "Not a problem. He's human."

"What does that mean?"

"It means he has only human methods of concealment. Which means that Max's finding him will not be a problem."

• • •   • • •

THAT NIGHT, LEO AND AVA WERE PRACTICING WITH KNIVES WHEN Rhys walked in with the phone. Malachi rose from the weight bench in the corner, but Rhys held up a hand.

"Damien," he said into the phone. "I'm with the others. I'm putting you on speaker."

"—long as you've swept for bugs recently," the voice came from the mobile phone that Rhys set on the counter in the large bedroom on the second floor where the workout room had been set up.

"I swept yesterday," Leo said, then he flipped two knives in quick succession. One hit the bull's-eye right next to Ava's last throw.

"Good. I'm looking in the corners here, so expect surveillance from the council. Be wary of any scribes who turn up unexpectedly."

"Why?" Ava asked as she threw another. It was a new set that Leo had found for her. Perfectly balanced.

"Ava?"

She could hear the smile in Damien's voice.

"Hey, Damien! Is Sari there?"

"Here," a woman's voice said. "How are you, sister?"

"I'm good." She smiled at Malachi, who was watching her with a smile of his own. He wiped his forehead with the shirt he'd stripped off earlier. "We're both good. Happy to be back."

"Good. I'll let Damien update his men. Then we should talk."

"Got it."

Ava turned back to the target she was sharing with Leo. It felt good to practice. Malachi was more of a dagger-fighting fan. Throwing knives wasn't something he enjoyed as much as Ava did.

"As I was saying, be wary of any unknown scribes."

Rhys asked, "Are we declining hospitality?"

"No. We can't do that."

Ava knew that would be a serious breach of Irin etiquette. Scribes were always welcomed by other scribes. No matter what. To go against that would raise alarms in Vienna and create enemies out of those who should be friends.

"Officially, I'm still here petitioning on the part of the watchers. I have letters from the houses in Berlin, Oslo, Budapest, and Paris. I'm warning the council about the rising threat, but I'm not having much success. They're loosening funds for repairs and rebuilding our house and other houses, but other than that, they're much more occupied with the Irina question."

Malachi asked, "The Irina question?"

It was Sari who responded. "The threat against Sarihöfn and the attacks in Oslo have finally spurred a response. I've been in contact with other havens. The leaders there are mostly of the same mind as I am."

"Which is?" Rhys was perched on the edge of his chair.

Sari paused. Ava held her breath.

"It's time," Sari said. "We can't ignore those calling for compulsion. If we're going to come out of hiding, it will be on our own terms, not the result of politicians threatening us. It has already started."

"I've heard," Rhys said quietly. "There are Irina showing up at scribe houses all over the world. The children and many of the others are still concealed, but more and more Irina are stepping forward and demanding a place at the scribe houses."

"The council must love that," Malachi said.

Ava put her knives down, no longer able to concentrate. "What can they do, though? They can't force Irina into retreats. Not when they've been hiding for so long. What right do they have? What—"

"No right, Ava." Leo put a hand on her shoulder. "But there are those who could make life difficult if they chose to."

"How?"

Sari answered again. "Most of us have mates who are active in Irin society. Soldiers. Watchers. Teachers. Right now, if a scribe has a mate and family, it is accepted that he might be gone for a time. Sometimes for a very long time. But if those in authority over them wanted to, they could make it impossible for those scribes to see their mates and children."

"They would break up families?" Ava asked.

Damien said, "They would make it sound like they are only thinking of the safety of those families. The problem is, the Irin council members who take the Grigori threat seriously are the ones most adamant that the Irina must be forced into retreats. And those who believe the Grigori are no threat are those who would allow the Irina to step forward on their own. In their own time."

It was Malachi who asked the question. "Sari, what do the Irina you speak to want?"

She walked over and kissed him on the mouth. "Yes, Sari, what do the *Irina* want?"

Leo and Rhys laughed, but Malachi just smiled and pulled her down to sit next to him.

Sari said, "Right now, we're trying to decide who should come to Vienna. We haven't had a ruling council for over two hundred years.

My grandmother is adamant that it must be reformed if anything is to be accomplished."

Rhys asked, "And what does the Irin Council think about that?"

"They're old men not used to sharing power," Leo said. "What do you think?"

Damien said, "They know it is inevitable. With Irina raising their voices again, they cannot ignore it. They're positioning singers who believe in compulsion to take positions of power."

"There are Irina who believe in compulsion?" Ava asked.

"Yes," Sari answered. "We are not of one mind. Nor do we have to be. But we've changed in the years since the Rending. There are too many who lost everything to the Grigori and the Fallen. They won't be compliant again."

They spoke of specifics for some time. Which council members were sympathetic. Which were hostile. Sari was passionate. Damien was fed up and clearly wanted to kill someone or something as soon as possible.

It was a full hour later before she and Sari could speak privately.

"You're not using your magic," Sari said.

"Sari, I—"

"I don't want to hear excuses. I want to know why."

Ava pursed her lips. "You're not my mother or my boss."

"I care about you, Ava. And your mate is one of Damien's closest friends. Your power is substantial, and whatever we may be facing, we need you to be able to control it."

She said nothing. How could she explain the threat she felt inside? It came from within. There was a darkness that lived in her. Ava had never sensed the same in Sari or Orsala or any of the Irina she'd met at the haven.

"I'm different, Sari."

"Do you think I don't know that?"

"Did Orsala—"

"My grandmother knows your power is not like the others. That doesn't make it dangerous unless you don't learn control. Are you shielding at least?"

"Yes."

"How about offensive spells? Have you practiced those? Malachi and Rhys can help you."

She clammed up.

Sari huffed out a breath. "You have to use your magic."

"I'm using it."

"Not the way you need to be."

She picked at the edge of the blanket in their bedroom. She could hear Malachi waiting in the hall, trying to give her privacy. She wished he would just come in.

"I have other stuff on my mind, Sari."

"What is more important than learning how to harness your power?"

"I don't know. Learning where it came from, maybe?"

The other woman was quiet, and Ava heard Malachi pacing. Frustrated, she sent out a tentative brush of power. It was hard to describe. A little like blowing air in his direction, but with her mind. A second later, she felt an answering brush of awareness, and he cracked the door open with a grin.

"You *called* me," he whispered, smiling.

She shrugged one shoulder and said, "I need to go, Sari. Malachi is here."

"How is he?"

"He's a pain in the ass sometimes. Right now he's very smug." Her mate kept smiling and lay down on the bed, putting his head in her lap. "But he's mine."

"You sound content."

She brushed a hand through his hair. "I am."

Malachi let out a rumble of pleasure and turned his face to her belly, putting an arm around her waist.

"I'm going to send Orsala to you."

Her fingers tightened in his hair. "What?"

"Ouch," he said. "Ava, really… ow."

"I just decided. This will be good! You were going to come here, but Vienna is unstable right now. I don't know how you'd be received. Instead, Orsala can go to you. Mala is here and restless. I'll send them both to you in Istanbul. Damien says Rhys is one scribe short for the house. Mala will more than make up for that."

"And she'll torture me."

"You're probably out of shape."

"Sari!"

"Let go," Malachi said with a grunt. "It's not my fault she's sending them."

"Tell Malachi I heard that," Sari said. "What are you doing to him?"

Ava was panicking. "Sari, I really don't think—"

"Damien is nodding. He agrees with me. I'll talk to her tonight, and we'll let you know when they will arrive."

Malachi untangled her frozen hand and sat up next to her.

"But I need to go find my—"

"Whatever it is, my grandmother can help. She needs something to do anyway, and that way she'll be able to continue your lessons like she was going to after Oslo. This is an excellent plan. Damien agrees."

"Sari!"

"I need to go. I'll e-mail with details later."

The phone was silent a second later, and Ava sat with her mouth hanging open. "I was ambushed."

"I was injured," he said, rubbing his scalp. "Sari's wrong. I don't think you're out of shape at all."

●　●　●　　　●　●　●

THE PHONE RANG LATE THAT NIGHT. SHE WAS IN MALACHI'S ARMS, and she reached across his chest to grab it before he could wake, putting it on silent as she checked the number. She didn't recognize it, so she answered cautiously.

"Hello?"

"Ava?"

"Max?"

"Your father is in Genoa. Well, a little town in that region. Not far from Portofino."

"Portofino?"

"He has a house there. An old castle he's renting."

She blinked, trying to clear her mind. "You've seen him?"

"Renata found him. He's not in good shape, sister."

She was still only half awake when Malachi took the phone from her.

"Send us the details," he said, rubbing her shoulders, which had gone stiff at Max's tone. "We'll leave tomorrow."

CHAPTER

THREE

Malachi opened his eyes, knowing he was no longer in Istanbul.

He dreamed, but Ava was not with him.

He was no longer in the forest of his mate's walks, but a room that resembled the ritual room of a scribe house. Wax candles dripped on the center table where coals from the sacred fire forced tendrils of heat through the room. Etchings marked the walls, ancient spells protecting the children of the Forgiven from harm.

And the black presence that stalked his mate lurked at the edge of his dreaming.

An epicene figure rose in the corner of the room. "I cannot reach her, but I can reach you."

Malachi turned, recognizing the voice that laughed in some shadowed corner of his lost memory. "Volund."

"Yes."

Malachi scanned the room, reassuring himself that Ava was nowhere near.

"She is not here," the angel said. "I have tried. He has shielded her from my sight. He excels in such things."

Malachi stepped closer. "Show yourself."

The slim figure rose and grew, abandoning the sculptural facade he showed the human world. Here, Malachi realized—in dreams—he could see the angel's true face. All traces of human flaw fled from Volund's visage. Blue eyes bled to gold. His skin, pale before, grew luminous as the moon. His hair, a sandy brown that would blend with the human masses, became true amber, translucent in the glow of the candles flickering in the center of the room.

He was utterly beautiful. A god to human sight.

Malachi was transfixed.

The angel's eyes glowed with barely restrained power, like the sun hiding behind a morning fog.

"Do you love me?" Volund stared into Malachi's eyes.

"No," Malachi said. "You do not want to be loved."

Volund smiled with closed lips. "No, I do not."

"What do you want?"

"I want to be feared. Worshipped."

"You were not meant to be worshipped."

Volund laughed, the cynical smirk marring the angel's handsome face, which melted back into a more human appearance. Stunning, but less otherworldly. And yet it was as if his power had simply condensed. Black energy licked along Malachi's skin.

This is a dream.

"If you think I have no power over your dreams," Volund said, "you are mistaken, Scribe."

"I am protected."

"By whom? Jaron guards your mate, though you know not his reasons." Volund's blue eyes danced. "You are nothing."

Malachi took a deep breath and closed his eyes, breaking the connection with the monster who taunted him and willing himself to return to waking.

"You are nothing." The voice was different.

Malachi opened his eyes, and the angel had departed. Left in his place, the phantom of the Grigori soldier he'd killed on the rooftop in Oslo.

Brage's expression held nothing of the arrogance he'd exhibited in life. His blue eyes were blank and hollow. His face was as beautiful as the day Malachi had slain him.

"We are nothing," Brage said. "Nothing."

"You are an illusion."

Then the corner of the Grigori's mouth turned up, and Malachi saw the wicked edge.

"Since when have dreams ever been illusion for those of our kind?"

"I am nothing like you."

Brage only laughed.

Volund appeared over his shoulder, his human face now a mirror of his son's. He embraced his child, stroking the hair back from his forehead and closing his eyes in sensual pleasure.

"I can be patient," he whispered. "Now that I have found you, I will find you again."

"Go away," Malachi said, stepping closer to the sacred fire.

"For now."

A spark of recognition showed terror on Brage's face, as if illusion had passed from his mind and stark reality intruded. The Grigori's eyes widened in horror. His mouth opened in a scream.

Volund pulled his child into the darkness and was gone.

Malachi bolted up in bed, a harsh gasp ripping from his lungs. He looked around the room, but there was nothing. No trace remained of the ritual room or the angel's darkness. He looked down.

Ava slept beside him, and she did not wake.

• • •   • • •

HE DIDN'T TELL AVA ABOUT HIS DREAM. MALACHI DIDN'T KNOW IF IT was a nightmare or a vision, and his mate had too many other things on her mind.

The train that took them along the coast of Liguria chugged steadily, stopping at the small towns along the route, exchanging a mix of humans for other humans varied in age and shape. Grandmothers going for a visit. Tourists with cameras. Hikers with backpacks. They came and went, and Malachi wished that he and Ava had reserved a private car. If that was even possible. She was firm in her belief that their best concealment was the routine of the mundane, so he indulged her.

Currently, he could not fault her reasoning. She managed to fit in with the humans with ease. She was the native, the tourist, the anonymous traveler with a small satchel and a camera. Unless he had the preternatural senses to feel her power, he never would have noticed her.

"Hmm," he mused, watching her as she snapped pictures out the window.

"What are you thinking?"

He was thinking about Volund's unexpected ability to invade his unconscious, but he didn't want to bring it up. Luckily, his mind could turn to pleasant things very quickly when he was with her.

"Do you really want to know?"

"Yes. I wouldn't have asked if I didn't."

It was true. Ava wasn't a woman who felt the need to fill the air with chatter. He wondered if years of traveling alone had trained it out of her or if the constant voices that had once plagued her were company enough.

"I am thinking… you're very beautiful."

He loved the slight flush she gave him when he complimented her. It made the offer of his praise all the more satisfying.

"You're the only one who's ever said that."

He was surprised, but not overly. Humans could be very superficial, and Ava's physical features were not the most astonishing thing about her. Pretty, but not uncommonly so. Clear skin. Dark hair. Her eyes were the most arresting part of her face, but only other Irin would recognize the unusual shade of gold as anything more than light brown or amber.

No, it wasn't her physical features that were remarkable. And Malachi loved that only he saw the secret of his mate.

Her beauty lay in her mind and her heart. Quiet strength and resilient humor were not things valued enough by the world.

"Hmm."

She gave him a quiet smile. "You always did that," she said. "Before. 'Hmm.' You'd be thinking something you didn't want to say, but I knew it was about me when you would say 'Hmm.'"

"I often think about you."

"That's probably a good thing."

They were sitting across from each other in the compartment. He put his foot on the edge of the bench beside her, enclosing them. Doing his best to block out the world. Ava set down her camera and slid a hand up his pant leg, her fingers playing along his skin.

"I think about you too," she said. "Some would say I'm obsessed."

"And you take pictures of me when I sleep. I hear the clicking in my dreams. It's borderline stalker behavior, really."

"It's settled then. We're both certifiable." She smiled and closed her eyes, sliding down in her seat and tilting her face toward the sun as it shone through the window. The weather was cool, but it was still sunny.

"So beautiful," he whispered.

"So handsome."

"Hmm." He nudged her hip with his foot when she laughed. "You just like my tattoos."

He'd seen a few humans on the train eyeing his arms when they sat down. He'd shoved up his sleeves because the compartment was warm, and his *talesm* were visible. It was a relief, living in a time when body modification was not as unusual as it had once been. Humans did all sorts of things to mark themselves now, so the intricate lettering on his arms was noticed but rarely remarked upon.

"Only yours," Ava said. "I was never a tattoo girl before I met you."

"No?"

She shrugged. "I never thought much about them."

"And you don't have any yourself."

"Only the ones you gave me." Her eyes sparkled with humor. "And those aren't for everyone's eyes."

Malachi supposed a more evolved scribe would try to suppress the surge of possessive satisfaction.

He wasn't that evolved.

Forcing back a smile, he glanced around the compartment. Since no one was paying attention to them, he decided to broach a subject he knew she'd been avoiding.

"Your shields," he said and felt the immediate tension in her fingers where they lay on his calf.

"Why are we talking about this?"

"Because we need to. I know you're still shielding yourself from the voices, but—"

"I thought you said that I could go at my own pace."

"You can. But I need to know what's happening in your dreams."

"Then what are you talking about?"

So it wasn't something she was doing. He hadn't thought so, but he wanted to be sure.

He glanced around again, then turned his eyes back to her. He'd suspected Ava had protection, but Volund's words confirmed it.

"During our dreams," Malachi said. "Do you sense it?"

"What?"

"The layer he's placed over you."

"Who? Jaron?"

"Yes."

She frowned. "I've sensed… something. But it's not something I've thought about much."

"He's shielding you," Malachi said. "I'm sure of it."

"From you?"

"No." From another, darker threat. "He's an angel. Jaron would probably be able to shove me out of your dreams completely if he wanted to. Or maybe not. I don't really know. As far as I've read, the Fallen do not enter our dreams. I don't know why Jaron can walk in yours, but I'm fairly sure he's shielding you."

He wished she would share what had happened on the rooftop in Oslo. There had been a break in time for him. Looking back, he knew that Ava and Jaron had some exchange, but he didn't know what had passed between them. As much as Ava shared with him, there were fears she hid. Malachi didn't even know if Ava realized she was hiding.

"If Jaron is shielding me from something, I don't know what it is," she finally admitted. "He's as confusing to me as he is to everyone."

I cannot reach her, but I can reach you.

Was he right to conceal Volund's intentions toward her? Malachi didn't know, but he didn't want to bring it up. It was one more problem for which he had no solution to offer.

Malachi shrugged. "The Fallen have never shown any interest in protecting humans as far as I can remember. I have no idea why Jaron is doing it."

"Not even their human lovers?"

"Humans are disposable to them. All humans."

"But he protects me." She frowned. "Maybe there's more to the angels than what you've been taught."

"I doubt it, Ava."

"But…" She frowned. "The Fallen and the Forgiven? They're all angels, right?"

"Yes."

"So what's the difference? Why were the Forgiven capable of compassion and not the Fallen?"

"I don't think you could call the Forgiven compassionate. They were just…"

"What?"

He shook his head. Some lessons were still crystal clear, even if he couldn't remember when or where he'd learned them. "The Forgiven gave up their place on earth—their offspring, their human lovers—but it was because they were cut off from heaven. They wanted to go back. It was for our sakes, but more for their own."

"So they were selfish to leave? Not sacrificing?"

"It was both. There had to be an element of sacrifice, because they were allowed to gift their children with magic. The Fallen were not."

"Don't the Grigori have magic?"

"Only the natural magic that comes from angelic blood. Which shouldn't be underestimated. But they don't know the Old Language as we do. So their magic is limited. It is our main advantage."

She was still frowning. "I don't get it, though."

"What?"

"Why don't the Fallen teach the Grigori the same magic? Wouldn't it make them more powerful?"

"I don't know if the Fallen want their children to be that powerful. Or even if they are able to teach it to them. They might not be able."

"You don't know?"

He shook his head. "They're Grigori. We don't engage them in conversation. We kill them."

Ava snorted. "For a race you've been at war with for millennia, you guys don't know much about your enemy, do you?"

"They're a predatory race. We know enough."

"Do you?"

He sat up straighter and lowered his leg. "What does that mean?"

She was looking out the window. "You know I'm no fan of the Grigori. But part of me wonders if the Irin don't choose to be ignorant about them. About their world. It's easier to dehumanize something you don't understand. Easier to kill someone you don't see as a person."

"There's a problem with your reasoning, Ava."

"Oh?"

"The *Grigori* are not human."

"No?" Her eyes swung back to his. "Think about it, Malachi. They're half human. Half angel. The Grigori are as human as you."

• • •　• • •

MALACHI STEWED SILENTLY FOR THE REST OF THE TRIP.

The Grigori as human as he was?

Hardly.

The monsters who had tracked Ava like an animal? Seduced and killed countless human women? Taken his own life? Flashes of memory haunted him, flipping through his mind in a litany of accusation.

Knives and blood. Knives were the only way to kill them and release their souls for judgment. And knives were messy, bloody weapons for fighting. Slices across his arms. His chest. He'd almost lost an ear once.

Knives and blood and dead, lifeless eyes. Not the Grigori. No, their bodies dissolved like so much dust, leaving the remains of their prey for others to find. Dead eyes, often open in surprise or rolled back in ecstasy. The Grigori were beings who made a mockery of love, the human women they hunted never suspecting that the glorious creature who touched them was actually sucking the life out of them.

A small, inconvenient voice in the back of his mind whispered, *You would too.*

His touch would be deadly too.

So the Irin didn't touch any but their own.

That was the point. It was what made them different. Made them the protectors, not the hunters. They were nothing like the Grigori.

He could hear Ava's voice. *But...*

The Grigori had no fathers or mothers as they did. Had no families. No training in magic. They had no Irina.

They had no Irina.

So what hope did they have?

And what monsters would the Irin have become with no hope?

He was silent when they arrived at the hotel. Silent when they made their way to their room. Silent even as Ava stoically put their things away, unpacking from the single bag they had brought, carefully arranging the room with the long practice of years living in hotel after hotel.

"I know you're mad at me," she said as he walked up behind her. She was standing at a small dresser, arranging their clothes. "It wasn't my intention, I'm just saying—"

"Shh." He bent down, wrapping his arms around her waist and kissing her cheek. "Ava."

"What?"

Her shoulders had been tense, but she relaxed as he held her and kissed her cheek. Her neck. They had few fights because they were still uneasy around each other. Both of them often retreated into polite silence, and he knew it wasn't right.

"I love you," he said, drawing her away from the bureau and into his chest. His hands traveled up her torso, slipping underneath the thin sweater she wore. He hungered for her skin. "You are my hope."

"Malachi—"

"You are. It is easy to forget"—he kissed the curve where her neck met her shoulder—"what I would be without you. There was a time when I was as hopeless as they were. I don't think the Irin are like the Grigori, but I will think about what you said."

"I'm not saying I want to be friends with them," she said, turning in his arms. "I just think there are things we could learn. Me, mostly. But maybe you too."

"You're right."

A teasing light came to her eyes. "You're so sexy when you agree with me."

"Am I?" He bit her lower lip as his hands ran back down to cup her bottom. "How about now?" he murmured against her lips.

"Say it again."

"You're right."

"Oooooh," she said. "Even sexier."

He grinned as he kissed her. He loved it when she teased him. When she laughed. It was happening more and more as time passed.

"You're my hope too, you know."

He paused. "What?"

"What was I before I met you?" she asked. "Lonely. Lost. Never fitting in anywhere. Ruining any relationship I tried to have."

"Human men would never have been good for you." A sudden spike of jealousy. No other man would touch her. Not as he did. His mate belonged to him alone. He picked her up and carried her to the bed.

"I know that now."

She let him roll over her, strip her clothing off so that he could feast on her. Breasts. Knees. Thighs. He bit the soft swell of flesh on her belly. No inch of her body was safe from his ravening mouth.

And she coaxed him with her words.

"I love your mouth," she whispered. "Love what you do to me. No one has ever made me feel like you do."

"Ava—"

"I was so lost without you." Her voice choked on the words. "So lost, Malachi. Only my dreams kept me sane."

He groaned and pressed his mouth to her breast, turning his head to listen to her pounding heart. To her, he had been gone. A painful memory. But to him, she had been a siren. His only touchstone in a world that made no sense. And he could only hold her in dreams.

Now she was real. With him. Not a dream. Not a memory.

Ava was everything.

"Come here." She pulled at his clothes, as hungry as he was. "I need you."

And when they made love, she dug her fingers into his shoulders. Anchoring him in their joined flesh, even as his magic flared. Reached for hers. He could see the glowing silver *talesm* on his arms.

"Sing to me," he whispered in her ear as they moved together. "Sing for me, Ava."

She remained silent, but he felt the curl of her magic wake, and her mating marks flickered in awareness.

"*Canım*," he said.

"Malachi." Her hands tightened in his hair.

"My hope, Ava. You are my hope."

* * *   * * *

THEY RENTED A SCOOTER THE NEXT DAY, CLIMBING UP THE HILLS OF the Italian Riviera where Jasper Reed had rented a secluded house. They told no one they were coming, and Malachi only hoped that the man who had disappointed Ava so many times would not do so again. It would pain his mate, and Malachi would be hard-pressed not to vent his anger on the human.

Ava leaned against his back, her cheek pressed against his shoulder as they drove over the twisting roads. The sun shone down on them, despite the bite of cold in the air. It was Italy, but it was still winter, and clouds were gathered on the horizon. But Ava had wanted to rent a scooter instead of a car, and he had indulged her.

The address Max had given them led them past a small village and up another steep hill. They came to a gate on the road with the number of the house. He could see it at the top of the hill. Ava opened an unlocked gate and began to climb. A steep fall of stairs cut into the hillside brought them to another gate, this one guarded by a solid man Malachi guessed was American. His stance said professional; his bearing spoke of experience. He was younger than Malachi but would be a reasonably skilled opponent if he were not human.

"Hey, Ruben," she said, her voice a little breathless from the climb.

"Ava." The guard's tone offered surprise, even if his eyes were invisible behind dark sunglasses. "I didn't know—"

"Yeah, I know I'm a surprise. You gonna let me in, or do I have to call him?"

"I..." Ruben hesitated, but then his shoulders relaxed a fraction and he opened the door. He glanced at Malachi, gave him a little nod, then turned back to Ava and took off his glasses. "He's not expecting company."

Malachi noted that he'd been assessed and filed away as Ava's bodyguard. It was incredibly strange to be among humans who just expected to have armed men following them around for security.

"Really?" Ava raised an eyebrow. "He's not expecting company?"

Ruben sighed. "Okay, he's not expecting his daughter. You know how he is. Ava, I wish..."

Malachi realized, quite suddenly, that this bodyguard was more than familiar with Ava. That he actually cared about her.

The guard had probably known her for years. He might even live in her father's household. Did she consider him a friend? They might have traveled together. Eaten together. How strange to live and travel with people you employed. Were they friends? Was true friendship possible when one was employer and the other employee? The thought added a new layer of loneliness to Ava's history.

"I know how he is, Ruben." She brushed a hand along the human's arm. "It's fine. Is Luis here?"

"Not right now. Went into town to do some stuff. There's no Internet up here."

"I bet he loves that," she muttered. "Do me a favor and don't call Luis, okay?"

Ruben's tone was pleading. "Ava..."

"Fine." She sighed. "Call your boss so you don't get fired. Is Jasper alone?"

"Right now? Yeah."

"No girls expected?"

Ruben shook his head. "Not until later."

"Got it." She took his hand. "This is Malachi. He's with me."

Ruben examined him with newly suspicious eyes.

That's right, human. I am much more than her bodyguard.

"Hey." He held out a hand. "I'm Ruben."

"Malachi." They shook hands, and Malachi was relieved the human didn't do the idiot measuring hand squeeze. That never ended well for humans. He did, however, make a point of meeting Malachi's eyes. The threat was unspoken but clear. The man considered Ava his responsibility.

They stared at each other until Ava said, "And it appears we all have plenty of testosterone. Ruben, let go. Malachi's my… boyfriend."

"Boyfriend?" Ruben was definitely surprised. He dropped Malachi's hand and stepped back.

"I really don't like that word," Malachi said.

"What should I call you? My lover? Husband? Ma—"

"Boyfriend is fine." He squeezed her hand, glanced at Ruben, then nudged her toward the door. "Don't you need to see your father?"

"You're so cute when you're annoyed," Ava said lightly, and he could read the tension in her voice. She was nervous and trying to hide it.

"Come on." He let go of her hand and put a steadying arm around her waist. "Ruben, where can we find Jasper?"

The guard's keen eyes flipped between them, but he said, "Probably out in the gardens."

"Thanks."

"Anytime."

Malachi let her guide them up another set of stairs, this one shorter than the last. When they walked through the last gate, the garden opened up to a graveled walkway lined with olive trees interspersed with flower-filled urns. Ava didn't stop to admire the view but went straight up the path, heading for the large house he could see towering over the gardens.

They passed the front door and the covered patio beside it, still following the path to the side of the house where he could hear the faint sounds of a guitar and the recognizable voice of one the most celebrated human musicians.

Jasper Reed was known for performing rock and roll, blues, and American folk music, but he'd collaborated with classical musicians and even written scores for movies. He was, without a doubt, one of the most gifted human musicians of his age. And when they finally rounded the corner and came upon him, Malachi knew his talent wasn't merely rumor.

The man sat on a low bench, guitar in his lap, several empty coffee cups on the table in front of him along with an overflowing ashtray. Several of the domestic staff watched him from a shaded doorway, one smoking, two whispering, but all of them with rapt eyes on the man.

Reed appeared to be in his forties, but Malachi knew he had to be older in human years. Dark hair like Ava's. A classically handsome, unlined face. And a soft voice laden with a practiced breathy rasp.

The music was pure in its simplicity. Seductive in its tone. His voice was quiet but seemed to suffuse the air around him until every human within its hearing was held in thrall. Even Malachi was entranced.

Ava stopped in the shade of a spreading oak, watching her father. And he was, undoubtedly, her father. She'd said she looked like her mother—and she did—but there was a quality of expression she shared with Reed. So much that Malachi wondered how anyone could have been ignorant of her parentage. Her face was yearning. Her power flared.

And was answered when the music stopped and her father turned toward her.

A crooked smile. "Ava? Baby girl, what are you doing here?"

Then Reed's eyes fell on Malachi, and the scribe knew without a doubt where his mate's power had come from.

Talented musician. Wasted drug addict. Delinquent father. Jasper Reed might have been many things.

But he wasn't human.

CHAPTER

FOUR

"Hey, Jasper."

Her father put his guitar down and held out his arms. "Come here! What are you doing here, Ava?"

She could lie to herself all she wanted, but when Jasper opened his arms, the little girl in Ava leaped with joy. The girl who'd never belonged stepped forward and embraced the man who had fathered her.

"Came to say hi."

"Why didn't you call?"

His arms were warm, and he smelled like sunshine and coffee and soap. He'd probably smell like cigarette smoke soon enough, but in that moment, she took a deep breath and enjoyed the feeling of his stubbled cheek against hers.

"Wanted to surprise you."

Jasper wasn't stupid. He pulled back and raised an eyebrow. "Since when?"

"Since Luis was being closemouthed about where you were. Why weren't you answering my e-mails?"

He scratched his cheek, the dark stubble hinting at some Mediterranean heritage he'd never confirmed. He didn't know much about his family, he'd always told her. But was it the truth? Or did he just not want to share?

"No Internet up here, baby girl. And I'm not sure where that phone is." He looked around, and Ava could see his eyes were bloodshot. Hard nights. He'd been having hard nights. She was surprised he was up and playing early with eyes like that.

Jasper had called her "baby girl" as long as she could remember. When Ava was a child, it had seemed a sweet endearment from a man she thought of as an uncle. It was only later, when she'd learned he was her biological father, that it had become the poignant reminder of how much he'd missed by being absent for so much of her life.

He'd stayed as close to her as Lena would allow and often crashed at their house in LA when she was growing up. It was to her stepfather's credit that the man hardly batted an eye. Then again, when it came to running the house, what Lena Matheson said was law. And she never gave Carl any reason to doubt that Jasper and Lena's romantic relationship was firmly in the past.

She patted his cheek. "You gotta keep your phone on, Jasper."

He winked at her and pulled out the pack of cigarettes he kept in his pocket. "But then everyone would call me. Maybe I need to get a phone only you have the number to."

"Might not be a bad idea," Malachi said behind her.

She turned to see Malachi watching them with wary eyes. She stood up and held out a hand for his.

"Jasper, this is Malachi. He's not a bodyguard."

"He's not? You brought your guy to meet me, Ava?" Her father looked strangely touched. "Really?"

"Yeah." She knit her hands with Malachi's, but his fingers were tense. Odd. Maybe he was worried. "Malachi's my—"

"Fiancé," he said. "Ava and I are getting married."

She turned to him and mouthed, *We are?*

He shrugged and turned his eyes back to her father.

"Damn, Ava." Jasper blinked, and Ava saw his eyes were wet. "Really? You're getting married? Your mom didn't tell me."

"We just decided a little while ago." Ava decided to go with it. It was probably the easiest way for her mom and Jasper to understand what role Malachi would play in her life. She didn't care about getting married, but her mom would. "Mom doesn't know yet."

Jasper cackled. "You better tell her. She'll be pissed if you don't. I'll wait to call her. Malachi, huh?" He stood and offered a hand. "Nice to meet you, man. Cool name."

"Thank you." Malachi shook his hand. "Nice to meet you too. Ava has spoken of you."

"I'd say it's all lies, but she's too honest, so I'll just offer a general apology for all past behavior." He sat down and looked around the garden. "Where'd they go?"

Ava thought he looked pretty good for being on a bender. But then, there was a reason she'd chosen to visit in the morning.

"Jasper, I wanted to ask—"

"Sit down!" He waved to the chairs across from him and craned his neck toward the house. "Sit. Those girls were just here. Gotta get you guys some coffee. Where'd you two meet? Malachi, you drink coffee?"

Ava sat. "We met in Istanbul. I was there on a job and Malachi—"

"You're Turkish, man?" Jasper drew on the cigarette again and nodded. "I can see it. Cool. Yeah. So what do you do, Malachi-with-the-cool-name?"

Ava barely caught the edge of suspicion in Jasper's eyes. It was odd for him to be protective, but then, she'd never brought a boyfriend to meet him. Never really had a boyfriend stick around long enough to matter.

"I'm in private security," Malachi said smoothly. It was a practiced lie; he'd implied the same thing to her when they first met. She supposed, in a way, it was true.

"Fuck," Jasper said with a snort. "I thought you said he wasn't a bodyguard, Ava?"

"Maybe I should have said he wasn't *just* a bodyguard."

Jasper laughed.

"Hey, they're the only guys who ever stick around," she said wryly.

"Carl didn't hire him, did he?"

"No."

"Good. All the guys Carl ever hired had a stick up their ass. Of course, Carl does too. So that's not really a surprise."

"Jasper…"

"Kidding. Kinda." He grinned at Malachi, who still sat silently, his expression a careful blank.

Malachi said, "I work for a private international firm based in Vienna. But I take my own assignments."

"So Ava's your assignment now?" Jasper's eyes were keen on Malachi.

"Yes."

"Good. Too many sick fuckers in the world." He lit another cigarette and looked toward the kitchen where one of the maids was bringing out another French press filled with coffee and two more cups. "Ah, there she is. And Ava, I never liked you hoppin' around all over the place."

"Yeah, you're one to talk."

"I speak from experience." He nodded toward Malachi. "I guess if you're gonna do it, good you have someone with you."

"Thanks. Jasper—"

"Hey." He interrupted her again while he waved the maid away and poured the coffee. "I wanted to talk to you about the Malibu house."

"You mean *your* house?"

"No. It's your house. It's been in your name for over a year now."

"Jasper, I already have—"

"Move your stuff from Lena's place. Live there when you're in LA. You can consider it my wedding present, if you want. But you need your own base, baby girl. Not a crash pad."

He refused to meet her eyes. It was an old argument, and one Ava didn't feel like having again. Jasper had already given her too much. The trust fund alone was in the multimillions. He had more money than God and was constantly trying to give her things. Cars. Jewelry. Houses. She didn't want that stuff. Didn't need it.

"I don't need a big house. I can stay with Mom when I'm in California."

He gave her his worried look. "This place—have you even been there?"

"Luis sent me pictures."

"It's quiet, Ava. I picked it myself. Secluded. Lots of acreage. Overlooks the ocean. You know…" He glanced away again. "Quiet. I know you need that."

And there it was. The knowledge she'd been skirting around ever since she'd found the Irin. Found the real reason she heard those voices in her head. Jasper had been one of the few she'd never had to hide around. She'd known, even as a child, that the man who heard beautiful music in his head—was tormented by it at times—would understand the isolated girl she'd been.

Jasper had known all along. Somehow, he'd known.

"Jasper."

His hand shook as he lifted the cigarette. He was getting worse before her eyes. The demons were waking up despite the warm Italian sun and the peaceful garden.

"Just take the house, Ava. I want to give it to you."

"Dad—"

"I told you"—his eyes flared as they met hers, a flash of gold behind the brown—"you don't have to call me that. I mean, you can, but… you don't have to. I never expected that. I know I wasn't…"

There was something going on. She felt Malachi's hand tighten on hers. "Jasper, I need to ask about your family. *My* family."

His face went out of focus for a second. When she blinked, it was back to normal. A trick of light and shadow. For a second, his skin had appeared luminous.

Jasper's voice was harder when he answered. "I told you I don't know much about them. Foster care, remember?"

He was lying. Ava knew it. She opened her senses to listen to his soul's voice.

Jasper's voice was the other reason Ava had always trusted him, even as a child. Though not as pure as Malachi's, it nonetheless had a resonance that had been soothing to her as a child. Jasper's voice had always made her feel safe. She'd put it down to him being an artist. He created beautiful music; why wouldn't it resonate from his mind?

Now that voice sounded broken. Halting.

"Malachi," Jasper asked the man at her side. "You have family?"

"I did. My parents are both dead now."

A hollow longing tone rang in his mind. "Sorry to hear that. My mom died when I was young."

A lie. Ava was positive.

Jasper continued, "That's why I don't know much about my family, you know? She was alone." He glanced at Ava. "On her own. Glad… I'm glad Ava met you."

Ava leaned forward. "Jasper, I wanted to know—"

"Nothing to know." He leaned toward her and cupped her face in his hands. "Beautiful girl. Beautiful Ava." His thumb brushed across her cheek. His fingers, thickly callused from years of playing, were warm. "You got a good guy now. I know he is. Because you'd never settle for less. And you're gonna get married. Maybe even have kids someday. And you'll be a kick-ass mama, 'cause that's what you had. A kick-ass mama. I haven't done a lot right in my life, but the one thing was picking a hell of a good woman to have my kid. So don't worry about the past. Look to the future, baby girl. Don't look for ghosts."

He knew. He knew something, but he wouldn't tell her. Maybe he thought she was prying, but she knew there was something; otherwise, why would he lie about it?

"Dad, why won't you tell me?"

He closed his eyes, and his voice was hoarse. "About what?"

"About your mother." She took a deep breath. "About Ava."

He drew back as if he'd been burned. "Who told you that?"

"I did," Malachi said. "We know your mother was named Ava, Mr. Reed. And we know that you made the records of her disappear. Why did you do that?"

A trick of the light again, and the scent of sandalwood and ash on the breeze. Ava sucked in a breath and it was gone. What was going on? Her father looked angry. Jasper was never angry with her. At himself? Often. But never with her.

"Jasper?"

"You had your man check up on me? Who's the 'we' he's talking about, huh?" He shook out another cigarette. "What the hell, Ava?"

"It was… I was curious—"

"You don't need to be curious about that shit. You don't need to know about my *maman*."

She saw Malachi tilt his head at the word.

Ava asked again, "Your mother? *Maman*? Is that French? Was she French, Jasper?"

He lit the cigarette with shaking hands. "I'm done. I'm not talking about this. Will you move into that damn house or not?"

"Jasper, I need to know."

"No, you don't. And I'm not talking about her." He lit the cigarette, and when his eyes met hers again, he was totally shut down. She knew she'd get nothing out of him.

"Dad—"

"I fucking hate," he whispered, "that you call me dad when you want something from me, Ava. Fucking hate that. I'd rather you call me Jasper. Rather you call me dickhead or bastard or one of the million names you probably thought over the years. I'd rather you call me any of that shit than call me dad just to… to get something from me."

The anger was always there, though she pushed it down. Forced it back. Chose to treasure what they had and what they could become. But it was always there. The lack of him simmered in her blood.

"I never wanted money," she said from behind clenched teeth. "Or houses. Or cars. Or anything, *Jasper*. I never wanted any of that stuff. But this? The one thing I've ever asked you. This you won't give me?"

He fingered the cigarette in his hand and reached for his coffee. Put it down.

"Ruben!" he yelled.

"Jasper, please."

Malachi stood up and moved behind her, but Ava stayed sitting, staring at her father, begging him to meet her eyes.

Ruben walked around the side of the house. "Yeah, boss?"

"Please, Dad."

Jasper ignored her. "Ava and her fiancé need to go. And find me a bottle of Grey Goose."

She shook her head.

"Unbelievable," Malachi said.

"Congratulations," Jasper said, lifting his eyes to her mate. "I'm fucking thrilled for her. And I can see how much you love her just by looking at you. I can see shit like that. I love her too. I know she's pissed at me right now, but she's the best thing in my life, and I'd do anything to protect her."

Malachi squeezed her shoulder and said, "Maybe the way to protect her is by telling her whatever you're trying to hide."

"She may think that, but she'd be wrong."

Her father's eyes finally met hers, and the haunted look was back. It was the look he wore sometimes when he looked at her mother. At her. The tormented part of Jasper Reed knew how much he'd lost by not being a good man. It was the same part that locked himself away from the world for months at a time and wrote some of the most achingly beautiful music Ava had ever heard.

"Love you, baby girl," he said to her. "Gonna work on your song when I get back to the studio. Promise."

As if she hadn't heard that promise a million times. There must be a dozen different versions at this point. She had never heard a single one.

"Sure. Right." She stood and took Malachi's hand. "Bye, Jasper. Take care of yourself."

Ava walked away from the man who had fathered her without looking back. She held Malachi's hand the whole time.

 . . .   . . .

HE'D SPENT THE HOUR SINCE HER UNSUCCESSFUL MEETING WITH Jasper holding her on the small couch in their hotel room. He hadn't said anything. Hadn't offered any words of comfort or anger or frustration, though she could tell he was worried.

Her concentration was strained, her emotions were strung out, and Ava was exhausted. Malachi's voice slipped through. Before she'd been able to shield herself, his voice sat in the back of her mind constantly. But like her father's, it was more like a steady background music than a jarring intrusion.

Reshon.

Soul mate.

"Imagine a person created for you. Another being so in tune with you that their voice was the clearest you've ever heard in your mind."

It was a voice that had come to mean everything to her.

And then it was gone.

Silence.

And for the first time, silence had made her scream.

For a time after he'd come back, Ava worried she wouldn't be able to hear Malachi as she had before.

She thought she'd lost him forever. Lost that connection forever.

Bit by bit, she was taking down the wall she erected around her heart *and* her mind. His voice slipped through more and more often.

In that moment, his voice hummed with concern. With love. But there was a dark thread that kept coming back over and over again.

Grigori.

"Why are you thinking about the Grigori?"

"Hmm?"

"Your head keeps whispering it. Over and over. *Grigori.*"

"I didn't realize. I'm sorry. Have your shields grown weak?" He put a hand on her shoulder, drew something there, and she immediately felt the surge of energy.

"Don't do that without warning me," she said, blinking as her heart sped.

"Sorry."

"They were a little weak, but—"

"Your father, Ava. I was thinking about your father. I don't under-stand him."

"I know. He's not much of a dad, but I knew that already."

"No, I mean, he's something…"

She turned when he stopped speaking. "What?"

"Don't pull away. I need to feel you." He slid his hand over her forearm to clasp her fingers. "He's other, Ava. He's not human. Not one hundred percent, anyway."

"But…" She frowned. "What do you mean? I mean, we figured he had some Irin blood, so why were you thinking Grigori? He's not… you're not thinking—"

"Your father is not Grigori. He doesn't smell it. Doesn't look it. But he's not human either."

She paused. "It's hard to wrap my brain around that when he's always just been Jasper."

"There is nothing 'just' about Jasper."

"Why do you say—"

"Think about it. He's in remarkable health, despite his lifestyle. He looks extremely young for his age."

"And he's a musical genius," she said. "Rhys said a lot of Grigori offspring are gifted in music. But he's not Grigori. You said so."

"No." Malachi sighed. "Rhys suspected bipolar disorder, and I'm tempted to think the same thing."

"And my mom would agree with you. To be fair, that might have nothing to do with Irin blood. A lot of artists have the same problems he does with depression and addiction. Hell, the whole world thought *I* was crazy for years."

"And you're Irina. So what does that make him?"

"Malachi, I don't—"

"He's not Irin," Malachi said, turning her so that she faced him but still holding on to her arm. "He's not… anything I've ever encoun-tered. How long were he and your mother together?"

"Awhile. Not a long while, but long for him." Ava searched her memory. "Months, I think. A few months." Which fit with her pattern of relationships before she'd met Malachi. Her longest relationship had been in the three-month range.

"An Irin scribe could never be with a human for that long."

"But he's not human, either." She thought about the odd flashes she'd had of him. The strange scent in the air. The gold in his eyes.

"There was something," she said. "Something new. I've never noticed it before, but—"

"You never knew what you were before."

She turned to him. "Do you think my dad has magic?"

"I think so, but it's not obvious." He frowned at the wall. "It's... covered."

"What?"

"It's like his power was covered. That's the way it felt to be near him. Sort of like you in your dreams."

"The same as my dreams?" She sat up straight. "*Exactly* the same?"

Malachi narrowed his eyes. "Yes."

"Do you think Jaron is shielding me *and* my dad?"

Malachi paused in thought. She could hear his inner voice going crazy. Words tumbled through his mind in a rush.

"If that shielding is a mark of angelic protection," he said, "then yes. Jaron or another one of the Fallen must be protecting your father."

"Could it be one of the Forgiven?" Her hope lasted for a moment until Malachi squashed it.

"It's not possible, *reshon*. The Forgiven are gone from this world."

"Are you sure?"

He nodded. "Unless one has chosen to fall again, they cannot come back here. Jaron has already shown a connection to you. It's possible he has one to your father as well. It is the most likely possibility."

"But why?" Ava asked. "Why would Jaron do that? My father has never... he's not involved in your world."

She felt his arms tighten around her. "*Our* world, Ava."

She nodded. "Our world. And he's not involved."

"How do we know that?" He turned her so he could look in her eyes. "Ava, he knows you're different. The way he talked about that house he bought for you. The *quiet*. The seclusion. If his mother was Irina—"

"How could she be Irina and have a child with a human?"

"I don't know. It might be possible. So many went into hiding after the Rending, Ava. If your grandmother was Irina and had a child with a human, it would be the first to my knowledge."

She rolled her eyes. "Yeah, well I discovered at Sarihöfn that there's a lot the Irin don't know about the Irina anymore."

"You may be correct. It could be possible—even likely—considering you exist."

"Would a quarter Irin blood be enough to let me touch you?"

He ran a hand up her arm. "I think that answers itself. It has to be."

She settled back against him. The sun had reached its zenith in the sky, and Ava felt drowsy. The room was warm and her mate stretched out on the couch, cushioning her body with his own. As upset as she'd been with her father, his refusal wasn't a surprise. It was easy to deal with disappointment when that was all he'd ever given her.

"What are you thinking, *reshon*?"

"I'm thinking… I like the thought of us getting married. It'll be easier to explain you to my mother if we marry."

"You know, you will not grow older now. With our magic combined, there will come a time—"

"Shhh." She pressed a finger to his lips. "I know. Someday, we'll have to disappear. For now, let me be happy."

He fell silent again and pressed a kiss to her hair. "Be happy," he whispered. "Despite everything happening around us, I am."

She watched the sun track across the room, dozing every now and then as she rested against him.

"I don't think she's dead." Her eyes felt heavy. "My grandmother. There was something about the way he spoke about her."

"If she's alive, *canim*, we will find her. I promise."

I promise.

Ava realized as she drifted off to sleep that to Malachi, those words meant something.

1.

J aron watched from across the crowded street. He had taken the
face of an old man and was holding a newspaper and watching
the humans pass in front of him as they strolled the ocean prome-
nade with family and friends. The winter wind gusted on the
Italian coast, but it did not bother the angel, only flapped the threadbare overcoat that covered his narrow shoulders.

Another old man came to sit beside him, holding a bag of warm
chestnuts.

"Does she know yet?"

"She's intelligent. She'll find the answers soon enough. And the
scribe is keener than I expected."

Barak lifted the steaming bag of chestnuts to his nose and inhaled
but did not reach for one. "Mikhael's offspring are often underestimated," he said. "Seen more for their physical prowess than their strategy.
This is a mistake."

Jaron nodded. "Mikhael is a great strategist. His prowess rivals
Yun's."

"Only when Yun is not working with you." Barak tugged on the
grey beard that covered his face. "I prefer the human eras that favor
facial hair."

Jaron lifted an eyebrow at his friend. "Do you? I detest them."

"You detest every human era anymore."

"Why do you think I'm doing all this?"

The corner of the old man's mouth lifted behind his beard. "Why, indeed?"

"Have you heard what your son is doing?"

"I hear everything." Barak's face wore a look of annoyance. "Which one?"

"You know of whom I speak. Have you traveled to Sofia lately?"

"No. Kostas is my brightest child in centuries. There is a chance he would sense me if I came close. I have others watching him."

"And do you approve of what he is doing, my friend?" Jaron was amused. "He would remake the world here, even as we seek to remake the heavens."

Barak watched a clutch of giggling female children pass by. They shouted and shoved each other, bumping into the knees of the two old men and shouting embarrassed apologies before they ran off.

Both of the Fallen watched them.

"Balance," Barak finally said. "In our arrogance, we have forgotten how the universe loves it. No world can exist for so long without balance."

"You're saying change is inevitable."

"Is that not what you're striving for as well?"

Jaron shrugged and the old coat slipped off one thin shoulder. "My goals are for myself. And my friends, if they desire it."

The other angel sat back, lifting the bag of cooling chestnuts again. "I have not yet decided."

"Decide soon, brother."

"Vasu will go his own way."

"I have seen it."

"And me? What have you seen for me?"

"I see nothing, because there is nothing yet to see."

"Hmm." The bearded man stood and reached over the bench, tossing the untouched bag of chestnuts in a bin.

Jaron caught Barak's hand, closing the wrinkled palm in his own. "This time, my old friend, we do not have millennia."

"I know this."

"You must decide soon."

"I know this as well." Barak squeezed Jaron's hand and blinked out of sight as the humans rushed by with unseeing eyes.

It was the way of things. Human sight was so very limited.

Though Barak had shifted away, Jaron's eyes were trained on the balcony where Ava and her scribe sat, drinking wine and watching the street musician who played below them. The musician was… not good. But Ava seemed to enjoy the performance anyway.

The scribe's eyes watched her but more often swept up and down the street, surveying the crowd, watching for threats. Jaron could tell the scribe did not care for his mate being out on the balcony, exposed to possible danger.

The angel approved of this. Perhaps Ava's unexpected call to heaven had manifested a boon for him. He still didn't fully understand why the Creator had allowed the scribe's body and soul to return, but that didn't mean he wouldn't take advantage. More than his own eyes would be trained on the woman if he weren't protecting her.

It wasn't time. There were still pieces to move into place.

Soon, time would run out.

CHAPTER

FIVE

Their return to Istanbul was easier the second time. Ava seemed less cautious and more relieved to be heading back to Turkey. They caught a morning flight and were driving to the scribe house by lunch time. To Malachi, it almost seemed as if she'd left her melancholy in Italy with Jasper. She was lighter. Smiling more.

"You're happy to be back," he said.

"Yeah." She smiled. "It feels like… coming home. With you. I missed it." She rolled down the window and took a deep breath of the air, only to wrinkle her nose at the smell of fish as they crossed the bridge. "Okay, I didn't miss that."

Malachi laughed and reached over her to roll the window up. "So no fish for lunch?"

"No," she said. "I want lamb and salad. Maybe some of those fried potatoes you make."

"Now *I'm* hungry." But happy. He enjoyed cooking for her, and her mood was infectious.

They reached Beyoğlu just a few minutes later, and when they walked into the house, Malachi heard fighting.

Immediately on alert, he held up a hand and put a finger to his lips. Ava dropped her bags and went to the closet, searching for the cache of weapons Leo and Rhys kept ready.

"Who?" she whispered.

He shook his head and held out his hand, catching the sheathed dagger she tossed him. Ava stuffed a throwing knife in her waistband and grabbed a short staff, falling in step behind him.

Malachi crept down the hallway, past the living room, and toward the closed door. The sounds were coming from the practice room, but there were none of the usual shouts and cheerful taunts of his brothers. Strained breathing and grunts. The clash of wood and bodies hitting the floor.

"Wait." Ava put a hand on his lower back. "I think…"

He turned and put a finger to his lips. "Wait here," he mouthed, tracing his *talesm prim*. He felt the wash of magic over his skin. His eyes grew sharper. His ears keener.

"But I think—"

In one movement, Malachi shoved the door open and rolled in, staying low as his eyes swept the room. Leo was on the floor in the corner, a woman straddling him with a staff across his neck. The big man was trying to throw her off, but she only pressed down harder, the muscles rippling in her lean brown arms. Leo scissored his legs in an attempt to flip her, but the woman pushed into it, angling the staff even harder against his throat.

Malachi heard his brother choking. He charged the woman, ignoring his mate's shouts from the doorway. With a bent shoulder, he tackled her to the ground, only to have her twist away before he could put her in a choke hold. Her staff came up and struck his temple, but he shook his head and brought up his dagger to attack.

"No!" Leo jumped between Malachi and the woman. "Malachi! Don't you remember Mala?"

Mala?

A faint memory from Oslo. Mala was one of Sari's Irina. A fierce warrior who'd lost her mate during the Rending and almost lost her own life in a battle near Lagos.

He shook his head. "Mala?"

"We were only sparring." Leo was panting. But grinning too. "She's amazing. Such skill with the short staff! I've never fought an Irina before. Are they all like this?"

Leo sounded as excited as a child at his Naming Day celebration.

"Mala!" Ava ran over, laughing as she embraced the dark-eyed warrior. "Please don't kill my mate. We just got home. We weren't expecting you."

The corner of the woman's full lips turned up. She embraced Ava with one arm, then pulled back, using her hands to sign.

"Slowly," Ava said. "I'm out of practice."

Mala signed again. Ava nodded, still grinning. "I'll tell him. She says you have a strong tackle, but you should work on your balance. Strength is no substitute for grace."

Malachi glowered.

"Hey." Ava held up her hands. "Don't kill the messenger."

His eyes shifted to Mala, who only looked amused. It was a welcome expression on an otherwise fearsome face. The Irina had been beautiful once. Was still beautiful. But her jawline was marred by horrible scars that looked like an animal had attempted to rip out her throat. That was why she did not speak. The Grigori had taken her voice.

Malachi held out his hand. "Well met, sister. You are a fierce opponent."

Mala bowed slightly, then turned to Leo. Ava translated when she started signing.

"I think… she says you rely too much on your size. A smaller opponent is often more… flexible?" Ava paused, watching Mala. "Nimble?" Mala nodded and continued. "She says you should practice dancing." Ava frowned. "Really? Dancing?"

Mala nodded vigorously.

"I can do that," Leo said with a grin. "But I'd need an Irina partner."

Mala picked up her staff and walked out of the room.

Leo said, "I guess that means she doesn't volunteer."

"I'll dance with you, Leo."

"Are you any good?"

"Not really. But at least you won't make me pass out, which is an improvement over most partners you're going to find around here."

"True."

Malachi sheathed the knife and tried to calm a heart that still raced. "Leo, do you still want to spar?" he asked. "I've been on a plane all morning and I'd love to stretch my legs."

"Of course." The big man picked up the second staff that was lying on the mat of the training room. "Ava, Orsala arrived with Mala."

Ava groaned and covered her eyes. "No."

Malachi went to her and kissed her temple. "She's probably with Rhys in the library, devising more magical torture for you. The longer you delay, the worse it will be."

"Save me," she said.

"I will battle Grigori for you, *canim*," he said gallantly. "I'll abandon heaven and cross continents."

"My hero!"

"But I will not interfere with that old singer's plans. Do you think I want to die again?"

She slapped his backside and walked toward the door. "Leo, kick his ass for me. He's getting way too cocky."

Malachi only laughed. "I love you, Ava."

Leo said, "I love you too, Ava. Good luck with Orsala."

"Both of you—useless!"

• • •   • • •

"MALACHI?"

He looked up from his drawing pad. "Orsala?"

The old woman smiled tentatively when she walked into the room. She wore the silver hair and lined face of an Irina who had stopped her longevity spells. Malachi had heard her mate had been killed years ago, so allowing herself to age and pass away was not unexpected.

"Am I interrupting?" she asked.

"Not at all." He pushed the sketches to the side. He had several *talesm* he'd been planning to scribe once they were back in Istanbul, and he needed to practice the characters. But sketching could wait. Malachi had a feeling she wanted to talk about his mate. "Is Ava—"

"She's fine. Resting, I think. She went to your room with a headache. I believe she was becoming frustrated."

He rose to go to her, but Orsala put a hand on his shoulder. "If I could have a moment…"

Malachi paused. "What is it?"

"She is very resistant."

"To using her magic?"

"Yes."

"I know." He took a deep breath. "She's afraid of what she can do."

She smiled, and warm creases formed around her silver-blue eyes. "I do not want to interfere. Or ask you to break her confidence. I want to help her."

"Let me talk to her again."

"Thank you."

"I warn you, though." He gathered his papers and turned to leave. "I will not pressure her to use her magic if she's not ready. My loyalty is to her, not any cause."

"As it should be," Orsala said. "You remind me much of my own mate. He was highly protective, even when I was at my strongest."

"It is when we are strongest that we often don't protect ourselves," he said. "Whatever her destiny is in this life, it is my job to defend her."

"For the Irina, I think the time has come for offense, not defense."

He shook his head. "I'm not talking about the Irina. I'm talking about Ava. I will not let her be dragged into a war of your making, Orsala. However much I may support your cause, her part in it will be of her choosing."

"She has not chosen this," the old woman countered, "but Jaron has. The Fallen has targeted her."

"And protected her."

"I know." Orsala stepped closer. "We need to know why. There is a darkness in her. A darkness to her magic that I have never seen before."

"I do not fear her darkness."

"Nor should you. But we need to understand it so we may understand her. She needs to understand herself, Malachi. If you do not fear the darkness, then do not shield your mate from it, either. Sometimes we must do exactly the thing that terrifies us most in order that we may live the life we were meant to have."

WHEN HE REACHED THEIR BEDROOM, HE KNOCKED. IT WAS THEIR shared room, but if she was exhausted—

"Come in, Malachi."

He pushed the door open. Ava was lying on the bed in a beam of sunlight, the sun catching red strands in her hair. Her eyes were closed. Her forehead smooth.

"Orsala said your head was hurting."

"I lied. Kind of."

He toed off his shoes and lay down next to her. "What's wrong?"

Ava rolled over to make room for him. "You know, I think this was what I missed the most when you were gone."

He said nothing. The fact that she was talking about her grief was extraordinary enough. He didn't want to interrupt her.

"I missed lying next to you. Just… that. Not sex. Not even your touch. I missed all those things, but it was just… you. Being here. Knowing that someone gave a shit about me other than my mom. Knowing you were beside me at night." She moved her leg over to hook it around his knee. "I could reach out for you if I needed you. Or just wanted you. When I had that… I'd never had that before."

He took a deep breath. "Sometimes I feel as if I'm a second mate. As if you grieved for someone entirely different. That you still grieve."

"I'm sorry."

"Don't." He rolled over and watched her face in profile. Her eyes were still closed. But now there were lines of tension on her forehead. He took a finger and smoothed them away. "Don't be sorry. You lost me, but I never lost you. I think I would go quite mad if our roles had been reversed. The man I am now has always had you. My memories began with you, so I never felt the pain you did. You were where I began, Ava. I was the lucky one."

She choked out a laugh even as the tears leaked from the corner of her eye. "You were the one who died."

"But that pain only lasted a heartbeat. Yours lasted for months. Please, don't hide your grief from me."

"I'm afraid," she whispered. "At night I wake up, and for a second, you're gone again."

"Reach out. You'll find me."

"I'm afraid if I reach for you, I'll find out this is a dream. That I'm caught in some kind of delusion. I don't know what's real in the dark."

He rolled over and drew her back to his chest, wrapping his arm around her waist. He called up the ancient magic that lived in his skin, allowing his *talesm* to glow. "Look, Ava."

She opened her eyes.

"When the darkness comes, reach for me."

She said nothing, but he could feel her fear.

"What are you afraid of? It's not just losing me again."

"I don't—"

"Don't lie." He tapped a finger against her temple. "I can tell."

"I think…" She put her hands over his and gripped them tightly. "I think my magic is evil, Malachi."

"It's not evil. I've felt it. It's beautiful."

"It's dark."

"Dark does not equal evil." He took a deep breath and felt her match him. They lay together, quietly enjoying the afternoon sun. "Is this because of what happened on the roof with Jaron?"

"It's more than that."

"Tell me."

Ava said nothing for a long while.

"I saw a black angel once," she whispered. "There was a Grigori attacking me in Norway. He'd broken into the room with another who'd gone after Mala. They were trying… I don't know what they were trying to do. Kill us? Capture us for Volund, maybe? But he was on me, and I'd made him angry by fighting back. His hand was on my throat."

Malachi forced his body to remain calm as he held her, but the rage bubbled beneath his skin.

"What happened?"

"I couldn't remember the spells, and I was so mad. I was *furious*. I'd lost you. Lost so much. And he was trying to take more. I felt this darkness well up inside me. It poured out of me. I opened my mouth, but I couldn't speak. It didn't matter. I could hear… wind. And then it was like the shadows in the room came to life. There was a figure. It felt like Jaron, but more. Darker. Heavier. There was no substance to it. Like a vacuum. And the closer I looked, the more it drew me in."

He couldn't help it. His arms tightened around her. "Ava—"

"Feathers," she whispered. "It sounded like feathers."

His stomach dropped, and his heart pounded. "What happened?"

She stared at the ceiling, lost in the memory. "I heard screaming, but it wasn't me. I think I passed out from his hand on my throat. By the time I came back, it was the Grigori screaming. His eyes were open. He was staring into nothing as if he'd seen it too. But it had captured him. It wasn't letting go."

Ava's voice dropped to barely a whisper. "He was so terrified. And I knew… He'd seen what I saw. But the shadow took him. I wanted him to see it, and he did."

"Ava, this was not…"

…your fault. Malachi couldn't say it. Because it might have been a lie. No one knew what she was capable of.

Thousands of you, Scribe. One of her.

"What was it?" She rolled over to face him. "That shadow? You know, don't you?"

He didn't want to tell her what he thought. But this was his mate. She'd know if he tried to lie or avoid the question.

"Death," he said. "You saw Death."

"How do you know?" she asked. "Maybe it was one of the Fallen. There are probably—"

"He is not one of the Fallen. He is Death."

She shook her head, dread marking her face. "No."

"Ava, I've probably seen him, even though I don't remember."

"Don't…" She sat up in the bed. "So, there really is an angel of death?"

He nodded. "Our books say he is neither Fallen nor Forgiven. He is Death. Some scriptures call him Azril. He comes for any with angelic blood. He is neither good nor evil. His job is to gather souls that have been released."

"And I called him?"

"No," he murmured. "I don't know. He serves no one but the Creator. But you saw him."

"But so did the Grigori. And I was the one dying, not him."

"Yes, he saw…" Malachi sat up next to her. "He saw what you saw."

"Yeah, I said that."

He took her hand. "Think about what you've done in the past, Ava. When you allow your magic to work."

She paused. "I see things."

"You see things," he murmured. "Why does your photography strike a chord with so many? Because they're not just pictures to you. Your camera is a lens into your mind. Your heart. You *show* things. I think your magic carries the same gift. What you see, you manifest in others' minds. When Jaron gave you a vision and you sang about it in Oslo, we *saw* it. Not just imagined it, we saw your vision in our own minds. You saw Death. And when you did, the Grigori did as well. And Death terrified him."

"How?" she whispered. "Who does that? Is that…" She frowned. "Is that Leoc? Leoc's gift? Orsala called me a daughter of Leoc."

"Leoc is a seer. He gave his daughters the gift of foresight." Malachi shook his head. "What you do is different."

"So where does it come from?" She pounded her fist on the bed. "Where do *I* come from?"

"Ava, it's not—"

"Dammit, Malachi! I need my dad to be honest with me."

"Ava—"

"No, really. I'm pissed. The more I think about my dad, the angrier I get. At first I was the sad, disappointed daughter I've been for years, but now? I'm just pissed."

"Your father—"

"My father *knew*. If his mother was the same as me, he's known for years that I heard voices. Maybe he knows about soul voices, maybe he doesn't. But he knew what was wrong with me, and he said nothing. Even just telling me he understood would have made me feel like less of a freak. But he was too selfish to do that for his own daughter."

He took her fist, spreading her fingers until he could thread them through his own. "We don't know—"

"He knew why I ran away from life. Knew why I could never have any real relationships. No home. No friends. No boyfriends."

"He might have been trying—"

"My dad *knew* what all the hovering and the bodyguards and the endless, *endless* psychological exams must have done to me. And he knew they wouldn't do anything to help. And he still said nothing."

"It's possible—"

"He. Said. Nothing."

Malachi stopped trying to calm her.

"And I know his mother is alive! I know it. And you know what? I bet he *knows* that I know it. And he's still lying to me. He's still keeping all these secrets."

She swung her legs off the bed and started pacing their room like an angry cat.

"I'm sick of secrets!" she said. "I'm sick of my dad keeping them and Jaron playing with me like I'm a pawn in his little games. I'm sick of being chased and hunted. I'm sick of acting calm when I really want to scream."

"I know." Deep down, Malachi was relieved that Ava was showing this much emotion about anything. She'd been too calm for far too long. She had a right to her anger. It was long overdue, and resignation did not suit her.

"I'm sick of it."

"I can see that." He tried to stop the smile, but she caught the edge of it.

"Are you laughing at me?"

"Absolutely not."

She stopped pacing. Her mouth hung open. Her hands were on her hips. Malachi felt the smile spread across his face.

"You are," she said.

"I'm not laughing. I'm thrilled."

"About what?"

He stood and faced her, putting his hands on her small shoulders. "I'm glad you're angry. Ava, I *love* it. You have every right to be. Take it. Use it. Force your father to be honest with you. Don't let him ignore you. The next time you see Jaron in a dream, question him. I can't, but you *can*. If he can reach you, then you can reach *him*. Don't let him ignore you. You want to find answers?"

"Yes!"

"Then what can I do to help?"

CHAPTER

SIX

"I don't tell you often enough," Ava said, love for him filling her up, balancing the anger. "I love you. You're strong and protective, smart and kind. You're just a… a very *good man.*"

"Thank you."

"I fell in love with the man I met in Istanbul. The mysterious one who touched me and made me feel like I was magic. And I grieved for the hero who sacrificed himself to protect me. But the man you are now? The man you're becoming? He's all those things. And he's more."

His eyes had lost all their humor. He reached up to cup her cheek. "Ava."

"You're a good man. And maybe I don't know who I am, but I know I'm grateful that you're mine. That I can find out who I am with you. And maybe help you find yourself too."

She stood on her toes and kissed him. Malachi reached down and lifted her up, swinging her around until they sat on the edge of the bed again, lips still locked. She pulled back and peppered his face with kisses until he was smiling. Until his dimple couldn't be hidden. Until he laughed. And Ava thought she might become addicted to the sound of Malachi's laughter. If she could find the answers she needed and live a thousand years with this man, she would never grow tired of hearing him laugh.

Then she was the one smiling when he threaded his fingers through her hair and kissed her deeply, teasing her tongue with his. He tasted spicy, like the peppers and sumac she had smelled from the kitchen during lunch. His shoulders were firm beneath her hands. His body commanding hers to give more. Deeper. His soul voice rang in her head, tuning her mind and body. She felt her magic rise up and settle against his.

He let out a gasp and pulled back. "Ava, it feels so good."

"More?"

"More."

She kissed him again. Heard the words in her mind. Pulled away to whisper in his ear.

"*Hanama*." She recited the simple spell, picturing what she wanted in her mind as she spoke. "*Da'adanama*."

Take of me, the magic whispered. *Give to me*.

His magic shot through her, and she could feel her mating marks burn as his arms tightened at the small of her back. Malachi's own skin was hot beneath her hands. Like a circuit sparked by her passion, their magic joined and fed them both, opening them to each other. No insulation. No barriers.

She could see his *talesm* glowing on his forearms. Could feel the ghost of them under her palms. Once, they'd covered his body, marking the territory of him like a map. She'd told him once that the lack of them didn't matter to her, but it did. Because they were part of him. Each spell carefully chosen and written. Not simply words a scribe had written to protect himself, but a guide to the man he'd chosen to become.

She wanted them back.

Cautiously, she bent to his ear again.

"*Ya davarda*," she whispered, the spell slipping from her lips. It should have been easy after all the times she'd recited it in her mind, but she was so afraid.

Remember.

It was a command she imbued with the deepest longing of her heart. For Malachi to remember who he was. And who he'd made himself to be.

"*Ya davarda, reshon*," she said it again, a little louder.

She felt the energy leave her fingertips and enter him. A slip of silk brushing against her skin. There for a heartbeat, then gone. Away from her. Into him.

"Ava!"

Malachi pulled back, his hands clenched on her hips so hard Ava knew they would bruise. His eyes were closed. The marks on his forearms glowed like fire fed from a sudden gust of wind.

She kept her hands on his shoulders, pressing down as if to keep them both from flying away. His face was clenched, but it was not in pain. His eyes darted back and forth beneath his lids. She felt a burning beneath her right palm and looked down.

Like living vines, his *talesm* crawled up his left forearm, joining and sometimes overwriting the spells he'd added after his return. The glowing quicksilver lines moved up his arm as she watched, twisting and turning. Traveling across and around his wrist, his forearm, his elbow, and bicep. His skin burned as from a fever.

The lines disappeared under his shirt. In their wake, his skin swelled and reddened, leaving ash-black ink embedded in his flesh.

Malachi's chest heaved for a few deep breaths and then fell still. His head fell. The magic seemed to leave him and retreat back into her.

"Malachi?" She squeezed his shoulders and he winced. Ava quickly pulled her hands away, but he did not open his eyes. She had felt him, shoulders rock hard under her hands. But she could also see the lines of red blood seeping through the white cotton of his shirt.

She tried not to panic. "Malachi?"

He opened his eyes, and Ava could see a gold fire ringing his irises. Then he leaned back and tore off his shirt. Fine wells of blood stained his entire left arm, crawling up to his collarbone.

"You," he panted, "did this."

"Are you okay?" Ava was trying not to freak out. She'd wanted him to remember, but though he didn't look angry, there was a violent expression in his eyes.

"Hurts."

"I'm sorry." She willed herself not to cry. She'd wanted him to remember, but his skin looked raw and wounded. She'd done this to him. Some of his *talesm* were back, but it must have been incredibly painful. "I'm so sorry."

"No," he grunted.

She tried to scramble off his lap, but he only held tighter, his hands digging into her hips. "Let me—"

"Not sorry," he said. His forehead was gleaming with sweat. The burning in his skin hadn't stopped. "Don't be sorry." He reached up and grabbed the back of her neck, forcing her mouth to his in a bruising kiss. Ava leaned into him. Relieved. Excited. She could feel the raw energy rolling off him in waves.

Adrenaline. Endorphins. Her mate's body had been hit with a massive cocktail of magic and hormones in the space of a few minutes.

She pulled away, gasping as his hands began to tear at her clothes. "Oh. Not angry."

"No."

* * *

MALACHI MADE LOVE TO HER WITH FURIOUS FOCUS, IGNORING WHAT had to be brutal pain on his left side. Ava just held on and let him vent the surge of power into her body. Over and over. He asked if she was okay. If he was hurting her. He wasn't. She was more afraid of hurting him, but he was insatiable and seemed to find as much satisfaction in her pleasure as in his own.

They took a break when the sun set, and someone—who wasn't brave enough to speak—knocked on their door, reminding Ava they weren't alone.

Malachi reached down, threw one of his boots at the door, and the footsteps hurried away.

Ava laughed into the shoulder that wasn't sore. His arm had already healed over, but it was an angry red.

"You're quite the beast today, aren't you?"

"It's your fault," he said, rolling onto his right side. "Do you know how much magic you woke in me?"

She tentatively touched his left arm. "A lot?"

"Yes. And Rhys was right."

"About?"

"I remember, Ava."

She paused, stunned that it had worked. "How much?"

"Most of my childhood. The earliest things." His eyes shone with tears. "I miss my parents again."

"I'm sorry," she said, stroking his cheek. He'd shaved that morning, but he was Malachi, so half a beard had already grown.

"Don't be sorry," he said. "I'm glad I miss them." He brushed the wet away from his cheek. "They deserve to be missed."

"How… What is it like?"

"You told me to remember, and it was like… a key unlocked in my mind. This door opened. And then inside that door, another door. And then another. I kept passing through each one, and it was as if the rooms they unlocked were infinite. Eventually, my brain just shut down. I remember everything through my school years. Rhys was there." Malachi frowned. "He may be my best friend, but by heaven, he can be an ass."

Ava burst into laughter. "He likes tormenting you."

"Still does." A reluctant smile crossed his face. "I suppose it was mutual."

"And your *talesm* grew."

He lifted an arm. "Apparently."

"That looks really painful."

"It is."

She winced. "I'm so sorry."

"Don't be. I wanted them back." He stretched his arm out and she could see the skin already healing around the tattooed flesh. "I feel stronger already."

"Then I'm glad."

"Good." He touched her chin until she looked at his face. The gold fire had retreated and his eyes were a beautiful, cloudy grey again.

"What is it?"

"I adore you, Ava. Your mind is fascinating. Your spirit humbles me. And your body feels as if it was made to fit my own. Even now that I have more of my memories back, my thoughts continue to circle you on a level that's borderline obsessive."

She blinked. "Wow."

"Know that. Understand it, because I'm going to say something that will likely make you angry."

She frowned. "Oh."

"You need to stop fooling around and work on your magic."

"What?" Her mouth dropped open. "But you said—"

"I know what I said. 'Go at your own pace. No pressure.' That was me being supportive and protective."

"I like you being supportive and protective."

"I don't think you need me to be supportive and protective right now. I think you need a kick in the ass. Because the magic I just felt has nothing dark or evil about it. You're scared of something that doesn't exist."

Yeah, okay. That made her a little mad. More than a little. He didn't know what she saw. Had no idea the shadows she felt lurking on the edge of her mind anytime the magic drew near.

"Until we know where my power comes from—"

"Ava, we may never know." He sat up and she followed him, facing each other on the rumpled bed. "We could search the world, question your father, wring answers from a fallen angel, and there is no guarantee we'll ever know why you were able to call me down from heaven. Or why you can show others things like the face of Death itself. We may not know any of it. Ever."

She had nothing to say, because he was right. She hated it, but he was right.

"What we do know," he continued, "is that your power is unique. It could be an incredibly potent weapon against those who want to hurt you. And you need to learn how to wield it like you just did with me."

She raised an eyebrow and glanced down at his naked body.

"Okay, maybe not *just* the way you did with me. You know what I mean."

She swung her legs over the edge of the bed and stared at the wall, unnerved by his honesty.

He was right. She'd felt the power when it left her. Felt the echo of it come back when they made love. It wasn't the dark shadow she'd felt in the past. The dark edge was still there, but it hadn't hurt Malachi, so she knew it wasn't inherently bad.

Could she use it to hurt?

Undoubtedly.

But she could also use it to heal. Her mate was in temporary pain, but his magic had been given a huge boost with the restoration of part of his *talesm*. The Old Language Orsala had taught her bent to her will, taking on her magic before she spoke it into life and power.

She had done this.

And she knew she could do it again.

Ya davarda, reshon.

It was a command. She'd told him to remember and he'd remembered.

How did Irina not become intoxicated by this power?

• • •   • • •

ORSALA EXAMINED MALACHI'S ARM, LIFTING IT TO SEARCH EVERY inch of the *talesm* that had reappeared.

"And these are what you remember?"

"As much as I can remember, yes. They feel right. If that makes sense."

"It does. These are your original marks. I can see the progression in expertise." She touched the skin that had already healed at his wrist. "A young man's marks here, for certain." Her finger passed over his forearm and elbow as Ava watched anxiously from her chair in the library. Rhys sat next to Ava as Orsala inspected Malachi in the full light of the window. "And then as we go up the shoulder… Yes, an obvious progression. You could be rather dramatic when you were young, yes?" She smiled at him, amusement twinkling in her eyes.

A faint flush stained his cheeks. "I was not always the most rational when choosing my marks."

Rhys said, "Still aren't."

"Shut up, Rhys."

"I can see a hotheaded boy in this arm," Orsala said, patting it. "But also the beginnings of a passionate, protective young man."

"Thank you."

Orsala turned to Ava, smiling. "You did this."

"I did."

Rhys nudged her arm, catching her eye with his mischievous smile. "And then they celebrated after. Loudly."

Malachi sent his friend a smug smile as he pulled on a shirt. "Jealous."

"Obviously."

He crooked his head and Rhys abandoned his seat next to Ava to go lean on his desk.

Orsala said, "I'd caution you to go slowly. When you unleash that level of magic, you're going to exhaust yourself. And each other."

Rhys couldn't smother the laugh.

Orsala narrowed her eyes at him, unable to hide her own smile. "While I'm sure some might find it amusing," she said, "I'd warn you to take your time. And also accept that one spell might not continue to be effective in the same way. It may be that a simple command to remember no longer works at some point. But you've taken the first step. You've started to heal each other."

Orsala reached down and took Ava's hand. "You are more open, I can feel it." She turned to Malachi and took his. "And you've regained some of your past. I can see your confidence returning. Your strength. I can feel…" She closed her eyes and drew in a deep breath, holding both their hands. "Your connection is almost tangible. I think your mating will be unlike anything our world has seen."

"I concur," Rhys said with a wistful smile.

"Be cautious," Orsala warned. "I want to work with you, Ava. Far more than we have been. Mala's physical training can wait for now. I do not think physical combat is your gift. I want to work on your magic."

Ava felt Malachi nudging her knee with his own. "I know. I will."

"And no holding back as you have been."

"I already promised this guy," Ava said, looking at her mate. "No holding back."

"I'll join you," Malachi said. "If she needs to practice spells, I'll be happy to help."

Orsala said, "I'd prefer to do this in Vienna with Sari, but we'll do what we can. When can you two go to the city?"

Ava exchanged a look with Malachi. "I need to get some information from my father before I go anywhere."

"Why?"

Malachi frowned. "To find her origins, of course."

Orsala looked at Rhys. "Isn't that something you can do while she's in Vienna?"

Rhys said, "I think Ava's father is the only one who knows the truth. My searches have come up with nothing."

"And my dad's currently in the middle of his mid-tour binge," Ava said. "He's not really all that coherent most of the time. Is there such a thing as a magical truth serum?"

"We can work on that if you think it will help," Orsala said. "But remember, truth is relative. He might tell you something he believes to be true, but there's no guarantee that his own perceptions are accurate, particularly if he's damaged his mind with drugs or alcohol."

"I'll take my chances. His memory has never been damaged, no matter how much he takes. Luis is right. How that man has managed to keep in perfect health is beyond me."

"Really?" The old woman stepped back and frowned.

"As far as I know. The drinking and drugs seem to work for him."

Orsala's eyes had lost focus. "I wonder…"

Ava waited for her to continue, but she seemed to have lost track of her thoughts. The singer wandered over to a stack of books on the library table and began to page through them. Rhys smiled at Orsala and came to stand in her place.

"I'll continue to search, but I don't know what other avenues to check."

Ava had a thought. "Rhys, speaking of Luis…"

"Luis Martin? I've checked him out. He's aboveboard. No criminal record. No links to our world that I can find."

"How about his personal property? Investments. That kind of thing."

"What about them?" Rhys frowned. "He's been a good financial manager for your father and seems very honest. There's no evidence of embezzlement or anything of the sort."

"Ah, but what about his own money?" Malachi smiled. "I know what she's thinking. We were looking for properties or payments in Jasper Reed's financial life that might indicate something about his mother. But did we check Luis Martin? If Reed truly wanted someone hidden, would he put it in his name or hide it behind someone he trusted implicitly?"

Rhys nodded. "It makes sense if he truly trusts Martin that much."

Ava said, "He does."

"Then I'll look into Luis Martin's financial life. I'll let you know if anything looks interesting."

"Thanks, Rhys."

Orsala called from the other side of the room. "Rhys, do you have a copy of *Gabriel's Old Tales*?"

"Which version?"

"The Hofstra translation is what I prefer, but any will do. Even one in the Old Language."

"I know I have at least one. Don't know about Hofstra…" Rhys led Orsala to the shelves, the two of them scanning the rows of books and muttering quietly back and forth.

"What are *Gabriel's Old Tales*?" Ava asked.

"Hmm? Oh. Children's stories." Malachi frowned. "Somewhat

frightening ones, as a matter of fact. I'm trying to think of a human equivalent."

"*Grimm's Fairy Tales*?"

"Perhaps."

"Fair maiden does something stupid and ends up eaten by a wolf or losing body parts and wandering hopelessly alone for the rest of her life? That kind of thing?"

"Yes," he said. "That kind of thing. My grandmother read some of *Gabriel's Old Tales* to me when I was a child, and I don't think I slept for a week."

"Nice."

"Now that I think about it, let's agree to never tell our children those kinds of stories, shall we?"

"We never finished the kid conversation, you know."

He reached over and put his arm around her shoulder, nuzzling his face into her neck. "You want my babies."

Ava felt herself melting. "You are confident, aren't you?"

"I'm confident because I know you want my babies. And you're a fierce woman who will make a tremendous mother."

"Mine was pretty great, even though my dad and stepdad were kind of useless."

"As our children will have the benefit of a superb father, you should have no concerns."

"What was Orsala saying about your confidence coming back?"

HER eyes opened in the darkness. She could sense her mate. He was by her side, unaware they were no longer alone.

Was she dreaming? She didn't quite know. All she knew was darkness and quiet. Peace filled her heart.

Darkness materialized from the shadows, but it wasn't Jaron. The rustle of feathers whispered in the air as the beautiful man leaned forward. His face emerged from the void of his hood, pale as the moon and holding an ancient, delicate beauty.

Ava felt no fear.

His eyes weren't the rich gold of Jaron's, but a silvery grey outlined by deep ebony lashes. His hair was the blue-black of a raven's wing; his face spoke peace.

Beautiful, immutable peace.

She put a hand on Malachi's shoulder and was surprised to feel the heat of his skin under her fingers. This was a dream, but it wasn't.

"I've seen you before," she said.

Death nodded, but he did not speak.

"You're not like the others."

He shook his head, a small smile playing across his lips.

"Am I going to die? Is he?" Her hand pressed into her mate's back, and Death's eyes followed her hand, resting on Malachi as he slept.

"No," Ava whispered, fear clutching her chest. "Please no."

Death flew to her side, pressing a warm finger to her lips. He drew her to his chest, and when he embraced her, a still, quiet voice whispered in her mind.

I am not here for you. Or him. I only see you together, and it fills me with a rare joy.

"You took him," she whispered.

I take them all. It is not often I am allowed to bring them back.

A sense of laughter in her mind.

Come with me, daughter. And I will show you secrets.

Death spread his arms and enfolded her in the night. His cloak was a blanket of stars, wrapping her in its depths as he surrounded her. She was weightless. Formless. And yet she still felt Malachi's strong shoulder under her hand as her soul flew with the black angel.

Come.

He opened his cloak and revealed a dark room. Three beings met there, cold and frightening in power. And though she stood in the center of them, Death held her shoulders, turning her around the chamber, and Ava knew they did not see her.

Listen.

The whispers came to her from behind a veil. Thoughts and voices tangled together. Ava knew they were speaking in the Old Language, but she had no trouble understanding.

"…troublesome child."

"Barak should have killed him."

"You killed Barak. Why… son still alive?"

They were indistinguishable by feature. She could only sense two beings with bright, glowing power and another clinging to one as a parasite to a host, feeding from the greater, though he did not know it. The Fallen were veiled, cloaking their power from the world and each other.

"…not long now."

"Watching. We must…"

"Scattered." Another voice drifted in and out. "…act now or they will discover them."

"There is no danger."

"There is every danger."

"If they find them—"

"If they find them, they will be reborn. The silent must remain hidden…"

Ava strained, but she couldn't hear more.

"…Irin will wake."

"A sleeping enemy does not trouble me."

"And Jaron?"

A pause. "Our brother does not have the strength to oppose us."

Something in the mocking tone of his voice reminded Ava of Brage, and she knew the speaker was Volund.

"He will make their army his own."

A growing sense of urgency. Wariness. Alarm?

Ava felt the black arms embrace her again just as Volund turned to stare into the void where she listened.

"Quiet, brothers." A long pause. "Azril, do you come among us?"

She dissolved, only to merge with her body again, her fingers still resting on her mate's back.

Warm hands clasped her face, though she could not see them. A cheek pressed against her own.

I cannot go to her, the angel whispered in her mind. *Though she calls me by my true name, I cannot reach her.*

The longing in his voice almost broke her.

"Who?"

Tell her I have not forgotten.

He was melting back into the shadows, and Ava still wasn't sure what was a dream and what had been real.

"Who are you talking about?" She crawled toward the darkness, desperate to understand. "Please! Who?"

Ava.

And he was gone.

CHAPTER
SEVEN

Despite their initial hope, searching through Luis Martin's financial information proved to be just as successful as searching Jasper Reed's.

"If anything," Rhys griped, "this is even more frustrating."

"Yes, he's a bit paranoid about privacy, isn't he?"

Malachi and Rhys were in the library. Malachi was waiting for Orsala to call him. She was doing meditation exercises with Ava in the sparring room. Then he would join them and they were going to practice defensive spellwork.

"It seems wrong to call him paranoid when we're hacking into his e-mail, doesn't it?"

Malachi shrugged. "Slightly."

"Oh well."

They continued to work, Rhys trying every keyword search he could think of to look for any mention of Ava's grandmother. Unfortunately, she was also named Ava, meaning that any search for her name hit on correspondence related to Jasper Reed's daughter and not his mother.

"He and Luis talk about her often," Rhys said. "I think her father thinks of her more than she realizes."

"Thinking of her and actually acting like a father are two very different things."

"Have you and Ava talked about children?"

"Briefly." Which wasn't something he wanted to discuss with Rhys. "What is that? He just mentioned a transfer to a Swiss bank."

"Shite." Rhys groaned. "Not that one. Their systems are archaic."

"But secure," Malachi said. "There's a reason why they're still as popular as they are. If Luis was making payments there, we need to determine what for."

"We're not going to be able to find out. Not from the bank. They still use paper. But let me…" Rhys tapped the keys rapidly. Screens popped up and disappeared faster than Malachi could read them.

"What are you doing?"

"I'm searching the exact dollar amount within his financial records. It wasn't a flat amount. $41,569.14 is not a random number. That's payment for something…" He tapped a few more keys and smiled. "Something specific. And monthly. Aha." Rhys sat back, a smile of satisfaction on his face. "I believe he pays that amount every month."

"How do you know?"

"Because he's transferred five hundred thousand dollars into that Swiss account every year for the past five years. Divide that by twelve and you have—"

"A little over $41,569? But why the single payment then? There must have been something unexpected that came up."

"Maybe it was just timing. That first payment was in December five years ago. A single month's payment before a monthly fee was set up? Automatically paid from the Swiss account probably."

Malachi sat back. "What costs that much for one person?"

"I think Reed—through his manager—is paying to keep his mother somewhere. A private institution, perhaps. Remember what Ava thought when we first met her? She thought she was insane. If Jasper Reed's mother was like Ava and living among humans, they might lock her up for hearing voices. That amount would fit with a private mental institution."

"And he'd hide her so thoroughly because he thought she was mentally ill?" Malachi was skeptical. "Wipe her from the public records? Hide her behind his manager and a Swiss bank account? That seems excessive."

"Unless she's violent. Dangerous. Or *in* danger from someone else."

It was possible.

"We need to search private mental institutions in Europe and the

US." He turned and saw Orsala standing at the door. "Search for any that cost that much on a monthly basis."

"Already on it," Rhys said. "See to your mate."

• • •   • • •

MALACHI SHOOK HIS HEAD. "No."

Ava's eyes were pleading. "But I can't practice defensive spells unless someone is attacking me." She spread her legs shoulder width apart and squared her shoulders. "Go on. I've rehearsed this a million times, but I don't know what I'll do in the middle of the actual spell. Orsala is here to stop me in case anything goes wrong."

Malachi crossed his arms over his chest. "While I'm duly terrified of your defensive abilities, *canim*, I'm more reluctant to attack you because you're my mate and I don't wish to hurt you. You may proceed without the attack from me."

Ava's jaw dropped. "Wow. Really? How old did you sound just then?"

Orsala said, "About four hundred years old. Ava, what did you expect? I told you it would be better to ask Rhys or Leo."

Malachi glared. "Absolutely not."

"Your friends would have no problem helping Ava practice."

"They would if they wanted to avoid injuries from me."

"Stubborn man!"

"I don't need an old woman's approval to protect my mate."

Ava held up both hands and stepped between them. "We're not doing this. I need to practice. This isn't a battle of the sexes. Malachi, you're my husband. Mate. Whatever. And I expect you to help me become stronger. I've tried unprovoked defensive spells, and they just don't work. I'm not getting that gut reaction I need to make them effective. So if you aren't willing or able to help me—"

"If there is no other option, then fine." Her matter-of-fact attitude convinced him. She was correct. To not help her become stronger would be to fail in his duties as her mate. "And we're getting married as soon as possible. If you prefer not to call me your mate, then I'll at least be your husband."

"Technically," Orsala said as she moved back to the wall, "she's not your mate either."

Ava's mouth dropped open, and Malachi said, "Yes, she is. Why in heaven would you say that?"

Orsala frowned. "Has she completed the mating ritual? I thought only you had performed it. Your magic doesn't reflect a mated couple."

Ava looked horrified. "I haven't." She turned to him. "What does that mean? What do I need to do?"

According to what he'd been told, Orsala was technically correct. Malachi had marked Ava before his death, but she'd never completed her side of the ritual, and he hadn't tattooed the mark that would make her claim permanent.

Ava was upset. "But we're dream-walking. And I... I feel you. I thought I was your mate. What we have—"

"Of course you're my mate," he said, soothing her. "We are *reshon*. Nothing can negate that. It's fine, *canim*."

"It's not," Orsala said. "He gave you his power, but you have not given him yours. Your mate will not heal fully until you do."

"But what do I do?"

Malachi marched over to the old woman. "She will not be pressured into this. This is between Ava and me."

"I'm not pressuring her. But you do her no favors. Mates carry each other's burdens. Do you think she is not able to carry yours?"

"That has nothing to do with it." And everything to do with Ava being as strong as possible. If she gave him her power, as so many Irina had before the Rending, then it was possible she would be weakened at a point when she might be vulnerable.

He turned to Ava. "We will complete the ritual in our own time. When things are safer for you."

Ava stepped to him. "Is she right?"

He was unable to lie to her. "I'm strong enough without borrowing your power."

Malachi saw Orsala shaking her head from the corner of his eye.

"It's not about strength or weakness," she said. "It's about sharing a burden."

The old woman strode over and, without warning, pushed Malachi over. Surprised by the old woman's move, Malachi lost his footing, falling backward on the mat. His shoulders bounced off the practice mat, his hands slapped down. He was up as quickly as he'd fallen, his fists clenched and his shoulders squared.

"What was that?"

"A point," Orsala said, circling the angry scribe. "I'm not stronger than you. Magically, perhaps, but I didn't use magic." She stepped closer and lowered her voice. "Trust me. You'd know if I did."

Malachi felt the press of her influence in his mind, but he refused to look away from her testing eyes.

The corner of her mouth lifted in reluctant approval. "You have the will of an ox."

"What is your point, old woman?"

"I'm not stronger than you, but you were not expecting an attack. You were unbalanced. Balance can be more important than strength, depending on the situation. If you and Ava are out of balance, then both of you are weaker. You are mates. Two halves of a whole. Learn from the foolishness of your fathers, Malachi of Sakarya, and do not make the same mistakes. Don't underestimate your other half."

Malachi looked at Ava. "I don't want—"

"I'm offering." Ava stepped forward. "I want this, Malachi. I've always wanted it. I didn't like you giving me your power to begin with."

"It was necessary." According to Rhys, she wouldn't have survived the battle in the cistern without his strength. Malachi had no regrets, even if it had cost him his life and his memories.

Ava turned away from him. "Teach me what to do."

Malachi crossed his arms again. "Not at the expense of your defensive spellwork."

"I can teach her both," Orsala said. "Have no fear, Scribe. Your woman will be protected from all sides. And now can we depend on your help to finish this lesson?"

Malachi looked between Ava and Orsala, knowing that at some point he'd lost the upper hand. He just couldn't figure out when. "Fine."

"Cool!" Ava said.

She grinned and Malachi couldn't be annoyed anymore. She looked too happy. He'd promised to attack her during her lesson, and she was thrilled.

"Gabriel's bloody fist," he muttered, bracing himself for the lesson ahead.

• • •   • • •

"I'M SORRY!" SHE KNELT OVER HIM, HIS HAND CLUTCHED BETWEEN hers. She might have said she was sorry, but she didn't look it. She looked thrilled.

Malachi wiped the trickle of blood from his lip and grinned. "Very good, Ava."

Without warning, he grabbed her by the shoulders and hooked his ankle around her knee, rolling them over so he was straddling her.

"*Vashahuul*," she whispered, freezing him for a split second. In that moment, she lifted her knees up between his legs and pressed up, throwing him off-balance. "*Vashaman!*" she shouted, amplifying the spell. He froze again. It didn't last long, but the split second he was paralyzed gave her an edge.

"Don't forget '*fasham*,' Ava!" Orsala shouted from the side of the room.

"*Ya fasham*," she hissed, and Malachi felt the wave of dizziness hit him immediately. The ground tilted between his feet.

Fasham. A simple word in the Old Language meaning "to tilt or unbalance" but in the mouth of an Irina, *ya fasham* was the command to fall.

He fell. Flat on his back, the wind knocked out of him.

"Now the staff. And remember, any spell can be amplified with *man*."

"Got it," Ava said, panting. She rolled to the side and grabbed the short staff that all Irina trained with. Malachi could remember his mother's. Always propped in a corner of the kitchen, it looked more like a broom handle than a weapon. But in the hands of a trained Irina—

"Ha!" It came down at the side of his head.

Narrowing his eyes, he reached out and snatched the staff from beside his head, giving it a swift tug and kicking his foot out to catch her ankle.

"Shit!" Ava yelled, losing her grip on the staff. Malachi spun it around and used it to vault himself to his feet.

"Did you mean to give this to me?" he said, taunting her. "Thank you so much. My mother had one of these. I felt it on my backside more than once."

She narrowed her eyes. "So you're used to taking a beating? Good. I won't feel too bad then."

"Ha!" He didn't try to stop her when she ran for the row of

weapons on the wall. She grabbed another staff and pounced, wasting no time before raining down a flurry of blows. She'd been taught well —by Mala, he was guessing—but her inexperience showed. He easily parried her blows, pushing just hard enough to challenge her without frustrating her. He allowed her to land a few blows before he took control.

"I thought we were practicing your defensive spells," he said.

"Seems a little unfair since I was beating you every time."

He laughed and brought the staff down, tapping her ankle and forcing her to the corner of the mat. She feinted right, and the end of his staff bounced up, striking her right in the stomach. She went down with a sharp groan.

"*Oof.*" She rolled on the ground, clutching her belly.

"Ava!" He tossed his weapon to the side and fell to his knees. "Ava, I'm so sorry. I didn't expect—"

"*Vashahuulman,*" she whispered, tensing under his hand. "*Ya fashaman. Aman!*"

The wave of dizziness swamped him, and when his eyes cleared, Ava was the one straddling him, a staff held over his neck and a smile on her lips.

"Did I ever tell you I went to acting camp?" she said. "We spent a whole week on how to take a fake punch."

Malachi grinned. "You are evil, and I am very proud of you."

"Thanks!"

THEY shared a shower later that afternoon before they went down to dinner. Ava was drying her hair and chattering about another spell Orsala had introduced to her that was supposed to cause instant nausea in any attacker. Messy, but effective. Malachi was listening with one ear but was distracted by examining the recovered *talesm* on his left arm.

"—for the spell. But that depends on me getting stronger, because that spell can only be used once I develop the ability to fly. Know what I mean?"

"Mmmhmm," he muttered.

She snapped her fingers in front of his face. "Hey, handsome."

He looked up. "Yes?"

"So you're cool with that, right? You can help me learn how to fly?"

He frowned. "What are you talking about? The myths about angels having wings are simply that. Myths. Ancient people had to rationalize angelic abilities somehow, thus the artistic depiction of... What are you smiling about?"

She tousled his hair. "You're so cute when you're being a nerd. But you should really listen to me instead of staring at your pretty tattoos."

"I don't remember writing them," he muttered, "but I seem to have been somewhat obsessed in my early years with sexual potency."

Ava burst into laughter. "Really? So that's all magically enhanced, huh?"

He closed his eyes and gave into laughter. "Apparently so. I apologize if you thought it was natural. I hate to disappoint you."

She was still laughing when she shoved him back and straddled his lap.

"Not disappointed, babe. Not even close."

He lay back and let her lean over him, tracing the line of her shoulder with one finger. She'd been softer in his isolated memories of her before he'd been killed. Her arms hadn't been lean with muscle. Her legs hadn't been quite as thick. Part of him missed the soft give of her flesh under his hand, but the other part was satisfied that his mate was more formidable now.

"Talk to me about the mating ritual," he said. "Are you sure you want it?"

"Why wouldn't I want it?"

He shrugged.

"A shrug is not an answer."

"I don't know," he said. "I worry. It's a permanent thing. Far more permanent than marriage."

"But you've marked me, right? I'll wear your mating marks forever."

"Yes."

"What did you write? What was your vow?"

He didn't remember the ritual they had shared, but he had examined her body when the magic held her, had seen the marks he'd written with his power. They glowed gold when they were intimate.

He felt the heat in his face. "There are many passages from Irin poetry we write during the ritual. Just like there will be many passages you will have to memorize to sing to me. You know—"

"But there's part that's just yours, right? The part that goes up my back and then over my shoulder to my heart? That's what Sari said."

"Yes." He traced the line of her back, seeing the words in his mind. He'd seen them countless times since. His own vow on her skin. A reminder of who she was and what he needed to be for her.

"What was it?"

"It was simple," he said, suddenly feeling inadequate. The words he'd written weren't enough. It wasn't often that he wished he was less of a warrior and more of a poet. "I must not have had much time. If I'd had more time—"

"What did you write, Malachi?"

"'I am for Ava,'" he said quietly. "'For her… my hand and voice. For her, my body and mind. Her strength in weakness. Her sword in battle. Her balm in pain. I am hers. Hers to cherish. Hers to hold. Hers to command.' That's what I wrote."

Malachi tried not to hear disappointment in her silence.

"I know it's simple—"

"You see that, *read* that, every time my marks glow?" Her voice was hoarse with emotion.

He traced a finger over her heart, following the words he'd written there. "Yes."

"So every time we make love, you are reminded of that vow. Every time you touch me"—she swallowed hard—"that promise is on my skin."

"It is Irin tradition. It's the way it has always been."

"And you don't want the same thing from me?"

Malachi dreamed of wearing her mating mark across his chest. It would be centered over his heart. And while the singer decided what words to include in her vow, it was up to the scribe to embellish those words and make them his own. His father's mating mark had been an elaborate illumination from his mother's German heritage. Scrolled flowers and birds marked the edges of her vow. He'd even broken tradition and added color.

And every time Ava faced him, her own promise would be written in his flesh.

"I want to wear your vow more than anything," he said with a pounding heart. "But I worry. Everything seems so precarious right now."

She sat up. "So you want me wearing your vow, but I shouldn't make any promises to you?"

"That's not… I don't mean it that way. You don't need to. I know you're my mate."

"Then you can take my mark, Malachi. You deserve my promise too."

"Don't you understand?" he asked. "You'll be surrendering some of your power. To me. But it's *you* that Jaron is tracking. It's you whom Volund has attacked. Ava, I don't want—"

"We're in this together." She spoke softly, but her voice was firm. "You heard what Orsala said. We work in balance or we don't work at all. We survive together, or we *don't* survive."

"If we'd been mated when I was killed, it could have killed you. It likely would have."

"You don't know that. Plus I'm stronger now. And you're not dying again."

"Ava—"

"Stop." She put a hand over his mouth and took a deep breath. "I'm serious. I don't really know how I brought you back the last time. I think it was beginner's luck. So don't even think about trying it again, because you'll probably just have to stay dead. And that's not acceptable, not even an option, okay?"

He saw that despite her attempt at humor, she was fighting off tears. Her strength humbled him again. Malachi peeled her hand away and said, "Okay."

"All right." She sniffed and wiped her eyes. "Discussion over. Let's talk about what kind of mating mark I have in mind. I'm thinking maybe some Nickelback lyrics. What do you think?"

He couldn't fight the smile. "Very funny."

"Maybe Beyoncé, if we want to go the more epic route." She traced something over his chest. "As for art, I'm cool with you just doing a little butterfly if you're worried about the pain."

He growled and flipped her over when she started to laugh.

"You are in so much trouble."

CHAPTER

EIGHT

"How can we practice like this and not…" Ava waved her hands at Orsala. "You know."

The old woman smiled. "Why are we able to practice spells without actually working them?"

"Yes."

They were going over the mating ritual in the library of the scribe house, taking advantage of the collection Rhys had been building. So much of the old library had burned in the fire the Grigori had set, but not all of it. Rhys was supplementing it with some of his own books and others that the scribes in Cappadocia had sent.

Most of the books had more information on written spellwork than spoken, but that was to be expected. Orsala and Ava could read and practice the poems she'd need to memorize for her mating ritual. Those were universal. But most of Orsala's teaching was verbal in nature.

"We're able to practice spells without actively casting them because…" The old singer frowned. "How to explain… Don't you feel the difference? You've worked various spells now."

"I have. I'm super careful about saying any words in the Old Language, though. The last time I did that, I brought my dead mate back to life, so… yeah, kind of makes me nervous."

"I suppose it would." Orsala paused. "There has to be… intention.

Purpose. I suppose a spell only works when you believe it will work. What words, exactly, did you say when you called him back?"

Ava took a deep breath. "*Vashama canem, reshon.*"

"Hmm." Orsala drew her hands together in front of her. "Not a command, then. A plea. To your *reshon*, specifically. A mourning cry."

"I'd heard it so many times."

"It's something we all hear if we're listening, isn't it?" Orsala's eyes filled with sorrow. "The soul cry at the loss of a beloved. A mate. A child. Irin and human alike. It's not a spell. Not exactly. Though I suppose any words spoken with enough power could be. That was our bargain with the Forgiven. They gave their daughters their voice. Their songs."

"What did they give their sons?"

"Glyphs." Orsala ran her hands down her arms. "Their *talesm*. But angels are not tattooed as our males are; their glyphs are part of their skin."

"So why did my words, which aren't even a spell, bring Malachi back from the dead?"

"I don't know," she said. "Perhaps because it wasn't a spell. It was a plea. To Malachi? To the Creator? Maybe it was simply an answered prayer."

Ava paused. "It wasn't because my power is different?"

"Your power is different and it isn't," Orsala said, leaning her elbows on the table. "It feels the same as all Irina power but... condensed. Your eyes are so gold. Your power so raw. Even untrained, you worked incredibly powerful magic. Your bloodlines must be very potent, whatever they are." There was a flicker of concern in Orsala's eyes, but then the old woman blinked and it was gone. "We should get back to—"

She broke off at the commotion near the doorway. There was a slam. A shuffle of coats and shoes. Low, urgent voices. Ava and Orsala rose to their feet just as the door burst open.

Maxim strode into the room.

Leo followed him. "But I don't understand—"

"Ava," Max said. He came to her, put his hands on her shoulders, and stared. "*Ava.*"

"Max, what is it? Why are you here?"

Orsala looked past them to the door. "Renata? What are you doing here?"

Ava put her hands over Max's and ignored the other voices in the room. She almost felt as if she were the one holding the massive man up. His eyes were focused on her as they had been the first time they'd met in the old scribe house, when Malachi had drawn the ancient words over her skin, marking her as one of their lost Irina. Max had stared then as he stared now.

Wonder. Confusion. Awe.

"Max, what's going on?"

"I can't…" His eyes pleaded with her. "I can't explain. You have to see."

"See? See what? What are you talking about?"

She turned when the door from the kitchen opened and Malachi walked in.

"Maxim," he said. "What has happened?"

Max just shook his head, still staring at Ava.

Renata walked further into the room and said, "We've just come from Bulgaria. The two of you—"

"He said nothing about Malachi," Max said.

"He is her mate," Renata said. "She's not going without him."

Rhys walked in on the commotion. "What in heaven's name—"

"You need to come with us," Max said. "There's something you have to see."

"In Bulgaria?" Malachi asked.

Max shook his head again. "I can't explain. You have to see. I didn't believe… didn't know. But now… It changes everything, Malachi." He squeezed Ava's shoulders. "Trust me?"

She nodded. Max had been instrumental in spiriting her away from Istanbul after Malachi had been killed. She knew he had dubious contacts in the outside world, but she trusted him implicitly.

"Malachi?"

Her mate said, "If you want to go to Bulgaria, we'll go to Bulgaria. Did you two drive here?"

Renata said, "Yes."

Orsala asked, "What's going on?"

"I want Mala to take you to the city," Renata said. "I want you with Sari and Damien. We'll send Ava and Malachi to you after we travel to Sofia."

Orsala narrowed her eyes but said nothing else.

Ava exchanged a look with her mate. Malachi shook his head, looking as confused as she felt.

Ava didn't know what was happening, but for the second time in her life, she had a feeling that everything had just changed.

⁕

"TELL ME AGAIN," RENATA SAID. "WHAT DID YOUR FATHER SAY ABOUT his mother when you confronted him?"

"Not much," Ava confessed as she sat next to Renata in the back of the car, talking about Jasper. "He called her 'maman.' Claimed she died, but I know he was lying. I could hear it."

"Hmmm."

"And not much else. There were a couple of times he looked…"

"What?"

"I don't know."

"What did you see?"

Her voice dropped. "He looked… different. I can't say exactly. Just different than he used to."

"Hmm." Renata sat back and folded her hands on her lap. "Interesting. We don't know enough, but it could fit."

"I really hate you guys keeping me in the dark on this."

"I know that, but if I tell you what I suspect, then I'll have to tell you everything." Renata waved her hand in a cutting gesture. "And if I tell you everything, you won't believe me."

"You realize that makes absolutely no sense, right?"

"It will after we get there."

"And where are we going?"

"To meet a man named Kostas."

"Does he know where my grandmother is?"

Renata shook her head. "I doubt it. But you might get some answers about *what* she is."

⁕

"MAX." MALACHI'S VOICE WAS A LOW GROWL IN THE FRONT SEAT. "What is this? I thought we were going to the scribe house."

"You have to trust me, brother."

Ava had never been to Sofia, the capitol and largest city in Bulgaria. It was only six hours from Istanbul but seemed farther when you climbed the mountains. Snow dusted the sides of the road in places, and the temperature had dropped from the damp and mild weather along the Bosphorus.

Ava asked, "Who's Kostas?"

"Someone I've known for a long time," Max said.

Malachi said, "The name sounds familiar, but I can't place it."

Max said nothing as Malachi carefully scanned the outskirts of the city where industrial areas sprawled. Wherever they were going, it didn't look close to the heart of the historic city. Commercial trucks and trailers seemed more common than cars.

"Tell me where we're going," Malachi said.

"To see Kostas."

"Damn it, Max!"

"You're going to have to trust me," he said, gritting his teeth. "I am limited on what I can say. I gave my word."

"Your withholding information makes me want to grab Ava and walk back to Istanbul right now."

Ava looked at the whipping wind outside the vehicle grabbing flurries of snow. "Maybe we shouldn't walk. I do know how to hot-wire a car."

Renata bit back a smile. "You are always full of surprises, my friend."

"Rebellious kid with lots of money and an overprotective mother. I had interesting friends as a teenager."

"I suppose so."

They turned onto a small road that led between a group of warehouses. Some of them were open, but most were closed. It was nearing midnight, and Ava rubbed her eyes to fend off the worst of the exhaustion.

Malachi must have caught the gesture, because he said, "We should find a place to rest. Do this tomorrow."

"It was difficult to get him to agree to meet with us. I don't want to delay."

They turned into a small parking lot in front of an older warehouse that looked more like a barn. It was freestanding. Not connected to any others, but still had the anonymous grey paneling they'd seen every-where else.

"I'm so tired," Ava said with a yawn.

"I don't like this," Malachi said.

"Trust us." Renata grabbed her hand as they came to a stop. "Stay with me and Malachi, Ava. Let Max do the talking right now."

They walked toward the door where a small window was glowing. It was the only light in the darkness. Not even a star appeared above them. The clouds had rolled in during their drive, and the night was pitch-black. Ava fell in step between Malachi and Renata.

Ten feet from the door, Malachi halted. "What the hell?"

Max turned and held up both hands. "I know what you're thinking, but you have to trust me. I would never lead Ava and Renata—"

"*What the hell?*" Malachi's voice echoed between the metal corridor of buildings and Ava heard the door open.

She looked beyond her mate and Max.

"Ava, get back in the car. Now!"

Renata held tighter to her hand. "Malachi, calm down. No one is going to hurt her."

There was a silhouette in the doorway. The man stepped forward, his lithe body moving with preternatural grace. As he stepped closer, Ava saw him and her heart almost stopped.

Pale, luminous skin set off eyes the color of the winter sea. Dark, curling hair fell over his forehead, touched by hints of the snow that had started to fall.

Beautiful.

Ethereal.

Grigori.

Malachi roared and reached for his knives as Ava stepped back.

Her mate rushed the soldier, who immediately countered with his own weapons. Malachi fought in a fury of knives and kicks, slashing the Grigori who fended him off with a short staff and a machete.

"Malachi, no!" Max was yelling.

Renata held Ava in an iron grip, keeping her from running to the safety of the car or joining her mate in battle. "Stay here and keep out of it."

"Stop," Max shouted. "Please!"

They didn't stop. Malachi had a deep gash across his cheek, but the Grigori looked worse. Still, the soldier fought with grim determination and focus. He winced and rolled away when Malachi knocked him to the ground.

Max, Ava noticed, was not helping. He was only shouting at the two men to stop.

"You have to listen to him," Renata shouted. "Malachi, stop!"

Four more men appeared in the doorway, hands clenched on their own daggers. One held up a gun.

"No!" Max yelled, rushing toward them. "He doesn't know!"

Renata left Ava and ran to Malachi, spinning him around and pulling him away from the Grigori. "Stop, you idiot, and listen!"

Malachi bared his teeth at Renata and lunged at the Grigori again, though the man was curled on the ground, barely moving.

Renata pulled him back and punched Malachi across the jaw.

"Hey!" Ava shouted, rushing forward. "What are you—"

"Don't you lose your head too," Renata said, swinging Ava around and holding her arms behind her back. "Look at them."

"Malachi—"

"Look at them!"

She looked.

Another Grigori stood in front of Max, his hands in his pockets. She could smell the sandalwood on his skin. His eyes surveyed the scene clinically as the soldiers rushed from the doorway and rolled their brother to his back to examine his wounds. Malachi was stirring, his hand reaching for his dagger, but Renata stepped on it and bared her teeth.

"Let. Max. Talk."

"Kostas said to bring the girl," the soldier in charge said to Max. "Not an Irin assassin."

Max said, "The scribe is her mate. She doesn't go anywhere without him. And you didn't leave me time to explain. I told Kostas to wait for my signal."

"Kostas does not answer to you." The Grigori's eyes narrowed. "And the butcher of Berlin isn't known for his understanding."

"Let me talk to him, Pietro."

"Fine. But get him under control. Or Kostas will refuse to allow any of you in." His lazy eyes flicked to Ava. "Maybe her."

Calm. Slight interest. But none of the grasping hunger she'd felt from the Grigori in the past.

There was something different in his gaze.

"Calm your mate, sister," the Grigori named Pietro said to Ava. "Then come inside."

Ava froze.

Pietro turned and followed the other Grigori, who had not attacked but only carried their fallen comrade into the dimly lit warehouse. Malachi stopped growling and rose to his feet, suddenly aware of the change in the air.

"Ava, what's going on?"

Sister?

He reached for her frozen hand as Ava's heart had begun to pound. "Ava—"

"I want to go in," she whispered. "I need to go in there."

She followed the strange Grigori without thought. Malachi fell in step behind her, still grasping her hand. She felt the blood sticky on his palm, but she couldn't seem to stop. Ava could feel the tension ratcheting up his arm.

As the Grigori led them through the building, various doors cracked open, but no one attacked them. No one even showed their face.

They made it into the cavern of the warehouse, a living area lit within the darkness. Low conversation flowed around the small group of men. No more than ten or fifteen were there. As they approached, they passed tables and chairs set up, old pallets and broken-down crates.

A man rose from the couch, his hands fisted on his hips.

His hair was long and pulled back to reveal another stunningly handsome face. Rich brown eyes and coffee-colored hair. Aquiline features that bore a hint of nobility, despite the grime and wreckage around him.

Max stepped forward and held up a hand. "Kostas."

"I said you could bring her. Not a scribe. He injured one of my best men."

"She is his mate. I told you she wouldn't come without him. And I saw him. No permanent damage was done. Please excuse me. This is my fault. I didn't prepare Malachi to meet you. I thought... I didn't know how much to say. It would be better to see."

Kostas's eyes flicked to Malachi, assessing him. "He is the one who returned?"

"Yes."

"Who are you?" Ava asked.

The Grigori's eyes shuttered. For a long moment, Ava waited to see what he would say, half of her tugging forward and the other half wanting to run. She lifted her shields and listened to the voices around her. Unlike the scratched voices she was expecting, these Grigori voices were touched with a resonance that reminded her of the Irin. But it was a jumble; her own mind was too scrambled to make sense of anything. She could only hear emotion.

Longing.

Anger.

Fear.

Ava looked around. She was surrounded by at least fifteen Grigori, but no one was coming after her. No one even approached. The normally seductive stares were wary. Cautious.

"As long as my people come to no harm, he may stay," Kostas said, then he narrowed his eyes at Ava.

Malachi stepped forward, blocking his gaze. "What is this place?"

Kostas smiled and, despite the knot in Ava's stomach, she reacted. He was so beautiful it was as if the sun had broken through clouds.

"Welcome to the heretics' house," Kostas said, giving them a deep bow. "The children of the Fallen your brethren have killed surround you."

"Oh shit," Ava said as Malachi tensed.

Kostas continued. "Allow me to officially extend my appreciation for your service." The gleam in his eyes was lethal. "We *very* much appreciate it."

"What the hell is going on?" Malachi asked Max.

"Wait."

The Grigori named Pietro stepped toward Kostas. "Boris and Roman checked the perimeter. They're alone."

"Good." Kostas looked toward a corner blocked off by crates. "Kyra, you may come out now."

A woman stepped from the shadows as Ava moved forward. She felt Malachi's hand on the small of her back; he stood steady and protective behind her.

She was tall and dark-haired; her long brunette mane was streaked with ebony. She turned her gaze, and Ava met eyes a mirror of her own. Glowing gold behind thick black lashes. She heard Malachi suck in a breath. The woman was beautiful. Incandescently beautiful.

Inhumanly beautiful.

Like the Grigori she stood beside.

"Ava." Kostas took the woman's hand. "I'd like you to meet my sister. Kyra."

Of course.

Of course.

Sister.

The memory of a dark angel's voice in her mind.

"Soon. You will know soon."

It was a startling, beautiful clarity, fresh as the sky after rain.

Kyra smiled at Ava. Her gold eyes were shining. "Did you think the angels only had sons?"

11.

J aron stood on the roof of a warehouse near Barak's son, watching
Ava in his mind's eye.

Of course.

"Did you think the angels only had sons?"

No.

There had always been others.

Barak appeared a second later. Vasu followed.

"She knows," they said together.

"Soon she will go to their city," he said. "And I will remove my
protection."

"Volund will be drawn out?" Vasu asked.

"He will come," Barak said. "He has his own interest in the
woman."

Vasu curled his lip slightly. "I still do not understand your
fascination."

"Not fascination," Jaron said. "She will draw him as nothing else
can."

Jaron opened his eyes to them as they watched the scene play out
among the sons and daughters of angels below them.

The Irin. Children of the Forgiven, their power glowing not with
the wild raw fury of Fallen children but the low, controlled burn of a

well-tended fire. Their magic had been honed. Trained. Tested. Their blood farther from the angels, they had used the knowledge the Forgiven had given them to become more powerful than those they fought. Male and female. They were a balanced race.

The Grigori. Raw fury and terrible hunger. Slaves to the Fallen. Abandoned to ignorance, their children raged against the human world with the fury of a child denied. Their sons, predators. Their daughters, a secret.

Born in fear. Terrible with untrained power. Forgotten. Disposed of. They called themselves *kareshta*. The silent ones.

Their fathers called them nothing. Those who allowed their daughters to live usually abandoned them to the madness of the human world. After all, female offspring were rare.

He'd never turned his mind to them, because for Jaron, there had only ever been sons.

Until there hadn't been.

"I sing sometimes when you're not here."

Broken.

His only daughter was so terribly broken.

"Your son, Barak," Vasu said with dark amusement in his eyes. "Kostas would remake the world we have built. There is power in that one. Are you sure he thinks you are dead?"

"Yes." Barak cocked his head. "He won't hear me. Whatever magic Jaron has laid over the woman protects me as much as it does her."

"Kostas is perceptive," Jaron said, "But he is not more powerful than me."

"Why do you shield her?" Vasu asked.

"I have my reasons."

Reasons only Barak knew. And his oldest friend only knew because he'd found Jaron in a killing rage sixty years before. A rage that would have swallowed the world unless Barak intervened.

Jaron had not taken a human lover since, and his line was dying.

He wanted it to.

Vasu, the most terrestrial of them, crouched down, clearly intrigued by the scene that Jaron showed them.

"I have never understood the fear of them."

"That is because you have never raised your daughters," Barak said.

Vasu shrugged. "If they run to the humans, the humans may have them."

"The humans consider them mad."

"What is madness but a form of wisdom?" Vasu murmured, his eyes still locked on the warehouse. "Once they were called seers. Holy women. They were revered in my territory. But Volund fears them. Hates them. Galal butchers them in the name of progress. Why?"

"They are of us," Jaron said, "but unlike us."

Barak said, "When the first Fallen daughters were born, they were killed immediately. Considered defective human offspring."

"Many still view them as such," Jaron said.

He remembered when Barak had stopped killing his female children. It was when the first pair of twins had been born. The two children grew to be some of his most powerful, though the daughter was always kept hidden from any he did not trust absolutely. Jaron was the only angel who knew Barak no longer killed or abandoned his daughters. Not that many didn't escape his control. Those, he left to the human world. Or he had, before betrayal had rent their world. Barak had also ceased siring children sixty years ago, for many of the same reasons Jaron had.

Yet Vasu knew nothing. He still stared at the warehouse, watching the scene as if it were performed on a human stage.

"Vasu," Jaron said.

Gold eyes looked up. Vasu's dark skin was colorless in the night, but his gold and black hair whipped in the wind. The gold reflecting the starlight, the black swallowing the darkness.

"What do you want of me?" he asked. "I do not want the same thing you do. I have decided."

"You will remain here?"

"Yes."

Barak stepped forward. "Are you certain?"

"Are you?"

Barak's eyes narrowed. "I am. If you remain, you will be alone."

"If we succeed, I will not be. There will be no more reason to hide, and my people will return to me."

Jaron said, "Killing Volund will not erase all your enemies, brother."

"It will erase enough of them," Vasu said. "Galal will be nothing without Volund's support. You have your vengeance, and I have mine."

"Enough," Jaron said quietly. "We are decided."

"We are decided," the three Fallen said, turning their eyes back to the cold warehouse on the edge of the mountains where the earthly realm had changed in the space of a single word.

CHAPTER

NINE

Sister.

Malachi's mind rebelled.

No.

It wasn't possible.

They would have known.

They *had* to have known.

How could they not have known?

He reached for Ava's hand, but she was already walking toward the woman called Kyra. Renata was at her side.

"Ava, don't!"

The Grigori around them had been calm, almost eerily so. But at his protest, they turned furious eyes toward Malachi, as if they were enraged at the interference. Max put a hand on his arm and he calmed.

"Renata is with her. She'll be fine. Kostas would never attack Ava, especially not in front of his sister."

Sister.

A sister.

"How——"

"They are Barak's children. Twins. Both their sire and mother are dead." Max lowered his voice. "Malachi, *surely* you can see."

He knew Max was telling the truth. It was the eyes. The woman's gold eyes were exactly like his mate's. She had luminous skin. Ethereal beauty. She was Grigori in female form.

Not Grigori.

Grigora.

"Max, it's not…"

"It is."

"But we would have known," he said. "There was never any—"

"Why would you have known, Scribe?" Kostas's eyes pierced him from across the room. "When does *your* kind stop to ask questions?"

Malachi ignored the Grigori and watched Ava. She was holding Renata's hand but reaching for Kyra. She looked over her shoulder, searching for him.

"Malachi?"

"I'm here."

"I…" Ava looked between Malachi and Kyra. Kyra and Kostas. "This is real?" she whispered, her eyes revealing her deepest fear.

He forgot the angry Grigori and walked over to her, bending to whisper in her ear. "This is real, *canim*. You're not dreaming. Does this feel like a dream or a vision?"

"No."

He squeezed her hand. "See?"

"Interesting," Kostas mused. "I wondered what she could do."

Malachi's head whipped around. He left Ava with Renata and Kyra as he stalked toward Kostas. "My mate is none of your concern."

Kostas looked amused, but Malachi said nothing else. He had no wish to confirm or deny anything about Ava until he knew more about whatever was going on. He glanced over his shoulder, but the women were locked in intense conversation in the corner of the room. The males around them had withdrawn, keeping watch but not interfering.

Malachi drew Max to the side. "How did you discover this?"

"I've known Kostas for years," he said. "We've traded information. Favors, at times. I knew there were others like him—Grigori free of their sires—but they're very secretive."

"And the women? Why did we never see them? Hundreds of years —thousands! How could a secret like this remain hidden?"

"How do we remain hidden?" Max said. "Human see what they want to see. And sometimes Irin do as well."

Malachi couldn't argue with that. He looked at the protective

Grigori soldier who stood near them. Watching his sister. Watching them.

The man was different than the others. All these Grigori were. There was none of the desperate hunger he associated with his mortal enemies. The men around him looked like Grigori. Smelled like Grigori. But… they did not act it. And Malachi wondered how it was possible. Was the presence of only one female so powerful to them?

"Your sister." Malachi walked toward Kostas. "There are others like her?"

"Yes. Though there have never been many," Kostas said. "If you're truly interested, I'll explain, though it probably won't improve your opinion of our race."

Malachi asked Max, "Do you trust him?"

"I wouldn't be here if I didn't."

Malachi crossed his arms and stared at Kostas. "Maybe you're different. But don't try to tell me most of your kind aren't murderers and rapists. I've witnessed the aftermath of too many attacks."

"I'd never claim to be anything but what I am," Kostas said. "But if it helps, the same angels trying to kill you would love to kill me as well."

"Why?"

"I'm an abomination," he said with a grim smile. "I should have died years ago when my father was killed, but I didn't. Volund, especially, hates that I even exist."

"Volund killed your father?"

Kostas nodded. "He wanted his territory. Barak used to control most of Northern Europe."

"That's all Volund's land now," Max said. "He was successful."

"How much do you know about us?" Kostas asked Malachi. "Other than what you've learned in your efforts to kill us, what do you know?"

"You have magic, but not like us."

"True." Kostas motioned them toward a number of ragged chairs. The Grigori who were sitting there moved away immediately. It was obvious who was in charge. "The average son of the Fallen lives for around one hundred sixty to one hundred eighty years. Nothing close to the Irin lifespan."

"But there are some who are much older."

Brage, the Grigori who'd killed Malachi in the cistern—who'd tried to take Ava from him—had been present during the Rending. He'd been at least two hundred and fifty years old.

"Our lives can be prolonged by magic—as the Irin's can—but only at the will of the Fallen. We exist for them. An angel who finds a particular child useful can extend his life indefinitely."

"Do they?"

"Rarely." Kostas leaned forward, his elbows on his knees. "Do you know what the Grigori are, Scribe?"

"You're sons of the Fallen. Half angel and half—"

"We're slaves," Kostas said with a bitter smile. "The Irin forefathers left, giving their children knowledge and freedom. The Fallen stayed and kept their children under their thumbs. We exist to serve them. We have no will other than theirs. No life beyond what they give us. If they call us, we come. If they command us, we obey. To do otherwise is unthinkable. We feed…" Kostas drew in a ragged breath. "We feed on humans because our touch hunger is voracious and most Grigori have no outlet other than the humans we're presented with when we are mere children. No mothers. No sisters. No mates."

"So you kill like monsters?" Malachi asked.

"We are never taught to care. We take what we want because we can. Cruelty is rewarded. Mercy or conscience is not."

"So why should I trust you?" Malachi asked. "How many women have you killed?"

Kostas's eyes froze. "Too many."

Malachi leaned forward. "And why should I not execute you here?"

"Because my men surround you," Kostas said. "They owe me their loyalty. And I cannot allow you to take my protection away from those who need it."

"How do I even begin to trust you?" Malachi said. "You could lie—"

"I love my sister." Kostas's eyes softened as he looked to Kyra. "I have always protected her. Even when my father was alive. I am far from guiltless, but she is the reason I've never surrendered to the total rage most Grigori feel. Her touch. Her life. Our father allowed us to stay together because I was useful to him, and I'm stronger with Kyra near me."

"Barak did not have an overly cruel reputation."

"Some angels are more lenient than others," Kostas said, turning back to them. "Some are negligent and don't care. But all of us exist at the whim of the Fallen. Free will only came to me once my father was dead."

Malachi checked on Ava again, but his mate was still huddled in the corner with the other two women, speaking in low voices. "Why have we never seen a female of your race before?"

"How do you know you haven't?" Kostas asked.

Malachi had no answer.

"Kyra and I were fortunate," he continued. "Barak doesn't kill his daughters at birth like most of the Fallen do."

A knot tightened in his gut. "Killed at birth?"

A hollow look came to Kostas's eyes. "The females have always been harder to control. Most angels consider their daughters too dangerous to live."

"Why?" Malachi asked.

"Think about it," Max said. "If we draw the Irin and Grigori parallel out, Grigori would be able to work magic if they could write as we do. If they were taught the spells."

"But the Fallen do not teach them," Malachi said, still profoundly grateful for that fact. Kostas the heretic might be controlling himself, but that hadn't changed his opinion of Grigori as a whole.

"Nor should it," Kostas said, looking at Malachi.

He tensed, realizing the man had heard his thoughts. "You're telepathic?"

Kostas shook his head. "Not truly. I hear whispers of thoughts every now and then. Barak's children sometimes do. If I'd had training from my father, I might know more."

"They offer you no teaching at all?" Malachi could hardly believe it. Knowledge was revered in Irin culture. Training started before children could speak. It was given in playful verses and songs from the time they were born. The teaching of magic was an Irin parent's primary responsibility.

"They do not teach us, or they cannot," Kostas said. "We don't know. I'm certain they wouldn't, even if they could. It would make us more powerful. And if we were more powerful—"

"You might be harder to control," Malachi said. "But why are your sisters considered more dangerous than their brothers?"

"They hear things," Kostas said, his voice low. "Sometimes they say things. Dangerous things they have no idea how to control. Many are unwell in their minds. Tormented by—"

"Voices," Malachi said, glancing at Ava. "If they are like our women, they hear the soul voices of humanity."

"Obviously your women have a way to control it. Ours do not. My sister… I try to keep her as isolated as I can. She wanted to come and meet your mate, though I advised against it."

"Ava was the same." Malachi offered that one comfort. "Before we found her. She survived."

Kostas took a deep breath. "I love my sister. I cannot remember a time when I did not. Even when my father was alive. Barak was… negligent. He didn't kill his daughters, but they were sent away. He had places that were mostly prisons. Those who escaped were left alone, but then they were at the mercy of the humans. Yet his negligence was still better than most of the Fallen. Many infant daughters, even if they aren't killed, die of neglect when their mothers give birth to male children."

"Why?"

"Because we kill our mothers," Kostas said. "Simply by existing."

Malachi tasted acid at the back of his throat.

"Don't you understand?" Kostas continued. "Your ancestors were forgiven because they recognized the truth: Angels don't belong here. Their children—all of us—never should have existed. We are abominations. They left because they knew that, so the Creator had mercy on the Irin. My people?" Kostas leaned back. "We received no mercy. We don't deserve it. We're all murderers before we can speak."

The man's self-loathing was so evident Malachi had a difficult time condemning him further.

Max leaned forward and said, "You fight to make things better, my friend."

Kostas gave him a rueful smile. "I would call you my friend, Maxim, but for your willful ignorance of the truth."

"It's not ignorance. I simply don't judge you as harshly as you judge yourself."

"I saved Kyra," Kostas said to Malachi. "I have been able to save a few others. I protect them. That is my penance for the lives I've taken. The harm I've done."

"How many women?" Malachi asked. "How many do you protect?"

"I don't trust you that much, Scribe. No matter who you are mated to."

"When I finally discovered it," Max said, "I knew I had to tell you. For Ava."

Malachi narrowed his eyes at Max. "You think Ava is Grigori?"

"No. Yes?" Max said. "I don't know. I see more in common than different."

Malachi's eyes turned to Ava and Kyra. He could see it, see the similarities, but he could also see profound differences. Ava didn't look inhuman, as Kyra did. Her skin wasn't as pale or as luminous. Her eyes were the same, but she was no ethereal creature. His mate had a delicate, yet earthy, beauty.

"I don't think she is, Max."

"There's something…," Kostas said. "Her eyes drew me at first. But I agree. Your mate does not look like our women."

"She's at least half human. Her mother is fully human, but her father is not. That may be the connection."

"Is her father Grigori?" Kostas asked. "Some of us are able to father children with human women. Some have enough control."

"He doesn't smell it. Or look it. Though there is something different about him."

"Reed's mother," Max said. "That has to be the connection. Ava's grandmother must have Grigori blood."

Malachi said, "We've been trying to find her, but we haven't had much success. Could she be one of yours?"

Kostas took a deep breath and frowned. "If she is, I'd have no way of knowing without meeting her. No records are kept in our world, particularly for females. The ones who survive are mostly in the human population because they're safer there."

"Safer?" Malachi asked. "Among humans who think they're insane?"

"They can't hurt humans as the males do, so they can often blend in. It's better than what faces them among the Fallen."

"Do you have any idea how many might be out there?" Malachi asked. "How many… Grigora?"

"The Fallen call them Grigora. They call themselves *kareshta*. The silent ones."

"Silent ones?"

"Those who make it through childhood learn to be silent. Not to use their voices. It's their only chance of surviving in our world."

Kareshta.

Kostas continued, "I would estimate only two—maybe three births in ten are female. The Fallen tend to create male children. Some have no daughters at all. Whatever genetics are in play, women are rare."

"Only four in ten Irin children are female," Max said. "We have no idea why. It's always been that way."

Kostas said, "Of that twenty percent, more than half are probably killed at birth. There could be hundreds. Thousands, counting all the minor angels. We have no way of knowing. Most of them are in the human world. Free Grigori like us who shelter the *kareshta* will only shelter those whose fathers are dead."

"What?" Malachi asked. "Why?"

"Security," Kostas said with a grimace. "If our sires are alive, they can find us. It doesn't matter where we go. Only those whose sires are confirmed dead are allowed. Almost all the women I shelter are my sisters. I cannot risk them. Too many of the Fallen are trying to kill me."

"Why?" Malachi asked. "Barak is dead. Why do they care what you do?"

"My mere existence is heresy. I'm the one telling the Grigori they can live without reducing themselves to murderous animals. That there *is* another way."

"But not a way the Fallen are happy about."

"How could they be?" Kostas asked. "In order for the Grigori to be free, the Fallen *must* die."

• • •   • • •

"I'M NOT *KARESHTA*," AVA SAID LATER AS THEY LAY IN BED. "I thought at first that I was, but I'm not."

They'd avoided the scribe house in Sofia, not wanting to explain their presence if it might compromise Max's promise of secrecy to Kostas and Kyra. Instead, they'd found a small hotel near the highway and taken two rooms. They were threadbare, but clean.

"You're not *kareshta*, but…?"

"There is something. Kyra feels familiar. Her voice sounds right, if that makes any sense."

"Her magic feels the same as yours."

"Yes, I think that's it."

Malachi hadn't said anything, but he'd sensed the same thing. More, Kostas's sister gave off the same nervous energy that Ava had been drowning in before she'd learned to shield herself from the soul voices of the humans around her.

He wrapped her in his arms, shaken by the truths they'd discovered that night.

For Malachi, it changed everything.

He was forced to see the Grigori in a new light. Yes, most or all of them were still victimizing humans, but they were also victims themselves. And some, like Kostas, appeared to be trying to change things. His black-and-white world had been thoroughly washed in grey. But in the confusion, his scattered mind focused on a kernel of hope.

If Ava had Grigori blood, how different could they be?

"You're not *kareshta*," Malachi agreed. "But it wouldn't matter to me if you were. You know that, don't you?"

"Yes." She snuggled deeper into his side. "I can hear you."

There was a dark edge to her magic. The visions that came to her were unlike anything Irina experienced. But Ava was good. Not perfect, but *good*. Her heart was warm and generous. She was protective. Courageous.

His.

She reached out with her magic, and it was as if small hands stroked him from head to toe. He shivered with wanting her, but Ava was too deep in thought.

"I think my grandmother must have been one of them. That might be why my father locked her away. Tried to hide her. Kyra said that many of the *kareshta* end up in mental institutions because people think they're crazy."

"That makes sense." He'd come to the same conclusion, but he knew she needed to work it out in her own mind.

"Yeah, it makes sense."

He felt her shoulders shaking before he heard her cry. "Shhh, Ava." He stroked her back, pulling her so tight to his chest that he was worried she would bruise. Her pain was a stab in the heart.

"They're out there," she said. "Others like me. Those are the stars in Jaron's vision. Out in the darkness, Malachi. So many of them. And so horribly alone."

"I know, Ava."

"We have to find them."

Could finding the *kareshta* be a way out of this never-ending war? Could Grigori society turn into something like the Irin? Kostas had said that those Grigori who had contact with their sisters were more stable. Had more control. If they could find more of the female Grigori —teach them to protect their minds—would it change their enemies as Kostas hoped?

What was the alternative? Endless, blood-soaked war? Generation after generation caught in the same vicious cycle? His own son continuing the slaughter of a people Malachi was starting to believe were more like his own than he wanted to admit?

The Irin Council's policy had remained unchanged for thousands of years. Scribes protected the human population from the Grigori, killing them any time they attacked. But with a few exceptions, the Fallen themselves were never targeted. Why? Malachi had always assumed they were simply too hard to kill. But could there be another motive for tacitly allowing them to exist?

What power would the council have without an enemy to fight?

"We need to go back to Italy," Ava said. "We have to find my grandmother. I refuse to let Jasper stonewall me. If she's like me, she's been living with voices her whole life, Malachi. There must be something I can do."

Ava's conscience would never allow her to let another live in the torment she'd faced for over twenty years.

"We'll go to Italy," Malachi said. "We'll find a flight to Genoa in the morning. I think it's only six hours or so with connections. We can be there by tomorrow night."

It was a good thing Max's forger was good. Their fake passports were getting more than a little mileage.

"Do you think my grandmother is in Italy?"

"Honestly? No. Italian hospitals are the first Rhys checked because your father tends to take his holidays there. None of them match the information we have. But we are going to Italy, and we are going to find her."

"How—?"

"We tried getting information from Jasper and got nothing." Malachi smiled in the darkness. "I think it's time to talk to the man who holds his keys."

TEN

They took a flight to Genoa the next morning and were driving by late afternoon. Ava had a hard time sleeping. Part of her wanted to find her grandmother, but another part wanted to be back in Bulgaria. Only Kyra's urging had allowed her to leave.

"Go. Find your grandmother. You know who and what she is now. You can help her."

Ava had wanted to start lessons immediately. She'd wanted to find the old monastery Kyra had spoken of where thirty Grigori women hid from the world and the madness that lurked on the edges of their lives.

Kostas and Malachi had refused. Kostas, out of distrust; Malachi, out of concern.

It was too soon, her mate said. They needed to think. Needed to plan. How could they risk putting Irin knowledge into Grigori hands? Ava knew Max and Renata agreed, even though they clearly trusted Kostas and Kyra more than Malachi did.

Her brain knew he was right, but her heart had other ideas.

For Ava, meeting Kyra had been like looking in a mirror. It wasn't her looks, because the woman's angelic beauty was nothing like her own. In fact, Ava was almost resentful she'd gotten all the mental anguish of Grigori blood without the excellent skin tone.

Oh well.

It was her eyes. Kyra said all the female Grigori had gold eyes like their angelic fathers, but it was more than that. The pain was the same. The constant stress of hearing. The ache of being *other*. Kyra, like Ava, had lived most of her life alone, though she'd been lucky enough to have a brother. She spoke of Kostas with a fierce and protective admiration, as if daring anyone to think badly of him.

Ava didn't think badly of the renegade Grigori. She didn't know what to think.

It was hard not to be wary.

While Kostas's men didn't exude the voracious hunger of the Grigori that had stalked her and killed Malachi, they were still clearly the sons of the Fallen. The seductive features were there. The scent of sandalwood that lured her. Their hunger was in their eyes, even though it wasn't layered with blind rage.

But they were also different from their brethren. Did they exude tension? Yes. But it was controlled.

"Ava?"

"Hmm?" She glanced at Malachi as he drove them toward Portofino.

"Why don't you try to sleep?"

"I'm too wound up."

"Try, *canim*. We don't know what this day will be like."

"More warrior lessons?"

He smiled, fine wrinkles appearing around his eyes. "Yes, like they taught us in school. Eat when you can. Sleep when you can. Fu—"

"I get it." She reached over and slapped a hand over his mouth. "Bad man. They didn't teach you that in school."

"The professors might not have, but the older boys did," he said as he peeled her hand away and kissed her palm. The smile fell from his face.

"What is it?"

"The Grigori have all this power—all this natural magic—and they have no control over it. I think it would be better to be human."

"Do you have to make it sound like that's the worst thing in the world? Being human? I was one, you know."

He gave her a raised eyebrow. Oh, those eloquent raised eyebrows her man offered.

"You know what I mean," he said. "If they were human, they'd have no magic, but at least they'd live a normal life."

She squeezed his hand.

"No mates," he continued. "No children, except those they sire by accident, and what kind of relationship would they be able to have with them? They've had thousands of years to be hungry with no relief. I'd never thought about that before. I cannot imagine the rage they must feel. To have so much power and no control. To live only to be a slave for the Fallen."

"They're no innocents, Malachi. They hunted me. They killed you. They've killed thousands of humans. They seduce them, rape them, and—more often than not—kill them."

"I know."

"And you feel sorry for them?"

"No." He paused. "Yes. Some. I feel sorry for some of them. Those who are trying to live peacefully but are caught on the other side of a battle they don't want. I feel sorry for the children."

"Do you think we can make the council see that?"

"I don't know."

They both fell silent.

When Malachi spoke again, his voice was low. "How will we make them see when I have trouble accepting it myself? Grigori killed my parents. Slaughtered our women and children. I cannot forgive that."

"Bitterness only hurts you," she said, echoing a lesson her mother taught her after she'd learned the truth about her father. "You can forgive without forgetting."

He reached over and played with a curl of her hair. "My wise woman. What would I do without you?"

"Have a peaceful, normal life?"

Malachi grinned. "Now why would I want that?"

• • •   • • •

SHE CAUGHT HIM STRAPPING TWO KNIVES TO HIS TORSO A FEW HOURS later. "What do you need those for?"

They'd settled into their hotel in Portofino and searched online to find directions to Luis Martin's house.

She knew going after Luis was a good idea. Her father's manager knew everything about Jasper's life and didn't trip her emotional wires. Rhys had found he was staying at a villa outside the harbor town a few towns over from Jasper. Malachi was confident. Ava was… unsure, but had agreed to follow Malachi's lead.

According to Rhys's research, Luis Martin used his credit card almost every night at a small tavern in the town. The card was swiped around eleven o'clock every time it was used. It matched what Ava knew about Luis's habits. He was a very predictable man.

"Malachi?"

"Hmm?"

"The knives? Why are you taking knives?"

Malachi ignored her. He finished settling the straps around his shoulders before he came to kiss her forehead.

"*Reshon*, how many times have you asked Luis for his help getting information?"

"Between the phone calls and e-mails? A lot."

"And has he given it to you?"

"You know he hasn't, but I don't want you to hurt him."

He chucked her under the chin. "Don't be silly. I won't need to hurt him."

"So why—"

"I just need to scare him a little." He reached into his suitcase and took out another knife, flipping it in his fingers before he tucked it in his waistband.

She walked to him, putting a hand on his forearm. "Babe, I really don't think—"

He stopped her mouth with a hard kiss. "Enough. He has information you need. Information you have a right to. You can reveal your power by using the spell Orsala taught you—"

She stepped back. Ava hadn't realized Malachi knew about the spell.

"Yes, I know about the spell. You can use that, but it risks Martin knowing you're not a normal human. That leaves me with the option of playing the brute."

"You're not a brute!"

He gave her a wicked grin. "I can be when I want." He put a finger to her lips when she went to object again. "Enough. We're doing this my way. We're getting the information. And I promise you, all Luis Martin will have is some soiled sheets and a bit of embarrassment. Happy?"

She probably should have objected harder to terrorizing Luis….

But it wasn't as if the man couldn't be a huge asshole when it suited him. He was Jasper's manager. Ava figured he probably had it coming.

* * *

AVA WATCHED MALACHI—DRESSED COMPLETELY IN BLACK—AS HE stood at Luis's door. It was a villa he'd rented for the month, but it appeared to have top-notch security. Ava recognized the logo on the keypad Malachi was fiddling with. Her stepfather used the same company for his homes.

"Babe, you realize this system—"

"Mmhmm."

"So I know you cut the landline, but—"

Malachi muttered something in Turkish, and Ava frowned. Leaning forward, she noticed the small wireless earbud he must have slipped in during their walk to the villa.

He was talking to someone on the other end. Probably Rhys.

"Yes. Tell me when," he said in a low voice. A few more seconds, then Malachi pushed a seven-digit code into the keypad, and Ava heard a small whooshing sound that sounded like a seal being released. He turned the knob and the door opened quietly.

"Dogs?" he asked her.

"He's allergic."

He walked into the house, holding her hand but moving ahead of her as he scanned each room.

"How did you get past the retina scan?" she asked.

"Rhys was able to override with an emergency password. We have five minutes before they call to confirm his safety."

"How did Rhys get his password?"

"Because Luis Martin had a folder on his home server labeled Passwords."

Okay, he was just asking to get robbed. Ava felt slightly less guilty.

They started up the stairs. Ava could hear someone snoring loudly.

"I feel like it should bother me more that you're so good at breaking and entering."

"Why?" Apparently, Malachi was no longer concerned with security. His voice was louder. He pulled out the earbud and tucked it in a small pocket of the vest he was wearing. "I've been doing this kind of thing for three hundred years. Trust me, it's a lot less messy than it used to be. I don't break and enter for personal gain. It's just a useful life skill."

"Useful life skills are starting a campfire, or… knowing how to tie really good knots."

"I know how to do those things too." He tugged her close and leaned down to her ear. "Give me one weekend without a world-changing revelation," he whispered, "and I'll show you my knot-tying skills."

The color rushed to her face. "Bad man. Very bad man."

He chuckled. "You wouldn't be saying that by the end of the weekend."

The snoring stopped and they both froze. There was a rustling sound before it started up again.

"Come on," Malachi said. "Let's get this over with."

The first doorway in the hall at the top of the stairs was cracked open. A shoe was lying right in front of it. Malachi pushed the door open while Ava kept her eyes closed, hoping Luis wasn't a nude sleeper.

"He's fine," he said, tugging her into the room. "And alone."

The hard-nosed negotiator looked far less like her father's pet pit bull and more like a normal guy when he was sleeping. His mouth hung open slightly. His hair was mussed from tossing and turning.

Ava sighed. "Okay. Time to scare the shit out of him. He's never going to return my calls again."

"Oh yes, he will." Malachi put one knee on the edge of the bed and leaned over Luis. Pulling out a long hunting knife, he put it under the edge of Luis's jaw.

"Luis Martin," Malachi said in a loud voice. "Wake up."

The snoring stopped, then the man's eyes slowly blinked open.

"The hell?" he muttered. His eyes widened when he saw Malachi, and he jerked up in bed, only to catch the edge of the blade and cry out in pain. A line of blood welled up from his skin and dripped down his neck.

Just then, the phone rang.

Oh shit.

Malachi was totally calm. "Do you recognize me?"

Luis's eyes darted between Ava and Malachi. "Ava, what—?"

"Eyes on me." The phone was still ringing. "You're going to answer the phone and tell them you're just fine. Otherwise, I'm going to hurt you."

"No fucking—"

"Yes, you will." Malachi reached up and wrote something across Luis's forehead with a finger. "Luis?"

"Yeah?" The man sounded dazed.

"Answer the phone."

"Okay."

Ava watched as her father's fierce manager followed Malachi's order like a well-trained dog.

"Yeah…" He was muttering into the phone. "Just tired. I don't know." Another pause. "Nah, I'm fine. Maybe kind of… drunk."

A few moments later, the phone was in the cradle and Luis's eyes were clearing.

"What was that? What did you do to me?"

"As you can feel, you should not attempt to move. Do you know who I am?"

Luis tried to nod but winced when the blade bit into his skin again.

"Answer verbally."

"Yes, I know you."

"Good. That will make this easier."

Ava was watching Malachi. He was very careful not to move the knife. As long as Luis didn't move, the edge wouldn't touch his skin. But the wily little man had always had a hard time sitting still for anything.

She started to warn him how jittery Luis could get. "Malachi—"

"Ava has questions for you," her mate said. "You're going to answer them. If you don't, I'm going to hurt you."

Ava could smell the scent of urine in the room.

"I see that you believe me," Malachi said. "That's good. I'm going to sit here while Ava asks her questions. Are you going to answer her?"

"Yes," Luis whispered, his terrified eyes flying to hers.

"Louder. So she can hear you."

"Yes."

"Are you going to take her calls from now on?"

"Holy fuck," Luis whispered.

The knife moved. "Answer the question, Luis."

"Yes. I won't avoid her calls." His voice was higher than Ava had ever heard.

"One missed call is fine. Two is not acceptable. Do you understand?"

"Yes."

"Are you going to block her access to her father?"

"Who are you?"

Malachi didn't move the knife—he moved. He leaned down closer. "You don't need to think about me," he said. "Are you going to interfere with Ava?"

"No."

"Good." He finally looked up and met her wide-eyed stare. "Ask now."

Ava stepped closer. "Luis, I'm so—"

She stopped when she heard a low growl. Malachi was glaring at her and shaking his head slowly.

Okay, no apologies.

She took a deep breath. "Is my grandmother alive?"

"Y…yes."

"Did you help my father erase her records?"

"No." He sucked in a breath when Malachi brought the knife higher. "I put him in contact with someone who did. But I didn't do it myself."

Ava took a deep breath and tried not to panic. Malachi was totally calm, but Ava was battling a nervous breakdown. It was one thing to fight through an army of Grigori soldiers who were trying to kill you. It was entirely different threatening the life of someone you'd had over for holiday dinners.

"Ava?"

"Okay, okay. Um… Luis, why did my dad hide her? My grandmother, I mean."

"I don't know." The knife moved a little bit up and Luis attempted to raise his hands. "I'm serious. I didn't ask. Jasper was always secretive about her. There's something wrong with her."

Malachi grunted and Luis backtracked, clearly free from the earlier compliant fog Malachi had put him under. "I mean, she's mentally ill! Or… something. I don't know. I think she's been violent in the past because I had to find a place that had housing for high-risk patients."

"Where?" Malachi asked.

Luis swallowed and looked at Ava, his eyes begging. "Ava."

"I need to know, Luis."

"He wanted to protect you. He didn't want you to think… I know there's some stuff about you he hides. Even from me. From everyone."

Malachi pressed the knife closer and the man whimpered. "I want a location. Where is she being kept?"

"It's in France. There's a hospital outside Albi. Catholic. Saint… Saint Cecelia's."

Malachi leaned down to the man, whispered in his ear, then stood. "Do you understand?"

"Yes." Luis's face was pale, the line of red blood dripping into the silk sheets that were rumpled around him. "Ava, I'm sorry."

How exactly did you say good-bye to the man whose life you just threatened, knowing you'd probably see him again?

"Um… It's fine, Luis. Take care of my dad."

"Jasper loves you, you know?"

"No, I don't know. I never did. Not from him." She walked over and took Malachi's hand. "Good-bye. And… sorry about the sheets."

CHAPTER

ELEVEN

Volund paced the room where Malachi dreamed.

Angry, Malachi thought. The angel was very angry. Frustrated.

The Fallen muttered words in the Old Language that Malachi couldn't catch. Bit out curses under his breath.

He didn't know what had happened to make the angel so enraged, but he couldn't help feeling satisfied.

Just as the feeling threatened to bring a smile to his face, Volund spun and forced Malachi's eyes to his.

Volund roared, and the rage rolled over him, searing his skin, stealing his breath.

"You cannot," Malachi choked out, "hurt me."

He gasped for breath. His mind knew this was illusion, though the dream state felt real. Ava was still nowhere in sight. He stood naked and stripped of every shield while the angel continued to rage.

Ash and cinders whirled around the ritual room, burning and scraping his skin until he could smell his own blood in the wind.

"You cannot hurt me," he said again.

Malachi opened his eyes and Volund was there, gold eyes wide with madness.

"She is mine!" the angel screamed.

In the next breath, Volund plunged the black dagger into his heart, and Malachi woke, gasping for breath, a hand pressed to his chest.

• • •   • • •

HE DIDN'T SPEAK OF HIS NIGHTMARE. SHE HAD TOO MUCH ON HER mind. Too many worries creased her forehead. He longed for a time when it could just be the two of them again.

Malachi wanted answers, but he also wondered whether Martin had sent them on another leg of an endless wild-goose chase. A mental hospital in France? Even if they found Ava's grandmother, what would they discover? Kostas hadn't painted a pleasant picture of female Grigori in the human world.

But Jasper Reed's money had provided an escape for his daughter. Perhaps it had sheltered his mother in a similar manner.

In the end, it was easier to drive to Saint Cecelia's than fly. They stayed one more night in Portofino before heading to France in the same rented car they'd picked up in Genoa. Nine hours of driving to reach an uncertain reception. Nine hours farther away from Vienna.

The converted chateau fifteen minutes out of Albi in the Tarn region of France could have been a luxurious country home or even an exclusive hotel. Rhys's search confirmed that it was neither of the two, but rather a very exclusive, very secure mental health facility run privately with a live-in staff and only fifteen to twenty permanent residents.

As far as caring for the mentally or emotionally troubled, it didn't get more comfortable than Saint Cecilia's.

Malachi turned into the drive, approaching the house through an allée of stately trimmed linden trees, their branches winter bare. They'd stayed the night in Albi before coming to the hospital that morning. Malachi called Max after they left Italy and told him their plans. They would leave the rented car in Marseilles and from there catch a flight to Vienna.

He was edgy. Mala had already taken Orsala to the city. Rhys and Leo had closed up the scribe house in Istanbul and joined them. Renata and Max were flying to Prague to check on an Irina safe house there before they joined Damien and Sari. All the former scribes of Istanbul were crisscrossing the continent with one destination in mind.

Vienna.

Kostas might have wanted his existence to remain a secret, but the Irin Council needed to know of the existence of Grigori females. The whole Irin world—especially the Irina—needed to know.

Because along with the inevitable dread of facing the council, Malachi also carried a mad hope.

The Irin race was dying.

Yet Ava had Grigori blood, and they had mated. More than that, he and Ava were *reshon*. Bound. Destined for each other by the Creator. And if he and Ava had a future together, anything was possible.

The Grigori had decimated the Irina, while the Fallen had thrown their own daughters to the chaos and darkness of the human world. If those women, the silent ones, could be found, it was possible they could be saved. Grigori and Irin alike. The very women the Fallen had shunned could be the salvation of the Irin race.

But what condition would they be in? Kyra had been fiercely protected by a devoted brother. Ava had never known she was anything but human. Malachi hoped that finding Ava's grandmother would give them a larger picture, especially regarding why she'd been targeted by two fallen archangels.

"You ready?" he asked her.

"Yes."

Luis Martin had called ahead and given the hospital permission to allow Ava and Malachi to visit. He'd also warned them that, from all reports, Ava Rezai was uncommunicative.

"Rezai," Ava mused as they parked in the gravel-lined oval in front of the house. "Persian?"

"I believe so."

"Jasper's Persian?"

Malachi shrugged. "His coloring is ambiguous. And we don't know. He could have taken after his father."

"Who is a complete mystery." She took a deep breath and unbuckled her seatbelt. "Shall we go visit Grandma?"

He took her hand, seeing through the bravado immediately. "You realize she might not speak. We might get nothing from her. And if we don't, we will continue on."

"We'll confirm she's *kareshta*, though. We'll be able to tell, don't you think?"

"I do." Her hand was so small in his. Such energy, such life in so small a person. "I love you. I'm very proud of you."

She squeezed his palm with her fingers. "Say that after I've made it out of here without embarrassing myself with tears."

And without another word, she opened the door.

Cold wind whipped around them as they walked up the path. Gravel crunched under their feet and Malachi could smell snow in the air. Before they reached the large wooden doors, one swung open and a woman dressed in a sage-green uniform waved them in.

"Ms. Matheson, yes?"

"Thank you," Ava said, stepping through the doorway and brushing her hair back where it had tangled around her face. "Yes, I'm here to see Ava Rezai."

"Of course. We were expecting you. This is good! Ms. Rezai doesn't receive many visitors."

Malachi followed them, touching Ava's arm as the woman—who looked like a nurse of some kind—led them farther into the entryway. There was a fire burning in a massive stone hearth, and two women sat near it, one in a soft white robe, the other in another of the green uniforms. Both were knitting and speaking softly. Past the large living area, a sunroom looked out over a clear blue pool and manicured grounds. Two men were sitting at a small table playing chess, one a patient, another an orderly or nurse of some kind.

Ava's eyes swept the room, searching for a sign of her grandmother.

"Ms. Matheson?"

"Please, call me Ava."

The nurse motioned down a wood-paneled hallway. "Ms. Rezai is not in the common area. Can I show you to the doctor's office? He wanted to speak to you before you see her."

Ava nodded. "Of course." She held out her hand and Malachi took it. Her skin was ice-cold.

They walked down the hall following the nurse, but Malachi didn't let his guard drop. There was something foreign in this place. Some energy teased his senses. Perhaps it was the echo of Ava's grandmother, but he didn't think so.

The nurse left them alone in a large office.

"It's nice," Ava said. "The house, I mean. It's beautiful here."

"It is."

"I guess if he was going to lock her up, it's good he put her some-place nice."

Malachi tucked a curl of hair behind her ear as they took seats in front of a large oak desk. "Don't think of it that way. It's possible she's been too damaged by the world. This place is quiet. Do you hear much?"

"No." She shook her head. "I listened when we first walked in, and I was worried the people here would be so sick their voices would freak me out, but it's not bad. Pretty quiet, really."

"See? This might be a restful place for her. Think of it as another kind of haven like Sarihöfn."

"Do you think—" She turned when the door opened and froze.

Malachi followed her eyes.

The unobtrusive form of Dr. Sadik stood in the doorway.

"Hello, Ava."

Malachi was on his feet in an instant, only to be pinned to the wall by the power of the Fallen.

Ava said, "Put him down, Jaron."

"Tell your mate not to try to attack me. It is annoying."

"You could have given us a bit of a warning. What did you do to the human doctor?"

"He is resting in another office," Jaron said, still wearing the appearance of the psychologist Ava had been seeing in Istanbul. He waved a hand toward Malachi.

He slumped down the wall at once, the pressure at his throat gone in an instant.

Jaron sat behind the human doctor's desk and spread his hands. "So you know."

Ava sat in the chair in front of the desk, glaring at the Fallen who'd been shadowing her for months.

"Yeah, I know. So that was the big secret? That the Fallen have daughters?"

"Trust me, it is a secret we have endeavored to hide for thousands of years."

Malachi stood behind Ava. He had no interest in sitting with the angel.

"Why?" Ava asked.

"They're uncontrollable. Unbalanced. Most do not have the physical strength of their brothers, so they're not useful. They've always been a problem for us, and they're considered a weakness."

Malachi was disgusted, yet hardly surprised.

"You act completely disinterested, but if that's the case, why are you here?" Malachi asked. "What's so special about Ava Rezai?"

For once, he sensed a reaction in the inhuman eyes of the Fallen before him. Jaron might have morphed his form into the shape of the harmless, middle-aged academic before them, but his eyes were the same. Frozen gold that shone with neither fear nor joy. But for an instant, there was a hint of something else. Had he imagined it?

Jaron ignored him and turned to Ava. "Why are *you* here?"

Her mouth dropped. "Because she's my grandmother."

"You already know the magic in your blood comes from your father through her. And you probably guessed she has Grigori blood. What more do you hope to learn?"

"I… I don't know. I just want to meet her."

Jaron slid forward, put his chin in the palm of his hand as he rested an elbow on the edge of the desk. "She might not speak. Would you leave here even more confused than you came? Will this ease your mind or torment it?"

"I don't know," his mate whispered, "but at least I'll know the truth."

"The truth…?" Jaron stood. "An interesting concept. You seek the truth, but will her truth be one you can accept?"

"I want to try."

"And you?"

Malachi looked up, realizing Jaron was talking to him. "What about me?"

"Why do you want to meet her? What do you hope to gain?"

"This is not about me, Jaron. It's about Ava."

"Yes." Jaron's eyes bored into his, and Malachi felt his body sway under the power of the angel's stare. "I have spent much of the past sixty years concerning myself with Ava."

He drifted off for a moment, his eyes lifting to the high windows that covered one wall in the doctor's office.

"Come," he finally said. "Let us meet her."

• • •　• • •

WHEN THEY STEPPED OUT OF THE OFFICE, MALACHI NOTICED THE quiet immediately.

There was no one in the house.

No chattering nurses near the large oak reception desk. No men playing chess. The fire crackled, but no one took up the knitting needles lying forlornly on the sofa.

"Where is everyone?"

"They're here and they're not."

Ava stepped forward and looked across the now-empty room. "Is this a dream?"

"In a sense," Jaron said. "More accurately, *they* are in a dream. A simple twist of time. When I call them back, they will have no memory that they didn't spend this time in the living area, going about their tasks."

Malachi felt his skin prickle. "You can just… make everyone disappear?"

"Not humans with angelic blood. But pure humans?" Jaron shrugged. "It's not without effort on my part, but I hardly consider either one of you a threat."

Malachi had never heard of such a thing. Never even conceived of it. Why was Jaron revealing this power now? He eyed the man with suspicion but followed him down one hallway and up a wide set of stairs. As Jaron walked, he grew, morphing into the form he'd taken the previous times he'd revealed himself to Ava. Close to seven feet tall, dark hair falling around a clearly inhuman face. He was an ancient god. An artist's mad dream.

And Malachi sensed he was still seeing only a fraction of the angel's presence.

It was on the third floor of the massive house that he stopped and turned to Ava. A long corridor stretched before them, empty like the rest of the house.

"Is your mind shielded?" he asked Ava.

"Yes."

Jaron cocked his head, clearly curious. "How?"

"It's like… a door. I can keep it shut or open it."

"Interesting. I always wondered. That door?" he said. "Keep it locked."

Malachi became aware of a growing power. It called him. He could hear the seductive voice in his mind. Twisted whispers of longing. Need.

Anger.

Whatever called to him was hungry.

Malachi heard a high girlish hum drift down the corridor. It was beautiful. He needed to find the voice. Hold it. Touch—

"Enough!" Jaron lost any human facade when he shouted, startling Malachi out of the trance. "Silence, Ava!"

Without another word, the angel strode down the hall. He raised a hand and a paneled door swung open. Malachi followed cautiously, holding Ava behind him.

"Do you feel it?" she whispered.

He nodded but didn't speak. He felt it. Like coals glowing under long-dead ashes, the voice waited. He hesitated at the threshold but felt Ava's hand at his back, urging him through.

When Malachi turned the corner, he saw something his years of training could never have prepared him for.

Blinding color filled the institutional room. It was as if he walked in an impressionist painting. Swirling seas and mountain crests. An achingly brilliant sunset covered one entire wall. On the opposite side, a blood-red eclipse hung, surrounded by black night and whorls of stars. Flowers filled one corner. Bones filled another. Twisted roots and looming trees. Layer after layer, the paintings filled the space, even crawling up the ceiling.

And in the corner, a woman sat, huddled on Jaron's lap.

Beautiful was too soft a word.

Her eyes were closed, and her cheek was pressed to Jaron's chest. When her breath stirred, the raised glyphs on the angel's skin glowed with a bronze light. Her hair was streaked with red and gold, her skin a dusky echo of the angel who held her. And on Jaron's face, an expression of such familiar tenderness that Malachi knew immediately why Jaron had been shadowing his mate her entire life.

"Come in," Jaron said in a voice touched with despair. "Come, Ava, and meet my daughter."

CHAPTER
TWELVE

"Daughter," Ava whispered, knowing immediately it was true. It had been there all along. Jaron's strange protectiveness. Watching her. Guarding her in his own way. And Ava's magic, far too powerful for someone completely untrained.

Of course she was strong. Her great-grandfather was an archangel.

She stepped closer, reaching for Malachi's hand to anchor her in the beautiful, frightening room. "She's my grandmother. But... she's too—"

"She stopped aging soon after she bore your father," Jaron said, stroking the hair of the woman on his lap. "Like our sons, our daughters do not age as humans do."

Ava stepped past Malachi, no fear in her heart. The frightening intensity that had bombarded her in the hall had leveled off the moment Jaron entered the room. "She's so beautiful."

"Once, she was the most beautiful creature to walk the earth. Her beauty rivaled the children of heaven."

A wave of longing washed over her. She wanted to touch. Wanted to hug. She was drawn to this strange woman her father had named her after, but she was also afraid. And Jaron showed no sign of letting his child go.

"Ava?" she whispered, crouching down across from her.

There was no furniture in the room except a bed bolted to one wall and a small table attached to the opposite wall. No mirrors. No windows. Plastic pots of vivid paint were lined on the table in precise color order.

Ava looked up and wondered how she had reached the tops of the walls and ceiling.

"I have no idea," Jaron said, guessing her question. "I've wondered that myself."

Ava looked back to him, surprised by the gentle amusement in his voice. "Does she know I'm here?"

Jaron pressed a palm over his daughter's temple. "She's aware, but she's resting right now. The only real peace she has is when I am able to visit her. Otherwise, she's quite mad."

"Why?" Malachi asked. "Is it because she has your blood? The woman we met in Sofia—Kostas's sister—wasn't like this."

"Why do you care, Scribe? She's the daughter of your enemy."

Malachi ignored the taunt and knelt down next to Ava, his eyes on the trembling woman in Jaron's arms.

"I have seen trauma like this before, Jaron, usually on the faces of Grigori victims. Who hurt this woman?"

Ava reached for his hand, strangely comforted by the anger in her mate's voice. The thought of someone hurting a stranger might not have roused another man's protective instincts, but Malachi wasn't other men. Even the daughter of a Fallen angel was someone to be protected.

He brushed a kiss over her temple and waited for Jaron to answer.

Jaron said, "Yes, she has been hurt. In ways you cannot imagine."

Her grandmother—it was hard to think of her as a grandmother when she looked the same age as Ava—twisted in her father's arms. Her mouth opened in a wordless groan.

"Who hurt her?" Malachi asked.

Jaron raised his eyes to meet hers, and Ava saw the truth in the rage and betrayal in his gaze.

"It was one of the Fallen," she said. "One of the others. Who else would be able to hurt your daughter?"

The angel nodded and let out a heavy breath, more human in that moment than Ava had ever seen him. "Unlike my brothers, I doted on my daughter with no thought of hiding it. I'd only ever had sons, then after she was born... I indulged her. She was quite spoiled."

Her grandmother's features twisted in pain before Jaron put a hand on her forehead and she settled again.

"Her mother was a lover I held in some regard. Atefah was descended from royalty. Beautiful. Spirited. A worthy lover for me. She survived the birth, mostly because I forced her to let my older sons care for their new sister. No princess was ever more pampered. Unfortunately, Ava's mother did not survive a second child. She died giving birth to a son."

"Did you love her?" Ava asked.

"Love?" Jaron frowned. "No. The Fallen are not capable of love. Atefah loved *me*. Quite desperately. I should have sent her away, but Ava was attached to her mother. So she stayed and died, along with the child. She was the last human lover I took and the only one who gave me a daughter."

"And that's why you care about Ava," Malachi said. "You may not call it love, Fallen, but I can see your regard."

"As others did," Jaron said grimly. "It was my own failing. Ava was the first being in thousands of years I held some… affection for. She amused me. If I have a personality in this realm, she reflected it. Perhaps that is why I care for her still." He looked up with sardonic eyes. "Everything is vanity, after all."

Vanity, maybe, but Jaron appeared to be fiercely protective. What idiot would have risked his wrath to hurt her?

"Volund," Jaron said, reading her frown.

Ava's eyes grew wide. "Volund?"

Jaron's daughter jerked in his arms.

Malachi picked up the connection immediately. "This is because of your damned rivalry? That was why he targeted *my* Ava. Why he killed me."

"It's about power." The gold fire in Jaron's eyes was a banked rage. "Everything is about power in our world. Volund was expanding his territory. He had eliminated his competition in Northern Europe. My allies. He had ambitions to hurt me, though I was a far more difficult target. He hurt my daughter to make a point. She was nothing more to him than a political maneuver."

"I don't believe you." Malachi's voice was low. "This was more than political."

"Perhaps it is more correct to say it *began* as a political move."

Jaron's hand tightened on his daughter's back. "But he became…
curious."

A knot formed at the pit of Ava's stomach.

Malachi asked, "About?"

"It was the Irin who gave him the idea."

"What idea?"

Jaron shook his head. "Volund—"

"Nooooo!" A shriek from the formerly silent woman startled them all.
Even Jaron.

She shouted and scrambled away from her father, huddling in a
corner, her eyes sweeping the room. She was frantic. Ava wasn't sure
her grandmother saw anything more than the demons in her mind.

"Stop!" she shrieked. "Stop it. Don't speak his name." The words
poured out of her, a river of tormented pleas. "Please, *Bâbâ*, no!"

"Ava—"

"Bâbâ, Bâbâ, no." A torrent of what sounded like Farsi poured from
her lips. Ava wasn't fluent enough to decipher it. But the strange energy
pouring from her grandmother was familiar. Ava knew she could reach
her if she could only catch her attention.

Ava crawled forward, ignoring Jaron's warning to crack open the
door in her mind.

"Grandmother?" she said. *"Ava."*

Their eyes connected.

Jaron's daughter held a trembling finger over blood-red lips. "Shhhh."

Ava listened, but the only thing she heard was a twisted cacophony
of pain.

Her grandmother stared at her, gold eyes transfixed on Ava's face.

"It's a secret," she whispered. "Like me. You can't tell a secret."

"You can tell me."

The tormented woman tore at the shining hair that fell over her
face and shook her head. "Demons play tricks," she muttered. "Don't.
Can't hide. Not even in my mind." A haunting singsong voice. "My
mind, my mind." A bitter laugh. "If I lose myself, not even he can find
me. Hide in the woods—don't dream! Don't sleep. He can't see the
visions I keep." A high, keening laugh. *"Bâbâ…"*

"I'm here, Ava." But Jaron stayed in place, as if touching his child
might hurt her. A low hum filled the air, and Ava's grandmother rocked
back and forth, hitting her head against the wall.

Ava moved closer.

Malachi said, "*Canım*, be careful."

"She's hurting herself."

The woman stopped rocking. Her eyes rose to Ava's.

She stared at her, and for a brief moment, Ava knew her grandmother was completely sane.

"Be careful," she said, her voice low and calm. "I cannot force him out. Do you understand?"

"I have your blood," Ava said. "Don't tell me. *Show* me."

Ava caught the dark flicker in her grandmother's eyes a moment before her vision went black. Her body froze and her muscles locked as her mind raced through the vision Ava sent her.

A lively street market in Beirut. A boy with seductive eyes.

Temptation.

"Just for the night. My father…"

Ropes. He had tied her. Why had he—?

Bâbâ!

Gone.

Where were her brothers? They were gone. Her father…

Why couldn't she feel her father? She could always feel her father.

"Let me see her."

A darker, deeper power hovered over her, blocking her from the light.

"Beautiful child…"

Such darkness.

Anger.

Pain.

"Mine."

NO!

It ripped through her. The tearing of innocence and hope and light and nothing—

Nothing would be light again.

He was in her.

In her body. Her mind.

The darkness trampled over the flowers of her soul and crushed them with his power and everything…

"Everything is dark."

"Ava."

No.

Violation was only the beginning.

"Ava."

Her dreams a torment. She ran but could not escape.

"Ava."

Hissing laughter bruised her mind.

The dark angel had marked her.

His laugher twisted as he called her mate.

He came again when she closed her eyes. Every night. Every day. Even when her body was taken back to her brothers, he was there. When the child was born, he was there.

His power lived in the child who bore the face of her nightmare.

Love and hate and light and darkness.

"You'll hurt him, Ava."

Take him away…

"Ava."

There was no escape.

• • • • • •

Ava rocked back, gasping. Hoarse cries broke from her throat. She could feel Malachi's arms around her, holding her steady as she trembled.

"Ava!"

The sound of her name only made her sob.

"Oh God!" She clung to Malachi. "It can't… she can't…"

Jaron pulled his daughter's shaking body into his arms. Her eyes were closed again, her mind shut down to anything but her sire's touch. And Ava knew from looking into her grandmother's mind that Jaron's presence was the only thing that gave her any kind of peace.

Because her dreams were nightmares she couldn't escape.

"Ava, what was that?" Malachi held her tightly, his arms almost crushing her ribs. "I couldn't see. You have to tell me."

"Mate," she whispered. A connection so deep and profound that had been utterly twisted by pure evil. "Volund didn't just attack her,

Malachi. He took her. He wanted to know… He raped her. And he *marked* her."

His hands froze. "No."

"He wanted to know if it was possible for an angel to mate with one of the *kareshta*. He was curious. So he marked her with his power and bound her to him." Ava choked. "He's in her dreams, Malachi."

"She dream-walks with the Fallen who raped her?" he whispered.

"She can't escape. He's there every time she closes her eyes."

There was dread in Malachi's voice when he asked, "Your father?"

"He's Volund's child. She tried, but she couldn't bear it. Jasper looks like Volund did when he took her."

The room had grown deathly quiet. Ava could only watch her grandmother, a woman locked in the torment of her own mind. She had sensed the darkness there as well. Volund's touch had marked her in more ways than one. There was violence and a burgeoning rage belied by the woman's still form. Jaron, she knew, could sense it. His eyes met hers as he held his child. He bent down to whisper something in her ear and Ava relaxed completely.

"She needs sleep," Jaron said. "She only truly rests when I am here."

"Why can't you help her?" Ava asked. "Heal her? Keep Volund from torturing her every time she closes her eyes!"

"I do not know how." He took a deep breath. "In thousands of years, no angel has violated his brothers' children the way that Volund did mine. She has even begged Death to come for her, but Azril will not. I do not know why."

"Why didn't Volund kill her?" Malachi said. "After he'd attacked her, why didn't he—"

"Whether he likes it or not, Ava *is* his mate. When Volund bound himself to my daughter, he didn't realize it would affect him too," Jaron said. "Perhaps it is her only power now, but she became his curse. He would kill her if he could do it without harming himself. But he cannot."

"You hate my father." Her instincts were screaming at her. "Because he's Volund's son."

"Yes."

"But you protect him."

"Yes."

"Why?"

"He's her son as well. She did not hate him. And... he has my blood."

"What is my father? Half Grigori. Half angel. How can he even exist?"

"How do any of our children exist?" Jaron asked. "They are the will of the Creator. Though if my master has a purpose for your father, I have not discovered it yet. Perhaps Jasper's only purpose was fathering you."

Ava tried to wrap her mind around it. "And Volund? Would he hurt my dad?"

"At first, Volund was interested in your father. I had to hide them both. He thought the child of an angel and a *kareshta* would be even greater than the Irin. But the child was far too unstable. He had power, but no control. More damning, Jasper has free will. I cannot control him, just like I cannot control you. Volund lost interest when he found out he could not control Ava's child."

"But he knows who I am."

"He learned when you came to Istanbul. He was watching me and found you. When you attacked his men in the cistern—"

"All I did was scream."

Jaron gave her a look that made Ava feel like an ignorant child.

"You unleashed power the Grigori had never experienced before," he said. "Our children live in fear of their sisters, because their voices hold power the Grigori don't understand. Volund's sons didn't know what you were. Your magic was dark like the children of the Fallen, but you were in the company of Irin scribes and they treated you as one of their own."

"So?"

"You attracted his attention, Ava. It was easy enough for him to discover the connection when he started to look. You have his blood, after all."

She shivered, and Malachi's hands soothed the goose bumps from her skin. "That's why he wants me."

"Yes."

"Why?"

"I honestly don't know. Nor do I care. He has become erratic." Jaron stroked Ava's temple. "Perhaps she torments him in his sleep as well. I can hope, but it does not matter. He cannot have you. Volund has taken enough of what is mine."

Malachi broke in. "Unbelievable. This is like two dogs fighting over a bone. Ava doesn't belong to either of you."

"Why?" Jaron asked. "Because she belongs to you?"

"She belongs to herself!"

"Enough." Ava stood and started pacing. "You can find me anywhere because I have your blood, can't you?"

"Yes."

"Can Volund? He's disgusting, but I am his granddaughter."

Jaron hesitated. "Unless I'm shielding you and you're shielding yourself, Volund can find you. The Irina magic you learned has helped immeasurably."

"That's why he couldn't find me in Norway."

Jaron nodded. "Your magic and mine, combined with the old singer's, made the haven the safest place for you."

"Until I left."

"The minute his Grigori spotted you, Sarihöfn became useless. I was the one who violated the wards there. You needed to leave."

She shook her head. "You've been playing me all along. And Malachi?"

Jaron waved a careless hand. "I owe your Irin mate no protection. He is not mine."

"Do you know how—"

"I have no idea how you were able to call him back. It was unexpected. But your blood holds the power of two archangels, and through your bond with this scribe, you were given the power of Mikhael's line as well." Jaron stared at her. "You *are* utterly unique, Ava. There are thousands of him, and only one of you. I do not care about him, but as long as his purpose helps mine, we are in accord."

Malachi said, "I would say the same of you, Fallen."

"Then we understand each other."

Ava rested against a flower-covered wall. "What *is* your purpose? What are you after?"

Jaron said nothing.

"I know," Malachi said, leaning against the bed, his arms crossed over his knees. "He wants to kill Volund."

"Yes," Jaron said.

"And he needs our help."

The angel's face was blank.

Ava asked, "Why should we help you?"

"Volund masterminded the Rending," Jaron said.

A vein pulsed in Malachi's forehead. "And you had nothing to do with it?"

Jaron smoothed the hair back from his daughter's face. "I didn't stop it, but I refused to use my sons to participate. I knew the Irin would kill many of our children, even in a surprise attack. Volund and his allies didn't agree. I suspect they had some deal with whatever Councilors had power at the time, though I hardly think the Irin knew the extent of his plans."

"You lie."

"Do I?" Jaron asked. "Are your elder scribes so incorruptible, son of Mikhael? Are they not hungry for power?"

"We are not Fallen," Malachi said.

Jaron only smiled.

"You didn't participate in the Rending," Ava said. "But you found me. You were looking for Fallen daughters in the human world. Why?"

"After the Rending, I began to see a way I could use the loss of the Irina to usurp Volund's power," Jaron said. "He had grown *very* powerful."

Malachi said, "It wasn't revenge for your daughter?"

"I didn't have a daughter then. I simply saw the females as an asset."

"How?"

"The Irin had lost most of their women. The Fallen had women it didn't want, some of whom still clung to their fathers out of loyalty. How better to gain power over our only adversaries in this world than by giving them the females they so desperately wanted? Females we could track. That we had influence over."

Ava's stomach turned. "You were going to use them like cattle. Pawns for your political games."

"Yes." Jaron's expression was unapologetic. "I was well on the way to putting my plan in place—ferreting out the Grigora who had filtered into the human world—when my daughter was born."

"Did you change your mind about using them?"

Jaron blinked. "No. I had no plans to use *my* daughter. She was to be protected."

Ava shook her head. Typical.

"What about me?" she asked. "Did you plan to use me when I came to see you in Istanbul?"

"You were unexpected. I had connections all over the world searching for women with Grigori traits, but I didn't expect my own granddaughter to be one of them."

"Why not?"

"Your human guardians had always seemed quite protective. The fact that they let you travel surprised me."

"I used Jasper's money. They really couldn't control me after I got that."

"Ah." A slight smile lifted the corner of the angel's mouth. "And we come full circle. Volund's son draws you into the game, no matter how much I try to avoid it."

"He's your grandson too."

Jaron's face grew cold. "He is an abomination. No one like him should exist. My daughter's torment will not be repeated."

"Of course not," Malachi said. "Because if you convince the Irin to take in the daughters of the Fallen, you know we'll protect them. We may not be perfect, but we value our women. And we won't let even the daughters of our enemies become victims."

Jaron cocked his head. "You're very predictable. It's useful."

"And to protect them, we'll even help you kill Volund."

"He did mastermind the slaughter of your innocents."

"Volund needs to die," Ava said, her eyes glued to the sleeping form in Jaron's arms. "He *has* to. Not only for killing you and masterminding the Rending. When Volund dies, your daughter might finally live."

III.

"What now?" Vasu wore the face of a petulant child. Thin and black-haired, he kicked at the post that stood innocently on the sidewalk.

Barak was walking along a curb, his arms held out for balance. That morning, he wore the face of a French schoolboy, waiting at the bus stop. "He's told them everything."

"What will they do?"

Barak shrugged his small shoulders. "They're flying to Vienna now."

Vasu scowled impatiently and a car traveling the road near them swerved on the icy road.

"Well, what can we make them do?"

"Nothing," Barak said. "They are not our children. They have free will."

"That was the Creator's mistake, giving the Forgiven's children free will. What was he thinking?"

Drifts of snow began to fall on the dirty sidewalk. Barak lifted his head to the sky and opened his mouth to catch one.

"Gifts given freely are more precious," Barak said, staring into the cloudy winter sky. "And our children are capable of love."

Vasu watched a girl walking along the sidewalk across the street.

She hurried, perhaps late for school. Her breath fogged in the morning air.

"What are we capable of?" Vasu said.

"Watching," Barak answered him as he stopped his movements to follow the girl with his eyes. "Waiting."

The car took the corner too fast. Barak heard the driver's panicked thoughts when he spotted the little girl in the bright green coat. She wasn't looking at the road. Hadn't noticed the ice. She was a child. She was thinking about her mathematics test.

The two boys watched impassively as the car spun in the road and jumped the sidewalk, crushing the little girl beneath its wheels in a sickeningly quiet thump. Shopkeepers rushed out of their buildings, crying and screaming. One wrenched the driver's door open. The human was pale and shaking.

"We watch and wait," Barak said.

Silently, Vasu crossed the street, stepping between the cars that had halted in the road. His hands were shoved in his pockets. Nobody noticed the solemn-faced boy in the grey coat as he crouched down next to the wheels of the car and reached out.

The little girl in the green coat smiled at him and took his hand. Standing next to Vasu, she watched the crowd with a small worried frown until the dark-haired boy tugged her hand. Then the two children walked up the sidewalk, Vasu holding her hand as old women cried over the dead child's body and sirens started to wail.

"And some of us still serve," Barak whispered as his eyes followed the archangel wearing the face of a child.

CHAPTER
THIRTEEN

Malachi closed his eyes and dreamed of Constantinople.

Cobbled walkways under his feet as he strode the paths his ancestors had followed. Sun-warmed stone and the smell of the river in his nose. The familiar streets were a comforting respite from the tumult of his waking hours.

Ava reached out and took his hand.

"Where are we?"

"When," he said, taking a deep breath and pulling her to his side. The heady scent of the spice market teased his senses. "*When* are we? These are my memories, *canım*. This is Constantinople when I was young."

Malachi heard the echo of horses clopping on the streets and vendors calling to bargain, but they were alone in the streets of the city he'd loved as a young man. The city where he'd met her.

"We're dreaming," Ava said, her face spreading into a smile. "We're in your dream instead of mine."

"I suppose so."

"I like it." She ran her fingers along the carvings of a wall as they passed, and Malachi could see the ancient words rise beneath her fingers like shadows reaching for long-dead eyes. "No, I love it. Your dreams are so much clearer than mine."

"I don't feel him here."

"Jaron? No." She turned and brushed a kiss on his cheek. "I like the privacy."

"So do I."

They walked for a while longer, enjoying the empty streets where the voices of long-dead residents clamored. He hadn't known dreams could be like this. It felt lighter. Brighter. Like a pleasant memory they could enjoy together.

"When this is finished," she said, "I want to come back here."

"To Constantinople?"

"Istanbul, remember? They changed the name a while ago, old man."

"So they did." He pinched her side and felt her squirm as she laughed, her body as real to his hands as if they were awake on the plane heading to Vienna.

"Why do you think we're in your dream and not mine?"

"Maybe because I'm remembering more."

"Are you?" She pulled him to a park bench along the Hippodrome, and Malachi heard the echo of wings as pigeons took flight. She pushed him down, then straddled his lap and faced him.

"What do you have in mind, *reshon?*"

Her words came shyly. "I want to sing to you again."

"Yes, please."

He waited, eyes closed in the sunlight as his mate put her hands on his cheeks and began a tentative song. It was an old poem he remembered his mother singing when she wanted to center herself. A focusing ritual before more complicated magic was sung.

"Relax," she whispered in English before she began the halting words.

Malachi resisted the impulse to correct her pronunciation as she sung the spell. He wouldn't interfere until something became dangerous.

Before, Ava had commanded him, a heady, forceful magic intoxicating to the senses. This time she coaxed. The words were lighter, more playful. A sunny, teasing spell that made him want to smile. Even the burn of the *talesm* on his shoulder and collarbone felt more like a tickle than a knife.

"Ava." He hummed her name when her lips tickled his ear. His hands smoothed over the curve of her hips, up her sides, and wrapped around her shoulders, drawing her body into his. Overhead, he heard the flap of bird wings again, but nothing in the sunny dream could distract him from the desire that coursed under his skin.

"Sir."

"Don't stop," he whispered into Ava's ear as her song died down.

"Sir, I'm afraid you have to stop."

That wasn't his mate's voice.

He came awake with a start, the disapproving flight attendant staring down at him and trying to block the view of the other passengers.

"Really, sir, if I wasn't sure you were sleeping…"

Malachi realized his hand was up Ava's shirt, her body splayed over his as they reclined in the airplane seats. Ava was still asleep, her hand heading in a southern direction as his headed north under her sweater. Though they had a blanket thrown over them, he realized they must have been giving the other passengers quite a show.

Slowly, he drew his hand away and nudged Ava over into her seat, ignoring her sleepy protests.

"I do apologize," he muttered.

The flight attendant took an impatient breath and opened her mouth—no doubt to offer some other warning—when her eyes widened in alarm. "Are you well?"

"I'm sorry?"

"Your chest. What happened?" She pointed down and Malachi caught the edge of blood welling up through the fabric of his collared shirt. "Do you need a doctor?"

"I'm fine." He reached for the scarf he'd shoved in Ava's purse. "I apologize. It is an old cut that must have opened as I moved. I'm quite all right."

"Malachi?" Ava blinked her eyes open. "Where are—" She saw the bleeding. "Oh, babe. I'm so sorry. Does it hurt?"

She sat up, and then Malachi had to deal with two females fussing over him.

"I'm fine," he protested. "It's nothing."

Luckily, the bleeding from his reformed *talesm* distracted the formerly annoyed attendant. She rushed away to retrieve some first aid supplies while Malachi tried to calm his body's natural reaction to the rush of magic and endorphins his mate had produced.

Ava must have caught the tent in his pants, because he saw her hiding a smile.

"You are in so much trouble when we land," he muttered.

"I'd apologize, but—"

"Don't." His command was hoarse. "Never apologize for that."

Her smile was wicked. "You may come to regret telling me that."

"Just as long as I come."

Her eyes widened. "Someone's in a mood."

Malachi growled and grabbed a handful of her hair, pulling her in for a brief kiss. "I want to disappear somewhere with you, not go to Vienna."

Her smile fell. "Me too."

"If we go back to sleep, do you think we can avoid the whole mess?"

"Probably not. And we might get in trouble with the flight attendant."

"Damn."

· · · ⚹ · · ·

THEY LANDED IN THE EARLY EVENING; THE SUN HAD ALREADY SET. Luckily, taxis weren't difficult to find. Rhys had e-mailed Ava an address near Judenplatz, within the Innere Stadt, the oldest part of the city. They would be within walking distance of the Library that served as the council chambers, but far enough away to afford privacy. They'd also be near St. Rupert's Church, one of the few places in Vienna Malachi felt didn't drip with ostentation.

"Has Damien told anyone about me yet?" she asked as they waited in the taxi queue. "Or about us?"

Malachi shook his head. "He's been trying to meet with different elders every day but isn't having much success. While Sari's presence in the city has caused some speculation, the Irina question is still being debated. The council is still treating the battle in Oslo as an isolated incident. And since so many of Volund's Grigori were killed, they consider it a victory."

Ava's mouth dropped open, but a car was pulling up. Malachi grabbed her hand and walked toward it.

He helped her into the taxi and loaded their luggage in back, happy that his mate packed with the economy of a seasoned traveler.

She'd already given the driver the address by the time he closed the door and settled into the cab.

"Volund wasn't even in Oslo," she whispered, well aware that most taxi drivers in the city would speak English.

"I know that," he said just as quietly. "But Brage was. And he was taken out. As Volund's oldest and most feared child, the council considers that a victory. Remember, they don't target the Fallen. In all my time as a soldier, I only remember hunting one angel. Grigori? Hundreds. But the Fallen are out of our reach. Of course, I don't remember everything, so don't take that as a complete picture."

"That's just…" She sputtered and shook her head.

Malachi could hardly argue with her. Underestimating the Grigori threat was ridiculous. And yet he was unsurprised that Damien hadn't found success. Watchers had been pleading for years to take a more aggressive stance against the Fallen, but it was a difficult argument in a city that hadn't seen a Grigori attack in centuries.

Now Jaron wanted Irin help to take out Volund. How he expected Malachi and Ava to convince the council of that was still a mystery.

Malachi was desperate for his memories. Without them, he was playing this game in the dark. He tried not to take his frustration out on Ava. It wasn't her fault he couldn't remember. And he still worried about pressuring her into the mating ritual. Though it would make him stronger, it could weaken her, and that was the last thing he wanted.

The fear of losing her was his biggest weakness.

Ava fell asleep on his shoulder just as they reached the Ringstraße. The days of scattershot travel around the continent had worn her out. He was tired as well, but he'd not be able to relax until he had his mate safe and was reassured that no harm would come to him while he rested. Their unpredictable travel had allowed them to remain anonymous for weeks. But now they were in Vienna. It was a spiderweb of politics, and a man only had to touch one wrong thread to attract dangerous attention from the wrong eyes.

◆ ◆ ◆　　◆ ◆ ◆

THE NEXT MORNING, THEY WERE LYING IN BED AND MALACHI WAS dozing in the grey dawn. The flat Rhys had let for them was small and tucked into a quiet corner of the neighborhood, away from the more lively restaurants and bars. He'd heard the crowds when he helped Ava to bed the night before, but the noise died down quickly. That morning, the only sounds that met his ears were the street sweepers and dog walkers below. The smell of coffee and bread drifted on the air, and his mate was curled safely into his side.

He was as content as he could be. Malachi had no idea whether Ava had traveled to Vienna before. She seemed to speak of more rural locations than urban, which would make sense with her previous inability to avoid the voices of the humans around her. As he lay there, smelling the bread and roasting beans from the *kaffeehaus* down the street, a few pleasant childhood memories intruded.

The first visit with his father to the Library where the elders met, the gallery above crowded as scribes clustered to observe the quiet work of their elders below. A tour of the archives that held the wealth of Irin history within its plain walls. Hearing his mother sing a story at the house of a friend, the walls echoing with laughter.

His mother had loved Vienna.

Perhaps they would have a few days to explore before Damien and Sari drew them into political maneuverings.

Probably not.

"Malachi?" Ava whispered.

"Hmmm?"

"Are you awake?"

"A little."

Ava's body didn't know what time it was. She'd woken after midnight, greedy for him. They'd made love with quiet intensity. She'd muffled her cries of pleasure in his shoulder, then fallen quickly back to sleep with his scent on her skin.

"I was thinking."

Malachi twisted a strand of hair around his finger. "Tell me, *canım.*"

"I can't stop thinking about my grandmother."

It was the first time she'd mentioned it since France. Malachi had tried not to bring it up. He'd come to learn she needed her silence. She'd speak to him when she was ready.

"What are you thinking about?"

She took a deep breath. "Seeing her was like a vision of all my worst fears made real."

Her power still frightened her. Ava had spent the majority of her life fearing her own mind, constantly questioning her perceptions. If she was ever to fully access her power, she would have to accept it, but accepting it meant not hiding from the darkness inherent in her nature.

Malachi had to remind himself how young she was. When he was her age, he was still in the middle of his training, the reality of battle years away. Ava had been picked up and thrown into a war that had been raging for centuries, and she'd lost the first battle when her mate had been killed. Both of them were still recovering.

"Your grandmother's mind was broken by violence," he said. "And by a continued violation she has no way of stopping." He put a palm to her temple. "You never have to fear that. The only one allowed in your dreams is me."

"Volund could get in."

"I don't think he could."

She rolled toward him. "If Jaron wasn't shielding me—"

"But he is." He kissed her forehead and whispered, "We will find a way to free her, Ava. Volund is powerful, but so is Jaron. There must be a way. And we'll find it."

She blinked away the shine in her eyes. "But his evil is still in me. And it'll never go away. I have his blood."

He knew a lifetime of fear couldn't be washed clean in a single year or with a single revelation. They were both works in progress.

"Do you remember our dream on the plane?"

"Of Istanbul?"

He nodded.

"Yes."

"That was your magic touching mine. Healing me. And there was nothing evil about that. That was beautiful."

"But—"

"I'm not saying you're all sweetness and light." He smiled when she narrowed her eyes. "I wouldn't want you to be. And you *are* Jaron's granddaughter."

He saw her shoulders tense, but he continued. "I do not fear it. Nor should you."

"Why not?"

"You hold power. And soon, you'll learn to claim it. Control it." The corner of his mouth turned up. "This city has not seen your like before."

A quiet knock came at the door.

Malachi brushed a hand along the *talesm* at his wrist and opened his senses. His ears recognized the familiar step. There was the scent of coffee and flour. And the irritated murmur when hot liquid spilled on skin.

"Get dressed. Rhys is here."

"Bossy." She rolled over and huddled under the covers. "I'm tired."

"That's because someone decided to be insatiable last night just when I was trying to get to sleep." He winked at her.

She threw a pillow at him and he laughed.

"Go back to sleep if you wish. We can go out for breakfast."

She peeked from under the covers. "You sure you don't mind? I just… don't feel like seeing anyone. Not yet."

"It's fine." He smiled. "We won't go far. Don't leave the apartment."

• • • ✦ • • •

RHYS MUTTERED THE ENTIRE WAY TO THE COFFEEHOUSE A BLOCK away.

"Don't know why I bothered bringing you an espresso—"

"Rhys, you brought me Starbucks." Malachi shook his head disapprovingly. "What were you thinking?"

"It's perfectly good coffee, and there's one right downstairs from my flat?"

"We're in Vienna." He pulled open the wood-and-brass door and the happy scent of roasted coffee, sugar, and flour assaulted him. "If I have to put up with the politics, I should at least take advantage of the coffee."

"Anything is better than that mud you make at home."

The waiter looked up from his newspaper and nodded toward a table in the corner. Malachi and Rhys both unwrapped their scarves and coats to hang them by the door. Winter had come with a vengeance, and icy wind bit his cheeks. A few flurries of snow had dusted the sidewalk the night before, but he had a feeling they wouldn't last.

"Why did I leave Istanbul?" Rhys asked.

"If it's hot, you complain about that. If it's cold, you complain about that." Malachi settled onto the leather-wrapped bench and shook out a paper someone had left nearby. "Is there any weather you do like?"

"England."

Malachi frowned. "Really?"

"In the spring."

"When the flowers are blooming, or do those give you sneezing fits?"

"Ha-ha."

"I'd forgotten how amusing your snits could be."

"You've forgotten pretty much everything about me, old friend." Rhys's eyes were sharp on his face. "Has that changed?"

"Some." Malachi leaned forward, glancing around the wood-paneled restaurant. "Is this place—?"

"It's friendly." Rhys nodded at an older gentleman who sat across the room sipping a cup. "It's owned by one of us."

"The waiter is human."

"But discreet and lacking in curiosity. Excellent qualities in a human, I've always found."

Rhys paused to give his order to the man. Malachi did the same.

"Now," he continued, "what has changed?"

"My *talesm* have returned to"—he leaned back and motioned halfway across his right pectoral muscle—"about here. A few more are scattered down my arm. And as my *talesm* have returned, I've recovered more memory."

Rhys's face was pale. "So you know about—"

"The badger prank was your idea, not mine. I cannot believe you tried to let me take the blame."

Rhys was affronted. "It was not! And if you hadn't started laughing, we would have got away with it."

"We were right little demons at school, weren't we?"

Rhys burst into laughter, and Malachi couldn't help but grin.

"We were," Rhys said. "Our poor mothers."

"It's amazing we survived to adulthood."

His old friend paused. "Your family marks?"

"No."

"I'm sorry, brother."

The tattoos his father had given him when he reached the age of thirteen hadn't reappeared. While they gave Malachi little power, they were part of his identity. A way of marking his lineage, given to him by his father. Because he'd not scribed them himself, he had no idea if they would ever return.

"It will be as it is meant," Malachi said. "I'm blessed that any have returned at all."

"Ava?"

"She sings to me. She heals me."

Rhys shook his head slowly. "Lucky bastard."

"I am." He lowered his voice again. "Has Max told you—"

"About the Grigora?" His smile fell. "He called everyone to Damien and Sari's as soon as he and Renata got into town. I'm still trying to understand how we could have missed something as big as this."

"They prefer to be called *kareshta*. Silent ones."

"Silent ones?" Rhys asked.

"Those who survived had to be."

Rhys slowly shook his head. "All these years, Malachi. How many have suffered? How many have been killed? They were the Fallen's first victims, and we knew nothing."

"How were we to know?"

"How could we *not*? It seems so obvious now. The Forgiven fathered daughters, why wouldn't the Fallen?"

"The stories only ever speak of male hunters. That's all we were ever taught."

Rhys was incredulous, barely noticing the human waiter who was back with their coffees and two glasses of water, along with a couple of small pastries.

"And we shouldn't have known better?" he asked. "Asked more questions? Our own scrolls speak of the mighty *men* of ancient times. Heroes, not heroines. And yet we know that the Irina were always there." Rhys leaned forward with bright eyes. "And I believe the early singers were with the scribes in battle as well. The Dacia manuscript—"

"This sounds like an academic argument I'm completely unprepared to have with you."

Rhys paused, his mouth likely ready to launch into an explanation of some ancient language interpretation Malachi had no interest in.

"That's… probably true," Rhys admitted. "But it may be relevant to the Irina problem."

"Can we stop calling them a problem?"

The corner of Rhys's mouth turned up. "Oh, I think they rather like being problematic. And you know where Orsala and Sari are going to fall on the Grigora—*kareshta* question, don't you?"

"Probably where Ava is."

"She *is* one, you know."

"She's part *kareshta*. It's…" He hesitated. It wasn't his story to tell. "It's complicated. You need to ask Ava."

Rhys's curiosity had clearly been sparked. "I will. Can I assume she also anticipates a large family reunion? Welcoming the *kareshta* into the arms of their Irin sisters?"

"She's more cautious than that. You have to remember, Ava has been in their place. She had no idea she was anything but human, and she had no control the way our women have. She thought she was insane, and I'm guessing more than one of the Grigori females is in the same situation. She sympathizes with them, but I think she's also more realistic about how damaged or dangerous some of them might be."

Rhys shook his head. "The main question is, can they be trusted? If what Max said is true, then any with living fathers can be tracked by the Fallen who sired them. They have no free will unless their sires are dead. We have to consider them security risks as well as victims."

"All the more reason to shift focus," Malachi said quietly.

Rhys glanced over his shoulder. "Are you saying what I think?"

"We must start going after the Fallen, not just the Grigori."

"A monumentally more difficult task," Rhys said. "And not one that will be popular with the council."

"Rhys." Malachi fought to explain. "The Grigori we met in Sofia— the ones Max has come to a truce with—they're not like the others. They're… more like us. Yes, they are wilder. Untrained. Hungry. But not mindless drones. With their sires dead, they had free will. They were struggling to control themselves, but they were *trying*."

"Not unlike the Irin now."

Malachi frowned. "What do you mean?"

"Surely you can see the parallels," he said, taking a sip of coffee. "We've been without widespread Irina influence for only two hundred years, and where are we as a society? Declining. Touch-hungry. More and more aggressive. We're completely out of balance. We need…" Rhys's voice grew rough. "Our race is dying without the Irina, and not just because so few children are born."

"Then we bring them back. On their terms, not because of some compulsion act dreamed up by old men. And we work to save the women we can, even if that means fighting with the council."

"You're ready for this fight."

"Yes."

Rhys smiled ruefully. "You're almost panting for it."

"And what if I am?"

"Yes." He drained his coffee. "You definitely seem more like yourself."

CHAPTER

FOURTEEN

"Welcome to Vienna," Ava whispered to her reflection. "Your father is an angelic bastard. Your grandmother was driven insane by the angel who raped her. Your great-grandfather is an archangel who kills things for you as tokens of his twisted affection. And somewhere in the middle of this, you mated a four-hundred-year-old man with amnesia."

She blinked and looked at the cat that had wandered into the apartment when she opened the door to its meow.

"How is this my life?"

The black feline only blinked guileless gold eyes.

"Do you come with the apartment?"

It gave a scratchy growl and jumped down from the dressing table where Ava had been brushing out her hair. It was clean and seemed well fed. She thought it must belong to someone in the building. As long as it didn't trash her stuff, she was fine with him hanging out. She liked cats and dogs; she just couldn't keep one herself because she traveled too much.

Ava sighed as she turned back to the mirror. She needed a haircut badly. And a pedicure. A massage would be a good idea, along with her regular medical checkups. She had a bunch of vaccinations that needed updating, and she felt like she'd put off the regular business of life for way too long.

She checked her phone. No e-mails from her mother or father, but one from Luis, asking how her grandmother was. Ava hoped he didn't feel like he needed to be chatty with her now because she was engaged to the guy who'd threatened his life.

That would be awkward. And frankly a little disturbing.

She shot him back a quick response and checked her calendar, only to realize she had a job coming up. In fact, it was a job she'd booked eighteen months in advance, right before she'd taken the assignment in Cyprus that eventually led her to Istanbul. She remembered it because she felt like the magazine was being overly cautious, booking her so far in advance to cover their summer beach spread for the next year.

Now the shoot was approaching and Ava had some decisions to make. She still had three months before she needed to be on location, but she couldn't cancel any later than six weeks out and not seriously piss them off.

She also realized that she and Malachi had officially been reunited longer than they'd originally been together in Turkey. She didn't know why that seemed significant, but it did.

She heard the key turn in the lock.

"Ava?"

"In the bedroom."

"Why do we have… a cat?"

"He wandered in," she said as Malachi entered the bedroom. "Seemed nice enough. Probably belongs to a neighbor." He leaned down to brush a kiss across her temple and flopped on the bed, only to have the cat jump up and sit on his abdomen.

"I don't think it likes me."

"Well, you are in his bed."

"I'm fairly sure we're the ones renting it."

"That reminds me, I need to get some money transferred to Rhys to pay him back."

He frowned. "Or don't, because the scribe house is covering it."

"Or let me do it, since I'm not worried about my budget? The house resources are probably strapped with the reconstruction."

"Ava, you don't need to do that."

She spun around in her seat. "Is this going to be a macho alpha-male problem for you?"

"Am I a macho alpha-male?"

"Yes. And I'm loaded. It makes more sense to let me—or let's be honest, my asshole of a father—cover the bill for stuff like this. It's a better use of resources. Besides, I'd probably be paying for a hotel and a guide—possibly a bodyguard—if I were traveling on my own."

He propped up on his elbows, his lips twitching. "Are you saying I'm your bodyguard and guide?"

"No." Her face reddened.

"Because I am very fond of your body. So guarding it isn't a problem."

"I'm just trying to help."

Now he was grinning. "You don't have to pay me though."

"Shut up!"

Malachi scooted off the bed and got on his knees, shuffling over to her as she sat at the dressing table. The cat gave an irritated yowl and abandoned the room. The stool she sat on was low enough that Malachi was level with her when he wrapped his arms around her waist from behind. She could see him laughing in the mirror.

"Am I your kept man, *canım*?"

"If you are, I feel like a lot more breakfast in bed should be happening."

"Mmmm." His lips trailed along her neck. "Now I feel this pressure to earn my keep."

"Coffee in bed, at least."

It was getting harder and harder to concentrate. The traitor cat had completely abandoned her. She should probably be getting ready for... something.

But he was playing with her. Teasing her. More and more of his personality was coming back. His humor. His bravado.

Ava fell in love all over again every time she turned around.

"All right, you've convinced me. I will take the job as your kept man. So..." He lifted her in his arms and turned to the bed. "Now it is time for work."

• • •　• • •

TWO VERY WORK-FILLED HOURS LATER, THEY MET THE OTHERS IN THE back room of a coffeehouse off Bäckerstraße. It was dark and smoky in the front room, the walls plastered with movie posters and flyers for avant-garde art exhibitions, but the small back room was bright and clean. The smell of coffee, beer, and sausages filled the midday air.

And Ava's friends, both scribes and singers, filled the room.

Suddenly she was fighting back tears.

Orsala sat in quiet conversation with a nodding Rhys. Mala was signing to both Leo and Sari, who was holding Damien's hand as he read from a tablet computer with a frown on his face. Max and Renata were there, even though both were pointedly ignoring the other by checking their phones.

Malachi unwrapped his scarf and hung it with the others tossed over a bench near the door.

"Ava, give me your coat and I'll—what's wrong?"

She turned, smiling. "Nothing is wrong. Sorry. Happy tears, babe." Her hands went to his cheeks. He'd let his beard start to grow, and she was getting used to it. It suited him. "You're coming back to me. And everyone is here. I feel like I've lived with this knot of fear in my stomach for months now, but I just… I know it's going to be okay. Somehow, it's all going to be okay if everyone is here."

He held on to her wrists and squeezed them as she smiled.

"I love you," he whispered, and Ava realized the whole room had gone silent.

She turned, and everyone was smiling at her.

"Hello, Ava." Sari stood and opened her arms. "It's good to see you, sister."

Sister.

Ava would only admit it to herself, but part of her had wondered whether the Irina would treat her differently now that they knew her blood was from the Fallen. She should have known better. Orsala embraced her. Mala pinched her bicep in mock disapproval. And Ava knew without a doubt that Karen would still bake her too many cakes and Astrid would still share a self-deprecating joke to break the tension.

They were her sisters. For the first time, her heart was light enough to enjoy it.

Malachi had his hand on the small of her back, guiding her to a chair near Damien, who looked up, tension plastered over his brow. Sari squeezed his hand, and he lifted her knuckles to his mouth, the easy affection between them another wound healed over in Ava's heart.

They looked like love to Ava. Tested. Broken. Mended. Faithful. Forgiven. She didn't know everything they had lived through, but if

Damien and Sari could recover from it, she was certain she and Malachi had a better-than-average chance.

"What's wrong?" Sari asked.

"Anurak has rejected my request for a meeting."

Sari looked shocked. "What? But he's been vocal about the reformation of the Irina council."

"I know. Perhaps he's feeling pressure—"

"If Anurak is the same scribe I once knew," Orsala said, "he's grown tired of *talk*. He's a taciturn man by nature, and I doubt he wants debate. I have a feeling he and many other older scribes simply want the Irina to step forward and claim their role in the Library."

"The Library?" Ava whispered to Malachi.

"The Elder Council meets in the Library. It's symbolic but also practical, as their primary job is interpreting Irin scripture and history and using those interpretations to resolve disputes."

"Where did the singers meet?"

"The same place. There are fourteen desks. Seven have been empty since the Irina elders fled after the Rending."

"A library?"

He shrugged. "It's a very *big* library."

"I thought I heard something about council chambers."

"I believe it is not unlike your court system. All the elders have their own offices and staff, but the actual decisions are made in the Library."

Well, Ava supposed there were worse places to run an entire society.

"But wouldn't meeting in a library favor the scribes?" she asked. "I mean, they're all supposed to be equal, right? Seven scribes and seven singers. But that's kind of a scribe thing, right? Written magic?"

Malachi frowned. "I don't understand."

"I mean, doesn't running the Irin world from a library mean the Irina are at a… tactical disadvantage?"

"No." He was shaking his head. "Irin scribes *must* be in the Library. That is where we draw our strength. But Irina…" Malachi smiled. "Irina singers *are* the library."

Oh. Well, that was cool.

Damien looked up with a rueful expression. "They can be quite superior about it."

Orsala chided him. "Just because you males are forced to rely on books and scrolls doesn't make your magic less powerful, Damien."

The watcher gave her an affectionate smile before he turned his attention to Ava. "It did create a rather major problem when the Irina elders went into hiding, though. While they could take copies of our scriptures with them as references, we had no access to Irina knowledge. It's one of the reasons there's been so much division since the Rending."

"I think Anurak is right," Sari said. "We need to stop debating. Irina elders should just walk in and take their place at their desks. No more debate. No more talk of compulsion. We'd have a voice on the council, and no one would be able to question it."

Mala shook her head and began signing. Sari translated as she signed.

"They would question anything not supported by the wives," Mala signed. "Sari and her supporters are not the only Irina in the city now. Whatever elder singers take their place in the Library must have legitimacy among all the Irina—even if there is dissent—or we lose all rights to challenge the elder scribes."

Max said, "I agree."

"So do I," Orsala said. "The problem is how we can elect our own elders when we're still so scattered."

"How are the elders chosen?" Ava asked. "I know they're chosen by the watchers of the scribe houses, but it's got to be more specific than that. I mean, we're talking about the whole world, right?"

Malachi put an arm around her shoulders. "One from each continent, for the most part. And then one seat that changes depending on population."

"So one from North America and one from South," Rhys said. "One elder from Africa. One from Europe. One from Eurasia—that one is up for debate every single election—and one from Eastern Asia and the Pacific region. That's six, and then when the seventh seat comes up for election every seventy years, it's decided based on population. Right now, there is an additional European elder on the scribe council, but the time before that, there were more scribes in Asia. It changes over time."

Sari said, "And the Irina are basically the same, but we tend to have different population concentrations. Our seventh seat has more often come from Africa or Asia."

"Okay, I get that it's complicated," Ava said. "But Sari, didn't you say the havens are mostly connected online?"

"We all have e-mail, of course."

"So…" She held up her smartphone. "Have elections online. Do it over the Internet."

"Online elections for elders?"

Max leaned forward, smiling. "You know, Ava has a good point. Human revolutions are fueled by social networks now. Don't you think the Irina could organize their own revolution on the Internet?"

Damien and Sari exchanged a look that told Ava they'd be talking more about it later. Yeah, so it kinda made her feel like a kid at the grown-ups table, but she had to remind herself that to these people she *was* a kid.

"Hey," she whispered to Malachi. "When are Irin considered adults?"

He was following what looked to be a quiet argument between Sari and Mala. "Full adults? Around sixty to seventy-five years. When we're finished with our training. Why?"

She flushed. Wow.

"So, you're quite the cradle robber, aren't you?"

Malachi turned to her abruptly. "What? No, I'm not."

"I'm not even thirty. That's like… a teenager to you guys."

She could see the flush crawl up his neck, even behind the beard. "You're human. You mature differently."

"But I'm *not* really human."

His shoulders were stiff and his posture screamed his discomfort. It was really a shame that Ava found teasing him to be so amusing.

"I mean, what would your mom say if she found out you were mated—and I mean well and thoroughly *mated*—to what she would basically consider a kid?"

He wiped a hand over his forehead. "Heaven above, please stop talking."

"So are we going to stop fooling around now?"

He groaned. "Ava."

"I'm just yanking your chain."

"You're going to have to speak up, because the mental lecture my mother's memory is giving me right now is rather loud."

She bit her lip so she didn't burst into laughter. "Malachi?"

"What?"

"Have you ever heard of Irin teenagers finding their mate before they're adults?"

"No."

"So, even though I'm young in your world, I'm thinking the universe decided I was an adult a while back."

He squeezed her hand and said, "I hate you a little right now. You know that, right?"

• • • • • • •

"The *kareshta*," Damien said after they'd eaten together.

Everyone turned to Ava.

"Hey, I don't have any inside information," she said quietly. She wasn't ready to share her grandmother's story. She'd talked to Malachi about it, and they'd both decided that until it became important, it wasn't something everyone needed to know.

"Did you find your grandmother?" Orsala asked.

"I did."

"And?"

"She's *kareshta*," Ava said as Malachi took her hand. "Jaron is her sire. She's his only daughter."

Renata said, "That's why he's taken an interest in you."

"Yes."

Leo asked, "Can he track you? Like Max said the other Fallen can track their children?"

"Yes," Malachi said. "But I want to point out he has tracked Ava from the beginning, and she's come to no harm from him. In fact, he's protected her more than once. Jaron's motivations are still murky—"

Orsala's eyes narrowed on Ava's mate as if she could sense the lie.

"—but for now, I do not believe he's a threat."

Rhys asked, "When do we tell the elders about them?"

Damien said, "When we know they're protected."

"You don't think the elders would try to harm them?" Rhys said. "Why—"

"We don't know how they'll react," the watcher said.

Max added, "And I told Kostas we would keep his secret. No place is more of a hotbed for gossip than this city. There are spies everywhere. I want to be cautious."

Malachi nodded. "And let's be honest. Not all the elder scribes want the singers to return. They like wielding total control over the council.

If the *kareshta* are taken in by the Irina, that could make them more powerful. They're first generation blood. If they were trained—"

"Ava is second generation," Mala signed as Orsala translated. "And we've all seen how powerful she is."

"She's also mated to a scribe," Sari said. "That focuses our power. The *kareshta* have no focus. The Grigori are their brothers; they have no mates."

"But they could," Leo said quietly. He looked around the room. "I'm not the only scribe who will think of this. I don't want to be selfish, but there are so few Irina." He paused and a red flush stained the giant's cheeks. "Ava and Malachi are mated. We know it's possible. To those of us without mates, the existence of these women offers us some hope that our *reshon* could be out there. That we will not always walk alone. Malachi is right. Many Irin may worry. But many will be motivated to help for that reason alone."

Mala put a hand on his shoulder and squeezed.

Damien said, "That's not selfish, Leo. When I look at Ava and Malachi, I see nothing one-sided about their relationship." Damien gave her a small smile. "We all need a place to belong."

"But we have to be cautious," Renata said. "These women have been lost for generations. Many died as infants or were discarded by the fathers who should have protected them. I think we all have the desire to help them, but they could also be a threat."

"I agree," Orsala said. "We need more information. I'm going to look in the archives, but right now Sari should focus on organizing elections and reaching out to the Irina in the city."

"The pro-compulsion sympathizers?" Sari scoffed.

"Yes." Orsala's tone brooked no argument. "Remember, some of those women you ridicule lost their children during the Rending. While you see compulsion, they see protection. Loss is a powerful motivator. Don't dismiss it. Or them."

Ava said, "I can help. I think. At least with the computer part. The organization."

"Thank you, Ava."

"And us?" Malachi asked his watcher.

"I want you to come with me to the Library this week," Damien said. "I know you don't have all your memories, but I need a new perspective. Rhys, I have a different project for you. Can you start looking through the police statistics here in the city?"

"Of course," Rhys said. "What am I looking for?"

"I don't buy that the Grigori have been absent from Vienna for generations," Damien said. "Though it makes the elder scribes look very good if any trace of attacks are silenced. We need to know the truth. Can you look in the human records?"

"Easily."

"Leo and me?" Max asked.

"I want you around the city. Keep your eyes out and tell me what you see. I want to know who has people here. Which elders have more than the average number of staff. Who's traveling lately and where."

"What do you suspect?" Leo asked.

"I'm not sure yet," Damien said with a frown. "For now, we should simply be cautious."

Sari said, "Mala and Renata, you can help with that, along with gathering information on the Irina who have showed up in the city. I want to know who is here and what their connections are. Are they mated? Do they have families? Where do their loyalties lie?"

"Of course," Renata said. "Consider it done."

• • •　　• • •

THE second time Death visited her, Ava wasn't as surprised. She sat up in bed when she heard him, rustling in the shadows of the room. The angel leaned forward, his black cloak falling from his head and his silver eyes piercing the darkness.

"You were talking about my grandmother before, weren't you? When you said you couldn't go to her."

He nodded.

"Why not?"

No answer, but the silver grey of the angel's eyes grew darker, like storm clouds gathering.

"It's not up to you, is it?"

Come with me.

"More secrets?"

Humor lit his face. She glanced down at Malachi, then slid out of bed.

Death embraced her again and she allowed it, sinking into his arms as he covered her with his star-filled cloak. In a heartbeat, they were sitting in a brightly lit hall. Ava couldn't decide if it was a church or a library. The walls were covered in tall bookcases, but the windows were filled with brilliantly colored stained glass. The whole room had a weight of holiness she couldn't dismiss. Church or library?

Both.

Death kept her shrouded as the room coalesced around them. Once again, there were muffled voices that came from a distance, as if she were eavesdropping in a hallway. Shadows became visible and formed in the room. It was Volund again, Ava now had the taste of his power from her grandmother's memories, and she struggled to control her immediate nausea.

"…tell your children to eliminate the threat."

"I am not one to waste my sons on foolish gambles. Didn't Oslo teach you anything?"

"It taught me that any with human blood are expendable."

A long pause.

"Are you sure of that, brother?"

A hissing sound, then a grunt in reply.

"Do not make the mistake of thinking we are equals, Svarog."

"You may be assured I do not."

Ava could tell by the tone of his voice that whoever Svarog was, he didn't think Volund was superior.

"The heretic has spies everywhere," a third voice hissed. "Even among our own people. More and more are listening to him. We must send a message. Once the city falls into our hands, any thought of rebellion will be quashed."

"And Vienna will be yours," Volund said.

"Yes," the one called Svarog replied. "That is our arrangement."

Ava could tell the angel wasn't one hundred percent certain of it, though.

"Grimold, are your children ready?"

"Yes. *All* of them."

"All?" She thought it was Svarog who spoke.

"All. If there are singers with them, they will not be a problem."

She tried to repeat the details to herself, knowing her memory of dreams could be sketchy. Volund and his allies seemed to be in some kind of strategy meeting, and Ava knew the information would be valuable to Malachi and Damien.

But the scene was too hazy. The figures never truly took shape. Ava only had a vague impression of them and their relative power. Two greater powers with a third attached to Volund. The voices faded in and out.

"Will I remember this?" she asked Death.

When you need to.

She sighed. "I love answers like that."

"Eliminate them and make it clear who killed them," Volund said. "It is past time that your allegiance became known. Unless you have something to hide, Svarog."

"Becoming your ally doesn't mean you are privy to my secrets. I do not trust you."

"Nor I you."

A slight pause before Svarog said, "Then we are agreed. I will take care of the heretic. Have you found her yet?"

"It is more than Jaron guarding her. There can be no other explanation."

"Another, then. She is more of a problem than we anticipated."

Ava turned to her angelic shadow and asked, "Are they talking about me or—?"

Before she could finish her sentence, Death enfolded her in his cloak and she was back in her bedroom, sitting next to Malachi who murmured once, then rolled toward her in sleep, pressing his face to her belly and wrapping his arms around her waist.

Death turned his back to Ava and walked back toward the shadows.

"Azril?"

He stopped.

"That's your name, isn't it?"

He slowly turned. Nodded.

"Why?"

His shining eyes moved from Ava to Malachi, then back again.

You are beautiful together. She would want to see such beauty.

When Ava blinked, he was gone.

CHAPTER

FIFTEEN

The next morning, Malachi dragged himself out of bed when he heard the sound of carriages clopping down the street nearby.

Ava's sleepy voice stopped him. "Babe?"

"I'm going to the Library, *canim*."

She burrowed farther. "So early. Wanted to talk to you about…"

"Ava?" He smiled when he realized she'd drifted back to sleep.

"I'm awake. Kinda. Funny dream. Why so early?"

"We have to go through the cleansing ritual first."

"Explain later, okay?

"I will." He brushed a kiss over her temple, then started toward the door. "You're with Sari today?"

"Mmhmm. Love you. See you tonight. I'll tell you then, okay?"

"Okay."

Malachi closed the door softly and paused, his palm pressed to the wood.

It was a little thing. The sleepy greeting. The recitation of the day's activities and the kiss good-bye.

Love you. See you tonight.

A simple thing. Infinitely precious.

And precarious.

Even with his memories returning, his world had never felt more uncertain. Fallen angels played with mortal lives as if they were pawns on a chess board, and an insidious threat lived in his mate's own blood.

Volund could find her anywhere.

Malachi hadn't had another dream since Italy. He was half-convinced they'd been nightmares of his own making. He hadn't told Ava. Every time he decided to share it with her, it seemed another problem or revelation came their way.

He leaned his head against the doorway and fervently prayed for the privilege of years. Years he'd be able to kiss her good-bye and come home to her at night. A lifetime of routines they would build. Everyday intimacies they would share.

Please.

Is a thousand years too much to ask?

For now… give me one.

His soul cried the unspeakable name of the one who had returned him to the mortal plane. He felt the yearning pull at his chest as the door opened. Then she was there, pressing a kiss over his heart. She leaned her forehead against his collar, wrapped her arms around his waist. She said nothing, but he knew she'd heard his voice. Her touch bolstered him; he grew taller under her small hands.

"I could hear you," she said. "Woke me up."

"I'm sorry."

"Don't be."

"I love you." He squeezed her tightly. "I'll see you tonight."

"I'll be here."

She stepped away from him and took a deep breath. "Coffee?"

"I'll get some with Damien on our way. I think he's probably waiting."

"Okay." She smiled, then cocked her head toward the door. "Really?"

"What?"

"You can't hear him?" She unlocked the hallway door and cracked it open, only to see the black cat from the other day slip in. He went to the kitchen and hopped up on the window ledge, staring out into the street.

Malachi shook his head. "We're not keeping him."

"That's so weird. Why would his owner even let him out so early? He doesn't look like a stray." She yawned and went to the kettle to heat water.

"Getting a cat through quarantine is a nightmare. If you truly want one, we'll find one when we get home."

"It's fine, babe. I won't get attached."

The "babe" thing she'd started had annoyed him at first, considering he was roughly three hundred and seventy-five years older than she was. Then… it didn't. It was Ava. His human-Irina-Grigora mate who called him ridiculous things like "babe" and said the word "dude" in actual conversation.

Maybe it was a California thing. He didn't care.

Heading toward the door with a smile, he called out, "I'll see you tonight."

"I'll… cook meatloaf or something."

Malachi turned. "Really?"

"No." She snickered. "I have no idea how to cook meatloaf."

"Chinese takeout it is."

"As much as I travel, Chinese takeout is my comfort food."

His eyes fixed on her.

"You have to go," she whispered.

"I don't want to."

A shy smile teased her lips. The cat growled at the window, pawing it before he looked over his shoulder.

"Go," Ava said. "The cat says Damien is here. Call me when you're done at the Library."

"The cat does not know that Damien is here." Still, he kissed her and walked out the door before he lingered any longer, walking down the stairs to find Damien waiting on the street, his breath frosting in the morning air.

He was looking up to the window of their flat. "Did you get a cat?"

"We're not keeping the cat."

"Huh. Coffee?"

"Please."

• • •　• • •

HE'D SATED HIS CRAVING FOR COFFEE, BUT MALACHI'S STOMACH WAS rumbling. He should have eaten a bigger meal the night before.

Hunger would have to wait. Liquids were permitted before the cleansing ritual but not food. The satchel over his shoulder held the linen wrap he'd wear, along with his ceremonial robe. They had both been in storage in Istanbul. Rhys had retrieved them before he came to the city. While scribe houses were more informal, Vienna was not. If he and Damien were to be permitted entrance to the Library, they would have to visit the cleansing rooms attached and enter in ceremonial garb.

"You've been doing this every day?" he asked his watcher.

Damien nodded as he drained his coffee cup. "Almost. I've managed to be granted audience with Konrad—whom my brother-in-law works for—and Kibwe. But both are already traditionalists in favor of restoring the Irina council. I need to speak with Anurak and Rafael. They're the swing votes. Currently, there are three elders who are openly in favor of compulsion."

The whole concept irritated Malachi. "Do they actually think they can force the Irina into retreats again? They don't have any control over them."

"No, but they have control over their mates. Other than a few deserters, the Irina in hiding are mated to active scribes who owe their own allegiance to the council. For the past two hundred years, the council has asked no questions when a scribe has left his post for a time—even if it's for years—"

"Somebody has to raise children if our race is going to survive. I can count on one hand the number of scribes I've known who've had children in the past two hundred years."

"Exactly. They've ignored it when a scribe has left his post when his mate was with child. Asked no questions. But what will happen to those mates if compulsion becomes law? They can make an issue of scribes leaving their posts if they want to. If the Irina they're mated to is not in a retreat."

"It's madness."

"It's control wearing the mantle of security. And some on the council are obsessed with it."

Malachi walked in silence, entering the maze of the palace complex along with myriad other workers and suited men as they made their way into the tangled streets and the network of passageways that made up the Hofburg Palace.

Massive buildings of every design—Gothic, Baroque, and Classical —surrounded them as he and Damien moved among the working population of the palace. Over five thousand humans worked in the

Hofburg complex, janitors and tour guides, clerks and government officials. It was the perfect hiding place for the Irin Library, and some version of the council had resided here for over five hundred years after having made a secret pact with the Hapsburgs. The empire had been lost, but the Irin had remained hidden with the help of their gold, influence, and magic.

Malachi knew that many of the suited men making their way into the government buildings wore *talesm* under their dress shirts. As a center of commerce, culture, and international intelligence, Vienna was the perfect seat of Irin power.

Damien knocked on an intricately carved wooden door hidden in the corner of a small courtyard. A buzzing sound followed and they pushed it open, only to be met by two scribes who were obviously part of the Library Guard. They wore suits and earpieces Rhys would be jealous of. They nodded to Damien with familiarity but still searched both their bags. Malachi turned in the pair of silver daggers he carried and received a receipt to retrieve them at the end of his business.

Damien was smiling when Malachi finally joined him.

"What?"

"You have caught the Guard's attention. They don't often see scribes carrying weapons here."

The Library Guard was one of the most prestigious postings a warrior could have, but it was also one of the least dangerous.

Malachi grunted. "Then they are complacent."

"Don't underestimate them."

The ground floor housed the cleansing rooms. Malachi breathed deeply of the steam and smoke when they stepped through the door. His heart swelled with longing. It had been too long since he'd been able to truly pray. While the political maneuvering was not how he would wish to spend his day, the ritual of the bath was welcome.

Stripping off his street clothes, he entered the chamber.

The bath's marble walls were carved with centuries of protective spells. Words dark with age. He could hear low prayers chanted from the far room as scribes who had already cleansed their bodies cleared their minds of earthly cares.

Malachi walked into the pool and took a deep breath before he immersed himself. Warmth, light, and love. Held in the water's embrace, he felt another door open in his mind.

"Like this?"

"Evet, oğul. *Just like that, Malachi.*"

Water sluiced over his small body as his father hummed a song his mother had taught him.

"*You have taken your first marks. Every year, we will do this now. To give thanks.*"

"*Every year?*"

"*It is tradition. Tradition is important.*"

Whispers drifted in the water, and there came a flash of light behind closed eyes.

Malachi floated.

Songs in the air.

A vivid sky cut with beams of gold light. Crystal waters and presence.

Holy and wholly.

His body feels no pain. His soul, no struggle. Body and soul are one. Complete joy. Complete peace.

Love surrounds him. Perfect love.

He cries with joy because he is home.

"*Son.*"

He is there. He is eternal.

This is what they long for.

Who would not long for this?

He is surrounded by love. Complete. Replete.

He needs nothing.

"*She calls you,*" *a familiar voice whispers.*

He hears.

Longing.

Need.

He chooses.

And like the angels before him, he falls.

Malachi rose with a gasp and lifted his eyes to see the carved marble and stone encasing him.

His body ached, his flesh a prison he'd never felt before.

In the space of a single breath, in the thin line between the present and eternity, Malachi remembered heaven.

He had danced in the presence of the angels. Welcomed as a beloved son.

"*Vashama canem, reshon.*"

He had come back for her.

But until that moment, Malachi hadn't remembered what he'd given up to return.

He didn't sense the tears on his face until Damien reached him. "Brother?"

"I'm fine." He wiped his eyes and dipped in the water again, brushing the wet hair back from his face and pulling the water from his beard. "I'm fine, Damien."

His watcher held Malachi with his eyes. "Tell me."

Malachi shook his head. How could he explain?

"I was in the heavenly realm for months, brother." He wiped the water from his face and moved to exit the bath. "Some memories I wish I did not recover."

"But why?" Damien followed him, and the men dried themselves with the linen towels provided. Their wraps had been placed on marble benches near the entrance to the ritual room. "You must have seen things—"

"It was perfect beauty. Perfect peace," Malachi said quietly. "And I chose to give it up. It was my choice, and I'm glad of it. But at this moment, it hurts."

He held the towel to his face and sat on the marble bench, staring into the steaming pool where the memory of heaven had been given to him.

Why?

"Choose."

He'd chosen Ava. He would still choose her.

Perhaps this was the answer to his desperate prayer that morning. Perhaps it was only the assurance that, no matter what the future held for him and his beloved in the earthly realm, something even more beautiful waited for them should they fall.

"I think I'd pull down heaven if that's what it took to keep you here with me."

"And I'd abandon it if you weren't there."

The memory snapped into place next to his vision of heaven. He and Ava, lying in bed after they'd made love. A different kind of completion, but no less beautiful. His mate, a daughter of the Fallen. Malachi, the son of the Forgiven.

"We were meant to be like this. Two halves of the same soul. Dark and light together."

Their union was a reflection of the peace he'd seen. Holy and wholly.

And Malachi finally realized what Jaron truly wanted.

Forgiveness.

He wrapped himself in linen and entered the prayer room, kneeling before the sacred fire and giving up the remnants of his pain as thousands of others had done before him. He left his sorrow and regret there. Burned slips of prayers in the fire. He let his soul mourn for what it had given up, while it caught fire with the vision he'd seen.

He'd left the heavenly realm for a reason. He was Mikhael's son, and he'd returned to earth to battle for the soul of his people.

* * *

THE IRIN LIBRARY WAS A PALACE OF KNOWLEDGE—EVERY RITUAL, every rule serving a purpose that had something to do with its preservation. Malachi and Damien wore linen shifts and ceremonial robes that dated back thousands of years. The linen, pure and undyed, was worn because it would not react to the ancient scrolls or manuscripts the scribes preserved. Baths served a spiritual purpose but also cleansed the environment of any pollutants or molds that could harm the books.

The first time his father had brought him here, Malachi had been thirteen years old and on the precipice of starting his training. A child in awe of the ceremony and solemnity, he'd bathed with other boys his age from all over the world under the watchful eyes of their fathers, passing the traditions on to the next generation of scribes. He'd received his family marks only weeks before, the first tattoos that had signaled his passage from childhood to adolescence.

That morning, he'd seen no boys readying themselves in the ritual room with barely concealed excitement. No fathers introducing the next generation to the sacred fire. No awe-filled eyes as they climbed the wooden steps to the scribes' gallery above the Library floor.

His heart hurt.

Malachi and Damien climbed the stairs in silence.

Seven scribes worked diligently below the gallery, assistants fetching them books or pens or ink, depending on what they were doing. Some were copying manuscripts. Others made notes in careful handwriting as they studied manuscripts or scrolls with silk-gloved hands.

Whispers filled the gallery. Quiet negotiations between secretaries and petitioners. While the work the scribes did below was sacred in nature, the Library was a political theater. Damien and Malachi were only two men in dozens who were visiting the Library that morning, hoping for an audience with an elder. They presented their petitions on paper slips passed to the secretaries. Those secretaries examined the petitions and decided which ones would be passed down to the elder on the Library floor.

The singers' gallery, on the opposite side of the room, stood empty but for three silent figures standing at one end, watching the elder scribes working below.

"Who are they?" Malachi asked.

"The mates of three of the elders—Jerome, Edmund, and Rasesh. They're the only Irina I've seen in the Library since I've been here."

His mother had once stood there. Had once sung there, joined by the chorus of her sisters.

Now there were only three.

The women also wore ceremonial clothing. Long linen shifts and robes, high-necked to warm the voices that held their magic. Their hair was freshly washed and tied back in simple plaits or cut short and clean around their faces. One woman stood out to him as the obvious leader.

"Who is she?" Malachi murmured. "The woman with short hair."

"Jerome's mate."

"She's powerful." It wasn't a question. Old magic surrounded her.

"Constance is also the most outspoken Irina proponent of compulsion."

What would lead such a powerful singer to give up so much of her self-determination? And if she was as powerful as she seemed, why wasn't she on the floor of the Library herself? Though Constance's youthful features glowed from the magic of her longevity spells, Malachi could see she was a singer of age and experience simply by the way she carried herself.

"She reminds me of Orsala."

"They are contemporaries, from what I've heard, though she is a daughter of Rafael."

"A healer?"

"A powerful one."

They paused at the counter where the papers and inkwells resided to let Damien compose the petition he'd give to Rafael's secretary. Rafael was the current elder from South America and, according to Damien, one of the swing votes in the council.

Malachi looked down, realizing what seemed off. "Where are the other desks?"

When he'd been a boy, the seven desks of the Irina elders had been in the center of the Library under the magnificent dome painted with scenes from Irin history. Now only the scribes' desks were visible. Skirting the perimeter of the bookcases, the elders worked. But the center of the Library was empty.

"There." Damien pointed his chin to seven empty desks tucked into the corners of the Library. "They were moved when it became clear the Irina council had fled. Stay here." He went to deliver his petition into the soft hands of the bureaucrat standing near the stairs leading down to the floor of the gallery. Unless an audience was granted, no one but the elders and their assistants were allowed on the floor.

Malachi could see two scribes making their way down the stairs already. One headed for Jerome. The North American elder was waiting for him, pale hands resting softly on the polished desk. Malachi couldn't help but see smug self-satisfaction on the scribe's handsome face. He glanced at Constance, who watched her mate from the gallery above with an inscrutable expression.

The other petitioner headed toward Anurak, the elder from Asia, who stood with a solemn expression and an outstretched hand.

The other elders continued their work, whether research, study, or manuscript transcription. Until their secretaries sent a petitioner to them, they would remain at their tasks. Quiet and solemn as political machinations twisted above.

It all looked so wrong. Malachi remembered thinking as a child that the Library floor looked like a star. The Irina desks in the center, radiating the singers' power out to the edges of the room where the solid desks of the scribes sat. That memory had been a dance of light and song. Had it only been a child's perception?

Damien returned to his side after delivering his petition to Rafael's secretary.

"Brother," Malachi said, "I have an idea."

"Oh?" Damien leaned against the railing and stared at the fresco on the ceiling. "Does it involve anything that will help pass the time? Because I've been staring at Leoc and Ariel's naked asses for more hours than I'd care to count in the past two weeks."

"Is there any way to make a call from here?"

"Of course. There are telephones in the hall outside."

"You want attention directed to the Irina problem, do you not?"

"Yes."

Malachi's eyes scanned the abandoned Irina desks along the edges of the room before they came back to Damien.

"Exactly how much attention would you like to attract?"

CHAPTER

SIXTEEN

It had been years since Ava had visited Vienna. At the time, she'd been on an assignment covering the numerous historic cemeteries in the city. She hadn't spent much time at the Hofburg other than when she passed through on the way to her hotel.

"What are we doing again?"

Sari flashed a grin at her. "Causing trouble."

"Oh, that sounds like a great idea."

Mala caught Ava's eyes and rolled her own, clearly along for the ride but not as enthusiastic as Sari was.

"Where's Orsala?"

"I believe she is the designated person taking the high road in this scheme. Therefore she's at the archives today."

"You know," Ava said, "this just sounds worse the more you explain it."

"It was your mate's idea."

"I love him like crazy, but you should know that Malachi"—Ava was out of breath trying to keep up with the two taller women—"can be a reckless troublemaker. Assuming Damien hasn't told you that already."

Sari said, "I knew I liked him."

"He got killed once. Just in case you've forgotten that part. Not too interested in repeating that experience, you know?"

"Nothing dangerous today," Sari said as they turned the corner into an empty courtyard. "Just tweaking the noses of some old men with superiority complexes and making a statement."

"Oh." They stopped at a door flanked by two potted hydrangea blooming a brilliant blue despite the winter chill. "Well, that sounds like fun."

Sari paused and turned to Ava. "You're not too American about nudity, are you?"

"Excuse me?"

"Communal baths. Do they bother you?"

"No." She shrugged. "I love the *hamam*, so—"

"This is actually quite similar. You'll be fine."

Mala and Sari rang a discreet bell, waited for the door to buzz, and pushed it open. Ava walked through to see a wide-eyed attendant and a suspicious guard who gave Mala a run for her money in the fierce department. She was tall and blond, carrying a staff that looked well used. She saw the guard eying Mala in particular, and Ava was grateful Sari had convinced her sister to leave her weapon at home.

The attendant stammered, "We were not expecting—"

"We have come for the ritual bath before we enter the gallery," Sari said smoothly. "It is my sister's first time in Vienna."

Ava didn't correct her. The guard eyed them warily before she searched their bags. Back at Sari and Damien's town house, Mala had given Ava a linen shift, strips of cloth to bind her breasts if she wanted them, and a high-necked robe. Ava had tucked all this in her old messenger bag and tried to sneak her camera in, but Mala had caught her and forced her to hand it over.

They left their shoes near the door and entered a marble bathing room that reminded Ava very much of the *hamams* in Istanbul. Grey marble benches lined the circular room. A seven-sided pool was in the center, and steam wafted into the air. It was humid and damp, lit only by oil lamps embedded in the wall. No electric light touched her skin as she undressed and stowed her bag in an intricately woven basket the attendant provided.

Mala and Sari disrobed beside her, obviously at ease with the ceremony of the bath. Ava simply followed their example.

"We bathe here before we pray," Sari said quietly. "The ritual bath is to cleanse your spirit and calm your mind."

Ava heard Mala take a deep breath before she immersed herself in the water. Sari hummed a quiet song as she closed her eyes and floated. Ava let the magic flow through her as she listened. She still didn't understand all the words of the Old Language, but she could sense the power behind them. Almost as one, the three women's mating marks lit on their skin as Sari's chanting grew stronger.

Mala's shone incandescent against her dark skin, no less beautiful for the mourning collar painted thick around her scarred neck. Sari's were a luminous glow against her pale skin. And Ava's shone clearly, the edges seared black against the olive tones of her skin. She looked down.

Her skin tone had always been a bit of a mystery, considering her parents were both fair. But with her father's family history being unknown, she'd never thought about it much.

"My grandmother is Persian," she said quietly.

"Ah." Sari tucked a wet lock of hair behind Ava's ear. "Yes, I can see that."

Mala signed something.

Sari said, "Mala asked if you look like her."

"Maybe a little. But she's much more beautiful."

Mala poured an almond-scented oil over Ava's hair, helping her to work it through the heavy mass while Sari rubbed her shoulders with a soap scented with amber.

"These are beautiful," Sari said, running a finger over Ava's shoulder where her mating marks gleamed. She could feel Mala turning her back to examine the marks there. "Malachi has a steady hand." She grinned as she ran the amber soap over her own skin. "Damien was so nervous on our mating night—I think a few of mine are barely readable."

Mala pointed to a faint mark on her hip as Sari and Ava turned to help her wash.

"Zander completely smudged that one," Mala signed as Sari translated. "He was so impatient. I'm amazed any of them dried properly before he attacked me." Mala smiled. "I was his first woman. His only woman. He was very eager."

Ava had never heard Mala talk about her lost mate, but in the darkness of the bathhouse, no topic seemed off-limits.

"My grandmother is in a mental institution," Ava whispered. "She's pretty much insane."

Mala signed with fierce movements. "She is not insane. She's only lived in the human world too long. We will find a way to help her."

"She is, though," Ava said. "More than me. It's a long story. I'll tell you. I promise. Just not today."

Sari took her hand and led her out of the bath after they'd all dipped in the water to wash the excess oil and soap from their bodies.

"We'll help them all," Sari said. "But to do that, we need standing again. That's partly why we're here. Come to the prayer room. Sing with me."

Ava did. She sat cross legged before a low fire, linking her hands with the two women at her side while Sari chanted a song that made Ava's heart fly. In that moment, she had no question where she belonged. No matter whose blood ran in her veins, these were her sisters. She belonged with them. She was made to sing these songs. Made to wear Malachi's marks on her skin.

She'd wandered for years, and now she was home.

•••   •••

"ARE YOU READY?" SARI WHISPERED AT THE DOOR THAT LED TO WHAT she called the singers' gallery.

"My hair's wet, I have no bra, and I'm dressed in what feels like a toga. This is not exactly the wardrobe I would have chosen to rock the world in, but I guess it'll have to do."

She felt Mala shaking with laughter behind her. Ava thought Sari and Mala looked like warrior goddesses from some cool sci-fi movie, while she looked like a kid playing dress-up. She needed platform boots, not felt-lined sandals.

"Just follow my lead. Don't feel like you need to say anything."

"Sounds good to me."

Sari pushed open the door, and Ava immediately felt every eye in the gallery swing toward them.

"Holy shit," she murmured.

It was a palace. No, it was a temple. Of books. Three stories of bookcases lined the walls, ladders and balconies built in to access what must have been thousands of shelves. She'd seen the Austrian National Library in this same palace complex, but it was nothing to the Irin Library.

The gallery across from them was crowded with scribes. She searched for Malachi but couldn't make him out among the crowd of men all wearing linen wraps and ceremonial robes similar to theirs but open at the neck.

"I guess everyone's in on the toga party," she whispered.

"Shh," Sari said.

The scribes' chests were bare, black *talesm* on display down the center of their robes, and Ava was relieved that Malachi's had mostly returned where they'd be visible. She had a feeling that more *talesm* equaled greater badass, and she didn't want her mate at a disadvantage.

Every eye was on them as they climbed the stairs to the gallery. Ava had never felt more conspicuous in her life. Just then, she caught her mate's smile. He was standing with Damien at the end of the railing, looking like the cat that had stolen the cream.

"Oh, yeah," she muttered, "this was totally your idea."

Sari ignored the shocked stares and whispers from the floor, heading toward the end of the gallery with Mala and Ava trailing after her.

"Constance," she said to the woman who waited there.

"Sari."

"I see we're once again missing our Irina elders from the floor today."

A slight smile crossed the woman's coldly beautiful features. "We are fortunate, then, that in the face of abandonment by our leadership, we have such excellent care from our mates."

Ava felt Mala tense beside her.

"That's an… interesting perspective," Sari said.

"Why are you here? You've been open in your contempt for the elder scribes before."

"I have no contempt for the office of elder, only for some who sit at their desks and try to 'unburden' me of my own self-determination."

"Don't put words in my mate's mouth," Constance said.

"The words in my own mouth have more than enough power," Sari whispered. "We've waited long enough."

With that parting shot, Sari strode down the steps and onto the floor of the Library.

Constance put out her hand and hissed, "You are no elder!"

Sari shoved it off and continued walking. "I never claimed to be."

Ava could barely breathe as Sari strode to the center of the room and spoke to the galleries on either side. "I am a singer of Ariel's line, and I request an audience with the Irina council."

Silence blanketed the Library.

The whispers from the scribes' gallery ceased. The muttering of the elder scribes stopped. Ava felt as if the entire room was holding its collective breath.

"I am an Irina singer," Sari said again, a little louder. "A daughter of Ariel's line. I request an audience with my representative on the Irina council."

Ava's heart was in her throat as she watched the fierce woman look around the silent room.

"Where is my council?" Sari asked. "Where are the elder singers who speak for me?"

Finally, a lone elder stood.

Mala shoved a small writing pad into her hands.

Konrad. European elder. Pro-Irina.

"Daughter," Konrad said with pain in his eyes. "I'm sorry, but your council has fled."

"No," Sari said. "My council was attacked."

Another elder stood. "Your council is in hiding."

Mala wrote again. *Jerome. North American elder. Pro-compulsion. Constance's mate.*

Sari stepped to Jerome's desk. "My council was protecting itself. Protecting its daughters when the scribes did not."

Furious whispers from the scribes' gallery.

Jerome spread his hands, a tense smile on his face. "And they do not trust us to protect our sisters even now?" Jerome raised his eyes to the scribes' gallery above him. "Does the Irina council not trust us to protect our own mates? Our daughters?" He looked back at Sari. "We *want* to protect them, and yet they hide."

She walked back to the center of the room. "And I *want* to speak to my council."

Jerome said, "I'm sorry, but your council is no more."

Sari raised her hands, standing in the center of the library, and began to whisper. Ava felt magic rise in the air. Dust motes hung frozen in the light that poured through the high windows.

No one breathed.

There was a low rumble, then with a mighty crash the seven desks of the elder singers slid to the center of the room, pulled by Sari's elemental power.

Papers and dust went flying. Furniture shifted as people ran to escape their path.

Sari stood motionless in the center of the floor, eyes traveling to meet the gaze of each elder as the massive wooden desks settled into place in a star-shaped pattern around her.

Ava released the breath she'd been holding.

"It's time." It was all Sari said before she left the floor of the Library and walked up the steps.

At the top of the stairs, Constance grabbed her arm.

"I see you like theater," the woman said. "You will come with me if you ever want to be welcome here again."

Mala stepped forward, but Sari held up a hand and shook her head. "Good. I've been wanting to have a little chat."

Constance and her two companions swept out of the gallery with Mala and Sari following them. Ava threw one more glance over her shoulder to see Malachi standing across from her, wearing a triumphant expression. Damien stood next to him, his face glowing with pride.

Ava gave them both a wide smile and followed her sisters out.

AT least if she was going to have coffee with the most passive-aggressive woman she'd ever met, she had her bra and shoes back on.

Ava sat in the airy sitting room of the town house near city hall. The neo-Gothic spire of the Rathaus was visible through the parlor window as Constance's maid served coffee and delicate cakes to the seven women in the sitting room.

"I'm glad we have this opportunity to talk," Constance said. "Perhaps we can come to an understanding."

"You're from the South," Ava said.

"Virginia." Constance nodded. "And you're American."

"I am. Los Angeles."

"How lovely."

Ava was pretty sure Constance actually meant the complete opposite. The singer turned her attention away from Ava and looked at Sari.

Renata had joined them, and she and Mala stood along the back wall while Sari and Ava took the couch.

"Well?" Constance asked.

"Well what? I have every right to demand an audience with my elders." Sari sat, her strong arms spread across the back of the delicate settee decorated in blue silk, which complemented the butter-yellow walls and cream molding of the room. Her hair was wild from the baths, her face ruddy from the winter air. Like the Northern fjords she hailed from, Sari was primal and beautiful at the same time.

Ava thought she looked like a Valkyrie at a tea party.

Constance had her own kind of power, though. She was the kind of woman Americans would call a "steel magnolia." She sat rigid in the chair across from Sari, unbowed by the other singer's presence. Her pixie-cut hair was utterly feminine and showcased high cheekbones and a strong jaw. Beautiful and cold.

"You know perfectly well our elders abandoned us," she said.

"Abandoned us?" Sari said. "Or were driven out of Vienna in fear for their lives?"

"I have been in Vienna for almost two hundred years," Constance said. She held a hand out to the woman at her left. "Helen has been here for one hundred." She nodded to the woman on her right. "Vania has been here for over seventy. There are many Irina living safely in our city."

"Then where are they? Why have none organized? Why have none stepped forward to try to reform the council?"

Tension was evident around Constance's eyes. "Because we believe our mates are correct. The Irina belong in retreats where we're protected. Not out chasing after Grigori like animals."

Renata said, "Did you hear that, Mala? We're like animals." She leaned over the couch and grinned. "Good. I like having teeth."

Constance's eyes narrowed. "Do not mistake bravado for strength. We have our own influence here. We've been working behind the scenes for years, trying to protect our sisters while you've been out throwing tantrums and killing angel spawn."

"What's wrong with killing Grigori?" Ava asked. "If they're attacking human women—"

"War is a scribe's job," Helen said, her voice crisply accented.

Renata stepped forward. "You ignorant little—"

"Enough!" Sari said. "I don't know what my grandmother was

thinking. You know *nothing*. You pretty birds sit in your gilded cages and play at politics while a war happens on the other side of the door. I have nothing to say to you when you are blind to reality."

Constance's chin lifted. "We have a good life here. If singers would accept the protection of their scribes, they would have a good life too. A *safe* life."

Childish chatter came from the hallway a moment before the door opened. A small girl, no more than five or six years old, bounced into the room, her honey-brown curls pulled into two pigtails on the sides of her head.

"Mama!" she cried and climbed into Constance's lap.

Ava saw the transformation immediately. All coldness fled from the woman's face.

"Lexi, what are you doing back from the park?"

"I was too cold. And we have visitors!" the little girl said, turning her sparkling eyes to Sari and Ava. "Hello."

Sari's yearning was an aching thing beside her.

"Hello," she said.

"Did you bring any children?" Lexi said.

"I'm sorry," Sari said softly. "I don't have any children."

"Oh." The girl's disappointment was clear. "Miss Helen's son comes to play sometimes, but he's so much older than me. Mama"—she turned in her mother's arms—"I want to see a baby. Does anyone have a baby I can play with?"

Constance ran a hand over her daughter's hair. "I'm sorry, Lexi. No babies are visiting today."

Lexi turned and confided to Ava, "I have lots of dollies, but babies are better, aren't they?"

Ava leaned forward, transfixed. "I suppose so."

"Go with Anna," Constance said. "We need to talk about grown-up things for a little longer."

"Okay." Lexi scrambled to the floor. "But come back if you have babies!" she called out as she left the room.

Silence followed her exit.

"There are still so few," Vania whispered.

"I understand," Sari said.

"I highly doubt that," Helen said.

Sari's voice was hoarse when she spoke again. "I was pregnant when our retreat was attacked," she said. "My mate was hundreds of miles away. I had… I'd lent him my power so he could fight in Paris. When the attack came, I was injured. My body could not—"

"They killed my son in front of my eyes," Constance said in an icy voice. "The Grigori animal sliced his throat in front of me and he bled over my kitchen floor while his friend held me down, choked my voice silent, and raped me. Thomas was seven years old, and the last thing he saw was animals raping his mother. Do you understand that?"

Ava's body was frozen in horror.

Vania reached for her friend's hand.

No one spoke.

"I only survived the Rending because of my mate. And Jerome was near death when he found me. He said the prayers for our son alone because no one else was left, and my voice was so damaged, I could not sing. I said nothing for twenty years. Nothing."

Sari closed her eyes. "Constance—"

"If I can save *any* mother from seeing that—save any child by rebuilding the retreats. Make them stronger. Make them safer—"

"There is no such thing as total safety," Sari said. "We both know that. *We* have to be stronger. *We* have to defend our children. Defend ourselves."

"We aren't capable of it. Are you so proud that you cannot acknowledge the truth? *We are not as strong as the scribes.*"

"Our power is different, not less."

"Don't you understand?" Constance stood. "Nothing can bring them back. No revenge will ever be enough. No blood can repay what we've lost. Don't you think I've wanted to hunt the animals who killed my son?" Her voice rose. "I could stop their hearts in their chests and pull the blood from their veins. I am a singer of Rafael's line. I could do those things and more. But that will not bring Thomas back."

Renata said, "You should be able to hunt them if you want. You have the right."

Constance shook her head. "Alexis is a miracle. We never thought…" She dragged in a breath and put a hand over her belly. "No one thought I'd be able to conceive another child."

Sari stood to face her. "And I may never have the opportunity to be a mother again. But if I do, I don't want my daughter growing up in fear."

"Your mate is a *legend*. Damien of Bohemia was a Templar knight, for heaven's sake! Don't you trust him to protect you?"

"It's not about trust," Renata said from the back of the room. "It's about using our own power. It's our job to protect them too."

Constance shook her head. "We are not meant for such things. We have a greater purpose. It is our job to rebuild our race. There is magic —healing magic—we can use to increase fertility. To build our families again. I've spent the past hundred years—"

"But that's our whole job?" Ava asked. "Having children to rebuild the Irin race?"

Vania narrowed her eyes. "You know nothing. I don't know where you come from, but every *true* Irina in this room would consider it a blessing to be able to bear a child. We're not like the humans."

Ava looked at the other singer. "I'm not saying motherhood isn't amazing, but that's it? That's all you do?"

"You're ignorant," Helen said. "I have heard the rumors. You grew up among humans. Be quiet and let others speak."

Ava rose to her feet. "*I'm* ignorant?"

Sari put her hand on Ava's arm. "We're done here. Orsala was right. I understand your position. I don't agree with it, but I understand. You deserve to have your voice heard too."

Renata's voice was an ice-cold blade. "Even if she's a fool?"

Constance lifted her chin. "Think that if it makes you feel superior. It doesn't matter to me. I'm not the only Irina who believes compulsion is the best way to save our people."

"I know," Sari said. "And as much as I disagree with you, I hope the Irina council speaks for you too."

"We have no council. We need none."

"That," Sari said as she walked to the door, "is truly ignorant. I'll tell you the same thing I told your mate. It's time. The elder singers are returning, whether you want them to or not."

"Then prepare yourself," Constance said. "The Irina of Vienna will not bow to your wishes. If you reform the council, you and your grandmother won't get puppets."

"Good." Sari opened the door. "We don't want them."

IV.

The man wore an impeccable three-piece suit when he entered the church. His dark hair was cut in the current fashion, and his silk tie was knotted firmly against his throat. After setting down his briefcase at the edge of one pew, he sat next to the ash-blond man in an overcoat who stared at the priest starting the evening mass.

"Where is he?" Barak muttered.

"Playing games."

Vasu entered from the back of the church, not dressed as a human businessman as the other two were, but looking more like one of the artists or musicians crowding the pedestrian street outside. His hair was pulled back in a knot, and he wore a rough beard that tangled in the scarf wrapped around his neck. He sat next to Barak, his physical body making audible noise his brothers avoided.

Jaron and Barak both turned their heads to their brother.

"What are you doing?" they asked as one.

Vasu shrugged. An irritating human habit he'd decided to adopt. "It amuses me."

"You did not ask my permission to track the girl."

"I'm not tracking. I'm watching."

"Enough." Barak's voice cut through their quiet argument. "Is he near? I've shielded myself so thoroughly in this city I'm having difficulty hearing at a distance."

"Is it still so important your children think you're dead?" Vasu asked.

"My reappearance at this stage would alter their actions. I want to see where things lead."

"I've shown you," Jaron said.

"Nevertheless." Barak watched a human mother and small child as they made their way up the center aisle. The child was small. He was fussing in the incense-laden air and his eyes were running. "Where is he, brother?"

"Hungary."

"Is Svarog in play?"

"He will be," Jaron said. "He has created too many vulnerabilities. Volund will use it to sway him to his cause."

"We shall see," Vasu said cryptically.

Barak asked, "What do you know?"

"Know? Nothing. But I have my suspicions." Vasu sat up straighter. "Grimold was never a surprise. He has long been Volund's puppet. But the status quo has been beneficial to Svarog."

"It has," Barak said. "But he knows he will not sway Volund from his path. He may decide backing him will serve his long-term interests."

"That makes little sense," Vasu said, "considering the probable actions of the scribes. This city is complacent, but not without strong magic. There are more mature Irin here now than there have ever been, and Mikhael's armory is here, along with their Library. The Irin blend in with the humans now. They control wealth and power. And their magic has been honed since Volund's last attack."

Barak said, "But they are still without their mates. Most of them are only a fraction of who they could be. And if the Grigora secret comes to light, the Irin will be on the offensive again. Their power will multiply with every mating. They will have purpose again, and a scribe with purpose is a dangerous thing. Volund knows he must strike now."

"The Irin council is not the primary problem," Jaron said, "It is no longer just the scribes we must anticipate. That much is easy. Their council is utterly predictable."

"The singers have returned," Barak and Vasu said together.

"And more are coming."

There was a new light in Vasu's eyes. "The songs have returned to Vienna."

Jaron longed for them. Not the echo of beauty in the Irina voices, but the true songs. He could still hear them, carrying across a crystal sea, rising into the endless sky where he had lived. Surrounding the throne. Jaron had once lived with their beauty in his veins. Their words remained embedded in his very skin.

Every moment. Every step he'd taken since the birth of his daughter had been with this purpose in mind.

He'd forgotten once.

But then his daughter sang to him, and Jaron had remembered beauty.

And he would have it back.

CHAPTER
SEVENTEEN

"I feel like we need to tell them." Ava was lying beside Malachi, enjoying the low morning light as they lingered in bed. He played with the ends of her hair, which were still scented with almonds and amber from the ritual baths the day before.

Malachi had barely been able to contain himself when he'd seen her enter the library with her sisters. Though she was slight, power had radiated from her. He'd heard the curious whispers in the scribe's gallery where he and Damien had watched Sari's powerful address.

"Who is she?"

"Such golden eyes…"

"Whose line?"

"…already mated? With whom?"

Malachi had wanted to crow, *Mine! She is mine.* Pride swelled from his chest as she held her head up against the curious stares.

Damien had stood solid and fearsome in the gallery as he watched his mate. Watched the elders near her with his hawklike stare. The soft scribes of Vienna had given the old warrior a wide berth when his *talesm* began to glow.

Such strong magic. There were few matings as powerful as Damien and Sari's left among the Irin. Every scribe in the gallery was in awe.

Malachi knew that, as the years passed, he and Ava would become stronger. Trials. Battles. Their power would grow until seeing the magic of one was the same as witnessing both.

He hungered for it. And her.

The echo of the Irina's desks hadn't even died before he was bolting from the gallery, but Damien stopped him on the stairs. Their mates were meeting with the Irina of Vienna, and Malachi would have to wait.

"Tell who about what?" he murmured, still half-asleep. He'd sated his appetite for Ava late into the night, intoxicated by the lingering magic on her skin and the scent of her hair.

"I think we need to tell our friends about my grandmother."

"Are you sure?" It was a sensitive subject, and though Malachi worried about Volund's ability to track Ava, he also had confidence in Jaron's protection.

"I don't feel like it's my story to tell," Ava said. "I feel like I'd be telling her secret. But I think the others need to know."

"How about this?" He rolled to his side and propped himself up on his elbow so he could see her face. "Talk to Orsala. Tell her. She will know if it is something that needs to be shared with the others."

"That's a good idea."

"I'm brimming with them."

She smiled and pushed his shoulder. "That was your idea yesterday, wasn't it? For Sari to create a scene."

"I think Sari likes creating scenes. And all the quiet machinations there annoyed me." He rolled to his back and pulled her onto his chest. "Where is the passion in our race?" he asked. "Where is the purpose? We have lost the fire of our mission. Become consumed with ancient lines and intricate interpretations. That is not what we were meant for."

"I thought the scribes' purpose was to preserve knowledge."

"It is. But I felt no love for it in that room. It was all routine and ceremony. No heart. No heat. And we are supposed to use that knowledge to fight the Fallen. To protect humanity. To help them. We cannot protect them if we can't see past our own walls."

"And the singers—"

"The moment the singers withdrew their magic from the human race, we put up walls. We let the fear of loss consume us. And in letting that fear rule us, we abandoned our purpose. We must change."

"Look at you." She smiled down at him. "A visionary."

"I came back for a reason, Ava. The two of us… we are meant for a purpose."

"The *kareshta*?"

"Part of breaking down walls is finding these women you've seen in Jaron's vision. We find them, we kill the Fallen who fathered them, and they will be free."

An odd expression crossed her face.

"What?" he asked.

"I think I'd better cancel that beach shoot in Spain. I don't think taking pictures of girls in bikinis is quite as important as saving the world."

He threw his head back and laughed.

"And we need to complete the mating ritual. I'll talk to Orsala about that too."

Malachi stopped laughing. "No."

* * *　　* * *

SHE WAS ANGRY WITH HIM, BUT HE COULD LIVE WITH THAT. WHAT HE couldn't live with was Ava with even a fraction less power. Eventually, yes. When the current battle was past. When they'd gone back to Istanbul and were able to rest. Then she could complete her half of the ritual.

"I cannot believe you're being so stubborn about this." She railed at him as they entered Damien and Sari's home. "Why do you even get a vote? This is *my* magic."

"Well, since I'm the one who has to tattoo the mark for it to be permanent," he said flippantly, "then I suppose you have no choice."

"I can always start singing when you're asleep. I'd be halfway through by the time you woke up, and you know you'd go along with it."

He stopped so abruptly she ran into his back. Malachi spun and gripped her shoulders.

"Don't try to manipulate me. If you did that—if you denied me even a moment of hearing your mating song—I don't know if I could forgive you, Ava."

She flushed. "Malachi—"

"Don't make threats about something that important. I would never do that to you."

He could see angry tears in the corner of her eyes, but she blinked them back. "But you'd deny me taking that step? Deny my own promise to you?"

"You know why."

"Because it's not safe? News flash: We're in a millennia-long war that shows no signs of dying down. There will never be a time when it's totally safe."

"She's right, you know," Rhys said from the doorway of the library.

Malachi said, "Shut up, Rhys."

"You're the ones making a racket in the hallway when I'm just trying to work." He shot a charming smile at Malachi's mate. "Hello, Ava, you smell amazing. The ritual baths suit you."

She smiled back. "Thank you."

He put a hand over his heart. "I would never deny your mark. Malachi is an idiot."

Malachi leaned against the wall. "I have now detailed fifty-seven specific and effective ways of killing you, Rhys. Would you like me to start listing them?"

"No need. I'm fairly sure your mate is thinking up a comparable list for you right now."

Orsala shouted from inside the library. "You're like children! Bicker bicker bicker."

Ava said, "I keep telling them—"

"You're as bad as the rest of them, Ava."

Malachi, Rhys, and Ava wandered into the library where Orsala was reading a scroll.

"Don't threaten your mate," she chided without looking up. "You would be furious if he did that to you. Rhys, stop antagonizing your brother. Malachi, stop being a stubborn know-it-all. I may have liked you better when you didn't remember anything."

Rhys knocked Malachi's skull with a fist. "There's still plenty of patchy spaces up here, Orsala."

Malachi punched him in the shoulder. Hard.

Ava wandered over to the old singer. "I'm sorry. He's driving me a little crazy this morning."

"That's their job, dear. Sari's grandfather was a menace." She looked up with a smile. "And yet we love them. What are you doing this morning?"

Malachi sat next to Ava and threw an arm around her shoulders. "We were hoping to speak with you privately, as a matter of fact."

Orsala's keen eyes grew even sharper. "Does this have something to do with your grandmother?"

Ava nodded.

"I knew it." Orsala said, "Rhys, that trip you were going to make to the archives. Do it now."

"But—"

"Now."

Muttering about bossy women, the other scribe left the room and shut the door.

"Before we start with anything else," Orsala said, "Ava and Rhys are both correct, Malachi. You need to complete the ritual. Now is as safe a time as any. There is little Grigori activity in the city, and Ava has become known to the Irin hierarchy. Rumors about her history are starting to circulate. She is quite obviously mated, but for the two of you to reach your full potential together, you need to be marked. It might also hasten the return of your power, which we need."

He looked down at his chest. "She sings to me. It's helping."

"It's not enough." The old singer leaned forward. "Stop being so stubborn! Let her protect you too. That is what the mating bond was intended it to be."

"I lost everything when I returned to earth. Ava was all I had. She says I help her remain sane against the voices? Her voice is the only reason I didn't lose my mind when I lost my memories." He felt Ava's hand curl into his, and he squeezed it tight. "Do you truly not understand why I don't want to take a chance?"

"You are holding her back if you don't. And holding yourself back as well." She held up a hand when he opened his mouth again. "Just think about it. Don't hold your mate back because you allow your fear to rule you. Now is not the time for defense, but offense."

Orsala's words were a mirror of his own. Only she was challenging Malachi personally, not the Irin race as a whole.

And Malachi had no defense.

Damn.

"YOU ALREADY KNOW THAT MY GRANDMOTHER IS JARON'S CHILD." Ava started the story after Orsala had called for coffee. "But… she is also Volund's mate."

Orsala sat back and her mouth fell open. "Heaven above."

Malachi kept his arm around Ava's shoulders.

"It was not by choice," she said. "Volund took her from Jaron's protection. He raped her."

"And he marked her?" Orsala said.

Ava nodded. "He wanted to know if it was possible."

"It is." Orsala blinked. "But there would have been no need for it to be violent. Volund is an archangel. He could have seduced—"

"He didn't," Malachi said. "I didn't see the vision she sent Ava until afterward when she shared it with me, but it was *not* a seduction. Volund wanted to terrorize her, and he did."

"I suppose…" Orsala's face was bleak. "I'll admit I suspected something of that nature, though I never imagined rape."

"What do you mean?" Ava asked.

"Your blood." She shook her head. "It never made sense for you to have so much magic with so little of your blood angelic. The Grigori sire children with human women, and they are not magical. Geniuses, yes. Great artists who are often unstable. Not like you. But you're not a normal Grigori—or Grigora in this case—child. You don't have one angel in your line, but two. Your great-grandfather and your grandfather. And both are archangels. It changes things."

"How?" Malachi asked.

Orsala looked at Malachi. "Do you remember when I had Rhys get the copy of *Gabriel's Old Tales* for me?"

"Back in Istanbul. Yes."

"The fairy tales?" Ava asked.

"They're not fairy tales in the human sense," Orsala said. "These are more like… legends. Folk tales, I suppose."

The story popped into his mind immediately, coming from the childhood memories he'd already recovered. "Of course," Malachi said. "'Adelina's Son.'"

"Who's Adelina?" Ava's eyes darted between them.

"'Adelina's Son' is a cautionary tale," Orsala said. "In *Gabriel's Old*

Tales, Adelina is a beautiful and gifted singer—the most treasured daughter of her village and a notable healer of Rafael's line. She appears in many of the tales and is always a very powerful character. But Adelina is also so beautiful that one of the Fallen—some translations imply Bozidar, others imply a lesser angel—fell in love with her and mated with her."

Ava asked, "And that can't happen?"

Malachi shook his head. "Not love. You heard Jaron. The angels are not truly capable of love. Emotion comes from our human blood, not the angelic."

"But it is a story, of course," Orsala said. "Not reality. The story says that Adelina was seduced by this angel and fell in love with him. They lay together and she became pregnant. At first, she was very happy. She sang that her child would be blessed above all others and would be a gift to the world. A child of heaven who would finally reconcile the Irin and the Fallen so we could live in peace."

"This is fiction, right?"

"Is it?" Malachi asked. "In the story, Adelina gives birth to a monster who consumes her as soon as it's born; his father has to kill it before it goes on to terrorize the world."

"Hey." Ava punched his arm. "My father is three-quarters angelic, and he's not violent or scary. Irresponsible and unstable, yes. But he's never hurt anyone but himself. And did they seriously read shit like that to you when you were kids?" She looked horrified. "I mean, that's just wrong."

Orsala patted Ava's hand. "It is a story. It's intended to frighten. And I think in this case it's intended to frighten young Irina away from ever being seduced by one of the Fallen. It's a taboo in our race for a reason."

"And no Irina has ever mated with a Fallen?" Ava asked.

Malachi and Orsala both shuddered.

"No," he said. "I can't even imagine the most rebellious Irina doing something so dangerous. We are taught to run screaming from the Fallen from the time we can walk."

"With stories about monster-babies, I'm not surprised. According to Jaron, it's never happened to one of the *kareshta* either. Just my grandmother."

"The Fallen are possessive of their offspring. Not loving, of course. But proprietary. For one of them to violate Jaron's child would be considered an aggressive act in any case. I'm guessing that for Volund to not only violate Jaron's daughter but then mark her as his own would be an act of war. He essentially stole her and tied her to himself."

"She dream-walks with him."

Orsala was at a loss for words for a moment. "That is… a torture I cannot imagine. And Jaron can do nothing to shield her?"

"When he's physically present with her, she's safe. Other than that? Volund can touch her mind any time she sleeps."

"Can Volund reach you?"

"Yes," Malachi said, "but not when Jaron is shielding her. And as far as we know, he's never lifted his protection."

"No…" Orsala's eyes went blurry. "He won't, of course. Not until he's ready."

"Orsala?"

She blinked and her eyes widened. "Jaron wants Volund."

"Of course." Malachi and Ava exchanged looks. "We've already told you—"

"Jaron wants Volund," she said again, rising to her feet and starting to pace. "He doesn't care about our war with the Fallen. He is at war with *Volund*. But Jaron's forces are depleted. According to rumors, his children are few. Jaron may be more powerful than Volund personally, but his army is not."

Ava frowned. "Yes, but what—"

"Malachi," Orsala said, spinning around. "In a battle, what is the most important step you can take to ensure victory before the fighting even starts?"

"Claim your ground," he answered immediately. "The combatant with a greater position can defeat an enemy more powerful than himself if he picks the right location." Malachi stood when the realization hit. "He's using Ava as bait."

"Jaron has picked his location," Orsala said, staring at Ava. "His and Volund's only blood tie is mated to an Irin scribe and currently residing in the most Irin-powerful city in the world. She's part of us now. A Grigori female mated within our race. Jaron knows we will fight for her."

The soldier in Malachi saw the brilliance of Jaron's move immediately.

"He's shielding Ava as he gathers his allies. And when he's ready…"

Ava's face was pale. "He's using me as bait to draw Volund here so the Irin will be forced to protect me and kill his enemy."

He could see the wheels begin to turn in her head.

Malachi said, "Don't even think about it."

She looked away from him.

"You're not leaving," he said. "That's not even an option, Ava."

Ava glared at him. "I'm putting an entire city at risk. It's stupid for me to stay."

"Where would you go that Volund and Jaron could not find you?" Orsala asked. "At least here we can protect you."

"And risk a battle in the middle of a major metropolitan area?"

Orsala frowned. "He will have thought of that. The Fallen have no desire to attract attention. In any case, Jaron's goals align with our own. Volund needs to die. He masterminded the Rending. He raped your grandmother. He has targeted females of both races for centuries. This is a battle we must fight."

"I agree, but I don't think the entire city of Vienna needs to be part of the carnage."

"So what are you going to do?" Malachi asked. "Run away?"

"Why should I stick around to be a pawn in their game?"

"Jaron is a powerful ally," Orsala said. "We've never worked with one of the Fallen before. Nor have they attempted to work with us. And yet it appears he wishes to do so. We should not dismiss him. Whatever plan he has will work to our advantage. If you leave, that could complicate things."

"And might possibly save thousands of lives," Ava said. "I should be in the middle of nowhere, where no one else can get hurt."

Malachi blurted out, "If you stay without arguing, I'll let you complete the mating ritual."

Ava's jaw dropped. "Unbelievable."

Without another word, she turned and left the room.

Malachi turned to Orsala. She was shaking her head. Her eyes pressed closed. His mother's mental voice had started to lecture him again.

"I can't help you with that one," Orsala said.

"Bad timing?"

CHAPTER

EIGHTEEN

"Ava, wait!"

She heard his voice, but she didn't stop. She'd grown comfortable on the streets here. There was no scent of Grigori in the air, and she'd learned to find her way around. She headed back to the apartment and didn't turn, even when she heard him getting closer.

"Ava, stop!"

He caught up with her a few blocks from the apartment.

"I'm sorry," he said, clutching her shoulders. "*Canim*, I—"

She shook him off. "And you accused *me* of being manipulative?"

"I know."

"No." She walked away, burying her hands in the pockets of her coat. "You really, really don't."

They were starting to attract attention, so they kept walking. Malachi fell in step beside her but didn't try to touch her again.

"Would it help if I told you I'd decided on it before you threatened to leave?"

She nodded. "Oh, so you were just holding that one in reserve for a moment when you needed to get your way."

"No. Not… exactly."

"Got it."

"I'd only just decided! Why are you trying to start a fight with me?"

"Nope. This isn't starting a fight. This is *fighting*. This is the two of us fighting over you being a controlling asshole."

It irritated her that she was walking as fast as she could, and yet he kept up with her effortlessly.

"Ava." He sighed.

She reached the front door and opened it with the key, ignoring how his hand reached out to hold the door for her. How he stopped to make sure it closed securely behind them. How he brushed a drift of snow from her shoulder.

Ava started up the stairs. The black cat was waiting at the door. It slipped in when she opened it and ran to the window to watch the street. Malachi followed behind her.

"What do I do to fix this?"

She was angry. Frustrated. Mostly, she was hurt. "I don't know. I honestly don't. It's supposed to be special. I've been memorizing all the songs for weeks now, so worried that I wouldn't be able to do things right. That I'd mess things up and embarrass myself. And you! And then… you don't want it. Do you know how that makes me feel?"

Rejected.

She didn't want to say it, because she knew he loved her. Knew he was proud to be her mate. But a lifetime of rejection from her father— from every man in her life—wouldn't disappear just by Malachi loving her. She wished it would.

Ava stripped off her coat and scarf, turned up the thermostat, and went to start the kettle for tea. She'd drunk so much coffee in the past few days she thought her stomach lining might start a revolt.

She felt his hands on her shoulders. Felt the roughness of his beard against her neck. "I want it."

"Maybe you're right. It's probably not a good idea. Not when Jaron is using me as bait. We don't understand Volund's connection with me. It might make you vulnerable too."

He wrapped his arms around her waist. "Please don't do this. It was stupid for me to say it then, but it doesn't mean I wasn't sincere."

"So you'll go through the rest of the mating ritual with me, but only if I agree to stay in Vienna?"

"You're not truly thinking of leaving, are you?"

She didn't say anything. She *was* thinking about it. Orsala and

Malachi could scheme all they wanted, but the fact of the matter was if Ava stayed in the city and people were killed in some massive angelic battle, she'd never be able to live with herself.

His arms tightened. "You can't be serious."

"If I leave, then who do they have to kill but each other? No Irin would be forced into battle—"

"And you'd be caught in the middle." He stepped back.

She turned slowly. "I am one person. We're talking about thousands—"

"We're talking about you! My mate. Do you honestly think I'd leave you unprotected?"

Ava said nothing. If she left, Malachi would have a hard time finding her, even with Rhys's help. She could go to her mother and Carl. If she asked Carl to make her disappear somewhere, he'd do it. He'd probably be grateful.

He put his hands on her cheeks. "Stop it."

"I'm not doing anything."

"You're leaving me in your mind," he whispered. "Don't do it. Don't you know I'd rather die than lose you?"

She shook her head. "I need to think."

"Enough!" He cut his hand through the air. "You're not going anywhere. I forbid it."

"Oh really?" She balled up the power welling in her chest and said, "*Ya fasham.*"

Malachi's eyes widened in shock as the unbalancing spell hit him full force. He reeled to the side and fell over. Ava stepped to the door and grabbed her coat and scarf. Then she threw another spell at him that Sari had taught her, and Ava knew Malachi's legs were going to be immobilized long enough for her to leave.

"Ava!"

Okay, his mouth could move.

"I'm going out for a walk."

"What did you do?"

"You're a smart guy, I'm sure you'll figure it out."

The cat had come to sit on his chest.

"Ava!"

She ran down the stairs and flagged down the first taxi she could find.

"Zentralfriedhof," she told the driver. "Gate two."

*   *   *   *   *   *

AVA DIDN'T KNOW WHY SHE WAS SO ATTRACTED TO CEMETERIES. MAYBE it was the quiet. For as long as she'd been alive, she'd found them soothing. She could walk among others, never feeling alone, but not plagued by the voices of the living. No matter what city she visited, she sought them out, content to linger among the dead while the living only tormented her.

The Central Cemetery in Vienna was one of the largest in Europe, containing the graves of many of Austria's most famous composers. Knowing what she did now about Irin history there and the Irina tie to music, the city's musical history made even more sense.

She walked the barren pathways toward the church, surrounded by grey headstones and the rare passing tourist. Some spaces were overgrown, but most on the central walkway were trimmed and many had freshly cut flowers, even in the dead of winter. It was one of her favorite cemeteries, a veritable city of the dead. Carefully tended, trimmed with lush gardens and populated by the marble figures of angels, poets, and mourners.

And Ava was freezing.

She tucked her scarf closer around her neck and wondered just how mad Malachi was going to be. Probably pretty mad.

It was the "I forbid it" that had been the last straw.

No. Just no.

He might have been hundreds of years older than her, but she wasn't a child to order around.

She turned left past the graves of famous composers, leaving Strauss, Beethoven, and Schubert behind as she searched for the gravestone that had become her first magazine cover.

It was a darkly sensual embrace emerging from stone. The male figure's hands possessive. Commanding. An odd sculpture to find on the grave of an obscure nineteenth-century writer. But it had spoken to her, the woman's face tilted up to her lover in surrender.

Ava remembered how she'd felt when she photographed it.

Longing. For possession. To belong to another utterly. To be precious. Needed.

She heard a hoarse chirp by her leg. She looked down to see the black cat from her apartment building sitting by her leg.

"What the—"

Before her eyes, the cat grew, stretching in the shadows of the evergreen trees that surrounded the old graves. He became a man with gold eyes, his dark hair streaked with amber. His lips were lush, the angles of his face and eyes speaking Eastern heat. Silk and spices. Hooded eyes lined with black stared down at her.

"Your lover holds you that way."

"Holy shit," she breathed out.

"No, Vasu."

"Who are you?"

He cocked his head, as if it should have been obvious. "Vasu."

Ava blinked. "Okay then, Vasu. *What* are you?"

"Isn't it obvious?"

Awe turned to irritation. "First Jaron, then Death, now you—"

"Azril? Has he visited you?" Vasu cocked his head. "How interesting."

"I'm really just wondering if I should run screaming at this point, or if you're a friend of Jaron's."

"I would not call your sire a friend, but he is my brother. And screaming would do you no good. If I wanted to kill you, I would have already."

Ava turned to look around. All the humans that had been in the vicinity—groundskeepers, carriage drivers, a few tourists—were gone. She was alone with the fallen angel in the long black overcoat who called Jaron his brother.

She narrowed her eyes. "Why were you pretending to be a cat?"

"Why not? Cats are very unobtrusive. I often pretend to be a cat."

"That's…"

"Ingenious?"

"Weird."

A smile lifted the corner of his lips. "You are amusing. I can see why Jaron and Azril are interested in you."

"Does Jaron know you're here? How did you find me?"

"I followed your taxi after I left the scribe. He is very angry with you."

"I bet." Ava took a deep breath, reassured that the angel didn't seem to be trying to kill her. "You must run really fast as a cat."

"No, I took the shape of a bird when you entered the automobile."

"Of course you did."

Ava started walking toward the church. Vasu fell in step beside her.

"You're not really going to leave Vienna, are you?" He sounded as irritated as Malachi had. "It will ruin everything. And I don't like being here."

"Vienna?"

"It's very cold."

"What am I ruining? Jaron's plans to use me as bait to draw Volund here and use the Irin to help kill his enemy?"

"I believe Jaron has every intention of killing Volund himself. The Irin are only useful to take care of the Grigori and lesser angels. You would be no match for Volund."

"There aren't any Grigori in Vienna."

Vasu's mouth ticked up at the corner, and he looked past her. "Are you sure?"

She smelled it when the wind kicked up. A hint of sandalwood on the air.

"What have you done?" she hissed. "Did you lead them to me?"

"Don't be ridiculous. Grimold's sons have been trailing you for days." Vasu opened his jacket and Ava saw a row of silver daggers. "Come, Singer. Choose your weapon. Or have you learned to fight with magic alone?"

She ripped two daggers from his coat and turned to scan her surroundings. The cemetery was still utterly empty except for the two men who stood at the end of the row, black against the limestone path. Ava turned and saw two more.

"They're tracking me?" she asked.

"There are two more by the gate where you entered. How fast can you run?"

"Not fast enough." She began whispering a spell of protection around her mind. She was mostly immune to Grigori seduction, but she didn't want to take any chances. "If they're just tracking me—"

"No." Vasu cocked his head. "They want you. For what, I don't know."

Ava started running. There would be few taxis near the main road, not as far out of the city center. But the tram line ran near the main road. If she could get out of the gate…

"What are you doing?" Vasu ran beside her. Or did he? The Fallen didn't even look like he was moving, but… he was.

"Trying to escape. I'm not stupid; it's six against one. Are you going to help me or what?"

"I can't really do anything to them unless they attack me. And they won't attack me. It wouldn't be courteous."

"Must be nice!" She could hear their steps coming closer. "Listen," she panted. "Really nice to meet you, but I'm kind of fighting for my life here, so if you're not going to help—"

"If you promise to stay in Vienna, I will help."

"What?" she rasped out a breath. "You too?"

She cursed the immortal lives of stubborn men everywhere.

"I want this to be over. I want to go back to Chittorgarh."

"I don't know where that is, but… fine. I'll stay here."

"You vow this?"

"Yes!"

"Excellent."

Then Vasu grinned—actually grinned—and it was brilliant, beautiful, and utterly cruel. Her body came to a halt and Vasu came behind her.

"Turn."

Ava spun and the two Grigori soldiers were right on top of her. The spell came to her mind immediately.

"*Shanda vash,*" Ava whispered, and she felt and heard the whisper of Vasu's voice overlaying hers.

The Grigori soldiers didn't just stop, they flew back as if thrown by an invisible hand.

"*Man.*"

"Good," he whispered in her ear. "Now sing with me."

He whispered again, and she moved, racing toward the Grigori, both blades in her hands. She could feel Vasu like a shadow at her back.

Magic hummed in her veins as she whispered the next spell. "*Ba dahaa.*"

Both men screamed, clutching their temples in agony as she leapt on them.

"Now," Vasu whispered, and she kicked one in the side, her body reacting as if she were a trained soldier. The thought was in the back of her mind that she wasn't entirely in control of her body, but when she heard the shouts of the other Grigori and the approaching foot-steps, she ignored it.

"Now, Ava!"

She twisted the head of one Grigori to the side, plunging the silver dagger into his neck. He began to dissolve beneath her, even as his friend tried to roll away.

Vasu pushed her toward him, whispering another spell in her ear.

"*Zi yada*," she hissed and the soldier froze.

These weren't Irina spells. Had nothing to do with what she'd been taught, but Vasu whispered them in her ear, the formless mass of him at her back, and she repeated his words, the dark power in her rising to the surface.

Not Irina magic. Fallen magic.

It came as easy as breathing.

"*Kareshta*," Vasu murmured as she plunged the dagger into the neck of the second Grigori. "Beautiful."

He rose as she did, turning and stripping off her coat so she could move. Her black shirt clung to her body like a second skin, and Ava ran toward the men who would pursue her, gold eyes flashing in rage, with Vasu pressing against her back.

They killed my son in front of my eyes… the last thing he saw was animals raping his mother.

Constance's pain was all she could hear as she threw her remaining knife, catching a Grigori in the eye.

"*Zi yada!*"

The Grigori collapsed to the ground and froze.

Another knife was in her hand, pressed there by Vasu's hand.

"Again."

Another dagger flung. Another bleeding Grigori on the ground.

He writhed as Ava ran to him, Vasu her shadow and the dust of the first two Grigori coating her lips.

The rage took her, spurred by the angel's voice in her ear.

"Kill him."

Ava didn't kill him cleanly. She stabbed the soldier in the gut twice, slicing up to his throat, slashing it as his blood spurted over her and tears ran down her face. Vasu's voice still whispered in her ear.

"They killed your sisters. Take your revenge. You deserve it and more."

She felt her gorge rise as she flipped the man over and stabbed him in the back of the neck.

"No more," Ava groaned.

"Finish it."

She plunged the blade into the neck of the fourth Grigori and waited, her hand frozen as the gold dust began to rise around her.

Vasu was in front of her, crouching down with fire in his eyes.

"The other two fled."

"Okay," she sobbed.

"That was beautiful, Ava."

Then Vasu leaned forward and gently kissed her on the lips.

The magic left in the space of a heartbeat, and Ava crawled to the bushes near an overgrown grave and threw up everything in her stomach. Vasu watched her with a curious expression.

"What do you feel? Guilt?"

"I don't know what I feel. I want to go home."

"Hmm." He stretched out next to her on the gravel path, ignoring the grit that must have embedded in his palms. He didn't move like Jaron did. This creature was at home in his body. "Where is home to you, I wonder? Not America."

Malachi.

Malachi was home. Wherever he was. However angry he was with her or she with him, Malachi was home, and she needed him.

"Fine," Vasu murmured. "I'll take you to the scribe."

A tug in her belly, and then they were in the entryway of Ava and Malachi's apartment. She'd lost her coat. Her hair was tangled around her face, and she was covered in blood.

"Ava!" Malachi ran toward her, eyes on the angel who held her.

Vasu winked out of sight, and Ava collapsed.

"What happened?"

He picked her up and carried her to the bedroom, but Ava put her hand on the doorjamb.

"Shower. I have to get it off."

"Is this your blood?" His voice was panicked.

"Their blood. Their dust."

She licked her lips and tried to spit out the grit that had collected there.

"Who was that?"

"Vasu. Jaron's brother."

"Did the Fallen do this to you?"

"Grigori," she whispered as he opened the shower door and started stripping the bloody clothes off her. "They're here."

* * * * * *

SHE CURLED INTO HIS CHEST, TRYING TO CRAWL INTO AS MUCH OF HIS heat as possible. Malachi had already called Damien and told him about the attack at the cemetery and Vasu's appearance. Rhys was digging into anything he could find on the archangel from the Indian subcontinent who was supposed to be dead.

"He wasn't dead," she whispered into his chest. "He... helped me. It was like he was in my body."

"*In* your body?"

"No, that's not right. More like he was... behind me maybe. Pushing me. I felt him with me the whole time. I moved so fast, Malachi. I've never moved that fast on my own. And he whispered spells to me. Magic I've never heard before, but it worked. Using those spells was as easy as breathing."

Malachi was silent for a minute, but his arms never left her. He'd wrapped himself around her and was holding her as if she might fall apart.

When Ava closed her eyes and remembered the blood spurting from the Grigori's throat, she felt like she might.

"But this Vasu didn't hurt you?"

"No, he helped. And the minute I thought about you, he brought me back here."

"So he could have taken you from there at any time?"

She nodded.

"Why?"

"What do you mean?"

"If he wanted to help you, why didn't he just take you away immediately? Bear in mind, I've never heard of a Fallen who can transport others, only themselves, so this might be unique to him. I don't know his power."

"I don't think he wanted to take me away. I think he was curious."

"Curious?"

"He made me promise to stay in Vienna, because he didn't like the cold. I have a feeling whoever Vasu is, Jaron is still the one in charge."

"He made you promise to stay in Vienna because he doesn't like the cold?"

"Yep. Whatever Jaron's plan is, this Vasu guy wants to get it over with."

"This sounds like a very odd angel."

She nodded. "He was the cat."

Malachi pulled away. "What?"

"The black cat who wandered in here? That was him."

Malachi cursed long and low.

"Hey, at least he got me to promise to stay in Vienna, right? You should be happy."

He squeezed her more tightly. "I don't care where we are. I only want you safe."

Ava's love for him was an ache in her heart. She kissed his chest, over his heart. Up his neck. Trailing her lips across his jaw.

"Kiss me," she whispered.

"Ava—"

"Please. I need you."

He met her mouth, his arms everything warm and real and safe. She was back at the cemetery, looking at the statue of the lovers, but it was Malachi who held her. Malachi who needed her. Malachi who was everything…

Everything.

She pushed him to his back, and his fingers dug into the small of her back as she crawled over him. When she sat up, he followed her, rocking up to take her mouth as Ava straddled his lap. She could feel him, hard and real beneath her, not a lover made of stone, but a man burning for her.

"Malachi."

"Want you," he breathed out, burying his hands in the waves of her hair, still damp from the shower. Her skin felt clean, but she hadn't felt whole again until he touched her. She dug her fingers into his shoulders as she felt the magic rise. Her mating marks began to glow in the dark room. His *talesm* shone with a silver light.

"*Reshon,*" she whispered. "My *reshon.*"

"Ava."

She threw her head back and felt the magic take over. The song hung in her throat, ready to be released.

Malachi put both hands on her cheeks, turning her face to meet his kiss. He drew back with a groan, the dark fire burning in his eyes.

"I'm ready," she whispered. "So ready. Please, let me sing to you. It's time."

Her mate wrapped his arms around her waist and nodded.

"Sing."

CHAPTER
NINETEEN

Volund lifted his head and raged against the heavens, shattering the frozen valley where he rested. A chasm split the earth, raining water, ice, and mud into the rift that formed beneath his feet.

"NO!"

The blood boundaries were falling. He could feel the power of his old rival's blood twine within the blessings of the Forgiven.

Jaron was winning.

In his mind's eye, he saw the black sun rise as light and dark magic melded together. And as the moon's shadow covered the sun, the light from the stars hidden for a thousand years blinked to life.

"Do not fear the darkness."

His scream reached the heavens.

* * *   * * *

MALACHI LAY IN THRALL TO HIS MATE. RISING ABOVE HIM, AVA WAS a vision in the dim room. Her hair damp against her shoulders, her skin dewy from the warmth of the shower and their shared heat. He braced himself, not knowing what to expect. Though he knew some of the traditions—the songs and litanies she had learned—the mating ritual happened only once in a scribe's lifetime. In this moment, he was as innocent as Ava.

He felt rather than heard when she started to sing.

"My beloved comes to me as the ground beneath my feet
Steadfast and faithful
The heavens direct our path..."

The words of the Old Language rose from her throat, her lips carefully forming the angelic tongue. Halting at first, then clearer as the magic took control of them both. Ancient instinct took over. He pushed the shirt she was wearing up and over her head, desperate to see his own vow written on her skin.

I am for Ava.

He released a breath when he saw it. Part of him was still transfixed every time it appeared over her heart. His finger traced the words he'd written. A memory locked in the black vault of his mind.

For her, my hand and voice.
For her, my body and mind.
Her strength in weakness.
Her sword in battle.
Her balm in pain.
I am hers.
Hers to cherish.
Hers to hold.
Hers to command.

The world around him ceased to exist. There was no city. No war. No angels or brothers or elders. Nothing could distract him from the purity of her voice. Her mating marks gleamed in the darkness as she continued to sing.

"My beloved holds me as the sky holds the moon
Vast and eternal
Our union is without end..."

Ava pushed his shirt up and over his head so they were both bare before the other. Her voice rose and fell as she sang the words legend said were given by the Forgiven to their children. The vows that bound them, not only in this life, but the next.

"My beloved warms me as the sun warms the earth
Sweet and rich
Our love mirrors the heavens..."

He felt the magic swell. The small electric lamp by the bedside flickered out and the only illumination was from the small window and the spells that lit their bodies. Tugged from his chest, the power spread over his skin, lighting his *talesm prim*, both old marks and new, before it traveled up and over, like a thread of quicksilver under his skin.

Malachi burned for her.

"My beloved is my own
First before others.
Before the bond of kin
Before mother or father
Brother or sister
Before the angelic host…"

He could feel her voice swell, reach a crescendo.

"This day I make my vow
I pledge my soul's magic to my beloved
In time of joy
In time of grief
In darkness and light
In life and death
This day I promise…"

And Malachi waited to hear the words she would give him, the words he would carve into his own skin in the ritual room, marking his body and heart as hers for all time. The words he would wear for the world to see that his mate had claimed him as her own.

"I promise," Ava whispered as she wrapped her arms around his neck, "to love you and protect you in every way I can. I will not let fear rule me. I will trust you with my heart and my song." He heard her choke back tears, and he pressed her cheek to his as she continued. "Because I called you in the darkest night of my soul. You heard me and you returned." She brushed a kiss across his temple. "You are my home."

She sat back and framed his face with her hands, looking into his eyes as she whispered, *"Da livkara bavatara ma."*

This scribe belongs to me.

The force of the mating spell drew a groan from his throat as it hit him, powerful and sweet. Ava's magic was blinding light edged in darkness. He closed his eyes as his back arched and the fire burned beneath his skin.

"Ava!"

"Stay still." She braced her hands on his shoulders as he leaned back and let the power of it wash over him. "Don't move. I can see them."

"I can *feel* them."

Pleasure and pain roiled in one intoxicating wave as the burning grew. He felt the knife dip into the fire and ink. The doors of memory slamming open in his mind.

Through the searing pain, he felt her. Through the flood, she held him. Her magic lifted him, turning his mind in circles as the invisible knife carved the ancient runes. Over his shoulders and chest. Down his arm and across his back.

"Touch me, Ava," he groaned. "Please."

"I don't want to hurt you."

"You won't."

He needed her to anchor him, because the flood of magic began to take him under. He could feel his power rushing back. It was like waking up after a vivid dream. Days and weeks and years tumbled in his mind, like the strands of an intricate tapestry tangling, unraveling, then forming something new. But the pattern was familiar. These were his years. His moments. His words.

They fell into his mind until their weight threatened madness.

Then…

One piece locked into place.

I heard you!

A hiss of steel and the bite against his skin.

Another piece locked.

"Do you have a name?"

A name?

"My name is Malachi."

Another and another and another.

Colored threads twisting in a hedgerow. Pine needles on the forest floor. Salt and cedar and wind in the pines.

In the crash of memory he became hers again.

"You make the voices go away."

A kiss.

One touch that had changed the world.

"You're not crazy, Ava. You're a miracle."

A miracle.

He didn't know what was real except for her.

She was real. The single voice in his mind.

"Come back to me."
So he did.

. . .   . . .

"MALACHI."

He heard her. Smelled the magic in the room like the lingering bite of ozone after a storm.

"Malachi?"

He blinked his eyes open and saw… everything.

Ava's hair hung around her face, a dark halo surrounding radiant gold eyes. Her mating marks still lit the room, and a sheen of silver reflected on her breasts. He looked down, then looked back at Ava. Her smile trembled on her lips.

"They're back."

He nodded. He could feel every inch, even the aching scars on his back where he knew his family marks had returned. But he couldn't take his eyes from her face. She must have given him new eyes, because his mate's skin was luminous.

"Does it hurt?"

Malachi paused. He knew that it must hurt. His brain registered the pain in his arms. But it was nothing to the pure jolt of power her mating song had given him.

"Will you say something?"

"No."

He sat up, wrapped his arms around her waist, and tackled her to the bed.

Ava gasped as he covered her. His mouth fell on hers in a ravenous kiss. He felt her breasts crushed against his chest. His hands tangled in her hair. Heat and magic and hunger swirled together in a vicious cocktail of need.

Malachi kissed her mouth, opening her lips with his tongue to taste her. Stroking along the lips that had worked such painful, beautiful magic. He bit her lower lip, sucked it into his mouth, and released it before he did the same to her upper.

One of her hands clutched his hair, the other dug into his neck, pulling him closer as her legs wrapped around his waist.

Jaw. Neck. Throat.

He let his lips linger at the rapid pulse in her neck as she gasped for breath.

Then his lips and tongue went lower, tasting the golden skin of her breasts, teasing frantic cries of pleasure from her. He bit the inner curve that tempted him, marking her with his teeth as he pressed up at the small of her back. He lifted her soft belly to his lips. He could feel his aching skin stretch and heal around the black ink that had reappeared, but the silver glow of the magic she'd given him was a pure current running through his body.

He pressed forward, taking her mouth again.

She was his. Every inch of her. Every breath. Every cry.

"Malachi, I need you."

His to cherish. His to hold.

He ran a hand down the curve of her waist to her hip, stroking back and squeezing the tight round muscle in the palm of his hand. He pressed up and in, holding her there as the scent of her arousal filled the room.

"Please," she whispered. "Please."

He released her mouth only long enough to tear away the loose pants she wore. Then he shoved down his own and he was over her, poised at her entrance.

"Ava," he commanded. "Look at me."

Gold eyes met grey.

"You are mine."

"Yes."

Malachi drove into his mate with one thrust, sinking to the hilt and allowing his face to fall into her neck on a groan.

He closed his eyes and saw it again, a gold sky streaked with light.

Holy and wholly.

Their union a perfect mirror of eternity as their magic met and twined together. Light and dark spun in an endless whorl.

FAST. THEN SLOW. FAST AGAIN.

"You're going to kill me," she panted after the second time they'd come together, and Malachi showed no sign of slowing down.

"Never."

Malachi teased her for hours, the potent cocktail of magic and endorphins forming a perfect storm of sexual energy. Ava was wrung out. Exhausted.

But he could also feel her happiness.

Her contentment was a balm over his soul. He could feel the magic she'd sacrificed to bond herself to him, but he refused to let fear spoil her gift.

"I love your vow." He stretched his arms over his head as she rode him.

She bent down, ran her lips over the flat, sensitive nipple surrounded by spells. Let her lips trail over the skin where he'd put her words.

"I will be proud to wear it," he said.

"I'm glad."

"I promise to always be a good home, Ava."

She paused and looked at him, her eyes stripped of every defense.

Malachi whispered, "A safe home. Always."

"I know."

"No matter where we go," he continued. "No matter what happens as the years pass, I promise."

He sat up, held her cheeks with both hands and watched her smile spread.

"I love you."

"I came back to you," he said. "I remember. It was a choice, and I chose you."

Ava's jaw dropped when she realized what he was talking about. "Was it beautiful?"

"Very."

"I'm so sorry."

"Don't. I told you," he said, rubbing his thumb over her trembling lip. "I'd abandon heaven if you weren't there."

"How can I repay that?" she said. "There's nothing—"

"There is no debt. Love is not a debt. It's a promise. And I promised you once that I'd be back. Don't you remember?"

"In the cistern," she said. "Before—"

"I promised." He smiled when he pinched her chin. "You only had to call me, *canim*. You may not have noticed this, but sometimes your mate is forgetful."

She laughed and laughed, and that too was a balm on his soul.

Because though Malachi had left her, he hadn't known to miss her in heaven. Not until she called.

Ava pressed a delicate kiss to his lips. "I'm glad you're back," she said against his mouth.

"I don't plan on leaving again." He rolled so she was under him. "And now I have a powerful singer as my mate."

She arched her back and ran her hands over his shoulders, along his biceps, and over the spells on his forearms until she could wrap her fingers around his wrists. "And I have a magnificent scribe who has claimed me."

He flexed his hips against hers and hummed in satisfaction when she moaned.

"You do."

"Make me yours again."

He leaned down, bracing an arm near her shoulder as he took her mouth.

"Always."

CHAPTER
TWENTY

S he watched him as he left for the Library. He'd woken before dawn to go and tattoo the mating vow on his chest. And though he would only be walking through the city center, he was strapping silver daggers to his body, taking every precaution before he left her.

"You're staring," he whispered. "You should go back to sleep."

"I'm not tired. And you're too beautiful not to stare at."

He smiled. It might have been just a little smug. But then, they'd both been voracious the night before. Ava guessed it was only the magic making her restless.

"Damien will be here in a minute," he said, sitting on the edge of the bed. "How do you feel?"

"I don't feel weaker or anything like that."

He tucked a piece of her hair behind her ear. "With Grigori in the city, I don't want you going anywhere alone. Normally we would have performed our mating away from everything. Taken time apart to give our bond time to mature so we would both be at full strength. We probably should have done it at my grandparents' house when we were there."

"We weren't ready then."

"No."

She took a deep breath and traced the line of a tattoo that peeked over his collar. "Do you really remember everything?"

"Yes. Including how stubborn you've always been. You pulled a gun on me once," he said with a grin.

"I thought you were a nefarious kidnapper. Bent on seducing me and stealing me away."

"That sounds like an excellent plan."

"Yes, let's do that."

He grabbed her hand and kissed it. "Until we can, I want you to be careful."

"The spells Vasu told me, they were pretty effective."

"Hmm."

She'd written down what they had sounded like to her, but he hadn't recognized the words. She'd told him the instant effect—both the excruciating mental pain and the paralysis they'd caused—and he'd been impressed.

"What are you thinking?"

"I'm thinking that the Fallen and Forgiven might have very different magic."

Ava frowned. "Isn't it all basically the same thing?"

Malachi shrugged. "Yes? I don't really know, to be honest. The Old Language is the angelic tongue, but you have to remember we only have what our ancestors were taught. We're talking about thousands of years of oral and written tradition following that. Irin magic has changed over time. I'm sure of it. It could be the spells Vasu taught you are words that have been forgotten. Or were never given to us at all."

"Well, I'm not forgetting them. If I can use those against Grigori—"

"I still want you to be careful. The Grigori advantage has always been numbers. In Vienna, that threat is mitigated because of the larger Irin population. At the same time, it's a city of bureaucrats and politicians, not active soldiers."

"I'll be careful."

He pressed a hard kiss to her lips. "Thank you, *canim*. That puts my mind at ease. I'm going to the ritual room with Rhys, but we'll be back as soon as I'm done."

She spread her hand over his heart. "So it's going here, huh?"

He nodded.

"Do I need to write it down for you?"

He shook his head. "I remember every word."

"Good."

Malachi stood and stretched his shoulders. "It doesn't hurt, but I feel them. I don't know how to describe it."

"You really remember everything?" She didn't know why she was having a hard time believing it, but she was. "Really?"

His smile turned wicked. "Yes. Even that thing you told me you like when—"

A quiet knock came at the door.

"Oh look." She jumped up and threw on her robe. "Sounds like Damien. You better go."

His low chuckle followed her out the bedroom door.

Yes, her mate was definitely back.

Malachi waited at the door until he heard Damien's quiet voice, then he cracked it open and greeted his brother with a solid embrace. Damien started in surprise until he pulled back and looked into his brother's eyes.

"You're back?" he asked. Damien's warm eyes turned to Ava. "He's back. Sister?"

Ava shrugged. "We completed our mating ritual. And when I gave him my magic, it just…"

Damien clapped Malachi on the shoulder. "And your *talesm*?"

"Complete." He patted his left chest. "Except for one very important one here."

"This is a beautiful day," Damien said. "I'll call Sari after you've left. She'll want to plan a mating feast for you."

Ava said, "That's really not necessary. I mean—"

"It is," Damien said. "Part of rebuilding our people is recovering our traditions. Sari and I have already claimed you as a sister. Please let us, Ava."

Ava threw her arms around the big man. "Thank you."

Damien kissed the top of her head. "I hadn't planned to let you go, you know. Just because he came back. You're our family now."

"Give me my mate," Malachi pulled her away from Damien. "A kiss before I go."

It was sweet, lingering, and long. Malachi paid no mind to his audience, even if that audience was his watcher and the man who'd claimed Ava as a younger sister.

He only pulled away when Damien started laughing.

"Go," he said. "Put her brand on your chest before you see her again. I'll keep her safe."

"Stay with Damien," he said, his hand on her cheek. "I'll be back soon."

She nodded and he slipped out the door.

Then Ava took a deep breath and turned to Damien. "Coffee?"

"Please. And you need to tell me about this angel you met. Malachi called, but I want to hear it from you."

"Fine." She started the water. "But I want to know about this rumor I heard about the Templar Knights."

"Damn gossiping Irina," he muttered.

HE WAS SILENT FOR A LONG TIME AFTER SHE DESCRIBED THE FIGHT she'd had with the four Grigori at the cemetery.

"All the humans disappeared?"

She nodded. "Jaron did the same thing once. He said something about them being in a dream."

"We know the Fallen can manipulate time and human perception. It must have something to do with that."

"Whatever his reasons, Vasu did protect me. I didn't even know the Grigori had followed me, and I'm usually pretty good at spotting a tail after years of having bodyguards when I travel. I'd let down my guard."

Damien shrugged. "Or he led them to you to see what you'd do. We have no idea what his motives could be."

"He was… oddly honest. I think he's an ally of Jaron's. He could have hurt me anytime he wanted. I'd let him in the apartment when he was a cat."

"A cat? Malachi left that part out."

Ava explained as she downed another cup of coffee and devoured the breakfast pastry Damien had brought. If it weren't for the typical voracious Irina metabolism, she'd blow up like a whale. The sweets in Vienna were out of this world.

"I've never heard of one shifting to an animal before, but that could be something unique to this Vasu. Perhaps the same talent that allows him to transport you over distances."

"Aren't angels basically the same?"

"No." Damien stood to get himself another coffee. "They were created to perform different duties, therefore they have different talents. That's why a daughter of Leoc has visions, but a daughter of Ariel has an affinity for the elements, like Sari." He lifted an eyebrow. "Can you move rocks and wood?"

Ava grinned. "That was pretty cool at the Library, huh?"

Damien's mouth lifted in the corner. "She was a vision. I was the envy of every scribe in that room."

"I love that you're not intimidated by her power. By how outspoken she is."

"Why would I be? It only makes me stronger." He sighed. "You lived in the human world for too long."

"I'm better now."

"I remember when I first met you."

"You were so suspicious."

"You were so jumpy."

They both smiled, and Ava was glad—as painful as Malachi's loss had been—that she'd found Damien.

She put a hand over his. "It's good to have a brother."

• • •　• • •

THE MATING FEAST AT DAMIEN AND SARI'S HOUSE WASN'T QUITE THE grand event that Ava had imagined. It was more like a really fun, really long dinner party with lots of speeches and blessings. Everyone stood up to say something really eloquent or really funny. All the scribes from the Istanbul house were there, along with Renata and Mala. Orsala, Sari, and Damien were the hosts. Sari and Damien's brother-in-law had also been invited. Gabriel was the mate of Sari's sister, who had died during the Rending. Ava could see the tension between him and Damien, but she didn't ask questions.

She was too happy.

Malachi was at her side. The passionate, intense man who had slowly been returning to her was back completely. He joked with his brothers. Held her close to his side all night. Teased her shamelessly and was quick to open his shirt and show off the new mating mark to anyone who asked.

He also watched every door and window like commandos might crash through at any time.

"Relax," she whispered to him when she'd gone to stand by the window and watch the moon. He'd drawn her away from the window without a word, distracting her with a kiss.

"What are you talking about?"

"You. You've been like… poised for action all night."

He slid his hand down to cup her bottom. "Well, if you'd like to leave now—"

"That's not what I'm talking about," she said with a laugh as she wiggled away. "You and Max and Leo looked all over the city today. And I know you've got some of your buddies outside right now. We're not going to be invaded by enemy forces."

His smile wavered. "We don't know that."

"What did Orsala find out about Vasu?"

"That he was supposedly killed by the archangel Galal over two centuries ago. But before then, he'd been an ally of Jaron's in Central Asia. He was also known as one of the more… human of the angels."

"How—"

"The legends say that Vasu was young—the equivalent of an angelic child—when the angels fell. He interacted with humanity more than the other Fallen. Humans in his area considered him a kind of god because he came among the population so much."

"Interesting. Well, he was different from Jaron. He, um…" She cleared her throat. "He kissed me."

"What?"

"It wasn't sexual." She put a hand on his chest. "It was after the fighting. I was in shock. And he was… curious, I think."

Malachi's face was stormy. "He kissed you?"

"I didn't kiss him back!"

"What did you do?"

"Well…" She paused, trying to remember the tumult in the cemetery. "I think right after that I crawled over to the bushes and puked. Probably not the reaction he was going for."

Malachi burst into laughter. "Probably not."

"Just relax," she said. "How many mating feasts are we going to have after all?"

"My mother had seven."

Ava blinked. "What?"

"Yes, one with her immediate family and new mate. One with my father's. Then the extended families host one. And of course, my father's family was in Turkey, so—"

"Wow, so…" She looked around the room. "Are we going to have to do a lot of these?"

"Not if you don't want to," he said. "We're not exactly the traditional Irin couple."

"No." She smiled. "We're just… us."

Rhys wandered over. "I feel privileged. The first mating of an Irin scribe and one of the *kareshta*. Doesn't this feel historic?"

Ava could see the scholarly excitement, but she had a hard time thinking of her own life as historic in any sense.

"Historic may be stretching things, Rhys."

"I don't think so," he said. "I want to know when Damien plans to reveal the existence of the Grigori women. We should all be in the Library for that."

Malachi seemed hesitant. "Do we need to? We promised Kostas our discretion. He has women and children he's protecting. Revealing anything to the elders could be dangerous at this point."

"But we must," Rhys said. "Not only could this change everything about how our race views the Grigori, but we may have trouble getting a mandate from the elders unless they know there is something to be gained."

Ava asked, "What exactly do you mean by mandate? In Irin terms."

Rhys said, "Think of it as… a rule of engagement. Officially, our mandate as scribes now includes protecting humans, killing Grigori, and hunting angels if they hunt us first. A watcher who deviates from that can be disciplined. His scribes could receive censure."

"So, officially, Damien and you guys have been breaking all kinds of rules."

"Yes," Malachi said. "But Damien is old and powerful enough that no one is going to question him too much."

"Did you know he was a Templar Knight?"

Both the men blinked.

"What?" Malachi said.

"This is awesome," she said. "I love knowing stuff you guys don't."

"Whether that's true or not," Rhys continued, "one of the reasons Damien has been petitioning the elders is to change the mandate of the scribe houses to include more offense against the Fallen—specifically Volund—based on the attacks in Istanbul and Oslo."

Malachi nodded. "He's not having much success."

"But the knowledge that there are Grigori women being victimized would be another motivation for taking action."

"Yes," Rhys said. "Leo was right. There are thousands of scribes without mates because there are so few women left after the Rending. The elders would not be able to ignore that. The Watchers' Council would force them to expand the mandate. They would see the *kareshta* as potential mates, as you and Ava are mates."

Malachi tensed. "You're saying that not only should we reveal the existence of the *kareshta*, but we should also reveal that Ava is of their blood?"

"Why wouldn't we?"

He squeezed her tighter as one of the scribes she didn't know came up to Rhys.

"We have a situation," he said quietly.

"What is it?" Rhys asked.

"There is a… I don't know what he is. He smelled Grigori, but he didn't attack." The guard sounded confused. "Just handed me a note to give to Maxim and ran."

"What did he look like?" Malachi asked.

The guard shrugged. "Like a Grigori. I would have killed him, but he came and left quickly. He looked to have a dozen men with him. I was prepared to call for help when he mentioned Maxim's name."

"Give me the note," Rhys said. "And wait here."

"Kostas?" Malachi murmured as they walked to a quieter corner.

"Possibly. Or a trap."

"Have you ever heard of a dozen Grigori walking through the middle of Vienna like that? We're only blocks from the Library."

"None would dare."

Except, Ava suspected, a heretic Grigori with nothing to lose. But Kostas had been adamant about secrecy when they'd met him in Sofia. What could have caused him to seek them out now?

"Ava?" Malachi reached for her hand and she took it. So much for reassuring him nothing was going to happen.

Rhys approached Max in the corner, who started and grabbed for the note his brother held out.

"Malachi," he called from across the room. "With me?"

Malachi nodded and tried to let Ava's hand go, but she held on tighter.

"I'm going with you."

"Ava—"

"He didn't hurt me before. He's not likely to do it now. And Kyra might be with him."

After meeting her grandmother, Ava was desperate to talk to the *kareshta* woman again.

Malachi paused, nodded. "Stay close."

"I will."

• • •　• • •

THE FOUR OF THEM SLIPPED OUT OF THE HOUSE AND DOWN THE stairs, turning right when the earlier guard nodded in that direction. In an alley, just off the main road, they caught the muted scent of sandalwood.

"Maxim," someone hissed from the shadows.

"Kostas?"

The man flew from the shadows and grabbed Max by the neck, tackling him to the ground.

Malachi and Rhys immediately flew to their brother's aid.

"Who did you tell?" Kostas shouted. "Who was it?"

"Kostas, I—"

"I trusted you!"

Ava saw the dozen Grigori standing in the shadows, but none went to aid their brother. They were watching. Waiting to see what Malachi and Rhys would do. Ava had the feeling that the minute any knives came out, all bets were off.

She saw Malachi reach for one of his daggers. "Malachi!" she cried.

Her mate pulled away from the fight to go to her, leaving Max, Kostas, and Rhys tumbling on the ground.

"Stop them!" she yelled. "Something's happened. We need to talk, not fight."

One of the Grigori stepped forward just as Rhys tore Kostas from Max's throat and stood between the two men.

"Yes, something happened," the beautiful man's face was twisted in rage. "One of you betrayed us. Betrayed our sisters. The children…"

Ava gasped and Malachi immediately sheathed the knife he'd been about to pull and put his hands down.

"None of us betrayed you," he said. "And we would never put your women in jeopardy. We've been trying to find a way to help."

"The monastery was attacked," Kostas panted out. "Old women. Children. They killed anyone who couldn't flee."

"No." Ava felt her knees give out.

Malachi caught her.

"Kostas," Max panted. "I would never—"

"No one knew where it was. We were so careful. We turned away dozens because we couldn't be sure their sires were dead."

Beyond the anger, Ava could see grief tearing up Kostas's eyes. The sickening rage of a protector who had failed.

"Who was it?" Kostas asked again. "*Who did you tell?*"

Max shook his head. "I don't know, my friend. None of us would put children at risk."

Kostas still glared. "Kyra was in the city with me. Sirius"—he pointed at the Grigori who had spoken up—"was the guard there. Most of his men are dead now. There were too many. Some of the older girls and women were able to escape with some of the smallest. But the oldest *kareshta* and some of the youngest…"

Sirius said, "We lost thirteen of our sisters and a dozen free Grigori. The monastery was compromised. They knew exactly how to attack."

Max said, "You've never taken me there. None of us knew where it was, Kostas. Think. This betrayal did not come from us."

"It was Svarog's men. Assassins from Hungary. We didn't even know they were in our territory." Kostas's shoulders slumped in defeat. "We didn't even know."

"The other women, are they safe?" Ava asked.

"For now," Sirius said.

"How many are left?"

"Eighteen. We need to find them a new place. Right now they're scattered among our brothers in populated areas. They can't stay there for long. It's not good for the little ones."

"I may know a place," Ava said. "But you'll need papers for them. It's not in Bulgaria."

The safe house Karen, Bruno, and Astrid had set up outside Prague was intended for Irina, but it could work for the *kareshta* as well. Ava was certain they wouldn't turn innocents away. She knew it was remote, but she had no idea how hard it would be to get papers for foreign women and children.

"It shouldn't be a problem," Max said. "I've already helped with IDs for them in the past." He turned to Kostas. "How could you think I'd tell?"

Kostas only shook his head.

Sirius said, "Kostas told me you were coming here to petition the elders. Some of them must know about the *kareshta*. We think some in Vienna are in league with the Fallen."

"Conspiracy theories," Malachi said.

"We have said nothing publicly," Rhys said. "Not even to our allies. These women are innocents. Most of the Irin—"

"Most of the Irin would kill them on sight, simply because they carry the blood of their enemy," Kostas bit out. "I have no faith in your mercy." He hung his head. "Nor should I expect it."

Ava pushed past Malachi and knelt by him. "I have Grigori blood. The scribes in Istanbul didn't turn me away."

Kostas lifted his eyes. "Did they know?"

"No. But when they found out, my mate didn't turn his back on me. None of them did. It will matter to some Irin, but not all."

Kostas shook his head.

"We're more than our blood," Ava whispered. "More than our pasts. We just have to make them see that. They need to see you and Kyra. See the good that you're doing."

"I'm not dragging my sister into this"—he looked around—"vipers' nest. Vienna would never be safe for her."

"You don't know that. And I think that decision should be left up to Kyra." Ava rose to her feet and held out her hand. "Stand up. Sitting on the ground angry isn't helping anyone. Brooding isn't productive."

Her irritation made the corner of his mouth turn up. "You remind me of her, you know."

"Then you should be able to predict how stubborn I can be. Come on," Ava said. "Come inside and let's figure out a way to fix this."

V.

Barak sat in his most familiar human form, watching the groundskeepers trim the bushes in the snow-blanketed cemetery in the middle of the Irin city. A conspiracy of ravens watched him from the bare branches of a lime tree arching over a family crypt where a frost-dusted woman sat with a scroll on her lap, staring into the heavens. Some melancholic mourner had placed a red rose there, and the despairing woman clutched it in her hand.

Vasu appeared behind him, also in his most familiar form.

"What has gotten into you?" Barak asked.

"I have decided this is amusing. Is he here yet?"

"No, but I've put the cemetery into a dream for when he comes."

"Why? I merely—"

His voice was cut off when Jaron appeared beside him in a rage.

Without a word, Jaron launched Vasu across the graveyard, his body hurled through the pillars of a memorial, which crashed with a massive thud, marble shards and ice flying through the frosty air.

Barak sighed. "You should have known."

Vasu countered, his human form disappearing in a blink, then reappearing behind his brother, clutching Jaron's shoulders as the two disappeared, only to reappear at the top of the church dome in the distance. Vasu threw Jaron off the tower, but the more powerful angel blinked out of sight and reappeared next to Vasu, shoving the angel off the blue-green dome and into the air where Vasu transformed into a large raven, one of his favorite forms.

The raven came to light on the tree across from Barak. The conspiracy took flight, leaving him alone and staring at Barak.

"I told you not to play games with her," the other angel said. "He is possessive of his daughters."

The voice that came from the raven's mouth was human, even if its form was not. "She's not his daughter."

Jaron appeared beneath the tree. "She is of my line, and she is mine. That is all you need to know. Play your games with your own blood, brother."

With a spread of wings, Vasu transformed again into the black-haired man with deep gold eyes. His black coat flapping behind him, he walked to Barak and sat down next to the weary angel.

"It was very informative to shadow her."

"You spoke knowledge to her mind," Barak said. "It has entered the world now. Are you aware of the consequences?"

"So our Master has not given us leave to tell our secrets to our children." Vasu rolled his eyes. "This would be important if I cared about staying in His graces. I do not."

Jaron hissed. Even Barak drew away.

"You tempt heaven, brother."

"I tempt nothing but the whims of the Creator. And since I do not aim to leave this realm, it is of no concern to me."

"Someday you will remember," Jaron said. "And you will curse this day."

"I will curse nothing. I am not capable of regret."

Jaron's mouth curled up at the corner. "We are capable of entirely more than what we like to admit, Vasu. For now, stay away from my daughter."

"She has given her magic to the scribe," Barak said. "This has never happened before. Their union is unique."

"It will not be for long. I have seen it."

"Was this your aim?" Vasu asked, his head cocked to the side. "A blending of Irin and Grigori magic? My brother, you have more heretical tendencies than I gave you credit for. My apologies for doubting you."

"I hate to disappoint you, Vasu. But I believe this serves the will of our Master."

Barak asked, "Why?"

"Azril returned the scribe."

Barak and Vasu said at once, "His Will be done."

"He desires unity?" Barak asked.

"If He did not, I would not have seen our triumph over Volund. Would not have seen our return."

"Redemption," Barak whispered, "was never my goal."

"But if it allows us to return," Jaron said, "I am willing to play on the side of the light."

Vasu crouched on the ground and drew his fingers through the snow, writing words that would disappear in moments as the snow began to fall.

"Svarog's children have routed your son," Vasu said, staring at the crystalline flakes. "They will be here in days."

Barak said, "Grimold's get have been here for months, playing quietly while Volund chased the Irina from his territory. Svarog has called his sons. They will drag themselves here—screaming in rebellion, perhaps—but they will come."

Vasu said, "Two armies are aligned against us, Jaron. Are you content to let your sons stay in hiding?"

"My sons have other tasks now. I do not need my army. I will take the Irin as my own."

"The Irina are here," Barak said. "Volund is foolish to underestimate them. They have no authority that constrains them as the scribes do."

"And we will use that to defeat him," Jaron said, brushing drifts of snow from his bare arms. The glyphs that marked his skin glowed with a faint silver light. As his daughter's magic had transformed with her bonding to the scribe, he felt his own powers changing. Melding into something he could not predict. A rush of emotion had reached him the night of their union. Feelings he had not experienced for thousands of years.

He found the experience disconcerting.

And if he had found it disconcerting, he could not predict how Volund would feel when he lowered the shields around Ava. Whatever strange magic their union had worked would hit his enemy full force the moment he could feel her blood.

Volund would be unbalanced, and Jaron would strike.

It would not be long now. The singers had returned. The scent of magic in the city had shifted.

"He knows we're here," Barak said. "How long must we wait? Their numbers grow by the hour."

"Not long," Jaron said. "Soon the council will be complete, and we will reveal ourselves."

Vasu looked up from the snow, a smile on his face. "Then we demons shall play at being heroes, and Death will visit us again."

CHAPTER
TWENTY-ONE

It wasn't, Malachi mused, a traditional end to a mating feast. But it seemed oddly appropriate for him and Ava.

Kostas and the Grigori who seemed to be his lieutenant, Sirius, were sitting across the dinner table from Damien and Sari. Orsala was on their right, and Gabriel on their left. Maxim sat next to Kostas, and Ava and Malachi had taken a spot at the end of the table, bridging the gap. Rhys and Leo stood in one corner with Renata and Mala. Both sides eyed the other with distrust, while the rest of the guests had joined the free Grigori soldiers outside.

The scent of sandalwood filled the air, and Malachi knew every scribe in the room struggled to restrain the ingrained instinct to kill the two men.

Gabriel was the first one to speak. "If this gets out, we will both be under censure, no matter what allies we have."

"The world is changing," Damien said.

"Not that much. This is too soon."

"I agree with you," Kostas said. "But this has been forced on us. Svarog's forces are coming to Vienna. Grimold's are already here."

Ava asked, "How do you know?"

"I can spot the signs," Kostas said. "If you look at police reports, there will be a slow build of attacks against indigents and prostitutes.

The winter weather helps conceal it. Most will probably be written off by the human authorities because of the cold."

"Are you sure?" Rhys asked.

Sirius answered him. "You can verify it with human authorities if you like, but I agree with Kostas. The Grigori here haven't been attacking Irin targets. They wouldn't dare. But Grimold is Volund's lapdog. His people have been here since Volund lost so many of his children in Oslo."

"We'll look," Sari said. "But that doesn't solve the problem of your women."

"Prague," Ava said. "Can you contact Astrid?"

Sari and Damien exchanged a look.

"It is an acceptable risk," Damien said. "But we must give them the option to refuse."

"They won't," Orsala said. "There are children among them."

"I thank you," Sirius told her graciously. The man's beautiful features were obscured by the obvious stress in the lines of his face. His accent marked him as Russian in origin, and he'd grown his hair and beard long. Malachi guessed it was to detract from the unnatural beauty of his race.

"The failure is mine," Sirius continued. "They are my responsibility. I will accompany them and provide whatever assistance your people require."

"There are scribes there who can watch over them," Damien said. "The location of our safe houses must not be compromised."

Sirius stiffened, and Kostas laid a hand on his second's arm. "Peace. We can work out the details later, and Kyra will be with them."

"We would never harm innocents," Orsala said.

"You would be wrong to think them all innocent," Kostas said. "Not all of our sisters are… well. Some are a danger to themselves and others. Part of Sirius's job is to watch those who are not wholly sane."

Sari said, "The children—"

"Some of the children are the worst," Sirius said quietly.

The silence was tangible as Malachi imagined children driven mad by the voices in their minds and the horrors they might have witnessed at the hands of their own sires.

Orsala asked, "Can they be restrained with magic?"

Sirius and Kostas exchanged a look. "Possibly. We have no magic that can affect them, but we are not Irina."

Orsala nodded. "I will go with the *kareshta*," she said. "That should be sufficient."

"Grandmother—"

"I've decided," she said. "The elder singers will be arriving within the week. I have nothing to offer in battle they do not have."

Kostas said, "The singers are returning?"

Sari paused, then said, "Many of them are already here. We've been in contact with havens around the globe. Of the seven former elders, three are still living and willing to take office. The other regions have sent representatives. The Irina council will be active within a week."

"That's when we should announce it then," Malachi said. "When the Irina council has taken their place in the Library."

"Announce what?" Gabriel asked.

"The existence of the *kareshta*."

Malachi felt Ava's hand tighten on his as the room held its collective breath.

"Who are you to make that decision?" Gabriel asked. "A censured scribe from Istanbul who was rumored to be dead. You show up in Vienna with a mate no one has heard of and suggest revelations that could disrupt the foundations of our race. *Who are you?*"

Malachi leaned forward. "I am the only Irin scribe in history mated to one of the *kareshta*."

No one had any response to that, so Malachi continued. "I am a warrior of Mikhael's line. And I've seen the dark edge of power in my mate. I don't fear it. I claim it. I *did* die. And I was returned from heaven for a reason. We met"—he reached out and took Ava's hand— "for a reason. *That* is who I am, and I will bear witness to it."

"We both will," Ava said.

Gabriel sat back, clearly still perturbed by Malachi's presumption. Malachi didn't care.

"And you may not agree with me." He looked around the table. "Any of you. But I think Kostas *and* Kyra need to be present at the Library when we tell the elders the world as they've known it has changed."

"No," Kostas said immediately. "I will not consent to allow my sister here when there are unknown threats against her."

"I agree with Malachi," Damien said.

"As do I," Sari concurred. "We can protect your sister."

Kostas still looked dubious. Malachi could hardly blame him. He was taking a great risk, making allies of those who'd spent their lives trying to kill those of his blood.

Renata said, "I will guard her as well. Practically speaking, the only threat to her would be other Irina, and we can handle them. No scribe would harm a woman in our company, even if she carried the look of a Grigori."

"But they'd kill me on sight," Kostas said. "You cannot argue with that. There is no possible way I could go to the Library. My scent would give me away in a second."

Everyone fell silent, forced to acknowledge the truth of his words until a lone voice at the end of the room spoke.

"I can mask his scent."

They all turned to see the dark form of an angel, chin propped on his hand as he rested his elbow on the edge of the table.

There were shouts of alarm. Weapons were pulled. Defensive positions taken. Malachi edged in front of his mate, but she sighed and pushed him to the side.

"Vasu," she said. "How long have you been here?"

"Long enough. I can mask the scent of Barak's son."

"Everyone relax," Ava said. "I don't think he's here to cause trouble. At least not the violent kind."

Malachi itched to reach across and plunge a silver blade in the nape of the angel's neck. It wouldn't kill him, but it would be very, very satisfying.

Vasu looked at him and winked. "Meow."

Only Ava's hand on Malachi's shoulder kept him from lunging at the black-haired angel.

"Explain," Ava said. "Why would you do it?"

Vasu sat up. "Obviously so I could see the look on their faces when they saw a Grigori in the middle of their precious Library," he said. "Also because it serves our purposes for our sons to be called into battle at this time. It would be better if they were not killed on sight. My children have already felt my call." He cocked his head and looked at Kostas. "So have Barak's, even if they do not recognize it."

The color drained from Kostas's handsome face. "No."

"Oh yes."

The Grigori stood in a rage, realizing his free will had only been an illusion. "No!"

Sirius stood next to him, his eyes tormented. "Why? We thought he was dead. Why would our father—"

"Calm yourselves." Vasu waved a hand at them. "Your sire has no intention of building his army again. He has other purposes in mind."

"He and Jaron want to return to heaven, don't they?" Ava asked quietly. "Jaron told me. 'I will tear the threads of heaven to return.' That's what he told me in a vision."

"Did he?" Vasu asked, all innocence.

It was a disturbing expression on a fallen angel.

"What is their plan?" Malachi asked. "How is Volund a part of it? What do they aim to do?"

Vasu looked him straight in the eye and said, "I have no idea."

And Malachi knew he was lying.

Rage boiled up. Months of frustration at being used like a pawn. Weeks of uncertainty, knowing his mate was in danger and being forced to rely on one of his mortal enemies to protect her.

Malachi flew out of his seat with a roar, only to find the chair Vasu had occupied completely empty. He spun, but the angel was already standing behind Kostas and Sirius. Bending down, he kissed both their foreheads then, with a wink at Ava, he disappeared.

Everybody in the room was frozen, then the shouts all came at once.

"And *these* are our allies?" Gabriel yelled at Damien.

"What did he mean? Does this mean Barak—"

"—how many Grigori is that? Are we supposed to fight *with* them?"

"—not know Jaron was speaking to Ava. Directly to her?"

"We still have no idea—"

Mala's staff crashed down on middle of the dining room table, and she threw out an angry sign.

Everyone fell silent again.

"That means 'Shut up,'" Ava said. "I know that one."

Orsala stood. "First things first. Damien, you are the oldest scribe in the room. Can you detect any scent of Grigori on our new... friends?"

Damien leaned closer, staring at Sirius and Kostas. Then he closed his eyes, stroked long fingers up his forearm to activate his magic, and inhaled one long breath.

"Nothing," he said, opening his eyes. "Not even with my *talesm*. They smell human."

Gabriel also leaned forward. "Astonishing."

"Well, he is an angel," Ava muttered. "Just kind of a weird one."

Sirius said, "Vasu was always known as a trickster. His sons are moody and unpredictable, but they worship him as a god."

"It's true," Kostas said. "He annoyed my father. His sons are madmen, but if Vasu calls them, they'll come without question."

Orsala said, "He's cloaked you for now. It's possible he's cloaked all his children. He mentioned Barak's children and his own. Can we assume Jaron's Grigori will be joining us as well?"

Everyone looked at Kostas. He shrugged. "Most of my father's children follow me now. I've killed those who wouldn't. Jaron's children are more mixed. The majority fled east after he lost Istanbul. A few tried to seek refuge with us, but we turned them away."

"Why?" Leo asked. "Wouldn't more free Grigori help your cause?"

"They weren't free, because I knew Jaron wasn't dead," Sirius said.

"How?" Ava asked.

Malachi returned to her side.

"Because he's been feeding me power for nearly fifty years," Kostas admitted.

Malachi saw Ava's eyes widen.

"Me as well," Sirius said. "Our father disappeared. Jaron was his closest ally. We had both stopped feeding from human women. We would have died without Jaron's help and the help of our sisters. We don't have longevity spells as you do. We're getting older."

Malachi didn't see it in their faces, but he saw it in their eyes. Both men looked exhausted.

"Jaron also directed *kareshta* to us through a doctor in Istanbul. Most had been living in the human world. They thought they were mad. We took them in if we could or found other safe places for them."

Interesting. Kostas appeared clueless that the "doctor" who'd been sending women to them was Jaron himself.

"Even after Istanbul, we knew Volund hadn't killed him," Sirius said. "He's one of the most powerful archangels in existence. But his children will never be free until he is dead. We could never trust that they were acting of their own will and not their father's."

Malachi felt Ava shiver at his side.

Though they couldn't affect her will, Ava would never be free until both Jaron and Volund were gone from the earthly realm.

Jaron wanted to kill Volund. Jaron wanted to return to heaven. If both those things were accomplished, Malachi's mate would be truly free.

Malachi said, "I don't know about his children, but for now our purposes align with Jaron's. So what can we do to help him?"

"Wait for the Irina council to reform," Sari said. "Then reveal the truth about the *kareshta*. And about Kostas and his brothers."

More silence as they took in Sari's words.

"Many will resist seeing them as allies," Max said. "Some will find it impossible."

Damien said, "Then we deal with that when it occurs. If the armies of three angels are descending on Vienna, then Mikhael's blood will rise. The Irin here are sleeping, not dead. They will take their allies as they come."

"And more Irina will come if they see the opportunity for vengeance," Renata added. "Plus, the opportunity to save sisters more lost than we ever were."

"Call Kyra," Sirius said to Kostas.

Kostas shook his head. "Brother—"

"Call her. You know it's the right thing to do. It should be her choice. And we cannot defend them ourselves. It is time to ask for help."

* * *   * * *

"IS IT JUST ME," AVA ASKED, "OR DOES IT SEEM QUIETER OUTSIDE THAN inside?"

"It's not just you." Malachi sat next to her in the corner of the library at Damien and Sari's house.

Three days after Kostas's appearance in Vienna, the *kareshta* had been hidden in Prague. Kostas and Max had moved swiftly to hide the women and children left from the attack in Bulgaria, and Sirius handed over their protection to Orsala, Mala, and the remaining singers of Sarihöfn. Kyra refused to stay in the safe house; she had returned to Vienna with her brother.

Now three singers stood in Damien's study, talking with Sari and arguing while Rhys, Leo, Ava, and Malachi looked on.

The seven elder singers had returned to Vienna, but as Sari warned them all, this was no puppet council.

Abigail and Carmina, the two most traditional of the council, were arguing with Sari over her decision to step aside for the European seat, leaving Constance the chosen favorite.

"Why have you withdrawn?" Abigail asked. She was a strong-boned woman from Newfoundland with a powerful voice. "You're one of the most respected singers in Europe. Many of my own people look to you as an authority."

"But I'm not a politician," Sari said. "I have other roles now."

Like the quiet plan Kostas and Damien were already working on to search for more of the lost *kareshta*. Sari, Damien, and Max were sending out inquiries to their allies across Europe, spreading the news and asking scribe houses to be on the lookout for women with Grigori traits, especially in areas where Fallen had been killed and might have left surviving children.

Minor angels killed each other with alarming regularity. And if their daughters were lost in the human population, they could be helped without danger of their sire's influence.

"She's not even European," Carmina protested. "She's American."

Carmina looked delicate, but Malachi had heard the singer carried Mikhael's blood. Her looks were probably deceiving.

"She's lived here longer than many natives," Sari said. "And her mate has family ties in France. She's a valid choice."

Abigail snorted. "She's a ninny. She'd lock every one of us in a retreat and throw away the key."

Daina, a dark-haired former elder from the Caribbean was one of the more moderate singers on the council and the only calm voice in the room. "She represents many of our sisters who carry this same view. Are they not allowed a voice?"

The singer's face was a stunning blend of African, American, and European blood. Malachi could tell she was very old. Her mate, a watcher of immense reputation, had left public life with her after the Rending. Rumor in Vienna was that Daina and Zamir protected one of the largest havens in the Western Hemisphere, somewhere in the southern Caribbean Sea. She'd been coaxed back to her former position in Vienna when South America had been given the seventh seat on the council.

"If you want to object to her seating," Daina continued, "object to the fact that her mate is one of the elder scribes. There is a reason it is avoided. A mated pair can hold too much power if they speak as one."

"Unfortunately"—Rhys decided to risk his input—"they both have political presences that are independent from the other. According to what Damien and I have been able to learn, they're not seen as a single entity here. They've had years to develop their own allies, and they don't agree on everything."

"They agree on compulsion," Carmina said.

Sari said, "Yes, but compulsion is not the only issue of our race. And on many of the others, Constance carries her own view and is admired for it. Further, she's seen as the leading Irina mind in Vienna. She's a medical doctor as well as a healer. Many of the women who've lived here since the Rending—"

"The ones who've lived in hiding?" Abigail asked. "The ones who allowed their mates to shut them up like prisoners in their own homes? Are we expected to take them seriously?"

"This is useless debate," Daina said. "She will be chosen. She will serve. You can debate with her in the Library."

Leo said, "Some of the elder scribes object to the council being reformed. They say it is not legitimate."

Daina waved him off. "I've heard the objections, but they are ridiculous. The Irin elders have never had a voice in choosing the Irina council, just as we have never had a voice in choosing their ranks. We will take our place in the Library in two days' time."

"They do object to us," Abigail said, her voice holding barely concealed pain. "Some object to our very presence in the city. My mother would be appalled."

"Let them object," Carmina said. "It is as Daina said. They have no standing."

"What do you think they will do?" Sari said with a wry laugh. "Bar us from the Library? They could try."

Daina said, "And they would fail."

"And how do you feel about compulsion, Daina?" Carmina lifted her chin. "You have not spoken about it since we've been here."

"I do not agree with compulsion," Daina said. "Nor do I agree with those who would throw our singers into war. That has never been our role. You risk throwing artists and teachers and healers into a war that has torn most of their families apart. Are you prepared to truly hear what those sisters have to say? It might not match your plans."

Sari said, "Some of those healers and artists have chosen different paths because of what happened during the Rending. Are you willing to stifle their desire to join this war?"

"Have they trained?" Daina asked. "Have they spent years in the scribe houses preparing for this as our mates have?"

Malachi leaned forward. "And what if there is a mission for which healers and teachers are the most qualified, Daina? What then?"

Daina cocked her head toward him. "I know of no such mandate. But I will be interested to hear you speak, Malachi of Sakarya."

Malachi leaned back after giving her a respectful nod. Daina was not a singer who liked others to make assumptions about her, and she would keep her own council. She reminded Malachi a great deal of his mother. He had a feeling that revealing the secret of the *kareshta* was the key to investing the more moderate Irina in their battle against the Fallen. After all, would women lost in the human world need warriors or healers?

Glancing over his shoulder at his mate who watched everything with perceptive eyes, he was reminded of who she had been.

Hunted. Tormented. Lonely.

Malachi guessed that most of the *kareshta* were much like Ava had been.

Had she needed a warrior or a healer?

She'd needed both.

CHAPTER

TWENTY-TWO

S he walked through the forest again, her feet muffled by the dead leaves on the ground, the bare branches of the trees forming a canopy overhead. She could feel her mate at her side, but she did not hear him. She heard only the sound of her own footsteps on the path.

And his.

Her blood recognized his presence now. Her power tied to his.

"Not only mine now," Jaron said.

"I know."

"You've completed your bond with the scribe."

"Yes."

"Are you… happy?"

Ava stopped and turned to Jaron, not understanding the expression he wore. It was the most human he had ever looked. "I am. He makes me happy. I feel complete with him."

Jaron nodded and continued walking. "I confess," he said as he walked, "I did not understand your connection at first. When you mourned him, it made me curious."

"Why? Don't angels mourn?"

"No." His hands were clasped easily behind his back. "I suppose some of us feel a sense of… longing for what we no longer have. That is a kind of mourning."

She knew he was talking about heaven.

"Do you think the Creator longs for you?"

Jaron paused, as if the idea surprised him. "We are His servants. We long for His presence alone."

"Even the Fallen?"

"Especially the Fallen. But longing, if frustrated for millennia, can easily turn to rage."

She stepped in front of Jaron, no longer afraid. "Why did you fall?"

He cocked his head, his brilliant gold eyes glowing in the darkness. "We were greedy. We were looking for something more."

"What?"

"Connection, I think. The love humans are capable of, it was foreign to us. And fascinating. We were seduced by it, only to find that it was not what we were created for."

"What were you made for?"

"Service."

He moved around her and continued walking in the moonless night. The light from the stars was the only thing illuminating the path.

"That seems harsh."

Jaron turned. "It is not for either of us to question the Creator. We see only the weaving of the tapestry, not its completion."

"So everything has a purpose? Is that what you're trying to say?"

Jaron bent down, pressing her cheeks between palms that were warmer than Ava expected. She lifted her gaze and met ruthless eyes.

"What I have seen, what I have shown you, is only a shadow of His mind. That was my gift. My purpose. To experience glory and show those who were less. I was… an interpreter. No human can know His mind. You would go mad."

"So I'm lesser than you?"

"Less and more, daughter. For you have been given the gift of free will, while I only experience the desire for what I have lost." He released her and stepped back. "I have used you, Ava. And I will continue to do so."

She drew in a shuddering breath. "And my grandmother? How is she?"

"Surviving." Jaron paused. "That has been her life for too long."

"If we kill Volund, will she heal?"

"I do not know. I only know she will be released."

"And if you return to heaven like you want?"

She saw the corner of his mouth lift. "I knew you would see it eventually."

"Is it possible?"

"I have seen it."

"Sometimes I see things because I want them too much," Ava said. "How do you know what is vision and what is real?"

"Why do you draw a line between them? One is the same as the other with enough will." He turned. Looked at her. "And the power to make it so."

"Oh God," she breathed out, stopping in the pathway.

"That is one of His names."

"That's why Malachi came back. Is that what you're saying?" She grabbed for his arm, stopping him from walking ahead. "Is that it? I dreamed it—I wanted it so much—that I made it real? Made my vision a reality?"

Jaron turned. "You are of my blood. And of Volund's."

"What does that mean?"

"Not even I can predict your power." He leaned down and whispered, "Be careful what you dream."

Her body was frozen. She felt her mate at her back as Jaron walked into the fog.

"How will this end?"

It slammed into her. The vision of the two eagles battling. Blood sprayed on her face as one fell, then the other, both pierced in the heart by the other's talons. They fell, but they did not hit the ground. A giant sword rose into the sky, its black shadow clawing the heavens with the teeth of a great beast. And when it pierced their breasts, the eagles turned into giants, and the darkness swallowed them whole.

AVA WAS STILL THINKING ABOUT THE VISION THE NEXT DAY WHILE SHE waited for Malachi to return from settling Kostas's men. She was making an effort to think of them as Kostas's men and not Grigori. The instinctive aversion was too strong, and she didn't want to offend Kyra, who was waiting with her.

The *kareshta* was nervous. She'd gone to Prague with the others to settle her sisters into Astrid and Karen's care, had spent some time with

Orsala, forming a rudimentary shield over her mind, but she still looked incredibly ill at ease in Vienna. The vulnerability made her otherworldly features somehow more human.

"Kostas and Sirius should be back soon," Ava said.

She nodded. "I worry about them."

"Malachi says that as long as they cover up and don't look too pretty, they should be all right. Their scent is completely gone."

"Good." She tapped her fingers and looked over her shoulder to where Rhys and Leo were trying very hard not to look at the stunning woman. Kyra had masses of long hair, a rich chestnut color streaked with darker shades of brown. Her skin was olive—a legacy from her human mother, who had been Greek—and her eyes were thick-lashed and gold. Ava felt small and plain beside her, and she could understand why Leo and Rhys had a hard time keeping their eyes to themselves.

She gave them a furious look and they went back to studying their books. "Sorry about them."

Kyra shook her head. Forced a smile. "It's fine. I'm sure I'm strange to their eyes."

"Oh, no. That's not it. You're just really, really gorgeous and—as old as these guys are—they're still getting used to being around girls."

Her eyes widened. "But... the Irina."

"Most that survived the Rending have been out of the public eye for two hundred years or so. If a scribe wasn't already mated, they weren't really welcome in the havens. So... most of these guys haven't seen a nonhuman girl in about two hundred years. Some of the younger scribes who were children during the Rending haven't *ever* seen one."

"Oh." If anything, that seemed to make her even more nervous. "That might explain the looks."

"Yeah, they can't really touch human women, so"—she leaned closer and whispered—"there are a lot of frustrated scribes out there."

Kyra blushed.

"I try to find the humor in the situation, even though it's not really funny."

"No." Kyra choked out the word. "It's not."

"You too, huh?"

Kyra looked around the library. "Is this appropriate to speak of?"

"Girl talk. Do I need to get some wine?"

Kyra shook her head. "That would not be advisable. I have no experience…" She cleared her throat. "Most *kareshta* are more attuned to the human world. Many have had relationships with human men, because of course, they thought—or continue to think—they are human."

"Like me."

"Yes." Kyra nodded, more comfortable now. "I do not have as much experience being out of… our version of havens. Because of my brother. And of course, most of his men are also Barak's children, so—"

"Oh my gosh, so you've been surrounded by like a thousand super-protective big brothers your whole life?"

She frowned. "A thousand would be hyperbole. But many half brothers, yes. Though I am older than most of them."

"That would pretty much kill any hope of a social life, huh?"

Kyra smiled and laughed a little. Rhys and Leo's eyes flew back to her.

Ava pointed at them. "Books. Now. Or I'll take her away."

They both averted their eyes, but she could see them sneaking glances.

"No," Kyra said. "No social life at all. Of course, hearing voices also dampens any urge I've ever had to be with a human."

"Yeah, I remember that part."

Kyra still carried the visible anxiety that Ava remembered so well. Her fingers tapped the arm of the chair and she was fidgeting madly, her foot tapping, her body shifting. Ava realized that though she was learning to shield her mind, the *kareshta* still felt the overwhelming excess of energy she channeled from the human souls in Vienna. Irina did too, but with more developed magic and regular contact with males of their own race, it was manageable.

For Kyra, who'd lived her life in purposefully isolated locations, the crowd of a city must have been a nerve-racking experience. And her brother, whose affectionate contact would help her manage her energy, had been gone for hours.

Going with her instincts, Ava glanced at Leo, then at Rhys. "Kyra?"

"Hmm?" The *kareshta* had been distracted, looking out the window.

"Will you trust me on something?"

"About what?"

She leaned forward and grasped the other woman's hand, releasing a burst of static electricity.

"Sorry," Ava whispered. "I know how you feel."

Kara's body grew deliberately still. "Do you?"

Ava nodded. "All these people. And you can still feel them."

"I am practicing the technique Orsala taught me, but being in the city is… difficult. Even here, where minds are more guarded and voices are softer, I hear things. There are just so many."

"And you're around new people, which makes you nervous anyway. Has the headache started?"

The slight tension between her eyes told Ava the truth even before Kyra nodded.

"I want to try something. Will you trust me that I would never do something that would make you more uncomfortable unless I thought it would help?"

Kyra was hesitant, but eventually she nodded.

"Hey, Leo?" Ava called.

The giant scribe was at her side in an instant. "Did you need something, Ava?"

Ava wrapped her arms around his middle, giving him a solid hug. Leo smiled and bent down, wrapping his arms around her and touching his lips to her forehead.

"I missed you," he said. "Malachi has been keeping you to himself since you arrived in the city."

Kyra's eyes widened, so Ava was quick to explain.

"Leo's a friend. When I lost my mate"—she squeezed him again—"he and Malachi's other brothers kept me sane."

Her lips parted in understanding. "You have… affection. Friendship. He is as a brother to you."

"Yep." Ava nodded. "Plus, Leo gives great hugs."

The big man smiled wider. "I do."

Ava laughed and saw that Kyra's face had softened.

"Do you need a hug, Kyra?" Ava asked.

It seemed like such a simple thing to her now, but she knew how hard it would be for Kyra. Human contact only made the voices worse, so Ava had learned to live in isolation before she knew what she was.

"I… I don't think…" The woman shook her head.

Ava stepped back, and Leo held out his hand.

"Give me your hand," he said softly. "If you like, Kyra. Just your hand."

Kyra held up a trembling hand, her fingers tense. Without a word, Leo grasped it and held it between both his hands.

She saw the deep breath he took, saw him close his eyes as her energy released. Malachi had once told her that touching Ava after they'd been apart for some time was like a surge of magical adrenaline.

Ava saw Kyra release a breath, saw the tension leave her forehead. Her restless tapping ceased at once. Her shoulders relaxed.

"You make the voices go away," Kyra whispered, staring at him in wonder.

Leo leaned forward, elbows on his knees and Kyra's hand pressed to his cheek, holding it there as his eyes fixed on her.

"Anytime you need me, Kyra. All you have to do is ask."

Kyra's eyes flew to Ava at his words. She could see the discomfort, so she simply took the *kareshta's* other hand and squeezed it.

"None of us are meant to be alone."

◆ ◆ ◆   ◆ ◆ ◆

"KOSTAS'S MEN ARE WELL TRAINED," MALACHI TOLD HER AS HE SHED his coat and began to take off the weapons strapped to his torso. "And Sirius is an excellent second, though it was obvious his mind was on the *kareshta* in Prague."

"I called Astrid today. They're doing really well, and Orsala has been a huge help. Bruno called some people, so there's about a dozen scribes at the house now along with some of the singers from Sarihöfn."

"I'll pass the message along tomorrow. It will ease his mind." He took a deep breath and collapsed on the couch, obviously exhausted.

Ava straddled his lap, drew his forehead to her chest, and began massaging his temples.

"*Sağ olun, canım.*"

"You're welcome."

His hands rested at her waist as she continued. She could feel the tension begin to release and he squeezed her hips.

"You spent time with Kyra today?"

"I did."

"Why was Leo's face glowing?"

She laughed. "I think a handshake from a *kareshta* is rather… invigorating."

"He didn't—"

"Just held her hand for a little while. She needed it. Don't you remember?"

He took a deep breath and turned his cheek to her breast. "I do now. You were like a live wire the first time I kissed you. It took all my self-control not to lay you down on that hill, strip you naked, and take you there."

"Yes, but then you got all honorable."

He grunted. "That didn't last long."

"Thank goodness."

She felt his smile against her skin.

"Ava."

"Hmm?" She loved being with him like this. Quiet and easy. The massive power of his body at rest against hers. She felt grounded in the best way.

"If we were not *reshon*, would you love me this way?"

She grabbed his hair and pulled him back to meet her eyes. "What kind of question is that?"

He shrugged. "One that plagues me, I suppose."

"Fishing for compliments again?"

"Forget I asked. It is a stupid question."

She tugged him back when he tried to move away. Then she bent and whispered in his ear. "I was fascinated by you," she confessed. "Long before you laid a hand on me. Your humor. The passion I could see in your eyes. Your *lips*. I wanted you to kiss me so bad."

She felt his dimple underneath her hand as he said, "In the Basilica Cistern."

"Yes." Ava pinched his ear. "I wanted to kill you when you stepped away and acted all professional."

"I *wanted* to kiss you. I felt so guilty about it too. I spent that entire night writing a new spell to put on my arm the next morning to help my self-control."

She crushed him to her, pressing her face into his neck. "I'm so glad I have you back."

"I'm glad to be back." His voice was hoarse. "I want this to be over so we can have a life together, Ava. I want a family. I want you to take me to visit your mother. I want to travel with you and show you the places I've been. I want you to be able to take pictures again. I miss your pictures."

"You just want me to stop taking all those nudes of you," she muttered.

Malachi laughed. "Maybe."

"Not gonna happen. You're too hot."

"I'm hoping if I take you someplace more scenic, I can distract you."

"You can try."

"Plus"—he drew back and kissed her lips sweetly—"I really do love watching you work."

"That's a relief. I've been feeling like I'm missing a limb without being able to carry my camera around." Though she could carry it around Vienna, it wasn't allowed in the places she most wanted to capture like the Library or the ritual bathhouse. She knew why, but it still irked her that the only camera she had there was the one in her mind.

"Soon," he said, and she could hear the heaviness in his voice again. "Whatever is coming, I think it will be soon."

"Because of my dream with Jaron?" She'd told him about it when she woke, and he'd agreed the vision of the two eagles was disturbing. Something teased the back of her mind. There was something she'd been meaning to tell him…

"Partly your dream with Jaron," he said, "and partly the activity we're seeing in the city. There are definitely Grigori attacks. Kostas's men have volunteered to start patrolling."

"Grigori fighting their own kind," she said. "What has the world come to?"

"A turning point, hopefully."

"Yes."

The next day, the elder singers would take their desks in the Library. Some in Vienna thought the rumors were only rumors. But as more and more singers flowed into the city, even the most stubborn scribes had been forced to acknowledge that something was in the air. Ava had seen singers in Irin-friendly coffeehouses. Seen more and more of them on the street as she ran her daily errands. Faces from all over the world, women with the distinctive thrum of power were starting to move in Vienna.

The air was so electric she had a hard time wondering how the human population didn't notice.

Ava looked at Malachi. "Are Kostas and Sirius ready?"

"They've decided only Kostas will go to the Library with us in the morning. Sirius will stay with his men."

"How are you going to get him past the guards?" she asked. "He doesn't have a single *talesm*. Won't he stand out?"

"Damien has a plan to get Kostas in *and* gain access to Mikhael's armory."

"Is that illegal?"

"Highly. Those weapons are passed out at the will of the council because they're so dangerous. You saw what that weapon did to Leo in Istanbul. Any wound from an angelic weapon can be deadly to a scribe or a singer. But if we're going to be fighting angels, we need them. We don't have the angel of Death on our side, waiting to gather their souls."

The angel of death.

Oh shit.

Now she remembered what she needed to tell her mate. What she'd needed to tell him for *days*.

"Malachi?"

"Yes?"

She paused, not certain how to proceed.

He squeezed her hips. "What is it?"

"Did I tell you I've had other dreams?"

"What do you mean? Our dreams?"

"No, they're… different. I'm not sure if they're dreams or not. I think they're more like visions."

"From Jaron?"

"No."

Not visions, someone whispered. *Visits.*

"Visits," she murmured. "I've seen Death. As in, the angel of."

Malachi frowned. "I know, *reshon*. You told me. In Norway—"

"Not in Norway. Here. I've seen him here. He… visited me."

She felt him tense beneath her hands. "What?"

"In dreams. But they weren't dreams. Or not exactly dreams. And I wasn't scared. He showed me things," she said quietly. "I thought it was just to reassure me. They didn't seem important. There was something about my grandmother. We talked a little about you—"

"Ava." His voice was frigid. "You were seeing *Death* in your dreams, and you didn't tell me?"

What could she say?

"It was only twice. And there was so much going on. We were traveling everywhere. Besides, I didn't know if you'd believe me," she muttered. "It hardly seemed real."

"What on earth would make you think that?" His voice creeped past irritation and rose toward anger. "When have I ever not believed you?"

"I don't know. Stop yelling at me."

"I'm not yelling!"

Ava gave him an arched brow, and he set her to the side and leaned forward, bracing his elbows on his knees. She could see his temper in the set of his shoulders.

"I'm allowed to be angry that you hid this from me."

"I didn't hide it. They just didn't… come up. Two dreams. In the weeks we've been traveling and plotting and fighting Grigori and discovering mind-blowing revelations. So much was happening that it didn't seem important when it was just about my grandmother."

"Why wouldn't I want to know about your grandmother?"

"But it's not…" She sighed. "I wasn't scared of him."

"You're making excuses."

She *was* making excuses. Mostly she was embarrassed that she hadn't told him before. She really had forgotten, and it made her feel like an idiot.

"These dreams, they were only about your grandmother? About me?"

She bit her lip, felt her heart race in her chest. Now she was the one whose memory was fuzzy. She had a new respect how Malachi had felt for months while he recovered.

"No. Not just…"

He took a deep breath. "What it is?"

"There was more in the dreams. But I can't remember."

Malachi frowned. "What more? Did you see Jaron again?"

"Not Jaron. I think I might have seen Volund."

Malachi swore and rose to his feet as he began to pace across the room. "Were you in danger? How could you not have told me, Ava?"

"I didn't remember Volund until now!"

He spun. "How could you not remember that?"

Why *didn't* she remember? Ava knew she wouldn't have kept something important from her mate. That was past forgetfulness and into negligence, so why...

"Will I remember?"

When you need to.

She hadn't forgotten. Not completely. Azril had hidden it from her.

"Stupid, know-it-all angels!" Ava leapt to her feet. "He hid it, Malachi. Just like Jaron. Azril hid it for some reason. I don't know why."

Ava heard laughter in the back of her mind and felt the memories push forward, timid creatures peeking from the corners where Azril had tucked them. The smell of incense. Muffled voices. Gold eyes and black energy.

"What do you remember?" Malachi put his hands on her shoulders. "Anything, *reshon*. It could be important."

"They couldn't see me. I saw... there were three of them. The three angels Damien was talking about. I don't remember all their names."

"Svarog, Volund, and Grimold?"

"I'm not sure." She shook her head. "I think so? It's not important."

"It *is* important. What did they say?"

She murmured, "'Eliminating threats. It's still not that clear. Something about the monastery, maybe?" Her heart ached. "If I'd remembered, we might have been able to warn them."

"They could have been talking about any number of things. Maybe Azril wanted... He doesn't have wants. Death only follows the command of the Creator. And if the monastery hadn't been attacked, Kostas and Kyra would never have come to Vienna."

She blinked. "You think Azril wanted them to be here?"

"Who knows what the angels want? Was there anything else?"

Ava searched her memories, wading through a cascade of images and voices. "Svarog," she said. "He and Volund don't like each other."

"That's not surprising."

"They *really* don't like each other. They want to take Vienna."

"It is the center of the Irin race."

A headache lurked as Ava struggled to make sense of the new images. She closed her eyes and thought back to the last dream. An image came to her a moment before the door slammed shut in her mind.

"They're here," she said with a gasp. "They're already in Vienna. They were in the Library."

She felt Malachi shiver.

"They were in the Library? Actually *in* it? What else? If there's anything I can tell Damien—"

"Something about the third one."

Yes.

For a second, she thought she caught the reflection of Death smiling through the mirror in the entryway.

"Is it Grimold? He is an ally of Volund's," Malachi said. "Though Volund is widely understood to be the more powerful."

"Yes. I think they called him Grimold. And there was something about his children, but…"

"Max and Kostas believe Grimold's children are the ones already in the city."

"But there's more. 'All of them,'" he said. There's something about Grimold's children we don't know. Something we're not expecting."

CHAPTER

TWENTY-THREE

Malachi tried to calm himself and sift through the new information Ava had given him.

It wasn't that he didn't understand how information could get lost in the chaos of travel and fighting. And really, the revelations Azril had given her were not much more than what they knew already. Mostly, he was irritated she'd concealed it. And he was worried by Death's fascination with her.

Ava rubbed circles over her temple. He wondered if a headache was building. She still looked confused, and Malachi was angry for her. To have your mind violated was a terrible thing. He'd never felt as helpless as he had when he'd lost his memories.

Convicted by the guilt in his mate's face, Malachi knew he had to confess his own omission, even though he'd been pushing it to the back of his mind for weeks.

"I'm so sorry, Malachi. I don't… I don't know how I forgot. It's just, my dreams are never clear and there's been so much—"

"Ava."

"What?"

He took a deep breath and spoke quickly. "I may have seen Volund in dreams. I didn't know what to think. Part of me thought they were only nightmares. But now I don't think they were."

Her mouth dropped. "What? How long?"

Malachi shook his head. "Weeks. I haven't seen him since Italy. He told me he couldn't get to you but he could get to me."

He could see her irritation spike.

"Why didn't you tell me?" she asked, unable to hide the anger in her voice. "You're angry at me, while you—"

"I didn't know if it was real or imagined. Not for sure. Why would I worry you if I wasn't certain? You were dreaming about *Death* and didn't tell me."

"His name is Azril."

"Oh, I'm so glad you're friends now. He's the angel of death, Ava. And I'm not going to apologize for trying to protect you."

"So typical! You try to shield me from worry as if I can't handle it. As if I'm still the grieving widow you found in Oslo—"

"I had no way of knowing they weren't just nightmares."

"You still should have told me. Even if you did think they were nightmares."

"Why, so you could worry too?"

"You really don't get this whole 'sharing the burdens' thing, do you?"

"Am I supposed to ignore my instinct to protect you?"

"No, but you're not supposed to protect me from *you*!"

It stopped him short, because it was exactly what he was doing. Malachi was protecting Ava from his own terror. His own fear. Because he didn't want her to know he felt weak.

"I'm sorry." He went to her and enclosed her in his arms. "I'm sorry, Ava. I didn't think—didn't realize. You're right."

She didn't offer any smart remarks, but she didn't return the hug, either.

"Forgive me?" he asked. "For doubting you."

Her shoulders relaxed and she hugged him back. "Only if you forgive me for being forgetful."

He huffed out a breath. "Why are we fighting about this?"

"I don't know."

"Then enough. I suspect Volund was trying to torment me since he couldn't get to you. But he wasn't able to hurt me in any way."

"And I don't know what Azril wants, but I'm pretty sure he's on our side."

Malachi's mouth opened, then closed. He finally said, "I'm honestly not sure what to do with that."

"Me either." She took a deep breath and stepped back. "Should we tell Damien?"

"Yes. About both of us." He walked toward the kitchen, bracing himself in the doorway. "He might be furious we're just telling him now."

"He's not the boss of me."

Malachi gave her a wry smile over his shoulder. "Well, he is of me. Nevertheless, with the schedule we've been keeping, he can hardly blame us for not remembering every dream we have."

"I'm sorry." Ava wrapped her arms around his waist from behind, pressing her cheek to his back. "I would never keep something from you if I thought it could help."

He put his hands over hers. "I know. And I have to remember, you're a woman who is accustomed to keeping her own secrets. I can't expect you to change that overnight just because you're mated to me. I've been part of a team for centuries. And Azril tampered with your mind. If anyone should have sympathy for that, it's me."

She squeezed his waist. "You're right. You're being such a jerk right now."

The laugh burst out of him. He pulled her around to the front and hugged her. "We're still new at this, aren't we?"

"Yeah."

"Don't worry." He kissed the top of her head before he released her and walked to the phone. "We have hundreds of years to get it right."

Hundreds of years. He had to believe it. The Creator wouldn't have brought them together again just to rip them back apart.

Would He?

MALACHI LINGERED IN BED THE NEXT MORNING AS LONG AS HE could, knowing that it might be days before he would have Ava to himself again. They made love quietly. Deliberately. He memorized her face in the morning light and whispered promises that he would see her soon.

"Soon," she whispered back.

Then she hid under the covers while Malachi slipped out the door, and he pretended he hadn't seen her tears.

Today was the day he would break all the rules.

He was bringing a Grigori into the sacred house, sneaking him into the halls of knowledge, and stealing ancient weapons from Mikhael's armory.

If his mother were alive, she would kill him. Or congratulate him. He wasn't sure which.

A year and a half ago, Malachi knew who the enemy was. He was his father's son. A scribe of Mikhael's line. Taking vengeance on the sons of the Fallen. He walked alone, with no mate and no family.

And then…

One moment in the market. One glance from a golden eye. Like a small rudder charting the path of a massive ship, the course of his life had turned with a single touch.

Ava.

He had died. He had lived. He held a mate in his arms and in his heart. Everything he knew about his race's history he now questioned. Everything he'd trusted could be a lie. He was fighting alongside his enemies to protect the one person he could no longer live without. He would play the pawn in Jaron's games and play the comrade to a villain, all so he could be a hero for the one woman who called him home.

There was no reason to feel peace as he walked through the snow-dusted streets of Vienna, but he did.

Damien, Rhys, Kostas, and an unknown scribe met him outside the town house.

"Are you ready?" his watcher asked.

"Are you?"

Damien gave him half a smile. "It doesn't matter anymore. It's time."

• • •   • • •

THE HOUSE THE STRANGER TOOK THEM TO WAS HIDDEN BEHIND A block of new construction on the other side of the river. They walked in silence, the empty scent of Kostas a void to Malachi's senses.

"You've told your brothers?" Damien asked the unknown scribe quietly.

A nod was his only answer.

"Do they know what he is?"

The strange scribe held up a single gloved finger. *One.*

"We thank you both for your help."

Malachi and Kostas exchanged a look, but he could see the Grigori was as lost as he was. Rhys walked behind them, texting with someone as they walked. When they reached the house, he remained waiting outside.

"Waiting for a call," was his only explanation.

They entered the warm house and stomped their feet, taking off their boots and coats before the stranger motioned them down a narrow hallway.

He was a big man, dark of hair and face, with features that spoke of the Eastern Mediterranean. Malachi realized that while he'd removed his gloves and overcoat, his hands remained wrapped and his neck was covered in what looked like linen strips. He walked in a shroud, silently motioning them into a room at the end of the hallway.

It was a ritual room, carved wooden panels bearing the spells of hundreds of scribes. Malachi narrowed his eyes and stepped closer.

"Of course," he said when he finally interpreted the passage over the door. "They're Rafaene scribes."

Kostas whispered, "What?"

Damien nodded. "Our guide is our friend Evren's son. He took vows in Spain last year, and his father intervened for us. I believe only he and his watcher know we are here."

"And they agreed to help us?" Malachi asked. "Rafaenes are removed from politics."

"But their mission commands shelter and protection of those in need."

Kostas asked, "What is a Rafaene scribe?"

"You need to take off your clothes," Damien said. "All of them. Every stitch. I'll explain as we wrap you, but the process takes some time and we don't have much of it."

The stranger motioned to Malachi and he went to him, taking bundle after bundle of fine linen clothes that looked like bandages and stacking them in a basket as Damien spoke to Kostas.

"All Irin males have the same schooling beginning at the age of thirteen. We are trained as both warriors and scholars, though after some time, it becomes evident where our particular gifts lie. Scholars tend to retreat to libraries or work in the business world. Warriors go to scribe houses to protect humans and hunt Grigori."

"Yes," Kostas said, "I'm rather familiar with those."

"For some," Damien continued, "particularly those of the angel Rafael's line, the cost of being a warrior comes at great cost. Rafael's line is known for their healing ability. For Rafael's sons, even though they are of great skill, hunting takes a toll. To help with this, the Rafaene order was established hundreds of years ago."

Kostas looked at the man stacking bundles of linen. "He is a warrior?"

"A deadly opponent I would not like to meet in battle, despite his age," Damien said.

Malachi saw the young Rafaene smile, but he did not stop his task, dipping each bundle of linen in the clear water heating over the sacred fire.

"Rafaenes take a vow of silence and eschew any unnecessary contact," Damien explained. "They wrap their bodies in clean linen to deprive the senses and maintain quiet as much as physically possible. The idea is to take those years of silence and sensory isolation to practice meditation so they do not lose their souls in battle."

"A respite," Kostas said, nodding. "I understand this. But why are they helping us?"

"They care for those in need, particularly the injured or mentally distressed. Evren, one of Orsala's peers, spoke to his son's watcher, explaining about your women—do not be afraid he will break confidence, he gave me his word."

Kostas tossed Malachi a grim smile. "I suppose the word of a silent monk is about as secure as it gets, eh?"

"I'd agree," Malachi said. "But they're not monks. Rafaene scribes take vows for seven years only. Then they are required to reenter the world. That is the maximum amount of time the council allows for meditation."

"But while they practice their vows," Damien said, "they live in compounds not unlike monasteries. Quiet, *safe* places where troubled minds might heal."

Kostas stood before them, naked to his skin. Malachi couldn't help but notice that despite the man's inhuman beauty, his body was scarred beneath his clothes. He'd either been damaged by angelic blades or been injured too profoundly to heal without marks. The heavy scars were a jarring counterpart to his otherwise perfect form.

"You're thinking of the *kareshta*," Kostas said, standing naked and yet still defiant. "You think they might find refuge in these places."

Malachi said, "There are Rafaene compounds spread around the world. It is an option."

Kostas looked doubtful as he watched the quiet man who had covered his head with a ceremonial wrap.

"Rafaenes protect those who shelter with them as part of their vows," Malachi said. "These are no soft scholars, but some of the fiercest warriors our race possesses. It is because of their skill and prowess in battle that they are most in need of retreat. They will defend those under their care to the death."

Kostas nodded. "I will speak to my sister. I need to be wrapped? Like him?" He pointed toward the silent scribe, who approached with a basket of linen.

The man nodded.

"They will not stop you at the ritual baths," Damien said. "Rafaenes are not common in the Library, but they do occasionally make an appearance. Because they live silently and in peace, they are not required to ritually bathe unless they have recently experienced battle. If you are dressed as a Rafaene, no one will stop you or question your lack of *talesm*."

Malachi smiled. "It's brilliant. As long as we can vouch for you and you have a letter from this house, no one will think twice. You won't have to speak. Rafaenes are even urged to refrain from eye contact."

Kostas looked at the silent scribe who held up a roll of linen, word-lessly asking to begin wrapping him. The Grigori nodded.

"Thank you, brother," Damien said.

The scribe said nothing, crouching to wrap Kostas, starting with his feet and working his way up the man's legs, covering every inch of skin in linen.

"I feel like I'm being prepared for the grave," Kostas grumbled. "How do they live like this?"

Malachi saw the silent one's shoulders shake, and he guessed he was laughing.

"It's not easy," Damien said. "Or healthy for us. At least not in the long term. That is another reason only seven years is allowed. Before the Rending, we were an affectionate people. Irin need touch to remain healthy."

"We are the same," Kostas said quietly. "At least that is what we have learned. My soldiers who care for their sisters—especially the children—are stronger. More stable."

"It is the way it was meant to be," Damien said quietly. "I begin to see that now. How could any race survive with no balance?"

Malachi said, "Far more is at stake today than the fate of the Irin Council."

*   *   *   *   *   *

THEY took a taxi to the Hofburg. Luckily, their heavy winter clothes covered the ritual wrappings, which were already making Kostas squirm.

"So this is what those uncomfortable underthings the women wear feel like," he grumbled. "I think I'd prefer to be naked beneath my clothes."

Malachi stifled a smile. "That's a little more information than we wanted, Kostas."

"Then you wear this next time."

"No need." He puffed out his chest a bit. "My *talesm* are complete."

The spiraling vows that Ava had spoken now decorated his left chest. It was a basic tattoo right now, only the words were finished. Malachi would embellish it at his leisure, but the core of the written spell was complete.

"Gabriel's blood, you're going to be obnoxious about that now, aren't you?" Rhys said.

Damien laughed. "Newly mated male."

"I did not congratulate you or Ava," Kostas said. "My apologies and belated good wishes. I'm sure this is cause for celebration."

"It is."

Rhys asked, "Your kind take no mates, do they?"

Kostas's face closed down. "No."

They arrived at the Library past the morning rush, but many scribes were still in the process of bathing when they entered. Damien had been correct. No one gave Kostas a second glance after he handed over the letter signed by the Rafaene watcher. While Malachi, Rhys, and Damien did their ablutions, Kostas quietly changed into the hooded robe Damien gave him.

As they left the baths, the watcher said, "Try to remain silent in company."

"Do I need to guess what the pockets in this robe are for?"

"You'll see," Damien said. "Follow us and do not speak."

The Irina Council was taking their desks today, and the news had spread. The scribes' gallery was packed. They could barely find room along the edges, and some scribes were forced to stand on the stairs.

"Do you see Ava and Sari?" Malachi asked, craning his neck to see across the room. Unlike their last visit, the singers' gallery was also crowded. Not packed, but Malachi could see many Irina watching as the seven chosen elders assembled at the top of the stairs.

The elder scribes waited below, some with sour expressions and others wearing wide smiles. Gabriel's employer, Konrad, was beaming.

"Do you see Gabriel?" Damien asked.

Malachi scanned the crowd nearest to the top of the stairwell where Gabriel would have his position as Konrad's secretary.

"There," Rhys said. "I see him."

Malachi bent closer. "Is he involved in this?"

"No," Damien said. "I simply hoped he would not miss the ceremony. Tala, his mate, was slated to take a council seat when she was killed. This would be… important to her."

Malachi was still searching for Ava.

"It is important to us all," Rhys said. "Damien, are you sure—?"

"I want you here," the watcher said. "Keep in contact with Malachi."

"Fine, just make sure the Luddite checks his phone."

"I'm not a Luddite."

Rhys rolled his eyes. "A higher score in *Angry Birds* does not make you technologically literate. Just keep your phone on. I'm going to stand with Gabriel."

Malachi glanced at Kostas, whom he could tell was bursting with questions he couldn't ask.

He was about to make Rhys's excuses when he saw a flash of dark curls along the stairwell.

Ava.

Malachi smiled. She was radiant in her robes, her hair not tied back as was traditional, but falling in soft waves down her back.

"There she is," Malachi said.

He saw her pull a thick shank of hair over her shoulder just as she drew something small and black from a fold of her robe. She crossed her arms casually as her hand twisted in the fall of hair. Her fingers…

She was holding something.

As her shoulders slowly angled toward the stairs, he saw it.

A tiny camera, no bigger than her thumb. If he wasn't looking for it, it would have totally escaped his notice.

Malachi sighed. "Damn it. The woman is incorrigible."

Damien turned. "What?"

"I'll tell you later." *Maybe.*

"They're almost ready."

He could see the seven women walking down the stairs. The rustles and murmurs of the crowd had stilled. There was only the sound of shuffling feet and excited breaths as, one by one, the seven elder singers took the desks that Sari had pulled to the center of the room.

Daina, the Caribbean singer, spoke in a resonant voice.

"The songs of the Irina have returned to our city. We greet our brother scribes at their desks." She nodded to Jerome first, who was closest to her desk, no doubt enjoying the grim resignation on his face. Jerome couldn't complain, Malachi decided. His own mate was on the council, a rarity in Irin tradition. It was doubtless a concession in his eyes.

"Clearly," Daina continued, "the dust on our desks is simply an oversight."

"Sisters," Jerome said. "We wel—"

"The Irina will sing," Abigail interrupted him. "And then we will talk of other matters."

Jerome's face turned an ugly shade of red, but Malachi enjoyed knowing there was nothing—nothing—the old scribe could do about it.

It was Constance who started singing, her clear alto voice piercing the air as she began the traditional greeting song.

As soon as she began, Malachi was thrown back to his childhood, to the gatherings his village had hosted and the songs his mother had led to greet visitors. He felt Constance's magic fill the room. The ancient magic of his mother and grandmothers. Of their sisters and daughters. Songs and verses that stretched back a thousand years to the first daughters of the Forgiven.

"We come," Constance sang.

The other women responded, *"We come."*
"The Irina raise their song
We sing of our Creator and his children
We, the daughters of the Forgiven
We honor them with our words."

One by one, the seven voices of the elder singers joined their sister, chanting their mandate in the Old Language, calling their power as the chamber filled with magic.

"We sing a song of Uriel,
Wisest of heaven's host,
Of Rafael, our healer,
He that searched for the lost,
Gabriel, messenger of heaven,
Gave our songs to us,
Ariel, beloved of the earth,
May our children lift you up.
We shout of the power of Mikhael,
The mighty fist of heaven.
And call to the heart of Chamuel,
As we serve beside our brethren.
Let Leoc open up our eyes
That we might seek our path,
Bring honor to our Creator,
And glory to his crown."

Kostas could not contain his quiet gasp. The strength of the Irina flowed through the room as the women in the singers' gallery joined in the chorus their elders sang. The scribes around him lit with power as the air of the Library charged. The mated singers across the gallery gleamed in the afternoon sun. Malachi saw Kyra raise her hood and stand back, melting into the crowd behind Ava.

"We sing of our fathers
We call to the heavens
We honor the gifts they have given
In thanks, the Irina sing:
Hear us, oh heavens, answer our song
We call on the power of our fathers
We call to our reshon…"

Malachi searched for Ava, only to see his mate looking right at him, her eyes shining with joy.

I love you, he mouthed to her.

I love you too.

He narrowed his eyes and pointed to his chest, letting her know he'd caught her with the small camera.

She only laughed and shook her head.

Incorrigible woman. He hoped she never changed.

The Irina were still singing when Malachi felt a tug on his sleeve. He turned. Damien nodded.

It was time.

CHAPTER

TWENTY-FOUR

Ava watched the three men slip out of the chamber while every eye in the scribes' gallery was glued to the Irina singing below. She'd never heard anything like it. Voice after voice, climbing and reaching. The Library soared with the ancient music of heaven.

She couldn't understand everything, but she didn't have to. The tone of their voices said it all.

The Irina had returned. They sang with the voice of the angels. And they would not be ignored.

Searching for reactions, Ava scanned the scribes' gallery. Most of the younger scribes stared in shock, the rumors of the elder singers no match for the reality. A few were openly scornful. Others only looked confused. But it was the oldest scribes, the ones who had allowed themselves to age, who caught her attention the most.

Malachi had explained to her once that most of the aging scribes she saw were men who had lost mates and children in the Rending and had chosen not to extend their lives with more magic. They didn't age as fast as humans, but eventually they would pass to join their families. For many, the time could not pass swiftly enough.

It was those scribes—the ones who had lost the most—who arrested her attention. Their eyes were bright. Their faces full of longing and joy. Heartache and resolve. For a moment, she remembered her own mourning, and she ached for them.

As the voices died down, the elder scribes were already rising to their feet.

Konrad was the first to speak. "We welcome our sisters and give thanks for their return." He walked over to Kanti, the elder singer from Africa, and embraced her. She smiled and spoke quietly to him. Obviously, the two were friends.

Jerome and Constance nodded to each other but did not offer formal greetings, and Ava wondered if the two were already fighting about something. Oddly enough, that was reassuring.

Sari, who was standing next to her, explained more to Kyra, whose hood was raised. The *kareshta* was trying to remain inconspicuous, though she'd garnered more than her fair share of looks among the singers gathered. No one, after seeing she was attached to Sari, stopped to question her.

"Konrad and Kibwe are traditionalists. They have been staunch Irina supporters and do not favor forcing us into retreats. Rafael usually votes with them but has been hesitant to expand Irina participation in the scribe houses. Like Daina, he questions whether Irina are suited for battle."

"And the others?" Kyra asked.

"Jerome is the leader of those who favor compulsion. He would vote to censure any scribe whose mate did not enter a retreat and register herself like an animal," Sari said with a growl. "Edmund and Rasesh vote with him, and they can usually gain Anurak's support. Though he has shown more independence lately. It is believed his mate lives quietly in Thailand and does not favor compulsion. That may be part of the reason he hesitates."

"Can the elder scribes really do anything now? The Irina Council is back." Ava smiled. "I mean… game over for them, right?"

"They can still force compulsion if they want to be nasty. They still run the scribe houses. If they invoke censure for noncompliance…" Sari shook her head. "It would be bad." She looked across the gallery. "They're gone. And now we wait."

• • •   • • •

MALACHI FOLLOWED DAMIEN DOWN THE HALL, HIS HEART RACING even if his body could not.

"Do you know where we're going?" he murmured.

"Yes."

Farther and farther they traveled into the labyrinth of the Irin headquarters. They passed quiet study rooms and meditation chambers. Offices and guard rooms. Most people didn't seem to take any notice of two scribes and a Rafaene wandering around the hallways. If a guard did catch Damien's eye, all they did was offer him a respectful nod.

Malachi wondered just how much more there was to know about his watcher. "Were you really a Templar Knight?"

Kostas's head came up. "Really?"

"That was a long time ago," Damien said. "We need to go down these stairs. Kostas, shut up."

The look the man gave Damien was priceless. Malachi wondered when the last time was that anyone had told the Grigori commander to shut up.

"That wasn't a 'no,'" Malachi said.

"You really do have a death wish," the watcher said.

"My mate would say, 'Been there. Done that.'" He couldn't stop the grin. He'd forgotten how fun it was to irritate the man.

They climbed down wood-paneled stairwells and into the belly of the Library. The hallways became narrower and the wood paneling ceased. What was left was stone and plaster chilled from the winter temperatures. One long hallway speared into the darkness, smaller passages running off either side. Every single passage looked identical, and every single door looked the same.

Old wood with intricate spellwork written in blood-ink. These were dangerous rooms.

"Here's where things get complicated," Damien said, turning left down one empty corridor and huffing out a frozen breath. "I have a theory. It will either work or bring down the whole of the Library Guard on us."

"That sounds promising."

Kostas said, "Can I speak now?"

"Yes. And to answer what you're probably wondering, no, there are no guards in this section. They would be redundant. Magic protects each of these doors. This corridor"—he spread his arms out—"leads to Mikhael's armory. The armory holds all the heaven-forged weapons the Irin have collected over the years. It has seven doors that correspond to the seven cardinal archangels. Malachi and I would go through Mikhael's door, except it is guarded against any Irin who does not have the password."

"What happens if you just try to break it down?" Kostas asked. "Could we get out fast enough?"

"It wouldn't matter if we flew. If we attempt to breach it without the password, these blood-spells would turn my own magic against me. The more powerful the scribe, the more dangerous the attempt. For someone my age, it would probably be deadly. For someone of Malachi's power, it would be debilitating. Even a child with his mother's magic would be harmed."

Malachi looked at Kostas and suddenly realized Damien's plan. It was ingenious. Or insane.

Kostas said, "I have no written magic. That's what you're thinking, isn't it?"

"You have natural magic, so it's not going to be painless," Damien said. "But it shouldn't kill you. The trick is finding out which door to enter. These spells were written specific to the Forgiven. Though our blood is mixed after so many generations, we all draw our magic from one cardinal in our background."

Malachi frowned. "And those with no cardinal in their blood?"

"It's rare, but if you found an Irin with no cardinal blood, he wouldn't be able to open a door."

"So it might just kick Kostas out?"

"Possibly. Or… kill him. I'm honestly not sure what will happen." Damien gave him a helpless shrug. "There is no way to break the magic. We can only hope to step around it somehow."

"And if I don't try it?" Kostas asked.

"Then we don't have any heaven-forged weapons. We will never kill an angel without a heaven-forged blade."

"Fine," Kostas said. "I will try this on two conditions. I claim one of these weapons for myself."

"Fine."

"And I will hear your vow—either of you, I don't care—that you will kill my father."

Damien and Malachi were both silent.

"Why?" Malachi finally asked. "Your father appears to be acting with us. As an ally."

"I don't care," Kostas said. "I cannot kill him. And until he is dead, I will not be free. Nor will my sister."

"But Kostas—"

"You have never lived as another's slave," the Grigori said with terror and rage battling in his eyes. "You do not know. I will have Kyra free of him, or I will walk out of here, find my sister, and you will never see us again."

"Done," Damien said. "Though I will pick the time. We cannot afford to lose an ally before we win the battle."

Kostas paused. "Fine. But I am not willing to wait years."

"You will not have to."

"Damien!"

"It is done, brother." Damien put his hand on Malachi's shoulder. "I will kill Barak, or I will die in the effort. Would you do less to kill Volund and free your woman from his power?"

No. Malachi knew that while Jaron might leave Ava alone for sentimental reasons he could not fathom, Volund would only use her.

"So," Malachi said. "We don't have three angels to kill, we have five. Lovely."

＊ ＊ ＊　　＊ ＊ ＊

AVA'S eyes were starting to cross from the tangle of voices on the floor. Debates were already happening as elders fought over the issue of compulsion. It was the only thing anyone wanted to talk about, even though Rafael, the elder from South America, had tried to bring up the growing violence in Vienna and the rest of Europe.

"I cannot condone this council's disregard for the evidence of violence growing daily against humans in our own city," he finally shouted, rising to his feet. "I had hoped—"

"You had hoped the elder singers would rush to support your concern for the humans," Konrad said, "though they have as little interest in it as the rest of us."

"Humans have always been violent toward each other," Edmund, the elder from England, said. "We protect them from the Grigori, but that is the extent of our mandate. It is not our job to hunt human predators."

"These are Grigori attacks," Rafael said.

Anurak, the Asian elder, said, "The evidence from the watcher in Oslo and Barcelona is compelling. But I see no evidence of Grigori here. There has been no Grigori attack in Vienna for a hundred years at least."

Ava leaned over to Sari. "How much longer do we keep our mouths shut?"

"Wait."

Abigail spoke up. "I have seen evidence of Grigori attacks. Even in Vienna, I have seen this. Those of you living too long in the city forget how devious our enemies can be. Do you think the sons of the Fallen will be so obvious?"

"Do not look to the headlines," Daina said. "Look to the stories the humans do not tell. It is the humans no newspaper will note that the Grigori target. And those people are missing in our city."

Silence fell over the Library. No one could discount an Irina elder of Daina's age and experience, and no one wanted to disagree with Abigail, either.

"If this is true," Jerome said carefully, "these attacks are even more evidence that the best place to protect our families is *within guarded retreats*."

The Library floor erupted in groans.

"This is not about compulsion," Abigail shouted. "You force your agenda—"

"We no longer have the luxury of debate," Rasesh said. "If the Grigori are upon us, we must take action to protect our most vulnerable."

"Who is vulnerable?" Gita, the central Asian singer, asked. "Me? Because it has been the *singers* of my region who stabilized the human population there after the Grigori erupted in violence over the death of their sire. The singers, not the scribes."

Rasesh stood. "You speak of an isolated incident—"

"The singers in Africa have been active for at least fifty years," Kanti said with a shrug. "The Grigori are on the decline because of it."

"Exactly." Konrad sounded bored. "Where are they? I see no Grigori. No Fallen. Our city is safe."

Ava frowned when the cacophony started to die.

Konrad stood up, emboldened by the sudden quiet. "With the return of the Irina Council, our enemies must know we are stronger than ever. We draw from the power of both halves of our race now. We can begin to rebuild our society. Why would the Grigori…"

He died off when he heard a low clapping sound.

Ava looked up to see where everyone's heads were pointing.

Vasu.

The angel was sitting on the railing of the balcony just below the organ pipes, slowly clapping with a wide grin on his face.

When he saw everyone's attention on him, he spread his hands. "Why do you stop? This is very entertaining."

•••   •••

DAMIEN, Kostas, and Malachi stared at the row of blood-stained doors.

"The Fallen have cardinals too," Kostas said. "Though only six were believed to be living, we know that's not true now. My father is one of them. Jaron and Volund are as well. Many of them have the same gifts as the Forgiven, and I am of Barak's blood."

Malachi nodded. "His purpose in heaven?"

"Barak was a guardian of the realm before he fell. He listened for unspoken threats. His gift is hearing."

Damien's eyes were sharp. "And you hear as he does?"

"Some." Kostas shrugged. "In bits and pieces. I have no control over the ability, but the magic is there."

"Hearing…," Damien murmured. "Malachi?"

"I say Gabriel's door," he said. "Irin in Gabriel's line have unusual skill in reading, but *Irina* of Gabriel's line can hear beyond the normal range. I'd guess Barak's magic is most closely associated with Gabriel."

"I'd guess the same."

Kostas said, "And I dislike the word *guess*. But I suppose it's worth a shot. Which door is Gabriel's?"

Malachi pointed to the second closest to the main passageway. The spellwork was complex. Layer upon layer of it, written in the black-red that marked them as blood-spells. For the Irin, blood mixed with ash from a sacred fire produced an ink of unmatched power. Indeed, it was the mix of blood and ash in their *talesm* that made the spells written on their body most potent. For written spellwork, you couldn't get more dangerous than a blood-spell.

And this blood-spell would turn a scribe's own magic against him. The more powerful, the more deadly.

Kostas stood in front of the door and took a deep breath. "What do I do?"

"Open it," Damien said quietly. "Just turn the knob."

The brass doorknob sparked when Kostas put his linen-covered hand on it. Malachi could almost see the slither of magic crawl up his arm, twining and testing the creature who dared touch it. Kostas's jaw tensed, but he did not break contact or cry out.

"It feels like a snake tearing through my innards," he forced out the words through gritted teeth. "How long?"

"I don't know," Damien said, carefully keeping his distance from the Grigori.

"What is it doing?" Kostas cast them a sidelong glance.

"It's testing you. I think. Trying to find where you belong."

"Good luck then," the man groaned out. "I don't belong anywhere."

He wasn't sure if the other man heard when Damien whispered, "I'm counting on it."

Malachi saw Kostas's knees buckle, so he stepped forward, only to have his watcher's arm throw him back.

"Don't touch him."

"He's falling."

"But he's not letting go."

It was true. Though Kostas was on his knees, his hand had not dropped from the doorknob. The brass glowed red-hot, and the spells on the doorway slithered over each other, ancient blood rising to life to take its turn testing the strange creature attempting to breach the passageway. The spells moved like living creatures, sliding closer to the doorknob and then slipping away after Kostas's body gave another jerk. Over and over, hundreds of years of blood-spells attacked the foreign intruder.

After more minutes than Malachi wanted to count, the crawling spells slowed. Kostas's body was still jerking, but he hadn't let go. His eyes were glazed over, and sweat soaked through his linen wrappings.

"How much longer?" he whispered.

Damien knelt down next to him. "Hold on, brother. When I tell you, you will give the command to open."

"Command...?"

"*Luoh*," Damian said quietly. "Say it now, Kostas. *Luoh*."

"*Luoh*," Malachi whispered along as Kostas groaned the old command.

With a heavy sigh, the reluctant door to the armory swung open.

THE whole Library stared at Vasu for silent seconds before the guards stationed at the foot of the stairs cried out and threw silver daggers at the angel.

Vasu simply disappeared and reappeared, now hanging on the tallest organ pipe. "That's not going to work," he said. "But do keep trying if you like."

Scribes across the gallery began leaping to the ground, some rushing toward the balcony, others running toward the singers' gallery where Irina had begun to chant over Vasu's laughter. Ava felt the terror in the air.

"What do we do?" she shouted at Sari while trying to shield Kyra from the wave of panic taking over the room.

"I don't know!" Sari looked across the Library, probably searching for Damien, but Ava had just looked and neither Malachi nor Damien were anywhere to be found.

"I think we need to—"

"Stop."

A single word froze the crowd, the room, and everything in it. Knives hung suspended in the afternoon sun. Papers rested in midair. Two scribes froze, their leap from the gallery halted by a single command from the one being Ava had never expected to see in the heart of the Irin Council chambers.

Jaron stood before the crowd, not hovering over them as Vasu did, but standing among them, a creature of such frightening glory that Ava heard some begin to weep. He made no attempt to veil himself. He had become giant. A creature of majesty and power, terrifying and beautiful at the same time.

"I am Jaron," he said, and though his voice was quiet, it filled every corner of the Library. "You will cease."

Silver daggers frozen in the air dropped to the ground. Papers fell, as did the scribes. But though Ava saw them moving, the violence had halted.

In the space of a heartbeat, another angel appeared. If Jaron's harsh features reminded Ava of a bird of prey, this being was a wolf. Silver-black hair hung thick around his face, and though his eyes were a glowing gold, his face reminded Ava of a winter lake. Calm and frozen.

Kyra let out a breath. "Father."

So this was Barak. He angled his head up to the singers' gallery. Kyra stepped forward, and Barak held up his hand.

But it wasn't only Barak who spoke.

With one voice, the two angels said, "Daughter, come."

It wasn't even a question. Jaron spoke, and Ava moved toward him. She and Kyra walked toward the top of the stairs, as the Irina around them whispered furiously and parted the crowd.

"No!" Sari shouted, trying to grab both of their arms.

"He lied," Ava whispered. Jaron had told her he couldn't command her, but she couldn't stop. She kept walking while Kyra wept, and Ava realized for the first time what the compulsion of the Grigori felt like.

Such exquisite torture.

Because nothing in this world, not the love of her mate or the strength of her will, could stop Ava from following Kyra down the stairs. Part of her didn't want to, but the other part wanted nothing else. Her eyes locked with Jaron's, and he was the most beautiful thing she had ever seen. She would do anything for him.

"No," Jaron said. "You will not."

She couldn't turn her head to look at Kyra, but she could hear the *kareshta* weeping, even as Barak made soothing noises to his child.

"I'm sorry," Kyra kept saying. "Forgive me, Father. I'm sorry."

"I do not want your sorrow," a tired voice came. "I never did, child."

When Ava reached Jaron, he turned her to face the crowd.

"This," he began, his solemn voice filling the room, "is the daughter of my blood." He put his hands on Ava's shoulders, and her mating marks lit under his power. "Wholly mated to a son of the Forgiven."

Ava felt every eye in the Library focus on her. She wanted to shrink, but there was nowhere to go. She wanted to hide, but Jaron would never let her. Whatever his purpose had been in keeping her safe, she knew it was for this moment.

"For thousands of years, we have hidden them," Barak said. "But no more. Your enemies gather while you argue over petty human concerns."

Jaron said, "Our sons took your daughters, so this day, we give you ours."

Ava saw the singers around the room flinch.

"Thousands of years they have lingered in hiding. Some killed by the hands of their brothers or fathers. Some mad with the voices you have managed to conquer." Jaron spoke to the gathered elder singers. "Find them and protect them. Add the strength of their blood to the wisdom of yours. Do this, and we will enact vengeance for the crimes against you."

Daina bravely took a step forward. "Why?"

"Volund approaches. He has made allies, even within your own ranks. If you are to wipe this enemy from the earth, you must stop fighting. You have been given the wisdom of the Forgiven. Use it for more than your own interests. Protect these vulnerable, and you will be our allies."

Jerome said, "We want no help from the Fallen."

Anurak stood. "Do not speak for those who have been silent, brother. What do you propose, Angel?"

"An alliance for now. Volund's sons linger at your gates. Grimold's get already walk among you. Walk outside and see what your city has become."

Ava looked at Sari, who rushed from the gallery along with several of the scribes from the opposite sides of the room.

Muttering and whispers filled the Library as Ava felt the eyes of the Irin fix on her and Kyra. She reached out for the other woman's hand, feeling her panic.

"Ava," Jaron said, leaning down till his mouth was at her ear. "It is time to show them."

"Show them what?"

"I show you what was has been, what will be, and what could be. Do not fear the darkness. Sing."

The vision rushed into her mind so quickly Ava knew she was only a conduit between the angel and the audience. Her mouth opened and song poured out. It was not the deliberate poetry she had studied, but a raw rush of tone and emotion. She didn't even recognize the words she spoke. In an instant, she saw the whole of Jaron's vision, and the scales fell from her eyes.

* * ◆ * * *

TWO DARK-HAIRED CHILDREN WITH GOLDEN EYES. A GIRL, LAUGHING AS butterflies swirled around her. A boy staring back at her with his father's petulance. An ink-black jaguar curled around the children protectively as a wolf and a tiger paced behind. The tiger bent to the girl, opening his mouth. The great beast closed his jaw around her nape as she continued to smile and pet its cheek.

Behind the delicate tableau, a great circle rose in the sky. A sun twisted with gold and silver. Higher and higher it rose until the moon covered its brilliance. In the sudden flash of darkness, a million scattered points of light became visible in the heavens, dancing tremulously in concert to a gathering song.

A bird of prey called as the darkness passed, its scream shattering the song of the stars. The jaguar leapt. It reached into the sky until its arms became the wings of an eagle that crashed into the attacking bird in the light of a blood-red eclipse. They battled, tearing each other's flesh as ash and blood rained down on a city of stones. Turning and twisting, the two battled higher as the wolf below howled and the tiger leapt on the jackals that were laughing in the barren streets.

Then both birds dropped, twisting into men of impossible beauty, and a jagged sword rose from the city of stone, piercing the angels as they fell.

* * ◆ * * *

AS THE LAST NOTE CARRIED OVER THE ASSEMBLY, AVA'S BREATH LEFT her and everything went black.

VI.

The three angels knelt beside her, Vasu brushing the hair from her forehead as delicately as a mother with a child.

"Will she survive?"

"Yes." Jaron's eyes swept the Library, but the assembly had shifted, a slight twist in dimension allowing him a last moment alone with her.

Though Ava still slept, he gathered the girl into his arms and rocked her as he had seen her mother do when she was a child.

Thirty years of watching over her at a distance. A blink of an eye. A sudden gasp of breath.

And yet.

Within her blood lay the secret.

"I know." Jaron bent to her ear, uncaring of his brothers, who listened in. "I understand why now."

Ava's eyes fluttered open. "Me too."

"What have you done to me, daughter?"

"The only worthy sacrifice is the one that hurts. How much do you want forgiveness?"

A drop fell on her cheek, and Jaron realized he was weeping.

"Will you tell her?" he asked his daughter's daughter.

"I'll tell her you loved her, and you wished you could say good-bye."

"I called her Ava because she was the voice of heaven to me. She called me *Bâbâ* when she was a child."

Ava put her hand on his cheek, and for the first time in thousands of years, Jaron felt it. He had been hollow before. Ava's union with the scribe—their impossible, unpredictable love—had altered his reality forever.

For the first time in his eons of existence, Jaron felt. "Now that I must leave, I find that I do not want to go."

"*Bâbâ*," Ava whispered, her voice thick with emotion. "Free her. Free them all. And return."

"Ava," he said. "Daughter of my blood." Jaron bent down and kissed her forehead, then he whispered in her ear.

She closed her eyes and nodded.

Then Jaron blinked, and Ava was gone. He stood and faced his chosen brothers: Barak, who would be with him until the end, and Vasu, who had chosen to stay behind.

"Do you understand what you lose, brother?" he asked Barak.

"Unlike you"—the angel's eyes held what Jaron now recognized as torment—"my magic mixed with the Forgiven's long ago. I am ready."

Jaron narrowed his eyes but asked no more questions.

"And you?" he asked Vasu.

"Someone has to stay behind and watch," Vasu said with a casual shrug.

"Do it," Barak said. "She is one of them now. Power surrounds her. Lower the shields and call him."

Jaron looked at Vasu. "Are you ready?"

The dark angel grinned a predatory smile. "Go."

CHAPTER

TWENTY-FIVE

Malachi held another knife out to Kostas, who tucked it into the cleverly sewn pockets in his robe. Damien was searching the armory for one specific weapon, but Malachi didn't know what it was. The chamber held case after case of blades of various eras and styles. Knives were most common, with throwing daggers a close second. Spears and swords hung on the stone walls. There were even a few crossbows and an ax or two. Malachi and Kostas were looking through the knives and hiding those they would smuggle out of the Library.

After a few more minutes, Damien came back bearing an intricately cut dagger. "Thought you might like to use this one."

"Why?"

He looked confused. "It's the one Brage used in Istanbul when he killed you. Too morbid?"

Malachi looked at the dagger, remembering the pitch-black blade the Grigori had balanced on his finger on the roof of the building in Oslo, then he looked back at Damien. "This isn't Brage's dagger. He carried it in Oslo. Ava gave it to Jaron when I killed Brage."

Damien's eyes went hard. "Are you saying this isn't a heaven-forged blade?"

Malachi shrugged. "I have no idea. But I know that's not the dagger that killed me."

"Dammit." Damien looked around the armory. "I wonder—"

"How many of these are actually heaven forged?" Kostas asked, picking through the rows of weapons. "Not all of them. Maybe half. Some of these are far too new."

"What do you know about angel blades?" Malachi asked.

"We all have our hobbies," Kostas said, picking up a rusted weapon that looked far from useful.

The Grigori brought it up to his face and breathed on it. Taking the edge of his own knife, he cut a long gash in his forearm, wetting the edge of one of his linen wrappings with blood before he took it and carefully wiped the blade. After a few minutes, he held it up again. The blade was a dull pewter in color, but the edge was sharp again, the blade now clearly lethal.

"Angel blades are best cleaned with blood. It restores them. If you're not sure if a blade is genuine, try that. A good rule of thumb is that anything forged in the past thousand years is probably a fake or simply something confiscated from an angel but isn't a heaven-forged blade."

"I thought all angels carried them," Malachi said.

"They're rare," Kostas told them, "even among the Fallen. Lesser angels usually can't keep them, so any blade taken from one of the lesser Fallen is probably just a sword. And of course, some of them don't need them. Guardians of heaven carry swords within their bodies."

Malachi and Damien both gawked.

"Unlike you," Kostas said with a grim smile, "my father is an angel. I do know a few things."

"I'll keep looking," Malachi said, turning back to the racks.

"Wait." Damien held up a hand. "I hear…"

Without warning, the doors to the armory groaned and swung open. Library guards rushed in, only to halt with wide eyes when they saw the two scribes and the man dressed as a Rafaene in the process of stealing weapons.

"Well," Kostas muttered, "this is awkward."

Damien stepped forward. "Brothers, we are—"

"Out of time." The captain of the Library Guard stepped forward. "I know who you are, Damien of Bohemia. The enemy is here. There are Fallen in the Library as we speak."

"Is it Jaron?"

"How did you know that?" the captain asked.

"Jaron is an ally. For now," Malachi said. "But there are others who are not."

The captain did not question him but nodded briskly and spoke to his men. "Distribute the weapons. Take one for yourself and others for the men under you, then head back to the Library and join those protecting the council."

Malachi saw Kostas swipe another blade. He must have had almost a dozen hidden in his robe. He tugged on the heavy wool and nodded toward the doors just as the captain of the guard turned back to them.

"I recognize you too, Malachi of Sakarya. I fought with your father. I will trust the son of Ilyas and Hanna would not betray his brothers."

"You trust rightly."

"Then go. We need all the able warriors we can spare," the captain growled. "This city has been soft for too long. Politicians and financiers are not warriors. They forget what it means to fear."

Damien, Kostas, and Malachi ran down the hallway as more guards flooded in. They ran up the stairs and out the main entrance, which was completely unguarded.

"Damien?" Someone shouted across the empty courtyard.

Malachi turned his head. It was Sari.

She came to her mate, completely out of breath. "The humans. They're gone."

"What do you mean, they're gone?"

Malachi walked toward one of the larger courtyards in the Hofburg, searching for the bustle of tourists or the honking of taxis.

There was nothing.

Cars sat empty on the small side streets. Horses snuffled and shuffled, waiting for empty carriages to roll.

"Heaven above," he whispered.

Who had done it? Jaron or Volund? More importantly, where was his mate?

He walked back to Kostas, Damien, and Sari, who were all frozen in the center of the courtyard.

"This is Jaron's doing," Malachi said. "Or one of the other angels."

"It's a city of ghosts," Sari said. "What have they done with them?"

"I don't think any of the humans will be harmed. They're just... away. More importantly, where is Ava? Which angels were in the library?"

Sari said, "It was Vasu first, then Jaron and Barak. I've just called Renata and told her, Rhys, Max, and Leo to meet us here. She checked the elder singers' homes this morning, and every one had been ransacked. The Grigori have been watching."

"They know the singers have returned," Damien said. "And your men, Kostas?"

"I'll call." The Grigori pulled his mobile phone from a pocket in his robe before he handed a gold blade to Sari with a wink. "That's for you. Matches your hair."

Sari frowned at Damien but took the blade. "Is this—"

"We'll explain later," Malachi said. "For now, let's head into the library. If the enemy has finally reached Vienna, we need a plan. And I want to see my mate."

*   *   *   *   *   *

AVA'S EYES WERE CLOSED, BUT SHE HEARD THE WHISPERED COMMAND.

"Go."

For a moment, she was still in her dream, then her eyes blinked open and three angels stood over her. Jaron and Barak she knew. The third was a frighteningly pale figure with icy gold eyes and face cut from pale marble.

"Yes," he whispered, and with his voice she knew.

Volund.

But Ava didn't have time to be frightened before Vasu was there. He wrapped his arms around Volund from the back, then with a wink, both angels were gone.

Jaron held out a hand. "Come and stand with your people."

"What just happened?"

"You are no longer under my shields," Jaron said. "Be wary. Vasu will keep Volund occupied for a time. You have no defenses against him except the words my brother spoke to you. Do you remember them?"

Ava nodded.

"Good. Use them if he comes near."

He began to walk from the room. Barak followed.

"Where are you going?" she asked. "And can't you just… blink away or something?"

Jaron smiled, and for once, it appeared to be a true smile. "Only

Vasu can do that without cost, as it is in his nature. For us, transporting takes power I would rather save for now. I am not, after all, a god."

"Oh."

Jaron looked around to the crowd of still-staring Irin. "These women and their kind are precious. Will you protect them?"

Daina stepped forward. "I give them my protection."

Jerome joined her. "As do I."

"Ava!"

She heard her name from down the hall. Jaron spared her a single look before he melted into the facade of her old doctor from Istanbul, then he and an older man with a beard slipped out of the hall as if no one had seen them transform.

Malachi stormed into the room, Damien, Sari, and Kostas on his heels. He ran down the stairs and caught her in an embrace.

"You're here," he breathed out in relief. "You're safe."

The elders around them were silent, but Ava could feel their eyes.

"So you are the scribe," Abigail said, "who mated with the daughter of the Fallen."

It was a little more complicated than that, but Ava didn't feel like explaining.

Malachi simply said, "I am. We are *reshon*."

She heard the concerned muttering around the room.

"What is your name, brother?"

"Malachi of Sakarya. Right now, we must—"

His words were cut off when a dozen solemn men marched into the library. The remaining scribes parted as they headed for the stairs and sped down, surrounding the Irin and Irina elders.

"Elders," the captain said, "we must make you safe."

"No," Carmina said. "We are the strongest singers in the city. We need to face this threat and defend our people."

"No, sister," Daina counseled, "we must make the council safe. For the Irina council to be wiped out now—just when we've finally reformed—would be devastating to our people. We will let the captain guard us and trust our sisters to play their part in the battle."

Several of the elder singers glared, but none contradicted Daina. They knew the woman was right.

Sari stepped forward. "We believe that Grimold's children are in the city. The human population appears to be gone. They have come for us."

"What do you mean 'gone?'" Konrad asked.

"Just that," Damien said. "They are not here. One of the archangels appears to have put the city in stasis."

"The whole city?" Jerome asked. "But—"

"It doesn't work on any with angelic blood," Ava said. "Jaron told us. So there may be humans with Grigori blood roaming around really, really confused. Other than that, yes, they can do it. I've seen Jaron do it before, and it may be something that other angels can do too. The humans aren't gone, they're just… elsewhere right now."

"Vienna is under attack," Malachi said. "The elder singers' homes have been invaded. We need to get guards checking any Irina safe houses in the city."

Constance stepped forward and said, "I will tell the captain where they are, but I only trust the Library guards."

Jerome sighed. "Constance—"

"The Library Guard or we stay in hiding," the singer said with an ironclad will. "These are not warriors. These are teachers and healers. And I will not trust these women to any but our strongest."

"How many?" Damien asked. "How many of your Irina are in the city right now?"

Constance glared at him, but then looked between him and Sari and relented. "No more than forty. Some are capable of defending themselves. But if we are overrun—"

"There is a Rafaene house in the second district near the Carmelite Church. Your sisters could take refuge there. The scribes would be bound to protect them."

Constance nodded. "They are mostly in the first district. That could work."

"Let the Library Guard protect you and the other elders," Damien said. "When my men get here, I will give them the task of helping your sisters to the Rafaene scribe house. No one will be able to touch them there."

"Very well," Constance said. "And the rest of us?"

The fourteen elders stood solemnly, watching the captain of the Library Guard.

"Come with me," he said. "We have defenses set up to protect the Council." He held out a hand when the secretaries and other assistants stepped forward. "Only the council."

A pale scribe asked, "But what should we do?"

"Fight," Malachi said. "Or stay out of the way of those who will."

◆ ◆ ◆   ◆ ◆ ◆

VASU MATERIALIZED IN MIDAIR, TOSSING VOLUND'S BODY INTO THE sculpture rising from the stones of the Graben. The normally bustling pedestrian mall was empty, thanks to Jaron's manipulations, and no one was there to hear the archangel scream.

"Did that hurt?" Vasu taunted. "Surely not. Surely an archangel has more fortitude than to be hurt by the petty constructions of man."

"You?" Volund roared and flung himself across the street, tackling the younger angel from his perch near the column of a nearby building. The stone cracked as they rolled into it, and the towering structure groaned. "Galal killed you!"

"Obviously not." Vasu laughed and blinked away, appearing to perch on top of the marble and gold angels of the plague column, the grand Baroque sculpture in the heart of Old Vienna some human ruler had commissioned to thank their god for mercy.

"Why do the humans make angels look like babies?" he mused. "It's insulting."

He ducked to the side as Volund leapt for him, his hands and feet crumbling the marble like so much dust as he crawled up the column.

"You do like to hear yourself talk, don't you?" Volund sneered.

"Yes." Vasu stood balanced on one foot at the very top of the twenty-one- meter column. "I'm very clever."

"You're very irritating. I'm going to kill you now, whelp. Then I will deal with Galal."

"You can try. But don't worry." His voice lost its humor. "I have my own plans for Galal."

From his perch, Vasu could see the shadows of Grigori slipping into the city. But he couldn't look long because Volund grabbed his foot, flinging him from the sculpture and slamming him into the stones below.

He'd forgotten how much impact could hurt in this form. How irritating. Still, it was better to be able to shift quickly.

Volund's lip curled. He stopped playing and drew a flaming sword from his side. "Do you remember this?"

Vasu's eyes gleamed. "Oh yes."

"I will slay you with it and feed your body to your children."

He ignored Volund but not the sword. "A Guardian's sword. Oh Volund, I should be afraid, shouldn't I?" He paused, looked his enemy in the eye. "And yet… I wonder."

"You won't have to wonder for long," Volund growled.

"Would Jaron trust me with her location?"

Volund froze.

"I could be there in a heartbeat." Vasu smiled. "Did you think your secret was safe?"

The other angel bared his teeth.

"I've always wondered what would happen if one of us killed her. Killed your *mate*." Vasu sneered.

Volund roared and swung his sword at Vasu. He flipped and spun, an expert with the angelic blade. And yet Vasu had been created to be a messenger of the heavens. His speed exceeded even the most dangerous of the Creator's guard.

"Would it hurt, Volund?" Vasu appeared behind Volund. "Would you bleed if she died?"

Volund turned and flung the blade at Vasu, only to have it come spinning back when its mark dissolved seconds before it hit.

"Is that why you hate her *so much*?" he whispered in Volund's ear.

And he was gone.

"Where is Jaron?" Volund spun in a rage, kicking the stone as shattered pieces of the old buildings rained down on the gracious streets below.

"You'd like to know, wouldn't you?" Vasu was perched on the plague column again, sitting on the head of a fat cherub, leaning his dark head against the gold. "You won't find him until he wants you. Just like you won't find your *mate*." He sneered the word. "But I can. Jaron hasn't hidden her from *me*, has he?"

Volund moved with lightning speed, leaping from the corner of his building and climbing up the sculpture. But it was not fast enough for Vasu, who blinked away again.

And appeared at the top of a building one hundred meters down the Graben. "Of course, maybe I already know where she is!" Vasu shouted. "Is that why you let Jaron hide her from the world? To protect yourself?"

With a roar, Volund jumped over the rooftops, raining stone and glass down on the street below. Just as he swung his body over the last one, Vasu grinned and blinked away.

Then he was at Volund's back, a heaven-forged blade pressed to the angel's throat. "I have no love for Jaron's blood. And your very soul would split in two if your mate died, wouldn't it? What a brilliant idea." He kissed the angel's cheek. "I think I'll go pay her a visit."

Volund grabbed Vasu's arm and swung him overhead. The younger angel grimaced. His eyes swam and his body made a sickening crack into the building. The ground shook below them as Volund began to bring the blade down.

Vasu only smiled and disappeared.

"WHAT IS THAT CRASHING SOUND?" AVA ASKED.

"I don't know, but I want you to listen to me." Malachi pulled Ava away from Damien and the others, who were shouting orders to the scribes who had joined them. The whole group had run out of the Hofburg and behind the riding school, taking the smaller side streets as they made their way toward St. Stephen's Cathedral, drawing attention away from the Library and toward a position they would be able to secure.

"Narrow streets and tall buildings," Malachi said as they jogged, "are not your friends. The plaza will be better. At least we'll be able to see them coming."

As they ran, Ava saw nothing but a few flickering shadows that quickly disappeared. More and more scribes joined them until their number included at least fifty. Also among their number was a collection of singers, most in groups of two or three. They whispered spells to surround the company, short staffs in hand, while the scribes surrounded them instinctively.

"Where is everyone?" she asked. "There are hundreds of Irin scribes in Vienna you told me. Where are they?"

"Politicians and financiers," Malachi said. "Most of these scribes have forgotten how to fight. Or they simply don't have the stomach for it."

When they reached the plaza, Malachi pulled her over to an isolated corner in the window of a pharmacy.

"When Leo arrives," he said. "I'm sending you and Kyra with him."

"What?" Her jaw dropped. "No, I'm not leaving you."

"You are. You and Kyra are too important. And you're not strong enough for this fight. I can't protect you and face this at the same time."

"Malachi, no."

"Listen—"

"Vasu gave the words to me. Spells I can use against the angels and the Grigori. I can protect—"

"Ava, we're not only facing soldiers." Malachi's voice dropped.

He turned them to face across the plaza and toward the Graben where the violent crashes and skittering footsteps had grown progressively louder. It was only then she saw them.

"I know you can kill Grigori," he said. "But can you kill *all* of them?"

Ava turned and saw Grimold's secret.

Slipping between shadows and jumping from balcony to balcony, the sons of the Fallen trickled into the square from streets and alleys and even from above. No longer distracted by the presence of humans, they focused on the scribes. There were hundreds of them, blending into the shadows and curling from the darkest corners of the street. They didn't come as an army but as thieves, their shadowed eyes watching the gathering of scribes in utter silence. They crouched in small groups or slipped from side streets as the Irin gathered at the foot of St. Stephen's Cathedral.

Especially the children.

Round-cheeked and slim. Fair-haired and dark. They crept like cats along the corners, trailing after their older kin with vicious smiles and hungry eyes.

"No."

His hands tightened on her shoulders. "Grimold is a monster. But so are these children."

"They're babies, Malachi."

"Babies"—his voice broke—"who would feed on you until you died. Babies you would have to kill to survive. Please, Ava. I do not want you here."

She could hear the agony in his voice, and she knew her mate had no love for this battle. Not when defeating their enemy meant the deaths of children. The Fallen's secret weapon was effective. She looked over the clutch of singers with Sari in the middle, holding Kyra close to her as the women around them chanted louder and louder. The barren, agonized expression on the singer's face and the terror in Kyra's eyes made her decision.

"I'll go with Leo," she whispered, then she threw her arms around his neck. "Please come back to me."

"I will."

Ava blinked away tears. "I won't be far. I want to be close enough that I can use my magic if I need to."

"I can live with that. Leo will find some place secure and out of the way of the worst of it."

A child watched them embrace, head cocked as a dog watches something curious. His feral gaze fixed on Ava, and she knew that Malachi was telling the truth. Though he wore the face of a child, Grimold's son was a monster.

"Where are Kostas's men?"

"They are hunting Grimold with Barak. If Kostas and his men can kill Grimold, his children—"

"Some of the youngest could be saved."

Malachi nodded. "That's what he's hoping."

Ava watched the street as more and more Grigori gathered. "Why aren't they attacking?"

"The Irina are holding them off. But we can't attack them in the middle of their protection, and the minute we leave the circle of their magic…"

She pulled away and pressed her forehead into his chest, kissing over his heart where her vow to him lay.

"Are you strong?" she whispered.

"Stronger than I have ever been, *canim*." He cupped her face, bringing her lips to his in a kiss that broke her heart. "I have your power in me," he whispered. "Your magic along with my own. Nothing will defeat me."

Ava saw Leo from the corner of her eye, so she squeezed them shut and gave Malachi one more kiss.

"I'm counting on it," she whispered. "Leo's here."

Malachi left her and walked to Leo, speaking low into the tall man's ear. Leo looked for Kyra, still frozen in the center of the singers' circle, obviously terrified. He nodded solemnly, then narrowed his eyes. She saw him shake his head once, but Malachi kept talking, putting his hand on Leo's shoulder, obviously trying to convince him. Ava was guessing Leo didn't want to miss the action any more than she did.

Though the singers' magic held, Ava saw the numbers of Grigori growing. If she and Kyra were going to hide, they needed to leave when their enemies were distracted. She saw Malachi walking over as Leo went to speak with Sari.

"When we break through, they will be confused," Malachi said. "Stay with Leo and use your magic to help him clear a path for Kyra. She has no defenses, Ava. You must help Leo get her away."

"I will."

She saw them walking over and knew she only had a few more seconds alone with her mate.

"I love you," she said. "At the end of the day, no matter what happens, I will never be sorry I was given the time to love you."

Malachi lifted her in his arms, crushing her to his chest. She felt the rapid beat of his heart as his body prepared for battle. Felt the pulse of magic over his skin as he kissed the breath from her lungs. His hand gripped the back of her head, holding her with painful possession for one precious moment before he made himself break away. Then he met her eyes and Ava saw the battle lust begin to rise.

"I love you," he said. "Stay safe."

Leo came, holding Kyra's hand and watching her. "Are you ready?"

She nodded. "Do what you have to do," Ava said. "Then come back to me."

He smiled and drew his knives. "Always."

TWENTY-SIX

Malachi watched Leo lead the two women to the edge of the Irin defenses. The attack would begin soon, but it was too dangerous for the females to run far. They'd be targeted immediately. Malachi and Leo's plan was to make a quick run to one of the nearby buildings in the initial rush of confusion. If they could hide in one of the upper floors, it would be the safest place. The majority of the Grigori were focused with preternatural concentration on the circle of singers in the middle of the plaza. Between Ava and Leo, Malachi hoped they'd be able to fend off any random attackers in the right position.

There were few scribes he trusted as much as Leo. Despite the man's affable demeanor, he was a fierce protector and a skilled warrior. His soft heart never blinded him to the realities of a fight.

But he was young. If Malachi could keep the man from the necessity of slaughtering children, he would.

He watched the small ones with dread in his heart, their perverse excitement more visible than their elders'. Grimold's children jumped and shouted, eager for the fight.

"A monster," Damien said as he came to stand with Malachi. "Not even Volund sends children to fight his wars."

"No."

"Be strong, brother. We'll try to disable as many as we can in hopes that Kostas's men will find Grimold in time, but do not let their faces fool you."

"I know," Malachi said. "Some will die."

It was inevitable.

Malachi saw Leo, Ava, and Kyra reach the edge of the Irin lines. With only a little push, the scribes in front of them would be the first into the battle. He saw some of the Oslo scribes there, along with others from Sofia and Berlin. The warriors had come to Vienna, and just in time.

Rhys, Max, and Gabriel were part of the core of scribes circling the Irina, guarding the women who sang out a circle of magic. Malachi could feel it move through the air around him but knew they must move out of it to kill their enemy.

"It's coming," Damien said. "They're pushing out and then we must go."

Malachi nodded.

"Do you have your blade ready?"

"Yes, Watcher."

"Be strong," Damien said. "And return to your mate."

Malachi touched his *talesm prim*, felt the power of his magic grow and swell, covering his body like armor. His marks glowed silver and his skin heated with excitement and power.

Sari let loose a loud cry, shouting a command into the sky, and Malachi felt the circle of magic pulse up and out. Grigori cowered before it, some falling from their perches on balconies and others covering their ears as they let out a wail.

Malachi charged.

He rushed past Leo and the women, throwing his knives at two Grigori who had spotted what they thought was easy prey. They fell down with knives in their throats as Malachi ran and threw an elbow in the face of another.

He felt the first knife slash across his arm, but his skin healed within seconds. With a loud grunt, he head-butted the soldier who had attacked him, sending him to the ground. From the corner of his eye, he saw Leo and Ava making their way toward a red-fronted building with Kyra between them, soldiers falling and writhing around them as he saw his mate's lips move. For a second, he saw the knife headed toward her throat, then Leo batted it away, pulling the arm of the Grigori who wielded it in one smooth motion, grabbing his head and twisting his neck until it snapped. The Grigori dropped to the ground and the three kept running.

Malachi lost sight of them in the fighting.

He let the power flow through him as he moved in instinctive rhythm. Punch, slash, kick, slash. His knife pierced the spine of so many Grigori soldiers he felt their dust coat his skin.

The crowd thinned, then thickened again, becoming more erratic. A knife pierced his groin, digging into the inside of his thigh as it reached for the artery there. He tugged the tiny attacker away. It was a child, no more than seven or eight, who wielded the silver knife that had struck him. The boy bit his arm and screamed, trying to scramble away, but Malachi shook him once, and he fell still. Then he clocked the child on the side of the head, sending him to the ground unconscious before he laid him on the side of the street, hoping he would not rise before Grimold was dead. Already too many small bodies had fallen, their diminutive outlines of dust staining the wet cobblestones in the shadow of Stephansdom.

And still they came, pouring down the streets and over the buildings. Hundreds of Grimold's children battled to take the city the Irin claimed as the scribes and a remnant of singers protected their home.

◆ ◆ ◆　　◆ ◆ ◆

"YOU!" VOLUND STALKED ACROSS THE BRILLIANTLY TILED ROOF OF the Stephansdom, headed toward Jaron. "Where is she?"

Jaron watched him coming, leaning against the base of one spire. "I don't know who you mean. My child? Your granddaughter? Which female do you fear today, brother?"

"But you would give her to Vasu?"

Jaron had long suspected that Vasu knew about Ava and Volund, but clearly the thought of another having access to his mate had pushed Volund into madness. His eyes were wide and raging. His form had lost all semblance of humanity.

He had to die, and Jaron had to kill him before his rage passed and he remembered his granddaughter.

Volund had already drawn the flaming sword from his body, so Jaron knew he would be weakened. Still, it was no easy thing to kill an angel of Volund's age. Jaron was depleted from shifting so many humans in the city. He was the only one of his brothers able to hold a dream for so long, and he had no weapon to match a guardian's sword. Only a consecrated blade would work.

All Jaron had was knives.

"I will kill you," Volund said. "I will kill you and your children. Take what is mine and—"

"She was never yours!" Jaron flew at him, felt Volund's blade pierce his shoulder, but he did not stop. "She is my child. She was *never* yours, thief." He and Volund rolled across the bright roof of the cathedral, then Jaron pushed back until the sword left his body, knowing he would not heal from the wound.

"I claimed her," Volund said, panting. "And she is mine. And when you are dead, I will find her and she will *torment me no more!*"

"If you want her," Jaron said, "then follow me."

He pushed off the building and launched his angelic form into the air, knowing that Volund would follow.

* * *   * * *

AVA WATCHED FROM A WINDOW ACROSS FROM THE STEPHANSDOM, THE great gothic spire of the cathedral knifing into the grey sky as the Irin and Grigori battled beneath it. Dark clouds hung over the normally bright roof, hiding it from human eyes. Thunder rumbled, though no lightning struck. And like a dark fog, the Grigori spread over the square, lurking as the shadows fell.

"There's no end to them," she whispered. Kyra was huddled in a corner, eyes closed, clearly in agony over the violence below. Ava had tried to enhance the woman's shields, but panic was her enemy. The only relief Kyra seemed to find was clutching Leo's hand with grim determination. Of course, when Leo had to let go…

"There is an end," he said, stepping beside Ava to look down. "And Malachi will survive."

His face was set, his eyes fixed on his brothers fighting below.

"You don't know that."

"Look." He pointed to one small clearing. "There he is."

Ava squinted. "Are you sure? How can you see?"

"I can't see his face. I know how he fights, though…" Leo's eyes shuttered. "The children are unexpected."

Ava turned her eyes away. "Am I a coward?"

"No." Leo placed a hand on her shoulder. "He needs you to be here, away from the blood. So that when he returns he'll remember what it is to be clean. Some memories you carry until you die. There is no reason you need to carry them as well."

"Leo—"

"I need you to stay with Kyra while I check this floor," he said. "Can you do that, Ava?"

She nodded. "Find me something I can use as a staff."

He grinned. "I'm sure there's a janitor's closet somewhere."

Ava gave one last glance to the fighting below the building, then she turned back to Kyra, opening the door in her mind to listen and keep watch as thunder sounded over the city.

◆ ◆ ◆ ◆ ◆ ◆

"THEY'RE ATTACKING THE IRINA," DAMIEN SAID, RUNNING UP TO him. "Fall back and protect the singers or we will have no shield."

Malachi looked over his shoulder, and he could see Sari and the others wielding their short staffs, batting back the children who had managed to sneak past their circle of magic. That must have been why Grimold had sent them. For some reason, the smallest of the Grigori seemed immune to the singers' power.

Children. His watcher was ordering him to kill the children.

"Damien—"

"We *must* protect the Irina. The small ones are immune to their magic."

Children.

He saw one holding two daggers, rushing at the legs of a singer who tried to kick him away. Blood bloomed above her knees, and Malachi ran toward them just as the child tried to plunge a blade into the Irina's abdomen.

Sari's staff lifted and struck, tossing the child away.

"Sari!"

Her tortured eyes met his. "We can't hold them back. I have no spells that work on them."

"Then defend yourself," Damien said. "*Míla*, you know you have no choice."

She nodded, even though tears filled her eyes.

There was no time to mourn. The Grigori children were unrelenting.

Damien glanced at the sky. "I do not see any sign of Volund."

"I think Jaron might be taking care of that problem. Grimold is directing his sons. We just need to hold them off until Kostas and his men find him."

Malachi was hoping it would be soon. And he really hoped they hadn't overestimated the skills of their free Grigori allies.

He hazarded a glance at the building where Ava hid before he fell back to his grim task.

• • •   • • •

"DON'T LOOK AT ME," AVA WHISPERED AS SHE WATCHED HIM AS HE retreated to defend the circle of Irina. "Pay attention."

Ava was sick to her stomach as she watched the vicious children with beautiful faces assault the Irin below.

"Why doesn't the magic hold them off?" Kyra asked, coming to stand next to Ava, her face pale and her eyes sunken.

"Maybe the magic is designed that way," Ava said. "Irina wouldn't want to hurt children."

"*I* want to hurt those children," she said. "Grigori children are more vicious than the adults."

Ava gave her a look.

Kyra said, "Harbor no illusions, sister. The female children can be just as frightening. There is a reason I was glad your friend Mala stayed with the group in Prague."

"He will hate himself. If only there was a way..." Ava blinked before she grabbed Kyra's arms.

Kyra looked at her like Ava had lost it. "What's wrong?"

"Their sires can control them, can't they?"

"The angels? Of course. But I don't know how."

"I know," Ava said with a smile. "I just have to get close enough."

"What are you talking about?"

Ava was trying to pry open a window. There was a balcony out there, and if she could get near enough...

"Vasu gave me spells. Words that knocked the Grigori on their ass when they came after me in the cemetery. I know the Irina probably created spells with safeguards to protect children, but I'm betting Vasu didn't."

Kyra nodded. "Try."

Ava finally stopped trying to pry open the window and just grabbed a chair.

"Stand back."

She threw the wooden chair at the window and it bounced off.

"Well… shit."

She heard Leo approaching and turned to—

"Not Leo!" Kyra shouted.

Three Grigori smiled, hungry eyes on Ava and Kyra.

"What do we have here?" one said. "Humans?"

"Humans with angel blood," said another. "Even better."

* * *   * * *

BARAK WAS RELIEVED TO ADMIT HE HAD UNDERESTIMATED HIS SONS. What he had seen as cowardice had clearly been something else. They had retreated, yes, but then they had regrouped. Grown stronger. More stable. A better-trained group of Grigori he had never seen. Kostas wielded authority like a true child of the Fallen. Violence was his currency. Praise rare. Discipline expected.

"It helps them," Kostas said quietly as they walked the rail yards in Simmering.

Snow blanketed the grey tracks. The bustle of humans was eerily silent. Though trains smoked in the station, no one boarded them. Nothing moved but the drifts of dirty snow that fell from the clouds above.

"Oh?" Barak said, mind on the strange swirling movement of the sky overhead.

"The discipline," Kostas said. "It helps the hunger."

Yes, that made sense. It had never occurred to Barak to teach his sons discipline. They were… incidental. Though he had ruled much of Northern Europe for thousands of years, he didn't have the patience for strategy. He'd held his enemies at bay with strength, and that had been reflected in his Grigori. Most were brutally handsome children with more power than brains in his opinion.

When Volund had outmaneuvered him, he hadn't been surprised. He'd been… resigned.

"They control everything better if they're disciplined," his son said. "Bodies and minds. Your death gave them hope. Their sisters gave them purpose."

"I do not wish to steal that."

"Oh?" Kostas asked. "So if we walk away now, you'll do nothing to call us back?"

"No. I'll just kill Grimold myself."

"Why are we here then?"

"Because he'll have his sons with him. The strongest—though none of his children are particularly that strong—he'll keep close by. I imagine with your newly grown goodwill, you don't want to set them loose upon the humans."

As if by signal, a clutch of Grimold's children leapt down on some of his men. They were quickly surrounded and killed. Their dust rose to the sky within seconds, and Kostas's men barely slowed down.

"No," Kostas said. "We do not want them loose."

Barak watched him from the corner of his eye. "I did not teach you conscience."

"No, I acquired it when I saw what killing humans did to my sister."

"Oh?"

His son was quiet for a long while. "She heard their terror. Even worse, their love."

"Ah." Barak shrugged, beginning to like the human gestures Vasu imitated. "And your brothers?"

"I have bent them to my way of thinking whether they like it or not."

Barak smiled as his son walked forward, surveying his men as they searched the train yard, exterminating any of the stray Grigori that were starting to creep out to meet them.

"We're getting closer."

"Yes."

"There are many," Kostas said.

"He finds them useful," Barak said. "Grimold has never been powerful. Only… prolific."

"Most of the Fallen have adopted that strategy. You did not."

"You and your sister are some of the last children I sired. I grew tired of human attention after that."

"Why?"

"The earth has little appeal for me anymore." The image of two small children drifted across his tired mind. He had thought they were brothers. Twins. They wouldn't remember him any longer. It had been too long. But the image of their small, blood-covered bodies held in his arms would remain with him through eternity. "This realm is so very brutal."

"And whose fault is that?"

"Humans," Barak said. "It has always been so. Be careful. Free will is a dangerous thing."

He was only looking a little. Sight had never been his strength. The Creator had given him the gift of hearing, so he used it now. Throughout the rail yard and the industrial neighborhoods of the district, he could hear the humans dreaming. Soft and soothing, their voices melded together in a murmur he'd become accustomed to over his thousands of years on the earth.

There were so many more now.

Perhaps that was another part of it. And another reason he wanted the daughters of the Fallen to find relief.

"Do you hear anything?" Kostas asked.

"Not yet, but I know Grimold is here."

"How?"

"His children are growing bolder." He nodded toward another small group of Kostas's men who surrounded two men twitching on the ground. "And because of what I do not hear."

"What is that?"

"Birds." Barak lifted an eyebrow and returned his son's incredulous expression. "They don't like Grimold. I have no idea why."

AVA DIDN'T HESITATE WHEN SHE SAW THE THREE GRIGORI SOLDIERS.

"*Ziyada*," she hissed the spell Vasu had whispered in her mind.

The first froze just as Leo burst into the room. He halted for only a second, then drove the point of his silver blade into the spine of the frozen Grigori.

"*Zi yada!*" Ava said again, louder. Another stopped. The third lunged at her, but Ava grabbed Kyra and threw herself out of his path. Within seconds, Leo had killed the two remaining attackers. One still twitched while the others stood frozen. Ava watched as they dissolved like statues melting into the sky.

"What did you do?" Leo asked.

"Fallen magic," Ava said. "Can you get a window open for me?"

Leo kicked the chair out of the way. "Will it work at this distance?"

"Hopefully?"

"It's worth a try." Then he stopped and turned. "But will it affect the Irin?"

Ava paused. "I don't know."

Kyra said, "It only worked one at a time on the Grigori. Maybe you have to direct it at each person."

Ava looked at Leo. "Should I try it?"

"If it freezes the Irin down there, they're dead."

"Especially since I have no idea how to undo it."

Kyra stepped forward. "Try with us."

"What?"

Leo nodded. "I'm Irin. She's Grigori."

"But—"

"If you knock me out and Leo's still moving," Kyra said, "you'll know it's safe. And if you knock both me and Leo out… just do your best. It can't last forever."

Ava eyed the open door.

"We'll barricade the door," Leo said, tossing her the short staff that looked more like a sawed-off broom handle. "You can protect us, Ava. But we need to try."

"Okay."

They pushed as much furniture in front of the door as they could. It was an older office, dusty from disuse and isolated about halfway up the building.

"What if I can't reach them?" she said, eyes darting to the fighting below.

"We try. That's all we can do," Leo said. "Now, Ava."

"Aim the spell at me," Kyra said. "Leo, stay close. They're fighting close to each other."

Leo stood behind Kyra, one arm around her waist. "Now."

Ava took a deep breath and focused on Kyra. She stared at her, felt the power grow in her belly.

"*Zi yada.*"

Leo caught Kyra when she fell.

"Did you feel it?"

"I felt it, but it didn't hit me. I just… felt it." Leo carefully placed Kyra on the floor, then ran to the window.

He yanked the drapes down, and Ava saw his thumb circle his left wrist. The power coursed over his skin as his *talesm* glowed for a moment. He held the drape up to the window, then with one powerful punch, the glass blew outward.

"Try now, Ava. The children are getting closer. You have to try."

CHAPTER
TWENTY-SEVEN

Malachi heard Sari shout as he cut through another small body. He'd already vomited everything in his stomach as he defended the Irina from the children's attacks. The Grigori boys darted around and under the blades of the scribes, and none of the Irina spells seemed to work.

He had slain hundreds in his long life. Felt his enemies' blood stain his face. Felt their death rattles under his hands and watched the life drain from their eyes before their bodies turned to dust.

But Malachi had never faced a fight like this.

His enemy carried the face of the innocent. He had to battle every instinct to protect as he beat them back. One singer lay unconscious in the arms of a scribe, her leg hacked off by one of the children. Other singers had wrapped their robes around their throats, trying to guard their voices from the relentless assault. He felt the blood drip where they'd jabbed their knives at his face and chest. Malachi was certain he'd lost part of an ear, trying to disable them without killing.

He'd knocked as many unconscious as he could, but there had been some who'd left him no option. The beautiful children knew their advantage and took it as their elder brothers attacked the Irin front line.

Struggling through the attack on the Irina, the scribes had been pushed to the gates of the cathedral, their focus now on keeping the

Grigori back as long as possible, hoping that more Irin would come. Hoping that Kostas's men would be able to kill Grimold. Without the angel's direction, the Grigori soldiers would lose their focus.

"Sari?" he called over his right shoulder. "What do you see?"

He threw two unconscious Grigori children away from the circle of Irina and turned. Sari was standing, her hands held up and her mouth hanging open. Two Grigori children lay at her feet, eyes open and bodies frozen.

"What is this?" she asked, pushing them with her foot. "They're not dead, but…"

"I don't know."

He looked up. Ava was hanging out a window, Leo holding her as she stared at the gates of Stephansdom. Her eyes were narrowed and he could see her lips moving. He felt their magic rise.

Another child dropped at his feet.

"Ava," he said. "She's using Fallen magic."

"It works on the children?" Sari said. "Do you know how—"

"I know the word, but not how to write it!" he said, flinging a child from his waist. "I can't write it, Sari, not even with my blood."

"Tell me!"

Tears were running down Malachi's face as he struck the arm of a Grigori boy who'd latched on to the singer at his left.

Mercy.

He was so small.

The boy's warm blood spurted on Malachi's face, but he would not let go of the Irina's throat. Another scribe's blade reached the child's neck as he bared his teeth. The Grigori froze; his eyes went wide. His mouth, soft with youth, hung open as Malachi fell to his knees, catching the child's body before it hit the ground. It shouldn't hit the dirty cobblestones. It wasn't right. None of this was right.

The child's unearthly gaze met Malachi's as he caught him. They stared for a moment, Irin and Grigori. Then the bright life drained out of his eyes just before the small body dissolved to dust.

"I can't," he groaned. "Ava, forgive me. I can't."

Mercy.

"Malachi!" Sari was at his shoulder. "Tell me the spell!"

The spell?

"*Ziyada*," he whispered. "Make it stop."

Make them stop.

Sari rose and flung her staff to the side. "*Zi yada!*"

A child froze mid-jump, then fell to the cobblestones at their feet. He did not move.

Other Irina heard and took up the spell, and the air rang with the shouts of Fallen magic as the Grigori children froze in their attacks.

Malachi looked up, searching for her, his cheeks wet with blood and tears. She hung over the window, her attention directed at the Grigori fighting the Irin scribes.

One by one, they began to fall, writhing in pain as their dust filled the air.

The scribes in the square rallied as their enemy began to fall back. Some of the children looked confused. A few followed their elders, though most continued trying for the Irina, even as their small bodies fell.

Malachi began to pick up the bodies of the fallen children, carrying them to the side of the cathedral so they wouldn't be trampled. He heard a shout and looked up. Walking down the Rotenturmstraße from the direction of the river and running behind the cathedral came a large group of the Irin. Led by a scribe in Rafaene robes, they walked with grim purpose and more than a few frightened expressions. Some of the men wore business suits that covered their *talesm*. Some wore scholar's robes. All carried weapons.

He heard the Grigori hiss and fall back from the edges of the plaza.

The Irin had awoken.

BARAK AND KOSTAS FOLLOWED THE RAIL TRACKS NORTH FROM THE Zentralfriedhof, fanning out as the tracks spread west of the freeway.

"He's here," Barak said.

Kostas motioned to Sirius, then the commander and six of his men spread their Grigori out in teams of three to five men, searching the rail yard which was empty of humans but teeming with Grigori assassins.

"Where?" Kostas asked.

"Quiet."

He let the profound noise fill him. Thousands of souls, tormented and peaceful, full of joy or sorrow. They surrounded him. Spread over him. Filled his mind and body until he could not separate himself from the voices of heaven. Then he reached out, looking for a single thread among many.

Gravel scraped along his senses.

There.

His eyes still closed, he drifted toward it, calling his children with him.

"Father, no."

A plea tugged at the edges of his mind. He opened his eyes to see Kostas before him, holding a black, heaven-forged blade to his throat. "Where did you get that?"

"Do not command us," he said through gritted teeth. "We will follow you, but do not take our will."

The fine blood vessels in Kostas's eyes had burst, and the Grigori's gaze was red and angry.

"Put it down, child—"

"Father—"

"—and follow me."

Barak strode over the rail yard, his form growing with each step. He reached into his body, pulling out the flaming sword of the guardians.

He had once been a protector of heaven, his purest joy in guarding the Creator and those who dwelt at his side. Then he fell into darkness, and the darkness had overcome him.

Do not fear the darkness.

He felt the sword draw from his flesh and gasped with the agony and ecstasy of it, for no angel carried a guardian's sword without pain. It fed on the blood of heaven's sons. Mortal hands could not touch it. And no angel would survive its strike.

"Grimold," he whispered. "It is time."

The angel met Barak with a hail of bullets shot from the hands of his children. Kostas's men sprang forward, attacking them as the angel fell on the archangel, his face flaming with rage.

"You will not do this!" Grimold screamed. "He has seen our victory!"

"He lied."

• • •   • • •

JARON LANDED ON THE ROOF OF THE OPERA HOUSE, THE BUILDING rattling under his feet as chips of stone went flying. Volund crashed into him, his blade arching through the air and glancing off Jaron's shoulder before he spun away.

"Where is she?"

"Grimold's sons are dying," Jaron said, ignoring Volund's question. "You are going to lose."

Volund laughed. "Svarog's men have not even arrived to join the fun! This battle is not over."

"No," Jaron said with a slow smile. "Svarog's children have not arrived. How curious."

Volund's smile fell, then he sneered again, rushing Jaron in a rage.

Jaron accepted the slashing blow to his arm, reveling in the pain as he felt his right hand turn to dust under the guardian's blade.

"What do you see now, you fool?" Volund shouted. "What vision did our Master send you? Did you see this, Jaron? Did you see your brother take you apart, piece by piece?"

He felt. For the first time in his millennia of existence, Jaron reveled in anguish. He fell to his knees laughing and shouting. Volund cocked his head, no doubt wondering where the solemn advisor of heaven had gone.

But Jaron saw.

He had seen the truth in his daughter's eyes, and it had made him yearn. Made him want.

Made him rage.

He had planned for decades, only to have his own machinations turned upside down by something as simple—as profound—as love.

Do not fear the darkness—his Creator had whispered to him once—*for it is only a shadow of the sun.*

Then Jaron, son of heaven, raised his eyes as his Master showed him the blade that would bring him home.

He jumped to his feet and ran at Volund, grinning when the guardian's sword pierced his belly. He wrapped his good arm around Volund's waist and jumped from the top of the Opera house, leaping into the storm as icy rain began to fall on empty streets.

••• •••

"AVA, COME BACK INSIDE."

"I can't." She could hear them, curling on the ground in utter pain. She could hear their screams.

And she loved it.

Ba dahaa.

She felt their suffering in her bones, but she would not relent. Ava fed the black void and felt her power grow. The hollow Malachi had drawn from was full, not with his own bright magic, but the black power that grew and flourished in her.

"Ava, come back."

"No."

She felt the glass cutting into her stomach, felt the sharp, icy rain at her back, and the tearing pain in her abdomen and legs.

Ava didn't care.

Ba dahaa.

Zi yada.

She could taste it. The sweet satisfaction of her enemies' cries. They screamed, their voices echoing down the city streets as the Irin cut them back.

"Ava!" Leo pulled her into the building and she spun, tearing at his face with clawed hands.

"Let me go!"

"They're winning!" He pointed to the streets below where Irin scribes and even a few singers had flooded the plaza, overwhelming the Grigori forces, many of whom were in retreat. "They're beating them back. You have to stop."

"I don't want to."

"You must!"

"No!"

"You are hurting Kyra," he shouted. "You have to stop."

She turned to the corner where the *kareshta* lay, no longer frozen but curled in agonized silence, her body twitching in the wake of Ava's magic.

Ava took a deep breath and pulled her power in. "No."

Leo knelt next to her. "I don't know what happened. But every time you hit one of the Grigori outside, she feels it."

"She can't filter them out," Ava said. "She's not strong enough yet. Hold her, Leo."

"I need to protect you too!"

"I've got it!" She glanced out the window. "And I think they have it too. Something is happening to the Grigori."

* * *   * * *

BARAK AND GRIMOLD WRESTLED, AND THE GROUND SHOOK BELOW them. Iron tracks buckled and popped, tossing railcars into the air as the sky let loose the hail that had gathered in the clouds. A great rumbling shook the earth as the train cars cracked together, drawn to Grimold's elemental power.

Barak felt his sons fighting around him, and for the first time in millennium he felt... pride. His child had resisted his draw. Once Barak was gone, they would be strong. Safe. They would not bring shame to his line. He wanted to pretend it did not matter, but he was a creature of brutal honesty, if nothing else.

He cared.

Grimold had no such pride. He drew his children to his side, throwing them at Barak like so much fodder. The guardian's sword sprayed dust as it slew them.

"Stop, Grimold. You kill them for nothing."

"I will kill you," the angel screamed. "Traitor!"

Barak stood, sword pulsing in the darkness. "That is the point."

Grimold stopped, his eyes narrowed.

Barak saw the twin railings coming from either side. His eyes met Kostas's for a second before his son ran toward his sire.

"Father!"

"I knew you would kill me," Barak said.

Grimold smiled.

So did Barak. "I always planned to take you with me."

Laughing, Grimold pulled the iron railings into his hands, the metal phosphorescent with angelic power. He brought them together, tearing Barak's head from his shoulders, and as he did, he looked down to see the guardian's sword sunk deep and glowing in the center of his chest.

He lifted his head to scream, but Grimold's voice was drowned by thunder as the two angels were sucked into the clouds.

* * *   * * *

JARON'S BREATH STOPPED FOR A MOMENT.

Barak was gone.

He landed on the green dome of Peterskirche, but he knew it wasn't high enough, and he was growing weaker.

Volund struggled, trying to get away, but Jaron's grip was like iron. He had no will to fight back, so he trapped his brother to his chest and ignored the spreading burn of the sword in his gut as Volund twisted and laughed.

He closed his eyes and, with the last of his strength, imagined the blade of heaven below him.

Father, let me fall.

AVA RAISED HER EYES WHEN THE THUNDER CRASHED. SHE SAW THE shadows of giants rolling in the clouds.

MALACHI LOOKED UP AS LIGHTNING STRUCK THE SPIRE.

"Impossible," Rhys whispered at his side.

JARON OPENED HIS EYES TO THE HEAVENS AND LAUGHED AS THE STARS danced over Volund's back. He felt his body falling and wondered what the humans below thought of his true form.

"No!" Volund screamed, though his blade bound them together. "NO!"

"The angel came upon them," Jaron whispered as the ground rushed up, "and they were sore afraid."

Then his back arched and he clutched Volund closer as the consecrated spire of the Stephansdom split them both in two.

CHAPTER

TWENTY-EIGHT

Fifteen hundred kilometers away, she screamed, beating her fists against the painted walls until her hands were bloody and broken. The humans rushed in to contain her, but she kept screaming. Then, as abruptly as it started, it stopped.

The woman known as Ava Rezai fell unconscious to the floor.

Vasu stared at her from the corner of the room as the humans raced in and tried to revive her.

Then he looked at Azril, standing by his side.

"She will live?"

Death nodded slowly and returned to Vienna.

AVA SAW THE SHADOWS, THEN LIGHTNING TOUCHED THE TOP OF THE spire, illuminating it for a fraction of a second before the vision was gone.

No thunder rolled through the air.

No rain fell.

She knew Jaron was dead.

Everything was quiet. The biting sleet that had fallen on the street below had stilled, and the air was almost balmy. Bodies, fallen bloody to the cobblestones, began to dissolve. Dust rose, so thick it resembled a golden fog rising from the street.

No bells rang. No birds flew.

Ava looked down to see Death walking among them. He stood over her mate and her heart stopped. Then Death looked up and met her eyes.

Not for many years, daughter.

Azril knelt and lifted an Irina from the ground, holding her up to heaven as her body dissolved and rose.

Another scribe. And another.

He ignored the bodies of the Grigori, except for the children. Gentle hands lifted them to the heavens, and their shadows passed by her as they rose.

So many.

Then the bodies were gone, and Death was too.

◆ ◆ ◆ ◆ ◆ ◆

QUIET GROANS AND SOBBING ROSE FROM THE STREET BELOW AS humans began to reappear in the plaza, walking as if nothing had happened. They ducked into brightly lit restaurants and bars, laughing with friends as street musicians played night music in the square.

Ava watched in a panic as dozens of scribes and singers scattered, whispering spells and touching *talesm* to hide themselves and the wounded from human eyes. The few Grigori who had survived scurried into the shadows, melting into alleys and side streets. Children woke and looked around in confusion, some of them dragged off by their brethren, others scattering to the streets to fend for themselves.

The dust of the dead still wafted on the breeze as the clouds cleared; stars shone in a pitch-black sky.

And the humans saw nothing.

"Ava, away from the window," Leo said.

"They don't see," she whispered, unable to tear her eyes from the busy, unthinking populace below.

"They never see," Kyra murmured, rubbing her temples. "My father is dead."

Leo looked at Ava. "Jaron?"

"Yes." She didn't know how she knew, but it was there. An inexplicable lightness in her mind. A weight off her shoulders. "Volund too."

"Are you sure?"

Ava looked at the street below. Scribes and singers had fallen in battle. Children of the Fallen were slain before her eyes. But the rain washed the blood away, and the bodies had dissolved into dust.

Within moments, the battle was a memory. Her own mate had disappeared.

"I'm not sure of anything anymore," she said. "I just want to go home."

She knew he was alive. The threads of magic connecting them had not broken. All Ava felt was an unspeakable sorrow deep in her chest.

"He's not answering messages." Leo was texting madly on his cell phone. "Damien and Rhys are going to the Library to check on the council. They think Sari is with Malachi, but they lost them after the battle. I'm trying to find out what happened to your brother, Kyra."

"Text Sirius," Kyra murmured in a daze. "Kostas is horrible about keeping his phone on. Just horrible."

Ava turned and leaned against the wall, sliding down until she was sitting on the ground.

"I don't hear any humans outside."

"This is an office building," Leo said, still texting. "It's nighttime, Ava."

Oh, of course it was. The moon was already in the sky, peeking through the clouds that had cleared away. Ava realized that none of the lights were on in the room. When they had entered, it had been daylight. How long had the battle raged? She couldn't grasp it. Hours? It hadn't seemed like hours.

Leo let out a relieved breath. "The council is safe."

Ava didn't care about the council anymore.

"Sari called Damien. She's taking Malachi back to their house, then home."

"Okay." She got to her feet and started to move the furniture from in front of the door.

"Ava," Leo said. "What are you doing?"

"I want to go home."

"There may still be Grigori—"

"Then I'm taking my broom handle"—she picked up the stick that was lying on the ground—"and I'm going home, Leo."

She could feel it building. Ava didn't want to break down in front of Kyra or Leo. She wanted solitude and Malachi.

"Okay, okay." Leo jumped to his feet. He started to help her clear the door. "Let's get you home."

* * *　* * *

WHEN THEY REACHED THE FLAT IN JUDENPLATZ, MALACHI WAS waiting on the steps of their building with hollow eyes and a black cat sitting near his feet. Rhys stood over him, haggard but wearing a smile.

"Go," Leo said. "I'll get Kyra back to Damien and Sari's."

Ava looked at Kyra, who nodded swiftly.

"Go," she said. "I'll be fine."

"Call me when you get back so I know everyone's safe."

Ava walked over and Rhys gave her a quick hug.

"All right?" he asked quietly.

"I will be."

"I'll leave him to you." He bent down. "He was protecting the Irina. And… the children. You know—"

"I know."

Her mate hadn't only killed soldiers.

Then Rhys, Leo, and Kyra ambled into the night and Ava held out her hand.

Malachi took it but didn't stand. He didn't look at her or embrace her.

"Go away, Vasu," Ava said.

So ungrateful.

The cat sauntered off, then turned.

They're dead, you know. You're safe now. Jaron made sure of it.

"Really?"

Truly.

"Thanks. I guess… thank you."

You're welcome. I'd forgotten how entertaining humans can be. I'll see you again, Ava.

She said nothing more to Vasu. Ava pulled Malachi to his feet and led him up to their apartment. When they got inside, she removed his clothes. He was wearing jeans; someone had thrown a jacket over him and pushed boots on his feet. The shirt under it was stained with blood.

Ava tore it off, searching for wounds.

"Not my blood," he said quietly. "It's not my blood."

She broke.

Pressing her face into his chest, she sobbed. Great, wracking, painful cries of relief and agony over the lives lost. For what she had done. For what he had been forced to do. He put tentative hands on her shoulders, but he did not embrace her.

"Ava." His voice sounded more fragile than she'd ever heard before. "I need to get clean."

She led him to the bathroom and stripped the clothes off them both. She would throw them away in the morning. Maybe she would burn them. Ava stood with Malachi under blistering hot water until it ran cold. She washed his hair for him and cleaned the dust from every inch of his skin. Then she led him to bed and crawled under the covers.

Neither one of them slept, but they held each other until dawn. And when the night had passed and Rhys had called to check on them both, Ava returned to him. Sometime after she heard the humans rouse in the streets below, she slept.

• • •   • • •

"I'M SORRY," HE WHISPERED, CLUTCHING HER IN THE FOREST AS NIGHT birds sang overhead. "I'm sorry."

"You did nothing wrong."

"I'm sorry," he whispered into her neck as she held him.

The forest was darker than it had ever been, though the oppressive fog around them had lifted. No moon shone in the sky above. The earth they rested on was bleak and cold.

"It's so dark," he said, his powerful body curled into her, shivering. "Why is it so dark?"

"It won't always be dark," she told him, running her fingers through his hair and down his neck, feeling the strength of him more powerfully for the way he bared himself to her. "I promise. The moon will come out again."

He said nothing, but allowed her to hold him.

"It's okay," she said, over and over again. "It will be okay."

She held him in the night, comforting him when she felt his shoulders shaking.

"You found me once," she said. "Do you remember? I was broken. You picked me up and you carried me."

"Yes."

"And you told me you would never leave me again."

"I'm tired, *reshon*."

"Rest then. I'll hold you."

He relaxed into her arms.

"Remember," she whispered, "it's only when the night is darkest that you can see the light of the stars."

He stretched her out and there was a soft blanket beneath them. The forest became a refuge, and she saw some of the sorrow leave his eyes.

"Sing to me," he asked her.

So she did.

VII.

"There you are."

Svarog turned when he heard Vasu's voice. The house in Wieden was empty. Had been empty for years, though Vasu had heard that the angel had kept a home and a mistress in the city at one time. He'd enjoyed tweaking the noses of the Irin Council—even if the council hadn't known it—only a few blocks from the famous Naschmarkt of Vienna.

Vasu wore his most comfortable human guise, a lean form native to the Indian subcontinent he called home. He was ready, so ready, to return to the warm climes of his home in Chittorgarh. He was ready to come out of hiding.

"And there *you* are, old friend," Svarog said. He'd taken on the appearance of an urban gentleman. His suit cut was immaculate. But then, Svarog had always liked his luxuries. "I knew rumors of your death must be exaggerated."

"Aren't they always?"

"It appears so. Both you and Barak were a surprise." His voice dropped when they spoke of the fallen archangel. "Jaron kept his allies close."

Vasu smiled. "Volund could have learned a lesson from him."

"Volund," Svarog growled, "was too proud to learn from anyone."

Vasu leaned against the banister in the spacious entryway. "And where are your children, my friend? I did not see Svarog's sons in the midst of battle."

The angel turned. "Where were Volund's?"

"Dead in Oslo."

Svarog raised a steel-grey eyebrow. "Exactly."

Vasu was delighted by the angel's trickery. Svarog wasn't an archangel. Like Vasu, he'd been quite young when he fell. And unlike many of his brethren, he still enjoyed the pleasures of human women. His progeny were widespread among Central and Eastern Europe.

"You double-crossed him. I'm delighted."

"I knew Jaron would kill Volund," Svarog said, looking out the window. "I never doubted that. And when he did, I was not going to lie among his sacrifices. My sons herded Barak's heretic children here. Then they returned to their homes. I would not waste my men for Volund's mad quest."

"And"—Vasu crept to Svarog's back, leaning his chin on the other angel's shoulder—"now that he is gone, it does leave such a delicious vacuum of power."

Svarog stared out the window into the cold grey Viennese morning. "So it does."

"And what will you do with it?"

"Nothing." Svarog paused. "For now… nothing."

Vasu stepped back and smiled as he shifted away.

"Liar."

CHAPTER

TWENTY-NINE

Ava and Malachi sat in Damien's study three days later with Damien and Sari. Renata, Max, Rhys, Leo, and Gabriel were also there. Orsala and Mala were still on the way from Prague.

Kostas was nowhere to be found.

"Where is he?" Rhys asked.

Max said, "He's taken his sisters and the women who were in Prague. They disappeared the night after the battle. I don't know where they went. He left Sirius and some of his other men here in the city to try to round up as many of the Grigori children as they could."

"They just left?" Leo asked.

Malachi wondered if Leo was more concerned with Kostas or his lovely sister.

Gabriel cleared his throat. "Trust does not come overnight."

"And what does the council say," Damien asked, "about the battle of Vienna?"

"We won one battle, but some act as if we won the war."

Malachi shook his head but said nothing. He shouldn't have expected miracles, even when they'd appeared in the sky over a major European city.

"And the *kareshta*?" Ava asked.

"They are drafting a mandate," Gabriel said. "It's still being debated, but it looks as though the scribe houses will be joining the hunt to find as many *kareshta* as they can. The elder scribes are not all in agreement, but the elder singers are unanimous. By next week, the daughters of the Fallen will be under the protection of the Irin race."

At least there was that. Malachi knew that ambitious watchers could use that mandate to go after the Fallen, interpreting the "protection of the *kareshta*" to mean freedom from the tyranny of their sires. He exchanged a quick glance with Damien and knew his watcher was thinking the same thing.

"And the free Grigori?" Max asked.

Gabriel's mouth firmed. "Like I said. Trust takes time."

"And us?" Sari asked, reaching for Damien's hand.

Gabriel smiled. "You know politicians. I expect any resolution will be months—if not years—away now that the Irina have their voice in the Library. Until then, our sisters will do as they want."

Max smiled. "Just as they always have."

"Good," Renata said. "I for one have things to do." She looked around the room. "I can't say that it's been fun. But… I'll see you when I see you." Then with one lingering glance at Maxim, Renata left the room.

Max bit his lower lip but said nothing.

Finally Damien spoke. "Are my scribes ready to return to their house?" he asked. "The brothers from Cappadocia have kept our fire burning, but Svarog's sons still live, and we have work to do."

Malachi was ready. So ready. Ready to hide away with Ava. Ready to rid his mind of the nightmares that met him every time he closed his eyes. For the first time since he'd returned, Malachi wanted to forget. But he knew the memories of the tiny lives he'd snuffed out would live with him for the rest of his days. He wanted to flee the city and never return, but he wasn't the only one who mattered. He looked at Ava, and she nodded.

"Ready, Watcher," Rhys said.

"Ready." Leo and Max joined him.

Damien looked at Malachi. He took Ava's hand and nodded.

"We're ready," Ava said. "Very ready to go home."

"And my mate?" Damien asked Sari with a smile.

"I can't leave Ava all alone with you males, can I?" Sari said. "Let's go home, Watcher. As you said, we have work to do."

Ava pressed her face into Malachi's shoulder, and he brought his hand up to cup her head, holding her close.

He wanted to return to Istanbul. But no matter where they were, with Ava, he was home.

CHAPTER

THIRTY

"Hope and purpose," he said quietly as they lay in bed.

It was early and the first call of the *muezzin* snuck in through the open window. Winter had passed. Istanbul hovered on the edge of summer. They woke every morning together, and Malachi never failed to ask Ava her plans for the day.

She had never been in Istanbul in the spring. It was beautiful. It felt like home.

He brushed the hair from her face, and Ava forced herself to open her eyes. She was lying nestled in the crook of his arm, one hand resting on his chest. She could feel his stubble catch in her hair and the warm, solid beat of his heart under her hand.

"What about hope and purpose?"

"It's what we were missing. What we got back when the Irina returned. And what will make us better as we look for the *kareshta*."

Things were changing. Maybe not as fast as Ava liked, but change was coming. Damien and Sari were regularly in Vienna, though Malachi refused to go back. The watcher and his singer had returned the night before with more news about debates in the council and a new air of vitality in a city that had once lost its passion for anything more than the status quo. Irina were visible again.

There were even a few reports of what Rhys called the Irin baby boom. Families were reuniting. Young scribes and singers meeting and mating. With all the changes, a new generation had begun. Ava hoped it was a safer and healthier generation than what had passed.

For Malachi, the ghosts still lingered. She saw the slight flinch when he spotted a group of children in the street. The shadows when he remembered what he'd been forced to do. The well of grief he carried seemed endless some nights. It pained her far more than any scar he wore on his body.

"The Irin needed hope," she said.

"Everyone needs hope."

Ava said, "And purpose? Protecting humans—"

"Is important. But empty. The Irin lived for a race we could never be a part of."

"Do you have hope?" She would battle an angel for this man. Walk through the darkest forest of grief. Give up her own life if she had to.

But she could not force his eyes to see the hope she kept wrapped in her heart if he didn't want to see.

"Talk to me," she said. "Please."

"I have hope, *reshon*."

"I'm scared sometimes," she confessed. "You scare me."

She pressed on even when she felt his body tense. "Not because of what you might do to others. I trust you more than anything. But what you might do to punish yourself for things you couldn't prevent."

"Ava—"

"It wasn't your fault, Malachi."

"I know that."

"Do you?"

He paused and in the silence, she felt his body begin to relax.

"You told me once that a wound doesn't heal just because it stops bleeding." She lifted her head and propped her chin on his chest. "And you gave me time."

"You needed it."

"And you need it now."

Malachi nodded.

"Okay," she said. "But here's the rule. Only one of us gets to be messed up at a time. Otherwise, we're seriously screwed."

The slow smile she loved spread across his face.

"Deal."

Yunan Province, China

"STOP IT."

"No." She grinned when she said it, clicking the camera when she snapped the picture.

Malachi had on his sunglasses, his face grim. He was in full body-guard mode, every inch the overprotective mate, and he was trying hard not to smile.

"You're supposed to be working, Mrs. Sakarya."

"I told you, you're too handsome to pass by."

She laughed as they followed the crew farther into the village. Dogs ran around their feet, and curious Chinese tourists watched them as the models and makeup artists arranged a small studio in the square.

The fashion shoot was not the kind of job she would normally take, but it was a favor for one of the few editors who'd continued to give Ava work after the eighteen-month break in her schedule. Conveniently, she was from LA. An explanation like "nervous breakdown followed by rehab" was hardly the strangest thing anyone had heard.

She and Malachi had been married in Malibu the month before, with her father and mother in attendance. Lena had been excited, thrilled to inform her friends about her daughter's exotic new husband and home in Istanbul. Jasper had seemed… better. Slightly more stable, but still a giant mess. He'd also lost about ten years to his face, Jaron's glamour dying with him. Luckily, he was in entertainment. Plastic surgery was almost expected.

That would work for now, but Malachi knew a serious conversation was inevitable.

Ava, by virtue of living in Turkey, was now on call for a lot more shoots in Asia, which kept her out of Los Angeles and away from curious eyes. Malachi was pleased. Ava… didn't really care. She still enjoyed her job, but she could take pictures anywhere.

And though they kept the mansion in Southern California, they lived in Istanbul, sharing a house with his four brothers and Damien's mate. It was crowded, but Ava was growing used to it. And when they periodically left for his grandparents' house in Germany or a random photography job, Malachi's people said nothing.

He watched her work, enjoying the sun on his face and the balmy air of Southern China. They were in the hills around Lijiang, and the weather was mild. The people were friendly, but he still kept an eye on the crowd. More were looking at the trio of American models posing with the old man in tribal costume, but a few had their eyes on his mate.

Because she was electric.

The anxiety, worry, and stress of living in danger had drained away, leaving Ava the woman she was born to be. Vibrant and curious. Funny and strong.

She had drawn him back from the edge of darkness more times than he could count. He still avoided children. Still flinched when he heard them laughing. The guilt assaulted him at the most unexpected times. He hated his weakness. Adored her strength.

"It will get better," she told him, over and over again. "We have time."

If Malachi wasn't quite healed yet from the mental anguish of the battle in Vienna, someday he knew he would be.

His mate—his wife—had told him so.

She spun as if she'd known he was thinking about her and captured the smile he couldn't hold back.

"Gotcha, handsome."

• • • • • •

HE ROLLED HER TO HER BACK AND MOVED DOWN THE BED.

"Yes," she panted.

"Yes?"

"Mmmm." Ava arched back, unable to say another word because the thing Malachi was doing should have been illegal. It probably was illegal in some countries.

He smiled against the inside of her thigh. "You have to be quiet."

"When you say you want to take a break from work, you really mean a break."

"I was feeling tense."

"Oh yeah? How's that going?"

"Better." Malachi's tongue circled her belly button and she groaned. "Much better now."

"I live to help work out your tension."

"Such a supportive mate."

He laughed quietly and bit her thigh before he lowered his head again. Then his arm wrapped around her leg and his hand pressed down on her belly and Ava wanted to move, but she couldn't and he—

The door crashed open. "Malachi, did you borrow the—*Gabriel's bloody fist!*"

Ava screamed, and Rhys spun around to face the open doorway as Malachi roared and came off the bed, throwing a blanket over Ava's body as she curled into a ball.

"What are you doing?" he shouted.

"Haven't you heard of locks? Locks, Malachi!"

"Try knocking, you bloody—"

"Get out of our room and close the door!" Ava yelled.

Malachi shoved his brother out of the room and slammed the door shut. Then he locked it and leaned against it for good measure.

She pulled the covers over her head again and tried to get the image of Rhys's face out of her mind. She pulled a pillow over her head too. It didn't help much.

Malachi sat on the edge of the bed. "I'm sorry."

She burst from under the covers and battered him with the pillow. "You. Forgot. To. Lock. The. Door!"

"I'm sorry!" She could tell he was trying not to laugh. "I'm so sorry. I was just… distracted. And there were a couple hundred years when privacy wasn't an issue."

She fell back on the bed and covered herself with the blanket again. "I live in a supernatural fraternity house."

"It's not that bad." He peeled the covers away and spooned her from behind. Ava tried to hide her head under a pillow, but he stole it. "*Canım?*"

"What?"

He kissed the back of her neck. "Does this mean you don't want to—"

"Go back to work before I stun you."

CHAPTER

THIRTY-ONE

Germany

H e woke with a start, the face of the child in the front of his mind. He sat up and put his head in his hands. This time when Malachi had caught the small body, the boy hadn't dissolved. Instead, his eyes had opened and he'd lunged toward Ava, leaping on her and tearing into her throat before Malachi could catch him.

"Babe?" her sleepy voice asked at his side.

"I'm fine."

"Come here."

"I'm fine."

"Come here anyway."

He lay down next to her and gathered her into his arms.

Maybe it was the winter wind that echoed outside the house, reminding him how it had shrieked through the Stephansplatz. Maybe it was the way the snow fell outside. He hadn't had a dream of the boy in months.

"Kiss me," she whispered.

"*Canim—*"

"It'll make the bad dreams go away. Promise."

Ava smiled up at him, so he kissed her, sinking into her mouth in relief.

She was here. She was alive. No one was after her, and Volund was gone.

His hands ran down her sides, cupping her hips as he brought her closer. And while the cold waves crashed outside, he made love to her. Long and slow with deliberate strokes that drew her pleasure out and forced his mind back to the beauty that was Ava and their union.

"I love you," she gasped as she came. "I love you so much."

Her mating marks shone on her skin and he read the words he'd written there.

I am for Ava.

Not for nightmares and death. Not for guilt and recrimination.

"For you," he said into her mouth. "I love you."

She held him after the pleasure wracked his body. Wrapped her arms around him and held on.

For Ava.

He was for Ava.

CHAPTER

THIRTY-TWO

"You're better," Ava said, smiling at her grandmother.

The woman looked more like her sister than her grandmother. The staff didn't ask questions, but she could see their inquisitive looks.

"A little more every day," Maheen said.

She'd asked Ava to call her by her new name the first time she'd visited after Jaron's death.

Why Maheen?

Someone called me that once. I liked it.

Ava didn't ask more. If her grandmother had chosen a new name for a new life, it was more than understandable.

She still lived in the hospital. Ava guessed she would live there for some time.

"You don't look like me," Maheen said.

"No. The eyes. I think that's the only thing."

"Grigora are more beautiful than human women," she said, her eyes drifting. "It's good you look human."

Maheen was not an easy person to talk with. Brittle pain leached into the air around her, though Ava could occasionally see echoes of the woman she might have been before her rape and binding to Volund. She hated Malachi's presence, and it had taken more than a little persuading to let her visit Maheen alone.

Malachi didn't trust her. Neither, if Ava were completely honest, did she.

The hospital said she hadn't been violent since the night almost a year ago when she'd started screaming and collapsed. She'd beaten her hands so badly they'd required surgery. She still struggled to hold one of the paintbrushes she was now allowed, but she was healing.

Ava hoped it was more than her hands.

"Is the scribe with you?" she asked.

"Yep. Waiting in the living room downstairs."

Maheen nodded, rocking back and forth a little in her seat.

"He won't come up."

"They were the monsters in the night, you know?"

"Who?"

"Irin scribes. My brothers would tell me stories. If I saw one in the market, I had to run. They never let me go anywhere alone." She laughed. "Except…"

Ava waited for a long while, but Maheen had drifted again. It was a pretty common occurrence.

"Grandmother?"

"You shouldn't call me that." Her head jerked toward the door. "You know they watch me."

Did they? Ava made a mental note to check. She couldn't see any cameras, but you never knew. Maheen was highly paranoid.

"Is he here again?" Maheen asked. "Did you bring him?"

"Jasper?" Ava hesitated to say. Maheen had refused to see Jasper the other two times they'd brought him. Ava kept convincing her father to give his mother another chance, but she could see him spiral each time his mother rejected his attempts to speak with her. According to Maheen's doctor, Jasper paid the bills, but he hadn't visited since Ava— *Maheen* had attacked him three years before.

"Yeah," Ava finally said. "He… He's waiting with Malachi. If you want—"

"Not today."

Not *today*.

Not *no*. Not *never*.

Not today. Which, in Ava's mind, meant there was still hope. Maybe it was a small hope, but that was better than nothing.

"Do you know anything about gemstones?" Maheen asked.

"Gemstones?" Ava frowned. "Not much."

"I studied history. I couldn't go to the university, but my father brought me books. Gemstones have fascinating history. Mythology…"

Her eyes drifted to the wall over Ava's head. They were sitting at a table having lunch in her room. Though her grandmother was allowed to walk throughout the estate now that her rages and seizures had calmed down, Maheen still preferred to live in isolation.

Her mind was a raw wound.

She resisted any attempts to learn shielding, explaining to Ava that she was used to the voices and it let her know when someone was approaching. The shield Jaron had forced over her at times had been stifling. She said it felt like a prison, and she didn't want another.

"Do you think you'll ever want to leave here?" Ava asked.

"I'll have to someday." She took a deep breath. "I've been preparing myself for months now. I've been here five years. I can only be somewhere for six or seven before they start to notice."

"You have time."

"It might be better…"

Ava waited, but Maheen was staring out the window now.

"No one's going to force you out," Ava said. "And there are places you can go if you want to leave."

Ava was thinking of the various scribe houses and libraries that had begun to open to Irina who wanted to rejoin Irin society, and a few *kareshta* who had found their way to them. She didn't know if her grandmother would be open to it, but she could try.

Maheen shook her head. "Not now. Not yet."

"Okay."

Their eyes met over the pot of honey-sweetened tea Maheen had requested.

"Thank you," her grandmother told her. "I know I'm not the easiest person to visit. I didn't even bake cookies."

Ava saw one of those rare glimpses in that moment. Fire and intelligence and humor. The spark of life that had woken an archangel and drawn the lethal attention of a predator.

"I know," Ava said. "You're really falling down on the grandmother thing."

Maheen barked out a short laugh. "I was a horrible mother too."

Her smile fell.

She didn't talk about Jasper.

"What do you do," Ava asked, "when you don't have visitors? Do you paint a lot? I like your canvases."

Maheen waved to a row of them stacked against a wall. "Take them. As many as you like. I run out of room."

"Thanks."

"I paint." Maheen nodded. "I read. I can enjoy music again. But mostly…" She took a deep breath and closed her eyes, an expression of utter peace falling across her face. "I sleep."

JASPER TOOK A DEEP DRAG FROM ANOTHER CIGARETTE AS THEY SAT AT the cafe in Toulouse. His coffee cup was empty. Ava was just glad it wasn't a wineglass. After all, it was only ten in the morning. Spring had come early, so they were enjoying the morning sun as Malachi talked on his phone in the small park nearby. Talked and paced. Paced and scanned the streets.

"That guy ever calm down?" Jasper asked.

"Kinda." She sipped her café au lait. "Not really."

"I'm starting to think he's more paranoid than Carl."

"Old habits are hard to break."

Jasper grunted. "I'm not complaining if it keeps you safe."

"It does." She nudged the ashtray with her own cup. "Is this all you're doing lately?"

"It's… ah, hell." He looked sheepish. "I'm trying. Whatever your man said to Luis sent him on some kind of crusade, but you know me, baby girl. I ain't ever gonna be father of the year."

"I just want you healthy."

He was. He would be for a long, long time, as far as any of them knew. Orsala had said nothing in Irina oral tradition spoke of humans with as much angelic blood as Jasper carried, and Rhys couldn't find anything in the archives either. The glamour Jaron had placed over Jasper had disappeared, leaving him looking more like her brother than her father.

He didn't ask questions. Mostly, Ava thought, because he didn't want to know the answers.

"How was she this time?" He scratched at the stubble on his chin.

"She's better," Ava said. "Thanks for coming. Again. I keep hoping—"

"It's cool, Ava." He nodded. "Yeah, you never know. I'm glad she's better. Is the uh…?" His finger lifted to tap at his temple. "That any better?"

"Not for her. Not yet. But I'm better." She glanced at Malachi. "A lot better."

Jasper could pretend they were normal. For now. But that wouldn't and didn't stop Ava from speaking the truth.

Words, she'd learned through experience, had immense power.

He'd have to learn eventually.

For now, they could drink their coffee and watch the flowers break open on the trees. Watch new life starting again and ignore the quickly passing years.

"I love you, baby girl." Jasper slid an open hand across the table. "Best thing I ever did in my life."

Ava put her palm in his. "Love you too, Jasper."

He wasn't much of a father, but he was hers. And Ava had realized he was the only part of her old life that would last into the new.

Malachi. Jasper. Maheen.

They would be her family.

She saw the car pull up and Luis step out, eyes flicking nervously between Jasper and Malachi.

"Do not know why your guy makes him so nervous." Jasper stubbed out his cigarette and patted his pockets. "I've seen Luis scare dudes twice Malachi's size, and yet that guy…" He shook his head. "No idea."

"Oh, you know," Ava said, trying to suppress the nervous smile. "It's probably the tattoos."

Jasper stood. "Ava, he's in the music business. Tattoos are like cardigans to us."

Ava threw her head back and laughed. Jasper took the opportunity to haul her to her feet so he could wrap his arms around her and squeeze. She hugged him back and relished the small kiss he planted on her head.

"Okay." His voice was rough when he let go. "Back to the studio."

"I'll see you in a couple of months."

"You better."

He was patting his pockets again. "I know I put it in here…"

"What?"

"Ah." He plucked a small USB drive out of the pocket on his chest. "There it is."

He handed it to her, bent down and kissed her cheek before he walked toward the car.

"Jasper?" She looked at the drive and took a few steps toward him. "Dad!"

He turned, grinning. Mischief lit his eyes. "What?"

"What is this?"

The smile turned wistful. "I finally got it right."

"Got what right?"

"It's for you, Ava." He slipped on his sunglasses. "It's your song."

Ava gripped the precious piece of plastic in her hand and watched him drive away.

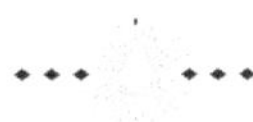

"CANIM?" MALACHI PEEKED HIS HEAD THROUGH THE DOOR OF THEIR room in Istanbul. Ava pulled off the earphones and set them to the side of the desk where she had her books spread out.

"Hey," she said. "What's up?"

He watched her, his heart shining out of his eyes. "Your song again?"

"It's beautiful."

"It is." He walked over and sat on the bed. "It's the best thing he's ever written."

"Yeah." She smiled and spread her hand over the history book she'd been reading. "It is."

She fell silent and he watched her.

"You have a secret," he whispered. "I can see it in your eyes."

"You must be magic."

"You have no idea."

She didn't say anything for a moment. Malachi just waited for her to speak.

"Do you know anything about gemstones?"

"Not much," he said. "Is this a hint?"

"No, I don't need a ring from you." She closed the book and went to him, straddling his lap so they were face-to-face. "Jasper is an ancient stone," she said, stroking her fingers along the close-cropped hair near his neck. "It's used for protection."

"Is that so?" he whispered.

"Yes." She laid her head on his shoulder as his arms came around her. "It's supposed to keep away evil spirits."

His hands tightened on her hips.

"She gave him the name Jasper to protect him." Ava closed her eyes and released a sigh. "She did it to protect her child."

CHAPTER

THIRTY-THREE

Malachi lay on the picnic blanket in Yıldız Park, his face soaking in the afternoon sun as Ava combed her hand through his hair and took pictures with her phone. A group of children shrieked nearby, the laughter almost piercing his eardrums.

"What are they doing?" he murmured.

"I think there's a squirrel." She laughed. "Uh-oh. And now there's a dog."

"*Özel dilerim!*" Malachi heard one mother call, apologizing for the racket.

"*Bir şey değil!*" Ava reassured the harried mother with a laugh. *It's nothing.*

She had picked up the language quickly after they'd moved to Istanbul. After living there over a year, she chatted with the vendor at the market and ordered from her favorite cafe with ease. Ava was still fascinated by languages, but most of her study was now focused on learning everything she could about the Old Language, particularly spells—like those Vasu had given her—that might have been lost.

She and Sari also corresponded regularly with Kyra, though the *kareshta* still lived in hiding.

He kept his eyes closed and imagined the scene as the dog barked and the children ran laughing into the trees. Their shouts and laughter had finally become a comfort. He loved his city, and human families were a part of it. A tumble of accents and languages flowed along the paths, though most of the visitors in the middle of the week were local. He heard a teacher instructing a drawing class several meters away, but no one came close enough to bother them.

Damien and Sari were away from the scribe house, visiting Orsala, who had taken residence in Cappadocia with Mala. The quiet scholars in Göreme didn't quite know what to do with the fierce Irina warrior, but Mala would not leave Orsala, so they learned to stay out of her way.

Officially, Malachi was in charge. But since Rhys was at the house, cranky because the air-conditioning was out again, Malachi was more than happy to escape. He and Ava had snuck out with a picnic basket, Leo giving them rude hand gestures as he waited on the phone with the repair company.

"Malachi?"

"Hmm?"

"There's something…"

He heard the catch in her voice and opened his eyes. She looked upset. "What is it?"

Ava shook her head. "I don't know how to tell you. I didn't expect…"

"Ava, what's wrong?"

Her cheeks were flushed. "Everyone said it wasn't likely, so—"

"What are you talking about?"

"I'm pregnant."

His heart skipped a beat.

"I know," she whispered, "with everything, it's not the best time. You still have concerns. I know that. And the dreams still… I need you to be happy."

"Ava." His heart was so full he thought it would pound out of his chest.

"I need you to be okay with this because I'm scared to death."

He wanted to reassure her. Wanted to tell her what a gift she'd given him, but the words wouldn't come.

So Malachi turned his face to her belly, wrapped his arms around her waist, and kissed the tiny life that grew inside.

Impossible, improbable life.

A miracle.

She bent down and leaned her head on his. "You're happy?"

He nodded. Then Malachi rose and took her in his arms, forcing himself to take deep breaths. It wasn't enough. He could feel tears in the corners of his eyes, but he could not be ashamed of them. He held Ava in his arms and let himself smile.

"You're happy," she said on a sigh, wrapping her arms tight around his neck.

He pulled away and kissed her face until she was laughing. Then he wrapped his arms around her and held her close, the wonder of what they had become a vibrant song in his heart.

"Sometimes, *canım*, words are not enough."

Continue reading in the Irin world with a bonus novella, *On a Clear Winter Night*, and a preview of THE SILENT, Leo and Kyra's story, now available in ebook, paperback, and audiobook at all major retailers.

And find out more about Elizabeth Hunter's **Irin Chronicles** at ElizabethHunter.com or
buy direct and save at Elizabeth Hunter Books.

ON A CLEAR WINTER NIGHT

Join Ava, Malachi, and their friends for Midwinter holidays in Prague. The Irin might not celebrate Christmas, but that doesn't mean Ava has to give up on the holidays. With her children on the way, nothing will stop the newest Irina from celebrating with her growing family. But will lingering doubts and worries about fatherhood let Malachi celebrate the way he wants?

CHAPTER
ONE

AVA LEANED INTO THE SOFA, shifting the unwieldy bulk of her eight-months-pregnant body farther into the embroidered cushions that decorated the couch. Malachi's eyes were trained on the television in a corner of the room, the black and white image glowing in the dim sitting room. The fire crackled in the hearth and early snow fell outside the window. A peaceful scene. Idyllic on a cold winter night.

But the jostling in her belly was just a bit much.

"Calm down in there," she muttered.

Malachi's hand drifted over to her, running a comforting hand down her arm and then lower over the swell of her stomach. He lifted the edge of her wool sweater and laid his skin against hers.

Instant relief.

The pulse of his power flowed over her like a warm wave. Spreading from her abdomen and up her torso, she felt her body calm, then the ache eased. The tension in her belly relaxed and the jostling slowed down.

She heard the last of the old dialogue on the classic Christmas film fade out and Malachi heaved a sigh.

"Really?" he said.

"What?" She blinked at him innocently. "Didn't they teach you that at the scribe academy? Everyone knows that every time a bell rings an angel gets his wings. Common knowledge, Mal."

He tried not to smile, but she saw the peek of his dimple through the beard he'd been growing since they arrived in the old farmhouse outside of Prague.

"You're ridiculous." He swung his legs up and stretched out, resting his head in her ever-shrinking lap. Then he turned his head to the side, lifted her shirt, and pressed a kiss to her belly.

Beautiful man. Ava's heart felt like it could burst when he did things like that. And he did. Often.

All Irin men were tactile by nature, feeding off the energy Irin women contained. They couldn't touch the humans they protected without hurting them. Touch was reserved for family, friends, and lovers, and before he'd met Ava, Malachi hadn't felt an Irina touch in hundreds of years. Since then, he'd been making up for it.

And once she'd gotten pregnant…

Well, if she hadn't derived so much mental ease from physical contact, she'd have been tempted to call him clingy. He was constantly with her. Leaving him to visit the small market in the village or run into the city with some of her Irina sisters was almost impossible. Malachi didn't want Ava out of his sight.

But the Irina needed Irin men just as much. The energy Malachi drew from her with his touch allowed Ava's mind to rest. Before she'd met him, she'd been a case study in anxiety. Socially isolated. Jittery. The energy she'd built up in her system, believing herself only human, had slowly been driving her insane.

Ava would never reject her mate's touch. They were, as bonded mates, truly two halves of one whole. And soon they'd be adding to their small family. Before Malachi, Ava never thought being a mother was even a possibility.

He glanced up and saw the tears in her eyes. "What is it?"

"You know me. I cry at the drop of a hat these days." She shook her head. "Nothing to worry about. Happy."

He reached an intricately tattooed arm to touch her face. "If they are only happy tears, that is acceptable."

"Acceptable, huh?"

"Yes." He pinched her chin. "I am your mate. Anything other than total happiness is unacceptable."

"We need to talk about your dictator voice, Mal."

The front door blew open and a booming voice filled the room. "Hello!" Bruno said with a shout. "It's almost as cold as home out there!"

Almost everything that Bruno said was a shout. The giant scribe had moved from his homeland in Scandinavia to start the haven outside of Prague with his mate Karen and several other Irina singers from the disbanded haven in Norway. He'd been less than happy with the "dreaded warm weather" in Bohemia. The light snowfall reddened his cheeks and made him look like a child with a new toy.

"Hello, sister." Bruno peeled off his jacket and put his boots by the door before he walked over and placed a hand on Ava's shoulder. "And brother! Hello, Malachi. I didn't see you there. What were you watching?"

"Christmas movies," Ava said with a smile.

Bruno frowned. "But Irin don't celebrate Christmas."

Ava threw her head back and moaned as Mal sat up with a know-it-all expression on his face.

"That's what I told her," he said. "But she insisted. I have been forced to watch *White Christmas*, Miracle on some street, and *It's a Wonderful Life*."

Bruno frowned. "I was surprised by how dark that one was."

"See?" Ava said. "Bruno watches Christmas movies."

Bruno shrugged. "I'm more of a Jimmy Stewart fan. That is how I learned English. But the bit at the end with the bell…"

Malachi said, "Thank heaven I am not the only one. Ridiculous. That child would start crying if she saw a real angel."

Bruno nodded. "Agreed."

"That's not the point," Ava said. "The point is that Christmas is… a wonderful holiday and there's no reason Irin shouldn't celebrate it. It's about family and good cheer and love for your fellow man. People give presents—"

"What do you want?" Malachi asked. "I'll get it for you."

"That's not the point." Ava shook her head and looked around the treeless living room.

The house in Karlštejn, forty minutes out of Prague, was cozy and beautiful. Snow fell on bare trees and evergreens blanketing the hills. It was the middle of December and the otherwise picture-perfect winter house had not a single red bow or pine bough. She'd been drooling over some of the glass-blown ornaments in the small village near the house, but she felt silly buying them because there was no tree.

Christmas had been one of the few bright spots in Ava's childhood. For much of the year, she'd been shipped off at this school or that camp. But at Christmas, her mother told her stepfather to stuff it, which usually meant Carl went skiing in Utah with his buddies, leaving Ava and her mother alone to celebrate the holiday quietly.

Lena would send the household employees away, making the mansion peacefully empty while mother and daughter decorated a small tree bought for Ava's room. Her very own tree. Not the large, lushly ornate tree that was for the benefit of guests, but one just for a little girl. Ava's collection of ornaments had been moved to her house in Malibu, but she and Malachi were hardly ever there.

Malachi leaned closer and peered at her face. "Now you are sad."

She sniffed. "I just like Christmas, okay? It's not a big deal. I know Irin have midwinter holidays, too. You celebrate the Winter Solstice, I heard Karen and Astrid talking about it yesterday. I'll learn those traditions over time."

"No," Malachi murmured. "I think this *is* a big deal. Canım, you must tell me these things. You have given up so much to be with me—"

"I gave up nothing." She grabbed his hand. "Nothing. You have given me everything. You and all your brothers. And my sisters. I have everything I need."

Home. Family. History. Purpose.

He nodded slowly. "But you also want a tree."

Well, when he put it like that, Ava felt like an ungrateful brat. "Malachi, I'm fine. I'm being silly."

"Memories are not silly. Traditions are not silly," he said. "We know that better than anyone."

Their first Christmas, Malachi had been a confused wreck. They'd been together, but most of his memories had been gone. He hadn't remembered the traditional foods or songs the Irin sang at winter solstice and Ava had felt lost, even as she tried for Christmas cheer. It had been the saddest winter she could remember. The next Christmas had been better, but still quiet. They'd been in Germany, but they'd both still been recovering from Vienna.

And now…

"Let's not tempt fate, all right?" She smiled. "We're blessed."

His smile was slow and sweet before he leaned over and kissed her.

"I am the most blessed of scribes," he whispered in Turkish. "To have you as my *reshon*. As the mother of my children. The heavens envy my fortune."

"Oh, you two," Bruno said with a big sniff. He wiped unashamed tears from his ruddy cheeks. "I'm so glad you came for Midwinter. It was too quiet with just us five."

Ava smiled at Bruno. He was like the really giant, really loud big brother she never had. She had lots of brothers now, but Bruno would always be one of her favorites. He and his mate Karen had been a solid island of comfort and safety when life had gone to hell.

"I wanted to be near Astrid when I deliver." Ava rubbed her belly where the football match had started up again. "Orsala taught me the songs, but I'm worried I'll forget on my own."

Ava had learned songs of protection to quiet the tiny mind of the daughter who would be born hearing the soul voices of the world. Songs to guard the son who would grow at his sister's side, learning and protecting the legacy of knowledge his father would pass to him.

Bruno shrugged. "I will confess my ignorance when it comes to babies. But I cannot wait to meet them."

Malachi and Bruno had been hard at work on the double crib for the tiny boy and girl nesting in Ava's belly. At least that was what Orsala claimed she was having. The old singer was certain there would be one boy and one girl arriving near the midwinter holidays. Children were rare among the Irin, but when they came, they were often in sets.

At first Ava had been completely overwhelmed. Twins? She'd never planned on having *any* children, much less two. Especially not two at a time.

But Malachi had been overjoyed to hear it, and the announcement of twins had caused so much rejoicing—and more than a few vodka toasts—in the scribe house in Istanbul that Ava knew she'd never be hurting for extra help. Damien and Sari, Max, Leo, and Rhys were all thrilled at the prospect of a baby in the house. Two babies meant they wouldn't have to share as much.

Ava and Malachi's children would be the first born in Irin history with blood from both the Forgiven and the Fallen sons of heaven. Unique beings among an already unique angelic race.

Despite her concerns, Astrid told Ava that hers was a completely normal pregnancy. When Malachi drew spells across her belly, the babies calmed. When Ava sang quiet songs to them, she could hear their tiny, unformed minds attuned to her voice. When Orsala looked to the future, she saw tranquility. When Karen dreamed, it was of laughter.

And so, with the comfort of her new family around her, Ava had found peace.

"Hurry with the babies, will you, Ava?" Bruno asked. "If you have them on midwinter, they'll be doubly blessed. And Karen will make so many more cakes."

Malachi smiled. "How are you not the size of this house, brother?"

Bruno puffed up his chest. "Who do you think chopped the wood in that fire? And cleared the driveway? She feeds me then puts me to work."

Ava said, "And you love it."

Bruno winked. "Of course." He sniffed the air. "Oh, gingerbread…"

He wandered toward the back of the house and the kitchen with the gingerbread while Ava shifted on the couch again.

So hard to get comfortable…

"Why did Bruno say the babies would be doubly blessed if they were born at midwinter?"

"It's tradition," Malachi said. "Any birth is very lucky. But babies born at midwinter are doubly lucky."

She frowned. "But it's the middle of winter."

"Exactly. The winter solstice is the shortest day of the year. So for the first part of their life, every day after their birth is just slightly longer than the last. A little more light every day as they grow." Malachi shrugged. "It's just superstition. It's the opposite for babies born in the Southern hemisphere during June."

"Weird. But kinda wonderful, too."

She leaned against his shoulder as Malachi began to rub the small of her back.

"Oof." The football game in her belly started up again.

"Soon," he whispered.

"Soon."

"Come, little babies," he crooned, putting a warm hand on her belly as the twins rocked and rolled. "*Baba* wants to kiss you."

He took Ava's breath away. After all the trauma of the last two years, she'd had no idea how he would deal with the realities of fatherhood. He had mental wounds she couldn't even imagine. But Malachi was eager to meet his children; Ava was the one who often felt unprepared.

"You're going to be such a good dad," she said.

He smiled. "But I have not been such a good mate, I think. Tomorrow, I get you a Christmas tree. And we will decorate it together. And when our children come, they can lie under the tree and look at the lights and the beautiful glass ornaments you have been looking at in the village."

The smile almost cracked her face. "Malachi—"

"But you do not need to give me any presents," he said as he kissed the top of her belly. "I think you have that covered, canım."

"I love you so much."

"Just promise me… no silly stories about angels with wings."

CHAPTER
TWO

MALACHI AND BRUNO STOMPED THROUGH the woods behind the house, looking for the perfect Christmas tree for his mate. He felt foolish that he'd overlooked her need for such human traditions as a tree and gifts. Brooke, the young teenage Irina who lived at the Karlštejn haven with her mother, had followed along with them, loping over the snow-covered hills with the ease of a country child.

"I used to walk like that," Malachi said to Bruno.

"Oh?"

He nodded. "My mother was German. We lived in a village there for most of my childhood before we returned to Turkey. There were forests all around us."

"And you've been a city boy since then?"

"I suppose so."

"Ava…, " Bruno started. "She likes the country, I think."

Malachi went alert. Did Bruno know something about his mate that he didn't? Was Ava unhappy in a massive city like Istanbul? He knew Karen and Ava spoke often.

"Yes," Malachi said. "She does like the country."

"But I think she often becomes frustrated with the pace here," Bruno said, smiling. "She must be bored."

Malachi relaxed. "She's anxious for the children to come."

"I can only imagine."

Brooke yelled from up the hill. "I think I found one!"

She stood above them, waving with a giant grin on her face. The girl had been born in America and had lived among humans for the first part of her life. She'd probably celebrated Christmas, too.

"Shall we go see?" Malachi said.

"I think we must," Bruno said. "I have a feeling Brooke is far more of a Christmas tree expert than we are."

They followed her footprints in the snow. The sturdy fir tree she was standing next to didn't reach over his head, but it was well-formed with short springy needles and a cheerful shape.

"This will make a good Christmas tree?" Malachi asked, walking around the fir.

"Yep," Brooke said. "I already checked. No bare spots. Well, one little one here, but we can put that against the wall."

"So we simply cut it down?" Bruno asked, reaching for the axe. "How do we stand it up?"

Brooke twisted her mouth in concentration. "I'm sure there must be tree stands in the village."

"We will cut it down and drag it back," Bruno said. "I'll clean it while you two go into the village for a stand."

"And lights!" Brooke said. "We have to have lights."

"Yes," Malachi said, "but we must let Ava pick out the ornaments. Glass ones, I think. Those are the ones she's looked at."

"Oh, they're so pretty!" Brooke clapped. "I was looking at them last week when we went into the city. They're all hand painted and have the most beautiful colors…"

Hearing Brooke chatter about the human holiday reaffirmed that Malachi must not have been paying attention to Ava's needs. Surely, anything that elicited this much excitement in a girl who'd only lived part of her childhood among humans must have been very important for someone like Ava who'd lived with human traditions her whole life.

Doubts began to eat him again. Most days, Malachi felt only elation at the thought of becoming a father. His own father had been a great man. His mother, a gentle force of nature. Like the forest, he thought, looking around the snow-dusted hills. His parents had been like the forest. Solid and safe. Sheltering him from the turmoil that must have hunted them as it did all singers and scribes.

Theirs was a society that existed constantly in war. Would his children know nothing else in their long life? What could the Irin be if they were not at war with the sons of the Fallen? Some nights he woke in a cold sweat, certain he'd be unable to protect them.

Brushing those fears to the side, Malachi held the treetop as Bruno cut the base, then he grabbed the lower branches and dragged the tree back down the hill. Brooke's laughing voice was the only sound for miles.

HOURS LATER, MALACHI WAS CHOPPING A PILE OF WOOD AND WAITING for his mate to return from the hospital in Beroun. Astrid, the healer Ava had first met in Norway, was also a medical doctor and the only person Ava would allow to deliver their babies. It was the reason they'd driven two days to reach the small haven in the Czech Republic.

So far, Astrid had reassured them that everything with the babies looked normal, but Malachi still worried. Part of him would have liked to force Ava into a human hospital, but he knew that the bombardment of soul-voices from the humans would drive his mate mad if she was in too much pain to block them out.

Her shields were very strong, but not instinctual like those born and raised Irina. She still had moments—especially if she was tired or sick —when her control over her abilities slipped. His mate was plagued by headaches if she went too long without contact from him, but she'd insisted on going to the local hospital without him.

Malachi probably frightened the nurses when he accompanied her for their weekly ultrasound. Last time, he'd been forced to leave his knives at home.

He saw the old Range Rover pull into the driveway just as he finished the last of the pile. He'd also scraped the thin layer of snow from the front walkway so Ava would not slip.

Malachi was told this much snow early in the year was unusual for Bohemia, but he wouldn't complain. Ava enjoyed it and it made her pale cheeks pink.

The first time he'd noticed her losing weight, he'd had to smother a jolt of panic. He had flashbacks to the wan faces of the human women impregnated by the Fallen, their Grigori offspring—mostly male— draining them of life even before they were born.

My son is not Grigori. My daughter is not kareshta.

Astrid had reassured him that Ava was as healthy as anyone

carrying two babies could ever be. Children stressed the body, and two caused more stress than one. She hadn't put on much weight during pregnancy, but not everyone did. Irina had very high metabolisms. The paleness was a result of morning sickness. She would be fine. The babies were fine.

"Everything looks good!" Ava called out as Malachi put down the axe and jogged toward them. "They're already playing football again."

Astrid came up behind her and draped a scarf over Ava's shoulders. "Stay warm, California girl."

"I'm fine."

Malachi tugged the scarf more tightly around her and enveloped his mate in a hug. He felt the children kicking against the firm muscles of his abdomen. "Behave," he said firmly to his mate's belly.

The babies ignored him.

He put a hand on her and traced a soothing spell over her belly. It calmed the children a little bit.

Heaven, to have that kicking coming from inside! Malachi couldn't imagine. It was bad enough when she snuggled into him at night and he could feel them kicking against his back or side, like tiny birds battering their cage. It was amazing they hadn't broken anything.

"Not long," Astrid said. "She's already dilated."

Malachi looked up with a jerk. "What? It's too early, isn't it?"

"Relax." Ava took his hand and pulled him toward the house. "Not for twins. Twins usually come early whether they're human or Irina births. Right, Astrid?"

"Yes," the healer said. "And she could be dilated for weeks without anything happening. It's nothing to be worried about. I was expecting her to deliver before midwinter, to be honest. Anything after thirty-six weeks will be fine." Astrid walked up and patted Malachi's chest. "And let us not forget their father is a very gifted scribe who is covering his mate with protection, and their mother is a very powerful singer who will be singing over them with her own magic."

"And they have the best doctor in the world," Ava said.

Astrid smiled. "That goes without saying."

Malachi said, "Ava, are you sure—?"

"No hospital," she said. "I told you, I'll only go if Astrid says I absolutely have to. Hospitals are horrendous for me. You know that."

"I know." He ushered her into the warm house, his arm still around her. "I have a surprise for you, canım."

"What is—oh!" Her face transformed. "Malachi!"

Brooke and Bruno had spent the past hours cleaning and trimming the tree, propping it in the bright red base they'd purchased in the village before they'd strung it with tiny white lights.

"Do you like it?" Brooke came running and gave Ava a sideways hug. "We found it today and Bruno cut it down and Malachi dragged it back and I put on all the lights. We got a few ornaments, but we saved them for you to put on. And you can get more of the pretty glass ones at the market! What do you think?"

He watched her as she took in the tree and the lights. Would it be enough? Should they have picked a larger tree?

"You guys, it's perfect," Ava said, her voice already sounding watery. "Oh my gosh, I'm going to cry again."

Everything made her cry these days. Movies. Taking pictures. A good joke. Sentimental magazine advertisements.

Everything.

"This is so lovely," Astrid said. "Don't cry, Ava. Why don't more Irin homes have a holiday tree during Midwinter? We should. It's a beautiful symbol."

"It's perfect," Ava said, sniffing. "Oh, Malachi, I love it. I can't wait to get more ornaments." Her hand came to her abdomen and she rubbed small circles. "You guys have to come out already. Your daddy got you a Christmas tree."

MALACHI watched Ava, Brooke, and Candace, Brooke's mother, as they decorated the tree later that night. They didn't have any of the intricately painted glass globes that Ava had been looking at, but they had cheerful red and green balls, and Karen had gathered her crafting supplies and spread some of the glass beads she'd collected on the table by the fire. The women were twisting wire and beads into stars and diamond shapes while Malachi watched and Bruno cooked chili in the kitchen.

Ava was laughing and teasing Karen about her superior beading skills. Candace and Brooke were telling Christmas stories from when they lived in Virginia. Malachi saw his mate glancing up, searching for him as she worked and laughed. The simultaneous air of vulnerability and steely strength marked her expression as she stretched up and rubbed her back.

He was her slave.

A fierce wave of protectiveness threatened to overwhelm him. Malachi had the urge to pick up his daggers and patrol the house. He wondered whether that damned fallen angel, Vasu, was still checking up on Ava.

Maybe he should have demanded all three of his brothers join them for Midwinter. Damien and Sari were at the scribe house in Cappadocia with Orsala, but he should have insisted on the rest of his brothers joining them. Max, Leo, and Rhys didn't have anything better to do. And were he and Bruno really strong enough to protect the house? What if—

Astrid banged a tall mug of mulled wine in front of him and sat on the other side of the table.

"You're brooding."

Malachi frowned. "What?"

"Are you still worried?" she asked more quietly.

He nodded, his eyes never leaving the delicate woman who had become his life.

"She's very strong, you know. And she's in excellent health. I know you're worried about her weight, but—"

"I would never ask you in front of her" —he switched to German, which he knew Astrid spoke fluently— "but the children... Their energy will be different. Their magic can't harm her, can it?"

"As the Grigori harm their human mothers?" Astrid shook her head. "You have to remember that though she was raised human, Ava *is* Irina. Or *kareshta*. It doesn't matter. Her blood is the same. Added to that, having two archangels in her genetic history makes her magic very powerful. She can handle this pregnancy, Malachi. The babies will not ask anything of her that she cannot give. You have no need to worry."

He sighed. "I think that is impossible."

"Probably." She patted his arm. "Drink your wine. The babies aren't coming tonight."

"And you're sure about the hospital?"

"For a hundred and fifty years, I delivered every baby at Sarihöfn in far rougher conditions than this, Malachi. There are two hospitals in easy driving distance, and I have more in my medicine cabinet to fight infection than I had in the whole of my infirmary a hundred years ago. If there is the slightest hint there is a problem with the babies, Bruno will get her to Beroun."

He let out a slow breath. "I'm being ridiculous."

"No, you're being an Irin father."

He gave her a grudging smile. "So we're all like this?"

"You haven't posted your brothers on the door and taken to wearing weapons to sleep. So you're not as bad as some."

"I was thinking about both those things," he admitted.

"And yet, I am not surprised."

CHAPTER

THREE

AVA LEANED AGAINST MALACHI, staring at the Christmas tree and listening to the bustle of activity as Karen, Bruno, Astrid, and Candace prepared for the midwinter feast. Irin lived all over the world, so midwinter celebrations were very diverse, but there were special songs and candlelighting ceremonies that were necessary for everyone.

It would be the first midwinter Ava spent with anyone besides Malachi.

"I love this," she said. "This is so cool."

"What were Christmases like when you were young?" He glanced over and smiled at Brooke, who ran up the stairs, laughing madly, with white flour covering her head as her mother chased after her, covered in flour herself.

Ava smiled at their retreating figures. "It was just my mom and me. She usually did something to make Carl mad so he'd go on vacation with his friends and leave us alone."

"Theirs is… not a healthy relationship, canım."

"Oh, I know." She stretched her toes closer to the fire. "But it works for her right now. I'm not getting involved. And in his own way, Carl takes care of her. And me. I think he's relieved I'm living in Turkey, though."

"Is your mother still coming in February?"

"Yep." She closed her eyes and buried her face in his shoulder. "I love the way you smell." The babies kicked her stomach. "Oof. So do our kids."

"Hmmm." Malachi stared at the fire as it crackled and popped.

"What?"

"Maybe next year we should invite your mother for Christmas."

Ava scooted up, trying to get into a more comfortable position. "You mean… in Istanbul?"

"Or Germany. We could spend midwinter in Istanbul and Christmas in Germany. Celebrate both holidays. Then Lena would be able to celebrate with her grandchildren."

Ava started to sniffle again.

"What?" Malachi laughed and pressed her face to his shoulder. "No, not again. Stop, Ava. You cried at the tissue advertisement on the television the other day."

"It was really cute!" She swiped at her cheeks. "And the mom was so sweet with the little boy and she just… I know. It's ridiculous. Ignore me."

He captured her lips and devoured them thoroughly. By the time he pulled away, Ava was breathless and her pulse was soaring.

"Never," he muttered against her mouth. "Never will I ignore you."

She slid an arm around his waist and pressed closer. "I *miss* you."

Sex had become very uncomfortable a few weeks before. For two people who had such a strong physical connection, going without it was difficult. They could do other things, but…

Malachi leaned down and whispered, "We'll have to be creative again tonight."

"Sounds good to me."

He gave her a wicked smile. "I enjoy being creative."

"And as for the Christmas and Midwinter idea," she said, "that sounds great. I'd love to do that. But I don't mind having Christmas in Istanbul. Or we could go to Malibu to meet her there. But I want the babies to be able to celebrate Christmas too. There's no reason we can't do both."

"Extra cookies."

Ava perked up. "There are cookies?"

"I'm fairly sure I smell some right now. Do you want to go look?"

"Yes." She held up her arms. "Okay. Hoist me up, babe."

"Oooh." Malachi stood and looked down at her, his hands on his hips. "I might need to call Bruno in to help with this."

THAT NIGHT, AVA WAS PUT TO WORK TWISTING THE SOFT *KRINGLE* sweet breads that Karen was making for Midwinter. She cut the dough at the table and twisted it into pretzel-like twists that would rise and bake in the oven. It was a tedious task, but she could listen to Karen and Candace talk while she worked and it allowed her to stay off her aching feet.

She looked up when Candace sat next to her.

"Hello," the quiet American woman said. "How are you feeling?"

"Good. Ready." Ava had never felt particularly close to Candace, even when she'd stayed at Sarihöfn. The soft-spoken brunette had lost her mate eight years before Ava had met her. Perhaps Ava's own grief at the time had been too new, but she'd avoided someone with wounds so similar to her own. "How are you and Brooke liking the Czech Republic?"

"We like it. Everyone is very friendly. Brooke is better with the language than I am. I still have trouble not thinking in English all the time."

"So you were born in America?"

Candace nodded.

"And your mate was American, too?"

"Canadian," she said quietly. "In Europe, the Irin travel so much, but in the Americas, villages were much more spread out. Ezekiel and I both came from very small communities. We didn't meet until just after the Rending. It was during that period when Irina were disappearing everywhere. I felt so… lost. All my family was dead. A woman from my village said she knew of a way to Canada. Her son was there with his mate, and she wanted to try to find them. She was very old. Powerful. I went with her because I didn't want to be alone."

"And you met your mate."

Candace nodded. The pain in her eyes was still so raw that Ava had to look away.

"I've been meaning to talk to you," Ava said. "I need help."

"Oh?" Candace's green eyes lit up. "What can I help with?"

Ava put her hand on her belly. "Well… this, I guess."

"Oh, but Astrid—"

"Is great. She's delivered a lot of babies. But you're the only singer I know who's actually given birth."

Candace smiled. "I suppose that's true. I hadn't thought about that. Zeke and I lived so quietly after… I grew up in a village with many births, so I didn't worry when Brooke was born. I had helped other Irina give birth when I was young. I saw my grandmother have her second baby when I was only ten."

Ava's jaw dropped. "But—"

"Some Irin siblings are decades or even a hundreds of years apart. Women don't lose fertility until they want to."

"Whoa." Ava tried to wrap her brain around it. "So your mother and her sibling—"

"It was a girl," Candace said. "My aunt was ten years younger than me, but she was one hundred twenty years younger than her sister. Something like that."

"Wow."

Candace shrugged. "That was normal for us. Irina weren't limited by time when they had their children. I was over two hundred when I had Brooke."

"And you had her at home?"

She nodded. "Just me and Ezekiel. We were hiding then, and he never trusted human hospitals."

"So…" Ava let out a long breath. "What am I in for?"

Candace smiled. "I think it's mostly like human birth. Traditionally, Irina don't use any drugs because the midwife or doctor will sing the pain away. Astrid is very good at it. It's our own kind of anesthetic. It will still hurt—there's no way to avoid that completely—but Malachi will be holding you, so—"

"Holding me? Holding me how?"

"A scribe sits behind his mate and holds her while she's in labor. I know that's not the normal thing for human hospitals, but it's very comforting. It puts your mating marks against his. Very powerful magic. Orsala taught you the songs for the baby?"

Ava nodded.

"It's the same for scribes. There are special spells Malachi will draw on your skin to help you give birth, and then those for the baby—babies!—when they are born." Candace's smile turned into a grin. "I'm so excited for you. Twins are so lucky."

Ava spotted a problem immediately. "But has anyone told Malachi what spells he has to write? None of his brothers or his Watcher are fathers."

Candace's smile fell. "I hadn't thought about that. And Bruno and Karen haven't had a baby either."

Ava felt a sense of panic. What if something went wrong because Malachi didn't know the right spells? What if her songs for her son and daughter didn't take because his half of the birth ritual wasn't correct? Would their daughter be tormented with the constant voices that Ava had experienced from the time she was a small child?

"Ava." Candace put a hand on her arm. "It will be fine. Orsala taught you the songs months ago. I'm sure someone taught Malachi, as well. He had his own father for many years. He probably learned them when he was young."

"But what if he forgot?"

"Scribes don't forget spells like that."

Ava let out a slow breath. "You're right. I'm probably worrying for nothing."

"Everyone worries. It's normal. Don't panic. It'll be fine."

THE DREAM SNEAKED IN ON QUIET CAT FEET UNTIL IT SAT IN SHADOW across from her. Ava opened her eyes to see the darkness sitting in the armchair across from their bed in the cozy library where Bruno had set up a bed for them.

Before her eyes, the cat stretched and yawned, transforming into a lithe, dark-skinned young man with a flow of black and gold hair covering his shoulders.

Ava blinked slowly. "I told you to stop doing that."

Vasu shrugged.

"Am I dreaming?"

"A bit."

"Why are you here?"

The fallen angel glanced at her belly. "They are unique."

A spike of anger. "They are none of your business."

"You're wrong."

A flash of an old vision.

Two dark-haired children. A girl with a golden gaze, laughing as butterflies swirled around her. A boy, staring back at her with his father's eyes. An ink-black jaguar curled around the children as a wolf and a tiger paced behind. The tiger bent to the girl, opening his mouth. The great beast closed his jaw around the girl's nape gently as she continued to smile and pet its cheek.

Ava opened her eyes with a gasp. "Is it you? The jaguar?"

Vasu cocked his head. "I do not see what you do, Ava."

Something about the vision set her at ease. Nothing about it spoke of danger. Vasu wasn't a restful presence, but she'd never felt in danger around him. Well, at least not danger *from* him. Vasu putting her in danger out of curiosity or boredom was another question.

"*Why are you here*, Vasu?"

"Azril sent me."

Ava sat bolt up and put a hand over her belly, ignoring the tearing pain in her back. "*No.*"

Vasu looked disappointed. "Really, Ava? You should know the angel of death doesn't always portend the physical. Azril lives in the space between. Transition. He intends no harm to you or your children. He has been watching you. You know he still keeps watch over your grandmother."

"Then why did he send you?"

Vasu cocked his head, as if listening to someone in another room.

"*Agatavyah boh.*"

"What?"

He frowned, as if still listening to someone. "Or... *ayatah agatavyah* if they are being stubborn."

"Vasu, what does that even mean?"

"Ask Azril. If you call him, he'll come. He just didn't want to show up and frighten you."

"So he sent you?"

"Yes."

Ava felt herself falling back into sleep, even though she wanted to keep badgering Vasu. "I think... needs to rethink his messengers..."

"'Please come' and 'Come quickly,'" Vasu said, his voice fading away. "He said you would know when to use them."

"Use what?"

She felt a shadowed hand press against her belly. It was warm. He smelled of the earth and green things. Of spices and rain.

"Sleep, daughter of Jaron. Their time draws close."

· · ·

WHEN SHE OPENED HER EYES, MALACHI WAS QUIETLY OPENING THE door to their library bedroom.

"Ah, sorry," he whispered. "I was just checking on you. I didn't want to wake you up."

"No, come here." She patted the side of the bed.

"Bad dreams?"

To tell or not to tell about Vasu's visit? She had to think about it some more. She didn't want to think about Vasu right now.

"Do you know the spells to write for the babies?" she asked, still half asleep.

Malachi stretched out on the bed beside her. "I do. I have studied them from books we had in the Istanbul scribe house. I wish…"

"You could talk to your father?"

"Yes. In times like this, I miss my father more than I can say."

"I understand."

Malachi helped rearrange the pillows under her belly, then laid his arm across her middle and rubbed large circles over her abdomen. Ava leaned back into his chest and felt him kiss the curve of her neck.

"I don't know why you're worried. You're going to be a wonderful father."

His hand paused. "I hope so."

"Tell me about your father."

The circles started again, Malachi sliding his hand under her shirt so his skin was next to hers.

"He was a very strong man but very funny. Everyone loved his sense of humor. Bruno reminds me of him a little bit."

Ava smiled. "Really?"

"Yes. But he was not as loud."

"I don't think anyone is as loud as Bruno."

Malachi's chest shook quietly. "My father was very caring. Very affectionate. Completely besotted with my mother. I would have been spoiled horribly as a child, but he put a stop to it. There was only one other child in our village, you see. And she was five years older. So it would have been easy for me to be indulged. But he was a very disciplined man and insisted that I must be, too. I think that's one of the reasons we moved to Turkey."

"So you weren't spoiled?"

"Yes. We moved to a village with more children. My mother missed her home, but it was a wise decision."

She drew a deep breath. "That'll be a challenge with our children. Everyone will want to make them happy."

"Leo will be the pushover."

"I don't know. Damien might be the stealth softie."

"Yes, you may be right."

Her whole stomach tightened with a strong contraction. She'd been getting them for days. Astrid said they could mean anything. They could continue sporadically for weeks or she could go into true labor tomorrow. Malachi buried his face in her neck and hugged her shoulders.

"My *reshon*," he whispered as she sucked in a tense breath, "I would bear this for you if I could."

"That's not the way it works," she said when she was able to breathe again. "I'm okay. What's the spell that feels like a spiral? That one helps."

"It promotes focus," he said. "The books say that one will help you during labor."

"That's good." She was feeling sleepy again. "You're going to be a great father. The best."

"Oh?"

"Yes, and I can prove it. One, you had a great dad, so you've seen it done right. And two, you're a wonderful husband. You take very good care of me, so why are you worried about what kind of father you'll be? You'll be even more protective of your children."

He was quiet a long time. "And you don't ever worry about me with the children? After what happened in Vienna?"

"Malachi." She tried to turn, but she couldn't move. She was so big and awkward. She reached back and put her hand on his cheek. "No. Never. I never worry about that. Because you are my *reshon*. Don't forget, I haven't only seen your face, I've heard your soul. I know how deeply you love them already."

She felt him relax behind her, only to start when the front door slammed.

"What the—"

He was reaching for the daggers on his side table when a booming voice yelled, "Happy Midwinter, sisters!"

Ava looked up at Malachi, whose scowl had turned to a smile.

"Is that—?"

"Merry Christmas, too!" a similar accent yelled. "Max, there are no presents under the tree. Aren't there supposed to be presents?"

A sardonic British voice replied, "Not if no one has bought any yet. Do you think they magically appear?"

"Well, we *are* magic."

A jumble of voices came in greeting as the three new voices were joined by the familiar throng.

"Canım" —Malachi looked down with a happy smile— "I believe we have been invaded."

Just then, a silence fell in the entryway, and Ava heard the reedy voice of an old man who couldn't have been more welcome.

She and Malachi both smiled.

"Evren."

CHAPTER

FOUR

MALACHI HAD NEVER IN HIS LIFE been more relieved to see the old scribe. Evren rarely left the ancient scribe house in Cappadocia. Most seeking Evren's wisdom came to him. But when Malachi saw the wise old man, he almost fell on his knees in thanksgiving.

"Brother," he said, bending to embrace him. "You have come to us and we are blessed."

"Brother Malachi." Evren patted his cheek. "I only hope I am welcome. Your brothers mentioned flying here for Midwinter, and since I had not had a chance to speak with you about the birth of your children, I asked to accompany them."

"You are welcome," Ava said from behind him. She'd wrapped herself in a throw from their bedroom and her hair was tangled, but when she waddled toward Evren, her face glowed. "*Very* welcome. Thank you for coming to visit."

"Ah, sister." Evren embraced her gently. "Your voluminous blessing has never felt more voluminous, has it?"

Ava laughed. "I'm so ready to get these kids out of here."

Malachi saw the babies jostling in her belly, clearly excited by the familiar deep voices of his brothers, who had spent most of Ava's pregnancy shouting at her abdomen "to talk to the babies." Max and Leo were already hovering over Ava, barely keeping their hands off her belly. Rhys gave her a gentle hug, then backed off to speak to Astrid.

"My *reshon*." He walked over, cupped her cheeks, and kissed her. "You are the most understanding of women. Back, back, back." He shoved his brothers away and led Ava to the sofa. "You will smother her."

"We missed you," Max said, stretching his giant frame out on the rug by the fireplace. "It was boring in Istanbul without you, so we decided to come here."

"And who is watching the house?" Malachi asked.

Rhys sat in a chair by the tree and batted a red glass globe like a curious cat. "Damien and Sari brought Mala and Orsala from Cappadocia to the city. Get them out of Cappadocia for a bit. I think Mala was getting edgy. They're keeping an eye on things."

Malachi relaxed. Grigori activity in their section of Turkey had been quiet, but it was always a risk. And with many humans fleeing war on Turkey's borders, that meant thousands of vulnerable humans could be prey for opportunistic sons of the Fallen. Damien, Sari, and Mala, however, were more than a match for any Grigori foolish enough to try to infiltrate Istanbul.

He turned to Max. "Heard from Renata lately?"

Max shrugged and said nothing, which likely meant the nomadic Irina was still in the wind. Malachi didn't know what to make of their relationship, so he didn't ask. He was simply happy to see them all. He put his arm around Ava and kissed the top of her head.

"Are you happy?" he asked quietly. "More people means more—"

"Noise. And voices. And stomping feet on the stairs. And mouths to feed." She looked up and grinned. "But it also means more people I love are here to celebrate with us. I'm happy. This is the best, babe."

"I'm glad."

THAT NIGHT, WHILE KAREN ROPED MAX AND LEO INTO MEAL preparations for Midwinter, Ava and Malachi met with Evren in the library. The old scribe pulled out a carefully wrapped leather-bound manuscript and opened it in front of Malachi.

An old ache eased in Malachi. "The *Hokman Abat*."

"I have brought you my own copy. There are notes written in the margins, but we'll go through all the inscriptions and possible variations. The sections on Irina birth and twin births I must confess to have not studied as closely because, of course, my mate was only having a son."

"Wow." Ava leaned closer and looked at the well-worn book. "So this is like… a childbirth manual for Irin dads?"

"Of course," Evren said. "For scribes, there are many tasks during the labor process. The spells are quite intricate."

"I have studied what I could," Malachi said. "But I am greatly relieved to have a scribe with practical knowledge to advise me before the birth. We should start right away. That is, if Ava can spare me."

"Of course!" She was smiling, and Malachi could not interpret the expression on her face. It was surprise, perhaps? A hint of amusement.

"What is it?" he asked.

"I love that the Irin have a birth manual for fathers. That's so cool."

Evren frowned. "Are you saying there is no similar manual for fathers in the human world? Granted, there are no spells that human men can do, but surely they have specific tasks while the mother is in labor."

"No," she said with an amused smile. "None that I know of."

"That's shocking," Malachi said with wide eyes. "How did fathers know what to do?"

"A few generations ago, human men weren't even expected to be with their wives while they gave birth."

Malachi must have looked horrified because Evren patted his shoulder.

"I think it is very different for women now in most of the world," Evren said.

"Were these humans under the impression that their women spontaneously reproduced?" Malachi sat up straight. "That is absurd."

Humans never failed to amaze him. Malachi could acknowledge that he never paid much attention to their mating or child-rearing habits, but he had no idea how a male could leave his mate unprotected while she was physically vulnerable. What if an enemy attacked during the hours of labor? Perhaps they had other security measures in place Ava didn't know about. That had to be the case.

"Luckily," Evren said, "you are having Irin children, not human children. While the labor will be difficult, I will help Malachi to perfect his spells to ease as much of your pain as possible and protect your children when they are born."

"Thank you, Evren." She hoisted herself to her feet. "I have a feeling you're going to be buried in here for the rest of the day, so I'll go help in the kitchen. Enjoy your book."

Malachi sprang to his feet and helped her to the door, then whistled for Rhys, who was lazing by the fire.

"Oh, for heaven's sake." Ava sighed as Rhys jumped up. "I'm having babies, not gradually turning into porcelain."

Rhys took her arm. "Are you sure they're not ducklings inside you? That's a formidable waddle, my dear."

"I can still hurt you, Rhys. All I'd have to do is sit on you at this point. You wouldn't be getting up anytime soon."

MALACHI AND EVREN STUDIED AND PRACTICED HIS SPELLWORK FOR days while Midwinter feast preparations swirled around them. As the hours passed and the solstice drew near, snow fell heavier outside the house, and Malachi saw Ava's usual enthusiasm narrow into an exhausted, steely focus. She slept often and ate little. She liked being in the middle of the feast preparations, but she didn't join in the conversation.

He knew in his gut that the children would come soon.

When she slept at night, she only dozed, and he knew she dreamed without him. Often, he would catch her dozing in a chair in the middle of the kitchen or on the couch and he'd have to scoop her up and take her to the library where he could watch her. The irregular contractions continued to come, but never progressed into true labor.

By the time Midwinter came, the forest around the house was blanketed with a thick layer of snow and the house was decked with holly boughs and candles. The Christmas tree, which had seemed so foreign to him at first, blended with the traditional Midwinter decorations and made his mate smile every time she looked at it.

Bruno had brought another table in from the barn where he did his woodworking, and the dining room stretched into the sitting room. All the furniture had been pushed back to the walls and the tables were piled high with fragrant soups, roasts, and savory pastries. The seven-branched candlestick they would light with short beeswax tapers was placed in the center of the table where it would burn until there was nothing but seven small flames to join the sacred fire Bruno kept burning in the meditation room.

It was every Midwinter feast he'd ever had, but better. Because for the first time, his mate and his brothers were together. His children would be born in a blessed house, surrounded by those who would give their lives for their protection.

Malachi felt the welling gratitude in his heart as he pulled Ava's chair out for her then sat next to his mate. He leaned down and rested his head on hers, wrapping his arms around her back and under her belly. She reached her hand up and put it on his cheek.

"This is good," she whispered.

"Very good."

"I think it will be soon."

"I agree. Try to eat something tonight. The soup would be good."

"I'll try."

"Ava?"

"Hmm?"

"I'm very proud to be your mate. I know you'll be a wonderful mother." He heard the sniffling and lifted his head. "Again?"

"I can't help it when you say things like that."

WHEN THEY DREAM-WALKED THAT NIGHT, THEY WERE ON THE BEACH Ava loved. It was north of Malibu, and the cliffs rose above their heads while the sun glistened on the ocean swells.

"Do you miss home?" Malachi asked.

She sank into the sand and pointed her feet toward the lapping waves. She was still pregnant in their dreams, but she moved with more ease.

"I don't miss home. Not exactly."

He sat down and immediately understood. "You miss your mother."

"Yes."

"You will see her soon."

She leaned against his shoulder and breathed in balmy ocean air. The salt and sand of the Pacific washed over them as they rested in the shallow surf.

He heard laughter in the distance.

"Vasu came to me," she said. "He had a message from Azril."

"Azril?"

She put a hand on his thigh. "Nothing to worry about. I think it was a spell Azril wanted to give me. He said I would know when to use it."

He gently rubbed her belly and heard the children's laughter come closer.

"This feeling, *reshon*. I have never felt such power. I would die for them. Kill for them. And I have not even seen their faces. This fierce love scares me."

"Do you think it was any different for your father?"

"No."

She lifted her face to his, and he kissed her.

"You were loved," she said. "Now you understand how much. We only fear the unknown."

"We all fear the unknown."

"But you—" She broke off with a gasp.

"*Reshon?*"

The laughter was in his ears, but his eyes never left her face. It was shock and fear and surprise and wonder. Every emotion flickered across her face.

She sighed and said, "It's time."

HE WOKE TO FIND HER STILL SLEEPING, HER BROW FURROWED AND HER stomach tight with a strong contraction. Malachi bent and kissed her awake.

"Mal," she whispered in a hoarse voice. "I… I think—"

"It's time, canım. Wake, my love. Our children are coming."

CHAPTER

FIVE

A VA BEGAN TO WHISPER the verses Orsala had taught her as Malachi helped sit her up in bed and put pillows behind her back. Astrid and Karen had already prepared the bed with special sheets and pads to help keep things clean. For a second, Ava wanted to throw everything Astrid had said out the window and demand a drive to the hospital.

Screw traditional Irin birth! She wanted antiseptic! She felt hot and uncomfortable. Her whole body ached.

But when Malachi pulled off her shirt and dressed her in the linen robe that would open at the back and front for skin-to-skin contact with her mate and children, she calmed.

She could hear the fire crackling in the sitting room beyond their door, and the low snores of their brothers. She heard another brother pacing outside the house, pausing at the lit window. There was a soft tap.

"Malachi? Ava?" Rhys called softly. "Is everything all right?"

Malachi pressed kisses to her shoulders. She felt her mating marks start to glow as Malachi walked to the window and cracked it open. The gust of crisp air cooled her skin.

"I think it's time for the babies," Malachi told his brother. "I'm going to wake Astrid."

"It's quiet out here. I'll wake her so you can stay with Ava."

"Thank you."

Ava heard Rhys stomping his feet on the front porch before the door opened. She closed her eyes and concentrated on the slow build of tension in her abdomen. She reached a hand out toward Malachi and he grasped it and slid behind her, stripping off his sleep shirt so he held her skin-to-skin.

He put his hands on her shoulders. "Do you remember the songs Orsala taught you?"

She nodded.

Malachi squeezed her shoulders and said, "Then sing, my love. I'll hold you."

Ava sang as the slow vise tightened around her middle. Just as she reached the peak, she felt Malachi draw a swirling pattern down her right arm and the pain eased. He rocked her through the last lines of the Old Language as she finished the first spell and everything tense in her relaxed. Her mind. Her heart. Her spirit rose.

Their babies were coming.

There came a soft tap at the door. Astrid's blond curly head poked through, her curls askew but her smile bright.

"It's time?" she asked.

Malachi said, "I heard them laughing in our dream. I woke to her contracting in her sleep. She might have been in labor for some time."

"Midwinter babies!" Astrid sang. "So much fun. I banished your brothers outside, Malachi. I think they might have issues with boundaries. Ava, is there anyone else you'd like to be here with you?"

"Candace," she panted. "But maybe not until later. I feel like this is going to take a while."

Astrid made all sorts of reassuring noises while she eased Ava back to check her progress.

"Everything feels normal."

Ava groaned. "Is it supposed to feel like a giant vise is trying to twist my guts out?"

"Yes."

"Awesome."

Malachi and Astrid spent half an hour in quiet conversation as Astrid timed Ava's contractions and confirmed that the greatly anticipated babies would indeed be born on Midwinter morning. Ava tried to concentrate on whispering her spells and not killing anyone making any noises.

"Twins born on Midwinter. So lucky, canım." Ava could hear the smile in Malachi's voice.

"Yeah," she groaned as another contraction began to build. "I'm feeling super-duper lucky right now. Thanks."

"Just remember," Astrid said as she watched the clock with a soothing hand on Ava's large belly, "you get a prize at the end of all this. In fact, you get two prizes."

Ava breathed out the songs Orsala had taught her as the pain came in ever-increasing waves. Magic filled the room as Malachi continued to press spells to her skin when he felt a contraction approach. Astrid was also whispering magic, but her focus was on the safe delivery of the children and Ava's well-being, not necessarily her comfort.

Even with magic, it was really hard work.

The sun rose and Candace woke with it. She brought a tray to Ava and Malachi's room with tea for Malachi and warm broth for Ava. She cracked the windows and aired out the room that smelled of sweat and ashes. As clean air swept into the room, Ava felt a renewed sense of purpose.

Her children needed to *come*.

She opened her senses and heard their minds. No words, but tiny murmurs and coos. New souls nearing transition into the world of men. Normally bright and innocent, her children's soft voices were tinged with confusion and fear.

Ava placed Malachi's hands on her belly and said, "They're frightened."

She sang, and Malachi drew along her skin as the glyph glowed in the morning light, gold shimmering on her pale, swollen abdomen. The contraction passed and the spike of fear from the children eased. There was still confusion, but it was quieter.

Ava laughed.

"What is it, canım?"

"Their voices," she said. "They sound so grumpy."

Astrid said, "I'm not surprised. It's quite crowded in there and now there's all this tensing and jostling. Come, babies…," Astrid cooed to Ava's belly and stroked a hand over the rise. "Come now, listen to your mama's voice."

Astrid started one of her healing songs, then motioned when it was Ava's turn to join in. It wasn't the smoothest singing she'd ever produced, but it seemed to get the job done. The next time Astrid checked her, she pronounced her ready to push.

AVA PUSHED. SHE PUSHED FOR HOURS. SHE PUSHED UNTIL ASTRID began to frown and small lines creased Candace's forehead. The gentle reassurances from Malachi were gone, and she could feel his attention focused tightly on Astrid.

"What does she need?" he asked. "Are there other spells I should be doing?"

"The children are not in distress," Astrid quickly assured him. "I've been listening to them as Ava has. There are no signs of trouble. They simply don't want to come out."

"Oh my gosh," Ava groaned. "I fail at pushing. This *sucks*." She felt hot tears well up. "Serves me right for mating with the most hard-headed man on the planet. Of course his kids are being stubborn. They're *his kids*."

"Canım—"

"Don't talk!" she snapped. "Just… no one talk. Unless you know a way of getting these kids out of here, you're not allowed to talk."

Astrid had a hand on her belly and felt the contraction building again. "Okay, Ava, get ready to push."

"Didn't I tell you not to talk?"

She could see Astrid fighting a smile.

"And no smiling either! This is not funny." She clenched her eyes shut and searched her mind for the gentle songs Orsala had taught her to coax the babies into the world, but they were escaping her. Ava wasn't in a coaxing mood anymore. Coaxing passed her by about an hour ago. She was approaching two hours of near-constant contractions, and while the babies were in no distress, *she was*.

"Okay, kids, time to get out of there." She pushed herself up and felt Malachi bracing her hips and shoulders. "Thanks, babe."

Because he was a wise man, her mate continued tracing spells down her arms and didn't say one word.

He said you would know when to use them.

Well, apparently Azril, the angel of death, knew her kids were going to be a handful. Maybe it was inevitable that children born from the union of two mortal enemies were always going to be trouble. She was ready for trouble. She was also ready to have her children leave the building.

Ava took a deep breath and closed her eyes as she breathed out the ancient words. "*Agatavyah boh.*"

Astrid stood up straight. "Ava, what was that?"

"Spell." She gritted her teeth and placed both hands on her belly. "Hold my hips," she told Malachi. "Lift them up a little."

He did and she groaned it out again.

"*Agatavyah boh!*"

"Ava." Astrid was starting to look concerned. "I don't know that spell, and I'm not sure you should be using it. You don't know what it could—"

"Stop," Candace said, speaking forcefully for the first time. "Look at her belly. Do you see?"

Ava couldn't see, but she could feel it. There was a painful roll and twist, and a small complaining whine in her mind.

Enough of this nonsense, the distinctly male whine seemed to say. *Let me out of here.*

"Oh." Astrid reached down and felt for the babies. "Someone pushed his sister out of the way. He's ready to come."

"So it is our *daughter* who was the stubborn one." Malachi finally spoke. "How very interesting."

"Oh my god, shut up!"

There was a great burning pain and Malachi pressed silver-lit arms around her. Their mating marks flared to life, lifting Ava past the pain, her mind arrowing in on the small soul being born into the world.

An angry cry and a triumphant shout from Candace. "Well done, Ava!"

A squirming warm body was placed on Ava's chest as Candace threw a blanket over the baby boy. Malachi was laughing, and he didn't stop, even when her body tensed for another strong contraction.

"Geron," Malachi whispered. "Hello, my wise boy. What a good boy you are."

Ava closed her eyes and took a moment to glory in the sound of her mate speaking to their baby boy.

Her son!

She started laughing, too. She laughed and she cried until the vise in her belly tightened again and a mutinous little voice batted against her mind.

Ornery little baby…

Vasu's words came back to her. "…*ayatah agatavyah if they are being stubborn.*"

Well, of course her daughter was being stubborn.

Ava cradled baby Geron to her chest, holding his tiny squirming body on her breast as she spoke firmly to her daughter.

"*Ayatah agatavyah*, Matti."

Another rolling turn.

"Oh, that stinker," Astrid said. "She turned faceup."

"Come on, kid. You don't have a choice in this." Ava pressed a firm hand to her stomach and mentally pushed her daughter with every bit of magic she controlled. She pictured the tiny stubborn girl exiting her body. Pictured her safe and sound and crying angry tears next to her brother. "*Ayatah agatavyah*, Matti!"

And there she was. Ava barely heard the delighted laughter of Malachi behind her or the happy clapping of Candace. Astrid was grinning and wrapping up Matti when she lifted her and Ava met her daughter's eyes.

Her little face was scrunched and scowling, but her eyes were fixed on Ava's face. Deep amber-gold eyes, and a shock of thick black hair. Ava could only shake her head and laugh. There was no more pain, no more exhaustion. She was riding high on adrenaline, magic, and pure joy.

Astrid put the squalling girl on her belly where Geron immediately wiggled closer to his sister. As soon as she felt her twin's touch, Matti quieted and nestled into him. Both babies turned their little cheeks to Ava's breast and let out a contented sigh.

"Look at that," Malachi said.

"She found her brother," Ava said with wonder. "Malachi… she's never ever been alone. Her whole life, her big brother has been right there."

"Ava…" He pressed a kiss to her cheek and she felt his tears against her skin. "I love you so."

"I love you, too. I'm sorry I yelled at you. That was rude."

"I think it was quite understandable, canım."

"Hello," she whispered to her children. "Look at you. I've never seen anything more beautiful in my life. I'm so glad I finally get to see you guys."

Matti and Geron snuggled closer together, Geron's arm curled tightly around his little sister's shoulders.

Malachi let out a long breath and shifted to the side, easing Ava back against the stacked pillows as Astrid helped her finish her labor. It was… not glamorous in the least. And Ava didn't care a whit. Candace brought a small tub of warm water over so she and Malachi could clean the babies. Ava was relieved when the bustle was finally over, the helpers had all left, and her children were nestled back into bed lying on Ava's breast as Malachi lay beside them.

"Heaven above, Ava, look at them." His voice was awestruck. "Look at you."

She couldn't hold in the laughter. "No cameras. Not allowed."

His face was luminous. "You have never been more beautiful to me. You are wondrous."

Ava couldn't say a word. She pressed her face into the curve of his neck and let him hold her while she cried the happiest tears of her life. Tears of surprise. Wonder. Amazement. *Relief.*

"They're so beautiful." She sniffed. "I thought I'd never get them out."

His chest rumbled with laughter. "I'm so very glad you did." He reached over and put his hand on Matti's head. "Matti, my daughter. You will give us trouble, I think, but also much laughter."

Ava brushed a finger over Geron's soft cheek. Without a doubt, her little boy—born only minutes ahead of his sister—was the more restful baby. He'd already searched out her breast to nurse, his hand curled around his sister's small fist. Matti had to be guided to Ava's breast, but once there, she latched on with gusto.

"I estimate," Ava said, gently tracing the curve of Matti's tiny ear, "that we have maybe a half an hour to ourselves before everyone in this house demands entry."

"I will fight them off if you insist."

"No," she said. "I don't mind. I don't think I mind anything anymore. I love them so much, Malachi. I never knew I could love anyone like this."

"Nor did I."

Sing, a voice inside her called.

And so she did.

Ava sang ancient songs of love and devotion, covering her children in the magic of the Forgiven. As she sang, their father held them, tracing gold talesm over their bodies with gentle hands, covering them with his protective magic as he kissed and held them both. The bedroom filled with ancient magic and new life. For a few minutes, Ava and Malachi rested, dozing with their children safe between them.

And as predicted, a half an hour later, the crowd descended.

EPILOGUE

"AHA!"

Malachi turned. "What?"

Max stormed over to him, a tissue paper crown adorning his blond head. "You're the one who stole Matti."

Malachi shook his head. "I would like to point out that she is, in fact, my daughter. If anyone is stealing her, it's you and Rhys."

Max bent down and held out his hand to the tiny girl, who immediately cooed and wrapped her little hand around the giant's finger. This one, Malachi decided, he would have to watch. She reserved her ornery moments for her mama and *baba*. For her aunties and uncles, she was the picture of innocence.

"She's just so cute," Max said. "Rhys and I were pulling Christmas crackers. Every time one exploded, she got the funniest look on her face."

Ah, his brothers. Teaching his tiny daughter the wonder of explosive devices when she was a week old.

"I am going to show her the Christmas tree," Malachi said. "Hopefully nothing will explode."

"And Rhys was going to read her a poem. There was something about the fat man and a bowl of jelly. I don't understand how anyone that fat could fit down a chimney."

"It's a myth, Max."

"But all myths have roots in reality," he argued. "So for the Santa Claus myth to develop as it has—"

Max shut up when the door to the library cracked open.

Ava asked, "Are you two fighting over the baby again?"

"No," Max said. "I was trying to understand why the Santa myth requires a very fat man as the central figure."

She frowned.

"And maybe fighting over the baby a little."

Malachi ignored his brother and walked over to his mate, who looked vastly more refreshed than she had when she'd lain down with their boy. "Hello, canım. Did you and Geron have a nice nap?"

She held out their son. "I did. I'll trade you. I just fed him. You change him and I'll feed Matti."

"It's a plan." He kissed the top of her head and took Geron and his full diaper before he handed off Matti. "Be good for Mama."

Ava took Matti back into their bedroom, and Malachi turned to Max.

"Here." He held Geron out. "Want this one?"

Max scowled and walked back to the kitchen as Malachi laughed and rocked Geron. "They always disappear when the diaper needs changing, my son."

Geron smiled, contented and milk-drunk, his little belly swollen. Astrid said the smiles were only gas, but Malachi wondered...

"Never mind," he said, pulling his face back from the tiny child. "That one was definitely gas. Let's get a clean diaper for you."

As they walked down the hallway, Geron stared wide-eyed at the walls. Malachi turned and noticed the ancient spells protecting the house rise to his view beneath the many layers of paint.

"Do you see that already, little scribe?" he whispered. "Someday, you will understand what that means. I will teach you."

As Malachi walked toward the laundry room where Ava had set up a changing table, he sang a silly melody he remembered his grandmother singing to him when he had been very small. Geron cooed with him, his voice surprisingly strong for a child only a week old. His eyes already saw everything.

Malachi wondered for the thousandth time what it all would mean. His son didn't only contain the blood of the Forgiven. In his children was mingled the blood of the Fallen *and* the Forgiven. Archangels and enemies. Powers he could barely grasp.

And yet…

Looking into calm grey eyes the exact color of his own, Malachi's mind and soul were at peace. Who could predict the will of the Creator or the machinations of the heavenly realm? He only knew that these children, these precious treasures, had been given to him and his mate to love and protect. And so he would.

With a clean diaper on his son's little bum, Malachi laid Geron under the Christmas tree on a soft blanket and stretched out next to him as his baby boy looked up in wonder at the sparkling lights that danced in the dim light and reflected from the brightly painted globes Ava had chosen. Quiet music played from the kitchen as Karen and Bruno prepared dinner for Astrid, Candace, Brooke, and all their guests. It was a crowded house, but a happy one. The first week of his children's lives had been filled with love and laughter and joy.

He heard the door to the bedroom open and Ava came into the room with Matti in her arms.

She laid their daughter next to her brother and cuddled into Malachi's other side. He put his arm around his mate, amazed by the fullness of his life. His *reshon* on one side and his children cuddling with one another on the other. Even a year ago, he could not imagine how much happiness one heart could contain.

"Happy Christmas, Ava."

"Merry Christmas, Malachi."

"It will be a blessed new year," he said with wonder.

"I think it already is."

THE IRIN CHRONICLES

The Irin Chronicles is now a seven book complete series, available in ebook, audiobook, and paperback from all major retailers.

The Scribe
The Singer
The Secret (Ava and Malachi)
The Staff and the Blade (Damien and Sari)
The Silent (Leo and Kyra)
The Storm (Max and Renata)
The Seeker (Rhys and Meera)

"We're all immortal, as long as our stories are told."

LOOKING FOR MORE FROM ELIZABETH HUNTER?

Whether you're a fan of contemporary fantasy, fantasy romance, or paranormal women's fiction, Elizabeth Hunter has a series for you.

The Elemental Mysteries

Discover the series that has millions of vampire fans raving! Immortal book dealer Giovanni Vecchio thought he'd left the bloody world of vampire politics behind when he retired as an assassin, but a chance meeting at a university pulls student librarian Beatrice De Novo into his orbit. Now temptation lurks behind every dark corner as Vecchio's growing attachment to Beatrice competes with a series of clues that could lead to a library lost in time, and a powerful secret that could reshape the immortal world.

Ebook/Audiobook/Paperback

The Cambio Springs Mysteries

Welcome to the desert town of Cambio Springs where the water is cool, the summers sizzle, and all the residents wear fur, feathers, or snakeskin on full moon nights. In a world of cookie-cutter shifter romance, discover a series that has reviewers raving. Five friends find themselves at a crossroads in life; will the tangled ties of community and shared secrets be their salvation or their end?

Ebook/Audiobook/Paperback

THE IRIN CHRONICLES

"A brilliant and addictive romantic fantasy series." Hidden at the crossroads of the world, an ancient race battles to protect humanity, even as it dies from within. A photojournalist tumbles into a world of supernatural guardians protecting humanity from the predatory sons of fallen angels, but will Ava and Malachi's attraction to each other be their salvation or their undoing?

Ebook/Audiobook/Paperback

GLIMMER LAKE

Delightfully different paranormal women's fiction! Robin, Val, and Monica were average forty-something moms when a sudden accident leaves all three of them with psychic abilities they never could have predicted! Now all three are seeing things that belong in a fantasy novel, not their small mountain town. Ghosts, visions, omens of doom. These friends need to stick together if they're going to solve the mystery at the heart of Glimmer Lake.

Ebook/Audiobook/Paperback

And there's more! Please visit ElizabethHunterWrites.com to sign up for her newsletter or read more about her work.

ABOUT THE AUTHOR

ELIZABETH HUNTER is an eleven-time *USA Today* and international best-selling author of romance, contemporary fantasy, and paranormal mystery. Based in Central California and Addis Ababa, Ethiopia, she travels extensively to write fantasy fiction exploring world mythologies, history, and the universal bonds of love, friendship, and family. She has published over fifty works of fiction and sold over two million books worldwide. She is the author of the Elemental Mysteries series, the Irin Chronicles, the Cambio Springs Mysteries, and other works of fiction.

ELIZABETHHUNTER.COM

ALSO BY ELIZABETH HUNTER

The Irin Chronicles

The Scribe

The Singer

The Secret

The Staff and the Blade

The Silent

The Storm

The Seeker

The Elemental Mysteries

A Hidden Fire

This Same Earth

The Force of Wind

A Fall of Water

The Stars Afire

The Elemental World

Building From Ashes

Waterlocked

Blood and Sand

The Bronze Blade

The Scarlet Deep

A Very Proper Monster

A Stone-Kissed Sea

Valley of the Shadow

The Elemental Legacy

Shadows and Gold

Imitation and Alchemy

Omens and Artifacts

Midnight Labyrinth

Blood Apprentice

The Devil and the Dancer

Night's Reckoning

Dawn Caravan

The Bone Scroll

Pearl Sky

Tin God

<u>The Elemental Covenant</u>

Saint's Passage

Martyr's Promise

Paladin's Kiss

Bishop's Flight

Tin God

<u>The Seba Segel Series</u>

The Thirteenth Month

Child of Ashes (2025)

The Gold Flower (2026)

<u>Vista de Lirio</u>

Double Vision

Mirror Obscure

Trouble Play

<u>Glimmer Lake</u>

Suddenly Psychic

Semi-Psychic Life

Psychic Dreams

<u>Moonstone Cove</u>

Runaway Fate

Fate Actually

Fate Interrupted

<u>The Cambio Springs Series</u>

Shifting Dreams

Desert Bound

Waking Hearts

Strange Dreams

Dust Born

<u>Linx & Bogie Mysteries</u>

A Ghost in the Glamour

A Bogie in the Boat

<u>Contemporary Romance</u>

The Genius and the Muse

Turning Up the Heat

<u>7th and Main</u>

Ink

Hooked

Grit

Sweet